POSH

BOOK ONE OF THE TEMPLETON FAMILY CHRONICLES

JON MALYSIAK

For Colin

| Preface |

Posh is a satire. It is intended to provoke. First and foremost, however, it is what I hope a cracking good story – one that will keep you turning pages while cringing at the gaffes of these truly (but loveably) awful characters. Very little is sacred in these pages. And I suppose to this end, it is not written for the easily offended. It certainly isn't blasphemous, or maybe it is? I guess it depends on the sensitivities of the reader.

Posh explores and explodes the most common tropes and stereotypes of the world in which we live today, through the lens of a privileged and decidedly white society. The Templetons exist in a world that is still very much alive today – a world that many would argue (and not without some justification) is antiquated and at odds with the more enlightened perspective we would expect from a socioeconomic and educated demographic that should know better. The fact that they don't know better is up for debate. Guy, Chloe, Edgar, Diana, and Penelope Templeton exist in a gilded cocoon of colonialism, sexism, racism, money, lineage, and power that even they (begrudgingly) concede puts them at odds with most of the rest of the world. As the reader will discover in this volume and in volumes to come, the Templeton brood will be dragged – kicking and screaming – into the 21st century. Some will fare better than others. Some will fare not at all. Copious amounts of drugs, sex, and alcohol will be consumed.

But I would also argue – perhaps controversially – that the Templetons and what they stand for are not the only cause for ridicule, offense, and concern. In 2023, we live in a world riven by a disturbing encroachment on our rights to freedom of speech, on our ability to disagree, to debate, to argue, to listen, and yes, to learn. This is a world where toxic masculinity exists – and must be dealt with – but, as evidenced by the most recent season of *Love Island* (and, yes, I'm aware of how ridiculous – and possibly undermining – that sounds), so does toxic femininity. How do we address that?

First and foremost, however, *Posh* is a novel, an entertainment. It is not a political statement or a polemic on the state of post-Brexit Britain. As an author, I am not taking sides. I said at the beginning of this preface that nothing is sacred. I stand by that statement. *Posh* takes the mickey out of everyone and everything.

It exposes us as the hypocrites we all are to a certain degree. There's nothing wrong with that. We just have to be okay with that truth. If you're not, well, then *Posh* is probably not the book for you. And that's okay too. You can just cancel me.

Lastly, I need to mention that *Posh* is a joint effort. It's my name on the cover, but my dearly beloved (and now tragically departed) brother Colin and I first dreamt up these horrible characters and these ludicrous plotlines together, as far back as 2014. Working on this (under the rather appalling title *Dangerous Machinations*), in what I didn't realize at the time were the last years of his all-too-brief life, brought us together in a way I don't think either of us could have anticipated. He's gone now – thanks in no small part to the insidious evil that was and is COVID – but his legacy lives on in these pages. *Posh* wouldn't exist today if it hadn't been for him. My grief is profound. This book is a tribute to him, to his *joie de vivre*, to his irony, and to his at times inappropriate sense of humor. I raise a glass in tribute.

Now fuck off and get reading.

That's the Templeton way.

PART 1

| GOA |

| 1 |

Disorientation was not something Guy Templeton related to. Hangovers: yes. Waking up not knowing where you were or how you got there: no. He'd had his share of benders over the years. Educated first at Harrow from the ages of thirteen to eighteen and then dual degrees in Russian and Economics at the University of Cambridge followed by a Masters in Business from the London School of Economics, Guy was well-versed in all things tipple- and bum- related and the consequences of whatever transpired while unapologetically under the influence.

While Guy's academic record—on paper anyway—looked positively smashing, if he'd been allowed to focus his studies on boozing, hazing, sporting, and whoring, he would surely have achieved all firsts across the board. But as it was, he knew he'd lucked out in not getting himself expelled after the first term at Harrow and every term at every subsequent school thereafter. He was, after all, a Templeton—a scion of one of England's most distinguished families, with a genealogy that traced back centuries. In other words, Guy was blessed. And while he'd never been one to tout his decidedly blueblood lineage, he also knew that being a Templeton meant some things were just given to you by virtue of the Templeton surname.

Of course, with this privilege came responsibilities—a detailed list of which his father, the much-esteemed Lord Carleton Templeton, never failed to enumerate *ad nauseum*—that, for Guy, became a kind of noble vise that, despite his desire and striving for independence, in all of his forty-three years he had never quite been able to shake. Privilege made Guy who he was. And yet, he couldn't help but think this same privilege would also prove his undoing.

Now here he was: lying facedown and naked on a bed he didn't remember climbing into, in a room he couldn't identify, with a pounding hangover exacerbated by the whirring of the ceiling fan above him, and the stale taste of last night's tequila and cigarettes (and something vaguely metallic) on his tongue.

Guy opened his eyes, closed them, and then forced himself to blink more fully awake. His vision was blurred. His face felt as though it had been pounded to shit in a boxing ring. His neck felt broken. And the rest of him, well, for a guy who had always defined himself by his athleticism—crew, cricket, equestrian, and footy—Guy Templeton suddenly and quite uncomfortably felt every bit of his early middle-age. It didn't suit him. And bloody hell, did he ache all over!

He reached over to the nightstand and fumbled for his phone. He tried to make his eyes focus but it seemed the more concerted the effort, the more insistent his body was on reminding him that he was no longer twenty-one, or thirty-one, or—fuck it!—forty-one. The reality was depressing. Defeating. It made Guy feel as though he might as well just pack it in. Despite the fact that he'd been born with a silver spoon in his mouth, he'd never been one to view the world through rose-tinted glasses. He had seen his share of hardship and he knew the world to be a dark and violent place. He didn't believe in God or redemption. People were who they were and would continue to brutalize each other because that's what people did.

Guy knew this put him at odds with most of his family—not the least of which his younger sister, Chloe, who still held fast to the belief that positive words, gratitude journals, and manifestations could and would change the world. But he had also seen things that most of them could never have imagined.

12:30 pm.

Where the fuck...?

Guy rolled over and forced himself into a sitting position. He rubbed his eyes and concentrated on bringing his surroundings into focus. The room wasn't bad. It had an open verandah that looked out onto a beach dotted with multi-colored umbrellas and a panoramic view of the ocean. A light breeze blew off of the water. It smelled of salt and coconut and curry. Guy remembered then. He was in Goa. India. He'd gone there to get away, to disappear from the world, to pretend—at least for the time being—that none of what had come before existed. Guy had meant to escape even as he knew he was too much of a realist to believe such an escape was possible.

He glanced again at his phone: three calls from Chloe and a WhatsApp imploring him to call or text her the moment he became available; two calls from two different numbers, both of which began with +7, the Russian country code; a text from Spencer that merely said "WTF?" and a text from Sunny Joy Whatever that made absolutely no sense whatsoever, just a jumble of letters followed by an exclamation point, a question mark, and a slew of happy face emoji that made him smile because, well, Sunny Joy Whatever was Sunny Joy Whatever. As jaded as Guy knew himself to be, Sunny Joy Whatever had more reason than pretty much anyone he knew (including himself) to see the world for what it really was, and yet the diminutive Bangladeshi managed to radiate optimism wherever she went.

With considerable effort, Guy launched himself out of bed and stood for a second or two with his bare feet planted on the rattan rug in the center of the room, willing himself to remain steady against the vertiginous rush that felt as though it would blow off the top of his head. He closed his eyes, breathed in and out through his nostrils, and pictured the ocean and the waves lapping against the shore. He visualized walking bare foot in the sand, the water rolling up to his ankles, pleasantly cool and warm at the same time. The breeze blew into the room through the verandah and played with his hair, gently drying the damp on his forehead, calming him. He breathed in again and brought his palms together, his fingertips lightly touching. He held the pose for fifteen seconds, just as his Nepalese yogi had taught him all those years ago, before opening his eyes and more fully absorbing the world around him. And yet he still couldn't remember anything about the night before.

Guy went into the bathroom, flicking on the light as he entered and stepped into the shower without bothering to check his reflection in the mirror. The water sputtered and spat before raining down upon him in a steady humid stream. He held his face up to the showerhead, opened his mouth and let the water bathe his suddenly aching jaw. He put his hand to his chin, noticing for the first time that it was swathed in a bandage that the water was now loosening.

What the fuck happened last night?

He turned off the shower without bothering to rinse himself and fumbled for the towel. He dreaded what he might find looking back at him in the mirror. Guy had been in more than his share of fights over the years—he was certainly no stranger to pain—but this was something different. Or maybe he was just starting to feel his age?

The mirror was steamed up. Guy used the back of his hand to wipe it clear and in doing so revealed a sight that was definitely not for sore eyes. Bruised and definitely bloodied, Guy peered at his reflection and took stock of last night's damage. The skin under his left eye was purple and swollen. There was a nasty cut just off his right eyebrow that looked as though someone had treated it with iodine but hadn't bothered to stitch it closed. His nose looked as though it had been knocked into a wall a time or two. His nostrils were caked in dried blood. But what alarmed him most was the series of stitches that peeked out from the soggy and crimson-stained bandage. He pulled it free to expose a gash that ran from the center of his chin, extending along the line of his jaw and coming to an abrupt end just beneath his left earlobe. The stitching was barely adequate. Guy knew that unless he had the wound properly attended to, it would leave a nasty scar.

If he'd been at all vain about his appearance, Guy would have made getting his face fixed an immediate priority. But as it was, he took rather smug pride in the physical evidence of his decidedly rough-and-tumble existence. He was posh to the core, but that didn't mean he had to subscribe to a diet of scones and fresh strawberries, at least not all the time. Wounds built character. Scars provided a map of one's soul. Never trust a bloke who hadn't had his lip split or his nose broken at least once, and if a tooth or two got knocked out in the process, well, Guy thought, so much the better. But whatever had happened the night before, even Guy conceded, was taking things just a tad too far.

And then he noticed the tattoo: an inky silhouette of a svelte yet pleasingly voluptuous woman that took up the length and breadth of his right bicep. It wasn't well executed but he knew exactly whom it represented and it was this that triggered at least a partial lifting of his amnesia:

Svetlana...

The Black Widow of Sochi.

Guy had had his share of women over the years but none of them held a candle to Svetlana Slutskaya. He didn't know what it was about her that held him captive. She was without question a looker, but lookers were a dime a dozen in Guy's world. He'd bedded more than his fair share—"Save a few for the rest of us poor sods," Spencer always joked—but Tsarina Slutskaya was in a league of her own. Even the most jaded couldn't resist a flash from the impenetrable darkness of her black kohl-dusted eyes. That's all it had taken for Guy to fall head over heels. Once Svetlana's spell was cast, there was no coming out from under it. Such was the effect she had.

Guy stood before his reflection, admiring of and yet repulsed by the tattoo, a now permanent reminder of the woman he thought he had finally escaped when he'd boarded the plane in Moscow in the dead of a Russian midsummer eve, feeling lucky to be alive while all too aware that as long as Svetlana Slutskaya existed somewhere in his universe, he would never be free. He traced the outline of the silhouette on his bicep as the memories flooded through a hazy caviar and vodka-infused lens.

He remembered the first time he'd seen her. They had been crossing Red Square from opposite directions on a January evening so cold that one almost had to prevent oneself from breathing lest the moisture freeze and blister one's lips with frostbite. Guy had spotted her long before she had seen him, or at least that was what she later had led him to believe. She was wearing a voluminous sable-lined cloak that caught in the wind behind her, giving the illusion that she was flying through the air on a carpet of snow. The collar of her cloak was turned up and her matching sable hat pulled down low over her forehead and ears so that only her eyes, nose, and lips were exposed. A wisp of black hair had blown loose from under her hat. Guy couldn't take his eyes off of her. They passed each other in front of Lenin's Tomb. The sidewalk was crowded and he stepped onto the curb to give her room, but not so much room that she didn't brush against him as she walked past. Her black eyes flashed in acknowledgment. Her lips pursed together as though appraising him in the three seconds of their first encounter. Guy's breath caught in his throat.

"*Spacebo,*" she murmured.

"*Nyet,*" he said in reply. "*Udovol'stviye moya.*" [No, the pleasure is mine.]

She smiled at him then, or rather the corners of her mouth twitched upward and the tip of her tongue darted between her lips. It was the most seductive thing he had ever seen. He wanted to grab the hem of her cloak and pull her hard against him, but his arms were frozen at his sides and Svetlana never broke her stride. He turned and followed her with his eyes, the image of her billowing cloak and the suggestive flick of her tongue burned deep into his imagination.

Their second encounter took place nearly a fortnight later at the Bolshoi during a performance of *Swan Lake*. The British ambassador to Russia—an old friend of his father's—had taken ill at the last minute and had asked Guy to accompany his rather unprepossessing eighteen year-old daughter, Cordelia, to the ballet. Guy had intended to spend the night playing roulette at the Casino Metropol but when the ambassador asked you to babysit his daughter you didn't say no. And, to be honest, he owed the old boy a favor or two.

Guy had first spotted the mysterious tsarina during the second act *pas de deux*. He and Cordelia were seated in one of the boxes typically reserved for foreign dignitaries and he happened to glance over to see if the ambassador's daughter was all right after she had brushed her gloved fingers across his forearm and shuddered during a particularly swoony phrase of Tchaikovsky's music.

"Don't you just love the ballet?" Cordelia gasped.

Guy coughed into his fist. Cordelia's hand traveled down his forearm to his wrist, her fingers teasing the hairs on the back of his hand. Even in the darkened theatre, Guy could see her brown eyes staring at him wide and moony, a band of perspiration dampening the edge of her trembling upper lip. And while Cordelia was anything but attractive—there was something of the nun about her—Guy couldn't help the stir in his groin. He crossed his legs, coughed again, and chastely patted the girl's hand while pulling his arm away.

"Shhh," he said. "Keep your eyes on the stage. You might miss something."

Just as he said this, he felt another pair of eyes upon him. He glanced over the top of Cordelia's head to the box adjacent to theirs and noticed, for the first time, the beauty from Red Square. She was sitting there, just on the other side of the partition, peering at him through a pair of opera glasses. Their gazes met. Guy re-crossed his legs as he felt himself stiffen, all too aware that Cordelia was still looking at him.

"Look!" he whispered while pointing to the stage where Siegfried had just embarked on a particularly impressive sequence of pirouettes. "Whoever said that ballet dancers weren't athletes?"

Cordelia sniffed. She followed Guy's gaze to the adjacent box, catching sight of the raven-haired Russian just as the woman was lowering her opera glasses and nodding her head in response to something the rather portly gentleman beside her was whispering in her ear.

Guy looked to see whether he could catch the woman's eye again but she had turned her attention to the ballet and remained focused as such through the duration of the act. At intermission, he caught sight of her just as she was leaving the box, her stout and very much older companion in tow and holding up the end of her glittering Swarovski-studded opera cloak so it didn't drag on the floor.

"Fancy a glass of champers?" Guy asked Cordelia without waiting for her to reply. He tripped over the leg of her chair in his effort to make it out to the foyer before the Russian had a chance to dissolve into the crowd. Cordelia had no choice but to follow, which she did with another of her thoroughly disapproving *humpfs* and a complaint (which Guy ignored) that he had stepped on her toe.

The lobby glittered with Moscow's elite. The effect was pure Tolstoy. Guy helped himself to two flutes of champagne from a passing waiter and handed one to Cordelia who accepted it without comment and proceeded to down it in one gulp.

"I'll have another, please," she said.

"You'll get me into trouble."

"With whom? With Daddy? I wouldn't worry about him, Guy. Daddy doesn't care what I do. Daddy doesn't care about anything except Tatiana."

"Tatiana?"

"His mistress. He doesn't think Mummy and I know but Mummy had him followed the other day."

Guy shrugged. "How am I supposed to react to that?"

Cordelia smiled in such a way that Guy supposed was meant to be alluring but coming from a pear-shaped eighteen year-old with a rather alarming case of rosacea, the effect was nothing if not ghoulish. Guy wondered how many glasses of champers she'd had before meeting him earlier that night at the ambassador's residence. He stepped back, bracing himself against the balcony overlooking the ground floor lobby. He feared Cordelia was coming in for the kill, but she merely came up beside him and leaned her elbows on the balcony railing while exhaling a long, plaintive sigh.

"If there wasn't so much cash involved," she said, "I think Mummy and Daddy would have divorced ages ago. But whatever. You're not interested in my boring teenage angst. You're a grown man. A *very* grown man."

Guy cleared his throat and looked about for the waiter. He snapped his fingers and another two glasses of champagne appeared before them. He handed one to Cordelia.

"Take it easy with this one," he said. "Pace yourself. I don't want your father accusing me of corrupting you."

"Would you?" she said.

"Would I what?'

"Corrupt me. I think I should very much like to be corrupted by you, Guy."

At that moment, as if on cue, the Red Square bombshell appeared just below them in the main lobby. Guy's breath caught in his throat. As impossible as it seemed, it was almost as though she sensed his presence. She looked up, her black eyes sweeping across the balcony in search of him. She stopped. The throng of bejeweled, champagne and vodka-swilling patrons seemed to collectively step back from her, isolating her. The Swarovski crystals that adorned her cloak shone in the light from the overhanging chandeliers. Their gazes locked. Guy gasped.

"Who is that?" he asked.

"Svetlana Slutskaya," Cordelia said, her tone betraying her disdain. "They call her the Black Widow of Sochi...among other things."

Svetlana raised her opera glasses and held them to her eyes. Guy gulped his champagne.

"Who is she?"

"It depends on whom you ask."

"What do you mean?"

"Officially, she's the widow of Miroslav Borosevic."

"The Chechen warlord."

"*Da.*"

"The one who died in that boating accident in St. Tropez what, like, three years ago?"

"The very same."

"And unofficially?"

"It was never definitively determined what caused the explosion."

"A hit then?"

"My lips are sealed."

"But you know something?"

Cordelia shrugged. She bumped her hip against his thigh. "I'm the ambassador's daughter," she said. "I know lots of things I'm not supposed to know. But ply me with enough champagne and I might start to reveal my secrets."

"Do you have a lot of secrets, Cordelia?"

"Corrupt me, Guy, and you might just find out."

The bell chimed to indicate the end of intermission. Guy blinked and Svetlana Slutskaya was gone.

"I must meet that woman," he said. "I'll do whatever it takes."

Cordelia knocked back what remained of her champagne and took his arm. "Officially I could tell you she's bad news," she said, pulling him away from the balcony and urging him back to their box. "She isn't received anywhere, at least not in official circles, which is why it's rather cheeky she's here this evening."

"Surely a woman who looks like that would never be banned from the ballet?"

Cordelia laughed. "You're a fool, Guy Templeton," she said. "An endearing fool, but a fool nonetheless. You just can't help yourself. I wish I weren't so damn attracted to toxic masculinity."

"Tell me everything you know."

"Then you must be willing to pay the price," Cordelia said, "and promise you won't hate me afterwards."

Guy bowed and gave Cordelia his most winning smile. He knew he was being bad, but as she'd said, he simply couldn't help himself. Beautiful or homely, dowager or ingénue, and utterly without regard to their persuasion or relationship status, Guy loved them all.

But the problem, as Guy saw it, was that he had yet to meet a woman whom he felt his true equal. It extended far beyond the bedroom or the broom closet, the Persian rug or the Turkish *hammam*. While rare was the woman who could match him thrust for thrust, such impressive (and, yes, frightening) creatures did exist and, when encountered, had at times even threatened to destroy him. In Guy's experience, even the most consensual of sex was a power struggle. The very nature of the beast meant someone was always on top and someone always below. There were only so many positions one could comfortably—and not so comfortably— accommodate. But rarer still was the woman who stimulated Guy well beyond foreplay (both verbal and physical) and the act itself (strictly physical). And while he was loath to consider himself a romantic in the traditional sense, as Guy found himself inexorably drifting toward middle age, the notion of finding himself in his late forties or early fifties still a bachelor held less and less appeal.

Guy wasn't looking to settle down. He was just looking for something he as yet couldn't quite put his finger on: not commitment per se (he doubted he could ever happily be a one woman man), but perhaps something a little more permanent. Until that woman arrived, however, there were girls like Cordelia— useful to him in her own way but not to be taken seriously—and women like Svetlana—fascinating, intriguing, and dangerous—who might prove too hot to handle but would definitely keep him engaged in the meantime.

The chimes rang again, signaling the end of intermission. Guy felt his palms sweat in anticipation of catching another glimpse of the Swarovski-bedecked femme fatale in the adjoining box. He wiped the perspiration on the sides of his trousers and forced himself to focus on escorting Cordelia back to their seats. He placed his hand on the small of Cordelia's back. She shivered.

"Your hand is cold," Cordelia whispered. "A reflection of the coldness in your heart, perhaps?"

"Be good," he said. "You never know who's watching."

"Yes, Daddy has spies all over Moscow waiting to catch you out."

"It isn't your father's spies I was referring to."

"Daddy can't keep me locked up forever," she said, a frosty petulance entering her voice that Guy found peculiarly alarming. "I'm not Rapunzel in some ivory tower."

"I never said you were."

"Although tonight I do feel a bit like Cinderella at the ball."

"Let me know when you find your Prince Charming," he said.

They were now seated once again in their box. The conductor assumed his position at the podium and beckoned for the orchestra to stand for applause. Guy glanced over to the box beside theirs only to be disappointed that the chair previously occupied by Svetlana Slutskaya now contained the rather rotund figure of an aging and rather Soviet-looking woman squeezed into a decidedly unflattering ball gown that revealed a bit too much flesh and an ample layering of talcum powder. She must have sensed him looking at her for, as if on cue, she turned and met Guy's gaze with a smile that was anything but enticing. Guy looked away. The fourth act was going to be intolerable. He needed a way out but he'd given his word to the ambassador that his daughter would be well looked after and he couldn't very well leave the girl without a chaperone, especially not after she'd promised to tell him everything she knew about the bewitching woman from Red Square.

The curtain rose on the fourth act of *Swan Lake*. The cygnets were graceful in their elegant tutus made to look like swan's feathers. Tchaikovsky's music swelled and soared. Guy tried to focus. He kept looking over to see whether perhaps Svetlana had returned—knowing as he did so that she was lost to him, at least for that evening—only to find her geriatric replacement ogling him without the subterfuge of opera glasses. He'd seen *Swan Lake* before. He knew the fourth act was relatively brief as far as ballets were concerned and that it seemed unfair to expect Cordelia to agree to leave before the dramatic final moments, but Guy also knew his limits and once he'd set his mind to a new conquest, there was very little that could persuade him from his cause, not even Tchaikovsky or the ambassador's daughter.

"Let's go," he said, bringing his lips to Cordelia's ear and making sure that his breath flushed hot against her already damp skin.

"But this is the best part," she whispered back, not daring to meet his gaze and yet melting closer to him. Guy knew she was putty. "You don't come to *Swan Lake* and not stay to the end."

"I do," he replied.

"You're impossible," Cordelia said.

They left without another word, sweeping out onto the mezzanine and down the grand staircase to the main floor with a fluidity that rivaled anything on stage. Once outside, Guy hailed their car. Sergei, the ambassador's chauffeur, wasted no time pulling up to the curb and making sure his boss' daughter and her chaperone were safely ensconced in the bulletproof luxury of the ambassador's late model Bentley.

"Where to?" he asked, his voice heavy with the accent of the Urals.

"Where to indeed?" Cordelia said, giving Guy's chest a teasing poke. "I only have until midnight, you know. At the strike of twelve my Bentley becomes a pumpkin and my Prince Charming little more than a boring government nobody."

"Is that what you think of me?" Guy couldn't help himself. "A boring government nobody?"

"You have until midnight to prove me wrong."

"I'd better get started then. Sergei, take us to Krasnyy."

"Yes, sir."

"Krasnyy? How very V.I.P. Can you really get us in?"

"You insult me. Don't ever do that again."

"Krasnyy it is then. Color me impressed."

Guy snapped himself back into the present. Don't go there. *Nothing good can come from rehashing the past.* He studied his reflection in the bathroom mirror and decided he didn't at all like the visage that stared back at him. It was old, worn-out, used. He hated that he couldn't remember anything about what had happened the night before: the crudely stitched and bandaged gash on his neck was bad enough, but the tattoo? Why couldn't Svetlana Slutskaya leave him well enough alone? When would it end? *Not until I'm dead.* As he stood in front of the mirror, sickened by the sight of Svetlana's silhouette on his bicep, Guy sensed that for the first time he might very well be in way over his head.

But he couldn't think about that now. His first order of business was to get dressed, get some food in his belly, and ask Spencer what the fuck was going on and why the fuck he had a gash in his neck that looked like it had been an attempted decapitation and why the fuck he couldn't remember anything about the night before? Spencer would know. And even if Spencer didn't want to fess up, Guy had ways of making certain that his best friend bent to his will. He was nothing if not resourceful.

When he emerged from the bathroom, Guy noticed a piece of paper on the floor that had been slipped under the door. He picked it up and peered at the handwriting:

Meet me on the hotel patio

—S.

Spencer. There wasn't a date or a time on the note and Guy had no way of knowing how long it had been since his best mate had left it for him, but it was as good an excuse as any to put on some clothes and begin the process of trying to put the pieces together of what exactly had not only transpired the night before but in however many hours it had been since he'd boarded that Aeroflot flight from Moscow—or was it Sochi?—and landed here in the beautiful but generic paradise that was Goa.

Guy rummaged in his suitcase for something appropriate to change into and settled on a rumpled pair of white linen trousers and a blue polo shirt that nicely hugged the contours of his chest without being too overt. A pair of non-descript but ridiculously expensive Dolce & Gabbana flip-flops completed the outfit. He was relieved (without really knowing why) to see that his wardrobe appeared more-or-less intact. He didn't remember packing it in the first place but it appeared he had done so in some haste. His clothes were tragically wrinkled— Chloe would not approve—and he wondered whether the hotel might have a decent dry cleaner on site.

He then spotted the messenger bag slung over the back of the rattan chair that fronted the balcony with the views of the beach. And Guy remembered this bag— or rather, what it contained—was of paramount importance. He unzipped it with unsteady hands and was relieved to find the cash in various currencies (mostly American dollars, pounds, and rubles), all as it should be, or at least all as he was able to recall. He unfastened one of the side pockets and found his iPad—good for checking the video highlights and scores of his team, Nottingham Forest—and his assortment of passports—U.K., U.S., and Australian. At least everything seemed to be in order even if his brain was still an utter scramble. And Goddamn did his neck hurt! He touched the jagged wound with the tips of his fingers, felt the uneasy and inconsistent stitching. He glanced at his fingers and was somewhat relieved to see that they came away dry. Of one thing he was certain—whatever had caused the gash in his neck was going to leave a rather nasty scar. *It builds character*, he thought, and Lord knew Guy Templeton already had plenty of character to spare.

Guy checked his mobile as he stepped onto the verandah and then down the terra cotta stairs that led to the beachfront café and patio. The place was packed with an international assortment of fashionably dressed holidaymakers and expatriate pensioners, most of whom were of a certain age and a decidedly Caucasian demographic, though mixed within this wholly homogenous crowd were the occasional Persian Gulf Arab and string-bikini-clad Bollywood starlet, each with their respective entourages in tow. Guy was thankful he hadn't lost his aviators in last night's fog. They provided him with a sense of anonymity that—even as he knew it was merely an illusion—reassured him nonetheless.

Chloe had sent him another WhatsApp—*Guy, this is your sister. Where are you? Why aren't you answering your phone? It's important.* His little sister was the only person Guy knew who still messaged in complete sentences with a schoolmarm's adherence to correct punctuation and spelling. As annoying as she was, Guy couldn't help but find her endearing. She was his baby sister, after all. She meant the world to him even though they rarely saw eye to eye about anything, especially not in regard to family, which was one of the reasons—one of many—that Guy spent most of his life as far away from them as possible. Chloe wasn't the problem, but it was impossible to separate her from the others—Diana and Edgar, not to mention their father—and as much as she was Guy's baby sister, Chloe was their father's youngest child even more.

He spotted Spencer Hawksworth sitting at a table at the far end of the café. The straw boater with the red and blue band was what gave his best mate away. There was never a moment when Spencer wasn't the epitome of Savile Row: an outfit for every occasion, all bespoke, all very properly British. Guy loved him like the brother he had always wished he had.

He felt the eyes of the café upon him as he wended his way through the rather close arrangement of tables and wait staff to where Spencer sat. He heard their gossipy and appraising murmurs. He felt their admiration and disparagement. He knew they knew who he was—the sunglasses could only disguise so much—and even in his decidedly vague state, the effect wasn't entirely displeasing. The Bollywood starlet pursed her gold-leaf-coated lips and blew him a kiss. Guy wondered for a moment whether he'd shagged her. She mimed for him to text her later. He shook his head and shrugged. She flipped him the bird and then snapped at one of her minions to give her a foot massage. Guy remembered that he had indeed shagged her. She'd given him a laundry list of positions. A contract had even been involved. In the end, it had all been rather tedious. Guy didn't mind high maintenance. He just didn't do crazy.

"Miss me much?" Guy said as he approached Spencer from behind and took a playful swat at his best mate's hat.

"You fucking wanker!" Spencer exclaimed, jumping up from his chair and folding Guy into a bear hug. "Where the bloody hell have you been? Do you know how long I've been trying to get a hold of you?"

"You and everyone else."

"Your mobile die or something?"

Guy took a seat opposite Spencer. He ordered a Tanqueray and tonic.

"What are you drinking?" He motioned to Spencer's glass. "That looks like orange juice."

"That's because it is orange juice."

"A screwdriver?"

"Are you kidding me? After last night? I don't think I'll dare touch alcohol ever again."

"You've said that before."

"Yes, well, maybe this time I mean it."

"Until the clock strikes five. Or four. Or..."

Spencer checked his watch. "Or one forty-five. Fuck it. I'll have what you're having."

"A G&T?"

"What? Since when do you drink gin? Was Mother Russia as bad as all that?"

"I think I have amnesia."

"It's called denial."

"Now you sound like Chloe."

"The voice of reason."

"Jesus fuck, it's hot!" Guy changed the subject. If there was anything between him and Spencer that could remotely be considered a sore subject, it was Chloe. His best mate and his favorite sister apparently had a history, however unacknowledged. Perhaps 'history' wasn't the best way to describe it. There hadn't been any histrionics, and as far as Guy knew everything had always been and still remained very civilized. Neither Chloe nor Spencer had ever really spoken to him about whatever had or hadn't happened and it simply wasn't in Guy's nature to ask. Growing up, the three of them had sort of been a 'thing.' Not in any overtly sexual way, but they had been inseparable. Many an English summer and darkest English winter had been spent in each other's company, both at the Templeton's Edwardian mansion in Mayfair and their ancestral estate in Dorset.

But Guy had always sensed that his best mate had designs on his sister. It just wasn't a subject he had ever cared to approach. He knew too much about—and, in fact, had participated in his share of—Spencer's various romantic and not-so-romantic escapades that he found something rather distasteful in the notion of Spencer and Chloe together in any capacity beyond the boundary of friendship.

And while he didn't doubt that Spencer's intentions toward his sister were anything other than aboveboard, in Guy's perspective, Chloe was still too innocent to have her purity tarnished by Spencer's slightly dodgy past.

To Guy, Chloe was the female ideal. She represented the very best of not just her gender but of humanity in general. With her passion for helping the Third World disadvantaged—Sisters Against Sweat Shops (SASS) her latest charitable endeavor—and her determined (and perhaps slightly myopic) opinion that there were still causes worth fighting for, Chloe Templeton was everything Guy was not. The fact that they were related, not to mention their closeness, never failed to surprise him. Chloe and Guy were indeed polar opposites yet because of this Guy felt he and his sister were each other's most dogged protectors, though this was likely to the detriment of their relationships with their siblings and any outsiders with whom they might become romantically linked. It was certainly a catalyst for the ongoing conflict between Guy and his father, another reality neither Chloe nor Guy had ever explicitly addressed.

Guy considered Spencer through his aviators. The chap was an unabashed toff. It didn't surprise him that Chloe had rejected his best mate's advances, if indeed that is what had happened. And while Guy knew Spencer to be a man of rare intelligence, he also recognized that it was all too easy to dismiss Spencer as little more than a posh twit whose substance barely ran skin deep. Still, where Chloe was concerned, whatever her reasons, Guy couldn't help but be relieved that the sixteenth century bells of the Templeton chapel would not be announcing the nuptials of Chloe Templeton and Spencer Hawksworth any time soon. Nor would they ever, if Guy had anything to do with it.

"I honestly don't remember a bloody thing about last night," Guy said, forcing himself to focus only on the present. The past—even the parts of it he didn't remember—was simply too treacherous. "How did I get here?"

"Very dangerously."

"That's not helpful."

"You're serious?" Spencer regarded Guy from beneath the shaded protection of his hat. "What's the last thing you *do* remember?"

Guy slammed what remained of his Tanqueray and tonic and snapped his fingers for another round.

"Why do I have a tattoo of Svetlana Slutskaya on my arm?"

"What?"

Guy glanced around the patio before rolling back the short sleeve of his polo to reveal the full extent of the Black Widow of Sochi's inked silhouette. Spencer's jaw dropped. Their drinks arrived. They knocked them back in a synchronous motion and Spencer motioned for round three.

"Something harder this time?" he suggested. "Shots?"

Guy shrugged, his hangover giving way to a not entirely unwelcome fresh intoxication.

"Tequila," Spencer barked to their server. "You're branded for life now. What on earth possessed you?"

"Like I told you, I don't remember."

"It's not a half-bad job though she might have done it with a steadier hand. I guess they don't teach coloring within the lines in Dhaka."

"This is Sunny Joy's work?"

"You insisted and she wanted to do something nice for you—bless—though I'm fairly certain a tattoo of Ms. Slutskaya was not what Sunny Joy had in mind."

"Why didn't you stop me?"

"Like I said, you were most adamant and I've learnt over the years that once Guy Templeton sets his mind on something, come hell or high water, nothing gets in his way. Besides..."

Their server returned with a bottle of Fortaleza and two shot glasses. Spencer poured for them both.

"Salut!" he said.

The tequila was smooth—too smooth, Guy thought—and went down like liquid fire.

"Ye gods!" Spencer shook his head and poured them another.

"You were saying?" Guy prompted once the shock of the first shot dissolved into the mind-melting beauty of the second.

"You were so far gone I thought it best to let you sober up in your own time, not to mention I had other—slightly more attractive—company to keep."

"Bully for you then."

Spencer raised his shot glass in an ironic toast before filling it up again. "Indeed," he said. "Goa is a bloody bachelor's paradise."

"I thought you were supposed to be looking after me?"

Spencer shrugged. "I'm only one man, and you've gone and pissed off some—how shall I say this?—very sketchy people. You're lucky you came out of last night more or less intact."

"What happened?"

"Obviously I left the bar before things got interesting. I'm afraid this business with the ambassador's daughter…"

"Cordelia?" The thought of her made the tequila rise in Guy's throat.

"Hell hath no fury like a woman scorned."

"What was I supposed to do? She's unstable."

"You took advantage of her."

"She's a child."

"I'm not saying that I blame you," Spencer said. "Where Svetlana is concerned, if I'd have been in your shoes I'd have chosen the Black Widow as well. I can't fault your taste. It's your tactics and your reason—or rather deplorable lack thereof—that I pose for debate. Listen to me, mate. Listen…"

Spencer poured Guy another shot and leaned forward.

"I don't think you quite appreciate the extent of the peril you're in. You've got some very bad dudes after you. And I can almost guarantee they won't be content with just breaking your kneecaps."

"She cheated me," Guy said. The fog was slowly starting to lift. He didn't know whether it was the Goa sunshine or the tequila that was helping to bring the past into greater clarity. What he did know was that his return to cognizance afforded little in the way of comfort and only exacerbated the sense that his predicament was, for lack of a better descriptive, dire in the gravest sense.

"I'm afraid she did far more than that, my friend," Spencer replied. "Unless you find some way to make good on the money you've essentially stolen from them, I don't see how you're going to get out of this colossal shit show with your head still intact. The Russians don't mess around. They're not any better than your average Islamist nutcase with a video camera and a butcher knife. Have you heard of the Wagner Group?"

The reality was making Guy's head hurt worse than it already was. He closed his eyes and ran his fingers through his hair. He wished for someone to blame even as it was all too obvious that he had no one to blame but himself.

"I can put in a few calls," Guy said. "Stall for time. A chap I know owes me a favor, maybe even two, if I'm lucky and he's feeling generous."

"Sorry. It's not going to happen. There's a very powerful cabal after you whose negotiation techniques are—shall we say?—rather infamously one-dimensional."

"But it's not my fault!"

"Oh, poor you. You're going to have to do better than that. You were played. And now we're all going to pay the price. Thank you very much."

Guy sank back in his chair. Suddenly Goa seemed a lot less like paradise.

"What am I going to do?" he asked.

"I might have suggested we chat with the ambassador and see if there are any strings he might be able to pull in Moscow, but I don't think I'd be off the mark in saying that's one channel I suspect is now rather permanently closed."

"MI-6?"

"Don't compromise me."

Spencer went to pour another shot but Guy shook his head and held his hand over his glass.

"I loved her," Guy said.

"Yes, I'm rather inclined to believe that you did. Still, it doesn't excuse the hash you've made of things. Until I figure out what the fuck we're going to do to get us out of this shit storm, I suggest you keep your head down. I'd tell you not to leave your room until I can arrange a safe house for you but I know you won't listen so I shan't waste my breath."

"Thank you."

"I will insist, however, that you stay away from karaoke bars and tattoo parlors. Last night was a spectacle that mustn't—and I repeat *mustn't*—be repeated for all the obvious reasons, not the least of which being I don't think I can stomach another rendition of *Total Eclipse of the Heart*. And Sunny Joy Whatever...dear God, the poor girl exploits herself without even realizing it. You owe Rajeev big time."

Guy snickered. "Then I'll resist the urge to serenade you," he said.

"It's really no laughing matter. You've checked your bag. The money's there?"

"Five hundred thousand cash...I think. Dollars, pounds, rubles..."

"You *think?*"

"It's all there. It hasn't been touched."

"And you know that for a fact, do you?"

Guy shrugged.

"I repeat: you know that for a fact, don't you? Nod your head and tell me you know for a fact that money hasn't been touched. Every last pence and cent is accounted for, yes?"

Guy nodded but the look on Spencer's face betrayed the fact his mate knew he was bluffing. The nod became a mournful shake of the head.

"Ye gods!" Spencer exclaimed, slamming his hand down on the table, much to the muted alarm of the café patrons around them. "At least tell me you've locked it in your room's safe."

Guy couldn't meet Spencer's gaze. He stared down at his hands like a guilty schoolboy about to get his hands whacked with a ruler.

"I cannot tell a lie."

"The fact you've left all that cash sitting around an unsecured hotel room not once but twice is bad enough," Spencer scolded, his voice, however, never once rising to the occasion. "Although looking at the bigger picture, I'd say there's a much greater problem on our hands. One that affects not just you, but me, and very probably everyone with whom you have ever come in contact."

"That being?" Guy muttered.

"You're losing it, mate."

Guy exhaled for the first time in several minutes. He picked up his glass and tipped it to Spencer for another shot of tequila. He was beyond drunk, beyond hungover. He felt numb...and the tattoo on his arm, like a particularly annoying harbinger of things to come, had started to itch.

"I'm fine," Guy tried to shrug it off. "I've just had a bad run of things lately." Guy threw back the tequila and was pleased to see that it hadn't lost its burn. "I'm over it," he said.

"Don't fucking bullshit me. A minute ago you were telling me you loved the bird and now you're speaking of her as if she was last night's news."

Guy glanced around them, catching the eye of the Bollywood starlet whose gaze he had felt on the back of his head from the moment he had sat down. She blew him a suggestive kiss. The rush of blood to his groin came as a welcome relief.

"I guess some things never change," Spencer said with a trace of disapproval, following Guy's gaze. "You're incorrigible."

"Nothing sticks to me," Guy said. "You know that."

"Yes, unfortunately."

Without breaking their gaze, the starlet snapped her fingers and held out her hand, palm up. One of her lackeys jumped to attention and placed her mobile phone on it. She began to text.

Guy's phone buzzed.

"I wouldn't if I were you," Spencer said as Guy read the starlet's message: *Room 472. 5 minutes. Don't keep me waiting.*

"You were saying?" Guy said as he thumbed a reply: *It just so happens I've been craving a little masala.*

The starlet languidly rose from her chair. Guy smiled. She clapped her hands before sweeping out of the café with her entourage dutifully in tow.

"Thanks for the chat, mate," he said. "Always good to catch up."

"You're joking."

"About the money," Guy said. "You know my room number. I'll meet you there in fifteen and we'll count it together properly."

"Fifteen?"

"That's the thing about Indian. A little goes a long way."

Guy's phone buzzed again. The starlet had sent him a picture.

"Bloody hell," he said. "Better make that twenty."

| 2 |

Spencer poured himself what little remained of the tequila and contemplated ordering a second bottle just for himself, knowing that with Guy, time was all too relative and that twenty minutes could easily turn into twenty hours—but thought better of it. He looked around for the server and in doing so caught sight of Rajeev approaching from the hotel lobby. Rajeev waved and smiled—his teeth a brilliant white against his golden-hued skin—and not for the first time Spencer was struck by the flawless beauty of the man. On looks alone, Rajeev Gupta could have been a Bollywood superstar, but instead Rajeev seemed content enough to run his seaside karaoke bars here on the balmy shores of the Indian Ocean while lending Spencer the occasional hand when business matters—both private and professional—required another set of eyes and ears on the ground.

"Looking good, *mere dost!*" Rajeev exclaimed as he arrived at Spencer's table, ivory veneers flashing. He sat down on the chair previously occupied by Guy. "Good to see you survived last night at least relatively unscathed. Mate, that was sick!"

Spencer nodded and decided he might as well order another round. He motioned to the server for another bottle.

"Where's Guy off to then?" Rajeev said. "I'd say he's looking more than a little worse for wear, but then Guy's always on the brink, isn't he? Fuck if I know how that bastard keeps going."

The server presented them with another bottle of Fortaleza and two new glasses. Spencer poured without asking Rajeev whether he was partaking.

"Hair of the dog?" Rajeev said as they clinked glasses and knocked back.

"Something like that," Spencer grumbled.

Rajeev beamed, his teeth positively blinding. Spencer couldn't look at him. He fiddled with the brim of his hat, pulling it down low over his eyes despite the fact that the sun was partially masked behind clouds. For reasons Spencer couldn't—or wouldn't—articulate, he found himself increasingly fidgety in Rajeev's company: the infuriating charm of the guy. His smile alone—Rajeev had once been a teeth model for an Indian advertising agency on a television advert created to encourage poor Indians to better oral hygiene—gave Spencer feelings that rather disturbingly resembled those he had once experienced whenever he saw Chloe: butterflies in the stomach, a mild to severe case of the sweats, an inability to form words let alone complete sentences. It was happening to him again now. The tequila helped but it could only cut the edge so far...

"I'm worried about him," Spencer stammered.

"Who? Guy?" Rajeev's smile was replaced ever so briefly with a flash of something resembling concern. "Other than ruining Bonnie Tyler for the semi-civilized world—and fuck, mate, that was awful, painful, I don't know if I'll ever recover!—what else has he gone and done?"

"He's losing it. Seriously losing it."

"What?"

"Have you seen his tattoo?"

"He got a tattoo?" Rajeev erupted in a burst of hearty laughter that was as infectious as his smile. "You don't say? Fuck me. Well, what of it? Lots of people have tattoos."

"It's not the fact that he got a tattoo that's the issue."

"No?"

"He's got a fucking silhouette of Svetlana Slutskaya on his arm."

"The Black Widow of Sochi?"

"Now do you see why this concerns me?"

Rajeev frowned, thought a moment, and then shrugged. "Not really. She's fucking fit. What's the problem?"

Spencer poured another shot and considered just taking the bottle and guzzling it down. Sometimes Rajeev was so goddamned opaque.

"You don't have any idea, do you?"

Rajeev shrugged. "I'm a simple man living a simple life in paradise," he said. "I don't ask questions. I don't know anything about Svetlana Slutskaya beyond what I've read in the society pages. That's my sister's world, mate, not mine. For all I know, Bips and Miss Slutskaya could be taking high tea at the Wolseley right this second. I don't know. I don't care. That's why Bipasha's in London and I'm livin' la vida loca right here. Now if I should be concerned that our mate got drunk and got a tattoo of the aforementioned Russian femme fatale on his arm or his arse or wherever the fuck you said, then you're going to need to enlighten me. Otherwise, I'll take my ignorance with a side of bliss, thank you very much."

The annoying thing about Rajeev was that he never took anything seriously. He'd always been like that. Even in school, Rajeev had projected a 'fuck-all' irreverence that, while certainly not without its charm, was more often than not bloody inconvenient. Of the three—Guy, Rajeev, and himself—Spencer liked to think he was the most 'present', the most 'woke.' He was the glue that held the boys together. Guy had the smarts and the looks but his libido tended to get the better of him, and usually with rather unfortunate results. The now infamous tattoo of Svetlana Slutskaya was only the most obvious manifestation of what was proving to be a disaster of international proportion.

And while Rajeev certainly had his uses—he was an invaluable officer in the field with a contact list second to none, not the least of which was his sister, Bipasha, a woman who could certainly give the Black Widow a run for her money: beautiful but deadly. How deadly Spencer couldn't even begin to imagine, although he'd read her MI-6 file and wondered whether Rajeev was as ignorant of his sister's predilection for the dark arts as he claimed —his inability to grasp the gravity of almost every potentially sticky situation (of which there were many) cast him as a bit of a liability in Spencer's opinion. Of course, Spencer's frustrations where Rajeev was concerned ran deeper than professional aggravation. A steady diet of repression had sustained him for forty years. He wasn't about to indulge an alternative...not now and probably (God willing) not ever.

And while Spencer knew he had his flaws—repressed or otherwise—he counted on himself to keep calm, carry on and muddle through. *See it. Say it. Sorted.* What choice did he have? He often thought he'd been born too late. Many a drunken idle afternoon had been spent wondering whether he mightn't have been happier working his way up the ranks of British India or holed up in Churchill's bunker smoking cigars with the great man himself whilst the Blitz rained down from above. Spencer Hawksworth was a man of God, king, and country in a time and place where these values seemed weighted with lesser and lesser significance. He hated that, hated that tradition was regarded with such low esteem, where basic kindness and decent, responsible behavior were viewed with suspicion and outright hostility. But even as Spencer conceded the alcohol made him a little sloppy at times, he craved order above almost anything else. And the more he sought a restitution of self-pride and morality, the greater his disappointment and the more pronounced his heartbreak.

"There's five hundred thousand in cash of various denominations stashed in a Louis Vuitton messenger bag in Guy's room," Spencer forced himself to attend to the matter at hand, leaning forward and lowering his voice in an attempt to press upon Rajeev the importance—not to mention confidentiality—of the situation.

"Five hundred thousand?" Rajeev exclaimed. "That's it? All this cloak and dagger shit for five hundred fucking thousand dollars? It's barely worth getting out of bed for. What's Guy playing at? Who's he low-balling?"

"It doesn't matter," Spencer replied. "All that matters is that it's accounted for and safely tucked away in a place where no one else can get to it."

"And I suppose that's where I come in?"

"Bingo."

"Crikey."

Spencer shrugged and poured them both another round. He and Rajeev slugged them back in one synchronous motion. Rajeev held his glass out for another hit. Spencer all too willingly obliged.

"You have to give me something here," Rajeev said. "I know you're a spook and all that but I have to look out for myself too, you know. Unlike you government twats I actually value my life. Why the fuck do you think I've pitched my tent all the way out here? It's not because I fuckin' love Mother India. I mean, I do but that's kind of beside the point, innit? I didn't go to fuckin' Harrow to run karaoke bars and tattoo parlors on the beach or to give refuge to fuckin' Bangladeshi fugitives on the run from human traffickers and sweatshop slave drivers, right? I mean, I know I just said this was paradise, but have you really taken a look around here, Spencie? You don't even have to scratch the surface to see this place is a fuckin' shithole."

Spencer didn't say anything. He knew the truth about Rajeev, or rather he knew why his best mate from Harrow had exiled himself to this particular sandy corner of the world. It was all in the file – the rumors confirmed: Bipasha Gupta was a force unto herself. He poured himself and Rajeev another round and waited for Rajeev to talk himself out. This was the routine. It didn't vary much. Rajeev gabbed and Spencer drank and Rajeev gabbed some more and Spencer drank some more and then when Rajeev had nothing left to say—when he finally realized that protestation got him nowhere, as it never did—he took a final giant gulp of whatever libation was most immediately at hand, they shook hands, and business carried on as usual. This was the routine and Spencer had long since mastered the art of patience.

"I need to give Sunny Joy a raise," Rajeev said.

"Then give her a raise."

"It's not right what those bastards did to her."

Spencer shrugged. He knew there was more to that story.

"She's a loyal employee."

"I've never doubted that," Spencer said. "She's a gem."

"Even though she really can't sing. But the crowds seem to love her. Especially the Australians for some reason."

"Fuck the Australians."

"So I'm just holding onto this cash? Putting it somewhere safe so the baddies don't get to it?"

"Pretty much."

"How long for?"

"Until I tell you otherwise."

"And who are the baddies this time? The usual suspects?"

"It's like 1985 all over again...except worse. Our parents had it easy."

Rajeev nodded.

"I assume the Black Widow has something to do with it?"

Spencer's mobile buzzed. He glanced at it.

Where's Guy? I've called and WhatsApped and texted multiple times and he still doesn't respond. I know you're there with him. Please. It's important. Tell Guy his sister needs to speak to him. Your friend for life, Chloe. XO.

"Your friend for life..."

"It's best you don't ask any more questions," he said. The bottle was empty. It was time to move on. Spencer worried he wouldn't be able to peel himself up off the chair.

"I get it," Rajeev said. "Never mind the fact that our mate almost fuckin' destroyed my place of business last night. But there's always been a bit of a double standard with you, at least where the great Guy Templeton is concerned."

"I'm sure I don't know what you're talking about."

But Spencer knew perfectly well. This was an old argument dating back to school days. As much as he'd integrated himself into *Tatler* society, where race was concerned, Rajeev carried a chip on his shoulder the size of the sub-continent. Of course Spencer had never really paused to consider what it might be like to be the only brown-skinned gentlemen in a room full of white-skinned toffs—he'd never been much for introspection—but as far as he was concerned, Rajeev looked to be doing pretty well for himself. Spencer was almost certain that if the roles were reversed, and he was the one living a life of leisure on the sandy beaches of a tropical paradise surrounded by beautiful Bollywood starlets, billionaire Arabian socialites and white Anglo-European supermodels, he'd find very little cause for complaint. If he were to delve even deeper—which again would have been highly uncharacteristic—Spencer might have observed that for all of Rajeev's post-colonial angst, Goa's most eligible bachelor came from a caste that had a history of subjugating its darker-skinned countrymen and sending its elite to England's most exclusive schools. When it suited him, Rajeev was whiter and more Anglo than Spencer or Guy or any of their peers combined. But of course such observations—while privately acknowledged—were never tacitly expressed, not if Spencer wanted to stay on Rajeev's good side and benefit from the man's not ungenerous largesse. If that made him a hypocrite, then so be it. The alternative was certainly less convenient.

"I'm going upstairs," Spencer said. "I trust you'll be on call this evening and that I can rely upon you to take care of what we discussed?"

Rajeev stood and gave Spencer an exaggerated bow. "As ever I am your most humble servant, *sahib*," he said.

"Get stuffed."

Rajeev's smile in parting lacked the warmth of their greeting. "May I remind you," he said, "that there's more of us in the world than there are of you. We've already risen up once. We'll rise again."

"And we'll always be there to pick up the pieces...until we're not."

Spencer winked, doffed his hat, and strolled along the verandah with an air of comfortable smugness that, in truth, was more feigned than genuine. In truth, he was feeling more than a little unnerved, and not solely because of Guy's seeming carelessness or the fact that he had documentary evidence that Svetlana Slutskaya and her merry band of Death Angels was on the move. What he hadn't told Guy was that of late he'd received a rather alarming barrage of WhatsApps from Chloe, none of which divulged any information other than a cryptic kind of urgency, all of which implored Spencer to tell Guy to call his sister post-haste. Had things gone a little less awkwardly the last time he'd seen his best mate's earnest but still undeniably fetching little sister, Spencer might have been inclined to pursue things with Guy in this regard a little more vociferously. In the moment, the money and Svetlana had just seemed of greater import.

And while Chloe had time and again demonstrated a rather uncompromising tenacity—which had taken her from the Amazon to 10 Downing Street, the United Nations, Sadr City, and Dhaka to the Knesset and back—in all the years Spencer had observed the dynamic between her and Guy (which while loving had never been without its contentious side) he had never known Chloe to pursue communication with her brother with the bloody-minded determination he now observed. Something must be up, he reckoned, something of dire importance. And yet he couldn't quite bring himself to respond, at least not now, not in light of what she had said to him that rainy London evening at Rules over bottles of French red after that dreary reception at the British Museum for the Crown Prince of some Godforsaken sub-Saharan kingdom, the night she had broken his heart… for yes, that is exactly what she had done with the same mercenary determination with which she sought to right the world's wrongs. Spencer knew he would never find it within himself to forgive her, and he hated himself for it, even now. Spencer was living proof that, despite the durable cliché, time does not indeed heal all wounds.

| 3 |

"You really are such a dear," Chloe said as Spencer helped her out of her rain-speckled Burberry raincoat and handed it to the coat check attendant before pulling Chloe's chair back and seeing her safely into her seat. "I don't know what I'd have done without you. You're my hero and my savior. I mean seriously. Whatever his virtues—and, believe me, the man is extraordinary. I could never take that away from him. Have you read his memoir? My God, the fact that he survived all those days living on nothing but the semi-digested cud of his family's dead camel—that he had to cut the fluids out of the camel's abdomen no less with little more than a flint, his fingernails and sheer determination—well, it's nothing short of a testament to the strength and power of the human will! No one appreciates that. It's shocking. It keeps me awake at night but we're such a consumer-oriented me-centric society that unless average and ordinary people like you and me stand up and insist that people like the Prince have a voice and their stories get heard, well, there's little hope left for humankind, is there?"

Spencer nodded and considered the wine menu.

Chloe went on: "But none of that detracts from the fact that, at least out of his element, he is a bit of a lech."

"Shall we order a bottle?"

"Oh, yes, please. But nothing too expensive. It just seems a bit extravagant to spend so much on luxury when there are so many people in the world struggling with the cost of living. I mean, I can't relate of course, but you have to acknowledge it's a worry...for most people, if not necessarily for us."

Spencer wanted to say that he didn't really consider a bottle of claret (and a decidedly mid-priced one at that) to be a luxury—a necessity, more like—but judging from what he sensed to be Chloe's mood he didn't want to provoke her, not when he had something very definite and perhaps life-defining to say to her, if only she'd let him get a word in edgeways. He merely nodded again and pointed to the selection on the menu when the server came round to take their drinks order.

"We'll have that one,"

"I'm sure he means well," Chloe said.

"Who means well, darling?"

Spencer noticed the slight twitch at the corners of Chloe's mouth, which he knew from experience meant she was on the verge of getting annoyed. He'd have to play it cool.

"The Prince!" she exclaimed. "Who did you think?"

Spencer shrugged. "Of course," he said. "The Prince."

"His Christian name is John."

Spencer shrugged.

"I'm sure it's a cultural thing. I mean the man has three wives! Who's to say he's not on the hunt for a fourth?"

"Indeed," Spencer said.

"I think his father had a total of seven wives before he died and he was ninety-something. The Prince can't be much over thirty-five."

"He's got a long way to go then."

"Precisely! And there's longevity in the family."

The server returned with their bottle and two glasses. Spencer stared at his cuticles and realized he couldn't remember the last time he'd had a proper manicure. He felt Chloe's gaze on him while the server went through the extended and overly elaborate ritual of uncorking the bottle. He wondered why she was so fixated on the prince with the unpronounceable surname.

The problem with Chloe, Spencer thought, is that she existed on a higher plane. What made her so admirable was her tireless devotion to righting the world's wrongs through her own personal efforts as well as through those of the various organizations and NGOs she belonged to, not the least of which was her foundation—Sisters Against Sweat Shops, more colloquially known as SASS— that Spencer himself had helped set up. It seemed to him that Chloe was so devoted to her work that it left little room for anything or anyone else.

In all the years Spencer had known her—going on now almost thirty—he suspected he could count on one hand the number of gentlemen in which Chloe had expressed even the remotest amount of interest, if even that. And it wasn't as though she hadn't had her fair share of suitors. He'd kept count, holding his tongue to the point of it being painful because giving voice to a 'thing' for one's best mate's kid sister just wasn't done. Not that he necessarily thought Guy would have a problem with it. Guy was fairly progressive that way. Spencer also knew of himself that he was a far superior candidate to any of the others. How could Chloe not respond favorably to him?

Yet, with so much going in his favor, Spencer had chosen to keep his feelings for Chloe unrequited. Perhaps it felt safer this way? Despite (or perhaps because of) his chosen line of work, Spencer Hawksworth wasn't someone who felt overly comfortable taking risks. With the world in such a precarious state—and so much of it out of his control—why tempt fate with what he *could* control when the status quo wasn't really all that terrible? Sure, he might never realize the aching love he felt for her, might never feel her heart pounding in unison with his against his chest, or taste her lips as they brushed across his mouth in the heat of a lover's embrace, or be able to run his fingers through her short, practical but always stylish Pixie-like hair as she surrendered herself to him heart and soul. But at least he had the fantasy. God forbid, he tell her how he really felt and find himself rejected. Spencer didn't think he'd be able to cope.

"Spencer?"

He looked up from inspecting his fingernails. Chloe was regarding him over the rim of her wine glass, her brow furrowed with a trace of what looked to be concern. She seemed relieved when he met her gaze, taking a sip of the wine and letting it linger in her mouth before swallowing. Spencer picked up his glass and did the same. They tasted the wine without speaking, the quiet between them strangely welcome—at least as far as Spencer was concerned, for it gave him pause to consider what he wanted to say to her and how best to say it. He sensed Chloe knew something was up as she wasn't particularly prone to extended silences, and while Spencer couldn't have said how long it had been since she had last spoken, something in her expression and the way she was staring at him—half-quizzical/half-amused (or was it alarm that registered on her perfectly porcelain face?)—betrayed that however long the silence, it was stretching well past her comfort zone.

"The wine's not bad," he said. "Fairly dry, not too fruity." He raised the glass to his nose and sniffed. "The bouquet is actually quite nice—cherry and the faintest whiff of dark chocolate. All in all, an extremely satisfying wine at bargain cost, no less. *D'accord?*"

Chloe took another sip—her eyes never leaving his—and considered it for another moment before swallowing. "It's corked," she said. "Are we really just going to sit here and talk about the wine all evening?"

"No…I was just…making an observation. It's a nice bottle of wine. It doesn't taste corked to me."

She rolled her eyes and looked out the window.

"I'm sorry, darling," Spencer said, suddenly feeling on the defensive. "Perhaps my palate isn't as developed as yours."

Chloe shook her head but didn't avert her gaze from the window. Spencer knew things weren't going well and that unless he acted quickly and with enormous delicacy, the opportunity could be lost to him forever. He took a rather more generous gulp of wine—alcohol never failed to bring him fortitude, corked or otherwise—but then he noticed, just as he was about to plunge right in with what had been plaguing him all evening, that a single tear had formed in the corner of her left eye. She sniffled and blinked and he watched the tear break and trickle down her cheek. He fought the hasty impulse to wipe it away with his serviette, an action that whilst well intentioned he suspected would be greeted with a fair amount of irritation given what seemed to be Chloe's present mood. Instead he remained quiet and finished what was left in his glass before pouring another.

"I don't know why I bother," Chloe said after what felt like an eternity.

"Darling, if I've said something to upset you, I really wish you'd tell me," he replied, sounding perhaps a bit testier than he intended. "I can't fix the problem if I don't know what it is."

Chloe shot him a look that told him he'd put his foot in it.

"This isn't about you," she snapped. "My God, you and Guy are exactly the same. You can't see past the ends of your noses."

"I'm only trying to help," Spencer said.

"I don't need your help."

Spencer reached for the bottle but was stopped short when he saw the look of anguish in Chloe's tear-smudged eyes. His hand gripped round the neck of the bottle but he couldn't move his arm to pour. He wanted to reach across the table and wipe the sadness from her eyes, tell her how much he loved her and how he wanted to devote the rest of his life to making her happy. It gutted him to see her so sad. But he was afraid. He wondered, as he often did in situations such as these, what would Guy do? His best mate never seemed at a loss for a plan of action, even if those actions weren't necessarily always the best course taken. At least Guy made things happen. Spencer felt of himself that he was too much a product of his class. While Guy seemed able to rise with effortless ease above family and environment, time and again Spencer felt stuck in the trenches of history. He had hoped Chloe, with her unflagging devotion to philanthropy and the betterment of the lives of the 'have-nots', might help him overcome what he had come to view as his tragic flaw. But lately it seemed his lifeline was slipping away. And what made it worse is that she clearly had no idea how much he absolutely relied on her to save him from himself.

"Go on," she said, motioning to the wine bottle gripped in his fist. "Don't hold back on my account. Far be it from me to stand between a man and his drink."

"When you say it like that..."

"Go on! Why pretend otherwise? And while we're at it, we might as well order a second bottle." She snapped her fingers at the server. "Excuse me. It seems we're having a liquid dinner tonight. Another bottle, if you please, and preferably one that's actually drinkable."

"Now you're making me feel bad."

"It's a wonder I don't become an alcoholic like everyone else," Chloe sniffed. "It seems *de rigueur* these days. I should feel positively outmoded without a drink in my hand. Maybe I really ought to take a cue from Penelope? Although, Lord knows, alcohol isn't my sister-in-law's only crutch."

"Is that what's got you so upset?" Spencer asked. "My drinking?"

Chloe fluttered her hand at him and returned her attention to the passersby outside. Spencer poured himself another glass—feeling ever so guilty for doing so—and decided to see if he could outlast her silence. He studied her profile and was once again struck by her perfection. Chloe Templeton wasn't a knockout—at least not by Guy's standards—but to Spencer, hers was a beauty that would withstand the test of time. She was delicate and pale but by no means weak. The tip of her nose pointed up with the slightest hint of impudence. Her lips were perhaps a tad thin—in later life she might benefit from a collagen injection or two—but, as they were now, Spencer imagined them to be perfectly kissable. Her eyes were a blue that changed to pale green depending on the colors she was wearing and her hair was soft and blonde with the faintest trace of red. Spencer had been horrified nine months ago when she'd come back from Mali—where she'd launched her foundation—with a completely shaved head. She said she'd done it out of solidarity with the poor African women and children she'd rescued from sexual slavery and sweatshops. Spencer had failed to see what shaving one's head had to do with anything, but he'd refrained from comment.

"I'm sorry," she said, breaking the silence, as he had known she eventually would. "I'm being unreasonable."

"Not at all."

"Penelope is the last person on earth I would ever look to as an example."

The server arrived with their second bottle. Spencer told him to leave it. He'd see to the uncorking when they were ready.

"The injustice of the world overwhelms me," Chloe went on, still not looking at him. She pressed her forehead against the window. "There's so much work to be done and I can only do so much. Of course I appreciate Prince John's contribution to SASS but I can't help but think his intentions aren't 100 percent above board and I'm certainly not in the market to be anyone's eighth wife."

Spencer nodded reassuringly and placed his hand over Chloe's on the table, resting it there ever so gently, secretly thrilling at the warmth emanating from her skin.

"And I'm worried about money and this damn fundraiser next month. I can't let our sponsors know how desperately we need cash and I've completely staked my reputation on the success of this foundation. Papa begged me not to do it. He told me it would be like this. He said it would only bring me grief because most people—at least most people with money—don't really give a shit about Africa (unless it's Malawi or somewhere equally godforsaken) or poor people. They feign interest and open their pocketbooks and jump onto the hash tag bandwagon when they think it'll give them a favorable mention in *Hello* and *OK!*, but when all is said and done, when a new 'it' cause arrives on the scene, they'll abandon me like last night's leftovers and move on to the next. Hash tag screwed. Are you going to open that bottle or are you waiting for me to do it?"

Spencer jumped to attention.

"And as if that wasn't all," Chloe continued, "Papa had a bad turn over the bank holiday."

"I'd heard," Spencer said. The cork gave a healthy 'pop!' and he poured them each an equally healthy glassful.

"Luckily Papa's cardiologist was one of our houseguests at the weekend so Papa was properly looked after. I couldn't abide that woman waiting to choke the last living gasp out of him. Diana just turns a blind eye."

"That woman," Spencer said. He hoped his tone matched Chloe's distaste. Lady Eliza – Lord Carleton's partner, for lack of a more appropriate term, and the true bane of Chloe's existence.

"And as for that pedophile. You know, she's not even a real nun?"

Sister Francine. Now there was a piece of work.

"I only came back to London for the event tonight, then it's back to Dorset on the train tomorrow afternoon. Carbon footprint and all that. I'm starting to think Sister Francine is the greater threat. I really do need to have a word with Diana."

"Tomorrow afternoon?"

Chloe frowned. "Why do you say it like that?"

Spencer shook his head. He dabbed at imaginary red wine splotches on the white tablecloth.

"Spencer?

"I never get to see you is all," he said. "If you're not in Africa you're in some remote village in the Northwest Province of Pakistan playing Russian roulette with the Pakistani Taliban or in some Syrian refugee camp in Turkey getting your picture taken pulling earthquake victims out of the rubble..."

"It's my job," she said, sounding more than slightly miffed. "It's what I do."

"I know. I know. I just..."

"And it's not as if you're so easy to pin down."

"You're right. I just wish..."

"What?"

It was now or never, Spencer thought. He wondered whether she had an inkling of the effect she had on him...

"The thing is," he stammered.

"Yes?"

"We've known each other for...how long would you say?"

Chloe shrugged and sipped her wine. "Decades," she replied. "As long as I've been conscious of time."

"Precisely."

"So?"

"So..." Spencer cleared his throat. She wasn't making it easy for him. He drained his glass and instinctively reached for the bottle, but Chloe beat him to it and held it away from him, just out of reach.

"This wine really is rather nice," she said. "I'm rather glad I ordered a second bottle. You hogged the first. I'm keeping the second for myself."

"I thought you said the first was corked?"

"This one's much nicer."

Chloe smiled and filled her glass almost to the rim. If she had been any other girl Spencer might have thought she was playing him. But as it was Chloe he couldn't help but think she was utterly unaware of the intoxicating effect she had on him.

"The thing is, Chloe," he began. "I can't stop thinking about you."

She laughed.

"No, really, I mean...I really can't stop thinking about you. It's like...it's like you haunt me: all day, every day, all night, every night. I can't get you out of my mind."

Spencer watched her smile fade and his heart sank. Chloe just looked at him, her brow poised between a frown and a not-frown while her eyes gazed at him with a look that wasn't exactly encouraging nor was it altogether dismissive. One hand gripped round the stem of her wine glass while the other held the bottle by its neck, hovering just over the tablecloth, as though frozen between decision and indecision. Spencer instantly regretted saying anything but now that he'd let the proverbial cat out of the bag, he could think of no alternative but to press ahead and hope the humiliation wouldn't be as severe as he imagined.

"I'm in love with you, Chloe," he said.

Chloe cleared her throat and darted a glance out the window.

"Well, that's...something," she said.

She poured herself a glass. Her hands trembled. Spencer leaned forward, intending to take her free hand and press it to his lips, but she pulled away. He grasped at her fingertips in what he knew was a futile attempt at ardor and then quickly desisted when she cleared her throat again and fiddled with the strand of pearls around her neck, looking everywhere it seemed but at him.

"Say something," he implored. "Surely, my feelings for you aren't completely unwarranted?"

"I don't know what to say," she said. "What does one say in situations like these?"

"Have I completely stuck my foot in it?"

"Well…" Chloe rather sloppily gulped her wine. "The thing is…your timing is really rather unfortunate. As you know…as we've just been talking about… Papa is…is…very unwell. SASS is such a struggle. I've got yet another round of fundraising because the first didn't go quite according to plan, and…erm…I was going to ask your assistance in locating my rather errant older brother because I haven't heard from him in ages, and Papa is asking that he come home, and you wouldn't happen to know where Guy is, would you? Let's talk about Guy, shall we? He's not answering my WhatsApps or my voice-notes. He never answers his mobile and I'm decidedly caught between a rock and a hard place because Papa is really quite insistent that Guy come home and I don't know what to do, and I think it's just best if we table this conversation forever. Would that be all right with you?"

Thud.

"Oh."

"You're very sweet, Spencer, and I am of course flattered that you would…that you would think so highly of me…in that regard—"

"But?"

"But I do think it's best we leave things between us as they are…as they have always been. We've known each other since we were children. I've come to regard you as…as family—"

"As another brother?"

"Precisely. And I ask you—I beseech you, actually—to find it within yourself to look upon me as you would a beloved younger sister."

"And if I can't?"

Chloe twisted the pearls around her finger with such an intensity Spencer feared the strand would break. He poured himself another glass of wine and downed it like a shot of not-very-good tequila. It left a rather nasty aftertaste.

"In that case then, I must ask that we downgrade our relations to that of business associates," she said.

"Really."

"You'll always have a special place in my heart, Spencer. Our families have too much shared history. And of course you're Guy's best friend so we're always going to be a part of each other's lives…which is why I need you to find my him—though

I suspect you probably know where he is—and tell him he needs to come home. You will do that for me, won't you? Regardless of whatever you may—or may not be—feeling towards me at this particular moment..."

Her expression was cold, steely, determined. This was Chloe the businesswoman: Chloe the internationally renowned philanthropist and socialite, accustomed to getting what she wanted when she wanted it, never mind the fact that without her family's deep pockets supporting her—and those of certain patrons, not the least of which was himself—all her charitable causes and foundations would have been dead on arrival. But Spencer didn't want to go there. He didn't want to resent her, though he did. He told himself she simply didn't know any better even as he knew, when one scratched the surface, that she wasn't much more than an entitled socialite. The flipside of love was hate. Spencer preferred not to hate Chloe Templeton, yet he couldn't help but feel she'd emasculated him. She'd manipulated his affection to the benefit of her cause, and the moment he'd outworn his usefulness, she cast him off. Not that that's what she was doing. Spencer wanted to believe the best of her. He had spent the greater part of his life, after all, head over heels in love with her. But if she could turn on him so easily, he wondered, had she only been using him all along?

"So we have an understanding then?" she said.

"About Guy?"

"It's only ever been about Guy," she replied. "Remind him he has a responsibility to this family. Tell him it's time he came home. We need to bring the family together. We need to rally around Papa."

Chloe raised her glass in a mini-toast before finishing what remained of her wine. Spencer did the same.

"Shall we order food?" Chloe asked. "I'm not at all hungry—too many canapés at that reception. But if you want to eat, by all means have at it. I know how you like your roast."

Spencer realized this was his cue to bow out with what little remained of his dignity. Yet despite it all he couldn't deny the fact that he was really rather famished. He knew Chloe was expecting him to do the gentlemanly thing and ask the server for their check, which he would have done had the atmosphere not suddenly (conveniently some might say) become permeated with the unmistakable scent of Chanel No. 5. He glanced up, ostensibly to hail their waiter, only to see the woman he knew to be the wearer of the classic perfume standing in the entrance of the restaurant in her calf-length Burberry raincoat, matching fedora perched on her head in its customary jocular tilt, fiery red hair flaming down to her shoulders, her lips pursed and painted a deliciously alarming shade of crimson.

Spencer's breath caught in his throat.

"Yvette!' he gasped.

"*Mon cher*!" Yvette strode toward their table, arms outstretched in front of her as though to fold the entire world in her embrace. Spencer stood up to welcome her. They air kissed in the French style and hugged. Her body felt snug against his. He gently squeezed her to him, finding himself instantly aroused by the taut litheness of her body, pleasingly framed by her black wool turtleneck, black skinny jeans, and brown knee-length riding boots. All she needed, he thought, was a crop to further exacerbate his fantasies. He pressed his nose to her neck and inhaled.

"*Comment vas-tu*?" he asked. "*Je ne savais pas que vous étiez à Londres*!"

"*Oui, oui. Je vais bien. Je vais bien,*" Yvette stepped back to appraise him from head to toe. "You look well," she said. "You've lost a bit of weight, *non*? I approve."

"And you look as *tres chic* as ever!"

Yvette tossed her head back and erupted in a throaty laugh that seemed to reverberate throughout the crowded restaurant. They were causing a bit of a commotion, but Spencer didn't care. Yvette Devereux certainly knew how to make an entrance.

"You flatter me!" she said. "I only just arrived this afternoon on the train from Paris and I'm afraid I haven't yet bathed."

Chloe cleared her throat. He'd nearly forgotten her.

"Pardon me," Spencer said, reluctantly forcing himself to turn his attention back to his dining partner who sat there with a tight and disapproving smile. "In the excitement of seeing you, Yvette, I'm afraid I've quite neglected to introduce my companion this evening. Chloe Templeton, this is—"

"Yvette Devereux," Chloe said. "We've met."

"Yes, yes...of course you have," Spencer spluttered.

Yvette extended her hand. "*Enchanté*...as always."

Chloe nodded and gave Yvette's hand a tepid squeeze. "*D'accord,*" she said before knocking back what remained of her wine.

Yvette laughed. Spencer couldn't help himself. The enmity between the two women was palpable and it rather thrilled him.

"It seems I'm interrupting your evening," Yvette said. "*J'désolé*. I won't keep you. I just happened to be passing by and saw you and had to pop in to say hello."

"Don't even think of not at least staying for a drink." Spencer commandeered an empty chair from the table beside theirs and placed it at a somewhat awkward angle next to his own. "Surely, you're not in such a hurry that you can't indulge us with the pleasure of your company for a glass of wine? Chloe and I were just about to order another bottle. Weren't we, Chlo?"

Chloe shrugged. "The more the merrier," she said.

"Well, in that case..." Yvette plunked down in the chair between them. She removed her fedora and ran her fingers through her hair so it splayed across her shoulders. Spencer couldn't take his eyes off the contrast between the pale white of the Frenchwoman's skin and the jet-black of her turtleneck. Chloe once again directed her attention out the window.

"How long has it been?" Spencer snapped his fingers at their server and mimed for another bottle. "Ages and ages."

"Three summers. Saint Tropez."

"Of course! That Russian bloke's party."

"Chechen. The yacht."

"Miroslav Borosovic."

"*Oui.*"

"And not long after that—"

"Poof!" Yvette clapped her hands together. "*Quelle surprise!*"

"Or not, depending on how one looks at it."

The wine arrived. Spencer waved the server away. "Allow me the honor," he said, brandishing the wine opener.

"Spencer likes to show off," Chloe said to no one in particular. She wouldn't meet Yvette's gaze. "Don't you, Spencer?"

Yvette smiled. "You must forgive me," she said. "Spencer and I have a tendency to get carried away when we're together. So many shared memories. I imagine it must be very inconvenient for you."

"Inconvenient?"

"What woman wants to share her lover with another woman, especially when the other woman has *une histoire* with the lover in question?"

"You're very much mistaken," Chloe snapped. "Spencer is very definitely not my 'lover.'"

"*Non?*" Yvette glanced from one to the other, her eyes wide, her lashes fluttering.

"Not for lack of trying," Spencer muttered. He ejected the cork with a satisfying 'pop' and poured. Chloe held her hand over her glass and shook her head.

Yvette laughed. "*Mes excuses*!" she exclaimed. "Forgive me. I just assumed."

"*Salut*!" Spencer said.

Yvette sipped her wine and made a show of letting it roll across her tongue. She held the glass to her nose, closed her eyes, and inhaled.

"*C'est bon, ne est ce pas?*" Spencer asked.

"Mmmm." Yvette took another sip and sighed. "*Ce est délicieux.* But then, I'd expect nothing less from you, Spencer. You've always been a man of exquisite taste. However *compliqué* the nature of your relationship, Chloe, it must be nice having such a refined man at your beck and call...and a civil servant to boot! Like James Bond, *ne c'est pas?*"

Chloe abruptly pushed her chair back and stood up. "I'm sorry," she said. "I just remembered I left some papers at the office."

Spencer frowned. "At this hour?" he asked.

"Yes."

"Can't they wait until morning? We're having such a nice evening—"

"You and Mademoiselle Devereux carry on—"

Yvette threw her head back and erupted with another burst of her trademark laugh. "You really do flatter me!" she exclaimed. "I haven't been *une mademoiselle* since at least before 9/11."

"Can I ring you a taxi?"

Chloe shook her head. "No, thank you. I'll walk."

"It's raining!"

"I survived the tsunami in Phuket. I think I can handle a bit of English drizzle."

"I don't like this, Chloe. I don't like this one bit. You're making me feel ungentlemanly."

"Enjoy your evening. And please, get ahold of my brother and tell him he must come home. If there's one thing you can do for me, Spencer, it's that. Good night."

Spencer watched Chloe hurry out the door. She stopped in front of their window and seemed to pause as though to compose herself before continuing on at a brisk clip. He polished off the wine in his glass without really tasting it. Yvette poured them both another.

"*Très intéressant*," she said after a moment. "*Ces machinations dangereuses!*"

"Come again?"

Yvette considered Spencer over the rim of her glass. If there was anything he'd learned about Yvette over the years it was that she was a woman of acute intelligence who, when push came to shove, typically had more than one ace up her sleeve, if not an entire deck. Yvette was nothing if not selective with what she shared about herself and her casework. He knew she'd put in her paces with the Marseille Police Department, rising to the rank of Chief Inspector in record time, an impressive feat made even more so by the fact that she was an attractive woman in a decidedly male environment. Of course, Spencer suspected, it didn't hurt that her father (now semi-retired in a village outside Nantes) was a Chevalier in the *Légion d'honneur,* awarded for his humanitarian work with the U.N. in Sarajevo in the '90s. A shrapnel-wound sustained during the siege had forced him into early retirement. As a young man, Claude Devereux had served in the French army, distinguishing himself on behalf of the *tricolor* in former French North Africa. An army brat, Yvette had spent her formative years in Tunis, Algiers, and Cairo before returning to France to attend the École Spéciale Militaire de Saint-Cyr where, like her father, she'd graduated at the top of her class. Now in her late-thirties, Yvette was an operative for the General Directorate for External Security in charge of keeping a tight lid on Islamic extremism both domestically and abroad, though this was of course strictly off the record and he had suspicions she also had business interests outside of the General Directorate.

Spencer had a grudging admiration for the feisty Frenchwoman. She excited and terrified him—excited because he'd never met a woman so self-assured and determined (both in the field and, it must be said, between the sheets) and terrified because she carried with her a reputation for being ruthless and, depending on whom one asked, of somewhat questionable ethics. They had had their share of run-ins over the years—of both the professional and horizontal kind. And while each of their encounters never failed to thrill him, Spencer always found that he was more than a little relieved when Yvette Devereux rode off into the sunset, her flaming red hair glinting in the rays of a setting sun. Over the years, he had also come to realize (and never fully appreciate) that when Yvette came to town, trouble was usually never far behind.

"Allow me to elaborate," she said, taking a sip of wine before setting her glass down on the table and patting her lips dry with the white linen serviette. Her lipstick left a crimson smear on the cloth. "*Il semble que nous sommes tous les deux à la recherche de la même personne.*"

"Really, Yvette, my French is a bit rusty," Spencer said. "And, admittedly, I am a wee bit drunk. Can we please stick to the Queen's – or rather the King's – English? I daresay you speak it better than I do."

Yvette glanced furtively about them. The restaurant was full. The din was loud and boisterous.

"But we are talking of sensitive matters, *ne c'est pas?*" she said. "It would be irresponsible of me to speak of such things when anyone around us might be listening to our *délibération, non?*"

"Frankly, I'm not sure I even know what we're speaking about."

Yvette smiled and shook her head. "Very well. I'll be blunt." She paused for dramatic effect. Spencer felt his heart start to race. He feared what was coming. "Guy Templeton is missing and I believe you know where he's hiding." She pronounced 'Guy' the French way: *Ghee.*

"I don't know what you're on about."

"Don't lie to me, Spencer. You're not very good at it."

"I'm not Guy's keeper."

"Even his sister doesn't know where he is. She asked you to tell him to come home. Why would she do that if you don't know where he is?"

"As the Americans say, I plead the Fifth."

"*Dieu merci, nous ne sommes pas Américains!*"

"English, s'il vous plait."

"How long have we known each other, Spencer?"

Spencer shrugged. "A long time," he said.

"*Exactement.* Which is why you know I always get what I want."

"What do you want, Yvette?"

"Where is Guy Templeton?"

"Who wants to know? Why does the French government have an interest in the whereabouts of an English national who, as far as I know, has no political affiliations, no ties to any terrorist organizations, and when one really gets down to it, hasn't the substance of a flea?"

Yvette poured herself another glass of wine. The bottle was near empty.

"I'll ask you one last time," she said. "*Où est Guy Templeton?*"

"Do you know what I think?" Spencer nodded to the server who presented him with the bill—a not untidy sum.

"*S'il vous plaît me éclairer.*"

"This isn't about Guy."

"*Non?*"

"*Non.* This is about his sister. Chloe. You're right, Yvette. We have known each other for a long time...a very long time. You've never forgiven her for what happened."

"Now I'm the one who doesn't know what you're talking about."

"Don't fuck with me, Yvette."

"*Seulement dans vos rêves.*" [Only in your dreams.]

Spencer handed the server his card. Yvette helped herself to the dregs of the bottle.

"It's well documented," Spencer said. "Your claim to fame. Your arrival, as it were...the only public blemish on your otherwise 'flawless' career. Those children almost died because of you, Yvette."

"*Je ne sais pas ce que vous parlez.*"

"If it hadn't been for Chloe, things would have gone very differently."

"*Oui.* I would have saved that poor girl's life. I would have brought her safely back to her parents."

"At the expense of eight other children! Eight other children whose lives were also being threatened in the worst way imaginable."

"I did what I had to do."

"Regardless of the cost."

Yvette shrugged. "I acted according to what I believed was right. I still hold to that belief. Chloe Templeton and others like her should leave law enforcement to the experts and stick to making posters and conning left wing millionaires into signing their petitions."

Spencer couldn't help but smile. While it bothered him to hear Chloe disparaged, he didn't necessarily disagree with Yvette's assessment of her. There was a time and a place for protest but even he had to admit Chloe often came a bit too close to crossing the line. He had warned her before—as had her father—that there were certain situations best left to the government, but Chloe had always possessed a formidable will and a rigid perspective where right and wrong was concerned. With Chloe, there was no gray area, and try as he and others had to get her to see otherwise, Chloe remained steadfast. It was no wonder Yvette and Chloe couldn't stand each other. They were two peas in a pod—albeit on opposite sides of every equation.

Spencer pushed back his chair and stood. It felt good to be up on his feet. He looked down at his watch—just past eleven-thirty. Bedtime, but that didn't necessarily mean he was ready for sleep. He helped Yvette into her coat and couldn't quite resist the urge to lean in and inhale her perfume. She didn't protest. He pressed himself against her. Spencer knew there was unfinished business between them. (There always was.) He knew her turning up at Rules that night wasn't mere coincidence. She'd intimated as much when she had asked him about Guy's whereabouts. The truth of the matter was he had a very vague idea of his best mate's comings and goings, but lately their communication hadn't been as consistent as in the past. The last time he and Guy had spoken they'd had a disagreement about some very unfortunate business pertaining to the British ambassador to Russia's daughter that still hadn't been satisfactorily resolved and, if things remained on their current trajectory, was threatening to turn into an international kerfuffle. Spencer had, of course, stepped in and tried to nip it in the bud before the media could ask too many questions. That's what he did best. But in doing so, he'd damaged the one relationship he'd always been able to rely on. He hoped it wouldn't prove irreparable. It certainly didn't help that, as a result, Guy had lately gone rogue. Personal feelings aside, Spencer had a duty to King and country. There were too many interests at stake. And the fact that Yvette Devereux was also looking for him didn't bode well. It didn't bode well at all.

"Where are you staying?" he whispered, pressing his nose into Yvette's ear. The smell of her was intoxicating.

"Tell me where Guy Templeton is," she said.

"*Coucher avec moi,*" he said.

Yvette pushed against him. His desire was painful. King and country aside, where matters of the flesh were concerned—at least as far as they involved Yvette—Spencer had difficulty restraining himself.

"Not here," she replied. "People are staring."

Yvette took his hand and with a quixotic smile led him out onto the street. The rain had stopped. Puddles reflected the yellowish glow of the streetlights. Spencer pulled Yvette toward him. If propriety hadn't been of such importance to him—at least when he was in London—Spencer wouldn't have thought twice about taking Yvette into the alley behind the restaurant and having her right there against the wall. They'd done it once before like that in the *Casbah* in Algiers. Afterwards they'd parted without a word. Two years had passed without contact. And then the kidnapping thing had happened and all hell had broken loose. But the damage had long since been done. Spencer felt it was time to rectify things.

"Your place or mine?" he persisted.

Yvette stepped back from him, her expression suddenly unreadable. She pursed her lips and tapped her forefinger against them. Her eyes sparkled even in the relative darkness.

"Where is Guy Templeton?" she said.

"I don't know."

"I don't believe you."

"When have I ever lied to you?"

She laughed. "When have you ever told me the truth?" she countered. "*Je sais. Je sais.* I know. It's simply the nature of what we do. We lie for a living, to others and—more often than either of us would ever care to admit—to ourselves."

Yvette adjusted her coat and pulled the fedora down low over her brow. The moment was passing. Spencer realized he would once again be going home alone ... or back to the office. The night was proving to be yet another failure: too much wine drunk, too much money spent, and nothing to show for it except a rapidly wilting hard-on and a bruised ego.

"I'm sorry you don't know the whereabouts of your friend," Yvette said, turning and walking slowly away from him. "It is most *incommode*. But I'll find him. The only question is, which of us will find him first?"

"Why do you need to know?" Spencer called after her. He didn't follow her. He knew there was no point.

Yvette raised her arms and answered him with an exaggerated shrug. "*Bon nuit, mon ami!*" she said over her shoulder before disappearing around the corner.

Spencer watched her go, poised between an urge to act on impulse and attempt to recreate the Algiers encounter and the slightly less impetuous—but no more assured—act of calling Chloe to see if she might be free for a nightcap somewhere near her office, if that was indeed where she'd been headed. But he decided instead to turn up the collar of his Barbour and walk in the direction of the Embankment. The rain had once again started to fall—a light but persistent drizzle that was more annoying than atmospheric. If anyone had stopped and asked him where he was off to at such a deliberate pace, Spencer would have been at a loss. *Nowhere in particular, he might say, or rather...nowhere in particular that I'm going to share with you.* Because, of course, Spencer knew exactly where he was going. And given the mood he was in as Yvette left him to fend for himself in the gathering wet and cold—broken-hearted and with his dick more-or-less in hand—Spencer could think of only one place that could restore (albeit temporarily) his lost sense of manhood. But exactly where—and what—this place was, well, in a line of work built on a bed of secrets, Spencer knew some secrets were simply too damaging not to keep...even from himself.

| 4 |

"I have a secret," Cordelia said.

They hadn't been at Krasnyy for more than forty-five minutes and already the ambassador's daughter was well on her way to getting sloppy drunk. At first it had all been rather amusing. Guy knew when he'd suggested they ditch the ballet and head to Moscow's most VIP nightclub that anything might (and probably would) happen. Unfortunately, however, he soon realized that he'd completely underestimated the amount the girl had had to drink. Innuendo was one thing, but when words became actions and the one doing most of the talking and acting was essentially the boss's daughter—who, whilst not quite jailbait, really wasn't all that much older—it didn't take long for Guy to realize that he was skirting the razor's edge.

He considered telling the driver to drop Cordelia at the ambassador's residence and then proceed on to the club alone, but one look at the girl was enough to convince him it was probably better for them both if he kept her well enough away from her father at least until she'd sobered up. And truth be told, if his intuition was correct—which it usually was even if his judgment was a tad off—he suspected he might actually need Cordelia as the night wore on. Thus, in the interim, he was willing to tolerate whatever nonsense she might throw his way—within reason— if it helped him to score the pot of gold he sensed was waiting for him at the end of the proverbial rainbow.

"Do you want to know what it is?" she asked.

"What?"

"My secret. Do you want me to tell you my secret?"

They were sitting in a banquette in the VIP section with an unobstructed view of the dance floor below. Russian death metal blasted from the high-tech sound system and the thump of the bass was sick and Guy felt it deep. His head was pounding from the champagne and vodka and the grinding almost dirty beat and he felt like he hadn't bathed in ages and he desperately wanted to fuck something hard while Moscow's elite bounced and thrashed with reckless abandon and grainy black-and-white images from snuff films projected on the ceiling and walls above and all around them. His eyes wouldn't focus and the stuttering strobe lights obscured both vision and identity. This was probably the worst place in Moscow he could have taken Cordelia—and he knew he'd pay for it later—but part of him really wanted to push propriety to its limit. He wanted to fuck with Cordelia if not fuck her outright, and if Svetlana Slutskaya turned up—as he fully expected her to—he would need Cordelia to finesse the introduction.

Seduction wasn't usually a problem for Guy. One look, one suggestive smile, one wink, a compliment however banal, was enough to charm even the most reserved of women straight into his bed. But Guy sensed Svetlana Slutskaya wasn't like most women. The way she carried herself—so self-aware, such *hauteur*—was indication enough that she knew what she wanted, what she was capable of, and when and how she wanted it. Guy knew he needed to be careful. He needed to play his cards right. He needed to be the submissive one—at least initially. But then he'd catch her unaware and the rest would be history.

However, until that moment arrived, he had Cordelia.

"If you tell me your secret," he said, turning to look at her and leaning close—too close—so she could hear him over the bass, "it won't be a secret anymore, will it?"

Cordelia grinned and sat back against the velvet cushions of the banquette. She grasped the bottle of vodka in one hand and raised it defiantly to her lips while the other teased the hem of her dress, pulling it ever so slightly above her knee while parting her legs this side of indiscretion. Guy forced himself to focus on her eyes, telling himself that whatever she did outside the periphery of his vision wasn't something he was a witness to and, therefore, couldn't be responsible for provoking. Technically, he reminded himself, she was of age. But he also suspected, despite her efforts to the contrary, that she was a virgin and he just wasn't in the market to be anyone's first. That's what he told himself anyway. Whether he could stick to his resolve was a whole different matter.

"I'm not wearing any knickers," she said.

"Is that your secret?" Guy asked, keeping his focus steady and strictly above the waist. "You'll have to do better than that."

"Do you want to see?"

"Not particularly."

"Why not?"

"Why do you think?"

"I don't know. Maybe you don't like girls."

"You're right."

"I don't believe you."

Guy shrugged. The music stopped. Sudden blackout and an eerie breathless silence descended on the club. His heart quickened. He felt a hand on his thigh. The silence lasted too long, though too long for a terrorist attack—perhaps a technical glitch? But no panic. Anticipation, yes. But no fear. Guy's pulse pounded in his ears. The hand on his thigh traveled up and up. His response was instinctive. He wondered if Cordelia had slipped something into his drink when he hadn't been looking, when he'd been scanning the crowd for a glimpse of Her. He was covered in sweat. He loosened his tie and then ripped it from his shirt. He was drowning. He needed relief.

And then a single spotlight: a blast of white light.

The bass: *Boom...boom...*

Electronic static. Artfully measured feedback.

Cordelia's fingers squeezed.

Boom...boom...

Guy blinked. His eyes slowly came into focus.

There she was: an apparition in the center of the dance floor swathed in black leather from veiled head to booted foot. Her face was upturned, pale skin stark against the harsh light. Her lips were painted black.

Her lips. Guy couldn't take his eyes off her lips.

The bass picked up speed: b*oom...ba-boom...ba-ba-boom...boom...* It was ferocious and primitive: an electronica *The Rite of Spring*.

Svetlana raised her arms in perfect time to the relentless, tribal pounding of the beat, and as she did so, she revealed the voluminous black cape she had worn at the ballet. It was attached to her wrists and as she lifted her arms above her head, the bass gave way to a shimmering synthesis of electronic pop and string arpeggios, and as she danced—seemingly oblivious to the world around her—the club erupted in a cacophonous roar that was both deafening and exhilarating and unlike anything Guy had ever experienced before.

"Slag," Cordelia snarled.

Svetlana commanded the dance floor as the lights swirled and the music seemed to transport her into another dimension. She danced with a choreographed precision that still managed to appear utterly spontaneous. Her eyes were closed and yet she stayed perfectly within her space as others filled in around her. She was a part of the EDM frenzy but separate from it, as though her movements were propelled by her own internal soundtrack.

"I've never seen anyone like her," he said.

"Humpf," Cordelia replied, removing her hand from his thigh and slumping back against the banquette with a dejected sigh. "I don't know what's so special about her. She's a bot."

"She's beautiful."

"If you like that sort of thing. I'm afraid I just don't understand men."

"You're young."

Cordelia pulled a face. "Not *that* young, Guy."

The song ended and the relative silence that followed was a relief to Guy's ears. Middle age was clearly taking effect. He stood up and leaned over the VIP balcony to get a better view of the emptying dance floor. Svetlana was nowhere to be seen. He was gripped by a sense of panic, an urgent need to find her. Guy knew it was madness, yet he couldn't help himself. He was bewitched.

"Are you looking for me?"

Guy immediately recognized the voice from their brief encounter in Red Square: a sultry purr that managed to be masculine in its timbre yet wholly feminine. He turned. There she was, standing in front of the banquette in a different costume to what she'd worn only moments before – a white leather jumpsuit that left nothing to the imagination. Her ebony black hair was pulled in a severe ponytail and held back by a leopard print scarf. She was even taller than he'd imagined, though her height was no doubt enhanced by the platform shoes she wore that resembled blocks of cement—very expensive blocks of cement. The contrast between her all-black get-up that had so attracted him at the opera and then just now on the dance floor, and this new look couldn't have been more dramatic. Either way, Svetlana Slutskaya was astonishing and he knew she knew it too.

He opened his mouth to speak, but no words came.

Svetlana smiled and held out her hand. Her nails were painted the same color as her hair and her lips.

"I'm Svetlana Slutskaya," she whispered, "though you probably know that already."

Guy took her hand and pressed it to his lips. It wasn't lost on him that her skin was cold to the touch.

"*Eto ochen' priyatno vstretit'sya s vami,*" he said. [It's very nice to meet you.] "*Ya Guy—*"

"Templeton. I know. And we can speak English. We don't want to alienate your little friend here. She's not looking very happy."

Svetlana turned to Cordelia who remained slumped in the banquette, arms folded across her chest, her bottom lip protruding in an indignant pout. Guy was almost embarrassed for the girl.

"What's wrong, little girl?" Svetlana asked. "Isn't it a bit past your bedtime? And on a school night too! Have you completed all your homework?"

"I'm not a child! I'm eighteen!"

Svetlana threw her head back and gave a loud throaty laugh.

"Allow me to introduce Cordelia Bingham," Guy said, finding not inconsiderable relief in the restoration of his powers of speech. "Ambassador Bingham's daughter—"

"*Da*. I know who she is too. I know everyone in this town...everyone worth knowing, that is. Are you going to buy me a drink or am I going to have to do it myself? I thought you English prided yourselves on your perfect manners. I have to say, I'm not so very impressed."

Svetlana slid into the banquette beside Cordelia who ignored her in favor of her mobile. A cocktail waitress appeared, different from the one that had served them before Svetlana's arrival, though equally as androgynous. Before Guy could place an order, a bottle of Dom Perignon White Gold was popped and two glasses were poured to overflowing. It was obvious Svetlana's presence had merited them an upgrade, though he shuddered to think at what cost.

"That's a two thousand pound bottle of bubbly," he said, more to himself than Svetlana, to whom price obviously meant very little.

"Only the best for Svetlana Slutskaya," she replied. "Or 'Lana' to those whom I favor."

"I hope one day I merit that favor."

"Hmmm." Svetlana sipped her Dom and traced her black-lacquered nail around its rim. "I'm very particular," she said.

"Whatever I can do to be of service."

"What about me?" Cordelia piped in, looking up from her mobile for the first time since Svetlana had joined them. She eyed their champagne with a look of hunger and childish resentfulness.

"What about you, little bird?" Svetlana leaned back against the cushions, elongating her body so that the white leather jumpsuit stretched and hugged her like a sheath. She tapped a finger against Cordelia's nose and traced her nail down the girl's cheek, teasing her lips before working her finger down Cordelia's chin and along the line of her neck. Guy watched the path of Svetlana's finger, in that moment finding himself more than a little envious of the eighteen year-old. He almost couldn't bear to watch. He drained his glass of champagne without tasting it and wiped his lips with the back of his hand. He noticed the cocktail waitress hovered over them, standing at attention, the bottle of Dom at the ready. Her expression was neutral. Her eyes were dead. He wondered what substance she was on.

"I would like some too," Cordelia whispered, her voice strangled in her throat. Svetlana's finger continued its journey, lingering over the girl's breasts, teasing her nipples through the filmy satin of her dress. Cordelia closed her eyes, gasped and squeezed her knees together. Guy crossed his legs and held his empty glass to the waitress for a refill.

"Good little girls don't drink champagne," Svetlana purred.

"Who says I'm a good little girl?"

"*Nyet*? Are you very naughty then?"

"Yes," Cordelia whimpered. "I try to be good but I have such dirty thoughts."

Svetlana laughed and rested back against the banquette, She drank her champagne with relish and held her empty glass out for the server to pour her more. "You're such a virgin," she said.

Cordelia looked utterly wrecked. Guy almost felt sorry for her. She pulled her dress down to her knees. Her eyes opened and then squeezed shut. She turned her head away, spent. Guy wondered whether he was expected to console her. He hadn't a clue what to say.

"We'll have another bottle," Svetlana said without looking at the waitress. "And get this girl a Shirley Temple."

"*Da*, madam."

Guy glanced from Cordelia to Svetlana. He couldn't tell whether he was horrified by what he'd just witnessed or indecently turned on. The poor girl was a disaster. She hugged her knees up to her chest and curled into a fetal position on the banquette. Her shoulders heaved. She buried her face in her knees and seemed to shudder. Svetlana beamed. Her black-painted lips parted to reveal twin rows of impossibly white teeth. The tip of her tongue slid along her upper lip. Her eyes flashed at Guy.

"Did you enjoy that?" she asked. "I think that you did."

"You're very cruel."

"Perhaps." Svetlana held her glass out and waited for the waitress to pour, her eyes locked on Guy's face, unwavering. "But cruelty is in the eye of the beholder, don't you think?"

"I thought that was beauty."

"Cruelty can be beautiful though, no?"

"Cruelty can also be just cruel."

"The girl wants you very much, but she can't have you."

"No."

"What a shame."

Guy shrugged. He sipped his champagne. Their gazes remained steady: a challenge of wills to see who blinked first. Cordelia whimpered and slowly, painfully, pushed herself up and out of her fetal position and sat upright, her hair tangled and matted across her face. Guy thought she looked like she belonged in a straightjacket.

"Look who's returned to us," Svetlana said. She snapped her fingers and the waitress jumped to attention with Cordelia's Shirley Temple, replete with maraschino cherry and paper umbrella. Svetlana took the drink and held it to Cordelia's lips. She gently, lovingly, brushed the hair from Cordelia's face and bid her sip the drink through its straw. Cordelia obediently did as she was told. "The little bird lives to sing again."

Guy knew he should have been appalled.

"What are you doing in Moscow?"

The question surprised him. But then, Guy was beginning to realize he needed to expect the unexpected at all times, especially where Svetlana Slutskaya was concerned.

"Business," he said.

Svetlana wiped Cordelia's lips with the tips of her fingers. Her thumb lingered and pressed itself between Cordelia's teeth. The girl's mouth opened and accepted Svetlana's thumb, her tongue eager and caressing.

"Hedge funds, yes?"

Guy nodded. "You've done your research," he said.

"There's a ball tomorrow night at the Mariinsky." Svetlana removed her thumb, leaned forward, and placed a delicate kiss on the girl's swollen lips. "You should come. I can introduce you to some very influential people. There is a lot of money here. I can make it happen for you."

"I don't have an invitation."

Svetlana laughed. She kissed Cordelia again, harder this time, biting the girl's bottom lip as she pulled away.

"As it's my birthday party," she said, "I can invite whomever I choose. I choose you."

"And what if I have other plans?"

"You have a lot to learn, Guy Templeton."

Svetlana gave Cordelia's cheek a furtive peck and abruptly—yet fluidly—stood.

"And you as well, my pretty little bird," she said. "You'll be Natasha at the ball. Would you like that, *"ptichka?"*

Cordelia nodded.

"But you must come early." Svetlana held Cordelia's chin and appraised her. "You have potential, but Mama Lana needs to work her magic before you can be seen anywhere near her ball. I'll send my driver to your school."

"But her father—" Guy felt it was his duty to protest even as he knew his words would have no bearing.

"I have it all under control," Svetlana said. "Her father and I have—shall we say—a history. He knows what is good for him. And I, in turn, know what is good for his daughter."

Svetlana didn't wait for a reply. She clapped her hands and was immediately escorted out by a pair of thuggish-looking bald-headed toughs with whom Guy, who rarely shied from a fight, felt it best not to make eye contact. He was now left with the ambassador's daughter who, sucking rather indecently on her Shirley Temple, looked utterly damaged even though some color had returned to her cheeks. Guy finished what remained of his champagne and waited for Cordelia to drain her glass. In Svetlana's absence, he became aware of his surroundings again, of the music (Italian pop) and the smell of weed, cigarette smoke, and sex. He experienced a flicker of guilt.

"We should go," he prompted. "You have school in the morning and it's well past your curfew."

Cordelia chastely placed her glass on the table and stood.

"That was delicious," she said.

"It was a Shirley Temple," he replied.

Cordelia shook her head. "I've never felt so alive. In that moment, when she was touching me: is that what making love feels like, Guy?"

"I wouldn't know," he said. "I don't make love. I fuck."

"Hmm. No, I suppose that's right. You're a brute."

"We should go."

"It was wonderful though, unlike anything I've ever experienced before. I don't think I shall sleep tonight. It's like a dream. What if I wake up and..."

"And?"

"And I discover she's only an illusion. But there's tomorrow night, isn't there? And she said...she said she'd make me like Natasha at the ball. I suppose that means you'll be my Pierre. But better looking. Much better looking."

"I've never read *War and Peace*," he said.

"Take me home, Pierre." Cordelia held her hand out to him. Guy thought for a moment she was going to swoon. "Natasha needs her beauty rest. She has a big day tomorrow."

| 5 |

Guy shuddered. The memory was painful. It drained him of his ability to finish and that just wasn't something that happened to him. He pulled himself out and up off the Bollywood starlet, rolled over and pushed her away when she tried to persuade him into another round. His jaw throbbed. The tattoo hurt even worse. *What the fuck am I doing? What the fuck is happening to me?*

"I have to go," he said. "This was a mistake."

"I haven't come yet," she said.

Guy clambered out of the bed, fumbled with his trousers, his shirt, pushed his fingers through his hair.

"Then use your finger," he directed.

"Fuck you, Guy Templeton."

Guy threw himself out of the starlet's room. Memories haunted him that he wished he could erase. He'd been tricked. It wasn't...it couldn't be his fault...what happened to Cordelia Bingham...he refused to take responsibility... But he couldn't help but blame himself, even as he knew he was at most an indirect participant. Not that that made things easier or lessened the guilt that weighed on him. At first, it had just been a game. At least that's what he told himself: a particularly risky game of cat and mouse where the roles kept changing and the rules were never quite what they seemed. He'd gone into it eyes wide shut. Svetlana had so dazzled him he'd simply lost himself in her web, which was of course exactly what she'd wanted. There was a reason she was called The Black Widow of Sochi. She mated and she preyed. Her late husband was only one of many, not the first and definitely not the last. No one was safe...not the least of which an impressionable eighteen year-old girl.

The late afternoon sunlight reflecting off the Indian Ocean blinded him as he stumbled out of the hotel and onto the beach. Guy had a vague recollection of telling Spencer he'd meet him back at his room...five hundred thousand in mixed currencies needed to be counted...concern that it wasn't all there. He wanted to forget everything, but the more concerted his effort to suppress memory's inevitable return, the more difficult ignorance became. Guy knew he was in trouble. He knew Spencer wouldn't have tracked him down to this remote tropical paradise if the situation hadn't been dire. He owed his best mate the consideration of taking his advice and direction. But Spencer couldn't know everything. He couldn't possibly understand the extent of how badly things had gone in Moscow. Guy's life had become a fuck-up of epic proportions and there didn't seem to be any solution.

Guy paused to catch his breath and stared at the ocean. There was a way out, he realized. It wouldn't fix the vicious circle he'd created but it was a surefire way of extricating himself from facing the consequences. It would be quick and relatively painless. He would just start walking, eyes fixed on the horizon, the water rising until it washed over him and filled his lungs. He'd surrender himself to the darkness, to the black that would engulf him, and sink. The mere notion of it made him feel better. How long could it possibly take? He glanced about him. This particular section of the beach was relatively deserted so there wouldn't be any witnesses, no one to play hero and run after him, swim him back to shore, pump the water from his lungs. The temptation was overwhelming.

And yet, the more he thought about it, the more Guy realized he wasn't quite ready. He needed more time to think, to brood. Perhaps another option would present itself? He was skeptical but he couldn't rule out the possibility. And for it to work he sensed he'd need to be a lot drunker. He wasn't sober by any means, but he wasn't blotto. He needed to be off his head. Like last night. If only he'd thought of it then, preferably before the tattoo!

So instead of walking out to sea, Guy continued along the beach. He tripped and lost his footing and fell face down in the sand, bumping his chin and further aggravating the pain from the gash in his jaw. His body ached to the point of numbness. He crawled and then forced himself back to his feet. He heard people around him—children laughing, parents calling out to them in Gujarati to stay away from the scary man. *That's what living a negative lifestyle does to you*, he translated. No one stopped to offer him assistance and for this he was strangely grateful. He wanted to suffer. He felt like a pariah. He didn't deserve to live. Poor Cordelia...

The canned din of an '80s pop ballad blasting from a karaoke machine jolted Guy out of his musing. The Bangles...*Eternal Flame*...sung bravely by a distinctly Asian female voice mangling the English to the point of rendering it indecipherable. Guy looked up from the sand and adjusted his sunglasses. Through the glare, he spotted Sunny Joy. She was center stage on the raised karaoke platform, teetering on six inch stilettos that were a size too big for her, dressed in neon sequined red hot pants and a Union Jack tank top. Her black hair was teased and piled high on her head, held in place by a pair of banana clips. As ever, she looked like a bargain-bin Imelda Marcos. If it weren't for the horrific scar—a lasting reminder of the acid attack—that cut a horrific path from the line of her scalp and across her right cheek, Sunny Joy might have been pretty. Guy had to give her credit. She tried. In a life all but destroyed by seemingly constant tragedy, Sunny Joy did her damnedest to live up to the promise of her name. To Guy, she was nothing short of a welcome ray of light.

She saw him before he'd reached the entryway into The Smiling Buddha Billiards Bar, another beachfront establishment owned by Rajeev that catered almost exclusively to British and Australian tourists. The place was serviceable at best. A few high-top tables scattered across a wood plank floor slightly elevated from the sand so the tide rolled beneath it. A hardscrabble bar where beer flowed on tap by rubbing an oversized smiling Buddha's belly, the aforementioned karaoke platform, and a single billiards table were its only accommodation. The place was a dive—as were all of Rajeev's properties—but it made money hand over fist, no doubt due to some backdoor dealings that Rajeev kept strictly backdoor. For what Guy needed at that moment, there was no better spot than the Smiling Buddha.

"Mister Guy! Mister Guy!" Sunny Joy had abandoned The Bangles and was making her wobbly way toward him. "Oh my God, Mister Guy, what happen to you?"

For someone of her rather diminutive size—especially when compared to Guy who was nothing short of 6'2—Sunny Joy was surprisingly strong. She grabbed his forearm with the grip of a professional wrestler while placing the other on the small of his back. In this way, she guided him up the steps from the beach and into the bar, all the while asking him if he was okay, did he need to go to the hospital, why didn't he call for her sooner. Guy found he could hardly speak. His throat was as dry as the sand and it was difficult to swallow. He surrendered to Sunny Joy's admonishments and allowed her to pull a stool out for him at the bar. He closed his eyes as she removed his sunglasses and subsequently gasped at the state of his face. She insisted that she call a doctor but Guy shook his head and asked instead for a beer.

"Mister Guy, don't you think you have drink enough already?" Sunny Joy clucked. She dipped the corner of a serviette in a glass of water and attended to the gash along his jaw, the bandage no longer adhering to it. "Oh my God, Mister Guy. Why you not take care of yourself?"

"I'm fine." He tried to brush her away but Sunny Joy was determined. She waved his hand away and continued to wash the wound with a painful intensity that only served to make him feel worse, though he didn't have the heart to tell her to be gentler. "I'll be even better with a beer."

"Who did this to you?"

"I thought maybe you'd know."

"I know nothing, Mister Guy. After tattoo, I close up shop and go home. Why you not take better care of yourself?"

Now he was becoming annoyed. Guy pushed her away a little more forcefully this time, not too rough but enough to get his point across. Not one to ever want to provoke him, Sunny Joy desisted with a disapproving shake of her head and another cluck just to let him know she didn't agree but wasn't going to push her luck. Guy had never raised a hand to her—he'd never raised a hand to any woman—but coming from her experience, Sunny Joy had long since learned not to trust any man not to use force against her. Men were brutes, even the seemingly kind ones. She took several steps back from him and went around behind the bar.

"Kingfisher, if you've got it," Guy said.

The bar was empty, which Guy found gratifying. The television above the bar was on and, much to his further satisfaction, it was showing a replay of yesterday's Nottingham Forest vs. Sheffield Wednesday football match, a playoff promotion. Football was in Guy's blood, almost literally. When he'd been a kid, his father had owned Sheffield Wednesday for a time, taking Guy up North from London on the weekends to see them play. These excursions to Sheffield were often the only occasions when father and son spent any quality time together. During the week, Lord Carleton was rarely at home. He had an empire to run and business interests to attend to that took him all over the world, and then, from the age of thirteen, Guy was off at Harrow and he and his father saw and spoke to each other even less.

Guy's memories of these weekend football excursions were bittersweet, at best.

Guy loved the buzz and atmosphere at the stadium, not to mention the excitement of seeing the game live. He thrilled at the chance to meet the players and ask them about certain plays, congratulating them when they scored and commiserating with them when they lost or when a bad call was made against them. And while all this indulged his lifelong passion for the game, his father constantly reminded him that the only reason he brought Guy along was to show him how the other half lived (albeit from the comfort and relative distance of the owner's suite) and to remind the boy that as a member of the privileged caste, he had a duty to look after those less fortunate than he. Money, class, and power were slippery slopes, Lord Carleton would tell him, all too easy to fritter away. Guy had certainly done his share of frittering—he discovered his rebellious streak at Harrow –and had been happy to leave the responsibility to Chloe and their two older siblings, Diana and Edgar, which certainly hadn't endeared him to anyone or made the family dynamic any less uncomfortable.

Sunny Joy rubbed the Buddha's belly and dispensed a pint of Kingfisher on the bar. He drank it without acknowledging her, intent on watching the game, forcing himself to concentrate on nothing but the sport and the taste of the beer as it washed down his throat. He caught a glimpse of her in his periphery, standing with her pudgy bare arms crossed at her ample bosom, hip cocked, tapping the toe of her stiletto impatiently on the wood floor. Like the steady monotony of a metronome, the sound of her toe hitting the wood echoed in the back of his consciousness. He couldn't bear it. He needed it to stop. He'd have to give in.

"Yes, Sunny Joy?" he asked, reluctantly dragging his eyes from the television to give her his undivided attention.

Sunny Joy shook her head and looked away, raising her chin and pursing her lips in a defiant pout. The toe tapping increased in both speed and volume.

"What do you want to say to me?" he prompted.

"It makes me sad."

"What makes you sad, Sunny Joy?"

"To see you like this. That woman...she does terrible things..."

"What woman, Sunny?" He knew full well. He instinctively covered the tattoo with his hand.

"Why did you ask me to make tattoo of her? I beg you not to, Mister Guy. I tell you it big mistake. But you insist. You tell me you love her. How you think that makes me feel?"

Sunny Joy's face scrunched up against the tears that ran down her cheeks, leaving a messy trail of black mascara and accentuating the scar that marred what once might have been a passably pretty face.

"She do terrible, horrible things."

"I know," he said. A roar came from the television. He looked up. Nottingham Forest was up by one. "There, there, don't cry. I was off my head drunk. To be honest, I don't even remember getting the tattoo. That's part of the problem."

"You're my moon and stars, Mister Guy," Sunny Joy said. She came around the bar, tottering on her heels, and placed her hands on his.

"And you're my Sunny Joy. As always...forever."

"Whatever!" She burst into an outsized bawdy laugh that never failed to alarm him, coming from someone of Sunny Joy's diminutive stature. She smiled and he smiled back and she wiped her tears and runny mascara with her fingertips. Guy wiped her nose with his napkin. Equilibrium had been restored.

"That's my name!" she bellowed, giving him a smile that looked so hopeful he found it heartbreaking. "Sunny Joy Whatever! Don't wear it out, Mister Guy."

Footsteps behind them marked the arrival of another patron. Guy gulped down what remained of his beer and slid the pint glass across the bar to Sunny Joy who gave him a disapproving look before rubbing the Buddha's belly again and pouring him another pint. Guy tried to focus once again on the game, but his concentration was disrupted by the presence of the tall Latin-looking stranger dressed in a Hawaiian shirt and khaki cargo shorts that had helped himself to the stool next to Guy's. This was the first thing that set Guy off. With the entire bar empty, why did this interloper have to sit down right next to him? Guy needed his space. But he wasn't in the mood for a fight. As it was, Guy already felt like death warmed over, not to mention the fact that another fight would surely send Sunny Joy over the edge and he just wasn't in the mood to deal with any more of her fussing. He knocked back his beer, chugging without tasting it, and nodded for Sunny Joy to rub the Buddha's belly once again.

"Soccer," the interloper said, his voice dripping with contempt.

This was the second thing that set Guy off.

"Excuse me?" he asked. "What have you got against football?"

"You're a Brit," the man said with a sarcastic smirk. "Figures. This town is crawling with them. I thought the Raj ended in 1948."

"'47," Guy corrected him.

"My mistake."

"Fucking American," Guy muttered. He hated Americans.

"Bar girl! Yo, Miss Saigon!" The American snapped his fingers. "What does it take to get a beer around here?"

Sunny Joy glanced warily at Guy. She touched the side of her face marred by the scar. He nodded to her. *It'll be all right. I'll shut this wanker down before he makes trouble.* She primped her hair, adjusted her Union Jack tank top, pulling it down just a little in an attempt to cover her midriff, before coming up to the bar and placing a cardboard coaster in the shape of the smiling Buddha in front of the American.

"Welcome to Smiling Buddha Billiards Bar," she intoned. "What I can get for you?"

"What are you offering?"

Guy cleared his throat.

"What beer you like?"

"How about we cut to the chase and just get freaky? Isn't that what's really going on here? I mean, this is Thailand, right? Phu-ket. Fuck it. Right?"

Sunny Joy frowned. She glanced at Guy again. He shook his head.

"This is India. This is not Thailand," she said, her voice starting to waver.

"Oh, my mistake. You people all look the same to me."

"Hey."

Guy pushed his stool back and stood, looming over the American, hoping his height would intimidate the arshole into backing off. But no such luck. The stranger challenged him, rising to his feet to reveal a height and build nearly identical to Guy's with the rather unfortunate advantage of youth. The guy scowled, his dark eyes flashing menace. He was clearly itching for a fight.

"You got a problem?" the American asked.

"Show the lady some respect."

"What lady? I don't see any ladies here."

"Back off."

"What, you mean that?" He motioned to Sunny Joy who had taken up a defensive position behind the bar. "She's a sex worker. Who the fuck are you?"

"Who the fuck are you?"

The American took a small step forward so he and Guy were now standing nose-to-nose.

"I don't think you want to fight me," Guy snarled.

The American grinned. "I don't think I have anything to worry about. You're looking to me like you spend most of your time on the losing end of a fist. Defend your masculinity a lot? Isn't that what you Brits do?"

Guy felt the rage.

"I'm giving you one last chance to walk away," he said.

"Or what?"

The American bumped his chest against Guy's.

"Don't push me," Guy warned.

Which of course was exactly what the American did. He head-butted Guy in the chest. The blow knocked the wind out of him and sent him reeling backwards, crashing into a range of high-top tables and chairs, sending them flying. Guy lay on the floor, unable to catch his breath. The pain was excruciating. He regretted not walking out to sea when he'd had the chance.

The American was hovering over him, fists clenched, ready to finish him off, and smiling almost maniacally.

"Get up, *puto gringo!*" he yelled.

Guy rolled onto his side. He couldn't drag himself off the floor. He reached for the leg of one of the bar stools that lay in pieces all around him and tried to grab hold of it, but the American's foot stamped down on his wrist, pinning it to the floor.

"I said, get the fuck up!"

Guy closed his eyes. He attempted to grab the American's ankle with his free hand but found he lacked the strength.

"You get off him! You hurting him! You hurting my friend!"

Guy opened his eyes in time to see Sunny Joy rushing toward the American, a billiards cue in one hand, the pair of six-inch stilettos in the other, ready to clobber him. Guy heard the cue crack across the American's back, but it was no match for him. The American backhanded Sunny Joy. She fell against one of the bar stools and hit the floor. The American turned his attention once again to Guy with the intention of finishing him off. But something stopped him. Guy squinted through the haze of his blurred vision as Rajeev gradually came into focus. His mate brandished a twelve-gauge shotgun, finger dangerously poised on the trigger, the barrel pressing into the space between the American's shoulder blades. The American had his hands up, but his face was still plastered with an ironic smile, flashing two rows of perfectly white veneered teeth.

"I am going to politely ask you to remove yourself from the premises," Rajeev said. "I am going to give you ten seconds. If you do not remove yourself from the said premises in the allotted time, I am going to pull this trigger. Trust me. You don't want me to pull this trigger."

The American's grin widened. With his hands still raised, he slowly turned. Rajeev prodded the end of the barrel into his back to give added emphasis to his threat, but when the American faced him, he lowered the shotgun. A look of disbelief washed across his face.

"Miguel," Rajeev said.

"Rajeev," the American replied. "*Mi amigo.*"

"What the fuck are you doing in Goa?"

Guy pushed himself up off the floor, using the broken barstool as a support. He felt the urge to vomit but held it in.

"What's going on?" Guy asked. "You know this wanker?"

Miguel laughed. Guy wished he'd bashed in the bastard's teeth.

"Rajeev and I go way back," Miguel said. "Don't we, Raj?"

"I wouldn't say that," Rajeev replied. He still held the shotgun, now aimed at the floor. Guy wanted to suggest he put it back where he'd gotten it from but given the turn in circumstances, he wasn't sure whether Rajeev might still have cause to use it.

"You've hurt my feelings, Rajeev. This wasn't the welcome I was expecting. I come in here for *una cerveza*, maybe *un pequeño coño*, and I end up being disrespected by this gringo *Inglés* and a shotgun in my back. What kind of establishment are you running here, Rajeev?"

"Rajeev?"

Guy felt his fight returning. He clenched his fists, ready to spring into action if and when Rajeev gave him the nod. Rajeev nervously licked his lips. He looked from Guy to Miguel and then back again. Sweat beaded across his upper lip.

"Put the gun down," Miguel directed. "There's no need for violence."

Rajeev placed it on the bar.

"Where's the dosh?" Miguel asked.

Rajeev looked shell-shocked. He wiped his hand across his mouth and brushed it against the back of his neck.

"I...I don't know..." he stuttered.

"¿Qué?"

"I don't know what you're asking me."

"Rajeev, what the fuck is going on?" Guy asked.

Rajeev shook his head.

Miguel took a step toward Rajeev. Guy took a step toward Miguel. For the first time since she'd been knocked to the floor, Sunny Joy stirred with a groggy whimper.

"I don't have to remind you," Miguel said. The smile had vanished. His expression was dark, threatening, indicative of all sorts of things Guy had no desire to imagine or experience. "I can shut down your operation with the snap of my fingers." He took another step forward, then another, until he was right up in Rajeev's face, pushing the latter against the bar. "*Yo podría romper ti.* [I could break you.]"

"Then why don't you?"

Miguel grinned. He leaned forward, bending Rajeev further back against the bar.

"*Tráeme los quinientos mil ... todo en efectivo,* [Get me the five hundred thousand...all in cash,]" he said. "*Por favor.* In the meantime, you owe me some R&R."

By this time, Sunny Joy had more-or-less recovered and was standing against one of the high-top tables, rubbing her cheek where she'd been struck. Miguel clapped his hands and stomped his feet like a flamenco dancer. He held his arms out to her for her to join him. She crossed her arms defiantly in front of her chest and shook her head. Miguel stopped.

"You," he said. "My back's killing me. You're not much good at tending bar but I assume that's not what Rajeev pays you for."

"No." Sunny Joy arched her back and re-crossed her arms. 'I don't like you."

"I'm not paying you to like me," Miguel said. "In fact, I'm not paying you at all. With a face as ugly as yours, it's on the house, isn't it, Rajeev?"

"Go on, Sunny Joy," Rajeev said.

"Mister Guy?"

Guy couldn't meet the fear in her eyes. He felt defeated. Broken. Full of regret, but full of questions, the answers to which he didn't think he wanted to know. He stared down at his feet as Miguel grabbed Sunny Joy by the elbow and pulled her towards the swing-doors into the back rooms that Guy knew was where Rajeev really made his money.

"Mister Guy! Mister Guy, please, no!"

Guy turned his back on her.

"And you, *gringo Inglés,*" Miguel said over his shoulder as he dragged Sunny Joy into the back room. "Don't get too comfortable. We're not finished."

The doors slammed shut.

Guy sat down hard on the floor at the edge of the bar, dangling his feet into the wet sand. The tide had come in.

"You have to leave," Rajeev said. "Now."

"What the fuck is going on, Rajeev? Who the fuck is that?"

"I don't know."

"That's not what you said earlier."

"He's no one. Someone I used to know."

"He seems to know an awful lot about you."

"It doesn't matter. You have to go. You've wrecked two of my establishments in less than twenty-four hours. You're banned. For life."

"All right. All right."

Guy eased himself down onto the beach. The water and wet sand felt pleasingly cool across his sandaled feet. Rajeev had him by the bicep—the tattooed one—and was pulling him away, back in the direction of his hotel.

"All you have to know," Rajeev said, "is the money is accounted for. I checked. Five hundred thousand. You don't have to worry about it anymore. We're keeping it safe."

Rajeev stopped and released Guy's arm.

"And another thing," he said.

"Yeah?"

"Chloe's here."

"What?"

"She arrived this afternoon while you were doing fuck all."

"Here? In Goa?"

Guy didn't think it possible but his day had suddenly gotten a whole lot worse.

"Something to do with your father."

"You've seen her?"

"Spencer and I ran into her in the hotel lobby. She said she's been trying to get a hold of you for days but you're not answering your phone."

"How did she even know I was here? I didn't know I was here until I woke up this morning."

"She contacted Spencie when she couldn't get through to you."

"Fuck."

"At any rate, she's here to get you out of Dodge. And maybe talk some sense into you while she's at it."

"Bloody hell."

"This is where I leave you. Some of us actually have jobs." Rajeev held his hand out. "Hopefully the next time we meet it'll be under a better set of circumstances. Although I daresay at the rate you're going you'll be dead before summer. But maybe that's what you want."

Guy shook Rajeev's hand. "You know I've always had a death wish," he said, trying to make light of what even he had to admit wasn't a particularly humorous situation.

Rajeev didn't look amused. "Take care of yourself, mate," he said. "And I'm warning you. If I ever see you around here again, I might have to sic Miguel on you for real. Understood?"

Guy didn't understand but he knew it was neither the time nor the place to argue or ask for an explanation. He squinted at Rajeev through his sunglasses and watched as his mate headed back along the beach toward the Smiling Buddha, not once looking back. While Guy had always known there was a lot about Rajeev's life that his mate kept in reserve, he'd never really stopped to consider what it was that Rajeev might be hiding, or why he chose to be so secretive. He supposed it had always been easier to turn a blind eye and not ask too many questions. Experience had long since taught him that too many questions led to trouble and secrets perhaps best left unrevealed. And if that gave the impression—as Guy knew it did—that he was remote or disinterested, then so be it.

But now, if Rajeev was to be believed, Chloe was in Goa. It shouldn't have surprised him. His little sister was tenacious if nothing else...and annoying as fuck once she set her mind on something. Guy had to remind himself that of all his siblings, Chloe was the only one who continued to give him the benefit of the doubt, and for this he was grateful because without her, Guy knew he would be utterly at sea. Chloe was his anchor, his foundation, and his conscience. He could choose to listen to her or disregard her, but she had never let him down, even as he knew that he in turn was nothing but a disappointment to her. Chloe was ever optimistic even when all the odds were stacked against her. And yet, she couldn't have picked a worse time to remind him once again that he wasn't an island unto himself. Guy knew, as he trudged back to his hotel looking far worse than she had ever seen him before, that he would have a lot of explaining to do.

| 6 |

Yvette wiped the steam from the bathroom mirror and evaluated herself. She looked good. *Tres chic.* The lingerie she'd bought from Fifi Chachnil before heading to Charles de Gaulle the day before (or however long ago it was) had been an inspired purchase. The black leather bustier made her breasts look fuller than they actually were (depending on the angle) and the matching black lace panties nipped and tucked her bottom better than any liposuction could ever do with none of the discomfort. She arranged her flaming red hair so it fell loosely about her shoulders, stylish yet spontaneous, the color nicely accentuating her freckled skin. She thought as she posed, running her fingers through her hair and piling it on top of her head, that she looked a bit like Rita Hayworth in the old movies she and Papa used to enjoy together when she was growing up and he had time to spare for her. She indulged in a little shimmy, delighting for a moment in how sexual and alive expensive undergarments made her feel, and thought (not for the first time) that in another life she might have enjoyed being a dancer at the Crazy Horse cabaret. The tease of burlesque never failed to arouse her.

There were days when Yvette wished she'd taken a different path in life. Not that there was anything particularly wrong with things as they were. She was good at what she did, very good in fact, if one evaluated the trajectory of her career. In almost record time she'd risen to the uppermost echelons of the French criminal justice system with more successful arrests and subsequent convictions of anyone she knew. Of course, it certainly helped that her father, Claude Devereux, was who he was, and graduating first in her class at École Spéciale Militaire de Saint-Cyr certainly didn't hurt. Yvette thrilled at the chase. In fact, she took tremendous satisfaction in cutting a swath through the sexist ranks of the French criminal justice system. She knew what people said about her and she told herself that she didn't care. But when she stepped back and really forced herself to take an unflinching look at where she found herself at the age of thirty-five with no husband or children—let alone a boyfriend—or even a permanent place of residence, Yvette couldn't help but ask herself whether she'd somehow gotten it all wrong.

The prospect of turning forty terrified her. What would happen? What would people say? The lads in Marseille had assumed she was *une lesbienne* but she chalked that up to jealousy on their part. She was a woman and she was their *inspecteur en chef.* Given the fact that most of these boys came straight from the *banlieues* Yvette couldn't really hold their sexism against them. She didn't excuse it, but she knew she couldn't really blame them either. But still, the comments and the catcalls, the leers behind her back when they thought she couldn't see them, the obscene gestures – after a while it collectively took its toll.

On the surface, Yvette knew she was a creature to be envied—undeniably beautiful, smart, and successful beyond her years. Yet looks and brains and chutzpah would only get you so far. She was tired of coming home to an empty hotel room or, when she wasn't on the road, a lonely bed-sit in the 17th arrondissement. Room service and tables-for-one in far-flung hotel restaurants and middle-class bistros had long since lost their charm. One-night stands with shady businessmen of dubious means and ambiguous marital status may still have elicited excitement in the throes of passion, but on le matin après, Yvette never failed to feel used and even slightly ashamed. She supposed her Catholic guilt had something to do with it—she still slept with the rosary her grandmother had given her as a first communion gift under her pillow every night—but the closer she got to forty, the more she realized she wasn't a woman who enjoyed being single. Her biological clock was ticking and despite her best efforts, there remained no potential suitors in sight.

Yvette released her hair and shook it down over her shoulders. She selected a lipstick from her make-up bag. And although the logo on the packaging struck her as trashy (and *très américain*)—a pair of messy and oversized lips that bore a striking and surely unintentional resemblance to another kind of lips—there was an irreverence about it that had struck Yvette's fancy. She applied it generously, for lipstick like this was certainly meant to be worn in excess, and decided after a quick appraisal in the mirror and a check that she hadn't gotten any on her teeth that she actually quite liked it. The color was brazen and made her feel a bit like a hussy, but (despite the jetlag) Yvette was in an adventurous mood.

She went into the bedroom where her vintage black Yves Saint Laurent pantsuit (circa 1967) was laid-out on the bed. She debated whether or not to wear the crème low-cut blouse beneath the jacket or to simply go with the bra, and decided in the spirit of the moment that the bra would more than suffice, in fact if anything it would probably help. The suit fit her perfectly and gave a pleasing silhouette whilst being both professional and sexy at the same time. This was to be a business occasion after all, though the man she was meeting knew nothing of her presence in Goa and, if the outcome of the rendezvous proved to her benefit, she was hoping to give him something beneficial in return. Yvette doubted he'd be able to resist. She'd never met a man who could.

Satisfied that she was about as close to perfection as she'd ever get, Yvette Devereux gave herself a final once-over in the mirror before completing her look with a pair of black Chanel sunglasses, black Louboutin slingback pumps, and her matching black Hermes clutch. If this didn't get her to mission accomplished then, Yvette thought, she might as well throw herself off the *Pont de l'Archeveche* when she returned to Paris. She didn't really think he would resist, but men were unpredictable—maddeningly so—and Yvette had come to expect—if not necessarily embrace—the unexpected in all aspects of her life, especially after *le grand fiasco* that had been Tahar. But she wasn't going to think about Tahar now. She wasn't going to think about Tahar ever.

Yvette went down to the bar in the lobby. She had some time to kill before her rendezvous and she wanted to stake out the scene and better familiarize herself with the surroundings. India didn't agree with her and Goa most especially. It was too hot. Perspiration was anathema to Yvette. She didn't even care for Saint Tropez in the summer, preferring the cooler climes of Paris in the spring or London on the cusp of autumn. Moscow in the snowy dead of winter suited Yvette just fine. She didn't doubt a psychiatrist would have a field day with her. Yvette had been to a therapist once, right after *l'incident* with Tahar, but she hadn't liked what the woman had said to her and had never returned. She'd been very vulnerable then. She hadn't needed the negative reinforcement.

She sat at the bar and ordered a Sancerre. The lobby was empty save for an obviously American couple checking in and a bellhop standing at attention at the front door. The atmosphere was stifling, the overhead fan providing little but welcome relief. Yvette knew she was overdressed and that she stuck out like a sore thumb but linen and madras just weren't her style and her wardrobe was too full to ever let them in. She opened her Hermes clutch and lit a Gauloises, her first cigarette in nearly twenty-four hours. The nicotine soothed her as did the wine when it was finally placed in her front of her by the bartender who looked and sounded Australian and who kept giving sidelong glances at her cleavage as though hoping to engage her in conversation (or, more likely, ask for her room number). Yvette found most men – Australian or otherwise – vulgar, but a part of her delighted in the attention. Yvette spread the lapels of her jacket just a touch: why not give him an eyeful of what he'd never have? she thought. There's no harm in letting him look.

POSH

Yvette sipped her wine and took a deep satisfying drag off her cigarette. Her body tingled. More than anything, she wished she had some weed. It wasn't something she did very often—in her line of work she couldn't very well find herself at the center of a drug bust—but every once in a while there was nothing quite like a spliff to take the edge off. The smell of it reminded her of her father. Some of Yvette's fondest memories were of sneaking a joint with Papa behind the shed in his garden outside her parents' stone cottage in the commune of Bourgneuf-en-Rez, or out in the small vineyard he tended on the days when he wasn't assisting the Nantes police force with surveillance work. They'd pass it between them whilst sharing a bottle of the local red and he'd tell her stories of his army days in Algeria and Tunisia and he made it sound so romantic even though Yvette knew it really hadn't been, at least not according to her mother, Madeleine, who always saw life through a very practical—Yvette thought, colorless—lens. Madeleine had once confessed to Yvette (in the dark time after Tahar) that if she had known before she'd gotten married what the life of an army wife in the colonies was really like, she would have made a very different choice. Yvette supposed it mustn't have been easy. She just had difficulty viewing her father objectively. Every man that entered her life—friend, colleague, or lover—was measured against Yvette's hero, and they inevitably, in one way or another, disappointed her. Expect perhaps Tahar.

No, she mustn't think of him. It was bad enough that her dreams were plagued by memories of those final terrible moments. To be in love with someone as much as she had been in love with Tahar only see him leave her in such a brutal way... it was beyond all comprehension. And so she drank and smoked and slept with suitably anonymous men and dedicated herself to her work with a passion and a drive that bordered on obsessive. No mission was too dangerous, no task too onerous. Yvette had seen the very worst of what the world could offer and she was determined to eradicate that evil from the face of the earth, even if she had to do it single-handedly, even if it killed her. For now that Tahar was gone, what else was there? *La vengeance.*

She glanced at the clock above the mirror behind the bar and debated asking the bartender for another Sancerre. It was early yet. She could afford to sit for a bit and contemplate exactly what she was hoping to accomplish from that evening's rendezvous. The hotel staff had proven very helpful and she'd tipped the concierge well. Her sources had him pinned to this exact location and Yvette knew that her target had been out for most of the afternoon. But more importantly, she also knew whom he was with. There were easier ways to go about getting what she wanted but Yvette had always enjoyed the game—the pursuit was what excited her most. She hadn't a doubt that in the long run she would come out on top, so why not have some fun along the way?

Just when Yvette was about to order a second glass of the Sancerre and enjoy another cigarette, the rather lackadaisical calm of the lobby was suddenly disturbed by an almighty *whoosh*! and a tsunami of spectacular energy. Yvette peered over her shoulder, making sure her Chanel sunglasses were perfectly poised at the end of her nose, and saw that the situation had gotten a bit more complicated. There in the lobby, not more than a few feet from where Yvette sat, was none other than Chloe Templeton. The bellhop that earlier had proven so helpful was now bending over backwards to accommodate LadyTempleton, who stood in the center of the lobby dressed immaculately (as always) in a floral print shift dress (by Miu Miu), sensible (but elegant) white Jimmy Choo pumps, and a straw hat with an oversized brim that she had pulled down over her eyes to block the waning but still potent late afternoon Goan sun. She held her mobile—replete with a Union Jack protective case—in one hand and a white leather clutch (also by Miu Miu) in the other. The bellhop hovered behind her with her Longchamp carryall.

"*Putain!*" Yvette muttered.

She snapped her fingers at the bartender. "My check, *s'il vous plait,*" she hissed, trying to keep her voice as low as possible lest she attract the very unwanted attention of the woman whom she couldn't help but view as her arch-nemesis.

"Are you sure you don't want another, Miss?"

The bartender leered at her. Yvette adjusted the lapels of her jacket, realizing then that she was practically falling out of her bra, and furiously shook her head.

"*Non! Non! Allez! Allez!*"

Yvette risked a glance at Chloe in the reflection from the mirror behind the bar. The Englishwoman was tapping frenziedly into her phone while pacing back and forth across the lobby, her heels click-clacking against the tile with a jarring regularity that set Yvette's teeth on edge. Everything about Chloe screamed of a particularly officious kind of entitlement that Yvette hated. And to make matters worse, the bellhop followed five paces behind her, bent forward at the waist in a subservient manner with her bag slung across his shoulder. Yvette fought the urge to scratch the woman's eyes out but couldn't afford the risk of her cover being blown, not when she was so close to her quarry.

"Hello? Hello? Yes, it's me again. I'm here. No, I'm really here. Yes, in the hotel. In the lobby. Yes, in Goa. Where do you think? I told you I was coming. I just arrived. No, I haven't checked into my room. There isn't a room. I didn't think to book. Yes, I know it's a long flight. Believe me, I know! We were late arriving in Delhi and my connecting flight was all screwed up. But, yes, I'm here now. Where are you? Are you with my errant brother? The reception's bad. I can't hear what you're saying. Damn it!"

Chloe started tapping maniacally at the touch screen of her phone, all the while pacing and cursing whomever under her breath. Yvette knew the chances of her escaping undetected were slim, and the longer the bartender took to ring up her bill, the worse her chances of escape. She couldn't afford to abort this mission. The outfit alone—purchased at a consignment shop on the Rue Daguerre—had nearly set Yvette back a month. And as much as Yvette enjoyed fresh *baguette et fromage*—for that had been all she'd been able to afford given the cost of vintage YSL—neither was worth the price of losing the opportunity to nab what very well could prove to be the first of several career-making arrests. Guy Templeton was big, but what lay behind him, Yvette knew, was even bigger. She was dogged and determined, a female Javert, though she hoped she wouldn't meet a similar fate.

"I'm sorry, Spencer, I lost you. The connection...yes, yes...I know...and no, I don't want to talk about that right now. The fact that you'd even bring it up, with the circumstances as dire as they are—yes...no, I don't think I'm overstating anything—well, let's just say that I didn't come thousands of miles to discuss the status of our relationship. No. I thought I made that perfectly clear. Thank you. I'll wait for you here in the lobby. Goodbye."

The bartender finally presented the bill. Yvette charged the amount to her room and signed without reading it, though she did see that he'd written her a cute note saying that he did room service until six a.m. if she got hungry in the middle of the night. Yvette looked at him, sized him up, focusing on where it counted most. She tossed her head back and emitted a suggestive laugh.

"I'd eat you up in two bites," she said, "and I wouldn't be satisfied."

He winked.

"The name's Patrick," he said.

Yvette smiled. "*Va te faire foutre, mon cheri amour*," she said. [Go fuck yourself, my sweet love.]

The bartender clearly didn't understand French.

Keeping her gaze fixed on the mirror's reflection, Yvette stepped down off the bar stool and scoped her escape route. Chloe had settled into one of the high-backed rattan armchairs that were scattered throughout the lobby, mercifully far enough away and situated at an angle that, barring any additional unforeseen obstacles, Yvette felt that her chances of ducking out without being spotted were surprisingly good. She tucked her Hermes clutch under her arm and was about to make a run for the hallway that led to the lifts when Spencer appeared, trailed by a not unattractive Indian gentleman whom Yvette thought she recognized from photos she'd seen on an Interpol watch list.

"*Putain!*"

If she didn't duck for cover and fast, there was little chance Spencer wouldn't spot her. Yvette adjusted her sunglasses and quickly scanned the lobby: four steps to her left and behind a rather conveniently arranged collection of chaise longue, were an array of potted palm trees. *Parfait!* Yvette managed to cross the tiled expanse in two steps and a rather heart-stopping wobble just as Spencer and his companion strode past the bar toward the chair where Chloe Templeton was holding court. Yvette felt the bile rise in her throat. She swallowed it back and adjusted the palm fronds to maximize their concealing ability. Yes, it probably would have made more sense to take advantage of Spencer's distraction and proceed to the lifts, but the scenario presenting itself was simply too intriguing to resist. She pressed a button on the side of the clutch and activated its specially fitted high-resolution digital recorder in the hopes of capturing whatever incriminating evidence this little impromptu *tete-a-tete* might provide.

| 7 |

"Bloody hell, Chloe!" Spencer exclaimed as he crossed the lobby, arms open wide, and greeted his best mate's sister with a decidedly awkward half-embrace. "I swear you arrived in record time. How do you do it? How do you fucking do it?"

He went for her lips but Chloe gave him her cheek.

"I'm a force a nature," she said.

"Bloody right you are!"

"Hello, Rajeev."

Rajeev bowed his head in a pose of mock subservience that made Chloe want to slap him. "Mum," he said.

"What's the going rate these days for sex workers fresh off the boat?"

"I'm not going down that road with you, Mum," Rajeev replied, keeping his head down, chin tucked into his chest.

"You're looking fresh as a daisy, Chloe," Spencer interjected in a desperate attempt to preserve a balance of amity between them. "Take advantage of the BA lounge during your Delhi layover, did you?"

"Or shall we talk about sweatshops? Slave labor? The exploitation of indigent minors? Or how about female genital mutilation, while we're at it?"

"Bloody hell, Chloe! This is a respectable establishment," Spencer hissed. "People don't want to hear about..."

Chloe looked at him, her expression set, cold, and uncompromising. "What?" she asked. "Hear about what, Spencer?"

"Whatever it is you're on about."

"No, Mum," Rajeev replied. He raised his gaze to meet Chloe's expectant stare, his dark eyes heavy with unmitigated loathing.

"And Sunny Joy?"

"What about Sunny Joy, Mum?"

"I trust she's still in your employ?"

Rajeev nodded.

"Tell her 'hello' from me. Unfortunately, this is going to be a rather brief visit, otherwise I'd check in on her and make sure she's not being unduly compromised."

"'Unduly compromised?'" Rajeev smirked. "Define that."

"Look it up."

Rajeev represented everything that Chloe despised, or if not everything, then a very significant portion. She believed there was an empirical order to the world, a rigid hierarchy comprised of both social and economic boundaries that were never meant to be crossed. Despite this, Chloe didn't see herself as particularly class-conscious—at least no more so than most everyone in her social circle, although she did concede her 'set' comprised of an elite grouping of individuals brought together more by shared socio-economics, schooling, and heredity than any meaningful commonality. And while she recognized there were limitations to being at the very top of the pecking order—the press wasn't always kind to her or to her various philanthropic endeavors (they had had a veritable field day with the name of her latest foundation, S.A.S.S [Sisters Against Sweat Shops]—Chloe held fast to the belief that her social and financial prominence gave her a certain responsibility to help those who couldn't necessarily help themselves, especially in those countries and communities still grappling with the residual effects of colonialism. What Chloe loathed more than anything—more than the trafficking and sexual enslavement of women in countries like Pakistan, Afghanistan,

Bangladesh, and India, more than the lack of modern and sanitary facilities throughout Southeast Asia within which to do one's business, and yes, even more than female genital mutilation—what Chloe loathed more than anything were the invariably brown-skinned men from these backwater countries who profited from the exploitation of their own kind.

Rajeev Gupta epitomized a particular kind of evil, one that she had devoted her life to wiping from the face of the earth. But what made Rajeev particularly vexing was that he'd grown up in the very same environment as Chloe and Spencer and Guy. He had benefited from everything Chloe and her kind had been spoon-fed from birth, raised under the same moral code, and given entry into a society that was almost exclusively reserved for people like Chloe, despite his country of origin, despite the color of his skin. In other words, Chloe felt Rajeev should have known better. He should have been her staunchest advocate, a devoted evangelist for her cause. He should have been out in the field amongst his people making sure all of Chloe's time, money, and heartache were being converted into tangible, measurable results. Instead, he seemed to take cruel satisfaction in mocking her—and not just her, but everything and everyone she represented—and going out of his way to thwart what she believed to be her life's work. Rajeev was an affront to everything Chloe stood for, and the fact that he gleefully scoffed at the very society that had raised him up from nothing (for he and his sister Bipasha had indeed come from nothing) made Chloe sick to her stomach. In her darkest moments, it made her feel that all her efforts were for naught. Once an interloper, always an interloper, Chloe thought. One had to have standards.

It certainly didn't help that Spencer and Guy seemed to hold Rajeev to some indecipherably exalted level of esteem. (Was it guilt perhaps? The white man's burden?) The two of them were his most passionate defenders whilst Rajeev, in turn, did nothing but sneer at them. Chloe had tried time and again to pull the wool from their eyes but they remained adamant, and after countless buckets of tears and bottles of Xanax, Chloe had simply given up. For as much as she loved her older brother—more than stuffy Edgar and certainly more than insufferable Diana—Chloe suspected Guy loved his mates more.

When there was so much else upon which to focus her efforts, Chloe resigned herself to the bitter reality that there were simply some battles she couldn't win and not everyone was going to love her the way she believed she deserved to be loved. Where Rajeev was concerned, Spencer and Guy were enablers, and in enabling Rajeev, they were striking at the heart of all Chloe felt she represented. It was nothing short of betrayal, but what could she do? She needed them—yes, she secretly conceded, she needed Spencer despite that awful scene at Rules a few days' back—for without them, Chloe knew she would truly be an island unto herself. She knew the loneliness would kill her and she didn't think she would have the strength to fight it.

"Spencer, where's Guy?" she asked, deciding it was best, given the present circumstances, to pretend Rajeev didn't exist.

"I don't know."

"What do you mean, you don't know? I told you I was coming. You told me he was in Goa. You told me you would keep an eye on him until I arrived. You promised me, Spencer. You promised me."

"I didn't expect you so soon."

"That's not an excuse!" Chloe sat down on the armchair and covered her face with her hands. She felt a migraine coming on and the last thing she wanted was to be sick in India. The infirmary in Freetown had been traumatic enough.

"You promised me. Why does everyone seem to break their promises?"

"Oh, come now, Chloe. There, there, darling." Spencer lowered himself to her level—a not inconsiderable effort given his height—and patted her shoulder whilst digging in his trouser pocket for a handkerchief, which he unfurled with a flourish and held to her nose. "Go on there, darling. Give it a good blow."

"What Spencer meant to say, Mum, is that he's just seen your brother and had agreed to meet up with him later."

Chloe blew her nose into Spencer's handkerchief and pushed his hand away. She knew he meant well but she didn't want to give him any ideas.

"Where is he now then?" she asked, feeling slightly better if not any more in control.

Spencer and Rajeev exchanged looks.

"He said he had some business," Rajeev said.

"I'm not speaking to you," she snapped. "Spencer, what business?"

"You know," Spencer shrugged. "Men's business."

"I don't know what you mean. What 'Men's business?' You're hiding something. What are you hiding? Why isn't he answering his phone?"

"The thing is," Spencer began, "Guy's not looking his best. He's in a spot of trouble...more than a spot really. He's in some pretty deep shit."

"What's happened? What's he done?"

"We can't tell you that. Or rather, we're still trying to figure it out ourselves.

Aren't we, Rajeev?"

Rajeev nodded and stared at the floor.

Chloe sensed another wave of anxiety threatening. She looked from Spencer to Rajeev and back again. She knew there was more that they weren't telling her. Once again she was being blocked. Once again she was being held on the outside when she wasn't the outsider. A pang of nausea stabbed her stomach. Her eyes muddled with a new onslaught of tears. She grabbed Spencer's handkerchief and blew her nose again.

"It's a good thing you're here actually, Chloe," Spencer placated, patting her rather chastely on the shoulder. "It's good that you've come to take him home. It's probably best that Guy disappear for a while."

"Disappear?"

"Or rather, remove himself from the equation whilst Rajeev and I sort things out. Quite convenient, actually."

"Papa is dying, Spencer!" Chloe exclaimed. There was no use holding back. "I don't see how there's anything convenient about that!"

"No, no, of course not, dear. Of course not. I didn't mean that. I didn't...well, you know what I mean. Don't you, Chlo? Don't you? You know I'm not good with words."

Chloe shook her head. She blew her nose a third time and held the sodden cloth out for Spencer to take. She closed her eyes, took a deep measured breath, and then exhaled while silently counting back from five.

"All right then," she said, a semblance of control having restored. "We haven't much time. Guy and I are booked on a flight back to Delhi at nine-thirty tonight and then a flight to London shortly thereafter. I need both of you to find him and bring him here. I'm not going to ask for any details about whatever this 'business' is you're referring to. If Guy wants to tell me himself, we've got more than enough time for that on the flight. But if I hear that you, Rajeev, have anything to do with it...well, you can be assured that I'll go out of my way to ruin you. You wouldn't last a day in prison in this part of the world."

She felt better—if not exactly relieved, then at least more on top of things than she had since boarding the first British Airways flight out of Heathrow however many hours ago. The important thing was, Guy was close and she was bringing him home. Equilibrium would be restored. And for all Spencer's failings, she did feel she could trust him...at least where Guy was concerned. He may not tell her everything—and part of Chloe felt this was probably for the better—but she knew Spencer loved her brother as much as she did, and while she often resented that love, she knew she could bend it when necessary to suit her needs.

"I believe you have your marching orders," she said, after taking another breath and forcing herself to relax. The knot in her stomach gradually unclenched.

"Absolutely!" Spencer clicked his heels together and offered a rather pathetic approximation of a salute. Chloe couldn't help but smile. "We're on the case."

"Go on then. I'll wait here."

"Are you sure you don't want anything? A drink perhaps? How about a g-and-t?"

"No thanks, Spencer. Just find Guy and bring him back to me."

"You can rely on us, Chlo," Spencer said. "We won't let you down."

"That remains to be seen."

Chloe sat back in the chair and crossed her legs with a demure flick, pulling the hem of her dress down over her knee. She was done. Spencer and Rajeev were dismissed. She watched them pass through the revolving door and then stop out front to confer before each heading their separate ways. It was only then that she noticed the bellhop still stood just off to the side, in the periphery of her vision, her carryall still slung over his shoulder. His presence annoyed her.

"You can go now," she said. "Thank you. Just leave the bag."

"Yes, Mum."

Just like Rajeev...

He placed the bag at her feet and she handed him a wad of cash, not bothering to check the currency. Money was money. It was then that she caught sight of a flash of red and a glimpse of impeccably tailored vintage YSL—Chloe knew her couture—dart out from behind one of the potted palms across the lobby and disappear into the elevator foyer. Chloe frowned: something about the hair and the way the woman held herself seemed familiar.

Her mobile buzzed. *Spencer's found him already?*

A text...not from Spencer:

Darling, it's been ages! Must catch up soon. So sorry about your father. Love SASS. I'm not worthy. Dying to get back to London. LA is killing me softly. Xoxo. Ash.

Chloe smiled. Ashleigh. Warm fuzzies elicited by fond memories of some uncharacteristically (for Chloe) wild nights. She looked up from her phone as the lifts closed. The redhead in the YSL pantsuit was already forgotten.

| 8 |

Spencer thought himself a reasonably forgiving man. He hated conflict and had pretty much structured his entire life around the Golden Rule: 'do unto others as you would have them do unto you.' It had helped him survive his father's all-too manic fluctuations between indifference and alcohol-fueled abuse, and had proven quite useful during the rather dark and lonely slog through public school (the hazing, the experimentation, the feelings of athletic incompetence) and uni. But it also—or so he believed—had proven a useful mantra as he rose up the ranks of public service to where he found himself today. It helped give him objectivity when he was dealing with the bad guys and a sense of fairness when meting out whatever tactics (or punishment) a particular situation required.

But lately, Spencer had started to wonder whether he hadn't gotten lazy, or perhaps he had just come to a rather late realization that the career he was in wasn't the one best suited to him. He worried he was at risk of becoming a patsy. This latest situation with Guy was disappointing. More than that, it was damnably outrageous. Intolerable even. For years, Spencer had always known (though perhaps hadn't been willing to admit) that for all their good qualities—and there were a few—Guy and Chloe Templeton were two of the most self-centered people he had ever met.

Guy, in particular, disappointed him. They had been best mates forever. Guy had helped him through the very worst periods in Spencer's life and Spencer, in turn, had always made sure to have Guy's back even when he found himself at risk of compromising his professional integrity. But as the years went on—and especially lately—Spencer wondered whether he wasn't outgrowing his childhood friend whose arrested development seemed very nearly lethal.

Of course, this wasn't unusual. Trust funds, inheritance, and good old-fashioned entitlement, if not managed correctly, had a way of making one feel infallible. The best of everything came too easily. But the life of Riley also made one susceptible to all sorts of financial and entrepreneurial misadventures, the consequences of which, as proven by this latest inconvenience with Guy, all too often played out to the advantage of no one.

Chloe wasn't any better, though Spencer was more apt to take a more forgiving view. At least she endeavored to use her wealth and social standing to some greater good. There was much to admire about her. She was tenacious, if nothing else, and passionate about her cause, though that passion, Spencer feared, more often than not verged on the autocratic. He appreciated her willingness to put herself at risk to promote the basic tenets of her philanthropy. But again, like Guy, she often did so without really taking into consideration the full measure of what she was getting herself into. And, as exhibited by her utter antipathy (and downright condescension) to Rajeev, Spencer sensed Chloe's moral code was firmly entrenched in an outmoded social hierarchy that bordered on, if it wasn't outright, racism. Of course, he could never tell her this, not if he wanted to preserve any chance in hell of getting a ring on her finger—and, despite the rather unfortunate and best left forgotten scene at Rules, he still believed that he could. Spencer was an optimist, though lately, pragmatism (or perhaps it was simply self-preservation?) was starting to get in the way.

The five hundred thousand was thankfully all accounted for. Rajeev had texted him from Guy's hotel room to say all was in order and that 'the job' was taken care of. Spencer thought it best not to ask questions as he felt his position was already rather dangerously compromised. Guy, of course, was nowhere to be found. He and Rajeev had then agreed to meet for a drink by the pool but an attack of nerves got the better of him and he suggested instead they meet for massages at the hotel spa. He hated being drunk at mid-day—it reminded him too much of his father—and he found himself gripped by an impending sense that things were going to get rather nasty sooner than he had perhaps originally anticipated. It also didn't help that Chloe was blowing up his mobile with increasingly emotive texts. He didn't begrudge Chloe her concern for her brother, but he also didn't appreciate the fact that the situation (or whatever it was) was now becoming less about Guy and everything about Guy's sister. On the chance that something was to go down with Svetlana here in Goa, the last thing he needed was for Chloe to put herself at risk.

He knew Chloe was on her way, and it would only be a matter of time before Svetlana and her entourage showed up as well. The texts from Chloe had started the day before with news that the great Lord Carleton had been taken ill and rather than rush him to the hospital in London, the incorrigible old bastard had insisted on being taken to the family estate in Dorset, because—as Chloe had texted—he wanted to die 'surrounded by hundreds of years of Templeton glory.' Chloe had argued against this. However, as per usual, Edgar and Diana (the two eldest of the

Templeton brood and probably the two with the most at stake in Lord Carleton's passing) had prevailed. So Edgar, Diana, Lord Carleton and all his attending entourage of nurses, doctors, and caregivers, had traveled to the family estate in Dorset in their private fleet of helicopters and town cars while Chloe badgered Spencer via mobile about Guy's whereabouts until Spencer had finally given in and told her. The next thing he knew, he had received a series of messages from her telling him that she was on her way to Goa on the next (commercial!) flight out of Heathrow via Delhi and that she expected Spencer to have Guy 'ready to go' the moment she arrived. Well, no wonder he was drunk before three and in desperate need of a massage! Who could really blame him?

The massage had been pleasant enough, if not as relaxing as he had hoped. Rajeev never failed to put Spencer on edge even though he was certainly always pleasant to look at, which might have been part of the problem. They shared a bottle of Moet and a plate of mangoes. Rajeev assured him everything was taken care of but that he expected to be handsomely rewarded at a later time of his choosing. Spencer knew better than to press for details. It was bad enough that he already felt compromised. He didn't need to feel dirty as well.

With his mobile blissfully switched off (or so he thought) and the bubbly percolating in his already saturated bloodstream, for the first time in days, Spencer allowed himself to drift. His mind floated on tropical breezes and azure skies over an ocean dappled with the sun reflected on its waves. He inhaled the scent of sandalwood and marigold blossoms and allowed himself to float wherever his imagination took him – Paris in the springtime, Yvette in a yellow raincoat channeling a young Catherine Deneuve, *The Umbrellas of Cherbourg...*

His mobile's ringtone shattered him into the present.

Rajeev: "Can't you turn that fucking thing off for five minutes?"

Spencer fumbled for his phone, feeling embarrassed and harassed. He waved the Filipino masseuse away who gave him a disparaging look but did what she was told. He squinted and looked at the caller ID:

Chloe.

"Hello?"

Her voice grated through muffled static: ""Hello? Hello?"

"Chloe?"

Spencer heard the words without really registering what it was she was telling him. He closed his eyes and willed himself back to the Tuileries Gardens, back to the delectable vision of Yvette in her yellow mini-raincoat, the rain, the swirling umbrella, the feel of her lithesome body pressed against his...

But Chloe was insistent "I'm here...in the lobby..."

"Here?" Spencer suddenly blinked awake. He propelled himself off the massage table, nearly losing the towel around his waist. *"Here* here? Or here where?" *Fuck.*

Rajeev was gesturing for him to do something (probably to go fuck himself), but between Chloe's voice in his ear assaulting him and his mate's unabashed nakedness distracting him, Spencer found himself at sea. The fantasy sequence in his head was gone—no more Michel Legrand, no more Technicolor—replaced by a vaguely nauseating feeling of vertigo that he couldn't seem to shake. He balanced his phone between his shoulder and his cheek while securing the towel more firmly around his waist. He understood about every third word of what Chloe was saying, and the more her voice grated in his ear, the more he was struck by a resentfulness he thought he had long ago overcome. *How dare she speak to him like this? Who did she think she was, ordering him around like a minion? No wonder Guy kept his family at arm's length! I would too were I in Guy's shoes!* Spencer fought the urge to hang up on her. But the longer she talked, the more he started to absorb, and then it finally sunk in: Chloe had traveled all the way from London to Goa for the sole purpose of retrieving her brother. And while Spencer knew that Chloe operated without an ulterior motive, he couldn't help but wonder if perhaps the fact that he was also in Goa had something to do with it, and that maybe—just maybe—she wanted to apologize in person for the way she had treated him that night at Rules. He wasn't going to hold out for an apology, but he wasn't going to go out of his way to accommodate her without one.

"It seems you and I have some unfinished business," he blurted without really thinking through what exactly he wanted to say. "Yes, that's right...we didn't exactly leave things on the best of terms when last we saw each other. Yes, at Rules...no, I think you were really rather rude... Before then...before Miss Devereux showed up...and no, I was just as surprised as you were... Of course, I didn't plan it. You're wrong about her...she's absolutely delightful. Hello? Hello, Chloe? What? Well, when would be a good time to talk about it? I never know with you... Okay, okay, down in the lobby...ten minutes. Fine. See you then."

Spencer felt the world was spinning off its axis. Individually, brother and sister were difficult to deal with in the best of times. Both of them together were a disaster. He indicated for Rajeev to get dressed, keeping his eyes averted and fixed on the ocean outside the window while he hastily threw on his clothes. His heart pounded at the thought of seeing Chloe without any preparation beforehand.

After all these years spent pining for her, only to receive polite indifference at best, one would think he'd know when it was time to move on to greener pastures. But Spencer was stubborn. He knew in his heart that he and Chloe were meant for each other. All he could do was remain stalwart in his devotion and wait her out. He'd whittle down her resistance until she realized there was no one better than he. And when that moment finally came, Spencer would be a happy man indeed.

Of course he was disappointed when he and Rajeev met up with her in the hotel lobby. Of course Chloe was singular of purpose. She was on a mission—to fetch her brother and drag him back into the Templeton fold—with neither time nor interest in anything beyond the successful completion of her task. Her antipathy for Rajeev was well documented, and Spencer supposed he shouldn't have held out too much (or any) hope that he might have a few moments of alone time with her to sort out the situation between her and himself. It was almost as if he didn't exist. He could have been anyone, little more than a glorified bellhop. It killed him that he fell so easily back into his comforting, bumbling self with Chloe, allowing her to walk all over him, appeasing her, wiping away her tears that he knew were more for effect than sprung from genuine emotion. And of course he told her he would do everything within his power to bring Guy back to her when what he really wanted to do was tell them both to fuck off for life.

Spencer often wondered what the exact moment had been when he'd lost his sense of himself. Had there actually been an identifiable moment, or had life merely taken its toll? He found himself staring at his reflection in mirrors without recognizing the person looking back at him. When had he gotten so old? When had his eyes lost their sparkle? When had he gone from celebrating life's rich proverbial tapestry to circling the wagons and peering at the world through a jaded lens clouded by bitter disappointment and a genetic pre-disposition toward alcoholic overindulgence? Simply put, when had he stopped caring? Strike that. The problem, he thought, was that he cared too much about people that couldn't have cared less about him. Take Chloe, for example. Spencer had always known that for all her philanthropic aspirations, Chloe was, at heart, a mercenary. As much as Spencer might have fooled himself into believing otherwise, Chloe Templeton was nothing if not her father's daughter, and Lord Carleton had a long-established reputation for being a right old shit, and (quite decidedly) not in any congenial way. Behind Chloe's outwardly demure and philanthropically focused exterior, Spencer had long suspected—even if he could never quite bring himself to fully admit—that everything she said and everything she did was calculated to bring her maximum benefit, regardless of how he or anyone might feel. Chloe Templeton was neither sweet nor particularly winsome. But she was rich and benefited from being Lord Carleton's favorite child. She knew how to play both to her advantage.

But Spencer played her game as though he didn't know any better. He held out his handkerchief for her in which to blow her nose. He dutifully wiped her tears away and gave her his shoulder to cry on even as he knew her crocodile tears were the size of the Nile. He didn't deny that removing Guy from the immediate premises was the best approach to the current situation, so in that regard, Chloe's arrival proved really rather convenient. At the same time, however, Spencer hadn't a clue as to how best to handle Guy's mess and he resented the fact that his life and what had once been a promising career in service to Her and now His Royal Majesty was irreparably derailed and dedicated only to covering his best mate's arse. It didn't make him feel good.

Spencer felt sloppy, jaded, debauched even. He didn't care, or perhaps he cared too much? He just didn't know anymore. He supposed in a way it was easier like this. Guy was never going to change, and as inconvenient and dangerous as this latest debacle was, Spencer didn't think it was anything he couldn't handle. The money was secure. Guy was being whisked back home, leaving him with Rajeev to deal with the fallout, which was easier to do with Guy out of the picture. When Svetlana Slutskaya and her squad of Death Angels descended—as Spencer knew they must—he was confident he'd be able to hold them off at least long enough to make sure Guy was relatively secure. And if his confidence failed him, Spencer had long ago resigned himself to the notion of an early death, for he also knew Svetlana and her protégé Ekaterina would devour him whole, leaving nothing—not even his bones—in their wake.

So he said all the right things and promised Chloe that he and Rajeev would find her brother and deliver him to her post-haste. She couldn't very well question him, nor did she seem to notice the anxious look he cast in Rajeev's direction that might have betrayed Spencer's utter lack of knowledge in regards to Guy's current location and thereby undermine his deceptively forthright tone. He and Rajeev proceeded with purpose out of the hotel lobby, through the revolving doors that deposited them on the beach, and then stood there huddled together, miming for Chloe's benefit what was meant to look like some sort of action plan was being discussed and then, as he and Rajeev marched off in opposite directions, was thus being enacted.

But Spencer then found himself suddenly distracted. A whiff of something in the air as he passed through the revolving doors: a fragrance that he couldn't quite identify yet knew was unmistakably connected to something or someone from his past. He turned back to the hotel entrance, checking to see that Chloe was distracted enough to slip past her when he re-entered and, following his nose, hurried rather stealthily to the lift foyer, frantically punching the 'up' button until the lift arrived and opened its doors to him. Spencer was consumed by the fragrance. Even in the lift, the scent was present—subtle yet intoxicating.

He pushed the button for his floor. The fantasy was returning. He closed his eyes and inhaled and then it came back to him: Chanel No. 5. How he adored the smell of Chanel No. 5! The lift doors opened and he followed the scent down the hallway to his room. He imagined Yvette in her yellow mini-raincoat and matching umbrella. He was in his fantasy of Paris once again, circa 1965. *Pourquoi pas?* And it was raining and after he and Yvette embraced and he twirled her around and they kissed and held their faces up to the drizzly Parisian rain—for Yvette had finally tossed the umbrella aside so they both could be baptized in the rain—they ran to his formerly discarded bicycle where the baguette in his bicycle basket was now soggy but the bottle of French red table wine was (improbably) still intact. He righted the bicycle and motioned for Yvette to climb on behind him, wrapping her slender arms around his waist, and he pedaled furiously toward the Place de la Concorde to his fantasy garret off the Champs Elysees where they ran up the stairs—six flights because the lift was broken—and entered his flat in a tumble of bright Technicolor magnificence and they made tender yet passionate love on his mattress on the floor in front of the easel and the stand upon which the early renderings of an abstract painting—for in his dream reality, Spencer had recently decided to indulge his inner Matisse—depicting Yvette (no less) in a decidedly tasteful yet languid pose. The camera tastefully pans up to the painted canvas as the strings in Michel Legrand's melodramatic score shrill in intensity and the screen fades to black. *La fin.*

Spencer fumbled with his hotel room key and pushed the door open, nearly falling flat on his face in the effort. She was here. The smell of her perfume: How he loved Chanel No. 5. It no longer mattered that he was meant to be rescuing his best friend or that what he had thought was the love of his life was impatiently waiting for him to procure results for her downstairs in the lobby. He cast reason out the window. Spencer didn't even think to wonder what the object of his obsession was doing in Goa of all places and in his hotel room no less. It didn't matter. He wanted nothing more than to be bathed in her perfume.

Yvette Devereux was waiting for him. She sat on the edge of the armchair facing the bed, dressed only in her Fifi Chachnil lingerie and black Louboutin pumps, legs crossed, cigarette in one hand held aloft so the smoke billowed in the breeze propelled by the ceiling fan. Spencer fell to his knees in front of her. She was his shrine. His icon.

"Yvette!" he exclaimed as he buried his face between her thighs. "*J'taime! J'adore! J'désire!*"

Yvette tossed her head back, her glorious red hair on fire in the late afternoon sun, and laughed.

| 9 |

Guy thought it better to try to sneak into the hotel from the back. The closer he neared the hotel, the greater his anxiety at being reunited with Chloe, whom he knew would barrage him with questions and recriminations and remind him for the umpteenth time that he was an ungrateful and irresponsible brother and the bane of not only her, but the family's, existence. The fate of the Templeton dynasty (not to mention its reputation) weighed heavily on his shoulders, as did the notion that even as he trusted Spencer and Rajeev's ability to clean up his mess, he wasn't so naïve as to think that a return to England to stay out of sight for however long would make the situation disappear. It would only prolong his eventual defeat, for Guy Templeton felt that nothing short of a miracle—or his suicide—could save him.

As he stumbled along the beach, hiding behind his aviators and avoiding eye contact with all who passed him, snippets of distorted memory started to return: flashes of insight devoid of any real context that enhanced his awareness of how fucked he really was. There was no way he could deflect at least partial responsibility for what had happened to Cordelia, though he held fast to his belief that at heart his intentions had been, while not exactly noble, not nearly as nefarious as many might believe.

Any fault of his may have lain in perhaps underestimating the power of Svetlana's attraction to the misguided and woefully impressionable young girl and underestimating the girl's vulnerability. As Guy preferred to see it, Cordelia had merely been a slave to her emergent adolescent hormones. Yes, he may have been a catalyst, but he certainly wasn't the smoking gun, regardless of Ambassador

Bingham's accusations. The ambassador's daughter was eighteen, after all, an adult – albeit an extremely sheltered one rather alarmingly prone (as it turned out) to behavioral extremes. But surely that wasn't his fault! If anything, Ambassador Bingham should have been held more to account, but he'd been too busy banging his Russian mistress to look after his own daughter. Guy had only been trying to do the ambassador a favor. So much for good intentions! Never again.

Of course, the whole fiasco had blown itself up into an international 'incident'. Guy knew enough about how government worked to realize it wasn't over yet. He was being set up for a fall. So he'd taken the money—all five hundred thousand of it, which really wasn't all that much in the grand scheme of financial thievery (especially where the Russians were concerned)—and run. But again, he'd clearly underestimated who and what he was up against, all of which brought him to where he found himself today, stumbling headlong into what he was certain was going to be an epic confrontation with his little sister that probably wouldn't bode well for any of the parties involved.

Chloe spotted him the moment he entered the lobby. She stood up from the armchair and then hesitated. Her expression registered an uneasy mix of relief and concern that ultimately settled on a crestfallen kind of disdain. Her eyes narrowed as she took in his battered visage and the woeful state of his clothes. Her lips drew into a thin line. Her hands anxiously clenched and unclenched the hem of her Miu Miu dress. Guy removed his sunglasses and squinted, the fading late afternoon light casting his sister in shadow. He couldn't move.

"Guy," she said.

He shrugged. Words caught in his throat. He didn't know whether he should go to her or let her come to him. He was overcome by a surge of emotion unlike anything he had experienced before. The weight of recent memory threatened to collapse him. He was paralyzed.

Chloe cleared her throat and smoothed the non-existent wrinkles down the front of her dress. She glanced about the lobby as though worried a *paparazzo* might pop out from behind the potted palm trees that graced the foyer and capture their reunion on film. She took a deep breath, mentally counting backward from five, before slowly, purposefully, crossing the marbled expanse that separated them, biting ever so slightly on her bottom lip. She folded him into her arms without a word. Guy melted. He buried his ravaged face into her shoulder as the sobs overwhelmed him.

"Let's go home," she said.

PART 2

| The Templeton Way |

| 10 |

TEMPLETON MANOR, DORSET, UK

The first thing Chloe did when she arrived at Templeton Manor was tell Imelda to run her the hottest bath imaginable and make sure her room was festooned with as many fabulous white tulips as Elena Grimaldi, the Tulip Queen of Amsterdam, could spare. She was desperate to be rid of the icky stench of travel and, truth be told, to have some much-needed time to herself away from Guy and his all-consuming gloom. He had barely spoken to her since they'd left the hotel in Goa, and any hope Chloe might have had of getting him to open up to her about his latest, and assuredly most egregious, transgression, she soon realized was a wasted effort. No amount of persistence was going to make him talk, at least not to her.

The whole situation was beyond the pale. Chloe loved her brother dearly, but time and again it seemed her devotion was thrown back in her face, leaving her to ponder whether what the others said of him was true, that Guy was a waster and a scoundrel and that they – the Family – would be far better off without him. But this went against Chloe's entire philosophy of being. The world was such a dark and scary place to her that turning one's back on one's own flesh and blood – regardless of whether such rejection was deserved – was simply too heartbreaking for Chloe to bear. It was bad enough that she had had to endure her mother's premature death only three short years ago – a shock and a grief that still had not left her – but to follow this up with closing her heart to her nearest and dearest next of kin would surely render her into a state of such emotional paralysis, Chloe was certain she would never recover.

Chloe felt deeply. In fact, Chloe felt so much she feared such feeling would one day prove her undoing. While she recognized that she had been born into a world of privilege – and with such privilege came distinct advantages, of this she was also aware – Chloe liked to think of herself as just another girl, no different from an average High Street shop clerk or City worker-bee with an exorbitant rent to pay and the responsibilities of any other reasonably well-adjusted single woman living the London dream. At least this was how Chloe preferred to see herself.

The reality, of course, was anything but. It wasn't that she was embarrassed by the size of her bank account or that she was titled (as opposed to entitled, a word Chloe would have banned from the English language if she'd been able), or that she frequently appeared in the pages of *Tatler, Vogue, Vanity Fair,* and the *Sunday Times* style section. She wasn't about to deny there were certain perks to being an 'It Girl.' Chloe just felt that in order to make a maximum impact upon the world, it behooved her to play down the trappings of her undeniably charmed existence and focus on her boundless compassion and approachability – for Chloe felt herself to be extremely approachable, much more so than her siblings and any of the other 'It Girls' in her social milieu. She believed her open face and welcoming aura inspired the less fortunate to come and seek her assistance and care. There was nothing Chloe loved more than to be enveloped in the arms of the tragic and poverty-stricken, preferably brown-skinned and thousands of miles from her home turf. The English poor didn't interest her. She couldn't relate. She wouldn't be caught dead in a town square, let alone an ASDA or a B&Q. Not that she necessarily related to Bangladeshi sweatshop workers, Sudanese victims of FGM, or ISIS widows stuck in refugee camps in Syria...she didn't. But she had a foundation (S.A.S.S.) dedicated to exposing and improving the plight of sweatshop workers in countries where such horrors existed, and to Chloe's (albeit limited) knowledge, sweatshops simply didn't exist in the UK, at least not anymore. If they had, perhaps she would feel differently. Probably not. Chloe Templeton's psyche was tempered by post-colonial guilt.

But no amount of compassion – real or otherwise – could help Chloe come to terms with what she feared was happening to her family. Guy was a disaster, yes, but if anything he was merely the tip of the iceberg. Chloe saw herself as the Titanic and the path before her was a veritable minefield of icebergs larger and deadlier than anything Guy and his failed business and financial ventures could throw her way. Of foremost concern (naturally) was what would happen once her father finally gave up the ghost, the inevitability of which seemed more definite with each day since his collapse. Chloe couldn't bring herself to think about how she might react when Lord Carleton finally expired. The very notion gave Chloe hives. She knew there would be a power grab: with so much money and property at stake, not to mention a business portfolio valued at least in the hundreds of billions, how could there not be? It wasn't that Chloe expected to benefit from Lord Carleton's death. (She wouldn't dare allow herself such mercenary aspirations!) She simply didn't want her father's legacy to fall into the wrong hands, namely those of an outsider, specifically those of one Lady Eliza Brookings.

Lady Eliza was the stuff of Chloe's waking nightmares. In this, if in nothing else, she and her older sister Diana were united. Yes, if what her mother, the late and much lamented Lady Fiona, had said about the circumstances surrounding Lady Eliza's entering their lives was true – that it wasn't an affair in the traditional sense, but rather a sanctioned "intervention" arranged by Lady Fiona herself to assuage her husband Lord Carleton's "voracious" sexual appetites – then, however much Chloe might object to such an arrangement on moral grounds, there was nothing illicit about Lady Eliza and Lord Carleton's relationship that Chloe could easily pin on Lady Eliza for wrongdoing. That her dearly beloved mother had been a saint, there was no question. That Lady Fiona would approve of, let alone help facilitate, such a distasteful arrangement out of love for her husband, Chloe's father, wasn't entirely outside the realm of possibility. Chloe preferred, however, to believe that her mother had been the victim of coercion, that Lady Eliza had had her sights on Lord Carleton for years, and had used Lady Fiona's illness as the impetus to pounce. Chloe didn't know Lady Eliza well, but she was certainly well enough familiar with her to know without a doubt that Eliza was an unscrupulous opportunist who would lie, cheat, charm and steal to get what she wanted, regardless of family, illness, or just plain old-fashioned propriety. And once Chloe got a notion in her head – justified or otherwise – there was nothing that could or ever would convince her to believe any differently. It was this uncompromising belief in the rectitude of her own judgment that Chloe felt was the backbone of her philanthropic success. She had yet to be proven wrong.

Chloe's mission to Goa had provided her a welcome distraction. She had been able to put any fears and misgivings she had about Lady Eliza on the back burner while she focused her attention on saving Guy. The fact that, in a sense, her mission had failed – for it was immediately clear that Guy had no intention of being saved by her or by anyone – hadn't bothered Chloe to the extent that it might have done, had present circumstances been any less fraught. She had merely used the hours spent airborne reflecting on how horrid the conditions had been in Goa and banging out emails to the S.A.S.S. board on how they needed to make the Indian subcontinent their next focus. The street children that had run alongside the hired car that had taken her to and from the airport had caused Chloe no small amount of angst.

"They aren't wearing any shoes!" she had declared to the driver, an affable but glum elderly gentleman dressed in an ill-fitting black suit that looked as if he'd been wearing it since Partition. He had merely shrugged and shook his head at her in the car's crooked rearview mirror as if it was of no consequence to him whatsoever that the street children were barefoot. "I mean, surely it isn't safe for them to be running around like that completely unshod? And why aren't they in school?"

"It is because they are poor, Mum," the driver replied, as if that was reason enough. "This country is filled with many poor people."

Chloe was indignant. "That's no excuse!" she exclaimed. "Where are their mothers, or if not their mothers, their *Aunties*? It's unconscionable. And can you please turn up the air conditioning? I'm melting inside my clothes."

"Sorry, Mum. My apologies. The air conditioning is not working. Roll down your window. There is plenty of fresh air outside."

"I most certainly will not roll down my window!" The heat, the smell, and the congestion had overwhelmed her. She felt like she was dying, and not for the first time Chloe asked herself whether being the family's moral compass was perhaps a more onerous task than she could handle.

It was this thought – this nagging undercurrent of self-doubt – that returned to her at an exponential intensity twenty-four hours later (or however long it was) after she had submerged herself in the scalding (but hopefully purifying) waters of the bath Imelda had drawn for her upon her arrival at Templeton Manor. Guy's continued silence about the situation from which she had rescued him silently infuriated her, as did his seeming reticence at the imminent death of their father. Was it reticence or just plain insolence? Chloe wanted to shake him. It had taken almost all of her remaining energy not to throttle him in the car on their long drive from Heathrow. Guy looked as though he had been through a war zone. It was embarrassing. No, more than embarrassing, it was humiliation. Chloe felt humiliated by Guy's appearance and even more so by his apparent lack of self-awareness ... or was it just old-fashioned bloody-mindedness? Chloe suspected the latter.

And, of course, the paps were staked out in the Terminal Five Arrival Hall snapping away with their cameras as they blitzed her with their intrusive questions. Chloe had a love-hate relationship with the press, as they did with her. You didn't get to be an "It Girl" without a certain amount of pandering.

"If I didn't know better," Chloe said to no one in particular once she and Guy were safely ensconced behind tinted windows in the backseat of the family town car, "I would almost think Penelope tipped them off. You know she's always so weirdly keen to get this family's name in the broadsheets, and she hangs around with that social media crowd with their perpetual air of desperation. Do you know what I mean?"

Guy shook his head. "Not really," he mumbled.

Chloe squinted at his profile behind her oversized Chanel sunglasses. "It might do you a world of good to be more aware."

"More aware of what?"

"I don't know." Chloe supposed she should be grateful that Guy was actually speaking to her now, but she could tell from the tenor of the conversation and how he wouldn't look at her, that the satisfaction to be parsed from the interaction was minimal at best. "Just more aware of whom you are...where you are...what you look like," she continued. "Appearance and perception are everything, Guy. We may not like it. And yes, I suppose it is a very shallow way to live one's life, but such is our lot. We have a certain responsibility to present ourselves in a certain way."

"And what way is that?"

"You might have cleaned yourself up a bit before we left the hotel." Chloe's irritation had been bottled up for too long. She was back in her home territory, her confidence subsequently restored. "I almost mistook you for one of those ghastly street *wallahs* that you can't seem to get away from over there. They're like pestilence."

"That isn't very charitable of you," he said. He rested his head back on the seat. His eyes were closed.

"Did you notice – you probably didn't because you don't notice anything – but did you notice that the children weren't wearing any shoes? They were running around like little monkeys with bare feet. Hundreds of them. I swear some of them followed me all the way from the airport to the hotel...and back again."

"They were hoping for a handout."

"Such a stereotype! Those children need to be in school. I fired off an email to the board about them on the plane."

"Which board? There are so many."

"S.A.S.S., of course! It'll be our next initiative: providing one pair of British-made shoes to every child in India. We need to expand our horizons beyond sweatshops."

"You're a true philanthropist, Chloe."

"I can't tell if you're being sarcastic."

"Mumsy would have been so proud."

"Yes." Chloe turned away and pressed her forehead against the window as her eyes welled up. She choked back a sudden onslaught of sobs. "I've been thinking about her a lot lately and wondering what she would say about all of this. You may not see it this way, Guy, but I think her death is what's caused you to lose your way."

"I haven't lost my way, Chloe."

"How else would you describe it? Just looking at you anyone could tell you've gone off the rails. I'm not going to pretend I understand anything about hedge funds or how any of that sort of thing works, but..."

"Then don't." Guy looked at her then. In his dark eyes there was a warning. Chloe shook her head and held the back of her hand to her mouth. She blinked away the tears that she knew she was helpless to prevent. She didn't want Guy to see her like this. She needed him to believe she was strong even though she often felt there was a lost little girl trapped inside of her. The fact that she hadn't slept in days – since Lord Carleton's collapse – certainly didn't help.

But she also knew her brother was soft at heart. Of any of her siblings, Guy was the one who – until lately anyway – had always been there to dry her tears and soothe her most nagging neuroses. She had long ago mastered the art of appealing to his sentimental side, a side of him few had ever seen, or at least that's what Chloe preferred to believe. And she, in turn, expected Guy to remain outwardly stalwart. Men weren't supposed to cry. She had never seen her father shed a tear, even at Lady Fiona's funeral. In fact, she had never seen her father express much outward emotion about anything, which she supposed some might see as a flaw – and perhaps a determining factor in why the Templeton brood were such emotional basket cases, each in their own way – but Chloe preferred her men strong and silent. Overt emotionalism was, in Chloe's opinion, the ultimate example of emasculation, and as such was profoundly unattractive to her, which she supposed was one of the reasons she found Spencer Hawksworth so cloying. But she wasn't going to think about Spencer now. If Chloe could help it, she wasn't going to think about Lord Hawksworth ever again. She blamed him in part for whatever was going on with Guy, despite his not unhelpful assistance in convincing Guy to go home with her. She dreaded seeing him at the Steeplechase. But then, there were a number of acquaintances Chloe rather dreaded seeing. What was it about one's past?

"Come here, little one, come here." Guy wrapped his arm around Chloe's shoulder and pulled her close. She fell against him as the floodgates opened and the tears she had suppressed for days rushed forward with an intensity that surprised even her.

"Oh, Guy, it's such a burden being me!" Chloe sobbed as she buried her face in his chest. His strength reassured her. "Everyone expects me to keep it all together... to be perfect...but the toll, Guy...the toll it takes on me. You have no idea. None of you do."

"There, there..."

Chloe suddenly paused to compose herself. There was no sense in calming down immediately. She wanted to enjoy the moment. Tears always worked with Guy.

"I should hate you," she said. "I do hate you. I do, I do, I do."

"You wouldn't be the first," Guy quipped.

His flippancy enraged her. Chloe pushed herself up to a more dignified position and slapped him petulantly – but lightly – across the face.

"You know I'm your only ally," she said, now thoroughly (and sensibly) recovered. "You should be nicer to me."

"I don't need you to fight my battles."

"You have no idea what you're in for. Everyone's gunning for you, Guy, even Papa."

"Is that why he's asked to see me?"

"I don't know." Chloe turned her back to him and stared out the window. The countryside passed in a blur. "There's talk."

"Idle gossip doesn't interest me, Chloe."

"It isn't idle," she protested. "That business with the ambassador's daughter. I can't bear to even mention it."

"An unfortunate misunderstanding..."

"Unfortunate yes, but hardly a misunderstanding. What they say you did to that poor girl...well, it's unconscionable. Mumsy must be turning in her grave. I mean seriously, Guy, what were you thinking? No, don't answer that. There's no reasonable explanation for such behavior. I feel dirty even thinking about it!"

"So don't."

"And then, of course, there's the other."

"What other?"

"That Russian. The oligarch's widow."

"You know about that?"

"The whole world knows about it!" Chloe forced herself to look at him. She no longer recognized the man staring back at her. "Are you deliberately being stupid, Guy, or are you really just that thick?"

"I don't want to talk about it."

"Well, you're going to have to talk about it at some point, so it might as well be with me. I'll at least give you a fair audience, which I can't say for anyone else. I just hope there aren't any scenes this weekend. The fact that we're having this weekend at all leaves a bad taste in my mouth. All of those ghastly people traipsing around our birthright while Daddy's upstairs on his deathbed…"

"You've always loved Steeplechase Weekend, Chloe," Guy said. "You look forward to it every year."

"This is an exception. Even Eliza agrees with me. But Diana insisted. I think she's just doing it to spite me."

Guy took her hand and rested it on his knee. She didn't resist. She hadn't the energy.

"It's good to see you, Chlo," he said.

"You're just saying that to shut me up."

Guy shrugged, but Chloe had warmed to him again. She leaned her head on his shoulder and closed her eyes. They sat like that in silence for the remainder of the journey. There was so much Chloe needed to know, so much that she felt it her duty to warn him against, but as Guy was often wont to do, he had drawn a line in the sand. His reticence was his shield.

Chloe was disappointed by the lack of ceremony when she and Guy arrived at the Manor an hour or so later. She found it awkward to have to ask Rupert to find Imelda to tell her that Lady Chloe wanted a hot bath and festoons of Elena's white tulips brought up to her room. Even Rupert seemed a bit embarrassed by the diminished staff. Chloe knew this was Lady Eliza's doing. Lord Carleton wasn't even in the ground yet and already his grubby paramour was trying to make her mark. Chloe would have to have a word with Diana as she couldn't quite bring herself to confront Eliza directly, at least not while her father was still alive. And besides, it really wasn't her place to do so anyway given that she was the baby of the family, and as she had never been able to quite figure out what Diana did all day, Chloe figured Diana had more time on her hands to get into the trenches with the she-devil. Chloe preferred to keep her hands clean and her mind occupied with changing the world one sweatshop – and now one shoeless Indian ragamuffin– at a time.

"How's Papa, Rupert?" she asked as she handed the family's longstanding butler her Longchamps overnight bag and hat. "Is he fit enough to see Guy? Diana said it was most important that Papa be alerted when Guy and I arrive."

"There's been a slight change of plan, mum," Rupert said, glancing (almost apologetically, Chloe thought) from Chloe to Guy and then back again.

"Speak up, Rupert," Chloe snapped. "Has something happened? Has Papa passed?"

"No, Chloe, your father is just resting." Lady Eliza appeared from around the staircase. "We've had quite an eventful day, but no need for worry."

"He's taken another turn?"

Lady Eliza's smile was fixed and severe. She brushed past Chloe without even acknowledging her and extended her hand to Guy. "Welcome home, Guy," she said. "Your appearance leaves something to be desired but I don't doubt a hot shower and a change of clothes will get you back to hearty and hale in no time."

"Hello, Eliza," Guy said. "I daresay you're right."

"Rupert, please show Guy up to his room and make sure he's comfortable."

"I can make my own way, Eliza. It's not as if I've not been here before."

Eliza pursed her lips and stepped back. She fiddled with the strands of pearls at her neck as she gave Guy an appraising once-over.

"Of course," she said. "I often forget you're a part of this family. We never see you, at least not in person. The tabloids don't count."

"Perhaps you can show me to my room after all, Rupert," Guy said after a pause. "This house is a labyrinth."

"Right this way, sir."

"Dinner's at eight," Eliza announced as Rupert and Guy ascended the staircase. "Formal dress. Cocktails in the front parlor at seven. And please be sure not to trip on the tulips as you go. It seems the Tulip Queen of Amsterdam has brought a little of the Low Countries to Templeton Manor this weekend. So much for Brexit."

Eliza then turned to Chloe, her eyes hard as steel. "Has Guy taken up boxing?" she quipped. "I'll have Dr. Raleigh take a look at him before he leaves for the night. I'm surprised they let your brother on the plane."

"What's going on?" Chloe asked. Lady Eliza's presence grated on what little remained of her already frayed nerves. "Where's Diana?"

"I'm not your sister's keeper."

"No, but you might as well be."

"Petulance isn't flattering," Eliza's smile was as hard as her gaze. "I imagine at one time it may have been cute...precocious even...but, how old are you now?"

Chloe opened her mouth to reply but no words were forthcoming.

Eliza beamed. "As I thought."

"You haven't answered my question."

"Your father has an announcement to make," Eliza said. "He'll be joining us at dinner. It's important that you and all your siblings are prompt and present because I don't know how much time he has. It's been very difficult, Chloe. I don't think you realize."

"I don't need you to tell me how difficult things are," Chloe said.

"Oh, but I think I do. And let me also tell you, dear Chloe, things are about to get worse."

"For you perhaps." Eliza's words had a chilling effect. As much as she preferred not to give them any credence, Chloe wasn't so naïve as to think there wasn't a kernel of truth behind what Eliza said. She was businesswoman after all, and – she liked to think – a fairly successful one, at least according to *Tatler*.

"A year from now you could very well be calling me your Messiah." Lady Eliza paused to allow her words to achieve maximum impact before turning away and heading up the staircase. "I trust you can find your room," she said over her shoulder. "Cocktails in the front parlor at seven sharp. Don't be late."

Imelda did well with the bath. When Chloe dipped herself into the claw-footed tub fifteen minutes later, she immediately felt her energy – and her nerves – replenished and restored. She lay back in the steaming water and closed her eyes. The tarnish of travel and family politics melted away. She felt almost human again. Even though the private jet had been available to her, Chloe had chosen to fly commercial, which she did every so often because it made her feel more 'accessible' and at one with 'the people.' Of course, she flew first class. Economy would have made her tear her hair out and ruin the delightful bob she had spent a small fortune on at the salon, but a girl (especially an "It Girl") couldn't be expected to completely deny herself at least one or two small perks: British Airways first class was one of them, cut and color at George Northwood was another ... and perhaps there were a few other indulgences that Chloe preferred to keep on the whisper. The paps certainly didn't need to know everything.

Chloe held her breath and slid deep into the tub until she floated in the detoxifying luxury of the Dead Sea's finest bath salts. There was too much for her to process, not the least of which was a flurry of text messages that had blown up her mobile from the moment she landed at Heathrow earlier that afternoon all the way through the two-hour drive to the house in Dorset, at least according to their time stamps. Chloe had left her phone in her carryall during the drive.

When she checked her messages upon arrival in her room while Imelda tested the temperature of the bath water, she found herself inundated by a tidal wave of passionate, yet vaguely menacing, texts from a certain R.H. who preferred – or rather, Chloe insisted – to only be identified by a first and last initial. R.H. had been invited to the Steeplechase without Chloe's knowing. R.H. was hot to trot and threatening to get even hotter upon their arrival at Templeton Manor the next morning. R.H. wanted to know if Chloe remembered (how could she forget?) those steamy Ancient Evenings they had spent together in Sharm-el-Sheik? (For the record, Chloe had been at the luxurious Egyptian resort attending a S.A.S.S.-sponsored conference on the trans rights of Palestinians.)

Chloe had never intended for their *liaisons dangereuses* to become quite so dangerous. She wondered if someone in the family knew. Lady Eliza? The woman seemed to have eyes in the back of her head and everywhere else, for that matter, but Chloe didn't think it was her father's lover. Eliza had only been on the periphery of their lives at that time. Chloe had justified her Levantine affair as a reaction against her mother's illness. She had been very, very discreet. Or so she had always thought. Diana perhaps? But what could Diana possibly hope to gain by exposing her in such a public way? Spencer? No, the fool was too blinded by his hopeless infatuation to allow for anything outside the purview of his rose-tinted glasses. Yvette perhaps? Hmmm. Now there was a thought.

Chloe held her breath until her lungs felt as though they were about to burst before she pushed herself up and above the water and came, rather reluctantly, back to earth. She rubbed the water from her eyes and nose and contemplated giving herself another dunk, when a gnawing sense that she was not alone suddenly gripped her and forced her eyes open.

"Darling," Diana said. She hovered over the tub in a silk *Chinoise* kimono that hung loose across her breasts. "I was worried for a moment you were drowning. I wouldn't have known what to do. I suppose I would have called Rupert. I don't know whom I would have called. The She-Beast has fired them all, you see. She told me today we've entered an Age of Austerity, like she's bloody Theresa May or Boris or that Hindu they've got at Number Ten now. I didn't dare remind her we were just a family – a family, mind you, that have been around for centuries – but then she wouldn't have listened anyway, so what would have been the sodding point?"

"Hello, Di," Chloe replied. "Are you drunk?"

Diana appeared puzzled for a moment. She shook her head and batted her hand in Chloe's general direction before taking a seat on the edge of the bathtub. Chloe crossed her arms in front of her chest and slipped down so the water rose to her neck. Diana had a singular way of making her feel exposed.

"I'm working on it," Diana said.

"I could use a drink myself."

"Cocktails at seven sharp. Dinner at eight. Chop-chop. No delay."

"Yes, I've been well-informed."

"How are you anyway?" Diana asked. "Such a long way for you to go for so little return. But then, that's your signature, isn't it? Our resident martyr."

"I do what I can."

"Yes, I suppose that's one way of looking at it."

Chloe waited as Diana leaned back until she was almost in the water herself. The kimono came undone. Chloe couldn't help but admire her older sister's trim physique. She hated that Diana seemed to grow in allure the older she got. Chloe hated even more the fact that she was flat chested in comparison, even though R.H. had told her again and again that her tits were "positively delicious."

"Do you remember," Diana slurred, "when we were children? Bath time? Do you remember how Mumsy used to gather us all up on Sunday evening after tea? And we'd all have to get in the bath together – you, Edgar, Guy, and me, right on down the line – and Mumsy would take the time to roll up her sleeves and wash our hair? I can still smell the fragrance of the shampoo she used."

"You and Edgar perhaps," Chloe said. "There's a ten year difference between us, Diana. I don't think we ever bathed together. And if we had, I've obviously blocked it from memory. The very idea of such a thing is triggering."

"You think I'm so old, don't you?" Diana adjusted the kimono to a more modest state and got up from the edge of the bathtub. "I was once young and pretty like you. There was a time when this face could have launched a thousand ships. But life and responsibility have a way of taking their toll. It'll happen to you eventually, Chloe. You'll wake up one day and see yourself in the mirror and you'll wonder, 'where has my youth gone?' And you'll no longer be cute. No one will want to take your picture or ask whom you're wearing at red carpet galas. All that you'll have left is whatever is in your soul. And if there's nothing there, well, in the long run, what will having been a three-time *Tatler* cover girl have gotten you?"

"Four-time," Chloe interjected.

"What?"

"You said three-time. I've actually been on the cover of *Tatler* four times...

no, five, if you count the Leibowitz group portrait at Ascot last year for their philanthropy issue. The others were solos."

"Five. Whatever."

The water had turned cold and the bath salts had lost their effect. Chloe hunched her knees up to her chest and hugged herself as her teeth chattered. It was painfully obvious Diana intended to make her as uncomfortable as possible, and as much as Chloe wished that she had the fortitude to stand her ground against her older sister, Diana somehow always managed to take the upper hand. A knock on the door followed by the entrance of Penelope, who was gotten up in an entirely gauche riding jacket and skin-tight jodhpurs and riding boots that belonged nowhere near a horse, further disrupted Chloe's longed-for serenity.

"Penny darling," Diana said, her tone cut with a rapier's edge. "My, don't you look equestrian. Did someone forget to tell you the Steeplechase isn't until Saturday?"

Chloe stifled a giggle in spite of herself.

"Hello, Diana." Penelope strode across the bathroom to where Diana stood appraising herself in the mirror. She went in for a hug but Diana merely turned her cheek for a kiss.

"Hi, Chloe," Penelope waved.

"I think you look smart," Chloe said. "Love your boots."

"Why, thank you!" Penelope looked relieved. Her American sister-in-law was really rather sweet, Chloe decided, in that uniquely American Midwestern way. But only in small doses. And only with generous gaps in between.

"Balmain?" Chloe queried.

"Belstaff!"

"Very chic. *J'approuve*," Chloe said.

"That means so very much to me, coming from you."

Chloe loved the flattery. "Nonsense," she said. "You're a very sexy woman, Penelope Templeton. You just need to own it."

"All you need is a whip," Diana said. "And a ball gag...and spurs."

"Be nice," Chloe snapped.

Diana waved dismissively at no one in particular and returned to her reflection in the mirror. She let the kimono hang open so her breasts were further exposed. She cupped them in each hand.

"Ladies," she prompted, "what do you think? Shall I get them pumped up? Is that what the boys want these days? Big tits and even bigger lips?"

"I'm allergic to silicone," Penelope said. "A few years ago...do you remember? After Walter was born and I went through that dry spell with Edgar..."

"How could any of us forget?" Diana rolled her eyes dramatically and cast off the kimono so she stood stark naked in front of the mirror. "The one thing I'll say about you, Penelope darling, is you're persistent in your paranoia."

"I'm not being paranoid," Penelope demurred. "And it's happening again."

"Here we go." Diana turned away from the mirror and strode to the bathtub where Chloe was veritably shivering. "Move over, Chloe, I'm getting in."

Chloe did as she was told.

"Oh," Diana said as she splashed into the tub beside her little sister, "it's like returning to the womb. Don't you feel closer to Mumsy, Chloe?"

"Look at you," Penelope said. "The Templeton sisters."

"Plus one," Diana added, not particularly kindly.

"You're both so beautiful." Penelope studied them with a look of such moony admiration that Chloe was almost embarrassed for her. "Maybe that's my problem. Maybe that's why Edgar can't keep it in his pants whenever that slag Rebecca is around. Maybe I'm just not English enough for him? It's that lovely translucent skin. Like paper."

"I told you," Diana sighed. "Take a lover. That's what men do. Why shouldn't you be able to do the same?"

"Rebecca?" Chloe asked. She lowered herself into the water so her chin dipped beneath the surface.

"Hastings," Penelope said. "She's front of house at Foraged. Edgar's shagging her."

"Oh...*that* Rebecca Hastings!"

"Is there another?"

"No." Chloe felt herself getting hot. She slid deeper beneath the surface but Diana's presence prevented her from going too deep. "I mean, I didn't know. She's shagging Edgar?"

"My life is ruined."

"And she's coming here tomorrow?" Chloe asked.

"With her husband."

"Who?" Chloe felt a desperate need to vomit.

"Nevin Cheswick?" Penelope explained. "The celebrity chef? You know. He was on Barracuda Bar. It was because of that show that Edgar snapped him up for Foraged. Well, him and Rebecca. They're a package deal."

"I had no idea," Chloe said.

"But I don't think they're actually married," Penelope continued.

"Nevin Cheswick is a tall drink of water," Diana snarled.

"He's very short actually," Penelope said. "He wears platform shoes for television."

"Chloe, darling, are you all right?" Diana playfully tapped Chloe's chin with her big toe. "You're looking rather jaundiced. Have we touched a nerve? Is there something you're not telling us?"

Chloe launched herself out of the bathtub with such a lack of subtlety she knew Diana would pester her about it for days. "No," she said. "Other than jet lag and the usual. I need a very dirty martini."

"Cheers to that!" Diana exclaimed.

"I'm feeling very much like the odd woman out," Penelope said. She attempted to perch on the edge of the bathtub but the angle wasn't right and her jodhpurs didn't allow for much bend in the knees.

Diana rolled her eyes and slid down beneath the surface, blowing bubbles as she did. Chloe wrapped her terrycloth robe close about her without bothering to dry off. She checked her look in the mirror as she dabbed talcum powder to her neck and elbows. Trust Diana to make a comment that threw her into a silent tizzy. She'd been on a plane for God only knew how many hours to a Godforsaken country where children ran in the streets begging for handouts without wearing shoes. If she looked a little "jaundiced" then who could blame her? But still. And then of course this nonsense with R.H. had her spooked. No, more than spooked. Chloe was petrified. What had she been thinking? She'd needed to unwind. R.H. had made her feel less herself. Dr. Tabitha Wainwright had advised her to calm down, to take a breath, to chill. (Easy for Dr. Tabitha Wainwright to say! She didn't have a foundation to run or women dying in sweatshops relying on her to save them from themselves and their circumstances!)

R.H. had taken Chloe outside of herself, had made her feel less like an automaton and more like a woman – a real woman with real needs and desires. People seemed to think that Chloe was some kind of machine: that she didn't feel, that she didn't crave. (How Chloe craved!) R.H. had given her so much. Their lovemaking? Out of this world. But then, Chloe often wondered if the reason for their stratospheric fucking had been less about skill than a sense that what they were doing was somehow verboten, and deliciously so. Chloe adjusted the robe and shivered.

"Diana," she said, "the She-Beast told me Papa was joining us at table. She said he has an announcement to make. Do you know anything about this?"

"What could I possibly know, darling? Eliza doesn't speak to me."

"We both know that isn't true." Chloe turned to the side and studied her profile. It was the lighting in the bathroom, she decided. "Eliza likes you best out of any of us. You didn't see how dismissive she was of me when Guy and I arrived. I could almost taste her contempt."

"I don't get it," Penelope said. Chloe suppressed the urge to roll her eyes. Her American sister-in-law actually got very little.

"Well, you wouldn't," Diana replied. She lifted herself out of the bath and paused to let the water ripple down her body before shrugging the kimono over her shoulders.

"I'm not sure I know what you mean."

"Sisters, please!" Chloe turned away from the mirror with a (even for her) melodramatic flourish. She was feeling peeved. The bath had been meant as a sanctuary and it had become, through no fault of her own, anything but. She wanted silence. She needed time alone to process and think. "If you'll excuse me, I'm going to retire to my room for a bit. I'm feeling claustrophobic and if I don't have some time on my own – five minutes! Five minutes! – I think I shall scream."

Diana tossed her head back and laughed. "Darling," she exclaimed. "You're such a fucking freak."

"You haven't seen Guy! You don't know what I've been through."

"Poor, poor darling. My heart bleeds for you."

Chloe threw open the bathroom door and stomped down the hallway to her bedroom. Her head pounded and her heart felt as though it was about to explode in her throat. Damn Diana for winding her up. Goddamn herself for letting her older sister get to her. Once she was ensconced in her room, Chloe launched herself onto her bed – the same bed in which she'd lain as a child – and closed her eyes. She wanted to escape. She'd do anything to get away: from herself, from her family, from this fucking dinner that she knew was going to be an abomination of epic proportions.

What was R.H. doing? Why the texts? Why the threats? Why take something that had been so beautiful, so perfect, and turn it into something dirty and debauched? And why the hell was she fucking Edgar? Chloe wasn't sure what was worse: the possibility that her dangerous liaison was about to be exposed or that her former lover had moved on from Chloe to her brother? This was new territory.

She wasn't sure how she was supposed to react. Should she even react at all?

| 11 |

I t was meant to have been simple: a quiet night at Mare Moto on the King's Road. Chloe certainly wasn't looking for anything. A night out with the girls from S.A.S.S. (Tamsin's birthday party actually), a couple dirty martinis, a harmless flirtation, nothing more. Chloe had been on the fence all day as to whether she would even attend. She'd always found Tamsin tiresome: striving above her station, competing with her for pole position in London society, constantly reminding Chloe that she was "someone", blah blah blah. Chloe shuddered. She found television presenters objectionable and Tamsin was the queen of the pack.

But like a loyal frenemy, Chloe had gone. She'd endured the rounds of Jagermeister, had suffered through the endless and endlessly inane chatter about Tamsin and Jack's struggles to get pregnant, about Tamsin's flirtation with a certain nameless Formula One driver who may or may not have been Luca Mariotti, about the difficulty Jack was having adjusting to civilian life post-Afghanistan: yada yada yada. Yawn. Tamsin wasn't objectionable so much as boring. But Cressida Parker had been there and Chloe wasn't too proud to admit that she'd always had a bit of a girl crush on *Posh* TV's grande dame (and lest it be forgotten, Guy's one-time runaway bride).

Cressida Parker had been in the midst of launching her first cookbook – Posh – of which Chloe had been one of a select few to have received an advance reader copy. The book read like a laundry list of proto-feminist metaphysical New Age woke-ism, filled with recipes and lifestyle tips designed to test and strengthen 'your inner feminine love child' and get further in touch with your 'pussy galore.' As far as she could tell, there was nothing posh about it other than the provenance of its author. Chloe wasn't much of a cook – making tea was a challenge – and the instructions (all that slicing, dicing, douching and purging) were nothing short of incomprehensible, but as Cressida was such a close family friend – and nearly a sister-in-law – Chloe felt it her duty to muddle through, if for no other reason than to be able to tell Cressida that her kale-and-olive oil-infused salt water enema was 'to die for' and the hymen placenta treatment made her feel like a virgin all over again. Sisters supported each other through thick and thin and Chloe was nothing if not loyal to her S.A.S.S. squad.

About two hours into the evening, with Chloe deep in the dregs of her third

Kir Royale and Tamsin demonstrating – yes, demonstrating – how the Formula One driver who may or may not have been Luca Mariotti had shagged her in the ladies' toilet at Novikov while Jack had been waiting for her at the bar, Cressida suggested they step outside for a quick fag and have some quality catch-up. Chloe wasn't much for cigarettes but Cressida was a chimney so she agreed as an alternative to telling Tamsin that what she was doing to Jack – a war hero no less – was an affront to the sisterhood. Of course, Chloe fancied Jack herself and Tamsin knew this, which didn't put Chloe in the best light as far as the overly enthusiastic television presenter was concerned. Best not to provoke a scene. It wasn't as if they were cast members of *Made in Chelsea*...at least not yet.

So Chloe dutifully followed Cressida outside and accepted the Camel Ultra-Light without question. Her hands trembled a bit – Cressida had that effect on her – but after a couple puffs, her nerves eased and she was able to look the head of PoshTV (and honorary sister-in-law) in the eye without blushing. Not for the first time, she wondered whether she should take up smoking on a more-or-less regular basis.

"What I wouldn't give to rip out Tam's cunt," Cressida said. Her voice was smoke-saturated and hypersexual. It never failed to give Chloe a thrill. "I mean seriously, right? Who the fuck does she think she is? I'd fire the bitch if I didn't like Jack so much."

"Jack is rather dreamy," Chloe said. The fag was making her head spin. She suddenly felt high.

"And it isn't as if I don't know who she's talking about. Luca Mariotti is one of Olivier's best drivers...nor is he particularly discreet," Cressida continued. "She'd be none too pleased to hear the things he's said about her. 'A common slag,' he called her but in that sexy Italian accent, which almost makes it sound like a compliment. If I weren't such a professional, I'd have half a mind to tell her myself. What I should do is recommend one of my tantric colonics. It's something she and Jack can do together. Olivier can't get enough of it. He can't get enough of me. You can read all about it on page 269 of my book."

"Hmm," Chloe didn't like the sound of a colonic, tantric or otherwise, not to mention the thought of Olivier Thibault having one. But who was she to tell Cressida anything? "I think I skipped that part," she said.

"And what about you?" Cressida let rip a glorious plume of smoke that wafted high overhead and shimmered in the streetlamps. "When's the last time you had a good old fashioned pig in the poke?"

POSH

That was the thing about Cressida Parker: she was as posh as posh could be, but she had a mouth like a chav. Her background was a bit of a mystery. One heard rumors, but then one always heard rumors and Chloe didn't like to speculate about people she actually liked. Everyone else was fair game.

"You make it sound so dirty!" Chloe exclaimed. She sucked hard on the cigarette and fought to suppress a cough.

"Sex is dirty, darling," Cressida said. "That's what makes it so delicious. Now answer my question."

Chloe didn't like talking about sex.

"I've been too busy," she replied. "Papa's not been well. He had a funny turn the other day at the football. He's fine but Dr. Raleigh said he needed to reduce his stress, which we all know is easier said than done, especially with Papa. Of course, it doesn't help that that woman is hovering over him at all hours of the day, waiting to pounce, and her creepy sidekick..."

"The nun?"

"It's almost as if Eliza is hoping to convert him to the papacy when she thinks we're not looking."

"She's fierce that one," Cressida said – rather unhelpfully, Chloe thought. "Is she Catholic?"

"She converted after things went pear-shaped with her son...at least that's the rumor."

Chloe shivered. The nicotine was getting to her, making her head feel all lethargic and ethereal. She was about to suggest they go back inside but Cressida was lighting a fresh cigarette from the butt of her first and it seemed churlish not to accept the offer of another.

"You still haven't answered my question," Cressida said. "But no matter. I'll have you know that I've taken it upon myself to provide a solution."

"A solution to what?" Chloe asked. The first cigarette had put her into a haze. The second created a fog.

Cressida made a dramatic show of checking her watch before looking up, snapping her fingers, and exhaling another epic cloud of smoke. "Right on schedule."

As if out of nowhere, accompanied by the sharp click-clack of impossibly high Louboutin heels, a vision of such porcelain beauty appeared before Chloe that a for a second – before she caught herself – she really did choke. Rebecca Hastings emerged from the shadows cast by the overhead streetlamps dressed in a paisley-print shift dress by BCBGMAXAZARIA that stopped at mid-thigh with sleeves that cut off at the shoulders and lifted in the breeze like fairy wings. Her Louboutin heels provided a razor-sharp line from ankle to calf and then on up beyond the hem of the dress. A pair of diamond drop earrings sparkled from each lobe. Her hair was piled high in a loose beehive that added to the illusion of Amazonian height. Her face was unadorned with the exception of a faint dusting of powder and a crimson slash across her lips. Chloe hastily tossed what remained of her cigarette into the gutter – first impressions were worth a thousand words and Chloe (for reasons she couldn't possibly begin to articulate) wanted to make sure Rebecca looked upon her favorably – and rummaged in her purse for a breath mint.

"My, my!" Cressida rumbled in her husky honeyed voice as she greeted Rebecca Hastings with a pair of air kisses and a sassy pinch on the derriere. "Aren't you looking scrumptious tonight? Mee-ow!"

"Darling!" Rebecca Hastings stepped out of Cressida's embrace and regarded Chloe with an appraising look that made Chloe's neck break out in hives. "And who, may I ask, is this? You look familiar. Are you someone I should know?"

Chloe felt like it was her first day in school.

"Of course she is!" Cressida put her arm around Chloe's shoulder and pulled her close. "Do you think I'd introduce you to a nobody? I know everyone and everyone I don't know isn't worth knowing. And Chloe Templeton is DEFINITELY someone worth knowing."

A flash of recognition flitted across Rebecca Hastings' dark eyes accompanied by a subtle twitch at the corners of her mouth: of surprise or discomfort or perhaps both, Chloe couldn't surmise. The look passed almost as quickly as it had come before Rebecca held out her hand and Chloe limply accepted it.

"Of course," Rebecca Hastings said.

"Chloe, meet the hostess with the absolute most-ess, and my first bestie-in-waiting, Rebecca Hastings."

"Nice to meet you," Chloe stammered. Her palms were sweating. She withdrew her hand from Rebecca's rather icy grip, and wiped it on her thigh.

"*Enchantee*," Rebecca Hastings said. "How funny. We travel in the same circles yet we've never met."

"Until now," Cressida added.

"Until now," Rebecca Hastings affirmed.

"You look familiar to me too," Chloe said, the effort to speak was proving almost beyond her.

"I should hope so." Cressida beamed with smug self-satisfaction. "Rebecca Hastings is the better half of – and soon to be better known, if I have anything to do with it – Britain's most dynamic culinary duo and, I might add, the stars of PoshTV's latest cookery show phenomena *Delicious*. We're still casting contestants but the outcome is pretty much pre-ordained."

"I know your brother," Rebecca Hastings said.

"Oh...which one?"

"The married one."

Chloe thought it sounded almost like a challenge. "Edgar," she said.

"Well, well," Cressida said. "Now that we're all acquainted, I think it's time I left the two of you saucy girls to your own devices. No one likes a third wheel."

In the time it took for Chloe to gather her thoughts and beg Cressida not to leave her alone, Cressida Parker bid her adieu (with a devilish wink) and hurried back into the restaurant. Rebecca Hastings cocked one hip and crossed her arms in front of her chest. Chloe coughed and was thankful for the fact that in the dark she didn't think Rebecca Hastings could see that her neck was bright red.

"Awkward," Rebecca Hastings said.

"A bit."

"You're very pretty."

"Thank you," Chloe gulped.

"You and Edgar have the same nose."

"I hate my nose." Chloe touched it reflexively.

"You look like a pixie," Rebecca Hastings said.

"I'm not sure what we're supposed to be doing now," Chloe said. She took a deep breath as she forced herself to organize her jumbled thoughts into some semblance of coherent speech. "I mean, I'm here for a birthday party. Do you know Tamsin? She's on PoshTV too. Tamsin & Jack. Home improvement or something like that. I don't watch it really. Of course, I don't tell Cressida that because she'll disown me or something, but I'd much rather be reading a book or working on my campaign."

"Sisters Against Sweat Shops."

"Yes!" For the first time since Rebecca Hastings had emerged from the shadows of the streetlamps, Chloe felt a surge of relief. "You know it?"

"I read the feature in *Tatler*," Rebecca Hastings said.

"It's rubbish really. The article, I mean, not the foundation."

"The camera loves you."

"Oh, I don't know about that!" Chloe laughed.

"I'd love to photograph you."

"Oh." Chloe felt the blush return, rising up her neck to cover her entire face. She suddenly longed for another cigarette. "You're a photographer too?"

"Amateur. I'm building a portfolio. Cressida keeps pressing me to exhibit, but..."

"Cressida has a way of..."

"...I haven't found the right subject yet. I'm still looking for my muse."

The way Rebecca Hastings said 'muse' sent electric sparks through Chloe's nerve endings.

"I'd love to see your work," Chloe spluttered before she could second-guess herself. "I mean...I don't mean to presume..."

"Shall we?"

"What?"

"My studio is just around the corner."

"Convenient," Chloe said.

"Rather." Rebecca Hastings' smile was somewhere between a smirk and a leer.

Chloe felt she was having an out-of-body experience. She wondered, as she walked with Rebecca Hastings to the chef-cum-amateur photographer's studio, whether Cressida had laced her Camel Ultra-Lights with something to take Chloe out of herself. *This isn't me*, Chloe thought as she waited for Rebecca to unlock the door of the storefront and flip the light on *I don't know who I am right now, but I know I'm not being me.* And yet, Chloe had long ago vowed that she was going to be open to new experiences, that her life as she had lived it these thirty-something years had been too sheltered – too provincial, in a way – despite her work with S.A.S.S. and everywhere that work had taken her. There had been a time when Chloe might have considered herself adventurous, even something of a free spirit. New York had been an eye-opener. Of course, she'd been younger then – just out of uni – and she'd had the benefit of Ashleigh's tutelage, which may or may not have been an asset or a disadvantage, depending on one's perspective. Chloe still wasn't sure herself.

But she was no longer a naïve twenty-one year-old who could perhaps get away more easily with the occasional indiscretion. Flash forward to the present, to her life now, and Chloe saw nothing but responsibilities – not least of all to her family, to S.A.S.S., to the media and her hundreds of thousands of followers online. And then there was Spencer…Spencer…what to do about Spencer? She couldn't think about him now, not when Rebecca Hastings was pouring her a whisky and she was standing in the middle of sterile white-walled gallery whose walls were adorned with the most stunning (and provocative) black-and-white portraits Chloe thought she had ever seen.

"Oh my," Chloe said as Rebecca handed her the whisky. "They're all…erm…"

Rebecca Hastings shrugged and knocked back her drink. "It's a celebration of the cunt," she said. "In all its unbridled glory. For centuries women have been taught to cover up, to repress their sexuality. Girls are told at a very tender age that they have two choices in life – they can either be the Whore of Babylon or the Virgin Mary. It's a fucking tragedy. That's why so many women reach middle age and give up. They realize they've lost themselves to the patriarchy, that they've been forced to abandon their sense of self, that they've been enslaved by paternalism and the responsibilities thrust upon them by the Phallus. I reject that. I hold up my middle finger and say 'Fuck you!' to centuries of male domination and captivity. My photography – my art – is designed to inspire women to throw off the shackles of their penis envy and embrace the beauty of their pussies. A woman's cunt is the most beautiful of all God's creations. It's time women come to terms with our power, that we harness the strength of our female mystique, and embrace the fact that our pussies are glorious. Pussy is power, Chloe. Don't ever let anyone tell you otherwise."

Chloe gulped the whisky with the desperate rigor of an alcoholic. It wasn't that she disagreed with the content of Rebecca Hastings's impassioned diatribe – in fact, had she been able to process it in her own time, she would have realized that much of what Rebecca said was in line with S.A.S.S.'s values statement. The foundation had, after all, been created to advocate for women's rights in Third World countries, and part of that brief was to educate disadvantaged and abused women on the importance of self-empowerment. But standing there, half-drunk and utterly disorientated for reasons Chloe was at a loss to articulate, she looked at Rebecca Hastings as though the woman was some kind of alien and that she was being indoctrinated into a subversive cult.

But that wasn't exactly true. What frightened Chloe – for yes, Rebecca Hastings inspired fear in her – was the simple fact that Chloe wanted nothing more at that moment than to be seduced by the feminist firebrand. Rebecca Hastings made her hot in places Chloe hadn't dared believe could tingle with such terrifying anticipation. She burned.

"Pussy is power," Chloe repeated. The words felt like revolution on her tongue. "Another?"

"Yes, please."

Rebecca Hastings took Chloe's glass from her and filled it to just below the rim. Chloe forced herself to sip carefully, lest the drink spill or she become utterly inebriated, or at least more so than she already was.

"How about some music?" Rebecca Hastings asked.

"Why not?" Chloe said.

She felt drawn to the black-and-white photographs, like a powerful magnetic force pulled her to examine each and every one and study their most intimate detail. She longed to touch the photographs, to trace her finger along each piece's lines and contours.

"I never realized," she said, more to herself than to Rebecca who was fiddling with the sound system on her desk. "I mean, each one is so different."

"Like the woman each represents," Rebecca Hastings replied. "Every woman is different. Every woman is unique. Every woman has her own kind of beauty. The same is true of her garden. No two flowers are the same."

"I guess it makes sense," Chloe stammered. The alcohol was making her flushed. "I mean...well, it's not like I've spent a lot of time thinking about..."

Bossa nova shimmered from the overhead speakers.

"Can I tempt you into a samba?"

Chloe pulled herself away from the vaginal portraiture as she felt Rebecca Hastings come up behind her. She nearly dropped her glass. Rebecca Hastings' body was so appealingly sinuous beneath her dress as she raised her hands above her head and let her body sway to the seductive Latin beats that Chloe couldn't help but feel compelled to move herself. She took a generous gulp of whisky. Rebecca Hastings removed the glass from Chloe's hand and set it down on the concrete floor. Her eyes were closed. Chloe took a deep, sustaining breath and decided to let go. The music infused her entire body. She and Rebecca Hastings touched without touching, each aware of the other's proximity and of what and where they were and of what and where they could so easily go. Chloe didn't dare. She gave herself to the moment with as much abandon as she could muster, which – she realized somewhat self-consciously – to an outside observer (or participant) might not seem like all that much.

The problem was (not that Chloe had ever really seen it as a problem – modesty and restraint were her modus operandi, those combined with an earnestness she had always found endearing) she kept herself so tightly wound that the effort to loosen up took considerable effort. Spontaneity terrified her, as did anything outside of her control. Spencer was always telling her to let down her hair and have fun. He never seemed to believe her when she tried to convince him that he needn't worry, which only led her to further believe that despite their best intentions with and for each other, theirs was a match not made to be. But there she went again: just as she was doing her damnedest to give herself over to the music and the delicious and dangerous eroticism she felt emanating from Rebecca Hastings' body, she couldn't help focusing instead on everything she wanted so desperately to control. *Face it*, Chloe, she said to herself as Rebecca's arms suddenly wrapped around her waist and their bodies danced as one, *you're an effing disaster*.

"I'm going to kiss you now," Rebecca Hastings whispered in Chloe's ear.

Rebecca Hastings' lips were hot. Too hot actually. There was a part of Chloe that wanted to be seduced, that wanted to throw caution to the wind and let herself be consumed by all of the very ripe possibilities Rebecca Hastings presented to her. But the dominant part of her, that which ruled Chloe's every thought, feeling, and action, urged her to pull away and return to the safety of the iron fortress within which she maintained her comfort zone. This wasn't the time to let impulse hijack her moral compass. She didn't know this woman. She had a reputation to preserve and protect. What had Cressida been thinking in throwing the two of them together? Chloe would have to have a word.

"I'm sorry!" she spluttered. "This isn't...I can't..."

"You can't or you won't?"

Chloe turned away and found herself confronted by what now appeared to her a grotesque image of a sizably overweight white woman's vulva bursting through the protective glass of its frame. Chloe clutched her stomach and fought against the rising bile that surged up her esophagus and threatened to spew all over Rebecca Hastings' photographs. She felt trapped. The walls were closing in on her: a thousand gaping vaginas mocking and taunting her inadequacy, her fear, her traditional sensibilities. Everywhere she looked were stark reminders of imprisonment and a sudden sense of self-loathing. What was happening to her? How had she allowed herself to come to this?

"I just need a moment," she gasped.

Rebecca Hastings threw up her hands in what Chloe could only surmise was frustration (or disgust) – which served to make her feel worse about herself and the situation – and went to the bar to pour herself another whisky.

"Cressida warned me it might be like this," Rebecca Hastings said. There was an edge in her voice that Chloe found unnerving, but more so was the suggestion that her best friend might have had something to do with this, as if Cressida and Rebecca Hastings had conspired to compromise Chloe's integrity. The suspicion of untoward behavior on Cressida's part gave Chloe a jolt that settled her stomach and made her feel more in control of her nerves.

"Cressida?" Chloe asked. "What do you mean, Cressida 'warned' you? Warned you about what? About me?"

Rebecca Hastings perched against the edge of her desk and regarded Chloe down the length of her nose. Chloe's instinct was to look away – she really ought to leave altogether but still she couldn't quite compel herself to walk out, at least not yet.

"Let's just say that our mutual friend is highly protective of you," Rebecca Hastings said. "It's really rather sweet, if uncharacteristic."

"I don't think it's uncharacteristic at all!" Chloe protested. "Cressida's always been there for me. She's like the older sister I always wished I'd had."

"You don't like Diana?"

"That's not what I mean."

"Penelope?"

"What about Penelope?"

"Edgar's wife."

"Yes, I know who Penelope is! What I mean is..."

"What?"

Rebecca Hastings crossed the expanse between them in two cat-like strides. Before Chloe could protest further – or find her way to the door – Rebecca's mouth was on hers. Rebecca's tongue pushed against Chloe's clenched teeth, forcing them apart as she pushed Chloe back against the wall. This time, Chloe was helpless to resist. Her body seemed to melt as she gave in to her unaccustomed desire.

And then they were apart once again. Rebecca Hastings returned to her desk and sat down leaving Chloe breathless and desperate for more.

"You've definitely got potential," Rebecca Hastings said. "I'll give you that. I think I should like to break you in. I think I should like to break you in very much."

To Chloe, it sounded like a rejection.

"I don't know what you mean," she stammered. "You speak a language I don't understand."

Rebecca Hastings smirked. "All in good time," she replied. "That's something else Cressida told me about you. She said you're very earnest."

"I like being earnest."

"Cressida finds it endearing. I, on the other hand, do not."

"It sounds like you and Cressida spend an awful lot of time talking about me." Now that she'd regained her power of speech – or at least her breath – Chloe felt less inclined to make a hasty departure. She decided she didn't like Rebecca Hastings. No, she didn't like Rebecca Hastings one bit. Yet she couldn't deny that she found the other woman intriguing. The kiss wasn't all.

"You like being the center of attention, don't you?"

"Not particularly." Chloe stopped herself. "I mean, I don't like friends talking about me behind my back. I shall have a word with Cressida."

Rebecca Hastings arched her back and swiveled in the chair. "What will you say to her?" she asked. It sounded like a challenge.

"What's it to you?"

"I don't like being spoken of behind my back either."

Something in the way Rebecca Hastings now regarded her made Chloe more uncomfortable than anything that had hit her with the kiss. She knew she should leave, but her feet were like lead on the concrete floor. Sweat trickled from between her shoulders down to the small of her back. It was moist and made her feel sick to her stomach. If she stayed she knew bad things were about to happen. Chloe could see it in Rebecca Hastings' eyes: cold, calculating, and yet utterly alluring.

"I think I should go," she said, but her words lacked conviction. She felt as though Rebecca Hastings could read her mind.

"I won't stop you."

Yet her feet – maddeningly – still refused to move.

"The door's that way," Rebecca Hastings said with a dismissive flick of her hand. Her stare, however, was anything but. Chloe struggled against the impulse to return the look with one of equal hauteur, but her face felt as frozen as her feet. She was hot and cold and clammy. Her heart raced.

"I don't think I like you very much," she said.

"Do you like everyone you fuck?"

"We haven't...I mean, I haven't..."

"No, but you want to."

"No!" *(A little too emphatic perhaps.)*

Rebecca Hastings didn't suffer fools. "If it makes you feel any better," she said,

"I don't like you very much either."

"Excuse me?"

"You're a prig."

"Then why don't you let me go?"

"I don't see any chains," Rebecca Hastings said. "You're free to go as you please."

"But I'm not, am I?" Chloe knew it was too late. There was no turning back now. Rebecca Hastings was a sorceress, and despite all better judgment, she was bewitched. "You've done something. You've spiked my drink."

Rebecca Hastings emitted a throaty laugh while releasing her hair from its up-do with a glorious flourish. "No, Chloe Templeton," she said. "I didn't spike your drink. I'd never pull such a mannish move. I'm not desperate.

"What then?"

Rebecca Hastings stood up from her chair. Chloe watched her approach with a long-legged, languorous yet purposeful, stride. Her eyes widened when Rebecca Hastings slipped out of her dress in one all-too-casual, all-too-experienced shrug. The woman's body was angular – like a Modigliani, Chloe thought – and perfect. Her breasts were pleasingly round and full, her nipples large and erect, like buttons. Chloe couldn't help herself. She looked down at Rebecca Hastings' thick and luxuriant bush.

"You don't..." Chloe gulped. She couldn't complete the thought.

Rebecca Hastings laughed. Her neck. Chloe wanted to kiss her neck.

"Au *naturel*, baby," Rebecca Hastings said.

"Oh, my," Chloe said.

| 12 |

Chloe's mobile buzzed. There was a knock on the door – less a knock than a sequence of harried and manic raps – that caused Chloe to jolt from the bed. She forgot for a moment where she was. She'd fallen asleep. Her dreams had been terrible, frightening, throwing her into a general sense of disorientation that didn't play well with her jet lag. *What time is it? Shit...quarter past seven.* There was a text waiting for her and a missed call. Chloe couldn't bring herself to see whom the messages were from. She instinctively knew – R.H. Chloe couldn't bear it. The past was becoming present. But then, the past was never really the past, was it?

"Chloe?" Guy. Another set of raps. "Chlo? You in there? You didn't fall asleep, did you? There's a whole shitload of people waiting for us in the parlor. The prodigal son and the Good Samaritan are expected. We mustn't disappoint, must we?"

"Fuck." Chloe didn't like profanity. She despised it, in fact, but sometimes no other words seemed appropriate. This was one of those moments. R.H. swore like a sailor.

"Chlo?"

She stumbled off the four-poster bed – hers since childhood – and nearly tripped over the loose-hanging tie of her terrycloth bathrobe.

"I'm coming!" she replied. "I mean..."

"Can I come in?" Guy knocked on the door again, more gently this time. "I can't face the madding crowd all on my own. I need you, Chlo. Are you decent?"

Chloe threw open her walk-in closet and surveyed its immaculately curated contents. Nothing suited her. *What an effing disaster!*

"Oh, so you're speaking to me now?" she quipped.

"Chlo?"

She settled for a tasteful (and thoroughly boring) navy blue and white print dress by L.K. Bennett. She'd liked the oversized sailor collar when she'd bought it, but now the dress just struck her as too – how had R.H. described her? – earnest. She needed a wardrobe upgrade. (Thank God, London Fashion Week was only a few weeks away!) The door flew open just as she stepped into the dress.

"I beg your pardon!" Chloe exclaimed. "Can't a girl get a little privacy in her own bedroom?"

She frowned at Guy's reflection in the floor-to-ceiling closet mirror. He was grinning at her in that irresistible way of his that always made Chloe's heart melt. She loved him. She really did. If only he weren't so obstinate. His black dinner jacket and white tie were crisp and pressed. He looked almost human again.

"I barely recognize you," she said.

"Dr. Raleigh had his work cut out for him," Guy said. "At least I have my looks to fall back on."

"Conceited so-and-so." All was forgiven, at least until the next time.

"Are we really going to go through with this?" he asked. "What say you we ditch the dog and pony show, hijack one of the cars, and give the fam' the bird? We can be in London in two hours' time. Table for two at The Wolseley? Drinks at Annabel's after? What do you say, Chlo? Up for a bit of fun?"

"It's fun that gets you into trouble," Chloe said even as she had to concede that

Guy's offer sounded infinitely more desirable than dinner and drinks with Lady Eliza at the helm. "Now zip me up and tell me I don't look like death warmed over, because that's how I feel."

"You look beautiful as always," Guy said. He kissed her cheek as he zipped her up.

She considered their reflection in the mirror. "Guy?" she asked.

"Yes?"

"What happened to you in Russia? You don't have to tell me now…"

"There's nothing to tell."

"There's always something to tell."

Guy turned away from her with an exasperated sigh. The easy thing for her to do, Chloe knew, was let bygones be bygones. She supposed much of what Guy got up to – or at least what she suspected he got up to – was his business and shouldn't impact her. The problem was, the things she had heard – speculations, rumors, and (unfortunately) some confirmed truths – did affect her because they affected the family, and Chloe took infinitesimal pride in the Templeton name and what it represented and, more so, keeping its reputation pure, or at least as pure as possible. It was one thing for Guy to be the black sheep of the family – for every family she had ever known had one, it seemed to be the English way – but quite another for him to be willfully tarnishing its reputation with indiscreet and irresponsible behavior. (Which, frankly, put her in a bit of a bind where R.H. was concerned. She couldn't very well be the one casting stones. But still. One had to have principles.)

"You do realize, don't you," Chloe began, as she stepped into a pair of 'sensible' flats and regarded herself one last time in the mirror, "that Ambassador Bingham will be arriving on the train from London tomorrow for the weekend?"

Guy was a master of the poker face.

"I had nothing to do with any of that," he said.

"That's like Bill Clinton saying he never had sexual relations with that woman." The more Guy obfuscated, the feistier she became.

"Cordelia Bingham is a grown woman," he said.

"She's eighteen! Less a grown woman than a child."

"She knew what she was doing."

"I can't do this right now." Chloe brushed past Guy on her way to the door. Her head was pounding. *Take a breath, Chloe. Get a grip.* She opened the bedroom door, then stopped, her hand gripped around the doorknob. "All I know is that the ambassador's daughter was found half-naked, wandering Tverskaya Street at four o'clock in the morning. She was drugged and her body bore signs of severe physical trauma. Those are the facts, Guy. There was nothing consensual about it, grown woman or not."

"And all I'm saying is I had nothing to do with whatever did or didn't happen to her."

"You deny the facts?"

"You don't know the half of it," Guy said. Something in his tone gave Chloe a start. She glanced at him over her shoulder and held his stare. His dark eyes chilled her. She struggled to catch her breath.

"I want to believe you," she murmured. "I really want to believe you."

"But you don't."

"I'm sorry, Guy," she said. The words choked in her throat. "Regardless of whether or not you are...were...*are* involved, what happened to that poor girl is an abomination, an affront to my life's work at S.A.S.S: white male entitlement of the most insidious kind. I can't just turn a blind eye to it, as much as I might wish I could. If I made you an exception– my dearest brother whom I love so very much – I'd be a hypocrite, and I simply won't give anyone that kind of ammunition against me."

There was nothing more to say. Chloe ignored Guy's proffered handkerchief and wiped her eyes again with her fingers as she strode down the hallway to the grand staircase. It broke her heart to say such things to Guy, but really, what else could he possibly have expected from her? As she descended the stairs and heard the din of family cocktail hour emanating from the front parlor, she reflected on the difficulty of her own situation. Of course, she was a hypocrite. She didn't need anyone to tell her that, nor did she need anyone affirming it. R.H. was a problem. Yes. But R.H. could be dealt with on the quiet, in a way that no one would ever have to know anything about. R.H. was a personal matter and nothing more. Guy, on the other hand, represented an issue much bigger than herself. She could try to mitigate the damage as best she could, but the Bingham scandal was writ large across an international canvas. The fallout could – and very likely would – have repercussions that would impact even those who weren't even remotely involved other than by personal acquaintance and association. It pained Chloe to no end, but she simply couldn't abide such instability in her life. She didn't think she had the strength within her to fight him on her own. It would have to be a collective effort. She'd need to rally the troops.

And yet, if only Guy were to come to her on bended knee, declare he was in the wrong and then confess everything to her so that she might see what she could do to help him, perhaps she could forgive and even – dare she think it? – forget. At the same time, however, she didn't think him capable and she feared getting her hopes up. But now wasn't the time. Her family awaited. She was late to cocktail hour, and if there was one thing that Chloe Templeton couldn't tolerate in herself or in others was being late...especially not to a party, even if it was a party she would rather not attend.

| 13 |

Lady Eliza Brookings was very well satisfied. So satisfied in fact that she almost had to pinch herself. How easily things were falling into place! Of course, there were challenges ahead, but none – at least from her current perspective – that struck her as insurmountable. If she played her cards right and maintained a level hand, there was no reason she shouldn't be sitting pretty on the veritable throne of Templeton Manor by the holidays, at the very latest. Or even sooner, if she kept her wits about her.

Diana had been an early concern, for Diana was ever-present. Of all the Templeton brood, Diana was the one who had stuck closest to home, no doubt believing that as the eldest, it was her duty to oversee the estate and her father's failing health in the aftermath of Lady Fiona's premature (and yes, tragic, even Eliza had shed a tear at her passing) death by cancer three years' previous. The oldest Templeton child was also – unquestionably in Eliza's mind – the smartest. Like Eliza, Diana Templeton was a natural born skeptic with an uncompromising eye for nuance and detail, especially where the family was concerned. Her painting was inscrutable, but other than that, Eliza could find very little to fault.

But of any of them, Diana was also the least welcoming of outsiders. Because she had led such a sheltered life, Diana possessed an innate distrust of strangers, and in particular those who for one reason or another were brought into the family fold. That Lady Eliza Brookings had been embraced first by Lady Fiona and then by Lord Carleton himself must have caused Diana no end of angst, because approval of Eliza had come from the very top, which of course Eliza used to her advantage and would continue to use until the threat went away, which (if Eliza had anything to do with it) would happen very soon now...very soon indeed. Patience was a virtue.

And, it seemed, Diana was coming round. Eliza knew that the key to Diana's heart (bruised as it was) was through appealing to her sense of need, an almost desperate desire to feel empowered. Eliza was well-acquainted with Diana's whole sorry story: the youthful rebellion, the love match that had long since turned sour – oh, the things Eliza knew about Duncan would surely put Diana in a straitjacket! – the miscarriage, and what was more-or-less its resultant self-imposed exile. On the outside, Lady Diana projected an air of dignified reserve that came inherent to those born with more than a silver spoon in their mouth. But inside, Lady Eliza knew, there burned a fire that if not properly contained could readily spiral out of control and consume everything in its path. Lady Eliza couldn't afford to let that happen, at least not until the timing suited her. Had circumstances been different – in another lifetime, in another world – Eliza might have thought to pursue Diana for genuine friendship. But in present circumstance, such would be the kiss of death, and Lady Eliza's talent for self-preservation was keen.

The others – Edgar (a lightweight waster who represented much of what Lady Eliza despised about the upper classes, and upper class men in general); Guy (the dark horse, unpredictable and therefore dangerous, but not so dangerous that a few well-placed kicks couldn't take him down for good); and Chloe (a spoilt, narcissistic dilettante if ever there was one) – really didn't pose much of a challenge. Once she took the reins – which she intended to do swiftly and unequivocally – they would either all fall into place or be knocked into oblivion. She wouldn't have to do much but sit back and watch them bleed their precious blue blood all over the Florentine marble floors.

Today had been the best day of Lady Eliza's life. And, she didn't doubt, tonight would prove even better. Of course, it was indulgent. Of course, there was a risk that Carleton would be too weak to move or that Dr. Raleigh would intervene and advise against putting such strain on Carleton's ailing eighty-two year-old heart. All of which was why it had been imperative that Father O'Callahan was smuggled into the manor that afternoon (in the wine delivery lorry from the village, no less!) while Diana had been distracted by her painting (and gin) and before the other children (and Elena Grimaldi) arrived from various and sundry. Lady Eliza knew that nothing was official until the conversion and the exchanging of vows, after which she had all she needed to effect the next steps of her plan. The only thing that could possibly have made the day any better, in Eliza's opinion, was for Sister Francine to have not missed her train from Watford on account of industrial action – inconvenient and disappointing, yes, but Eliza was not completely insensitive to her spiritual advisor's recent health issues. Cancer was insidious and unfortunately all too democratic. First Lady Fiona…Eliza didn't care to think about it.

She stood apart from the others in the corner of the parlor by the rococo fireplace, watching them gathered about the room in their various poses, each playing their various parts, and contemplated the scene with an intense scrutiny as though she was in the audience watching an utterly daft but still oddly compelling play written by Noel Coward perhaps (*The Importance of Being Earnest*) or a novel by Evelyn Waugh. *Brideshead Revisited* – one of Lady Eliza's favorites for all its Catholic handwringing – seemed particularly pithy. The clock on the mantle struck the quarter hour. Fifteen more minutes before Carleton was rolled into the dining room and the real festivities would begin. The atmosphere teemed with tension and tulips. Even Eliza had to concede that Elena's floral creations – while not exactly to Eliza's taste – were things of wonder. She would have preferred that Elena stayed in London, for The Tulip Queen of Amsterdam wasn't family and what was about to transpire that evening was strictly Family. But to protest too vociferously would have risked jeopardizing the stealth with which Eliza had planned the evening. She couldn't afford to raise too much undue suspicion, not when she was so close, not when victory (finally!) was so near at hand. It was probably just as well that Sister Francine had missed that train.

Lady Eliza allowed herself a few moments of focused reflection. It hardly seemed possible that the past five years had played so well to her advantage. While the Templeton family – and everything they represented – had always existed in Eliza's periphery, it wasn't until that fortuitous church bake sale in a village outside Watford (of all places) where Eliza first came into contact with none other than Lady Fiona herself, the Templeton's famously virtuous, kind-hearted, and much-admired matriarch. The bake sale was a local affair, an effort to raise funds to fix a leaky roof in the village Catholic church, and Eliza – whose only son, Trevor, had just been convicted of drug-smuggling in Harare and was facing an uncertain future in one of Zimbabwe's more notorious prisons – had turned to the church for spiritual and emotional sustenance. Her husband – Lord Chester Brookings – had died in dubious circumstances in a Bangkok massage parlor in the bed of a barely legal Thai bum boy years previous, leaving Lady Eliza in the unenviable position of sorting through her late husband's equally unenviable financial situation and an extended family (her husband's) that had never accepted her and turned further against her the moment Chester's body had been discovered with his throat cut and his scrotum stuffed in his mouth. (As if she'd had something to do with it!)

POSH

With the fortune Eliza had counted on to see her through old age tied up in probate and her son for all she knew rotting away in prison, Lady Eliza returned to the sanctity of the Catholic Church she'd abandoned by necessity the day she had accepted Lord Chester's marriage proposal. The Brookings family estate was based in Hertfordshire and the village – a quaint old place dating back to the 16th century – lay conveniently on Brookings land. With a decrepit spinster sister-in-law from hell breathing down her neck every minute of the day spewing invective, not to mention a rebellious house staff deliberately thwarting Lady Eliza's every instruction, Eliza found herself walking to the village each morning at sun-up to soothe her beleaguered soul in the front pew of the modest stone church and its disproportionately imposing wooden crucifix.

For the first several weeks of her pilgrimage, she encountered no one. The village was like a ghost town and the church a relic from pre-Reformation times. She wouldn't have been at all surprised had it been haunted. But then, one early November morning, Lady Eliza arrived to find to her not inconsiderable consternation that her worship was to be conducted in the presence of another: a woman of rather plain countenance and stout proportions pushing the outer edge of middle-age, dressed in a matronly khaki knee-length skirt, white blouse, and sensible brown shoes. She looked up with a sharp glare when Lady Eliza entered – the single oak door creaked mightily with age – and held her gaze as Eliza hurried down the center aisle to her customary seat in the front row.

Eliza found the woman's presence disconcerting. She squeezed her rosary as she went bead-by-bead through her daily cycle of prayers, but the peace that usually descended upon her was absent that day, and she couldn't help but blame the other woman – the interloper – for intruding upon her meditation.

Eliza didn't dare address the woman. She shunned the very notion of making even tentative eye contact. But she felt her in the pew behind her, listened to the woman's mouth-breathing, and found herself counting the seconds of each inhale and exhale and the seconds in between. The woman felt very close, as if she was hovering over her, tracking Eliza's every move, waiting for an opportune moment to descend and punish her for daring to occupy the same church and pray before the same crucifix. Eliza had half a mind to get up and run, but where would she go? It was too early to return to Brookings Farm and Chester's sister, Dulcinea – Dulcie for short, to everyone except Eliza – would only just be rising from her bedchamber. She was trapped. She simply had no other choice but to stand her ground and focus on the prayer rotation. Eliza wrapped the beads around her fingers and squeezed until they cut into her palm.

"That's one way to achieve stigmata," the woman whispered. Her lips brushed Lady Eliza's ear. Her breath was stale and hot. Eliza gave a start.

"Excuse me?" she asked, staring at the crucifix, refusing to break concentration.

"If you're not careful, you'll break it," the woman said, "which would be such a crying shame, wouldn't it? Them's look expensive."

"I bought it at the Vatican." Despite her misgivings, Eliza found herself drawn into conversation. The woman's voice – flat and nasal – had an hypnotic effect upon her, or perhaps it was simply the fact that it had been so long since another person had engaged her in conversation, that Eliza craved the interaction. "I had it blessed by the Pope."

"Well, aren't you fancy?" There was an edge in the woman's voice, but it wasn't entirely unkind. "Did His High Holiness also invite you to tea?"

"Yes, actually." Eliza regretted saying it the moment the words left her lips. "I was a little girl. My father was in the diplomatic corps. He was posted to the Vatican. Years ago."

"You're Lady Eliza Brookings."

Eliza turned. The woman was on her knees in the pew behind her, so close they nearly knocked heads.

"I beg your pardon?" she asked.

"Of Brookings Farm," the woman continued. "Such a shame about your husband. It must be awful. But then, husbands can be awful, can't they? My Seamus ain't awful. He's just dull. I'd take dull over awful any day. And your son…"

"I think I should be going." Eliza stood up to leave but the woman's hand was cold and forceful on her shoulder. She had no choice but to remain.

"I seem to have forgotten me manners," the woman said. "Let me introduce myself. I'm Esther. Esther Mulroney, though me friends call me Essie. You can call me Essie too, if you'd like."

"Essie…"

"Essie and Eliza. It has a certain ring to it, don't you think?"

"What do you want?" Eliza snapped. There was something about the woman – Essie – that chilled her, and it had nothing to do with the draftiness of the old church. Over the years, Eliza had grown accustomed to the occasional loony accosting her in the street. Her late husband had certainly had his detractors, especially since the scandal, and while she supposed the general public had a right to their opinions – and to a lesser extent the right to express these opinions – Eliza preferred to be kept ignorant of them when and wherever possible.

When the Bangkok story broke, MI5 and MI6 had encouraged her to hire a security detail, but Eliza had scoffed at such a notion as alarmist and (more to the point) an unnecessary hassle. Eliza considered herself perfectly capable of handling whatever came her way – though she did agree to a course of martial arts self-defense training taught by a former member of the SAS. She was her own woman – she always had been – and she wasn't about to let a little scandal (however salacious) interfere with her sense of independence. But every once in a while – a very long while – a passing stranger's comment or look or a particularly slanted article in the broadsheets – usually *The Guardian* – or on the BBC would catch her off-guard and Lady Eliza Brookings of Brookings Farm would find herself on the verge of very much losing her tightly wound composure. This was one such moment.

"Oh, Lady Eliza, I think you misunderstand me," Essie hissed. "If my presence offends you, I apologize, though I daresay I mean you no offense."

Eliza hesitated. As much as instinct screamed for her to take her leave, she found to her surprise that she didn't disbelieve the woman, even as she detected what struck her as a sinister undercurrent in the apology. She gripped the rosary in her fist and willed herself to calm down, at least long enough to hear Essie out. She supposed it was the very least she could do.

"No offense taken," Eliza said.

"The thing is," Essie continued, her hand still resting on Eliza's shoulder, "I've seen you coming in here day after day and I must say, it has been a very long time since I have witnessed such a potent display of what I can only describe as true faith. You strike me as a believer in the most devoted sense. That's rare in these troubling times...very rare indeed. And highly commendable, I might add."

"You've been spying on me?"

"Not spying exactly...observing."

"Why haven't I seen you? The church is always empty when I come. I think that's why I return. I like the solitude. I'm not sure I'd come back if I knew I was being...observed."

"Which is precisely why I've remained...unobserved," Essie said. "Until now."

"I don't understand."

"I needed to see, I needed to be sure, that you were devout – a real Christian – before I revealed myself to you. If you only knew, Lady Eliza, if only you understood where I've been these past many years – the emotional journey has taken a toll – my sister, you see, Frannie…"

Essie broke off as the words seemed to suddenly catch in her throat. She coughed into the back of her hand and waved away Eliza's instinctive gesture of concern. After a moment or two, Essie appeared to regain her composure, and continued on as if there had been no interruption:

"Let's just say the Lord has seen fit to challenge me," she said, "and it is not for us to question His divine mystery but rather face it with eyes open and arms spread wide as we carry on, armed with the power of our unflagging faith, marching through adversity, marching in step as soldiers of Christ."

Looking back on that moment all these years later, Eliza recognized Essie's profession of faith (for there was no other way to describe it) as a turning point in her life. The ardent belief, the absolute righteousness with which Essie Mulroney spoke these words struck Eliza as nothing short of a crusader's call to arms. It stirred feelings she had long held at bay, for reasons she couldn't articulate. And while the fear remained – for yes, there was something fearful in Essie's zealotry – Eliza found herself inspired. It was as though she had spent countless years in the dark only to find herself now coming into the light. A weight felt lifted. She could breathe again.

"I'd like you to join us, Lady Eliza," Essie said. Her eyes burned with intensity. The hand on Eliza's shoulder was hot. "Francine and me. We're only just the two of us, but we're growing. And what we lack in numbers we make up for in strength."

"Join you in what?" Eliza gasped. Her skin where Essie touched it felt as though it was on fire, but the warmth was anything but threatening.

"Tea."

"Oh."

"You don't drink tea?"

"Yes…I mean…of course…I mean, I was expecting…"

Essie laughed. "All in good time, Lady Eliza," she soothed. "All in good time. Frannie's waiting for us at the tearoom down the lane, in the event you and I were favorably disposed…"

And so Eliza followed Essie out of the church and down the lane that bisected the village between the churchyard and the one or two antiques shops that comprised the village's high street. She felt as though she was floating, not entirely in control of her actions, but rather more than willing to allow herself to be led by this strange woman of such powerful religious conviction, which needless to say was entirely out of character, as Eliza had never allowed anyone or anything take possession of her in such an all-consuming way, not even Chester, God bless his poor perverted soul.

The tearoom was empty when they arrived ten minutes later, save for the presence of a middling-sized woman dressed head-to-toe in black wool – black turtleneck, black skirt, black stockings – and heavy black buckled shoes with thick rubber soles. A single gold chain, from which dangled a delicate crucifix, stood out amid such austerity as a testament of her vehement faith. Her black hair was cut short as though it had only recently been shaved to the scalp. Eliza found the woman's appearance nothing short of extraordinary – oracular even.

"Frannie," Essie hissed as they swept into the tearoom to the table where Sister Francine had been waiting. "She has come. Lazy Eliza is in our midst."

Sister Francine's expression was stoic. She acknowledged Lady Eliza with a terse nod before pouring them each a cup of tea from the porcelain teapot that graced the center of the blue-and-white checkered wax tablecloth.

"Darjeeling," she said. "It soothes a weary soul."

"Thank you," Eliza replied.

"My sister's just been in the clink," Essie said, filling the heavy silence as Sister Francine poured equal measures of tea into each of their cups. "She only got out last week."

"Eighteen long years," Sister Francine rumbled. "And let me tell you, everything they say about prison is true."

"I've no doubt," Eliza said. She thought of her son, Trevor, somewhere down there in South Africa, or was it Zimbabwe? She couldn't keep track. Trevor wasn't particularly good at keeping her informed. He'd always been a bit of a wild one, ever since he was a toddler. Eliza had done the best she could for him. It hadn't been easy raising a child in a house as cloistered as Brookings Farm. Chester wasn't much of a father – or a husband, for that matter. He much preferred the tropics of Southeast Asia to the agrarian landscape of Hertfordshire. Business had kept him away for weeks, sometimes months at a time, forcing Eliza to endure months of isolation in a house alone with their suspicious staff and his younger sister, Dulcinea, a mad cow of a woman whose smothering devotion to her brother had often triggered alarm bells, though she had never dared give voice to her concern. The birth of Trevor in her fifth year of marriage had been a blessing and a curse.

"One thing I will say," Sister Francine continued. She took a healthy slurp of her tea and smacked her lips together in evident satisfaction. "I missed me a good cuppa."

"I can only imagine," Eliza said. Now that she had moved from the gloomy confines of the church and out into the real world, the almost religious fascination she had experienced with Essie and her strangely hypnotic words had lost a bit of their luster. Tea had never been Eliza's refreshment of choice. Coffee better suited her temperament – boiling hot, black and unadulterated. She liked the burn of it down her throat.

"But it gave me time," Sister Francine said, "to think. To reflect upon my life and where I went wrong. He was such a dear sweet lad, was Liam, was my boy. We loved each other. I loved the other children too, but Liam was special, y'know what I mean?"

"I have a son too," Eliza blurted. It seemed appropriate that she should share. "His name's Trevor. I don't see him all that often anymore. He's a bit of an wanderer. Like his dad, I suppose."

"Chester, Chester, the child molester," Sister Francine intoned.

"Really, Frannie!" Essie interjected, placing her cup down on its saucer with a mild clatter that spilled tea over the rim and onto the checkered tablecloth. "What have I said? What have we talked about? You can't just go around saying everything that comes into that cluttered head of yours. You're not in prison now. You have to be cognizant of other people's feelings. Where's your sense of propriety, for Heaven's sake?"

"It's all right," Eliza said. Her words surprised her. She supposed she was meant to take offense but nothing much upset her anymore. Life had made her hard. "I'm not offended. There's an element of truth to it. Besides, I've heard it all before – from the media, my own family even. My husband was a deceitful, secretive man and he got what was coming to him. I daresay death was preferable as I can't see him surviving behind bars. He needed his freedom. I thought, after what happened ... after I went to Bangkok to identify and repatriate his body ... I thought I might finally have a taste of freedom too. But no, it appears I'm doomed to endure my own kind of prison in perpetuity."

"That's because you have bars around your heart," Essie said.

"Have you been to Brookings Farm?" Eliza laughed. Humor wasn't really her thing either, but her outburst had embarrassed her and she wished to cast it off. "It's like something out of Dickens, or worse. My warden is a crazy old bat who stalks around the house dressed in a moth-eaten eighteenth century dressing gown and Marie Antoinette wigs that she keeps on mannequins all around her bedroom like oversized dolls. I can only escape when she's 'resting.' Of course, Dulcinea blames me for Chester's death like she blames me for everything."

"Oh dear," Essie said. "I don't think I like the sound of that."

"Them's demons at work." Sister Francine raised her eyes from the tablecloth for the first time since Eliza had sat down and gave her a look of such fierce antagonism Eliza very nearly feared for her life. "The Devil's play."

"How about another cuppa?" Essie lifted the teapot and poured Eliza another round. "Are you hungry, Lady Eliza? Shall we order some cake? They've a nice treacle tart here. Or a tasty Battenberg perhaps?"

"No, thank you, I'm fine."

"You'll have to excuse my sister," Essie chattered while pouring herself and Sister Francine more tea. "As Frannie said, eighteen years is a very long time and it's only been a week. We must be supportive during this process of acclimatization. We must be like Christ. Frannie is Lazarus. She's been raised from the dead."

"Born anew," Sister Francine added.

"Indeed," Eliza said. She paused. "I'm sorry...erm...I'm not exactly sure why I'm here, to be perfectly honest. I thought..."

Essie placed her hand on Eliza's hand. Her fingers stroked Eliza's knuckles. Her expression was beatific, her touch warm. "You're quite the anxious one, aren't you?" she said. "It shows you're a woman of action. Frannie and I have waited for so long ... one could say we've been waiting for eighteen years..."

"Eighteen long years," Sister Francine emphasized.

"But what does any of this have to do with me?" Eliza asked. She was beginning to feel a bit desperate. "I don't know how I can help you if I don't know what it is exactly that you want."

"A voice," Essie said. "A presence. You travel in circles Frannie and I could never hope to access."

"You know rich people," Sister Francine added, which Eliza immediately realized was more to the point. "Cash."

"What Frannie means is..." Essie twittered nervously before Sister Francine interrupted her:

"I know what I mean, Essie. Don't be putting words in me mouth!" She slammed her fist down upon the table.

"There's ways of saying things that aren't so direct."

"I speak the truth. If Lady Eliza don't like the truth, then she can bloody well fuck off back to the posh twats at Brookings Farm!"

"No, no, I understand," Eliza said. She found the dynamic between the sisters fascinating. "I understand perfectly. The thing is...and this is me speaking truthfully now...I don't have that kind of cash. At least, not readily to hand. My husband's finances are rather complicated. We're still working with the lawyers and – well, you know what that's like..."

Sister Francine and Essie both gave her a look.

"Or maybe you don't," Eliza stammered. "I forget sometimes that other people's lives aren't quite as complicated as mine."

"But you have access," Essie said. "You have connections."

"Well, yes, I suppose I do. I'm just not sure what you need the money for, is the thing."

Essie pushed her teacup to the center of the table and out of the way. She rolled up her sleeves and leaned forward, resting her elbows on the table in a gesture that said she meant business. Eliza couldn't help but mirror her actions. Sister Francine ran the edge of the tablecloth deep under her thumbnail and seemed to fixate on the blood that pooled there as a result.

"It's early days yet," Essie began after glancing around the tearoom to ensure there was no one else within earshot. The place remained empty. "But I began to describe it to you in the church. Frannie and I have started an organization, an army if you will."

"What kind of army?"

"An army of Christian soldiers." The longer Essie spoke, the more emphatic she became. Spittle flew from her lips. "There's evil amongst us, all around us: an insidious, dark, and invasive evil that will take over the world if we don't actively arm ourselves against it."

"Oh," Eliza said, for there was very little else she could think of to say.

Essie continued: "Frannie has visions," she said. "She's seen the apocalypse."

"The four horsemen," Sister Francine interjected. "Nay, but they wasn't men."

"And these four horsemen...or whatever they were: what did they look like?"

Sister Francine's eyes grew wide. "You've seen them too?"

"No!" Eliza suddenly rocked back in her chair, nearly tipping it over, such was the force of Sister Francine's stare. "No, I mean I'm curious. What you're describing sounds extraordinary. Tell me more."

"Hmmf." Sister Francine crossed her arms and slumped in her seat. "You ain't taking the mickey, are you?" she asked. "I don't take too kindly to folks taking the mickey. I had enough of that sort of disrespect in prison, before I showed 'em what's what."

"I would never, I swear," Eliza said.

"Frannie's visions speak to the future." Essie drew Eliza's hands back into her own. "They show what's coming and what could be if we don't act. The problem is, it takes funds to raise an army like what's needed. And unfortunately, Frannie and I, well, it's not like we've got money trees growing in our garden. We don't even have much of a garden. Just pavement."

"Have you spoken to anyone else?" Eliza asked.

Despite all better judgment, Eliza found she couldn't dismiss the two sisters or their cause, however dubiously articulated. She needed something to hold onto, something that inspired her to get out from under Dulcinea's hateful recriminations, and put some distance between herself and Brookings Farm. It was certainly true what she'd said about the state of her finances. But what she hadn't said was that more than seventy-five percent of the money she and Trevor were supposed to have inherited was tied up in paying off debtors and mysterious business ventures Chester had set up in Bangkok, Hanoi and Kuala Lumpur, businesses Eliza reckoned were never meant to see the light of day, buried as they were so deep in the Dark Web.

She needed to get away from all that. She needed to start anew. Eliza had an eye for opportunity. As long as she'd been married to Lord Chester, however, Eliza had had to contain the entrepreneurial part of herself, and while she hadn't been submissive exactly, she'd definitely repressed what she considered her acute intelligence. But now, with her husband dead and buried and Brookings Farm almost assured a similar fate, Lady Eliza was in desperate need of an exit, and – early days or not – Essie and Francine were showing a promising amount of potential. They were just a little rough around the edges.

"No," Essie replied. "You're the first. We have to be careful, you see. There's a certain *demographic* what might think we're mad. Frannie and I don't exactly make the most prepossessing pair now, do we? Prison obviously takes its toll and as for me, well, I've never been much of a looker. I got married when I was but sixteen and marriage is like its own kind of prison, you know what I mean? So much for wedded bliss and all that palaver. Don't get me wrong. Seamus isn't a bad man. I suppose he loves me in his way. But he's a man of a certain age. And men of a certain age, if you don't keep a close on eye on them, tend to get a little wayward, you know what I mean?"

"I do." Eliza was reminded of that horrible, sweaty, stinking afternoon at the police station in Bangkok. The superintendent – through the translator – had tried to warn her ahead of time, but Eliza had dismissed him with a wave. She knew what was waiting for her beneath the white sheet. She knew it would be unpleasant. Eliza wasn't immune from unpleasant. But the monstrosity that uncovered itself – the pure savage evil of it – had been more than even Eliza could have imagined or prepared for.

"Sometimes," Essie said, "a man needs to be reminded who's boss."

A sex crime, that's what the police superintendent – speaking through Eliza's translator – had said it was. Her husband was the victim of a particularly brutal sex crime, perpetrated by a Thai drug cartel funded by the Russians, who employed local street hustlers to lure wealthy Westerners into massage parlors and sex clubs where they'd then be robbed and killed, the money subsequently flowing back to the bosses of the cartel. But there was more to it. The superintendent wouldn't elaborate, but reading between the lines, Eliza knew her husband, Lord Chester Brookings, hadn't been just a random British tourist picked off the street. The way in which he'd been killed – the barbarism of it – was sheer butchery: split open from pelvis to throat (with a machete, the superintendent had said) and gutted like a stuck pig. There was a point being made. Eliza didn't argue with the police. She reckoned it would only be lost in translation – unless, of course, the police were in on it – and she'd only end up frustrating herself beyond what she was willing to expend of her energy, limited as it was. The facts as they were presented to her simply didn't add up. She worried that Trevor might somehow be involved too, but she refused to let herself go there.

"Do you have a name?" she asked, anything to distract from the dark places her mind insisted upon taking her. "It would seem to me that if you want to attract attention, you need a name that people will respond to, that they'll remember. Something catchy."

"The Movement," Sister Francine said. Her tone was hollow, her voice flat.

"The Movement? Hmm." It wasn't exactly what Eliza had had in mind, but then, no other ideas came to her either.

"Do you like it?" Essie squeezed Eliza's hands with an enthusiastic flutter. "Frannie and I brainstormed. We wanted something simple and direct."

"No bells or whistles," Sister Francine added. "Nothing fancy or posh. I can't be doing with posh."

"It's very austere," Eliza said, "if not a bit ambiguous."

"Which gives it an aura of mystery," Essie said. "'Aura' – is that the right word?"

"Ambiguous, or whatever you call it, is good," Sister Francine elaborated.

"Keeps 'em on their toes. Keeps 'em guessing."

Eliza nodded. "The Movement," she said again. "It has a certain ring. And you're not likely to forget it once you've heard it."

"Exactly," the sisters chimed in unison.

Eliza sat back in her chair and appraised the two women. Essie was the verbal one, but it didn't take an expert on emotional intelligence to recognize that Sister Francine was the brain behind the operation. While it would be important to cultivate both, the ex-con was the one she needed to keep the closest eye on. There was an element of unpredictability in Sister Francine that attracted Eliza. Lord Chester Brookings' widow liked being kept on her toes. Essie was far too cloying for her taste, too easy to please, too much a representative of her class, or rather what Eliza deemed the woman's class. While she might be necessary at the moment, Eliza was fairly confident that Frannie's more traditional sister would soon prove expendable, regardless of whatever it was The Movement was meant to do.

"If I'm going to help you," Eliza said after a pause, "we'll need to start with a plan. I assume you've thought this through?"

"Like a business plan?" Essie asked.

"Something in writing that we can show potential investors," Eliza continued. "You can't very well expect anyone to give you money if they don't know what it is they're signing up for."

"We're saving the world!" Sister Francine pushed herself up from her slouch. "We're ridding the planet of vermin. We're spreading the fear of God to the heathen, to the unbelievers. It's as simple as that."

"No, actually it isn't that simple." Eliza struggled to keep the exasperation out of her voice. There was no use in antagonizing Sister Francine, at least not until she – Eliza – had taken the upper hand. "We have to be careful how we present ourselves. Your enthusiasm and devotion are commendable, and passion can take you a long way, but without structure, without a readily identifiable platform, passion and enthusiasm will only take you so far. Money's tight these days. People are more...austere – even 'posh' people. At least the ones I know anyway."

"Listen to the lady, Francine," Essie urged. "She knows what she's talking about."

"Go on then." Sister Francine settled back in her chair with her arms crossed against her bosom.

"Here's what I propose." Eliza was speaking on the fly, but the longer she spent with Essie and Francine, the greater her confidence in what she believed she could offer them. However well-intentioned the sisters may have been, clearly neither had much of a head for business, or rather not business as Lady Eliza knew it. And while she'd never run a company, she'd certainly sat on her share of boards and rubbed shoulders with an elite crowd of captains of industry to know how the moneyed elite operated and what it would take to break through their notorious tight-fistedness.

It was after three when Eliza and the sisters stood up from the table and shook hands on their new partnership. She'd given them a homework assignment to be completed in time for their next meeting the following morning. The sisters were to define a vision statement while Eliza gave herself the rather unenviable task of going through her late husband's business contacts with the aim of putting together a list of possible donors to the cause. She proposed a social gathering – something low-key and traditional in keeping with The Movement's message of austerity: a bake sale at the church where she and Essie had first met.

Essie said she was friendly with the priest and could easily bribe him with a special batch of her 'parish famous' Hot Cross Buns in exchange for keeping the community garden behind the church open after the 10am service. "He's desperate for parishioners," she'd intimated as she and Sister Francine left the tearoom arm-in-arm, "and a bit of a tipple. Do you know what I mean?"

Eliza was content to the let the sisters sort that out for themselves. Of course, she knew that rooting through Chester's voluminous Rolodex ran the risk of exposing her to all sorts of unpleasantness about which she'd rather remain ignorant. But, she supposed, she couldn't very well continue with her head buried in the sand forever, and if there was even the slightest possibility that Trevor – the son she increasingly felt was running away from her, or from something – was involved in any capacity with her late husband's 'business,' it was best to dig as deeply as she could in an effort to perhaps save him from a similar fate as his father.

When she returned to Brookings Farm late that afternoon, she found Dulcinea in the front parlor deep in the midst of what looked to be a very complicated tea party involving trays of sandwiches with their crusts cut off, their best silver tea set, and her beloved mannequins, all arranged in a circle and adorned with fluffed and powdered wigs. Lottie, the downstairs house/kitchen maid – and, Eliza suspected, her sister-in-law's primary confidante – stood in attendance, sans wig but dressed in one of Dulcinea's ancient white dressing gowns with her face made up like a porcelain doll. The sight gave Eliza the shivers. She tried to tiptoe past, but Dulcinea – whose aural capacity missed nothing – jolted to attention in her wheelchair and snapped her fingers.

"Oy! Oy!" Dulcinea crowed. Her voice was ravaged by emphysema, but still managed to carry like a clarion bell. "Not so fast. You're missing my tea party."

Eliza paused in the hallway to collect herself before stepping reluctantly into the room. The trick with Dulcinea was to let her have her initial outburst and then duck out when she went to catch her breath or was wracked by one of her violent, phlegmatic coughing fits. Lottie curtsied but her expression – even obscured beneath an obscene amount of powder – was defiant.

"Hello, Lottie," Eliza said.

"Mum," the maid replied.

"Where've you been?" Dulcinea spun the wheelchair around to face Eliza and rolled it a few feet towards where Eliza stood in the doorway. "We've been waiting all day for you. We have guests, you horrible woman. You horrible, nasty, disgusting woman!"

"I've been out," Eliza said. For as much as she knew her sister-in-law wasn't in control of her words or actions, the venom with which Dulcinea hurled her insults and accusations still had the power to leave a mark. Eliza didn't think she would ever be immune to them.

"Traipsing around the village like a common tart," Dulcinea spat. "Hitching up your skirt and spreading your legs for any Tom, Dick, and Harry. You hussy! You slut!" She hacked up a ball of phlegm and shot it toward Eliza who only just managed to step out of its path. This was familiar territory too. "One of these days you're going to come a cropper. Mark my words! The village will string you up on that oak tree outside the church and you'll be left there hanging to rot until the crows come and pluck out your scabby nethers. Mark my words!"

"Lottie, when you've finished in here, please make sure my sister-in-law is properly bathed and fed and put to bed," Eliza directed. "And please also remember to leave Dulcie's wheelchair in the hallway outside her bedroom before you put her down for the night. Last night there was an almighty ruckus. It isn't safe for Dulcie to roll around the house until all hours of the night. She might hurt herself, or – God forbid – roll herself down the cellar stairs."

Lottie's expression was cold and unblinking. "Yes, Mum," she replied with another slight curtsey.

"You'd like that, wouldn't you?" Dulcinea cried. "You'd like to see me down those stairs with my neck broken. You whore. You slag. Just like my poor, dear, poor, poor, poor, dear, darling sweet Chester. I've started an investigation, I'll have you know. I'm going to expose you for the grubby gold-digging slut that you are. I know what you're about. I spotted it from the moment you first walked into our lives. You don't fool me. Jezebel!"

Eliza sighed. "Your tea's getting cold," she said as she stepped into the hallway and closed the door, wishing that she had a key she could lock and then throw away.

Without bothering to freshen up – the sooner she dug into her research, the sooner she could retire for the night – Eliza let herself into Chester's office off the first floor library and locked the door behind her. She draped her scarf over the handle so as to obscure the keyhole. Eliza had caught Lottie in the past peering through keyholes and standing with her ear pressed to doors where she had no business being. Eliza knew she had the power to fire the whole lot of them – Lottie was only one example – but where that would leave her with Dulcinea wasn't something she was keen to consider.

There were reasons for Dulcinea's madness. Eliza wasn't so hard of heart that she didn't on the rare occasion experience moments where she actually felt something akin to sorrow for the old bat. Chester's younger sister – junior by five years – had always been spoiled and selfish. "Indulged" is how Chester had always described her, even in the early days of their courtship when Dulcinea would descend into fits whenever Chester brought Eliza round to Brookings Farm. There were indeed moments of dramatic psychosis, but these usually passed once Dulcinea was fobbed off with a sweetie and packed off upstairs to the nursery where she still maintained her Victorian dollhouse and childhood rocking horse. This alone should have been indication enough that all was not quite right with the young woman, but the Brookings family was very much of the strong and silent ilk – Dulcinea aside – and to discuss anything that may have crossed into the personal was strictly *verboten*. In fact, Eliza remembered being told by Chester's mother, Lady Josephine – a dead ringer for the late great Queen Victoria if ever there was one – that there were certain topics related to the family that were off-limits to strangers, making it very clear (by inference, of course) that despite any possible future relations Eliza might have with the matriarch's son she would always be considered an outsider.

Eliza had taken it on the chin. She hadn't any choice. At that time, the only thing that mattered was Chester's ring on her finger and a place in Chester's bed. Anything else was superfluous. Eliza had been raised to believe that marrying into a family as illustrious as the Brookings was her sole reason for existing. The social (not to mention financial) livelihood of her own family depended on the successful nuptials, with a brood of children – preferably male – to follow very soon thereafter. That she was being sold at the tender age of twenty-one into an institution – for Brookings Farm and everything it represented had very much been an institution – that valued her as little more than an indentured servant, hadn't entered into her consciousness, at least not in those early years of what she had thought was blossoming first love.

Of course, Eliza had had her concerns almost from the outset. While she had more-or-less forced herself to turn a blind eye to Dulcinea's tantrums all the while she and Chester were merely courting, once she moved into Brookings Farm after a month-long honeymoon at the Brookings plantation outside Nairobi (an experience that in itself should have given her pause), whatever questions she may have had about her husband's younger sister – and the level of their attachment – could not be put off so casually. Eliza came to realize that Dulcinea's behavior was less a product of over-indulgence than the result of what Eliza could only describe as an alarming obsession with her brother, Eliza's husband, Lord Chester, that seemed almost to be encouraged – if not endorsed – by Lady Josephine.

The latter had certainly wasted no time letting Eliza know that she objected to their union, but in those initial months that then became years, Eliza had yet to find her voice. When she had tried to engage Chester in discussion about their less than ideal family arrangement, Chester reminded her that she had known what she was getting into the day she agreed to be his wife, when in truth, while Eliza hadn't exactly been in the dark, she'd never imagined the extent of the ties that bound Chester to sister and mother, a bond he prioritized over any obligations he may have had to anyone else, least of all his new wife.

And yet, despite these misgivings, Eliza had continued to do her best to remain optimistic of mind and light of spirit. Her job as she understood it was to be the best wife she could possibly be to Lord Chester and to provide him an heir within the first year of their marriage. It wasn't as though her husband was deliberately unkind to her – a bit formal perhaps and never one for public displays of affection. But that was all right with Eliza who, still in her early twenties in those years before Trevor's birth, was of rather modest temperament, raised to be a good Catholic girl with nary an inkling of sin. Of course, she'd converted to Anglicanism before marriage, perhaps (if she was honest with herself) not as willingly as she'd let everyone believe. In fact, there had been a time in her late adolescence when she'd even considered becoming a nun. The simplicity of a monastic lifestyle had appealed to her then, devoid as it was – or at least so it appeared to her – of the burdens endemic to modern life in a society that seemed to be changing (and not necessarily for the good) at the speed of light. This was the late Sixties, after all. But to have sworn herself to a life of servitude to Jesus Christ would have deprived her family – aristocratic of name and lineage but rather barren of funds – of a means to support itself in the fashion to which they were all accustomed. Eliza was an only child. The responsibility for that upkeep was hers and hers alone.

However, as time went on, Chester's seeming reticence devolved into a kind of isolation. He spent less and less time at Brookings Farm, choosing instead to look after the plantation in Kenya for weeks and sometimes months at a stretch, leaving Eliza alone with a mother-in-law who despised her (for reasons Eliza couldn't fathom) and a sister-in-law whose "indulgence" turned to verbal cruelty punctuated with the occasional physical assault.

The first altercation had taken place late one night in the second year of Eliza's life at Brookings Farm. Chester was away as per usual in Kenya. Lady Josephine was in London, which meant Eliza was forced to fend for herself against Dulcinea and a staff who seemed poisoned against her from the moment she'd crossed the threshold as Lord Chester's wife. As a result of her husband's frequent absences and the anxiety of being cooped up in a house whose maudlin interior had last been updated sometime in the mid-1840s, Eliza had developed a rather severe case of insomnia. She had taken to reading the Bible by candlelight in an effort to gain a semblance of emotional sustenance from the stories of men and women whose challenges made her own seem trivial by comparison. Usually the remedy worked, with her falling asleep sometime between three and four in the morning, only to be woken at the crack of dawn by the crowing of the rooster Dulcinea kept as a pet in the adjacent chicken coop.

The fact that she had only just closed the book, snuffed out the candle (for electricity was only to be used sparingly), and settled under her comforter when the bedroom door opened and Dulcinea charged into the room brandishing a pair of fabric scissors in one hand and a lantern in the other, like some Gothic wraith out of a story by Wilkie Collins, was probably what saved her. Eliza didn't like to think what might have happened had she been deep in slumber.

Dulcinea attacked with intent to kill. Eliza leaped out of bed and warded off her sister-in-law's frenzied blows with her pillows before escaping into the corridor and screaming for the staff to come to her rescue. When none were forthcoming

– although she could feel their presence behind conspicuously closed doors – Eliza ran out into the courtyard and didn't stop running until she reached the still-sleepy village. Not convinced she was out of harm's way and unable to bring herself to look behind her for fear that Dulcinea was in close pursuit, Eliza went door to door, knocking and screaming for help. Not one door opened to her. Not one light switched on. Eliza felt as though she was in the midst of some Lady Josephine-inspired conspiracy to have her done in. How convenient that would have been for her and, with Josephine in London and Chester in faraway Africa, how utterly untraceable!

Having exhausted herself and with no sanctuary in sight, Eliza collapsed to her knees in the churchyard and fell asleep amidst the tombstones. She had never felt so cold or desolate in all her relatively young life. But Eliza was nothing if not resilient. The village may have rejected her – out of fear of Lady Josephine or out of pure indifference, Eliza didn't know – but Eliza refused to be cowed. The attack had terrified her, yes, but in an odd and unexpected way, it had given Eliza a newfound determination to overcome whatever the tenants of Brookings Farm might throw her way. And with this renewed strength coursing through her body, Eliza picked herself up off the ground and strode back to Brookings Farm with a conviction that anyone who happened to see her in light of what had happened in the early hours of morning would have found astonishing.

When she returned to the house, Dulcinea was sitting at the dining room table eating toasted soldiers and runny egg, some of which had dripped onto the frilly bib Dulcinea wore whenever she was at table. Her expression bore no indication of alarm at Eliza's entrance, but rather a moon-faced indifference that Eliza found inscrutable but not atypical. Rather than round on Dulcinea in a furious rage – which might have been her instinct had she been anyone else – Eliza calmly pulled back a chair and sat opposite her husband's troublesome sister. She poured herself a cup of tea, willing her hands to remain steady, and sipped the hot brew while the silence hovered between them.

"Do you have something you want to say to me, Dulcie?" Eliza asked.

Dulcinea's eyes darted over Eliza's face before settling on the mess of yolk and crumbs on her plate.

"Dulcinea?" Eliza said. "Answer me when I speak to you. Is there something you want to say to me?"

"Nay," came the insolent reply.

"I don't believe you."

Dulcinea shrugged.

"You tried to kill me last night," Eliza continued. "You do know that I could have the police come and arrest you, don't you? They'd try you for attempted murder and you'd be locked away for the rest of your life ... that is if they don't hang you."

"Nay," Dulcinea said.

"Is that what you want? Do you want to hang? I don't imagine that would be very nice, though I suppose it's better than prison, not that Brookings Farm is anything to write home about."

"I hate you."

"Oh, she speaks!" Eliza clapped her hands in a mock ovation. "Well, I don't like you very much either so I suppose the sentiment is mutual."

"Mummy hates you too."

"There's a surprise!" Eliza scoffed. "The thing is, Dulcie, and it's something you and your mother are just going to have come to terms with: I'm not going anywhere. I live here now. Your brother married me. And when your mother passes, I shall have run of this house. Do you understand? So if I were you, I'd make a concerted effort to be nice to me. The only alternative you have is the clink or, if I'm feeling compassionate, I can always have you committed to the asylum. I hear they have vacancies."

"Mummy wouldn't let you!" Dulcinea looked up from the dregs of her breakfast with a scowl that betrayed the full force of her hatred.

Eliza was unfazed. "Mummy isn't here now, is she? She's in London."

"He doesn't love you, you know."

Even though Eliza knew better than to place too much trust in the words of Chester's sister, these latest struck a mark, as they spoke to a suspicion – no, an insecurity – she had that perhaps the marriage had indeed been a mistake. It wasn't natural for a couple, in what still should have been the halcyon days of their union, to be separated like this for such extended periods of time. Unless, of course, Chester was running away from her. The last thing Eliza wanted was for her husband to have felt pressured into marrying her. Yes, her parents viewed the nuptials as a business transaction. And yes, she had gone into the marriage knowing that by doing so she was securing her family's social and financial position for as long as she remained Lady Eliza Brookings, which she had intended to be for the rest of her life and the lives of her children, and so on and so forth. Yet, the longer Eliza resided at Brookings Farm in the absence of her husband, whose very presence had served as a buffer against the idiosyncratic disparagement of his mother and sister, the more she began to question the foundation upon which her marriage was built.

She started to feel as though she had volunteered to be the butt of a rather nasty and distasteful joke. She knew she should go to the police after this latest and most egregious episode with Dulcinea, or at the very least, she should check herself out of the madhouse for the time being and insist that Chester return to England post-haste. But Eliza chose to do no such thing. Instead, she decided to take matters into her own hands if for no other reason than to prove to Lady Josephine – and yes, to Dulcinea as well – that she was a strong, capable, independent woman who wasn't about to take guff from anyone. Still, there was a kernel of doubt, the trace of a thought that perhaps this wasn't the time to take a principled stand. Maybe what she really should do was run?

"And how do you know that, Dulcinea?" Eliza asked. She poured herself another cup of tea. Mercifully, her hands had stopped trembling.

"He told me."

"Who?"

"Who do you think?"

"If he hates me as much as you say, why would Chester have married me? That doesn't seem a very logical course of action, now does it?"

"You don't know anything."

"No, clearly, I do not, but I suppose you'll enlighten me?"

Dulcinea hesitated. She played with the corners of her serviette and spun her plate in a slow, meandering circle, all the while maintaining Eliza's gaze. Her blue eyes were wide, vacant, yet vaguely sparkling. Her mouth drew into a tight, narrow line. Eliza willed herself not to break focus. She couldn't allow Dulcinea to sense how troubling she found this turn in the conversation. What secrets were about to be revealed? She steeled herself against the worst without really knowing what the worst could be. Intuition told her it was probably best that she remained ignorant, but the masochist in her was all too desperate to know.

"Ask Mummy," Dulcinea broke Eliza's gaze and focused on the serviette, bringing it up close to her eyes as though studying each individual microfiber.

"Ask Mummy what, Dulcie?" Eliza's resolve had started to crumble. She placed her cup on its saucer with a mild clatter.

"Ask Mummy about Deirdre," Dulcinea whispered. "About what happened to her."

"Deirdre?"

"About what they did to her."

The conversation had gone too far. Dulcinea launched herself out her chair and ran out of the dining room, leaving Eliza to process this latest revelation on her own. Without knowing anything about this Deirdre beyond the fact that she knew whomever this woman was, she could possibly be the key to unlocking a Pandora's box lodged deep within the inner corridors of Brookings Farm. Yet, Eliza also knew that she needed to keep her cards close and her wits firmly about her, which meant she couldn't go into confrontation mode. Clearly, Dulcinea had spoken out of turn. It didn't take a master of subterfuge to know Deirdre wasn't a name Eliza was ever meant to hear. Patience could only serve to Eliza's benefit. Still, Eliza was unnerved.

Chester returned from Kenya not long after. Whether Dulcinea had said anything to Lady Josephine who had then summoned her son back to Brookings Farm, Eliza didn't know. In the weeks and then months that followed, life assumed a more orderly, if not normal, pace. The somewhat distracted affection that Eliza had grown accustomed to in hers and Chester's months of courtship reappeared to the point that she started to wonder if perhaps she had imagined Chester's emotional distance. For all intents and purposes, Chester now presented himself as the ideal husband. He surprised her with weekend trips to London, breezy summer holidays in Capri, and extravagant shopping excursions to Paris so her wardrobe stayed up-to-date. His lovemaking was ardent – though mechanical – and it seemed for a time that he couldn't get enough of her. And Eliza, who for so long had been starved of his touch, wasn't about to question this unexpected but mostly pleasurable manifestation of his devotion.

On their third wedding anniversary, in the midst of a blissful sun-and-sex-fueled fortnight spent sailing off Sorrento on the private yacht of one of Chester's business associates – whose identity, Eliza realized much later when things had started to go pear-shaped again, he had refused to reveal – Chester surprised her one morning with a breakfast in bed of Prosecco, burnt scrambled eggs, and oysters that he'd selected himself from one of the local fishermen. Chester joked that he wasn't much of a cook ("*Pardon the eggs, darling.*") but he hoped she would at least appreciate the effort and that he had been assured the oysters were guaranteed their aphrodisiacal powers.

"Darling, I love oysters!" she had exclaimed rapturously, throwing her arms around him before feeding him one of the dozen half-shells. "They're divine!"

They slurped the briny meat from the shells between kisses and nibbles and generous glugs of Prosecco, feeling decadent and indulgent and very glamorous.

"I love you, *mi amor!*" Chester said as he pushed her back on the bed.

"*Ti amo, morito mio!*" Eliza replied.

"*E io ti amo, mia moglie!*" Chester responded in kind. "Let's make a baby."

Just under seven months later, Trevor Christopher Gaylord Brookings was born. What should have been a happy occasion proved traumatic as the birth was premature, induced by a freak riding accident that nearly cost the lives of both mother and unborn child. While Eliza had to concede that she had no business atop a horse so advanced into her second trimester – or jumping, for that matter – she was a skilled equestrian, and the accident itself (as an investigation soon proved) came as the result of tampered stirrups and not anything Eliza herself had done wrong. Both stirrups had simply come away from the saddle mid-jump, causing her to be thrown over the neck of her horse and onto her back, breaking the fence and rendering her unconscious.

Despite the inauspicious circumstances of his birth, Trevor Brookings proved as resilient as his mother who, the doctors said afterwards, should have died from internal injuries at the scene of the crime. For Eliza was convinced the accident was a premeditated attempt at murder, masterminded she had no doubt by none other than Dulcinea, whose behavior towards Eliza in the months leading up to the accident – post-pregnancy announcement – had been nothing short of pathological.

Of course, Eliza had no one to whom she could turn. When she and baby Trevor were finally released from the hospital six weeks later, a wall of silence and bitter, though unspoken, recriminations seemed to form an unbridgeable schism between herself and Chester. His affection was now as absent as his presence at Brookings Farm. Their relationship, which had seemed so full of love and promise in the months between Dulcinea's first attempt on her life and the "accident", reverted back to its previous dysfunction. Confined to her bed with little access to the world outside Brookings Farm, with a husband whose absences grew in frequency and duration with each passing month, a mother-in-law who clearly resented her survival, a sister-in-law bent on her destruction, and a shadowy, sinister staff that acted as prison wardens, Eliza feared she was going mad. Even the nurse the family had hired to look after Trevor seemed too keen to prevent any time Eliza might have had to bond with her newborn. It was bad enough that Trevor refused her breast – preferring instead that of the nurse or, as Eliza later discovered to her horror, Dulcinea – but what really frightened her was the vacancy she sensed in Trevor's blue eyes when he looked at her and the way his scrawny little body twisted and squirmed as far away from her as possible whenever she tried to hold him. It was as if she repulsed him, or, perhaps more to the point, as if that was how he had been trained.

Many a lonely night passed in her draughty bedroom on the third floor of Brookings Manor. Deprived of both husband and child, Eliza was left with little to do but ponder what had become of her life. There might as well have been bars on her windows and a lock on her door, so utterly confined did Eliza feel. Through it all, two questions persisted: Who was Deirdre? And what had happened to her? Eliza couldn't help but wonder if the fate of this mysterious figure was in some way connected to the "accident" and its aftermath. Not once had she confronted Chester with these questions, nor had she ever dared to raise the subject with Lady Josephine or Dulcinea, the very root of the mystery. But enough was enough. She had to know or else risk losing her mind.

One blustery mid-March evening, Eliza ventured from her room to join mother-and-sister-in-law for tea and petit point in the first floor conservatory. She half-expected Lady Josephine to find an excuse to keep her on the third floor, but no such attempt was made. The three women sat and drank their tea in a silence broken only by the sound of the wind howling against the shutters and the steady tick-tick-tick of the metronome on the piano that, at least according to Chester, had a soothing effect upon Dulcinea's nerves. Mother and daughter were intent on their individual embroidery while Eliza – who found the hobby a little too arcane for her tastes – pretended to concentrate upon a book of Wordsworth's poetry. Baby Trevor had long since been put down for the night.

Before long, Eliza grew restless. She couldn't sit there another minute with the incessant ticking of the metronome clawing at the back of her head, nor could she endure the frenzy of her own imagination. And although she had scripted and rehearsed how she intended to phrase the question, she thought it best to throw tact to the wind and dive in headfirst.

"Who is Deirdre?"

Lady Josephine looked up from her petit point. Her eyes squinted and the corners of her thin-lipped mouth twitched while Dulcinea remained focused on her stitching.

"What?" Lady Josephine asked.

"Deirdre," Eliza repeated. "Who is she?"

The pause belied Lady Josephine's words: "I don't know what you're talking about," she snapped.

"That's funny," Eliza persisted, closing the book and setting it on the cushion beside her. "I could have sworn your daughter mentioned her to me. Not recently, no, but not so long ago. Isn't that right, Dulcie? Do you remember our little chat?"

Dulcinea's face was buried in the embroidery. She emitted a muffled cough but gave no other sign that she had heard Eliza's question.

"Leave her alone!" Lady Josephine tossed her petit point aside and made as if to rise from the settee but Eliza's hard stare held her in check. "Dulcinea doesn't answer to you. She doesn't answer to anyone but me, her mother," she bellowed. "You know she's damaged. You know she's prone to flights of fancy. Dulcinea is as brainless and full of stuffing as a rag doll. Deirdre doesn't exist. She's a figment of Dulcinea's twisted imagination and nothing else. I never want to hear that cursed name mentioned in this house ever again! Do I make myself clear? Never again!"

"Then was it a figment of *my* imagination that Dulcinea entered my bedroom in the middle of the night and threatened me with a pair of fabric scissors?"

Lady Josephine's back arched as she drew herself up to her full height and loomed over Eliza in the center of the room. "How dare you?" she thundered.

"Was it also a figment of my imagination that the stirrups on my saddle were loosed so that they broke away while I was in the midst of a jump?"

"You horrible woman!"

"You can call me all the names you like," Eliza said, "but the fact remains, your daughter tried to kill me at least once that I can prove. She can't deny it."

"Do you have witnesses?"

"God is my witness."

This last statement proved more than Lady Josephine could bear. She lunged and backhanded Eliza across the face. The force was strong enough to draw blood, but was no match for Eliza's determination. She remained steady, her hands primly clasped in her lap, an island of calm in the face of Lady Josephine's rage.

"Papist!" Lady Josephine cried. But the edge was gone. Having already worked herself up to the slap, she was now bereft of any additional means of release. So she just stood there, fists clenching and unclenching at her hips, rocking from side to side – quaking – as Eliza merely shrugged and picked up her book. In truth, Eliza's ears were ringing and she worried Lady Josephine's blow had knocked loose one of her teeth, but she wasn't about to back down or show the slightest sign of vulnerability.

Dulcinea giggled.

"If I weren't a Christian woman," Lady Josephine said, "a *true* Christian..." She turned on her heel and strode out of the room. "Come along, Dulcie, it's time for your bath."

"Mummy lies," Dulcinea murmured when her mother was well out of earshot. "Mummy knows."

"Mummy knows what?"

"Mummy took Deirdre. I saw her."

"Took her where, Dulcie?"

Dulcinea held the petit point to her face and played peek-a-boo with it, covering first one eye and then the other, laughing like a child.

"Took her to the place where the bad little girls and boys go."

"Tell me, Dulcie." Eliza got up from the sofa and sat down beside Dulcinea on the settee. "Where is that place? Can you show me? Can you tell me how to get there?"

Dulcinea lay back on the settee and placed the embroidery over her face. She shook her head and drew her knees up to her chest until she was curled into a fetal position.

"I've never been," she said.

"But Deirdre's there?"

"Yes. Deirdre...and the others."

"Others?" Eliza leaned close to Dulcinea. She gently pulled the petit point off the young woman's face, which Dulcinea then covered with her hands. "What others, Dulcie?"

"The others Mummy took away." Dulcinea rolled off the settee then and onto the floor before pushing herself up to her feet. "I have to go," she said. "It's time for my bath."

The interview had come to a close. Eliza knew there was no point in further pursuing this line of questioning. And while there was still so much she needed to know – questions upon questions without any answers – she felt that perhaps she and her sister-in-law had in some perverse way grown closer. Perhaps Dulcinea was more in control of her faculties than Eliza had previously given her credit for? She wouldn't necessarily bet the farm on it – not yet anyway – but the hint of a suggestion was there. Was Dulcinea playing her? Could Eliza play her back? It was still too early to tell. Regardless, of one thing she was certain: there were bad things afoot at Brookings Farm: very bad things.

An understatement if ever there was one. Lady Eliza shuddered. And yet, somehow she had persevered. Not only persevered, but thrived. For look where she was now – at the very pinnacle of her life's ambitions: the wife of one of England's most revered (if not always respected) bluebloods, at the helm of a dynasty and at the top of her game. Of course, there was still much work to be done. Lord Carleton wasn't dead yet, for one, but getting his ring on her finger and the marriage officiated had been of most pressing importance – that and getting him to agree to the conversion. And the will. Yes, the will could still prove difficult.

As Eliza sipped her champagne and surveyed the family tableaux in front of her – assessing the Templeton children, their dubious spouses (Penelope that is, for Duncan claimed he was held up with business in the City and would be round in the morning), and Lord Carleton's dreadful grandchildren – she wondered (not for the first time) if Lady Fiona's intent had been to position Eliza where she was now. Eliza preferred to think so, for the alternative cast her as someone not all that removed from the person her new stepchildren accused her of being. But then, what did it matter what Diana, Edgar, Guy, and Chloe thought of her? What power did they really have? Sure, they could involve their various lawyers – as they probably would – and litigate until the inheritance was gobbled up by legal fees. But in the end, she would still be the one in control.

Eliza glanced at her watch: ten more minutes until the festivities were due to begin. She'd checked upstairs with the nurses to ensure everything was set, that Carleton was prepped and mobile, that he'd been fed and washed and dressed in the tartan dressing robe, pajamas, and slippers she had set out for him. Eliza had even asked the barber up from the village to give Carleton a haircut and a beard trim. Her new husband wasn't looking well. His pallor was wan, his eyes jaundiced, and the weight he'd lost these weeks since his collapse was really rather inauspicious, but the fact he was still alive and at least semi-coherent was all Eliza needed to enact the final part of her plan.

Did Eliza love Lord Carleton? She scoffed at the idea. Was it even possible to love a corpse? Before the collapse, before the diagnosis, when she'd first laid eyes on him at Ambassador Bingham's residence in Belgravia – on the occasion of the reception for the Russian foreign minister – and Lady Fiona herself had introduced them (not long after their initial meeting at the church bake sale), what a fine specimen Lord Carleton had presented to her then! Tall, athletic and still very spry for a man in his twilight years, dressed impeccably in his Tom Ford suit and black tie, Lady Eliza Brookings had felt something that might have been mistaken for love. An awakening of her long-dormant sexuality was probably more accurate.

At seventy-seven, Lord Carleton proved himself an ardent and agile lover, unlike Chester who had never been much good at fucking even at the best of times. And then, of course, the repulsion she had felt after the truth – long suspected – had finally come out. Deirdre had merely been the tip of the iceberg. The place where bad little girls and boys went had been real. Too real, in fact. The effect upon Eliza was such that for years she'd never wanted to have sex again, and the thought of having any more children – not only in regards to Chester, but with any man – was nearly as repulsive to her as the existence and reality of Deirdre's hiding place. There was still unfinished business, but everything in good time. Eliza needed to get her house in order before she could move on to anything else.

"Chloe, darling." It amused her how the Templeton brood made such a production out of avoiding her. Even Diana was keeping a measured distance, pretending to be engaged in a whispery and no doubt superficial conversation with Elena Grimaldi, the queen of superficiality herself, never mind her blasted tulips. But Chloe was the worst offender. The youngest of Carleton and Fiona's children had a face Eliza wanted to slap. With her precocious pixie haircut that made her look like an overgrown Peter Pan and lips pursed and primped to look like rose buds, Chloe Templeton represented a certain kind of privilege Eliza couldn't stomach. But if provoked, however, (and Lord knew how easily Lady Chloe could be provoked!) she could be relied upon to provide at least ten minutes of passable entertainment. All it would take were one or two well-placed barbs and the waterworks would soon overflow.

Chloe regarded Eliza with suspicion as Eliza made her way across the parlor to the grand piano, behind which Chloe stood whilst tapping frantically at her mobile, and around which later that evening – in an attempt to tamper down the inevitable post-announcement pandemonium – Eliza would suggest an old-fashioned family sing-along to celebrate a new era in the Templeton dynasty.

"Chloe, darling, just a gentle reminder of the new rule we have in this family about mobile phones," Eliza said with a smile designed to enrage its recipient. "They are not allowed at family gatherings. Please put it away or I shall have Rupert confiscate it for the duration of the evening."

How Eliza enjoyed watching the blood rise up Chloe's snow-white throat and blotch her impertinent little face!

"Who are you to tell me anything?" Chloe replied with such an utter lack of conviction Eliza knew she'd hit her mark. "You're not my mother. You never will be my mother. And if you so much as try to take her place, I won't let you."

Eliza rolled her eyes, her smile fixed and lethal. "So we're going there again, are we?" she asked with an exaggerated sigh. "How boring."

"We're all against you, you know. And if you aren't careful, we'll expose you for what you really are. All I have to do is call our solicitor and then it's curtains for you."

"Well then, I'm happy to relieve you of the effort," Eliza said. "I'm very well-acquainted with your solicitor and your financial advisors, the head of your security detail, as well as each of your father's business associates, shareholders, and the board of trustees. So there's really no need for you to call anyone. A new day has dawned on this family, Chloe, and I'm afraid there's very little you – yes, even you – can do about it."

Chloe's phone buzzed. Eliza watched as Chloe suppressed the urge to check it. The phone buzzed again. Chloe looked apoplectic.

"If it's that important, I suppose you can take it in the hall," Eliza conceded, although she herself was curious as to the identity of Chloe's mystery caller. Whoever it was, the person was obviously causing her youngest stepdaughter no small amount of discomfort. "Anything to spare me your amateur theatrics. You have exactly five minutes before the dinner bell."

"No."

Chloe shook her head and attempted to hide the offending mobile in her pocket, only to realize (somewhat awkwardly) that her L.K. Bennett sailor frock lacked one. She placed it on the piano bench instead, from where – Eliza suspected – Chloe would take it up when left once again to her own devices. Perhaps she'd enact a ban on all technology in Templeton Manor once Lord Carleton was well and truly on the other side? The notion, though most likely unenforceable, gave Eliza a twitch of glee.

"Are you sure?" Eliza asked in her most cloying voice. "I realize business stops for no one. Far be it from me to come between you and a magazine cover."

"It's nothing." Chloe could barely bring herself to look at her. Eliza bit down hard on the inside of her cheek. "Just an old friend of mine in London whom I haven't seen in years. I honestly don't know why she's texting me. She probably saw the *Vanity Fair* piece and wants to cash in on the fact she was someone I used to know."

"Like they do."

"People are such sycophants." Chloe was sweating. Her face was the color of a particularly ripe beet.

"Yes," Eliza replied. "Indeed." She glanced again at her watch. Less than three minutes to go. She scanned the room to make sure all the necessary players were present and well lubricated. Although Eliza wasn't much of a drinker – she'd had more than her fill of alcohol in the days and weeks after the Deirdre debacle, not to mention Chester's death and Trevor's arrest – she appreciated how it added an additional layer of tension to the family environment. People became less inhibited and more prone to speaking their minds. She had a feeling there would be an awful lot of truth-telling that evening once the bombshells had been dropped when she would sit back – stone cold sober – and enjoy the fruits of all that she had wrought.

Her gaze alit upon Guy who looked infinitely better than he had that afternoon, though he still possessed a rough-and-tumble countenance that Eliza felt at odds with their surroundings. Having grown bored of Chloe, she passed on from the piano to the alcove by the window where he stood with one hand shoved in the pocket of his suit trousers, the other nursing a brandy, while Penelope appeared to be talking his ear off about some banality, Eliza supposed, in her thoroughly affected, pseudo-Continental accent. Penelope's voice made Eliza want to rip her throat out.

"Would you mind?" Eliza inserted herself into the space between the two and turned her back on the offending American, leaving Penelope with little recourse but to take the hint and find someone else at which to natter.

"Eliza," Guy said.

"You clean up well," she replied. Eliza wasn't entirely immune to Guy's rugged charm. "Dr. Raleigh's a miracle worker, though I suppose it helps to have good genes. You and your siblings have certainly been blessed in that regard."

Guy shrugged. Eliza despised diffidence, especially in men.

"My mother was a very beautiful woman," he said.

"Yes, she was." Eliza paused. "Even on her deathbed she was exquisite. We all pale in comparison."

"Something tells me you didn't come here to talk about my mother."

"Just like your father. You cut right to the chase. It's a pity you don't resemble him in other ways." Eliza waited a moment to let the slight sink in. Guy's expression was stoic. She couldn't read him, but then she reminded herself: the man was a gambler —not a very good one, but clearly he had mastered the art of the poker face. "At any rate, before we go in to dinner, I wanted a quick chat. As I've told your sisters, there are going to be some necessary changes that I don't doubt won't go over very well, but it's the times we live in."

"So I've been told," Guy said. He wasn't giving anything away, which only made Eliza's job more difficult, though she hoped the satisfaction after would be sweeter for her efforts.

"The thing is, Guy," Eliza persevered, "your father is very disappointed in you. You may not realize this – Lord knows your father isn't the most expressive of men – but he's always thought the world of you – as do I – which you've never seemed to appreciate. Now don't worry, I'm not picking on you exactly – your other siblings are no better – yet it must be said that your father's disappointment in you is perhaps more acute because he's placed so much more faith in you as a son. I realize that five hundred thousand pounds is a mere drop in the bucket when you've grown up with all the privileges you're accustomed to ... but it isn't just five hundred thousand quid, is it? There's millions behind it, not to mention certain criminal elements involving shady characters of ill-repute, who – at least according to my sources – are of a distinctly Russian persuasion."

Eliza paused again. She peered up at Guy to see if her words had provoked even the faintest glimmer of effect. Perhaps she detected a hardening of his stare, a subtle tightening of his jaw, a greater rigidity in his posture? Beyond that, he gave away very little. She glanced at the door, expecting Rupert to show up with the dinner bell. If Guy wasn't going to satisfy her with a verbal response, there was very little for her to do but carry on until he did.

"Of course, I understand that these things happen in business," she continued. "High stakes beget high risk in exchange for hopefully high return. And Russia, with all its natural resources – not to mention certain moral and ethical flexibilities – is an obviously attractive target to a businessman such as yourself."

"Go on," Guy said. Eliza felt a twinge of glory deep in the pit of her stomach.

"All I'm saying is, the failure of your hedge fund, not to mention the very public collapse of that pipeline deal – and yes, I know about that too – doesn't lend itself to a particularly favorable impression, at least not in this challenging socio-economic climate. Add to that the palaver with the Ambassador's daughter – ruined for life now, I should think – and it amounts to a rather distasteful set of circumstances that make you a liability this family can ill afford."

Eliza felt the fire simmering just beneath the veneer of his surface calm. These Templeton children were so easily provoked. But it wasn't as though she was saying anything that couldn't be proven. And whilst she didn't want to criticize Lady Fiona's parenting without Carleton's first wife present to defend herself, Eliza recognized in her stepchildren the faults wrought by a permissive hand. Lady Fiona had been too good to be true. Even Eliza conceded that the woman had been a saint. The first time she ever laid eyes on Fiona – at the church bake sale – Guy's mother appeared to her bathed in an angelic glow that seemed to follow her wherever she went.

Eliza had been overwhelmed by the good that had radiated from her predecessor and infused her every word and action. Normally, Eliza would have been nauseated by such genuine selflessness, looking for and exposing the cracks wherever she saw them. But it hadn't taken long for her to realize that Lady Fiona was indeed flawless, the fact of which both maddened and relieved Eliza. Maddened because it went against Eliza's perception of the world – but who could blame her after years of being a virtual prisoner within the dismal walls of Brookings Farm, where the basest forms of perversion were not only allowed to thrive, but seemed to have no end? – and yet, oddly relieved because within Lady Fiona's unflappable virtue lay the kernel of a recognition that there was still much that was good in the world, even as Eliza allowed herself a healthy dose of skepticism.

The children, however, presented no such redemption.

"How any of that is of any concern to you, Lady Eliza," Guy said, his voice containing within it an edge that Eliza was only too keen to test, "is beyond me. If my father wishes to reprimand me that is certainly within his right, but it is also within my right that that discussion takes place in confidence – without third party influence."

"Well, all I can say is time will tell."

Eliza beamed up at Guy with her tightest smile and patted his arm as she walked away. She looked at her watch – it had now gone five minutes past eight – as the first rumblings of panic started to make their presence felt. Eliza believed in precision. She lived her life by a rigid schedule, at the heart of which was punctuality. Rupert was to have rang the bell for dinner at precisely eight o' clock. The doors into the formal dining hall were meant to have opened, and the family was then to have made its way to the table, at the head of which Lord Carleton was already to have been seated in his wheelchair. This is what had been discussed and gone over. What could possibly be the reason for such delay?

Lady Eliza didn't care to speculate. Carleton had given her a scare earlier. After all the paperwork had been signed, the prayers recited, and the vows exchanged, Eliza had rather hastily – perhaps too hastily – banished Dr. Raleigh, Father O'Connell, and the attendant nurses to the anteroom off Lord Carleton's bed chamber. She'd locked the doors and pulled the heavy damask drapery across them so as to muffle sound and prevent anyone from spying through the keyholes. (The scars from Brookings Farm ran deep.) Carleton lay in the bed, propped up by an assortment of overstuffed pillows and cushions, a duvet tucked and folded over his waist. He regarded her through his cataract-coated eyes. His mouth hung open. His breathing was labored and raspy, betraying the phlegm that ravaged his lungs. She had insisted Dr. Raleigh remove the oxygen mask during the exchanging of vows. The doctor had protested – saying it was the only thing keeping Lord Carleton alive – but Eliza had a way with the doctor. He knew better than to go against her. He had acquiesced.

Divested of the entourage, Lady Eliza wasted no time. She slipped her undergarments off from beneath her skirt before climbing onto the bed and straddling Lord Carleton with a dexterity that belied her age. He wasn't hard – Dr. Raleigh had warned her against administering such treatment after Carleton had first fallen ill – but Eliza had trained herself to work around this inconvenience. It wasn't ideal (and there was actually very little physical satisfaction she derived from these encounters) but Eliza believed that a marriage wasn't a true marriage until the act of consummation, and who knew how much time was left before the new bride became a widow? She positioned his member inside her and went to work. For yes, it all felt like work to her – a process she was only too happy to endure. It didn't take long for Carleton to respond. He may have been on death's door, but he was still a man. It never failed to amaze Eliza how little effort it took to appeal to a man's base needs. Sex was instinct. But to Eliza, sex was also transactional.

She felt him working his way into a frenzy beneath her. His breathing grew more strained. The veins at his temples threatened to burst through his skin. He was with her and apart from her. But his eyes – despite their filmy covering – were fully engaged. Eliza hovered over him. His hands reached up and weakly attempted to caress her back in an effort perhaps of tenderness. Eliza grabbed them and held them down on the mattress. She pushed with all her might to restrain him. She closed her eyes and imagined herself as a young woman in the early days of her courtship with Lord Chester – before Deirdre, before Bangkok, before she recognized Brookings Farm for the house of horrors that it really was. She remembered Lady Fiona, seeing her for the first time at the bake sale, looking at her and wondering how such altruism could possibly be real. She reflected on those early conversations – the honeymoon phase when one went to such (needless) lengths to present oneself in the best possible light...and then Lady Fiona's diagnosis, which at the time had affected Eliza more than she cared to admit. For she hadn't intended for them to become friends. Essie and Sister Francine had warned against letting emotion come into the equation. She had tried, but Lady Fiona had been so ingenuous and so welcoming of Eliza's friendship – especially in those dreadful months of her illness – that Eliza couldn't help but be seduced.

She would never forget how nervous Lady Fiona had seemed that afternoon when the trajectory of Lady Eliza's life changed forever. They had agreed to meet for tea at Liberty on one of the rare occasions when both she and Lady Fiona were in London at the same time. Several weeks had passed since they had last seen each other – when Fiona had first told Eliza of her diagnosis, the morning after the Ambassador's reception – and Eliza had been a bit hesitant about seeing her new friend, fearful of what Fiona might look like, unsure of whether she could handle any additional emotional upheaval, especially in light of Trevor's recent arrest in Harare and the media's subsequent hullabaloo. Oh, the field day they had had with it, coming so soon after Chester's death. The questions they asked her, as if one had anything to do with the other! Of course, she privately conceded the speculation was entirely reasonable, which only made the whole nightmare that much more difficult.

Eliza had been tempted to cancel. Despite its isolation, Brookings Farm afforded her the relative anonymity she craved then, but to have done so might have run her the risk of never seeing Fiona again, and now that Lord Carleton was within her grasp – however tenuously – Eliza needed to insure her position in his periphery so that when Fiona finally passed (as mercenary as this made her sound) she could be there, amongst the first to offer him a shoulder to cry on. With this in mind, she accepted Fiona's invitation.

Luckily – and to Eliza's vast relief – the ravages of Lady Fiona's cancer were not outwardly apparent, despite the Hermes scarf she wore as a kind of turban around her head, no doubt to mask the effects of aggressive chemotherapy. Fiona was already seated and waiting for her in the tearoom, a pot of Darjeeling and a plate of *macaron* in place on the table.

"I'm so sorry I'm late," Eliza said as she swept into the tearoom with a breezy conviction she didn't feel. "Please forgive me. I hope you weren't waiting long."

They air-kissed and Eliza sat down. "It's gotten rather tricky avoiding the paparazzi, although you would think by now I'd have mastered the art of evasion!"

Lady Fiona smiled and took it upon herself to pour them each a cup of tea. Her hands were steady, Eliza noticed, which for reasons she didn't quite understand made her feel slightly better about everything.

"Darjeeling," Fiona said.

"My favorite," Eliza lied. She was indifferent to tea, Darjeeling or otherwise.

"Yes, mine too." They sipped their tea in a warm silence. Lady Fiona held her cup just beneath her nose to inhale its slightly bitter aroma. She closed her eyes and sighed before bringing the cup to her lips and swallowing. "It soothes the soul," she said. "How are you holding up anyway?"

"I feel I should be asking you that," Eliza replied.

"I'm as well as can be expected, I suppose," Fiona said. "Some days are better than others. Today is one of the good days."

"I adore your scarf." Eliza felt she was stabbing for words in a barrel of fish.

Fiona beamed at her and self-consciously adjusted the scarf. "This old thing?" she laughed. "It was one of the first presents Carleton ever gave me. Paris on our honeymoon. I haven't worn it in years!"

"It's lovely."

"Thank you for meeting me."

Fiona placed her cup back in its saucer. Eliza held her breath. A pall seemed to descend across Fiona's face. She suddenly appeared frail, as if the effort of greeting her and pouring the tea had expended what little energy Fiona had managed to muster. *This isn't right*, Eliza thought. *This isn't fair...*

"Of course," Eliza said.

"It happens sometimes. I'll go hours feeling all right, or if not all right exactly, then functional, just very tired. I apologize."

"Can I get you anything?"

Fiona shook her head, paused, and then took a deep breath before looking up at Eliza with an almost defiant glimmer in her eye as though she was determined to present a brave face to the world despite her all too evident pain.

"I have everything I need," she said. "However...may I ask a favor of you, Eliza? We don't know each other well and I would completely understand if you tell me no. I wouldn't be offended. It's just that I feel so close to you. In the short time we've known each other...I feel as though...what I mean to say is...I do so admire you."

"Don't be silly!" Eliza protested. The aura that seemed to emanate from Lady Fiona made her claustrophobic. How was it possible that Lady Fiona could be so perfect, so good? "I've done nothing to deserve your admiration. I'm really rather unremarkable."

"To the contrary! You're so brave. Were I in your shoes, well, I don't know how I would cope. Do you even recognize yourself in the press, in what the media says about you? In what the media says about your late husband, and now your son. As a mother, I can't imagine how you don't just fall apart. If I were you, I daresay I'd never leave the house let alone open a newspaper or turn on the telly."

"I carry on," Eliza said. Fiona's effusions were beginning to grate. To distract herself, she poured another cup of tea and offered the same to Fiona. "It's the English way."

"I wish I'd met you earlier. I feel there is so much I could have learnt from you."

"You said you had a favor to ask?" The question sounded harsher than she had intended. Lady Fiona flinched. The pall drifted across her face again and then faded. She smiled, but Eliza thought it looked strained.

"I hate to impose."

"Nothing you would ask of me could ever be an imposition," Eliza said as though to assuage any offense she may have caused.

"You're too kind." Lady Fiona took a sip of tea and regarded Eliza over the rim of her cup. "Carleton was very impressed by you at the reception. All the way home and for days after, he couldn't stop singing your praises. He doesn't impress easily."

Eliza blushed in spite of herself. She couldn't appear too eager. "Well, I don't know why," she replied with an incredulous laugh. "If anything I felt a little off my game that night."

"To the contrary. You lit up what's typically a very drab affair. Ambassador Bingham isn't exactly the most scintillating conversationalist and he's an even drearier host." Fiona leaned forward over the table as though drawing Eliza into the utmost of confidences. "Believe me, Carleton and I have known the Binghams for years. My husband's business dealings with Tony go back long before he became Ambassador."

"Your husband certainly seems to know a lot of influential people," Eliza replied for lack of a more fitting response. She was getting impatient.

"Yes," Fiona said after another weighted pause. "It's easy to lose track. He's an excellent judge of character and he doesn't suffer fools, which is why I know his enthusiasm for you is genuine."

"Your husband seems like an extraordinary man. You're lucky to have him."

"He's lucky to have me." It sounded to Eliza like a correction, or a reprimand. Eliza wasn't sure how she was meant to respond. "Men are difficult, especially husbands. And the more money, power, and influence they have, the more extreme their needs. Wouldn't you agree?"

Eliza thought of Chester, lying there in the coroner's office, naked, split from belly to neck, his guts splayed out.

"My experience doesn't relate itself well to others," Eliza said. "After twenty-something years, you think you know someone and then overnight you discover the man you've called your husband has a predilection for underage Bangkok bum boys who like to play with machetes. Unlike your husband, Lady Fiona, I'm clearly not a good judge of character."

"Oh dear," Fiona said. She clasped Eliza's hand on the table. Her skin was cold. Eliza suppressed the urge to pull away. "I'm so sorry. How insensitive of me! I didn't mean to imply..."

"No apologies necessary," Eliza said, though she couldn't help but feel judged. Defensiveness had become instinctual. "My husband – my *late* husband – was a victim of circumstances beyond my control. It is probably for the best I was kept ignorant."

"Yes, yes, of course. You poor, poor dear."

"You said you had a favor to ask of me?"

"I hope I can speak frankly." Fiona squeezed Eliza's hand. Her eyes widened and assumed an earnest cast that Eliza would have found irritating in any other person, but she knew Lady Fiona was sincere. "Sister to sister."

"Of course."

"My husband...Carleton...has – how should I say this? – a rather healthy appetite...if you know what I mean."

Eliza had an inkling. "I'm not sure that I do, actually," she replied. "He struck me as very fit when I saw him that night. But, of course, black tie has a very slimming effect."

Fiona frowned. "Yes, his doctors have always said he has the body of a thirty-five year-old...and the drive to go with it."

"Oh." With her free hand, Eliza fiddled with the pearls at her neck.

"The thing is," Fiona continued, seemingly oblivious to any discomfort the topic might have provoked, "before I became ill, Carleton and I always had a very robust sex life. Well into our sixties, we'd make love sometimes three or four times a day. It's one of the reasons we've stayed married for so long. Lately, though, we've had to accommodate. As I'm sure you can imagine, my energy isn't what it used to be ... while Carleton's, by comparison, is at an all-time high. He's a walking erection..."

Fiona laughed. Eliza shifted uncomfortably in her seat. She longed to pull free from Fiona's grasp but didn't dare.

"Carleton is so patient with me," Fiona said. Her smile was bittersweet. "This illness was unexpected, for both of us of course, but for Carleton especially. He's always been a man for whom there are solutions – money and power open many doors. But in this case, I'm afraid there's nothing he can do except pay to keep me comfortable and cared for. I feel I'm letting him down."

"I'm sure that isn't the case," Eliza said. "It's very clear that your husband loves you very much."

"How naïve you are!" Fiona shook her head, but not unkindly, which only served to make Eliza feel that much more inadequate. "Carleton's love for me isn't in question. Our love is eternal. What I'm talking about is Carleton's libido. It isn't healthy for a man of Carleton's temperament to be deprived of his most basic needs. And sex, for a man like Carleton, is oxygen. It's the air he breathes."

Eliza needed a moment. She slipped her hand out from under Lady Fiona's grasp and sat back in her chair. What was Fiona asking of her? And why her? Of course, Eliza supposed she shouldn't look a gift horse in the mouth. The fact she had made such a favorable impression on Lord Carleton at the Ambassador's reception had been her exact intent, her only reason for attending, not to mention the fact that Essie and Sister Francine had been most adamant. They had reminded her in no uncertain terms that The Movement depended upon the unlimited coffers of families like the Templeton's, at least in these initial stages.

And yet, reading between the lines – all this excruciating detail about Lady Fiona and Carleton's intimacies – Eliza couldn't help but wonder if she was being set up for something she wasn't prepared to consider. Moving in on a man for tactical purposes after his wife had died was one thing, but to have such strategy not only condoned but suggested by the man's dying wife was quite another. Had Eliza's motives been so obvious? Had Fiona suspected her intentions all along? Eliza began to doubt whether she had perhaps overplayed her hand, which then made her call into question every move she had ever made. Had Chester's death and Trevor's recent arrest affected her in ways she hadn't expected? Was it time for a complete reassessment of her strategy?

To give herself time to quell the whirling thoughts in her head, Eliza raised the teacup to her lips and went through a pantomime of blowing the steam away in a pretense of cooling it down before sipping delicately – as she had seen Fiona do – and letting the sweetly bitter taste settle on her tongue. Fiona's gaze was unwavering. Eliza had indeed underestimated the woman. There was a determination behind the sweet she'd missed entirely.

"I've made you uncomfortable," Fiona said without the slightest trace of apology in her voice. "I just felt it was important to tell you where I'm coming from. Perhaps I misinterpreted the basis of your interest in my husband?"

Eliza nearly dropped the cup. "Excuse me?"

Lady Fiona's expression softened. She smiled. She had the advantage. "All my life, people have underestimated me," she began. "Women in particular, but men too. Being faithful to one's husband, one's family, and one's moral code doesn't have to equate to subservience. As Carleton will most assuredly tell you, I have never bent to his will. I may smile and look as though I'm permanently -- some might say, blissfully – in soft focus, but I've always known who my friends and enemies are and I've always been correct in my assessments. Believe me, you don't stay married to a man like Carleton Templeton without knowing how to play the game."

"What am I?" Eliza asked. Now that she had gotten past her initial surprise, she found she quite enjoyed the 'new' Lady Fiona that sat before her. "Friend or foe?"

Fiona paused. The smile remained fixed. She bit into one of the *macaron* and chewed slowly. Eliza recognized the tactic for what it was.

"Friend," Fiona eventually replied. "You're too amateur to really pose much of a threat. I can spot women like you a mile away: constantly striving, scheming: every step, every word, every sentence you utter so carefully constructed. You think you're being subtle but your motives are written plain as day across your face. Don't get me wrong. I don't hold it against you. You've had a difficult run of things. With limited resources at your disposal, of course you're looking for a man to support you going forward. Chester was obviously a disappointment. But we live, we learn, we carry on. There's not much to do beyond that, is there?"

"Since you've decided to be blunt," Eliza ventured, "what is this favor you want to ask of me?"

"Yes, the favor. I think you'll actually be doing yourself a favor as well."

"It no doubt involves your husband?"

"Indeed."

"Well?"

"After I'm gone, I want you to make yourself available to him."

"I'm not a prostitute."

Lady Fiona rolled her eyes. "Don't force me into clichés," she said. "Carleton needs a strong woman behind him. He's had his affairs – his peccadilloes, sexual and otherwise – but he's always had me there, guiding and supporting him behind the scenes. Once I've passed on, there's no one else to step into my place. I love my children – they are my heart and soul – but unfortunately, they're all rather useless, however well intentioned. I'm their rock."

Eliza considered Fiona's words. There was no denying their appeal. And given the conversations – the scheming, the machinations – she had had with Essie and Francine, it would seem that all of their plans were falling neatly into place. Still, Eliza had cause for concern. The Templeton children were notorious – insular and overly indulged. Trevor had known Guy at uni, not well as he had only traveled on the periphery of Guy's elite circle but well enough to observe and form the opinion that the man was nothing more than a privileged waster. The very worst, Trevor had said.

Of course, Eliza had always suspected that part of Trevor's issue with the Templetons had to do with the fact that their doors were closed to him. Trevor had been born with a silver spoon in his mouth. But unlike those of his peers, Trevor's spoon had been tarnished.

She missed Trevor. She regretted they had grown so far apart. Africa held no appeal for her. She hadn't been back since her honeymoon. Yet Chester had loved it so and, it seemed, Trevor shared his father's passion for the chaos of its teeming cities and the majestic expanse of its countryside. With Chester gone, all Eliza had left was her son, who for reasons she recognized but preferred not to consider wanted nothing to do with her. Was it her fault that Trevor had followed in his father's footsteps? Had she inadvertently pushed him away? Was it too late to make it up to him, to breach the cavernous gap that had sprung up between them? Regardless of whatever plans she had concocted with the sisters to get herself in Lord Carleton Templeton's bed – for The Movement, of course – Eliza's first priority had to be her son. She needed Trevor back. She needed him safe – in England—where he belonged. Perhaps Fiona's "favor" might benefit not only Lord Carleton and The Movement, but Trevor as well?

"Does Carleton know we're having this conversation?" Eliza asked.

"Of course not. He must never know."

"And what if he rejects my advances?"

"Carleton has never rejected a woman in his life," Fiona replied. "I shouldn't think he'd suddenly have a change of heart once I'm gone."

"Your children?"

"They're terrified of their father. They'd never go against him."

"Children have a nasty habit of being greedy."

Fiona arched an eyebrow. "Speaking from experience?" she asked. "It's no secret that you and Trevor are...'estranged'."

"Whatever issues I may have with my son aren't any of your concern."

"Carleton could help you with that, you know," Fiona persisted. "One of his best friends from the army has pull with certain officials in Nairobi. If you'd like, I can have Carleton get in touch with him. There's no need to wait until after I'm dead. Hamish owes me a favor or two."

"Hamish?" Eliza didn't want to appear too eager but at the same time she felt Fiona was offering her a lifeline. The only question, of course, was at what price.

"You may have heard of him: Hamish Tavistock. He's rather famous."

"The Australian entrepreneur?" Eliza had indeed heard of Hamish. His fame – if the *Wall Street Journal* and *The Financial Times* were at all accurate in their reporting – was based more on infamy than admiration.

"Mogul," Fiona corrected. "You know him then?"

"*Of* him," Eliza said. The cogs in her mind were whirring.

"Most of what they say about him in the press is true," Fiona said. "Some of it's exaggerated, of course, but then Hamish has always had a knack for spin. He's a legend in his own mind, but still a legend. I've always had a bit of a soft spot for the old coot."

"In other words..."

Fiona laughed. "I never kiss and tell," she said with a wink.

Eliza couldn't help herself. She laughed even as part of her felt she was signing a deal with the devil. Lady Fiona surprised her.

"I'll put in a word," Fiona said. "Now I really must dash. Chloe, my youngest and dearest, is hosting a fundraiser this evening at the RA for her new foundation: something to do with sweatshops in Bangladesh, of all things! I'm not feeling at all up for it, but Chloe insists I attend. And I suppose I do owe it to her. She's worked so hard to get this far and as I won't be around to see it blossom, the least I can do is be there for her tonight. I must pop over to Harvey Nick's now and hope I find something halfway presentable to wear. I've lost so much weight! Really, Eliza, the things we do for our children!"

Fiona stood up from the table and patted Eliza's hand in farewell. "This has been such a delight," she said. "I'd say we should do this again but it's rather difficult to plan ahead when any day might be my last. Goodbye, Eliza, and good luck. You'll need it."

Eliza never did see Fiona again. A news bulletin on the BBC website a fortnight later announced that Lady Fiona Templeton had passed away in peace at the family's estate in Dorset, surrounded by her husband, their children and grandchildren. And now – three years later – here she was presiding over the death of one of England's heretofore most eligible widowers, surrounded by the very same children and grandchildren, though not her own. Eliza had to pinch herself. It was an effort not to gloat.

But she was worried. Her instructions had been that Carleton was to be wheeled down to the dining room at eight o'clock sharp, not a second before, not a second after. Here it was, well past the hour, and no Rupert with the dinner bell. Eliza had never been one to panic. Things seemed to have a way of working out, yet never before had the stakes been quite so high. Should she try to slip out of the parlor and see from whence the delay stemmed, or should she remain in the room, relatively composed, and wait for Rupert's signal? The longer the wait, the more she wished she had insisted that Sister Francine find some alternative means of transport down from London. As much as Eliza was loath to admit, she had become dependent on the loathsome ex-nun. Sister Francine's quiet – some would say sinister – stoicism had a strangely calming effect upon Eliza, inasmuch as she was able to look beyond the fact that the woman was little more than a pedophile. (*Chester, Chester, the child molester!*) Eliza shuddered at the memory. How low she had fallen, but beggars couldn't be choosers. And now that she was officially Lord Carleton Templeton's wife, Eliza relished her newly exalted position. Her begging days were finally behind her. At least, that's what she was counting on.

And then, just as the first tendrils of self-doubt began to make their presence felt around her throat, the double-doors into the parlor swung open and Rupert appeared in his immaculate-as-ever butler's costume and white patent leather gloves. (How Eliza loved a man in white patent leather gloves!) The Templeton's ancient and long-serving butler cleared his throat and the chattering din ebbed to a low, nearly indistinct, rumble.

"*Mesdames et Messieurs*," Rupert announced with the soft tinkling accompaniment of the bell, "dinner is now served, if you please."

As the family made their way out of the parlor, Eliza lingered behind. A sense of dread overcame her. She was fearful of what might await her in the dining room.

"Is there a problem, Rupert?" she whispered.

"A problem, *Madame*?" Rupert sniffed. The old curmudgeon wasn't exactly subtle about his dislike of her.

"You're late," Eliza hissed. "I said eight o'clock. It's gone nearly past the quarter-hour."

"Yes, *Madame*, a delay but only slight."

"Slight or not, why was I not informed? Is Lord Carleton all right? Has he taken another turn?"

Rupert remained steadfast. He wouldn't look at her, which only served to infuriate Eliza further. "All things considered, Madam," he said, "Lord Carleton is doing about as well as can be expected. Beyond that, I cannot tell you."

Lord Carleton's "turn" earlier that afternoon had caused Eliza no matter amount of anxiety. That he had nearly suffered a stroke in the midst of consummation had certainly been less than ideal. She'd misinterpreted his gasps for cries of passion, which had only served to intensify her own. It wasn't until Carleton flailed out at her – arms and legs akimbo – in a desperate attempt to retrieve his oxygen mask (nearly tossing Eliza onto the floor in the process) that Eliza realized she had perhaps pushed him too far. (*Thank God all the necessary paperwork was already signed!*) Once Carleton's oxygen had been restored and his breathing returned more-or-less to normal, Eliza paused a moment to gather herself – no point in presenting a spectacle to the good doctor – and checked her look in the mirror. Her complexion was pleasingly flushed, her hair ever so fashionably tousled, her skin relatively free of age-betraying wrinkles. Eliza was quite satisfied with her appearance. While not quite the blushing new bride, she felt she certainly gave Lady Fiona a run for her money.

Of course, Dr. Raleigh wasn't fooled. When she'd finally summoned him and the attendant nurses, the look he gave her was all the proof she needed of where his loyalties lay. Lady Fiona may have given her the opportunity of a lifetime, but it hadn't prepared her for the often-blatant disparagement of the first Lady Templeton's inner circle – an endless and ever-revolving door of family, friends, staff, and hangers-on. Eliza, who took considerable pride in her obsessive attention to preparation, kicked herself for having come up short where Lady Fiona's legacy was concerned. But that was all about to change. She took comfort from the fact that soon – very soon – the great Lord Carleton Templeton would become the *late* great Carleton Templeton and everything that had once been Lady Fiona's – and she meant *everything*! – would finally and irrevocably be hers.

She began to see The Steeplechase as an opportunity – her "coming out" as it were, her "debut." It was imperative the next seventy-two hours went off without a hitch or another scare like she'd had with Carleton in the bedroom. *Note to self: no sex allowed.* It was a terrible shame, however, that she'd never be able to conceive. What a thumb in the eye that would have been to Lady Fiona's insufferable brood! The very idea gave Eliza gooseflesh. Still, she contented herself with the knowledge that she did have one ace up her sleeve. Trevor. How important her distant and ne'er-do-well son had become to her, again thanks in no small part to Fiona and Carleton's perhaps largely unintended largess. How sly she had been! How masterfully she had played them both! And Hamish? Well, Lady Fiona's suggestion that she involve the florid Aussie businessman in her effort was the cherry on top of a very decadent sundae.

"I don't appreciate your impertinence," she said. In actuality, Rupert's diffidence mattered very little. He'd be gone at the end of the weekend, as would the rest of the staff: needless expenses all of them, drains on Templeton Enterprises' balance sheet that they could ill afford. But one step at a time. "Tell Hortense to hold off serving the amuse bouche until I give the signal. Lord Carleton and I have a very important announcement and we don't wish to be interrupted by servants hovering overhead clattering silverware. Am I understood?"

"Yes, Madam."

Eliza took a series of deep, clearing breaths and straightened the invisible creases down the front of her new Badgley Mischka evening gown. The frock had been an indulgence – an extravagant splurge whose price tag flew in the face of everything Eliza purported to believe – but given the enormity of the event it was meant to commemorate, Eliza felt the dress a worthwhile expense. She could always sell it at the village consignment shop if Sister Francine objected too vociferously. On second thought, perhaps it wasn't such a bad thing after all that Sister Francine was stuck in London?

Eliza forced a tight smile and assumed a proudly erect posture as she strode into the dining hall en route to her seat on the Templeton throne. There they all were – the whole sodding lot of them, arranged in their places around the grand candle-lit, crystal and silver-bedecked dining table, aglow beneath the chandeliers, so smug, so arrogant, so prime for knocking down, one-by-one, like bowling pins. The sight of them all together made Eliza's stomach churn. She swallowed the bile that rose in her throat. How she hated each of them and how she relished that hatred! So much mutual antipathy in one room – for she knew the children secretly (and not so secretly) despised each other almost as much as she despised them – that it made Eliza's eyes tear-up with nearly orgasmic joy. And the little monsters – Rain, Charlotte, George, and Walter: shiny and spit-polished miniature clones of their abominable parents. There was a special place in hell for precocious children like Edgar and Penelope's offspring. (*The place where bad little girls and boys go.*) Eliza would delight in sending them off there. All in good time, she said to herself as her gaze swept across the room, *all in good time.*

Lord Carleton presided at the head of this veritable Last Supper looking as regal as a wheelchair-bound octogenarian on the verge of death could possibly be expected to look. He was dressed exactly as Eliza had instructed – pressed white shirt, black tie, Armani dinner jacket – with a heavy tartan blanket neatly tucked over his lap. That his mouth hung open and his expression was slack didn't give Eliza too much cause for concern. She just needed him to sit there and perhaps hold her hand while she spoke for the both of them, and once the announcement was made, she'd instruct the nurses to wheel him back to his bedchambers where he belonged. After the announcement, it really didn't matter what Lord Carleton did. Her plan was already set in motion regardless of whether he hung on for one more hour or the entire weekend. Much beyond that, however, would be rather inconvenient. Perhaps he could be hurried along?

Eliza made a big production of tucking in Lord Carleton's blanket and dabbing at the corner of his mouth where the drool was starting to show. Dr. Raleigh had assured her that Carleton hadn't suffered from a post-coital stroke as she had feared, but she could see he was clearly the worse for wear for all his nuptial exertions. When he was sufficiently sorted, Eliza took the helm at the head of the table. She raised a glass of champagne to her lips and wet her tongue just enough to feel more loquacious. All eyes were upon her. She felt their loathing and distrust, their willing her to fall on her face and make an utter arse of herself. Eliza looked forward to not giving the Templeton children any such satisfaction. This was her moment. All her life had been leading to this. She was damned well going to make the most of it and rub the shit deep into their smarmy and privileged faces.

"Thank you all for being here tonight," she began, her gaze slowly taking each of them in, one at a time, lingering just long enough to make them squirm. "With all of this weekend's activities I thought it best to save this evening for family time. And while you aren't family, Miss Grimaldi, it would have been inhospitable of me to chuck you out to fend for yourself tonight, especially as you have so generously graced us with your overabundance of tulips. You've brought a little bit of Holland to our stodgy English home."

"Thank *you*, Lady Eliza," Elena nodded and bowed her head. Her smile was taut and toothsome. Her teeth were blinding in the glow of the chandeliers and candlelight. Eliza wanted to take a sledgehammer to them. "It was the very least I could do. *Dank je.*"

The sarcasm wasn't lost on Eliza. She took note and stored it away for future use.

"Your father and I have an important announcement to make." Eliza sensed her nerves starting to get the better of her. She gripped the champagne flute and forced herself to take another steadying sip. Now that the moment was upon her, it was easier if she looked above and beyond them, at her reflection in the gilded mirrors on the opposite end of the table, behind where she would have sat Sister Francine if the rail unions hadn't gotten in the way.

"I should like to start by saying that I love your father very, very much." She could only hope the words sounded sincere. Eliza had rehearsed this. Essie had once told her that her natural speaking voice was brittle and that whenever she tried to inject emotion into her tone, it came off as disingenuous and strained, which turned people off. Eliza had taken Essie's words to heart even as she had a few of her own she might have tossed Essie's way had Sister Francine not been standing there. The sisters were a difficult and tricky twosome. Essie she could do without, but Sister Francine was her rock. They came as a pair. They couldn't be separated.

"I can't express enough the joy your father – and grandfather – has brought me these past two years." It was good to acknowledge the grandchildren: the stuck-up nine year-old prissy little missy that was Rain; the gormless Walter, who at only six years of age was already the spitting image of his father, Edgar, an infantile waste of space if ever there was one; and the twins, three year-olds George and Charlotte, named after the Prince and Princess of Wales's children, and dressed just as precociously. (Oh, how desperate their mother, Penelope, was to be the perfect English wife! The American turned Eliza's stomach, but perhaps – if Diana proved a disappointment – she could be molded? After all, they were both outsiders. Perhaps they shared a common bond? The jury was still out.)

"Now I know that some of you – all right, let's be honest, *all* of you – look upon me as the very worst kind of interloper—"

"Gold digger more like," Chloe said.

The little bitch...

But this was Eliza's night to be magnanimous. "Gold digger, then...if you prefer," she said.

"I don't prefer," Chloe persisted. She'd obviously been on her drink. "I'd prefer that you not be here at all."

"Chloe, really darling, this isn't the time," Diana said.

Lady Diana to the rescue. Best to move on, stick to the script. There would be time enough for accusations later.

"It's fine, Diana, but thank you," Eliza replied. She took another sip from her champagne. Her hands were sweating. "Yes, I am an outsider. Yes, I'm not nearly as posh as all of you. I have had a difficult life. I married very young and very foolishly. My parents needed the money and I was sold off – yes, we'll call a spade a spade – I was sold off to a man I didn't understand, a man who didn't love me, a man that, despite all of my best intentions, I didn't love in return. You all know what happened to my late husband, just as you all know what happened to Trevor, my son, who could have been and, I hope and pray, *can be* the one good thing that came out of mine of Chester's union.

"I need you all to understand something. I did not rise to this occasion on my own. It wasn't something I planned. It was your mother, the wonderful and saintly and blessed Lady Fiona, who came to me, who asked me in her very last weeks – days even – to look after your father when she was no longer able to look after him herself. So you can call me all the names you want – interloper, gold digger, opportunist, believe me I've heard them all – but the fact remains that my presence in this family was sanctioned by your mother before she died. I am here because of her."

"You're lying," Chloe again. The girl was really starting to try Eliza's nerves even more than usual. Her chin was already quivering which meant the waterworks were only moments away.

Eliza braced herself. She was still only in the preamble of her speech. She glanced at Carleton. His expression hadn't changed. Eliza wondered if he was even cognizant of his surroundings. Perhaps her need for sexual consummation had been premature? She needed Carleton engaged. She needed him to support her against his children.

"I realize this is difficult for you, Chloe," she said. "But I would hope that eventually you're able to get past your inherent – and perhaps understandable – bias, and make peace with the fact that I am only here because of your mother. And that I have only the very best of intentions for your father and for all of you. Carleton, is there anything you wish to add before I continue?"

Of course, he didn't respond. A bubble of saliva expanded and burst between his lips. Eliza felt nauseated. She nodded for one of the nurses to wipe his mouth dry with a handkerchief before clearing her throat to give herself time to steady the trembling she knew underlay her voice. What was supposed to have been her moment of triumph was devolving into her worst nightmare.

"Is Papa all right?" Chloe pushed back from the table and ran to her father's side. She knelt on the floor beside the wheelchair and clasped Carleton's hands in her own. "Papa, it's me. It's Chloe. Papa, are you all right? Can you hear me, Papa?"

Carleton blinked. For a moment, it appeared he was with them: aware of Chloe fiddling with his blanket, wiping the drool from his lips, adjusting the lapels of his dinner jacket, straightening his tie. Eliza wanted to scream. She wanted to tell the spoiled little strumpet exactly what she thought of her, of all of them. Chloe was stealing her spotlight. In all of Eliza's preparations with the sisters, the hysterics started after the announcement, not before. Goddamn Carleton for not adhering to her playbook! Goddamn – no, *fuck* them all.

"Chloe, please sit down," Eliza said, instantly regretting her choice of words the moment they passed from her lips.

The tears were in free fall. "Papa? Papa, can you hear me? What is he...?"

Carleton's mouth opened. A rattling emerged from the back of his throat. His eyes widened and blinked and then widened again. He looked from Chloe to Eliza and then back to his daughter, seeming to see her for the first time. His hands moved on his lap.

"Yes, Papa?" Chloe persisted. "What do you want to say? Please, everyone, quiet! Papa is trying to say something."

The Templetons – children and grandchildren – appeared to rise from the table as one unified mass. They surrounded Carleton, pushing Eliza to the periphery, casting her aside as the outsider they all believed her to be. Eliza knocked back the contents of her champagne flute and snapped her fingers for another glass.

"Don't crowd him," Dr. Raleigh said over the din of semi-hysterical chatter. "Please, everyone, give your father some space."

Eliza couldn't see Carleton through the wall of black dinner jackets and evening gowns that now separated her from her husband. She drank deep from her glass and relished the fizzy burn. She hadn't planned to get drunk that night, but now intoxication seemed the only logical course of action.

And then she heard Carleton. Her breath caught in her throat. He was speaking. He was with her after all. Eliza stepped forward. She pushed her way through to Carleton's wheelchair. Chloe was still on her knees at his feet, her face pressed into his lap, sobbing. The others were gathered round him, all leaning forward en masse to hear the words Eliza had planned to say to them herself. Defeat was turning into glory. The old coot wasn't so far gone that he couldn't fulfill his duty to her.

"Children..." Carleton stammered. "Lady Eliza and I..."

Speak, Carleton, speak! Eliza was nearly beside herself.

"Lady Eliza and I..."

"Yes, Papa, what?" Chloe lifted her head from his lap and wrung his hands. Eliza thought she looked like a snot-nosed banshee with her mascara running down her cheeks.

"Lady Eliza is your mother now."

Stunned silence. Eliza assumed her position behind Lord Carleton's wheelchair. She placed her hand on his shoulder and squeezed it hard to the bone. *Thank you,* she mouthed.

Eliza now had the confidence of Valhalla. "What your father is trying to tell you," she began in a voice of almost stentorian clarity, "is that this afternoon, he and I were married which, of course, makes me your stepmother."

The room erupted. Eliza maintained her grip on Carleton's shoulder as she watched the various pantomimes in front of her. Chloe leapt up from the floor and turned on Eliza, fists raised, arms akimbo. Eliza steeled herself for the inevitable rain of blows. Her smile was cold but she felt warmth in the comfort of her satisfaction.

"You're lying!' Chloe screamed. "It's not possible. It isn't true! It can't be true!"

"But I'm afraid it is," Eliza replied.

Chloe lunged but Guy held her back. She buried her face in his chest and pounded him with her fists.

"Now, look here," Edgar interjected. His face was beet red and with his chest puffed out in his ill-fitting shirt and jacket, Eliza thought he looked like an overstuffed penguin. "What's this all about anyway? You can't possibly...I...I demand a word alone with my father. I need an explanation. You're a Papist!"

"I am Catholic, yes," she replied. "And proudly so." The warmth traveled through Eliza's arms and legs. Whether it was elation or the alcohol or a combination of both, Eliza didn't know. But the sensation was extraordinary. She'd never been happier. "As is your father. Father O'Connell oversaw the conversion right before he officiated our marriage. I have all the paperwork upstairs, if you require proof."

Chloe came up for air. "How dare you!" she cried. She struggled against Guy's grip but he continued to hold her fast, for which Eliza supposed she was grateful. "There's no way Papa would ever agree to this. You've bewitched him – you and that horrid nun who's always hanging about, lurking in corners and giving everyone the evil eye. The two of you cast a spell on Papa. You've corrupted him!"

"Really, Chloe darling, you're being hysterical…as per usual." Diana entered the fray looking slightly bored, or (more accurately) too drunk on a mixture of gin and champagne (and whatever else she'd snorted) to be all that bothered about anything. "This isn't the Middle Ages. Catholics aren't burnt at the stake anymore…at least not in this country."

"You're taking her side?"

Diana gave Eliza a withering look before putting her arm around her little sister and pulling her gently out from Guy's embrace. "No, darling, of course not," Diana said. "But what's the sense in ramping things up from zero to sixty? Papa's a grown man. He has a right to live his life how he chooses. We may not agree, but it's his choice, not ours."

"How can you say that?" Chloe shrilled. "Don't you see what she's doing? Don't you see what she's done to Papa? He's like a…he's like a vegetable."

Despite her words, however, Chloe (mercifully) allowed herself to be led back to her place at the table. Eliza took a breath, nodded her gratitude to Diana who quickly looked away, and indicated for yet another glass of bubbly. The bombshell had been dropped to predictable results. Now all that was left was for Eliza to keep the reins firmly in hand and remind them – and herself – who was boss, if it still wasn't apparent.

"Thank you, Dr. Raleigh," she said with a thick smile. "You can take Lord Carleton back up to his room. I've asked Hortense to serve him his dinner there. No doubt he'll be more comfortable in his bed, where he belongs."

She could tell Dr. Raleigh didn't like her either. It was all too obvious that his perspective was skewed by his long-standing loyalty to the family. Eliza considered it a good thing that she wouldn't be in need of his services for too much longer.

She wondered what she could do to hasten Carleton along.

Once the doctor and his entourage had removed Lord Carleton from the premises, Eliza assumed her seat at the head of the table. The Templeton children, their respective spouses (conspicuously minus Duncan), the grandchildren, and – not to be forgotten – Elena Grimaldi returned to their former positions around the vast and ostentatious table. They could cry foul all they wanted, but at heart, the Templeton brood were nothing if not traditional in their very English sense of propriety. At least when it concerned The Firm, decorum must be preserved at all costs. Eliza couldn't help but smile to herself. How quickly their smug self-satisfaction was about to change!

Eliza tapped her salad fork against the rim of her champagne flute. The crystalline ring brought an immediate if unruly silence to the dining table.

"Now that you've had time to recover from the shock," she began with a light-hearted but seriously weighted laugh, "and before we're served the first course, there are a few cautionary words I wish to share with you.

"I want to start by expressing my utmost gratitude for one amongst us who doesn't receive half the respect she deserves. You dismiss your eldest sibling as inconsequential. Don't pretend that you don't. I know it. You know it. And believe me, Diana knows it. But I assure you, without Diana's devotion and support, your father would already be six feet under. And what a mess that would be!"

Rumblings of protest. Eliza held her hand up to silence them. They – albeit reluctantly – obeyed. (Sister Francine would be so proud!)

"So I just want to take a moment to personally thank Diana for being such a friend and ally to me through this very difficult time. Whilst all of you were gallivanting around the world, spending and wasting and losing your father's hard-earned money, posing for magazine covers, or serving third-rate food and overcharging the gullible sycophants who comprise your social milieu, Diana was here in Dorset in this cold and draughty and thoroughly unfortunate house, tending your father, changing his bed pan, bandaging his bed sores when they became infected, and dutifully, unselfishly providing me with the resilience to stand up to the adversity we both knew I would face, not only tonight, but for the rest of my life.

"So I wanted to take a moment to raise a glass to Diana. For your loyalty and your unswerving commitment to this family I can't thank you enough."

What were they going to do? They couldn't not raise a glass to their eldest sibling. Eliza beamed as she held her champagne flute out in front of her and waited for the others to do the same. Diana glared at her across the table. Yes, Eliza conceded, she had rather overstated Diana's value, and it wasn't lost on her that by making an example of Diana she was alienating her from the rest of the clan. But within Eliza's praise was a warning. Eliza needed Diana at Templeton Manor. Diana was the buffer, the conduit, and the voice of reason to the rest of the Templeton children. And Diana, Eliza knew, didn't have much choice in the matter. For what was she really? Without Templeton Manor and all its *accoutrement* – including Templeton Enterprises – Diana had nothing. She was nothing. Her husband, Duncan – so conspicuous in his absence that evening – had his fingers in more pies (quite literally) than the poor woman could possibly imagine. If Eliza had the capacity to feel compassion, she may have felt a twinge for Diana. But cheating husbands were a dime a dozen, and Duncan, at least according to Eliza's sources, was a master baker.

So they raised their glasses and saluted Diana who nodded and graced them with her customary tight-lipped smile while Chloe nattered away in her ear, Edgar coughed his Harrovian indignation, and Guy just watched with a glassy-eyed kind of detachment that, for reasons Eliza couldn't articulate, made her want to smash her glass across his face. Penelope, the American, just went through the motions like an automaton. Oh, how desperately she wanted to fit in! How imperative her need to be accepted! Eliza thanked her lucky stars she'd never felt so pressing a desire to be relevant. And Elena Grimaldi, well, this was the stuff that social media was made for! In a way, Eliza supposed, there was a benefit to having the self-proclaimed Tulip Queen of Amsterdam there as a witness. Eliza didn't really know Elena, but she certainly knew *of* her and even more of the Dutch woman's extended social circle. Elena could prove useful to the cause. With the right amount of persuasion, Elena Grimaldi could be bent like the stem of a week-old tulip in need of fresh water.

"As for the rest of you," Eliza continued, "enjoy this weekend because, I can assure you, there will be no more Steeplechases, no more shooting parties, no more multi-thousand pound tabs at The Groucho Club or Annabel's or The Ivy. And yes, I've seen the credit card statements. All of them. The era of decadence has come to an end. As I've told Diana, this family is in dire financial straits. We cannot sustain ourselves at this rate, which means there will be sacrifices expected of each and every one of you. Oh, you can scowl at me all you want, Chloe, and mutter hateful things about me under your breath, but the fact remains, without austerity you'll all end up in the poorhouse. Any questions?"

"I say," Edgar stammered. His face was flushed and pinched like a schoolboy who'd been instructed to stand in the corner of a classroom with a dunce cap on his head. "I don't see why you have to be such a bloody bitch about it."

"Edgar!" Penelope slapped his arm.

"I'm just saying," he replied. "It's not like you can just waltz in here, fuck our father into his deathbed, and then expect to lay down the law. I mean really. Who are you anyway? One hears rumors."

"Yes," Eliza said, "one does."

"What exactly do you mean by that?"

Edgar was clearly blitzed which, Eliza felt, gave her the upper hand.

"I have no secrets," she said. "I tell no lies. My conscience is clear. I shan't give you the satisfaction, Edgar, of stooping to your level. You do your mother an injustice."

"Don't speak of our mother!" Chloe cried. "She's turning in her grave because of you."

"No," Eliza said, "on the contrary. Your mother would be so ashamed to see how your wretched behavior has blasphemed her good name. She saw it coming before she died. She said as much to me the last time I saw her. God rest her hallowed soul." For effect, Eliza punctuated her words with a robust Sign of the Cross.

"I'm Catholic too, you know," Elena said. "Lapsed, but Catholic."

"Name me a Catholic who isn't lapsed," Eliza replied, "and I'll canonize you."

Elena raised her glass in a hearty toast. "*Proost!*"

There was nothing for the Templetons to do but take Elena's lead, for who could deny such exuberance? Eliza beamed at the Tulip Queen as she drank from her champagne flute. She was beginning to change her perception of the self-made Dutch aristocrat. She'd ask for some time alone later, on the weekend, in the midst of the festivities. Eliza immediately thought of Trevor.

And so, thanks in no small part to Elena Grimaldi, the evening settled into a tense but civilized rhythm. Dinner was served – Hortense really was an excellent cook, Eliza observed. Such a pity she would have to be let go! – and the wine flowed. Eliza watched the charade from her helm at the head of the table. The dynamics were fascinating. She felt secure in her superiority, and yet, she wasn't entirely at ease. The delay before dinner had unnerved her, as had Carleton's sudden burst of eloquence. While Eliza appreciated her new husband's affirmation, she knew she couldn't trust it – or him – any further than she could throw Dulcinea down the cellar stairs. (Well, she'd done it, but not without considerable effort.)

Ever the eternal skeptic, Lady Eliza couldn't help but wonder whether Lord Carleton had somehow double-crossed her at the last minute. She needed to know, but she also knew she could never let her new family see the panic that had now taken hold of her. She'd have a word with the financial advisor after the weekend. She'd call Sister Francine later that night. Eliza hated how the ex-nun could assuage her insecurities with little more than the sound of her drink-heavy voice.

After dinner, when all were too intoxicated to remember or care that they hated each other, the Templetons – and Elena Grimaldi – migrated back to the front parlor where Chloe was persuaded by her siblings to lead them in an old-fashioned, properly Victorian, sing-a-long on the pianoforte. After much coaxing and cajoling, Chloe assumed her position at the instrument and accompanied herself in a set of rousing and nostalgic English folk ditties and defiantly Anglican hymns that reached their apex with a particularly earnest rendition of "Jerusalem" followed by – at Guy's insistence – the Sheffield Wednesday fight song. It was at this moment when Rupert tapped Lady Eliza on the shoulder and informed her that a young woman was waiting in the entrance hall, having asked to speak to Lord Carleton.

"Who is she?" Eliza asked, fear overwhelming her already frazzled nerves.

Rupert shrugged. "She's but a girl," he replied. "A wee slip of a thing."

"Why didn't you tell her Lord Carleton was indisposed?"

"It's pouring down rain outside, Mum," Rupert said, as if this was any reason. "She's chilled and soaked to the bone."

"We're not expecting anyone until tomorrow. The invitation explicitly stated…"

"With all due to respect, Mum," Rupert said. He leaned down until his lips nearly brushed Eliza's ear. "From the looks of her, I'd say she's not here for the Steeplechase."

Eliza followed Rupert out of the parlor with a mounting sense of unease that certainly wasn't helped by the crashing of lightning and thunder outside. It was a miracle the roof hadn't caved in. She'd check for leaks later.

"Thank you, Rupert, I can take it from here," she directed upon entering the hall, whereupon she encountered the unexpected guest looking quite as the butler had described her. "May I help you?"

The girl was young, Eliza estimated not much older than twenty, and dressed in a sodden flannel shirt, denim shorts that were much too short for Eliza's liking, and combat boots that looked as though they could outfit an entire army. Her long dirty blonde hair was plastered to her face from the rain. The hall was encased in shadow, yet even in the dark, Eliza could sense an energy and a heat that spelled nothing but trouble.

"I'm looking for Lord Carleton," the girl said. She arched her rather prominent eyebrows as she gave Eliza an undisguised onceover. Her voice was gruff but unmistakably posh. "Where is he?"

"And you are?"

"None of your effing business," the girl snapped. She wandered about the foyer, dripping water all over the newly polished marble floors, as though expecting Carleton to be hiding from her behind the tapestries on the walls. "Is he here?"

Eliza's instinct was to show the girl the door, but something in the stranger's demeanor held her back. Without knowing her name or the nature of her business with Lord Carleton, Eliza felt the need to handle the girl with kid gloves. The dread – if not paranoia – that had been gnawing away at her all afternoon and evening increased tenfold. Whatever the motive behind this most unwelcome and inopportune visit, Eliza was certain that it didn't bode well. She wondered whether Chloe had something to do with it.

"Lord Carleton has retired for the night," Eliza said. "Is he expecting you?"

"I need to see him."

"Well, you can't just show up here and..."

The girl flipped Eliza her middle finger as she pushed her way down the hall toward the front parlor where the strains of the Elton John standard "I Guess That's Why They Call it the Blues" reverberated from the piano. Eliza hurried after her, panic now gripping her. Where was Rupert? Why had he left her to handle this crisis on her own? For all she knew, the girl was armed and dangerous. Their lives could be at risk. This was a disaster. If she survived the next few minutes, Eliza determined to throw Rupert out into the rain that very night. Forget waiting until after the Steeplechase to divest Templeton Manor of its staff. They could all go tonight! That is, of course, assuming she survived...

"Excuse me!" Eliza said, knowing full well her words would have little effect. "Where the hell do you think you're going? This is a private gathering..."

But it was already too late. The girl threw open the double doors into the parlor and strode into the room as though she owned the place. Elton John came to an abrupt stop. All eyes turned toward her with one collective gasp.

"My name is Contessa Templeton," the girl declared. "Which one of you wankers is my father?"

| 14 |

Contessa ("Tessa") Templeton arose from the eiderdown depths of the four-poster bed, yawned and stretched to her near six-foot height before throwing open the shutters and stepping out onto the balcony that faced the paddocks where preparations for the Steeplechase were already in full swing. She couldn't remember when she'd slept so well. She was naked and utterly unabashed by the attention she attracted from the stable hands shoveling manure in front of the stables, well within sight of her perch on the balcony. Tessa loved her body: every soft, narrowly curvaceous inch of it was a cause for daily celebration. As God had blessed her with perfect genes, she felt it was nothing if not her duty to share her beauty with one and all. To do otherwise would have been selfish.

Satisfied that she had given the boys below a suitable greeting, Tessa returned to her bed and luxuriated once again in the plush and inviting warmth of the comforter. Things had gone better than even she had anticipated. Tessa was, by nature, a pragmatist. Of course, it helped that she lacked any sense of inhibition. Tessa simply didn't care what people thought of her. She was body and sex positive. If people didn't like her, she had no problem telling them to fuck off, which she did often and often with great enthusiasm. So while a lesser mortal might have quaked at the notion of crashing a party at one of England's most celebrated estates, Tessa Templeton saw the whole thing as little more than a particularly cheeky lark: an excuse to get out of London and enjoy a posh few days in the countryside on the family's expense account.

Not that Tessa's reasons for showing up like she had were without merit, for there was serious intent behind them. She believed with all her heart that Lord Carleton was her father. Her mother had sworn by it. And while there had never been any DNA tests to prove the veracity of her mother's claims, the black-and-white photo of a laddish Carleton Templeton that her mother had kept in a silver locket given to her as a Valentine's gift by the young lord was all the proof Tessa needed that she had as much of a right to the inheritance as any of his other – albeit perhaps more legitimate – children. The paternity test could come later. For now, it was achievement enough merely to be in his house and acknowledged by his family...*her* family. Everything else would work itself out in time.

A tentative knock on the door announced the arrival of Chloe, who strode into the room before coming to a rather abrupt stop at the end of the bed. Tessa smiled and pulled the comforter up under her chin until her toes peeked out the other end. Chloe had been the most welcoming of her the night before, taking Tessa under her wing and making sure she had a hot bath and dry clothes and a decent meal from that night's leftovers. She had shushed the others' protestations – especially those of Eliza, the dragon lady, whom Tessa soon came to understand was Lord Carleton's new wife, though this was currently up for debate – and appealed to their Christian sense of charity, taking in a lost and lonely soul from the cold. The fact that she was neither lost nor lonely, Tessa decided, was probably best left uncorrected.

"Did you sleep well?" Chloe asked. "I haven't woken you, have I? I didn't want to disturb you but it is rather late in the morning and I was worried you might have caught a chill. Are you quite comfortable?"

Tessa stretched for effect. The comforter came loose. Chloe's eyes widened as her face flushed and she adjusted her focus to a presumably safer point out the double French doors while Tessa arranged her hair to fall loosely down over her bare shoulders and chest.

"Deliciously well," Tessa said. "Like I've been freshly shagged."

"Well, that's good enough then, I suppose," Chloe replied. She coughed into the back of her hand and cleared her throat. "Do you drink coffee or tea? I'll ring downstairs and have a pot brought up for you. Breakfast?"

"Liquid is fine."

Chloe looked at her then without really looking at her. Tessa smoothed out her hair. "Sorry?"

"I'll have a Bloody Mary if 'downstairs' can manage it," Tessa said. "With lots of Worcestershire. I picked up the habit in America. Mind if I smoke or is that not allowed?"

Without waiting for a response, Tessa rummaged in the pocket of last night's flannel – now nicely washed, pressed and folded at the end of the bed – and was relieved to find that her pack of Marlboro Reds and lighter were both in their proper place. She lit up before wrapping the comforter around her and dragging herself out of the bed and back out onto the balcony, beckoning for Chloe to follow, which Chloe did with mincing haste. The stable hands whistled and catcalled. Tessa gave them a wave and a bit of a flash before sitting down and enjoying her first smoke of the day.

"I'll warn you," she said, "I'm a handful."

"Clearly," Chloe replied. She sat in the opposite chair. "You've made quite an impression."

"I'm a model. That's what I'm paid to do."

"You're a model?" said as if it was the most exotic profession Chloe had ever heard of.

Tessa shrugged. "It's aspirational."

"Have I seen you in anything?" Chloe pounced. "Have you been in *Vogue*? I adore Anna Wintour, but not Edward Enninful so much. I don't think he liked me. How about *Elle*? *Women's Wear Daily*? I've been in *Tatler,* you know. And *Vanity Fair*. I'm not a model, though. I'm an It Girl. Have you heard of S.A.S.S.?"

Tessa blew an indulgent ring of smoke into the air and watched it dissipate.

"I've done my homework," she said. "As for modeling, I've shot some stuff you've probably never seen, nor should you, if you know what I mean."

Chloe frowned. "Not really," she said.

"There's a band in LA ... the Duke's Boys ... I was a back-up dancer in one of their videos. And there's an artist in Paris I kind of hooked up with before he fucked me over by posting a bunch of stuff I'd done with him online. No big shit but not the kind of thing you want an agent to see...at least not a legitimate agent, at least not when you're still in the aspirational stages of your career."

"You mean like a sex tape?"

Tessa laughed. "There's more than one," she said. "A goddamned trilogy. Would you like to see it?"

Chloe hesitated a moment before replying. Her voice faltered and seemed to catch in her throat. "No," she stammered. "That's private."

"Honey, it ain't private if it's on the Internet."

"No one's ever called me 'Honey' before."

Tessa threw her head back and exhaled another indulgent stream of smoke. "Whatever. Anyway, I'm kind of proud of it. With better lighting it might have been performance art."

"But don't you feel exploited?"

"Babe, I'm the one on top. What cheesed me off is that he didn't ask before posting."

"And if he had?"

Tessa shrugged.

Chloe's eyes looked as though they were about to pop from her head. "Really?"

"Seriously?" Tessa asked.

"I'm a good girl. I don't have experience with such things."

"Ha!" Tessa tossed her pack of Marlboro Reds to Chloe who caught them on the fly. "That's what all the really bad girls say."

"I'm not a bad girl," Chloe protested. She fiddled with the pack of cigarettes. "I'm 'aspirational.'"

"Cute," Tessa said.

Chloe finally managed to open the pack of cigarettes, pulled one out, and placed it between her lips. Tessa was ready with the lighter.

"I don't smoke," Chloe said.

"And I suppose you don't swallow either?"

Chloe shrugged. "Are you really my father's daughter? No one believes you, you know. You should have heard what Diana said about you last night after you'd gone up to bed."

"That frigid cow? Fuck her."

"How do you know she's frigid?"

"Have you never been on the Internet?" Tessa asked. "Wikipedia?"

Chloe shook her head.

"It's like an encyclopedia about anyone and everyone worth knowing anything about."

"I thought that was *Tatler*." Chloe exhaled a languid stream of smoke. "Anyway, we're not talking about Diana. I love Diana. I really do. She's my big sister and all..."

"But?"

"What does Wikipedia say about her husband?"

"Duncan?"

Chloe nodded. "I'm sure you've noticed he's not here. Duncan's never here. He's a bit of an odd duck, if you ask me."

"Where is he?"

"London, or so he says." Chloe took another contemplative pause. "They're all looking at us, you know."

Tessa waved to the stable boys down below. They did more than wave back. Chloe blushed at their enthusiasm.

"I think I rather fancy a ride," Tessa said. "Could get me a mount?"

"I don't fraternize with the help," Chloe replied.

Tessa laughed. The comforter fell loose.

"I have to go." Chloe jumped up from the chair and vigorously stubbed the cigarette out underfoot. "I trust you can find own way downstairs? The

Steeplechase is tomorrow and we've got loads of people coming in from all over the place. It's all rather overwhelming, if you ask me. And I suppose it's inappropriate given Daddy's condition, but we do this every year and people would ask too many questions if we cancelled. Although, just so you know, I wasn't in favor of the last two years, but tradition must prevail. Are you staying with us long?"

"Have I already overstayed my welcome?"

"No...it's just that, I didn't notice you'd packed anything...clothes and whatnot. And we're kind of funny around here about..."

"Clothes and whatnot?"

Chloe blushed. "I think you're making fun of me," she said.

"On the contrary." Tessa winked. "I think I rather like you."

"And I think I rather like you too," Chloe replied. "You're like the little sister I always wished I'd had. Regardless of whatever happens, I do so hope we can be friends."

Tessa smiled. Chloe rather preciously excused herself with a promise to check in on her later before leaving Tessa once again to her own devices, which Tessa preferred anyway. When she finished her cigarette, Tessa stood up and let the comforter fall, giving the stable boys one last look before she returned to the bedroom and donned the flannel shirt and denim shorts from the night before. She conceded that Chloe had had a point. If she was going to last the weekend – and beyond – she needed more appropriate attire, especially for The Steeplechase, which anyone who knew anything about anyone knew was the Social Event of the Season, if not the Year. She'd have to borrow (or steal) from someone's wardrobe. Tessa didn't fancy Chloe's fashion aesthetic – too conservative, too prissy, too Chloe– but then Chloe was also too short. At nearly six feet, Tessa was used to being sartorially challenged. She'd have to get creative.

In the meantime, she decided to go for a meander. The sun was bright despite last night's storm and she soon found herself wandering the grounds and its many horticultural intricacies. The temperature was unseasonably warm. Tessa didn't like being hot. A decorative pool with a fountain in the midst of it beckoned. Tessa shed the flannel and denim and plunged in. The pool was deep and pleasingly cold. When Tessa resurfaced, she discovered she wasn't alone.

"Well, hello," she said.

Guy stood above her at the edge of the pool dressed in Orlebar Brown swimming trunks and a t-shirt that hugged his pecs. Tessa liked what she saw.

"Hullo," Guy replied.

Tessa liked what she saw...a lot.

"Are you going to just stand there and perv me," Tessa taunted, "or are you going to actually take that fucking t-shirt off and join me? You could lose the shorts too. I certainly wouldn't object."

"What exactly are you playing at?" Guy asked.

"Fuck," Tessa said. She loved nothing more than a good swear. "Are you all really so fucking uptight? I had you pegged for a good time."

Guy stripped off the t-shirt and shorts and jumped in. The water splashed. Tessa hoisted herself out of the pool.

"It seems I've forgotten my towel," she said. "I hope you don't mind. But then, we're family, right? And the sun is so hot, maybe I'll just lie down and dry off over here."

She stretched out in the grass. Tessa knew the effect her body had on men.

"You haven't answered my question."

Tessa pulled a cigarette from the pack in her shorts. "Give us a light, love," she said.

"You're something else," Guy replied.

He climbed out of the pool, lit Tessa's cigarette, and helped himself to one before stepping back into his Orlebar Browns and sitting down beside her on the grass. Tessa covered her eyes with her arm. She felt him trying not to stare at her tits, which only made her want to torment him all the more.

"Sometimes my body gets me into trouble," she said.

"Do you get into trouble often then?"

Tessa peeked at Guy from the crook of her arm. "Often enough," she said. "When it fancies me."

"What do you fancy?"

"You're old enough to be my father," she said. "It's good for both of us that you're not."

"I'm not your brother either."

Tessa shrugged. She arched her back and slowly lifted herself up off the ground to a seated position while balancing the cigarette between her lips.

"You don't know that," she said.

"It's easy enough to prove."

"You surprise me. I'd have thought – given your reputation – you liked things a little taboo. After all, I'm not much older than Cordelia."

Guy looked away. Tessa smiled.

"You thought I was her, didn't you?" she goaded. "Last night when I came in and you were all sitting around the pianoforte singing songs like you were the fucking Von Trapps. *The Sound of Music* happens to be my favorite film. I always wanted to be Liesl."

She shifted onto her knees. "*I am sixteen going on seventeen, I know that I'm naïve...*" she sang in a baby doll voice.

"Stop it."

Tessa playfully slapped his arm. She saw him clench and unclench his fists. He still wouldn't look at her.

"What's wrong, Guy?" she asked. "Have I touched a nerve?"

He stood up. She felt his desire, his rage.

"It's okay, bro," she said. "I know I look like jail bait, but I am legal."

"The sooner you pack yourself off to wherever you came from, the better. I don't want trouble...at least, not your kind of trouble."

"But I'm the best kind of trouble there is," Tessa replied. "Besides, it's too late. Chloe's invited me to stay for as long as I like. She's so nice. She's made me feel so welcome here. I've always wanted a big sister like Chloe. To decline her invitation now, after I've already accepted, would just be rude. And as proper manners seem to account for a lot around here, I don't want to start off on the wrong foot. It's bad enough the others hate me."

"Chloe's a fool."

Tessa admired the outline of his member beneath the swimming shorts. "But you don't hate me though, do you?" she simpered.

She raised herself up onto her knees so she was level with his mid-riff and ran her finger along the waist of his shorts. Guy slapped her hand away, not hard but forceful enough to push her back onto the grass with a light thud.

"Ouch!"

"And cover yourself up, there's young children about." Guy tossed the flannel shirt at her.

Tessa lay back in the grass, but took the shirt and put it on, though she left it unbuttoned.

"Typical male double standard," she muttered. "And if anyone were to say anything, I'd tell them you started it. On second thought, you're looking a little long in the tooth. Desperation doesn't suit you. It just makes you pathetic."

He walked away. Tessa lit another cigarette and pondered what to do next. She was bored. She supposed she could look for Lord Carleton and demand he acknowledge her as his love child – one of many, Tessa didn't doubt, if the rumors were true, which she had no reason to suspect they weren't – but the idea of forcing a confrontation so soon after her arrival made her nervous. It carried with it the risk that things could go very badly if he refused to give her the time of day, and she'd find herself right back where she'd started: thumbing a ride back to London and relying on the kindness of strangers in strange and uncomfortable hostels. The last one had had bed bugs and a perpetually plugged-up loo.

No, Tessa Templeton didn't fancy that, not one bit. She liked the trappings of luxury. Last night had been the first time in she couldn't remember how long that she'd slept in a proper bed. No, she wasn't about to jeopardize this much easy comfort, at least not until the situation became untenable.

Tessa decided to continue her exploration of the house. The grounds were too vast and the outdoors didn't much suit her temperament. The notion came to her then that in the event Carleton rejected her, there were so many rooms in the house that she didn't doubt she could easily find her way back inside and live there quite unnoticed by the rest of the family, at least until she'd sorted her next move.

She wasn't unaccustomed to a certain level of stealth. She'd been a thief before – breaking and entering was a specialty – and street smarts had always come to her aid in the past. She might as well suss the place out now as insurance against the future. But she also didn't much fancy the prospect of squatting. She'd done that before too. She had the scars to show for it.

The house was abuzz with preparations for The Steeplechase. Tessa had planned the weekend well. She passed unnoticed through a staff entrance on the lower level and found herself in a mudroom adjacent to the pantry off the restaurant-sized kitchen. The atmosphere was warm and dense with the aromas of freshly baked bread and all sorts of culinary delicacies that caused Tessa's stomach to rumble and highlighted the fact that, aside from the leftovers Chloe had prepared for her the night before, she hadn't eaten a proper meals in days. She wasn't above sneaking into the kitchen to help herself while the cooks' backs were turned, but just as she was about to kick into stealth mode, a flurry of high-pitched shrieks, childish giggles and the patter of running feet arrested her. Tessa pressed herself against the wall just in the nick of time as Penelope and Edgar's two eldest children, Rain and Walter, followed close behind by the toddling twins Charlotte and George – pudgy little arms and legs flailing every which way – nearly ran her over as they barreled down the narrow hallway and past the kitchen.

"Oy!" Tessa exclaimed. "Watch where you're fucking going! This ain't

Silverstone, you know!"

But the children ignored her as they carried on to parts unknown, with little Charlotte and George doing their damnedest to catch up. Tessa lit a cigarette and took a deep drag. Her nerves were easily jangled. She didn't particularly like children.

"Did you just swear at my darlings?"

Tessa looked up as Penelope rounded the corner – out of breath and looking thoroughly worse for wear.

"Those rug-rats are yours?" Tessa asked.

"I beg your pardon?"

Tessa rolled her eyes. "You're 'the American', right?" she asked, exhaling a stream of smoke in Penelope's general direction. The ceiling was low and rather medieval. Penelope made a grand show of coughing and waving the smoke away as if it was the most offensive thing she had ever smelled.

"I'm *Lady* Penelope. And yes, those are my children you've offended."

"You should teach them not to run indoors. They nearly ran me over."

"I hardly think so," Penelope said. She scrunched her nose and squinted up at Tessa through the lingering haze of bluish smoke. Tessa squinted back. She noticed the American's eyes were bloodshot, her pupils dilated.

"Are you high?" Tessa asked.

"Excuse me?"

Tessa leaned down until she was eye-level with Penelope.

"You're dilated," she said. "Your pupils. I can spot a junkie a mile off. I've always thought you had that look about you. There's only so much magazines can Photoshop. And then last night you just seemed rather twitchy."

"'Twitchy?'"

"When was the last time you had a fix?" Penelope opened her mouth as though to protest, but Tessa had her. She smiled. "It's all right," she said, "I'm actually rather relieved. Everyone in this fucking joint just seems a little too uptight, like all of your crusts have been cut off or something. I've always thought the crust was the best part. Do you know what I mean?"

Penelope shook her head and tried to step around Tessa, but she was no match against Tessa's height and casual but thoroughly imposing bearing.

"I ask that you kindly let me pass," Penelope muttered. "My darlings..."

"So what is it?"

"What is what?"

"Looking at you, I'd say painkillers – Oxycontin? Vicodin? Tylenol with Codeine? Pills are so convenient, aren't they? No mess to clean up. No track marks. Am I right or am I right?"

Tessa expected more of a fight, not that she was looking for one. The encounter with Guy by the fountain had left her dissatisfied and, truth be told, she regretted not arranging a drop-off with Ahmed before she left the hostel in Whitechapel. Ahmed was her dealer. He was a little too eager-to-please which Tessa found annoying but she couldn't deny it was awfully convenient, except when it wasn't.

"No," Penelope said. "I mean, maybe a Vicodin every once in a while..."

"Mummy's little helper?"

Penelope shrugged.

"What else?" Tessa pressed.

"What do you mean, 'what else?'" Penelope paused. "Sometimes I'll have a white wine spritzer...or Prosecco...champagne if I'm feeling particularly tense. Or a dirty martini. Or three. But that's it. I swear. I don't know who you think you are or where you get your ideas, but you can't just accuse people of things without knowing anything about them first."

Tessa stepped back to give Penelope space. She feared the woman was on the verge of passing out, so tightly wound she seemed.

"I know lots of things," Tessa said, "about lots of people."

"Are you threatening me?"

Tessa sensed Penelope's fear and decided then to give the American a hall pass. "You know what I think?" she asked. "I think we're both kindred spirits, except I've learnt to celebrate mine while you bury yours beneath other people's bullshit. Be free, Penelope – oh, I'm sorry, Lady Penelope. Be free, *Lady* Penelope. Be free. Sometimes it's okay to fly like a bird."

Penelope drew herself up to her full height, which was still several inches shorter than Tessa. She puffed out her cheeks and flicked her hair back over her shoulder in a gesture that Tessa supposed was meant to be defiant but came across as just petulant.

"Now if you'll excuse me," Penelope said.

"It's Spice, isn't it?"

"What?"

"Look, this isn't my first day. I've been around the block more than once – lots of different blocks actually. I'm a *flaneur*, if you know what I mean."

Penelope just stared at her wide-eyed and dazed as though the wind had been knocked out of her. Tessa decided she didn't hate the woman as much as she expected. In fact, she didn't hate the woman at all.

"I'll keep your secret safe," she said with air quotes around the operative word, "but seriously, dude, you're a hot mess."

"I'm harried," Penelope replied. "Try having four young kids, a career, and a husband who's fucking the hostess right under your nose – in your own goddamned restaurant – before you start lecturing me on what you think I am. And do you know what's worse? I'll tell you. That slag is coming here this weekend. She's coming here with her husband who's not really her husband. How fucking convenient is that? Fucking Edgar invited them here, knowing full well how I feel about her. Convenient for him too! My life is a fucking disaster. So if I need a little pick-me-up – a little Spice, if that's what you kids call it these days – then who can fucking blame me?"

"Right on, sister!" Tessa held her hand up for a fist bump. Penelope looked at her like she was crazy and then slowly, reluctantly, tapped her knuckles against Tessa's. "Now don't you feel better? Keeping all that rage bottled up inside isn't good for you. You need to let it out. Have you ever been to therapy?"

Penelope shook her head. She lowered her gaze to the floor. "Therapy isn't going to stop my husband from fucking his hostess," she mumbled. "Or inviting her here for the weekend."

"I'll show her what's what."

"It's not as if you can do anything. This is Edgar's house, not mine. I have no power here. I'm not really one of the family. I'm nothing but a vessel. As long as I keep popping out the little snot-nosed fuckers every few years my place is secure. Until, that is, he finds someone else: someone younger and prettier and *English*. That's been made abundantly clear."

"What's her name?" Tessa insisted.

"Rebecca!" Penelope spat. "Rebecca Hastings."

"Rebecca Hastings." Tessa let the name linger. "How proper. How very Sloane."

"Yes, isn't it just?"

"VeHry!" Tessa placed a reassuring hand on Penelope's forearm. She felt Penelope flinch.

"Leave it to me," she said. "Rebecca Hastings is going down."

"No…really…you can't!" Penelope spluttered. Her already gloomy countenance darkened further. She clutched Tessa's hand on her arm. Her expression was panicked and imploring.

"No, really, I *can*," Tessa said. *"I will."*

"What I mean is...it's taken care of, or rather...forget it. I don't why I said anything to you. I don't even know you. I mean, you could be anyone. I don't for a fact believe you are who you say you are. Or maybe I do? I don't know. Just... please...leave me be."

With that, Penelope hurried past Tessa in pursuit of her children, who could now be heard jumping up and down an unseen staircase and screaming nursery rhymes (in French and Mandarin) to each other in full voice. Tessa watched Penelope go. She didn't attempt to detain her, knowing from experience that a woman as distressed and hopped-up as Penelope could be detrimental to one's health if not handled with care. If the streets had taught Tessa anything, it was the necessity of self-preservation. Regardless of anything else, she had to look out for number one.

But the encounter with Penelope had given Tessa hope. The American was a walking disaster, but Tessa saw enough in her that could be cultivated for Tessa's own benefit. She realized she might have overplayed her hand naming the source of Penelope's addiction. Tessa had seen what Spice could do. Ahmed had tried to push it on her once, and once was all Tessa needed to convince her that Spice was some really fucked-up shit. If Penelope knew what was good for her, she'd steer well clear of it. Unfortunately, Tessa suspected, Penelope was already too far-gone.

Tessa continued her meander. What she wanted now was a drink – preferably several – and a bit more exploration. The house itself no longer interested her. Tessa's appetite for mischief knew no bounds. She now set her sights on finding Penelope's husband – Lord Edgar – and getting to the bottom of this Rebecca Hastings business. It wasn't as though Tessa objected to the second oldest Templeton heir on moral grounds. From her experience, most men couldn't keep their dicks in their trousers and those that could struck her as shady and best stayed clear of. But in Penelope, Tessa had been surprised to find a kindred spirit, and based on her name alone, Rebecca Hastings sounded like the kind of woman with whom Tessa would enjoy getting into the ring and knocking around for a few bouts. She had a mean left hook. Without even seeing her, Tessa figured Rebecca Hastings wouldn't last five minutes, let alone thirty seconds. How she loved a good fight!

The entrance hall was a scene of civilized chaos. She lingered behind one of the bannisters of the grand staircase to listen and observe. The vantage point was excellent, especially as the hall was festooned with every variety of flowering horticulture known to humankind, mostly of the Dutch variety, care of the indomitable Elena Grimaldi who strutted to and fro across the marble in a pair of stiletto-heeled cowboy boots, barking orders to the various florists and caterers and workmen in a patois of Dutch, English, and utter posh-ness. Tessa peered between the branches of a potted tulip tree that stood a full six to eight inches taller than her. She was confident she couldn't be seen, having long ago mastered the art of hiding in plain sight. Tessa Templeton was nothing if not a cipher.

It didn't take long for her stealth to be rewarded. In the midst of Elena Grimaldi's tulip whirlwind, a smartly dressed woman of statuesque bearing with long brown hair tied back in a ponytail like a horse's mane appeared in the open front doorway with a short (in comparison), rather disheveled, nebbishy man with thick-framed hipster glasses and a ruddy complexion that immediately marked him – at least as far as Tessa was concerned – as either a poet, a chef, or a drunk – or, most likely, a combination of all three. Of course, Tessa knew without a doubt that this pair was none other than the illustrious Rebecca Hastings and Nevin Cheswick. It had taken a moment for Tessa to place Rebecca's name with the face, and now that she had, she understood why Penelope was in such a state. Edgar was clearly punching above his weight. Tessa would enjoy knocking him down.

"Just wait here while I find Edgar," Nevin said. "You'd think in the very least he'd have sent someone down to greet us."

Rebecca Hastings rolled her eyes as she took in the OTT surroundings with a pinched and thoroughly disapproving grimace. "So naff," she said. "Every day I thank my lucky stars we didn't let that Grimaldi woman anywhere near Foraged when we were choosing the décor. Can you imagine? Horrors!"

"The problem with you, darling," Nevin Cheswick said with a louche flick of his hand, "is that you just don't like other women. Admit it."

"*Au contraire,*" Rebecca Hastings replied. "You just like other women too much."

"*Touché.*"

"Now run along, darling, you're boring me." Rebecca Hastings took out her mobile and starting tapping away on the touchscreen. "Find Edgar and ask him where the hell he expects us. He promised us pole position, but I didn't realize we were working in a fucking greenhouse."

So this is the illustrious Rebecca Hastings, Tessa thought, *live and in person.* She adjusted one of the branches to get a better angle and hoped her position wasn't too obvious. She couldn't risk exposure just yet, not when she suspected things were about to get juicy.

Tessa was desperate to know whom Rebecca Hastings was texting. There was an urgency to the woman's actions that, Tessa suspected, signaled something not quite licit, like a secret rendezvous with another woman's husband – Edgar perhaps? Tessa was certain that, if indeed Rebecca Hastings and Nevin Cheswick were married, theirs was a business affair, for it was all too obvious – at least to Tessa – that Nevin Cheswick was pansexual. And it wouldn't at all have surprised her if Rebecca Hastings herself was somewhat poly where sex was concerned. Not that there was anything wrong with such an arrangement. *Au contraire.* Tessa didn't believe in boundaries.

Rebecca Hastings' phone beeped with the arrival of an incoming text: a reply perhaps from Edgar, an illicit assignation, to which the hostess with the mostess tapped out a furious response. Her posture was rigid, her pacing back and forth across the entrance foyer indicative of a certain angst, a certain flustered and/or impatient disposition. Tessa shifted her weight from one bare foot to the other, warding off pins and needles. She wished she had thought to bring her mobile. If ever there was an opportunity for blackmail photos, now was certainly the time.

Rebecca Hastings suddenly looked up from her phone. She stood rigid, her expression strained. She flicked her tongue across her painted lips to moisten them. Tessa held her breath.

"You're early." A voice that Tessa recognized, a face she could not see. Chloe. On the staircase above her.

"Actually we're late," Rebecca Hastings replied. "Nevin doesn't do early."

"Well...hello."

Chloe came down the remaining stairs. She walked cautiously – gingerly – toward Rebecca Hastings. The two women embraced with air kisses on either cheek. *The plot thickens,* Tessa thought...

"Is that how it's going to be?" Rebecca Hastings asked.

"What do you expect?"

"Give me some fucking credit, Chloe. It's the least you can do."

"I didn't invite you here. I thought I made it perfectly clear the last time."

"No, Chloe," Rebecca Hastings said. "No, you didn't. Nothing is ever clear with you. You're just like your brother in that regard. Actually, the two of you are rather similar. It's frightening."

Tessa leaned in. She silently pleaded with Chloe to turn around. Despite her cool veneer, it was obvious that Rebecca Hastings was rapidly coming undone.

Tessa wondered whether she ought to tell Penelope.

"You can't keep texting me like this," Chloe said. "You're acting like a stalker. It demeans you."

"I could go to the press," Rebecca Hastings replied with a cold, but altogether desperate, smile. "What a field day they would have. In fact, I don't even have to do that. The press is coming to me. Thanks to Penelope, everyone who's anyone in the media – social and otherwise – will be here this weekend: Tamsin, Bree, Maximilian Porter, even fucking Cressida Parker. BNN, Posh TV, the fucking works. I would say, Chloe Templeton, you're in very hot water...very hot water indeed."

Chloe turned away with a start and a sniffle. Her eyes welled with tears. Tessa worried for a moment that Chloe could see her. If she moved, surely Chloe would be alerted to her presence and her cover would be blown. But, thankfully, Chloe was too beside herself to notice anything beyond the end of her pixie nose. The youngest Templeton daughter – bar Tessa – took a moment to compose herself while Rebecca Hastings stood tall and waited as though she had all the time in the world, her posture erect, arms crossed, hip cocked, nostrils flared. If Tessa had been forced to place a bet, she'd wager on the front-of-house at Foraged.

"I'm not going to have this conversation with you now," Chloe eventually said. She remained facing Tessa and the tulip tree, her back to Rebecca Hastings – now more composed and elegantly defiant. "There's too much risk here. The walls of this house have ears and CCTV is everywhere. I'll text you later. I'll meet you somewhere outside. The stables perhaps. Or the boathouse. Somewhere we can be alone."

"Thank you," Rebecca Hastings said with a deference that Tessa found unbecoming. "That's all I want. I've missed you."

Chloe sighed. She squeezed her eyes shut and opened them again. They were dry. She turned on her heel so her back was to Tessa once again. "We'll talk," she said.

The front doors opened. A rather foppish-looking, though certainly not unattractive, gentleman dressed in proper country house shooting attire – replete with Hunter Wellingtons and a tweed jacket – entered on the arm of a woman whose flaming red hair, beret, and Burberry overcoat epitomized an awesome but understated and distinctly French hauteur that rocked Tessa's world. It wasn't lost on Tessa that the moment was ill-timed and uncomfortable for all parties involved. Chloe's breath caught in her throat. Tessa felt her wince. The toff coughed discreetly into the back of his hand. The redhead tossed her hair and peered down her nose at both Rebecca Hastings and Chloe. Rebecca Hastings tottered rather awkwardly to the side. Tessa fought an impulse to make herself a part of the scene.

"Chloe," the toff said.

"Spencer," Chloe replied. "Yvette."

"Chloe," Yvette said with a condescending smirk that nearly sent Tessa into ecstasies.

"Have I seen you somewhere before?" Spencer said to Rebecca Hastings, who shrugged and looked somewhat helplessly at Chloe, who scratched the back of her neck and shook her head. "Yes, of course! You were on that cookery show. Well done, you! Well done! That final episode, well, I was on the edge of my seat! I certainly know who to go to when I need my cannoli stuffed. Right, Chloe? Do you remember?"

"I don't like cannoli," Chloe sniffed. Tessa wondered if it was obvious to anyone but herself that Chloe was beetroot red from neck up and seemed to be perspiring rather profusely. "But you know me. I'm just so busy saving the world one sweat shop at a time that I hardly have a spare moment to read a book let alone keep up-to-date on what's on Posh TV or who's stuffing who's cannoli."

"We were on BNN actually," Rebecca Hastings said. Her tone was sour. She looked just as uncomfortable – if not more so – as Chloe. "*The Great British Restaurant* was BNN's first foray into scripted reality. It was such a long time ago it's hardly worth remembering. Nevin and I are appreciative of the attention, of course, but we'd rather be known as great British restaurateurs than former reality TV stars."

Tessa nearly choked.

Spencer was nonplussed. "Well, all the same, it's an honor to meet you," he said with a put-on flustered sort of deference that instantly repelled Tessa, who preferred her men on the rougher side of Sloane. Guy was the perfect example.

"I read Ian Corcoran's review," Yvette said, her French accent taking prominence over her words. It was like watching a bad TV soap opera from the 1980s, Tessa thought. "If I recall correctly, he said something about Foraged [*For-ahhged*] being the worst kind of insult one could ever inflict upon one's palate – willingly or otherwise. Of course it does not surprise me. Everyone knows the best restaurants in the world are in le France, *n'est pas?*"

Rebecca Hastings visibly bristled.

Spencer coughed into the back of his hand and made much of being jovial.

Tessa wanted to slap him. Chloe looked like she might. Yvette's smile dripped sex, superiority, and sarcasm. Tessa wanted to be her.

"I must say, however," Spencer said. "these flower arrangements are to die for."

"Elena's been working all night and all day on them," Chloe replied, no doubt grateful for the change in subject.

"Elena Grimaldi?" Yvette sniffed. "She's here?"

"You should have seen the house yesterday," Chloe continued, addressing no one in particular except perhaps the floor. "When Guy and I arrived from Heathrow it was almost like being at the tulip festival in Amsterdam."

"If you like tulips," Yvette said. "Of course, I prefer *fleur de lis*."

"The old boy's here?" Spencer asked. "And how is he? I must have a word."

Chloe shrugged. "You know Guy," she said.

"We saw Sunny Joy," Spencer said. "I meant to tell you in Goa before you left, but you just whisked him off, like you do."

"What's happened to Sunny Joy is shameful," Chloe said. "The vicious circle..."

"Well, she's quite the spunky little thing," Spencer forced an awkward laugh. "Never without a smile and a ping pong ball."

"I have to find my husband," Rebecca Hastings said. "It seems once he gets with Edgar he forgets he has a wife. Excuse me."

Her departure clacked on the marble of the hallway floor.

"Yes," Chloe said. "If you'll excuse me. It seems I have a bit of a headache. Must be the jet lag. I need to lie down. Spencer. Yvette."

"Chloe," Spencer and Yvette said in unison.

Chloe ascended the staircase.

Tessa was dying to exhale.

Spencer turned to Yvette. "Shall we?" he asked.

"I need a moment," Yvette replied. "If you don't mind."

"Are you all right? I thought you looked a little piqued in the car."

"I'm fine. I just need *un instant*."

Spencer frowned. He produced a handkerchief from the inside pocket of his tweed jacket and proceeded to dab Yvette's forehead with it. She flicked the handkerchief (and him) aside.

"*Arret!*" she exclaimed.

"Sorry, darling. It isn't morning sickness, is it? You're not preggers, are you? Fuck me, that would be awful!"

"*Non.* I am not pregnant. And at least now I know where you stand."

"I only meant that...well...the timing and all..." Yvette shot him a withering look. Spencer tucked his hands into his trouser pockets and cleared his throat. He rocked back and forth on his heels. "I'll go have a word with Guy."

"*Oui.*"

"We're cool, yeah?"

Yvette nodded. Tessa could tell the Frenchwoman was anything but "cool." Something in Yvette's demeanor gave Tessa pause to wonder whether her presence behind the tulip tree had been detected. She didn't know how much longer she could maintain her camouflage.

"*Aller!*" Yvette commanded.

Spencer did as he was told. Tessa slowly started to exhale.

"Color me impressed," Yvette said. She stepped toward Tessa's tulip tree. "I have to admit, I wondered how long you were going to be able to keep up *le silence.*"

Tessa froze.

"Come out, come out, wherever you are," Yvette Devereux said. "You may have fooled the others, but you cannot fool me. Yvette Devereux is *un caméléon,* a master of a thousand disguises. I saw you the moment I walked through the door."

Tessa stepped out from behind the tree. She felt stupid, intoxicated, hot. Yvette's smile was condescending. Tessa had to give credit where credit was due.

"I am not worthy," Tessa said.

"Who are you?"

"Contessa...Tessa for short."

"Tessa."

Tessa nodded.

"And who sent you...Tessa?"

"No one. I mean..." Tessa hated when she was caught up short.

"*Oui?*" Yvette shook her head. "Non."

"I'm just a girl."

"Is it Singer?" Yvette asked after a contemplative pause. "Did she send you here to spy on me?"

"Singer?"

"The Agency."

"I don't know what that is," Tessa spluttered.

"But you *do* know who I am?"

"No. I mean, you told me your name...I think..."

"Why were you hiding?"

"I wasn't...I mean, I..."

"Don't lie to me. I am better at this than you. Did Dr. Joanne Singer send you to spy on me?"

"I don't know who that is. I'm Tessa Templeton. I arrived from London last night."

Yvette stopped her pacing and looked at Tessa with an inquisitive frown. "Templeton?" she asked.

"Yes."

"You are related to...?"

Tessa shrugged. "I'm here to claim my share of the inheritance," she explained. "Lord Carleton is my father...at least I think he is...that's what my mother said anyway."

"And your mother is?"

"Dead."

Yvette gave herself the Sign of the Cross. "*Mon Dieu*," she said.

"And you're Yvette Devereux," Tessa continued. The initial shock of Yvette's interrogation had worn off. Yvette's Louboutin heels meant she and Tessa now stood at eye level. Each woman appraised the other, neither certain whether they liked what they saw, but both acknowledging they were in the presence of another formidable female who, if nothing else, deserved at least a modicum of respect.

"*Oui*," Yvette replied, "although if I know what's good for me, I should neither confirm nor deny that."

"We never had this conversation," Tessa offered with an ironic smile.

Yvette turned on her heel and started to pace the entrance hall with slow and contemplative strides. Tessa watched her and waited. Instinct dictated that she remain quiet and let the other woman make the next move. She sensed that her destiny was somehow tied to the redheaded Frenchwoman.

"You're very tall," Yvette eventually said.

"I'm a model."

"Everyone wants to be a model these days."

"I guess I'm just waiting for my first big break."

"Lucky for you," Yvette said, speaking more to herself than Tessa, "I look after some very tall women."

"Are you an agent?" Tessa asked with more hope than she was accustomed to showing.

"*Oui*, in a manner of speaking."

"Can you get me a job?"

Yvette stopped. She peered at Tessa as though seeming to see her for the first time.

"*C'est possible*," she said. "You have potential."

"Thank you."

"And one can never have too many eyes to the wall or ears to the ground."

"What do you need me to do?"

"Can I trust your discretion?"

Tessa nodded.

"This is a very dangerous business," Yvette said. "Just like that, your life could be at risk. You need to be a survivor."

"I grew up on the streets," Tessa replied. "And I once dated a professional kick-boxer. Well, we weren't really dating, but he showed me some moves."

"*Tres bien*. Are you staying for The Steeplechase?"

"I guess so. I mean, I kind of live here now, at least until the Dragon Lady kicks me out. But I think Chloe likes me so I'm golden."

"A wolf in sheep's clothing, that one," Yvette said. "She's a snake."

"Yes, I can see that now."

"And Guy?" [Pronounced in the French way, as *Ghee*.]

Tessa felt herself flush.

Yvette smiled knowingly. "He has made an impression, *non*?" She winked. "*Il est tres sexy, n'est pas?*"

Tessa didn't speak a word of French, but luckily, she didn't need to be a language expert to catch Yvette's drift.

"*Oui*," she said.

"I think you could be of use," Yvette said after a thoughtful pause. "I've been tracking Guy for a while now – from Moscow to Goa and everywhere in between – but he's onto me. You, on the other hand – you're an enigma. Even to me."

"I never show my hand."

"Stay alert and await my orders. This weekend could prove sticky in more ways than one, especially once the Ambassador arrives. I may need back-up."

"Ambassador Bingham?" Tessa asked.

"You know him?"

"Of him. Because of his daughter..."

"Cordelia. There's more to that story..." Yvette appeared to drift off before suddenly snapping once again to attention. "So I can count on you? A pretty face and a fit body are useful, but without stealth and cunning, they are nothing. *N'est pas?*"

Tessa wasn't exactly sure what she was agreeing to, but whatever it was, it sounded better than wandering aimlessly around a draughty old manor house for hours on end with nothing to do. And she liked Yvette. It was important to her that she made a good impression. Tessa sensed Yvette Devereux could prove a worthy ally, for she suspected Chloe wasn't the only wolf in sheep's clothing at Templeton Manor that weekend.

"When the time comes," Yvette continued, "I will call for you. In the meantime, it is best for both of us if no one knows we have met. *Entendu?*"

"*Oui,*" Tessa replied.

Yvette regarded Tessa one last time before tossing her head back and emitting a throaty laugh of such bawdy abandon that Tessa wasn't sure whether to be aroused or terrified or a combination of both. She settled for somewhere in between. Without another word, Yvette Devereux turned on her heel and marched down the hallway, leaving Tessa once again to her own devices, at least until she was called upon to serve.

Tessa Templeton had never been so sure that coming home had been the right thing to do.

| 15 |

After the third shot of single malt, Guy started to feel almost human again. His whole body ached, despite the relative wonders of Dr. Raleigh's treatment the night before. Guy's pain had less to do with the past and present – for what's done is done – and everything to do with what lay ahead. And while he held firm to his conviction that the unfortunate business of the Bingham Affair – as the media had dubbed it – was 1) overhyped, and 2) had nothing whatsoever to do with him, despite his rather unfortunate (and yes, perhaps, suspicious) proximity to the girl in question, the notion of seeing Ambassador Bingham again was not something Guy relished.

What made the situation tricky was the fact that if he hadn't elected to take Cordelia to the club that night after the ballet, none of what subsequently occurred would have happened. He'd been goaded into it by the girl herself. Guy adamantly believed this. Could he have insisted he take her back to the ambassador's residence after the ballet? Yes, of course. Had he? Well, no, not really. The allure of Svetlana

Slutskaya was too powerful, and beautiful women were (admittedly) a weakness. But what was missing from the press coverage – and investigation – was the fact that Cordelia Bingham was not some innocent child that had been groomed for exploitation. Despite the demure façade – for he knew better than anyone it was a façade – the ambassador's daughter had known exactly what she was doing. And, at the time – at least in Guy's albeit foggy recollection of events – to have denied her that night might have put himself at even greater risk. Unfortunately, it was her word against his, and in the court of public opinion the odds were heavily stacked in her favor.

He stirred the whisky with his finger and sat in one of his father's favorite armchairs in the bay window facing the rose garden. How had life come to such a pass, Guy asked himself. It was bad enough his father was near death – Dr. Raleigh had said the end could come at any moment – but this business with Eliza was beyond the pale. And then there was the issue of the five hundred thousand, the hedge fund debacle, and whatever additional trouble was awaiting him on the other side of the Continent and, perhaps more immediately, within his own home. Chloe was furious with him. Guy did and did not agree that her anger was justified. His little sister had always been prone to catastrophising and rather costly flights of pseudo-philanthropic fancy, but her latest behavior –and all too ready condemnation of him – was something new and disturbing.

In the past, Guy had always been able to rely on Chloe to take his side against the others. When they were younger, each had made a grand game of "Guy and Chloe vs. The Firm." Diana had always been too old, too remote, and too rooted in archaic family tradition, while Edgar only ever seemed to care that he was part of the family when it suited him, which was usually only when the checks were cut to fund his various (mostly ill-timed and ill-fated) business ventures. And as for the in-laws: Duncan always tried too hard to be on the right side of Lord Carleton, and Penelope was too high-strung and too overtly status conscious to develop much of a relationship with anyone. Chloe had been his rock, his bulwark against the shifting allegiances and judgments of the others. But now, Guy feared The Bingham Affair had caused her to join the dark side, leaving him irrevocably defenseless and alone.

The door opened as Spencer entered. The two best friends greeted each other with a hearty affection that belied the fact they had only last seen each other forty-eight hours earlier.

"You're looking worse for wear, as per usual," Spencer said as he stepped –

somewhat self-consciously – out of the embrace, "though I must say a fair sight better than in Goa."

Thank God for Spencer, Guy thought, his only friend in the world...

"Last man standing," Guy replied.

"Tell me about it. And you're already into the drink, I see. Good man. I may have a wee dram myself, if you don't mind."

"Be my guest."

Spencer helped himself to the bottle before sitting opposite Guy in the bay window. The two sat and drank in silence. Outside, caterers were setting up tents.

"I say," Spencer began and then stopped.

Guy anticipated the worst.

"I suppose we should talk at some point – not now, I mean once things have settled in a bit – about, well..." Spencer knocked back his whisky and got up to pour himself another. "How's your father, by the way?"

"Dying, if he's not dead already," Guy said. His friend's behavior annoyed him. Spencer had never been good at getting to the point. "As you well know, nothing comes between this family and Steeplechase Weekend. I shouldn't be at all surprised if the old man gave up the ghost in his sleep last night and was put on ice until Monday."

"That bad, eh?"

Guy shrugged. He wondered how much Spencer already knew. The awkward formality of this conversation grated on him.

"Chloe seems fairly distraught," Spencer ventured.

"Chloe feeds on distress," Guy said. The sound of his voice left a bitter taste. "You should know that by now better than anyone."

"Still she's a trouper."

Guy finished his whisky and remained silent.

"The money's secure...in case you were wondering," Spencer continued. "Rajeev's always good in a pinch. A fine fellow when he wants to be. It's a shame about certain of the old boy's associations, but then family's family. That's one thing we don't get to choose. Saw him in London last night, by the way, tearing it up with his customary elan. He's a quite good DJ too. That shit he plays in Goa doesn't do him justice. Must say though, I was surprised to see him. He hadn't said anything to me about coming to London...not that I'm his keeper or anything. Saw the sister too. Bipasha. She's something else. Yvette doesn't care for her, but then, whom does Yvette care for? I'm beginning to think she doesn't care much for me either."

"You obviously have something you want to say to me," Guy cut in. He launched himself out of the chair and brought the bottle over. "Spare us both and just come out with it. You're irritating the fuck out of me."

"There may be some trouble this weekend," Spencer said after a measured pause. "Obviously I can't share my sources – or anything in detail – but suffice to say, a certain someone may have followed us here from Goa."

"Svetlana?"

"I can neither confirm nor deny the identity of said individual," Spencer continued as he poured what remained of the bottle into his glass. "It's enough that I've told you anything at all. The powers-that-be would have my balls if they knew I'd even divulged this much. It's what happens when you work in government. Your life is never really your own, which I imagine isn't so much unlike marriage, and because of which I will most likely remain a confirmed bachelor 'til the end of days."

"She's here? In England?"

"What have you gotten yourself into, Guy? What have you done?"

Guy stood up and went to the window. He pressed his head against the glass and watched as a sudden gust of wind blew one of the tents down to the ground. "I fell in love," he said.

"No, it's more than that," Spencer said. "You played Russian roulette and you lost. And now, because of your indiscretion, everyone close to you is going to pay the price, whether they're directly involved or not. Cordelia Bingham is merely a harbinger of what's to come."

"I didn't harm that girl!"

Guy felt as though he was choking. It was like there was a noose around his neck that was slowly, methodically, cutting off the oxygen into his lungs.

"But you facilitated the introduction, Guy. You were specifically entrusted with the responsibility of making sure no harm came to that girl. And what did you do?"

"Svetlana was at the ballet. How was I to know she'd be there?"

Spencer's tone was cold and uncompromising, the voice not that of a best mate, but a government hack: "I'm not talking about the fucking ballet, Guy," he said with a tinge of exasperation. "Sod the fucking ballet. I'm talking about *after*. The birthday party. The ball. You were there, representing Her Majesty's government in the capacity of chaperone to the British Ambassador's daughter. Given all that came to pass, Guy, how can you expect anyone to absolve you of responsibility?"

Guy knew at that moment he was defeated. He closed his eyes. He wanted to be sick but he couldn't (wouldn't) give Spencer the satisfaction of witnessing his distress.

"It pains me to say this," Spencer droned on, "and please don't think it's easy for me. You're my best mate, and you always will be. But as your mate, it would be irresponsible of me to pretend as if there isn't a serious issue here. I've already spoken outside my jurisdiction so this will be the last I'll speak of it unless ordered otherwise. But I implore you to consider very carefully the gravity of this situation."

Spencer paused. When Guy didn't reply, he pressed on with a weary sigh: "Ambassador Bingham is scheduled to arrive later this afternoon. He's going to expect a face-to-face. Have you thought at all about what you're going to say to him?"

"I've got nothing to say," Guy said.

"Wrong answer."

"I've already been hung, drawn, and quartered in the court of public opinion." Guy turned away from the window and returned to the chair. "What am I supposed to do?"

"You could apologize, for one."

"I've done nothing to apologize for."

"For fuck's sake, Guy!" Spencer exclaimed. "I'm trying to help you! At least do me the respect of trying to help yourself. My neck's on the line here and possibly my career. Do I really mean so very little to you?"

Guy shrugged. There weren't words...

"You're just as bad as Chloe," Spencer said. "Two peas in a sodding pod. You fucking Templetons only think of your fucking selves. It's all very disappointing – very disappointing indeed."

"Where is she now?" Guy asked.

"Who?"

"Cordelia."

"She's being looked after."

"Where? By whom?"

"I can't tell you that."

"Why?"

"Why do you think?"

"Do they think I'll try to find her?"

"Really, Guy, I can't say. The Ambassador is angling for a shot at Number Ten in the next election. If he becomes PM – and I'm not saying he will, but *if* – your family could find itself out of favor. Your father certainly hasn't helped. Some of his more recent business endeavors – not to mention, shall we say, acquaintances – raised quite a few eyebrows in NW1. Of course, the man was in mourning and we're all entitled to a grace period in the aftermath of the death of a loved one– however," Spencer leaned forward and tapped Guy's forearm for emphasis, "I don't have to tell you that that rather unfortunate 'to do' over the replica of Westminster Abbey, and the suspected mastermind behind it, caused quite the hullabaloo, not to mention a collective questioning of your father's sanity."

"I don't know anything about that," Guy muttered. "I was out of the country."

"It doesn't matter. You're still on the board."

"That's Diana's purview. Have you spoken to her?"

"There's a perception in certain circles that your father has come under the influence of something not unlike a religious cult. Again, I can't share the details of what I know – or rather, what I've heard – but there is chatter. Let me ask you. How much do you know about Lady Eliza and an organization that calls itself The Movement?"

"Other than the fact that it seems she is now my stepmother, I know very little. And as for The Movement – or whatever you called it – never heard of it. If you have concerns, Spencer, I suggest you speak to Eliza directly. You're in her house now."

'Oh,' Spencer said. "I see. When exactly were the 'happy' nuptials?"

"Yesterday, or the day before." Guy waved his hand dismissively. "We're all rather still reeling from the shock."

"You're being serious then."

"But that's not all," Guy said. "There's a girl."

"Oh, Guy, not another girl!"

"A *young woman*. She showed up here last night claiming to be my father's daughter."

"Really? How extraordinary! Is it true? I mean, I suppose it would be easy enough to prove."

"She's trouble," Guy said. He remembered the way Tessa had looked at him – naked, the water glistening on her skin – and how she had touched him.

"They always are."

They sat in a boozy silence. Guy considered opening a fresh bottle of his father's whisky, knowing that nothing good would come from such action. It wasn't even noon yet and already he was feeling the lethargic stupor of a single malt buzz on top of the dregs of last night's hangover.

"Whichever way you look at it," Spencer said once the quiet had extended well past either of their comfort levels, "you're fucked."

"Thanks for the vote of confidence."

"I'm just being a realist, and I suggest you be the same. This whole unfortunate Bingham affair has put all of you – justified or not – under the lens. None of you are exempt. And if you know what's good for you, Guy, you'll at least try to make amends with the Ambassador. He probably won't accept your apology but at least we'll have it on record that you made an attempt."

"I'll say it again. I have nothing to apologize for."

"Then I really can't help you." Spencer launched himself out of his chair and lumbered rather unsteadily to his feet. *He's always been a lightweight,* Guy thought. "Please consider what I've said to you, Guy. If not for your sake, then for your family's."

Spencer extended his hand in parting. Guy ignored the gesture. The significance of this was lost on neither of them.

"If I hear anything more about Svetlana," Spencer said, "I'll let you know. In the meantime, well, I guess I'll see you around."

Svetlana...

| 16 |

The birthday ball at the Bolshoi. How excited Cordelia had been! How foolish! In retrospect, Guy supposed he had underestimated the extent of her naïvete. She was an innocent at heart, her attempts to exude an air of sexual sophistication little more than a mask for her rather woeful lack of experience. Guy couldn't blame her for trying to push the envelope. The girl lived in a cocoon, exiled from the world within the confines of the ambassador's residence, and a pawn in her parents' ongoing and increasingly rancorous domestic drama. Friendless, sexless, and alone, it was only natural that the eighteen year-old would seek to press her luck with an attractive, decidedly single, older man. And while Guy held fast to his belief that Cordelia's ravishing was entirely of her own doing, he conceded that perhaps he should have been more insistent that he take her home rather than extend the night after the ballet to the Krasnyy, which was where everything had started to go a bit pear-shaped. But he hadn't been thinking about Cordelia. He hadn't been thinking about anything other than Svetlana Slutskaya, so completely had the Black Widow of Sochi bewitched him.

He had watched from the balcony as Svetlana escorted Cordelia down the grand gilt staircase and into the swirling mob of black tie and jewel-bedecked guests on the floor below. Cordelia looked like a Russian princess in her borrowed white chiffon gown with diamonds stitched in intricate yet subtle designs throughout the fabric that shone in the light from the chandeliers. The girl's hair was styled in a sweeping up-do, held in place by a tiara of such delicate beauty Guy feared it would shatter at the slightest touch. He had to give credit where it was due: Svetlana had transformed the ambassador's daughter to such a degree he hardly recognized her. The only thing that gave Cordelia's natural homeliness away was the slightly bow-legged way she walked in the unfamiliar silver and gold ballet slippers, which might have had more to do with her inability to hold her liquor than discomfort with the shoes themselves. Of course, her appearance – however transformed – was still overshadowed by the staggering yet effortless beauty of Svetlana herself, who acted with the grace and manner of the perfect hostess, floating in and among her hundreds of guests as though on the wings of an angel, yet still managing to be perfectly attentive to Cordelia, who anyone might have mistaken that night for Svetlana's younger, slightly less endowed sister. Guy enjoyed the display.

"Are you having a good time?" he asked when Cordelia came up for air hours later and joined him on the balcony. She glowed.

"It's magic!" she exclaimed. "It's everything I imagined it would be and more. I feel like I've stepped back in time and into the pages of Tolstoy, like Anna at the ball with Count Vronsky...or...or Natasha with Bolkonsky."

"You look like Cinderella," he said.

"As long as my carriage doesn't turn into a pumpkin at the stroke of midnight!"

"There's no chance of that. It's already gone past one."

"Has it?" Cordelia beamed. "I don't ever want this night to end. Ever, never, ever! I hardly recognize myself. I really can't thank Svetlana enough. I know people say the most horrible things about her – and I've said a few of those things myself – but after tonight I'll never say another word against her. Never again, I swear! Cross my heart and hope to die!"

Guy couldn't help but laugh at Cordelia's earnest exuberance. He took two glasses of champagne from a passing waiter and gave her one.

"Shall we toast?" he asked.

They clinked glasses. Guy sipped his wine while Cordelia gulped hers down with relish.

"And what about you?" she asked.

"Me?"

"You really are most peculiar, Guy Templeton. I've had my eye on you all night, you know. Even when it looked like I was otherwise engaged or trying to figure out the intricacies of my dance card, I was always aware of where you were."

"I've been right here," he said.

"Yes, I know."

"Keeping an eye on you."

Cordelia tapped him playfully with her fan. "Don't lie to me," she said. "You only have eyes for Svetlana. I don't blame you, I suppose, but it is a little discouraging."

"Discouraging?"

"I'd rather hoped you might have eyes for me. All this time, and you haven't even asked me to dance."

"You've been busy. It would have been rude to cut in."

"Now you're just feeding me a line." Cordelia turned away from him with a mock pout. He helped himself to another glass of champagne.

"I don't dance," Guy said.

"I don't believe that for a second, and neither do you. I bet you're an exquisite dancer, better than all the boys down there. The number of times I had my feet stepped on tonight...well, it wasn't as if I could complain or anything. Beggars can't be choosers. But don't expect me to believe for one moment that you don't know your foxtrot from your polka."

Guy took her hand. "You've been warned," he growled as they descended the staircase together and merged with the waltzing revelers on the main floor.

He knew he was playing with fire. From the way her eyes sought his gaze as they twirled around the floor to the way she gripped his hand, Guy was all too cognizant of the power he had over the girl. How easy it would be, he thought, to seduce her. He felt her sweat through the gown when he placed his hand on the small of her back. Her body was on fire aching for him, he thought, not without a rather smug sense of masculine – albeit toxic – pride. As they danced amidst the glittering crowd – many of whom belonged to Russia's noblest classes (not to mention, most corrupt) – Guy found himself wondering what it would be like to fuck someone as inexperienced as Cordelia Bingham. Would the experience measure up to her expectations? Would he satisfy or – God forbid – disappoint? The pressure was extraordinary, the temptation even more so.

The dance ended with a polite round of applause. Cordelia clung to Guy's hand while his continued to linger on her back, his fingers splayed so they stretched across the swell of her buttocks beneath the chiffon. The feel of her aroused him.

"Well?" he asked, more than a little out of breath, but not from the exertion of the dance. "What's your verdict?"

Cordelia looked at him in a delirious rapture. "I feel as though I'm on gossamer wings," she gasped. "Dancing with you is heaven, Guy Templeton."

"How do I measure up?" he asked. "Against the others?"

Cordelia placed her free hand on his chest and pressed herself against him. He knew she felt him wanting her, wanting her to want him. "I told you. The others were just boys. I've already forgotten them," she whispered, her lips hot against his cheek. "You're a man, Guy Templeton. A real man. There's no comparison."

The orchestra played the opening strains of Tchaikovsky's "Waltz of the Flowers."

"Another round?"

"And another and another," Cordelia swooned. "I want to dance all night."

Guy could feel every contour of her body beneath the gown. He imagined her naked. He fantasized the smell of her, the taste of her. The fantasy was like madness. It consumed him until he lost track of everything around them. The dance floor was a mosaic of light, perfume and sound. Guy worried he was losing his way.

"I need some air," he said. "Do you mind?"

He didn't wait for Cordelia's reply. It was imperative that he escape, that he put as much distance between himself and the Ambassador's daughter as he possibly could. The situation was too fraught. One wrong move and he knew his life – his position and his standing, both within the family and without – might be ruined forever. And yet...

Cordelia followed him outside. The air was bracing. He hoped the contrast would sober him, knock him back to his senses.

"Are you all right?"

She was behind him. Her hand on his shoulder. Guy tried to shrug her off, but her hand remained. He needed space.

"Guy?" Cordelia persisted. "What's wrong? Are you having a heart attack? Do

I need to call an ambulance?"

"No," he said, waving her off, "I'm fine. I just need a moment."

"Shall I get you some water or something?"

"No, really, Cordelia, I'm quite all right. You needn't stay out here with me. Five minutes and I'll be good as new. "

"Is this your way of trying to get rid of me?"

"Sorry?"

Guy looked at her then. She stood against one of the columns with her arms folded in front of her chest, her bottom lip protruding in a pout like a petulant child. The illusion was gone.

"You don't fool me, Guy," she said. "Svetlana warned me about men like you. She said you were all cut from the same cloth. Still, I haven't given up all hope yet. I'm only eighteen, too young to be jaded like you old farts."

She giggled and launched toward him, pushing herself from off the column and into his arms. She would have fallen had Guy's reflexes been any less. Her body molded itself against his. She gazed up at him, batting her lashes like the femme fatale she no doubt imagined herself to be.

"Kiss me, Guy," Cordelia said. "Kiss me."

Before Guy could react, her mouth was pressed against his, her tongue forcing its way through the barrier of his teeth. The reality was nothing like the fantasy. Guy tried to push her away, but Cordelia held fast, stronger than he had given her credit for. They staggered back against the column, her lips locked on his – hungry, desperate, searching. Guy found himself responding as only moments before he had vowed not to. Resistance was futile. He asserted control, grabbing her hair and pulling her head back. The tiara fell to the ground.

"Is this what you want?" he asked. He grabbed her buttocks and hoisted her up so her legs straddled him as he pushed her against the wall. He unzipped his trousers. "You like it rough, do you? Huh? Is this how you want it?"

Guy reached beneath the under-layers of her gown. If this was what she wanted, he thought, who was he to refuse her? But then, he felt her hands on the back of his neck became fists that she used to pommel him. She pushed him away, shaking her head, and dug her knees painfully into his groin. He released her. She slapped him. There were no tears. Cordelia merely stepped a safe – but not too safe – distance away from him, and casually smoothed the creases down the front of her gown.

"Slow down, Mister," she said, emphatic but with little actual vitriol. "No wonder you're single and stuck here chaperoning me. If I were you, I'd be seriously rethinking my playbook. This isn't 1985."

"I wasn't...I thought..."

"Some girls actually like to be courted before the other stuff."

He rubbed his jaw where Cordelia had slapped him and zipped his trousers.

"You played me," he said.

"I can't believe you actually just said that. You disappoint me, Guy. I had you pegged for a gentleman. A rogue certainly, but a gentleman rogue."

"There's no such thing," Guy replied.

And then she was there: Svetlana, emerging from around one of the columns, with a look of imperious satisfaction plastered on her immaculately painted face.

"Oh, but I beg to differ," Svetlana cooed. She put her arm around Cordelia's shoulders and pulled her close. "Are you all right, *detka*? Did the big bad wolf try to eat you?"

Cordelia shook her head, her eyes wide and adoring.

"Oh, look! You've lost your crown." Svetlana picked the tiara up from off the ground and placed it on Cordelia's head. She fussed with the girl's hair. "You're really rather pretty," she said, "if you lose a bit of weight and make more of an effort."

"Thank you, Svetlana."

"*Tsaritsa*," Svetlana corrected.

"*Tsaritsa*."

Cordelia curtsied.

Svetlana smiled. Her eyes were steel as her gaze shifted to Guy. "I think you need to leave," she said.

"I'm her chaperone," Guy replied, knowing as he said this how ridiculous he sounded. "I stay or she goes home."

"Really?" Svetlana laughed. "Surely, the irony is not lost on you? This poor girl's rapist calling himself her chaperone? Priceless. And yet so typical, *nyet*?"

"Well, technically, he didn't...I mean, he stopped before..." Cordelia said.

"*Molchat'*!" Svetlana exclaimed. "Never contradict the *tsarista*!"

Cordelia lowered her gaze. The pout returned. Her lower lip trembled. "I'm just saying," she mumbled.

Svetlana adjusted the voluminous cape around her bare shoulders. "Very well then," she said. "If that's your game, I can play it too. I'm having an after-party at my townhouse. Consider this your invitation. My footman will text you the details."

"It's late," Guy said. "The girl has a curfew."

"The 'girl' has a name!" Cordelia cried.

"Your father..."

"My father thinks I'm at a pajama party at my girlfriend's house," Cordelia said. "He's not expecting me anytime soon. Have your footman text me the details, tsaritsa. I am delighted to attend, with or without my 'chaperone.'" She stuck her tongue out at Guy. He tamped down the rage.

Svetlana looked from one to the other with an imperial hauteur befitting of her title. Her gaze rested on Guy.

"It's a dangerous game you're playing." She swished her cape as she turned for the doors. "Pyotr will text you the where and when."

Cordelia smiled. "It appears you've underestimated me, Guy," she said with a sly wink after Svetlana had gone. "My parents have always been too busy fighting each other to pay me much heed. I've learnt to fend for myself."

"You don't know what you're getting yourself into."

"Oh, but you're mistaken." Cordelia went up to Guy and brushed his cheek – slowly, caressingly – with the back of her hand. "I think it's you who's all at sea."

Guy couldn't deny there was some truth to what the girl said.

Pyotr's text arrived shortly thereafter. Before Guy could protest or otherwise attempt to dissuade Cordelia from replying – an effort he knew would prove futile given he'd already overplayed his hand – he found himself sitting with the ambassador's daughter in a 19th century troika manned by two footmen (one of whom he assumed was Pyotr) dressed in matching black and gold brocade waistcoats and breeches, and powdered wigs. Their faces were obscured by Venetian carnival masks: one with a long nose that resembled an extended phallus, the other adorned in peacock feathers. The collective presentation made Guy fearful of what portended when they arrived at Svetlana's townhouse.

"I love Moscow at night!" Cordelia exclaimed as they passed in front of the Kremlin on their way along Ostozhenka Street. "Is there any other city in the world quite so romantic? I challenge you to name me another."

She nudged his knee with her slipper.

"Paris," he offered. It was easier to play along than not.

Cordelia wrinkled her nose and sniffed. "Full of frogs," she said. "And their personal hygiene leaves something to be desired."

"Venice."

"It's sinking and smells like a sewer. And Italian men? Sexist and drowning in latent homoeroticism. *Bunga bunga*, indeed! I'll give you *bunga bunga*."

"New York."

"Americans."

Guy shrugged. "London then," he said.

Cordelia pursed her lips and paused to consider. "There's no place like home. I'll give you that. But Englishmen are such boors. I swear they prefer their own company to that of women."

"I'd say that's probably true of most men," Guy replied. "English or otherwise."

"Are you a misogynist, Guy? Daddy is. That's why he and Mummy fight so much. She's an independent woman, you see, though perhaps not independent enough. If she truly had the courage of her convictions, she'd leave him and go trans like she's always threatening. What do you say to that?"

"I have nothing to say. It's none of my business."

The troika stopped in front of a tall brick and stone building in the Art Nouveau style with mansard roofing and French windows illuminated from within by multitudes of candles perched atop elegant candelabras visible from street level. Pyotr alighted from the carriage and held the door for Cordelia while his henchman tended the horses.

"*Spacibo*, Pyotr," Cordelia said. She beamed at Guy as she took his arm, her round face glistening with anticipation. "Isn't this enchanting?"

"I'm not much for house parties," Guy said.

"Pish posh pish! And I'm not much for boring old fuddy-duddies!"

Arm in arm, Guy and Cordelia ascended the stairs up to the oversized double front doors, which opened at their approach. A butler – masked in the same style as Pyotr and his sidekick – appeared in front of them bearing a silver tray upon which rested two masks and two flutes of champagne.

"I do so love a masquerade!" Cordelia exclaimed as she raised the mask to her face and tied it in place. She drank the bubbly with relish. "Anything can happen. Nothing is taboo. Catch me if you can, Grumpy Pants!"

Cordelia ran off with a giggle that struck Guy as vaguely maniacal. He knocked the champagne back and reached for another before following the ambassador's daughter into the darkened interior. The flickering candles cast menacing shadows on the walls and ceiling that only served to enhance the Grand Guignol effect of the masquerade. Everywhere Guy looked, masked revelers were taking full advantage of their masked anonymity. Indeed it seemed, as Cordelia had said only moments before, nothing was taboo.

Guy tried to focus on Cordelia just ahead of him. He knew he couldn't afford to let the girl out of his sight. Regardless of how experienced (or inexperienced) she regarded herself, this was no place for someone of Cordelia's age and character to be left on her own. Guy cursed himself for not putting his foot down, for not insisting they return to the ambassador's residence. But Cordelia had outplayed him. It seemed she fancied herself in some kind of an alliance with Svetlana that she would no doubt use against him if he prevented the girl from getting her way. How easily he'd been duped, he thought, and now he was forced to deal with the consequences of his stupidity.

Cordelia glanced over her shoulder to see if he was watching her. Her cheeks were flushed and her skin was dewy with a glow that Guy thought made her look feverish. She tilted her chin back and giggled. With Svetlana backing her, there was very little he could do to overcome what he couldn't help but concede had been a staggering lack of judgment. Guy blamed Svetlana more than the girl for he knew the ambassador's daughter was desperate for approval. He knew there would be a steep price to pay. The night was young. There was far more damage yet to come.

"Grumpy pants! Grumpy pants! Come and catch me, Grumpy Pants!" Cordelia sang out over the din of a string quartet playing Mozart, the clinking of glasses, and the unmistakable sounds of sexual conjugation. With another childish laugh, Cordelia ducked out of the hallway and disappeared into a room that, when Guy caught up to her, was in the full throes of orgiastic revelry.

"This isn't a game, Cordelia," he whispered. "Let me take you home before someone gets hurt."

Cordelia's breath seemed to catch in her throat. Guy feared she might swoon. A white stallion had been led into the room, its eyes wide with terror. It pulled hard on its reins as it stamped and pawed at the floor.

"What do you reckon the horse is for?" Cordelia asked. Gone was the tease, the flirtation. "The poor thing looks scared out of its wits."

A masked woman dressed in an early 19th century ball gown appeared. Two footmen, similarly clad in Napoleonic attire, stood on either side of her. They stripped the woman of her gown and raised her up, naked, as though making an offering of her to the stallion.

Cordelia gasped.

"Come on, Cordelia," Guy urged. He didn't dare touch her though his impulse was to take her arm and drag her away from the bestial spectacle. Words would have to suffice. "Now."

"I want to watch."

"I'm serious, Cordelia. Let's go."

"You've forfeited the right to tell me what to do," Cordelia said. "Svetlana said I don't have to listen to you. She said my mind and my body are my own. No man can take it or control it against my will."

There was a collective gasp as the stallion reared up on its back legs.

Guy grasped Cordelia's elbow. She pulled away and slapped him before running out of the room, leaving Guy with very little recourse other than to follow her. The hallway teemed with guests in various states of undress. He'd lost sight of his charge. Cordelia seemed determined to elude him.

"Over here!"

And there she was: the ambassador's daughter standing at the foot of a spiral staircase. Guy pushed himself through the crowd, desperate now to capture her, to lead her to safety, or at least out of this seventh circle of sexual hell. But just as he reached her, Cordelia once again slipped out of reach. She hitched up her gown and ascended the staircase at a pace and with a dexterity that surprised him. Guy nearly tripped on the stairs. At the landing, Cordelia stopped and turned to face him. She took off the mask. Her eyes were bright in the light from the chandeliers. Guy thought she looked possessed.

"Come on, Guy Templeton," Cordelia taunted him. "Don't think I'm just going to give myself away to you for free. The *tsaritsa* said the Female Apocalypse is at hand. She said I was its handmaiden."

"Svetlana's wrong," Guy replied. He hated that he was out of breath. He despised the fact that Cordelia had him by the balls. "She knows you're easily led. She'll tell you anything because she knows you don't know any better. Quit the game, Cordelia. Let me take you home."

"You're just jealous: jealous and depraved. And, I might add, pathetic. You're a pathetic old man, Guy Templeton, and a perv. Catch me or deny it."

"And then what? I catch you and then what happens?"

Cordelia shook her head. She held her index finger to her lips. "Shhh," she whispered. "Someone's coming."

A child of not more than seven or eight appeared on the landing behind where Cordelia stood. She was dressed like a miniature Marie Antoinette, her wig a mess of powdered and pouffed curls that rested high atop her head. She pushed her way past Cordelia and ran down the stairs with a childish abandon that would have been reckless had she not appeared so self-assured. When the child reached the bottom of the staircase where Guy stood, she paused and looked up at him. The moment couldn't have lasted more than a second or two but, for Guy, it was as though his life passed before his eyes. He staggered back against the circular bannister and tugged at his collar. The girl pointed a stubby finger at him, her accompanying laughter mocked and beguiled. Guy tried to grab her hand but the girl proved fleeter of foot. She hopped the last remaining stairs before running down the hallway. Her laughter thundered in his ears. Guy wondered whether he was going mad.

"What's wrong?" Cordelia taunted him from above. "You look as if you've seen a ghost."

"That child," Guy gulped. He couldn't grasp what he'd seen. "Who is she?"

Cordelia shrugged. She tossed her mask at him and bounded up onto the landing. In that split second of his hesitation – distracted as he was by the sudden appearance of the child – Cordelia rendered herself out of reach. The ambassador's daughter disappeared into the fog of iniquity that permeated the townhouse and, with her, the last vestige of hope Guy might have had in maintaining at least a tenuous hold on that night's proceedings. For in Cordelia's place at the top of the spiral staircase, Svetlana now appeared, dressed in a black crepe gown with an elaborate train that followed at least sixty feet behind her, and a matching feathered headdress of black swan feathers held in place by a ruby-studded diadem. Guy felt her eyes on him, imperious and commanding. He looked up but his vision was blurred. His hands shook. He gripped the bannister, which felt disconcertingly slippery in his sweating palms.

"Svetlana!" Her name choked in his throat.

"*Tsaritsa*," she corrected. "Your queen."

"Who is that child?"

Svetlana slowly descended the staircase toward him. The path before her parted as the train swept aside all others between and alongside them.

"My daughter," she said. "Feminina. She looks like me, don't you think? She's young but I have high hopes for her."

"That's impossible," Guy said. Something was wrong. His heart pounded. His throat constricted. He clutched the bannister in a desperate attempt to steady himself as Svetlana came to a stop on the step above him. Her gown fluttered in an artificial breeze.

"What is impossible?" Svetlana asked. "The fact that I should have a daughter? I am human after all...and a woman. I concede, however, that there are those who have exaggerated my power by assigning me laughably super-human attributes more appropriate to the pages of trashy fantasy novels. Contrary to popular belief, I do not command my army from the back of a dragon."

"Her father?"

Svetlana shrugged. "He is gone," she replied with a dismissive wave. "A ball of fire took him from me. I was almost destroyed but I have come back from the brink. You look surprised. Is it the notion that someone like me might suffer from a broken heart that causes you to reconsider what you think you know of me? I have known great love in my life, but I have also known great sorrow. I exist in the netherworld of the human soul. In a world that was once filled with light, I now exist only in shadow. Feminina is my beacon. She reminds me of all that once was but now can never be."

Nothing Svetlana said made sense. She may as well have been speaking Russian. Guy's head throbbed. He felt himself curling down into the floor. Svetlana hovered above him. Her diamond-studded slippers were now at eye-level. He coughed and choked on the bile that rose in his throat. He feared he might vomit.

"What's happening?" he gasped. "What have you done?"

"Thank you for delivering the ambassador's daughter to me," Svetlana said. "But you really have overstayed your welcome. It is time that you left. Thank you, Guy, for your service. *Spacebo*. Feminina will show you the door."

Her toe connected with his chin and sent him reeling backwards down the staircase. Each step bumped painfully as he tumbled head over heels. He heard laughter above and around him, a thousand different voices mocking him in unison, taking Svetlana's lead. When he came to a stop on the floor below, he opened his eyes. The girl – Feminina – stood over him. Her face was distorted and framed by the ringlets of her powdered wig. She held out her hand.

"Come with me!" Feminina said.

Guy saw his hand reach up to take the girl's. Her grip was surprisingly strong. She pulled him to his feet, and with a hop and a giggle, Feminina led Guy to the door.

"Courtesans and courtiers!" Svetlana's voice thundered behind him, bouncing off the walls and ceiling like an echo chamber. "The moment you have been waiting for has finally arrived. It is time. Let the ravaging begin!"

| 17 |

Guy jolted awake. He was slumped in the chair by the window overlooking the rose garden. The bottle lay on its side on the floor at his feet. He blinked. Chloe stood over him, her eyes dewy, her pale face flushed with concern or aggravation, or perhaps a little of both. She flicked water in his face.

"What?" he spluttered. "What the fuck?"

"You're drunk!" Chloe exclaimed. "It's barely past one and you're already totally soused! I can't believe this. I can't believe you."

Chloe picked up the bottle with an exasperated sigh and pointed at it. "Daddy's best. He's not even in the grave yet and already you're plundering his liquor cabinet. Really, Guy. Have you completely lost all sense of propriety?"

Guy pushed himself up out of his slouch and cracked his neck.

"I must have fallen asleep."

"I'll say. Snoring like a miserable old drunk, no better than a football hooligan after last call!"

"Where's Spence?"

"Entertaining the ambassador. He sent me to get you sorted."

"Bingham's here?" The name and the significance of it immediately sobered him.

"He's early," Chloe said. "He showed up an hour or so ago with his entourage and instantly set about looking for you. The fact that you were indisposed set him right off."

Guy rubbed his eyes with his knuckles and forced himself onto his feet. The room spun. He wobbled. Chloe steadied him.

"Spencer bought you some time," she said. "Chalked your absence up to jetlag. It's a lame excuse, if you ask me, but it seemed to work."

"Where are they now?"

"On a tour of the stables. Spencer and his Gallic paramour are showing them around as everyone else seems conveniently indisposed. It never fails to astonish me how I seem to be the only person in this family who realizes there is no 'I' in 'team.' No wonder I'm always the one taken most advantage of."

"You're a peach," Guy said. He didn't care whether the sarcasm was lost on Chloe or not. His head was pounding. Lord Carleton's reserve single malt was definitely not something to be messed with.

"You should be nicer to me, Guy," she said. "Depending on what happens with the ambassador, I may be the only thing standing between you and the poorhouse or jail."

"Maybe jail will do me some good?" he quipped. Guy took a step forward and wobbled. Chloe held him steady. "Might build some character."

"We've characters enough in this family," Chloe replied in earnest. "We've certainly enough characters in this house this weekend. I mean really. What was Diana thinking, inviting Ambassador Bingham here after everything that's happened? It's like she's asking for trouble."

"Diana's always loved drama. You forget."

"She needs an occupation. I don't know what I'd do without S.A.S.S. Can you believe it, Guy? That horrid so-and-so who's now slept her way into being our stepmother had the audacity to tell me – well, perhaps not in so many words – that S.A.S.S. was being re-evaluated in light of austerity? I mean, who the hell does she think she is? It's that witch, I tell you, and her old crone of a sister. I can't decide for the life of me which is the worst of them. They're like Rasputin."

Chloe's voice nattered on in the far reaches of his fogged-up brain. It took all of Guy's strength to put one foot in front of the other. Surely, it was in no one's best interest for him to reunite with the ambassador in his current state? What good could possibly come of it? Guy supposed – albeit grudgingly and with very little conviction – that Bingham had every right to vent his antipathy to the man he held responsible for what had happened to his daughter. And yes, what had happened to Cordelia Bingham that night was heinous beyond description. But punishing Guy for being perhaps a bit negligent in his duties as chaperone didn't strike Guy as the best channel for the aggrieved father's energy, not when Svetlana Slutskaya was still out there, free to poison the earth with bitter and seemingly unstoppable impunity. Of course, it didn't help that the woman's profile was now permanently inked on his bicep. He couldn't let anyone see, least of all his little sister. That would indeed send her over the edge and – no doubt – him with her.

"I thought I'd park you in the Blue Room," Chloe said, "until the ambassador returns from his tour of the stables. Spencer said he'd bring him there after."

"I need a moment," he said when they reached the doors of the Blue Room, the estate's reception hall for members of Parliament, other government dignitaries, and otherwise Very Important Persons. Chloe's hand remained gripped on his forearm. "I don't think the ambassador would take too kindly to me puking my guts up on his Harris Tweed knickerbockers." (Ambassador Bingham had a well-known predilection for antiquated country weekend attire. He wore it like a fetish.)

Even Chloe found it hard to suppress a smile. "No," she agreed with a mischievous twinkle in her eye, "but it might do him some good, the stuffy old fart."

Guy closed his eyes and took a deep breath. He felt slightly better. The walk from the library had done him good. He almost felt prepared for whatever might come his way once the double doors were opened.

"Oh, and Guy?" Chloe hesitated. "One more thing. It seems Tucker O'Donnell decided to show up early for the weekend as well."

Guy felt the blood turn cold in his veins.

"I don't think he's traveling with Bingham," Chloe continued. "They arrived in separate cars. But I think Tucker's sniffing around for a story."

"About me?" Guy asked.

"To be honest, I don't know. The timing just seems a little suspect."

"And Cressida?"

"She and Olivier aren't due until this evening, but then, no one seems to be adhering to protocol anymore. Who knows when they'll show up?"

Chloe released his arm in preparation for opening the doors.

"Stand up straight, Guy," she said. "You're slouching. Chin up. You need to confront the ambassador on his level. Despite recent behavior, you are still a Templeton ... at least until Eliza and her coven declare otherwise." She winked. "That's a joke."

"Lead on," Guy said.

Chloe opened the doors with a regal flourish. The funk of cigar smoke and brandy made Guy's already bloodshot eyes water.

"Hullo, Guy." Tucker O'Donnell stood before the arched windows overlooking the main drive, snifter in one hand, cigar perched jauntily in the corner of his mouth. The legendary newsman was kitted out in head-to-toe Barbour, looking so English it made Guy's teeth ache. "Chloe."

"Hello, Tucker." Chloe went to him with an exaggerated politesse that only further rendered the scene a charade in Guy's estimation. (Blimey, how he hated the bastard!) Chloe and Tucker exchanged air kisses. "So nice to see you again."

"You lying little bitch," Tucker said with his customary air of feigned insouciance. "You hate my guts for what I wrote about you and your little foundation after that rather suspicious 'accident' in Dhaka. Given the opportunity you'd have me stuck like a hog in a Hawaiian luau with my scrotum shoved up my arse. Don't look so shocked, Guy. Your little sister and I go way back. Don't we, darling?"

"You're right," Chloe sniffed but not without an air of catty amusement. "I hate your guts. But I do so love to hate you, Tucker."

"Let me count the ways," Tucker said with a strangled chuckle.

Guy didn't like the way Tucker's hand lingered on Chloe's ass, nor did he much care for the way his sister didn't seem to mind being groped by the old school journalist who, while perhaps not quite old enough to be her father, brought to mind a rather lascivious favorite uncle. *I've been away too long*, he thought. *Or perhaps there's more to Chloe than what meets the eye? We all have our secrets.*

"As much as I hate to leave you," Chloe said, peeling herself from Tucker's immediate proximity with a blush and coy little laugh Guy saw right through, "I'm sure you and my brother have lots to catch up on before the Ambassador crashes your reunion."

"Bingham's a bore," Tucker said with an exuberant yawn. "Can anyone really blame his wife for fucking half the Duma? She's not even discreet about it. Like mother, like daughter."

"I'm sure the ambassador sees things a bit differently, not to mention his daughter," Chloe said. She rolled her eyes and winked at Guy as she headed for the doors. She even seemed to walk differently around Tucker, Guy observed, not that he'd ever really paid attention before. "Tata, gents. I'm off to make myself useful for a few hours before everything really starts to unravel."

"Saving the world again, are we, Chlo'?" Tucker asked.

Chloe laughed. "One sweatshop at a time," she said. "It's a rather thankless task, but someone's got to do it."

"Moscow Mules on the terrace later," Tucker called after her as she opened the double doors and disappeared into the hallway. "In honor of the ambassador's daughter." He held Guy's gaze over the rim of his glass as he downed what remained of his brandy with gusto. "Your sister is some piece of ass," he said. "The ones who pretend they don't know it get you right where it counts."

"For fuck's sake, she's my sister," Guy said. His impulse was to deck the bastard but prudence held him at bay. He still ached from the thrashing he'd received in Goa.

Tucker sucked on the cigar and blew a contemplative stream of smoke while studying Guy through the haze. "Are you going to tell me what the hell happened in Moscow or are we just going to stand here all afternoon pretending we like each other?"

"I don't like you," Guy said. "I'm not pretending."

"Oh, come off it, Guy. What's past is past. As much as you may think otherwise, I had nothing to do with all that runaway bride palaver." Tucker poured himself another brandy without bothering to ask Guy if he'd like one. "Cressida's a smart cookie," he continued, "though not nearly as smart as she fancies herself. But smart enough to know – without any meddling from me – that you were always going to be a losing proposition. She got out while she had the chance. Not that I think Thibault is any great prize, though I do hear his Formula One investment may finally be paying off. The bookies are saying Luca Mariotti's the one to beat this year. His win in Baku was pretty damn impressive."

"What do you want, Tucker?"

"Yes, yes, that's right. Cut to the chase. You're just like your father, at least in that regard if in no way else. How is the old man anyway? I hear he's finally come a cropper."

Guy clenched and unclenched his fists. He forced himself to take deep breaths.

"No matter." Tucker smacked his lips. "I've a feeling our interview is going to be cut short, so we might as well jump in head first with a heave and a ho!"

"There isn't going to be any interview," Guy said, measuring each word as he said them. "You're mistaken."

"Not even for Chloe? Surely, you don't want to disappoint her? She had such high hopes."

"Chloe set this up?"

Tucker shrugged and swirled the brandy in his glass. "She thought it might help. And you know me, Guy. I simply can't resist a damsel in distress, especially when said damsel is as fetching as your little sister."

"I wasn't there," Guy said after a pause. "I left before anything happened."

"Without Cordelia."

"I think I was drugged. I don't remember much of anything that night."

"Are you saying the Black Widow slipped you a roofie?"

"I don't know. I'm just saying I don't remember."

"Well, that's awfully convenient, don't you think? Though selective amnesia is rarely a convincing defense."

"Am I on trial?"

Tucker shook his head and chewed on the soggy end of his cigar.

"What's Cordelia say?" Guy asked.

"Nothing yet apparently. Her jaw's wired shut and she refuses to give a statement, which of course begs the question: Who is she protecting – you or the Black Widow? Then, of course, there's also the brother."

"Brother?"

"Anatole."

"I don't know about any brother. Svetlana's?"

Tucker shrugged. "It's a family affair," he said. "My sources tell me he's actually the one calling the shots. You have to admit it's all rather suspicious."

"I don't think I like your angle."

"Inquiring minds want to know. Better me than the ambassador. Again, according to my sources, he plans to challenge you to a duel this very weekend. A steeplechase and a duel all within forty-eight hours. Quite extraordinary, if you ask me. I do so hope the ending's not a disappointment. No one likes an anticlimax."

As if on cue, the double doors flung open and Ambassador Bingham strode into the room hemming and hawing like a bull charging towards its matador. "There you are, you scoundrel! You rapscallion!" he exclaimed as he rounded on Guy and prepared to take a swing. "Thought you could hide from me, did you? Hmm? Speak up, boy, or forever hold your peace!"

Guy braced himself for the impact of the ambassador's fist, but Spencer was two steps behind and grabbed the ambassador's arm before any connection was made.

"Whoa there, Nelly!" Tucker said with a chuckle and a bemused shake of his head. "Now that's what I call an entrance."

The ambassador struggled against Spencer's hold but ultimately couldn't break free. "That bastard ruined her!" he cried, jabbing at the air with an accusatory finger. "He's ruined my Cordie!"

Guy almost felt sorry for the man...almost, but not quite. He nodded his appreciation to Spencer who nodded back. The gentleman's code between them was strong. "Let him go, Spence," Guy said. "The bloke has a right to express his anger, however misdirected."

Spencer released Bingham, who collapsed to his knees with an anguished howl.

"There, there, old boy," Spencer said. "Surely, it's not as bad as all that? A few scrapes, a couple of broken bones. It's not ideal, I'll give you that, and running half-naked through the streets of Moscow at four a.m. may raise a few eyebrows, but…"

"Shut it," Guy mouthed.

"'A few scrapes?'" Bingham asked, anguish quickly replaced by a renewed fury. "'A couple of broken bones?'" He pulled himself up from the floor and turned toward Spencer, fists clenched and ready to strike. "You have no bloody idea what you're talking about! My daughter was brutalized. She'll never have children. She'll never live the life she was born into. She's damaged goods, you buffoon! What man will ever touch her again?"

"How about a brandy, Bings?" Tucker offered. "It seems we could all use a bit of liquid fortification, don't you think? Who's with me? Guy? Spencer?"

"Here, bloody here!" Spencer agreed. He ducked around the ambassador to join Tucker at the bar. "I meant you no offense, Mr. Ambassador. Of course, what happened to your daughter is an unspeakable tragedy, to be sure. All I meant is that things could be a whole lot worse. She's on the mend, yes?"

Guy accepted his drink from Spencer and tossed the amber liquid down without tasting it beyond the burn. He sat in the high-backed armchair in the window and pressed his head against the cushion. All he could think about was the need for a discreet means of escape.

"I suppose," Bingham replied with a grudging scowl as he allowed Tucker to lead him to the chaise opposite Guy at a safe enough distance on the other side of the room.

"No harm no foul then," Spencer continued. "It seems to me that all of our efforts would be put to better use in catching the baddies who did what they did to your daughter instead of harboring untoward and unhelpful animosity toward Guy, who I will concede displayed a shocking lack of judgment on the night in question. I mean really, dear chap, whatever were you thinking?"

Guy shrugged. What could he possibly say? Spencer was a horse's ass but he was nothing if not diplomatic. MI-6's finest.

"I want to assure you, Mr. Ambassador," Spencer continued to placate, "MI-6 is on the case. Svetlana Slutskaya and her army of *Death Angels* have been on our radar for quite some time. We're working day and night with our allies in Europe and in the States to make sure she is not only contained, but eliminated altogether. These kinds of operations are very complicated and often take more time than you, me, or any of us would like. There's often collateral damage, under which heading – unfortunately – your daughter seems to have fallen."

"Is this on or off the record?" Tucker asked with a wry smile.

Spencer blinked. "Sorry?"

"Don't answer that," Guy cut in. "It's a trap."

"Really, Guy? You cut me to the quick," Tucker said. "A man has to earn his keep somehow. I'm only doing my job."

"I think I'll have another brandy," Spencer said as he hopped up from his seat.

"Your companion," Tucker continued. "The redhead with the *va-va-voom* tits."

"Yvette?" Spencer gave himself a healthy pour before polishing it off with an alcoholic gusto. "Fuck me, that's strong!"

"*Oui, oui*," Tucker said. "Mademoiselle Devereux, *n'est-ce pas?*"

"She's not my companion," Spencer replied a little too hastily to be convincing.

"But you came here together, *non?*"

"Spence..." Guy warned.

Spencer lingered at the bar. He poured another finger or two of brandy and contemplated it before raising the glass to his lips.

"She's a friend," Spencer mumbled.

"In the spirit of cross-Channel collaboration," Tucker said. "My sources have her pegged as an operative at The Agency. Would you care to comment? Strictly off the record, of course."

"Like I said, she's a friend. Nothing more."

"Because if it were to be anything more," Tucker pushed, "well, I don't need to tell you that some might interpret such a *liaison* as a potential conflict of interest, especially where state secrets are concerned. But I trust you've thought through all of this and have the approval of your superiors in Vauxhall..."

"We're out of brandy," Spencer said.

Guy got up and crossed to the doors. "This 'interview' is over," he said. "Mr. Ambassador, again, I am truly sorry for what happened to Cordelia. If it makes you feel better to blame me for whatever part I may have played in the regrettable actions of that night, then I take full responsibility. You trusted me with your daughter's care, and I betrayed that trust. For that, I apologize."

"Well said," Spencer replied. "If we had any more brandy, I'd raise my glass."

"We'll get more brandy," Guy said.

"These questions aren't going to go away," Tucker said. "Better they come from me – a true friend and patriot – than other of my less circumspect colleagues in the Fifth Estate, whose names shall – at least for the time being – remain unreferenced."

Tucker stood and held his hand out to the ambassador who regarded the gesture with a befuddled frown. "Mr. Ambassador, have you anything more to say? I'd heard earlier you were itching for a duel. I trust your bloodlust has since been assuaged?"

"Never!" Ambassador Bingham shook his finger at Guy but with much less vehemence than that with which he had entered. "It's blood that makes a man strong. You mark my words, Guy Templeton. We haven't seen the end of this. My darling Cordie will be avenged for what you've done. Mark my words, indeed."

"Mr. Ambassador."

Guy gave the ambassador a deferential – if mocking – bow as the older man was dragged out of the parlor on Tucker O'Donnell's arm. Just as Bingham and Tucker entered the hallway, Yvette appeared from behind a coat of armor. She glanced first at Spencer and then Guy with a twitch of her nose and a rather flustered toss of her hair before arranging her face into a smile of such welcoming solicitude as the ambassador and journalist approached that Guy couldn't help but wonder where the Frenchwoman's loyalties truly lay. Had Tucker been onto something, after all? It seemed they were all treading a dangerously fine line.

"*Mademoiselle.*" Tucker stopped to kiss Yvette's hand.

"*Messieurs,*" she replied.

"I was just telling Spencer it's a wonderful thing to see our Anglo-French alliance blossoming in such an open manner," Tucker said with an expansive gesture toward Spencer who cleared his throat and stared down at his shoes. "But I'll tell you the same thing I told him. Tread carefully. You never know who's taking notes."

"To be sure," Yvette said.

"*A bientot,*" Tucker said. "I do so hope to see more of you this weekend. And by more, I mean *more.*"

"*D'accord.*"

"What the hell were you doing?" Spencer asked once Tucker and the ambassador were safely out of earshot.

"I panicked," Yvette replied in a seething whisper. "I was conducting surveillance and when the doors opened, well, it would have looked suspicious if they'd caught me there with my ear pressed to the door. That suit of armor was all there was between me and almost certain exposure. *Bonjour,* Guy."

"Miss Devereux."

"You're spying on the ambassador?" Spencer said.

"Not spying exactly. Keeping an eye on him and an ear to the ground. And it's not the ambassador I'm interested in anyway."

"Then who?"

Yvette gave Guy a wary look before drawing herself up to her full height and shaking her head. "Do not ask me questions, Spencer, the answers to which you know I cannot give. You have your orders. I have mine." Yvette caressed his cheek with an apologetic smile. "That journalist is right," she added. "It would behoove us both to tread carefully. There are spooks all around. And that goes for you too, Guy. No one's secrets are safe. Now if you'll excuse me."

Guy watched Yvette glide down the hall. He felt Spencer tense beside him. "You sure know how to pick 'em," he said. "No wonder Chloe goes into fits whenever that one's around."

"Well, at least Yvette's on the right side," Spencer snapped. "I don't suppose you've managed to get that tattoo on your arm erased since last I saw you? If Bingham catches sight of that – or anyone else for that matter – you're toast, mate. *Burnt* toast. And there will be nothing I can do to save you. Now, how's about that brandy?"

Guy followed Spencer back into the reception hall. He couldn't argue with the facts. He realized he was in no shape to dispute anything Spencer told him. His position was precarious – both within the family and without. Were he to find himself without Spencer's defense, he would have to recognize the reality that he hadn't a leg to stand on. And yet, Guy refused to concede defeat. As time went on, he knew he was more in the wrong than right, at least as far as Cordelia Bingham was concerned, but he clung to a belief – more a shred than anything else at this point – that eventually the truth would out and he would be absolved of any and all guilt, though he wasn't at all sure anymore for what he was being held accountable.

There was so much he still couldn't remember – namely, how he'd managed to get from Moscow to Goa with a traveler's bag containing five hundred thousand in currency of mixed denominations. Nor could he recall how he'd gotten back to his hotel in Moscow the night of Cordelia's "ravaging." The only logical explanation was that he'd been drugged. But who would believe that? Guy had counted on Spencer, yet even this historical reliance now seemed tenuous at best. (And just who was this Anatole?)

It appeared he was rapidly running out of allies. Guy didn't like to think what might happen should his luck abandon him altogether.

| 18 |

Chloe needed a moment. More than a moment, actually, she needed several. In fact, if she could have had her druthers, Chloe Templeton would have preferred to hide herself away in her room for the next thirty-six hours and pray that come Monday morning no permanent damage had been done and she could go back to London and throw herself into S.A.S.S. or whatever else she was meant to be doing, and put everything else behind her...including anything and everything to do with Tucker O'Donnell and – perhaps most especially – her brother Edgar's front of house hostess, who it seemed was now not only intent on stalking her via text and social media but –and most unacceptably – within her own house as well.

The situation was untenable. And what made matters worse – for they could only get worse – was that despite all her best intentions, Guy seemed to be fulfilling every single doubt and suspicion she had ever had about him. There was only so much more she could take. Even It Girls had their limits.

The main problem, at least as Chloe saw things, was that she wasn't sure which issue she was meant to prioritize. It was the classic battle between her head and her heart, raw emotion versus cold hard pragmatism. Chloe had always viewed herself as a pragmatist. Her worldview was black-and-white. That's how she had been raised and, until very recently, she had never seen any reason to change her perspective. But it seemed the older she got, and the more life experience she acquired, her trajectory was forcing her to re-evaluate not only herself and what she could almost have sworn was her destiny, but also (and most problematically) the rather uncooperative realities of the world and the people around her.

Like Tucker, for example. What they had shared, at least as far as Chloe was concerned, had been fleeting at most, the product of a very specific time and place, not designed to be replicated in any other environment beyond that wherein the "indiscretion" had originally taken place. The same held true for Rebecca Hastings, though Chloe conceded that where Rebecca was concerned, the state of affairs between them wasn't nearly so cut-and-dried. Their night together at Rebecca's studio had never been meant to continue beyond the confines of that one very finite encounter. Yet, the whole experience had been so enlightening that Chloe found she couldn't help herself. The attraction she felt for Rebecca Hastings – and yes, Chloe admitted she felt an attraction – had less to do with sex (though it had been very good) and more to do with a certain kind of empowerment that Chloe had never experienced in any of her more hetero-normative interactions – Tucker O'Donnell notwithstanding – which only made her dilemma all the more complicated, for who was Tucker O'Donnell really and what was he meant to represent? That she wanted to have sex with her father? Surely not! The very notion caused Chloe's stomach to flutter (again, not in a good way.) But if not that, then what?

The aging newsman was exciting. Tucker O'Donnell was like a swashbuckling adventurer – a modern-day Ernest Hemingway, for lack of a more imaginative comparison – who represented a certain kind of carelessness that ran counter to everything she thought she believed. He'd caught her unawares at a time in her life where she was still trying to find herself post-university. New York had been a blank canvas. She'd never been to the Big Apple, which was why it seemed like the perfect escape at the time. And it had been perfect, in its way, though perhaps not quite in the way Chloe had originally imagined. The people she had met and the relationships she had forged during those wild and impressionable eighteen months had proved the most formative of her life. Tucker had certainly played a role, though the jury was still out in terms of his lasting impact. She preferred to trivialize him. It was easier that way. It absolved her of any guilt or responsibility. Chloe didn't see herself as a home-wrecker, although Tucker's wife would certainly have viewed the situation differently. And besides, Chloe hadn't even known the man was married – well, not initially anyway, which in her reasoning minimized the moral compromise.

Okay, whom was she fooling? Of course she'd known Tucker O'Donnell was married. He had been very much married to none other than Stella Macintosh, the Texas oil heiress, celebrated DC socialite and Republican Party fundraiser – several years his senior – whose cocktail parties at her Georgetown townhouse were said to have been legendary. Chloe had just found it more convenient to claim ignorance of anything about her lover outside the confines of their deliciously tempestuous (not to mention frequent) rendezvous in various 5-star hotels across Manhattan's Midtown and the Upper East Side. To have acknowledged the existence of Stella would have meant coming to terms with the fact that she was willfully placing herself in the rather morally compromised role of The Other Woman, which ran counter to Chloe's perception of herself, which she simply couldn't abide.

She supposed the same held true of Rebecca Hastings. And while it afforded Chloe a specter of relief to believe she wasn't the guilty party in either case –

ever the seduced, never the seductress – she knew her innocence was nothing more than a self-deceiving façade. Chloe couldn't help herself. She liked the unattainable. The forbidden gave her a rush, at least until it all caught up with her, as it inevitably did: hence, the awkward situation she now found herself in with Tucker and Rebecca Hastings. Oh, the damned inconvenience of it all!

And then there was Spencer. Chloe supposed of any of them, she cared most for the hapless MI-6 agent. For a time she believed she might even have loved him. Perhaps she still did? But the problem with Spencer was that he was simply too good to her, too good for her, and where was the fun in that? Except it now appeared that Spencer was indeed very much an item with Yvette. Chloe had known for ages that the Frenchwoman was her most serious rival. And of course, given their shared history, Chloe couldn't help but suspect Yvette had positioned herself in Spencer's life in the way she had for no other reason than to rub the Dhaka fiasco in Chloe's face. Had the roles been reversed, Chloe couldn't honestly say she wouldn't have done the same. They were both fierce, sexy, and intelligent women. It was an inevitability of human nature that they should hate each other. For Chloe hated Yvette Devereux with a passion that – had she allowed herself to consider it more introspectively – should have given her cause for alarm. But then, Chloe had never been particularly introspective. It was easier to remain in denial and blissfully unaware. It wasn't that Chloe was clueless. She just preferred to believe herself impervious. What had Papa always said of her? She was a higher form of life. If Papa said so, well then, it had to be true. Though lately, Chloe was beginning to wonder whether her father's judgment wasn't quite as sharp as she had always been led to believe.

"Got you!"

Chloe startled out of her musings to find herself alone in a particularly isolated corner of the first floor hallway with none other than Rebecca Hastings, whose very presence seemed so predatory that Chloe found her terrifying.

"There's no getting away from me now," Rebecca Hastings said. "I'm never letting you go."

Rebecca stepped out of the shadows and pushed Chloe back against the wall. Her lips pressed hard and searching upon Chloe's mouth. Chloe clenched her teeth and turned her head away. She willed herself to remain steadfast, but the all-too-familiar ache between her legs had returned to remind her that the desire – however repressed – was still very much alive.

"Stop it!" Chloe protested. She fought against the yearning. She pushed

Rebecca away and tried to escape down the hall, but Rebecca's hand gripped her wrist and prevented her from fleeing. Chloe forced herself to take a breath. She knew hysteria wouldn't serve her well. Best to be rational. Best to reason. "I meant what I said earlier," she began, though it was obvious such words would only fall on deaf ears. She had serious doubts she even meant them herself. "It was a thing – a London thing – and now it's over."

"I can't stop thinking about you," Rebecca Hastings persisted. Her lips were hot against Chloe's ear. "And I know you feel the same. We're too good together. We're meant to be."

"No! We're not meant to be. This isn't right. It isn't natural. I was vulnerable and you took advantage of me. End of. I'm sorry you mistook it for something more. But I really can't do this. You need to stop."

But Chloe knew she was stuck. The fact was, after that first encounter in the gallery, Chloe had found herself returning night after night over a period of several months. She had relished the secrecy of it. It had been as though she had stepped outside of her normal life and assumed a new identity that couldn't have been further removed from the girl the world recognized as Chloe Templeton. A bit of the New York excitement had returned. It had taken until that first night for Chloe to realize how much she missed her New York existence – however brief – of so many years ago. In Rebecca Hastings, Chloe had rediscovered deep within herself an alter ego. Rebecca Hastings knew it. Chloe couldn't lie.

"You're my muse," Rebecca Hastings said. "I need to feel your fire again. I can't create without it."

Rebecca Hastings bit Chloe's earlobe – not painfully, but with just enough of the old sting that Chloe found herself falling back all too easily into old habits. Chloe grabbed Rebecca's hand and pulled her through the nearest open doorway and into a room that served as a mudroom of sorts off of the greenhouse. Lips searched. Hands groped. Fingers pried. Buttons flew.

Chloe felt her self-control slipping through her fingers, abandoning her with each popped button of her blouse. Rebecca's hands were cold on her breasts. She shivered and pushed Rebecca away.

"Not here," she said. The blouse was ruined. She held it together with one hand while the other struggled to straighten her skirt. "Anyone might walk in. I told you to wait. I told you we'd meet later in the boathouse. Why couldn't you wait until then?"

"I'm obsessed!" Rebecca Hastings said, reaching out to apprehend Chloe who took several steps to put herself safely out of harm's way. "I can't stop thinking about you." She paused. "I want to leave Nevin."

This was really beyond the pale. Chloe turned. She didn't know whether to laugh or to be afraid. "Surely, not to be with me?" she exclaimed, perhaps with more ridicule than she had intended.

"I don't love him. I'm miserable."

"What about Edgar?"

Rebecca's eyes widened. "What do you know about that?" she snapped.

"Nothing. Everything." Chloe shrugged. "I don't know. I'm very confused. This is all so new for me. Please don't take offense when I say this, Rebecca, because none is intended. But…"

"Don't do this." Rebecca attempted to take Chloe's hands in her own but once again Chloe pulled away. "I don't think I can live without you. I mean that. My life with Nevin is hell. It's a pantomime for the cameras, for the press. And yes, it was good for my career. I don't deny that. But I want to move on. I'm an artist, Chloe. I want to live my life the way I want to live it … the way God intended for me to live it. Don't you understand?"

Chloe frowned. Her bottom lip started to quiver. She bit down. This wasn't the time for tears. It wasn't that she was completely without compassion for there was something unexplainable in Rebecca's pleas that moved her. She just preferred – at that time and with this particular person – not to be moved.

"Not really," she said. "I've always known exactly what I've wanted. And I know right now without a shadow of a doubt that I don't want you."

Rebecca Hastings gasped. "Bitch," she said.

Chloe took a deep breath and straightened her posture. Her default urge to cry hadn't left her exactly, but having stated her intent, she felt better.

"Obviously the situation this weekend isn't ideal," Chloe said. "I'd prefer that you leave, but I know that you don't really have that option, and the questions raised by a premature departure, quite frankly, aren't worth the drama."

"Then what do you propose?"

"You stay out of my way, and I'll stay out of yours."

"And if I don't?"

Chloe came to within an inch of Rebecca until the women were standing nose to nose. She dug her nails deep into her palms. There was no way in hell she was going to let Rebecca Hastings know the depth of her terror.

"Things could end very unfortunately for you," Chloe said.

"Is that a threat?"

"You drag me into the gutter, Rebecca, I'll respond in kind. Never cross a Templeton. You'll always lose."

Before she could doubt her resolve, Chloe marched out of the mudroom and into the hall. She clutched the torn blouse to her chest, fearful of the questions anyone who would chance to see her now might ask. She felt herself collapsing inside. The tears she had struggled to restrain in front of Rebecca threatened to push through the floodgates. She stopped and leaned against the wall for support, half-expecting Rebecca Hastings to follow her and further their confrontation. Her strength was gone. In a second round, Chloe knew without a doubt that Rebecca Hastings would take the upper hand.

She squeezed her eyes shut and silently counted back from ten.

"Angel, darling," an unfamiliar voice approached her in the dark. "For what reason shed you these tears?"

"Excuse me?"

A man suddenly appeared in front of her: tallish – but not much taller than her – with vaguely Germanic features somewhat undercut, she thought, by a rather weak chin and an overbite. Chloe knew she had seen him somewhere before, but couldn't place where. His appearance threw her. There was a reason she never ventured into the back wing of Templeton Manor. Legend held that it was haunted, but Chloe didn't believe in ghost stories. The man who now stood before her though seemed strangely – disconcertingly – ethereal.

"You are too pretty to be so distressed," he continued. "May I?"

From out of nowhere he produced a crisply pressed white handkerchief that he opened with a flourish and held to her nose. Instinct dictated that she blow.

"*Das ist besser,*" he said. "Tears are *nicht gut*. Tears we do not like, no?"

"Who are you?" Chloe asked. Words escaped her. She was too bereft and bewildered to even think. "Have we met before?"

"Xander am I." He held out his hand.

"Xander?" His skin felt clammy to the touch. She fought the urge to shudder but something about him warned her against doing anything that might give him cause for offense.

"The P.A. of your brother," Xander said by way of explanation. "From London this morning I arrived. *Ach*! What a journey. Upon National Rail you really cannot rely. Not if on time anywhere you want to get."

"I'm Chloe," Chloe said. "Of course you probably know that already."

"*Die kleine Schwester*," Xander smiled.

"In the flesh." Chloe forced a smile. She didn't know whether to warm to or be repulsed by the oddity that stood before her. He seemed harmless, yet she sensed a sinister impulse within him that caused her to maintain her guard. "May I ask what you're doing back here? It's just that this part of the house isn't exactly well traversed. It's supposed to be haunted, you see."

"To the shadows is Xander most attracted," Edgar's PA replied. "To light come the most interesting things where exists the darkness most. *Verstehen Sie*?"

"No, not really." Chloe paused for a moment to reflect. "Are you a spy then? There seem to be an inordinate number of spooks gathered here this weekend. Or maybe I'm just paranoid and should start seeing a psychiatrist? I feel I'm losing my grip."

"Talk to Xander, *meine Geliebte*. In Xander place your trust."

Chloe's instinct screamed at her to find an escape route, but despite the fact that Xander struck her as positively reptilian, she found she couldn't tear herself away. The effect he seemed to have on her was almost hypnotic. Or perhaps she was merely desperate for someone new to talk to?

"I have this issue, you see," she began, not wholly sure of which issue she wanted to address first or whether it was a good idea to address any of them at all. "Well, actually, there's more than one...issue, that is. I'm a bit of a basket case at the moment, which I'm sure you'll understand is not very convenient when one must maintain oneself in the public eye as much as I'm expected to. Reputation is everything in my world. One false move – even the faintest trace of vulnerability – can set my work back irreparably. And with me, you see, it's all about the work. I *live* for my work, Xander. Take that away from me and I might as well be baking cookies in Watford...not that there's anything particularly wrong with baking cookies – or Watford for that matter, although I've never been to Watford...and come to think of it, I've never baked cookies either...I've just never had the time... nor the inclination, if I'm perfectly honest."

Chloe felt herself becoming hysterical. Her mind raced with a catalog of all the things she'd never done before – all of them perfectly acceptable and perfectly middle-class, but for reasons Chloe couldn't articulate the thought of baking cookies seemed utterly at the bottom of the dustbin for her, and the more she got caught up in this thought pattern, the more she started to feel that straight to the bottom of the dustbin was where she was heading if she didn't pull herself up short fast. She felt Xander's hand on her arm: cold but oddly reassuring. She liked his quiet and his evident lack of judgment. The fact that she didn't know him from Adam also helped. Perhaps he was that new person she had been craving without knowing it? Perhaps Edgar's personal assistant could somehow become her new best friend? Maybe she was getting a little ahead of herself...

"Breaths you must take," Xander soothed. His thumb caressed the back of her wrist. "Here for you is Xander. To Xander you may tell everything."

"Yes," Chloe replied. She breathed deeply through her nose and exhaled. The rush of oxygen to her brain felt enlightening.

"Better do you feel? In your nose through, out your mouth...in your nose, out your mouth..."

"Yes," she said after several repetitions of this breathing pattern. "I suppose this is what's called mindfulness?"

"Full of the mind, yes...but not too full, you see. The mind calm must be."

"You have the most extraordinary speech pattern," Chloe said. "I can't place it. Are you German?"

"Xander a citizen of the world be," he said. Then, abruptly: "Saying were you?"

"I think I'm having a nervous breakdown. Or perhaps I need to be more circumspect in my choice of lovers? Scratch that. I'm not a slut. I've never chosen a lover in my life. They all choose me. Perhaps that's the problem? I've always believed that I'd be perfectly happy sequestering myself in a nunnery. Like the ambassador's daughter, for example, although not exactly like her because what happened to her was, well, there are two sides to every story but I don't think I'd much like...whatever, you know what I mean."

"Indeed," Xander cooed. His thumb pressed into her wrist.

"No one knows that I know Miss Bingham has sworn herself to the church. You must keep that to yourself."

Xander placed a finger to his lips. "Assured is my discretion," he said.

"All I'm saying is that my love life seems overly complicated and utterly not of my doing. And this business with Rebecca Hastings..."

Xander's ears twitched. "Rebecca Hastings?" he asked.

"Do you know her? Of course, you must know her. She works for my brother."

"More than just work for your brother does she," he said. "Xander knows. Xander hears. Xander sees. Your lover she is too?"

"No!" Chloe tried to pull her hand away, but Xander's grip on her wrist tightened, not violently by any means, but the force was unmistakable. Chloe peered at him through the shadows of the hallway, suddenly feeling ever so slightly afraid. Sensing this, he lightened his touch, but didn't release her hand. She didn't resist. "I mean, not in any way that was planned, or meant to be anything more than it was."

"An inconvenient woman she is..."

"Yes, I suppose." Chloe wondered if Xander could read her mind. His intuition unnerved her. "I don't want anything bad to happen to her. I mean, I wish her no lasting ill will. Obviously she's mentally unwell, unstable...the woman probably doesn't know any better. She told me just now she wants to leave her husband – or whatever Nevin is because even that's a bit nebulous – for me. For *me*! I mean, really. Can you believe that? Whatever gave her the impression that I'm anything other than hetero-normative? I mean, the very notion is absurd, right?"

Xander shrugged. He continued to caress Chloe's wrist. His fingers found the pressure points in her hand.

"The problem is," Chloe continued, "Rebecca Hastings is not a rational human being. Obviously. You know her. What do you think?"

"Troublesome Xander finds her," he replied, raising Chloe's wrist to his nose and sniffing it before releasing her hand and stepping back. "Creed?"

"What?"

"Wearing Xander's favorite perfume you are. Creed. Very sexy Xander finds it."

"Yes," Chloe said. She rubbed her wrist where Xander had held it. She knew she was most likely imagining it – Edgar's personal assistant had such a way about him that Chloe wasn't sure whether to be allured or repulsed – but her skin suddenly felt hot, like he had burned her with hot pincers or a branding iron. Chloe peered down at her wrist, relieved to find that it remained unmarked but more unnerved by him than ever. "Creed. I wear nothing else."

"Rebecca Hastings too."

Of course! Chloe had forgotten...

"Well, I can assure you, I was wearing Creed long before Rebecca Hastings," she snapped. "This scent was made especially for me by Monsieur Creed himself: *le père, pas le fils*. We have a special relationship."

"Not all special relationships exclusive are it seems."

"What are you talking about?"

The longer Chloe stood in the hallway with Xander, the more she felt herself spinning out of control. It was true that she wore a blend created especially for her by the estimable French *parfumerie*. But it was also true – because she and

Rebecca had once discussed it post-passion in the room Rebecca kept behind her studio – that Monsieur Olivier Creed (*le père*) had created a commemorative scent for Mademoiselle Hastings years ago when she'd been an 'It Girl' herself in Paris and on the international equestrian circuit. One of the things that had fascinated Chloe about Rebecca at the time of their affair had been Rebecca's stories of her childhood devoted to ponies and dressage and training for the British Olympic Equestrian team. It was only after her dreams of gold and glory at the 2008 Beijing Olympics were shattered in a horrifying riding accident during team qualifiers that Rebecca Hastings reinvented herself as a top chef, or rather a top hostess. Rebecca's life made Chloe feel inadequate and trivial, envious even. S.A.S.S. was no comparison.

Xander's fingers touched her wrist again. Chloe startled.

"*Meine Geliebte,*" Xander cooed. "All right is everything? Offended thee hast Xander?"

Chloe shook her head and shuddered. It was time to remove herself from the situation and return to whatever it was she was meant to be doing. She just didn't know what. Place settings. Yes, place settings for the dinner that night. She'd even had the stationary shipped all the way from the boutique she liked on the King's Road – embossed and engraved in gold leaf with hand-painted equestrian figures to celebrate the official start of the Annual Templeton Steeplechase Weekend. She supposed Rebecca Hastings – Little Miss Olympian Wannabe – would get herself all got-up in her bespoke riding outfit and flaunt herself about the premises like Chloe didn't know what. The very thought made Chloe's skin crawl. The rage started to boil. *Deep breaths, she told herself. In through the nose, out through the mouth...*

"I'm fine," she said, knowing she sounded anything but. "I just remembered what I'm supposed to be doing. Well, I mean, I'm supposed to be doing lots of things but this one thing in particular, you see. The dinner tonight. It has to be perfect even if Papa isn't well enough to enjoy it, let alone notice my efforts. Excuse me. Very nice chatting with you, to be sure."

She tried to step around Xander but the space between and around them seemed to constrict as though both were being sucked through a vortex. She stepped one way, there was Xander. She stepped the other way, again, there was Xander. If she didn't get around him, Chloe worried she might scream.

"About *Fraulein* Hastings," Xander said.

"Yes?"

"Xander has power to make said inconvenience – as say they – disappear."

The finality of it stopped Chloe in her tracks. "Excuse me?"

"Seems to Xander that *Fraulein* Hastings is inconvenient to many, not just you." A trace of a terrible smile twitched across Xander's thin lips. The tip of his tongue flicked from between his teeth. "Seems to Xander it would most *convenient* be if *Fraulein* Hastings were to be removed from this inconvenience that is so inconveniencing to so many."

"That sounds rather forbidding," Chloe gulped.

"Yours is the choice, Friend Chloe. To act or not to act. For *Fraulein* Hastings, no choice is had but to be or not to be: the question that is."

"Are you suggesting what I think you're suggesting?"

Xander held a forefinger against his lips. "Shhh," he warned. "Safe our secret be."

"I really need to go."

Chloe pushed Xander out of her way and scurried down the hallway back in the direction from which she'd come. She felt Edgar's assistant's eyes bore into her long after she'd removed herself from his line of sight. He didn't bear thinking about. What he'd said about Rebecca Hastings – what it seemed he had implied from whatever it was she had told him (Chloe couldn't remember) – made her feel as though she was in some way complicit in whatever dark behavior Xander had up his sleeve, at least where the troublesome – *inconvenient* was the word – former equestrian-cum-artist-cum-chef-cum-seductress was concerned. Surely, he wasn't implying anything violent! That was the last thing the family needed – a mysterious death at the Steeplechase, a criminal investigation, something right out of the pages of Agatha Christie! No, such a scenario was untenable! And yet...and yet...

Chloe sequestered herself in her bedroom suite (nearly knocking over Tilly the laundry maid in her haste) and poured herself a shot of Beefeater gin from the bottle she hid in the secret drawer of her vanity – the drawer where she also kept her vibrator, Valium, and occasional diary – while allowing herself the space to really consider Xander's words. Of course, things would be easier were Rebecca Hastings not quite so much in the picture. She was one of those women who were just too perfect and too aware of their perfection. And while Chloe knew she had her critics – some of her best friends in the media hadn't always been so kind – Chloe liked to believe of herself that at heart she was just a regular girl who had been blessed with decidedly irregular privileges. Which was why she had long ago devoted her life to helping those less fortunate. Could Rebecca Hastings lay such claim?

As far as Chloe was concerned, Rebecca Hastings was the very worst kind of celebrity. It wasn't as if RH had ever been particularly successful at any of her multitudinous endeavors. The Olympics didn't work out for her so she'd done the next best thing and gone the reality TV route. Cookery shows were a dime a dozen, and she'd just been fortunate to have been paired off with Nevin Cheswick. Chloe didn't believe for a second that Rebecca Hastings had had any part in the creation of the Victoria sponge that had won them the competition. (Or the cannoli.) Chloe knew this for a fact because none other than Cressida had told her. But Chloe wasn't one to kiss and tell, at least not with those kinds of kisses. Speaking of which, perhaps it really was best that Xander, or whoever that wraith-like being in the hallway had been, work his black magic and make Rebecca Hastings disappear? Or if not disappear entirely, then go away for a while. Everyone needed a holiday, and the poor dear really did seem stressed. Chloe tipped back the gin and shivered at the thought.

"Can I come in?"

Penelope. Chloe closed her eyes and pressed the glass against her forehead. *Lord, give me strength*, she thought. *From one inconvenient woman to another...* She wondered for a fleeting moment if Xander might be able to do something with this one as well.

"Hello, Penelope," she said with an unconvincing smile.

"I'm not interrupting anything, am I? You're not having a private moment or something, are you?"

"This is Templeton Manor," Chloe said with a sigh, "there are no private moments here."

"Well, in that case."

Penelope strode into the room and closed the door behind her. *Oh dear.* Chloe poured herself another generous glass of gin. "Would you like some?" she asked. "I'm afraid it'll have to be straight as I've nothing to cut it with."

"Yes, please."

Chloe poured. They clinked glasses. They drank.

"Well?" Chloe said.

"I have to ask you something," Penelope started in with barely a breath after she'd downed nearly half the gin in her glass. "That girl."

"Which girl?"

"The imposter – the one who showed up last night claiming to be one of us."

"Tessa."

"Do you think that's even her real name?"

"I have no reason to think otherwise."

"Oh, Chloe, you're too trusting." Penelope tipped back what remained of her drink and held the glass out to Chloe for a refill. "You always want to believe the best of everyone."

"Not really," Chloe said, though she supposed Penelope's observation was more accurate than not. "There are lots of people I don't like."

"Well, I don't like her."

"We don't know her well enough yet to judge. If you ask me, she seems rather fun."

"Fun?"

"And I think we could all use a bit of levity around here, especially now."

"Eliza's having fits," Penelope said after a contemplative pause. "She thinks Tessa's a plant."

"A plant? Eliza's paranoid."

"I find in this case I may be inclined to side with her."

"Traitor," Chloe said, perhaps with a bit less venom than she'd intended. The gin had a mellowing effect. "It seems to me, Penelope, you of all people should be a bit more – shall we say? – accommodating."

"I beg your pardon?"

"Of outsiders, I mean. It's not as though any of us welcomed you with open arms when Edgar brought you to us."

"Your mother was always very nice."

"Only because she was relieved Edgar had brought home a girl."

"Meaning?"

Chloe rolled her eyes. The conversation was getting tedious, or perhaps she was just easily bored?

"You know what people say about Spencer, don't you?" Penelope asked.

Yes, in fact, Chloe did. She turned away from Penelope and went to the window. She pressed her forehead against the glass and noticed that it was raining. *God help them if it rained on Steeplechase Weekend.*

"They say he's a closet homosexual," Penelope hit her point home.

"I don't care what he is," Chloe said. She closed her eyes. This was not the time for tears. "He's my friend."

"I'm just saying," Penelope said. "Some say the same about you."

"What?"

Penelope shrugged.

Rebecca Hastings...

"Have I struck a nerve?" Penelope asked. "Oh my."

"You don't know what you're talking about."

"Edgar's not gay," Penelope snapped. "If he was gay, then he wouldn't be fucking his hired help."

"Rebecca Hastings."

"I hate that bitch," Penelope seethed.

"Yes," Chloe said. "I do too. More gin, Penny?"

She poured. They drank. A sort of equilibrium seemed to have been restored.

"I suppose we can take heart in the fact that we're not alone," Penelope said. "Our antipathy for the UK's favorite hostess seems to be quite liberally shared."

"Oh?"

"Tessa said she'd help me out."

'Tessa?" Chloe frowned. "Just a moment ago you were intimating you didn't trust the girl, and now you're saying you're allies?"

"She gets me."

"Well, that's one of us then," Chloe said. The bottle was nearly empty. She wasn't feeling generous.

"It would seem to me," Penelope continued, "that you and I could both stand to benefit if a certain something happened to a certain someone whose name perhaps it's best we do not mention in this particular conversation."

Chloe was intrigued and mortified at the same time. She squeezed her hand around the glass to prevent it from shaking.

"If you catch my drift," Penelope said.

"Who told you I'm...you know?"

Penelope blinked hard, her eyes wide, like a deer caught in headlights. "We should change the subject," she stammered. "I didn't realize you'd be so..."

"So...what?"

Penelope stood up and began to pace the room. "You know how people are, Chloe, how people can be," she said.

Chloe tipped back what remained of the gin, barely enough to wet her lips, and cast the bottle aside. She felt drunk. Mid-afternoon intoxication struck her as oddly liberating. She wanted to say things, push the envelope just a bit with her sister-in-law, get into trouble. The lack of inhibition scared her, but only just. She felt outside herself. Chloe leaned her head back against the chair and regarded Penelope through half-closed eyes. She was sleepy and manic and alert all at the same time. The push-pull between the extremes played games with her head.

"There's more to me than what meets the eye, you know," she said, more to herself than to Penelope. "One of these days I'll give an interview that'll knock the pants off the establishment. I'm quite debauched. I know you don't believe me, Penelope, but it's true. Guy's not the only one in this family who likes to have a good time. You should have seen me in New York. I got up to all sorts of things. Ashleigh and me. I hardly recognize myself now. Being an It Girl is a full-time job. And I can't help but wonder, what's it all for? I'm terrified I'll end up like Diana."

"Or Eliza," Penelope said.

Chloe gulped. She squinted hard at her sister-in-law and tried to think of something particularly cutting to say, but nothing was forthcoming. Her mind was a gin-soaked fog. She knew she'd have a ghastly headache, which didn't bode well for the evening's festivities – the Steeplechase Ball to mark the official opening of Steeplechase Weekend. All Chloe wanted to do was sequester herself in her room, crawl into a tight ball, and sleep. She and gin did not take well to each other.

"Do you think it's true?" she asked. "About Eliza and Papa? I mean, has anyone verified it, asked to see the documentation – the marriage certificate or whatever – or are we to just take it lying down like obedient little children?"

"That's for Diana and Edgar to decide," Penelope replied. "It would seem like an awful lot of bother if it wasn't true."

"I can't believe Mumsy would have condoned this." The more Chloe dwelled on what had become of her late mother's legacy, the more incensed she felt. The injustice of it was too much. She bolted out of her chair with a single-minded determination that wasn't unlike that which she felt when confronted with Third World poverty and disease: little brown-skinned children running through the streets of Goa without shoes. Injustice was injustice regardless of where one found it.

"I can't allow this!" she declared with a clear-eyed sobriety unlike any she'd experienced in recent memory. "That usurper must be stopped."

"Quite," Penelope said. "What do you have in mind?"

"Do you stand with me, Penelope? I'm counting on you."

"No one's ever counted on me for anything," Penelope said. "What are we standing for again?"

"I'm not going to allow Eliza and that papist cult of hers to destroy all that Mumsy did for this family. We must nip evil at the root and drive a stake right through the heart of it. Templeton Manor and Templeton Enterprises must be protected against all imposters – both within and without. But I can't do it alone, and I really can't rely on Edgar or Guy to storm the barricades for me. "

"You want my help?" Penelope hurried to Chloe's side and took the younger woman's hands in hers. "Does this mean you think of me as one of the family now? Am I one of you? You know that's all I've ever wanted: to be accepted by you. I've always loved you so!"

Chloe pulled her hands free but didn't back away. She felt quite euphoric. "Sisters have to stand up for each other," she said, "even if that sometimes makes for strange bedfellows."

"I'm at your command."

Chloe nodded. She needed time away: time to think, to plan, and to strategize. "Keep your eyes open," she said, "but don't be suspicious about it. Hide in plain sight, but never let Eliza out of *your* sight. This weekend isn't optimal, too many people coming and going, too many opportunities for Eliza to elude our attention. But when all of this is over, Penelope, we must be prepared to strike."

"Of course."

"This is our little secret. You mustn't tell anyone, especially not Edgar."

"Diana?"

Chloe shook her head. "Leave Diana to me. I fear she's gone to the other side. It might be too late."

Chloe grasped Penelope and pulled her close. She looked into her sister-in-law's eyes with an intensity that brooked no compromise. She had never felt so prepared to go into battle as she did at that moment. Perhaps too much gin in the afternoon was a good thing after all?

"Are you sure you're up for this?" she asked.

"Yes!" Penelope gasped. "Oh yes!"

"Because once we set this wheel in motion, there will be no turning back. If you betray me, Penelope, it will be a betrayal not just of me, but of this family, and I shall dispose of you in much the same way I intend to dispose of Eliza. Is that clear?"

Penelope acquiesced with an earnest nod. Her eyes were feverish. Chloe felt the American's pulse through her skin. This alliance was either an act of extreme foolishness, Chloe thought, or one of exceptional brilliance. Only time would tell.

She certainly had her doubts.

"Go on then," Chloe said. "We've got the Social Event of the Year ahead of us. As representatives of this family, we're expected to shine. Prove to me that you're more than just an aberrance. Prove to me that you're deserving of your title and of the Templeton name."

"With pleasure," Penelope said with a fervid curtsy. "I won't let you down."

Chloe turned and went to the window. The sky was darkening and the wind had picked up again. She noticed the viewing stands and VIP box were in the midst of being installed across the green. The sight of them gave her a not unpleasant shiver of anticipation.

"And one other thing," she said over her shoulder.

"Yes?"

"Let me know if you hear anything more from or about Rebecca Hastings this weekend. She may be of more immediate concern than even Eliza."

"Yes, Chloe."

An inconvenient woman indeed, Chloe thought as Penelope shuffled out of the room and quietly closed the door.

| 19 |

Dr. Joanne Singer watched as the barkeep poured her the perfect pint. She was particular where her beer was concerned, just as she was particular about everything in life, and she wasn't about to let the man behind the bar shortchange her of even one drop of Guinness just because she was an American and he thought he could get one over on her. No one got anything over Dr. Joanne Singer. Her attention to detail – some might call it OCD – had served her well over the years. She had risen the ranks of the CIA, the NSA, and now The Agency in record time. At the age of forty-seven, Dr. Joanne Singer had broken through the glass ceiling of the American intelligence corps and wasn't about to rest on her laurels or let any upstarts push her from her roost. It was a difficult game she played, but as far as she was concerned, hers was the only game in town.

The barkeep – young, tatted, and built like a bulldozer (exactly how Dr. Joanne Singer liked her men) – pushed the pint glass across the bar. She scooped it up in her hand with nary a beat and took a deep, satisfying draught, not coming up for air until the glass was empty. She set it down on the bar with a hearty sigh and wiped the foam from her lips with the back of her hand.

"Keep 'em coming!" she barked. Dr. Joanne Singer loosed the fiery corkscrews of her auburn tresses from the confines of a tight bun and shook her hair free. "Sometimes, you just gotta let your hair down, Miguel," she said to her companion who sat beside her at the bar, rather unenthusiastically nursing his first gin and tonic of the afternoon. Dr. Joanne Singer intended to drink him under the table.

"Do you think that's wise, Dr. Singer?" Miguel "the Chihuahua" Rodriguez asked. He nodded to the pint glass as it was being refilled. "We have only been here thirty minutes and already that's your third pint."

Dr. Joanne Singer liked her earnest Latino deputy despite his rather boring adherence to sobriety on the job. She knew he was easily shocked. She also knew she could fire him at the drop of a hat. It was one of the perks of being Dr. Joanne Singer.

"I think what you need is a tequila," she said. "G&Ts are for pussies."

"Really, Dr. Singer, I am fine."

"Then what's the fucking problem?" she asked. The barman finished her latest pour. She accepted it with a wink that suggested more than appreciation of his bartending skills. She hoped he read between her lines.

"Loose lips sink ships," Miguel said. "It is my understanding that we traffic in highly classified information. It would behoove us, I would think, to remain cognizant of the importance of one's sobriety when handling these very important matters. Wouldn't you agree, Dr. Singer?"

"Sometimes, Miguel, you're a real fucking drag."

Miguel shrugged. "I'm just doing my job."

Dr. Joanne Singer knew he was right. She hated him for taking the wind out of her sails. The Guinness suddenly didn't taste nearly as good.

"He's late," she said, changing the subject. "That's not like Agent Hawksworth. If he's nothing else, he's punctual."

"Do you think he suspects anything?"

"Don't get your panties in a twist, Agent Rodriquez."

"I'm just saying..."

"We're just going to give him some friendly, professional advice," Dr. Joanne Singer said with a slightly peevish sigh. "Spencer Hawksworth's a twat and a wanker but I respect him. I respect his office even though Six would be nowhere without us. Don't forget, Miguel, America's the greatest goddamned country in the world. They need us more than we need them. It's time we make America great again."

"How do you think he'll take it?"

"I don't give a shit how he takes it, Agent Rodriguez. I'm not paid the mucho dinero to give a shit. He can take it up the ass for all I care...and apparently, he has. Agent Devereux is no use to us if she's constantly on the verge of compromising this operation. The UK may be our ally, but there's a limit to how much 'special' we put into the 'special relationship.'"

"I can't argue with that." Miguel nursed his gin and tonic. "Maybe I'll have that tequila after all," he said.

"Good boy." Dr. Joanne Singer snapped her fingers and indicated for the barkeep to pour her deputy a Patron. "You train well for a Chihuahua."

Dr. Joanne Singer didn't care to admit it to herself – let alone to her deputy – but she was getting nervous. Spencer Hawksworth was fifteen minutes late and time wasn't on their side. Of course, it would have been preferable had he been able to slip her an invitation to the Steeplechase – as he had promised – but at the last minute he'd contacted her to say that Ambassador Bingham had brought an entourage with him that may or may not have included Tucker O'Donnell, a man that Dr. Joanne Singer knew all too well. She didn't trust journalists, but journalists who happened to be ex-lovers – especially the kind of ex-lover that Dr. Joanne Singer knew Tucker O'Donnell to be – were best kept at a distance. Tucker had too much shit on her. She'd been young and foolish and desperate to kick-start her career. Tucker had been married and all too keen to come to her assistance. Damascus had nearly set her on fire.

It had been ages since she'd even thought about her ex-lover, and now here he was all buddy-buddy with the UK Ambassador to Russia whose daughter was at the heart of one of the worst diplomatic crises since the end of the Cold War. As if the containment of Svetlana Slutskaya and the march of her Death Angels wasn't challenge enough, Dr. Joanne Singer had to deal with the hot mess of the ambassador's daughter as well. Of course, she knew in her heart the two crises were linked. She just lacked proof of the connection.

"How's Magdalena?" she asked. She needed to think about something other than the Female Apocalypse while waiting for Spencer, whose uncharacteristic tardiness was making her a little too hot under the collar. Agent Rodriguez didn't need to see his boss sweat, at least not under these circumstances. "Still popping out babies and hiding illegals in East LA? What's she gonna do when the wall finally goes up?"

Miguel knocked back the tequila and nodded to the barkeep for another.

"You're not allowed to ask questions like that, Dr. Singer. I could report you to HR."

"Fuck HR. And fuck political correctness. Fuck woke. The U.S. of A. has gone to shit because of fucking woke liberals like you and your ilk." Dr. Joanne Singer felt the alcohol going to her head. She knew she needed to rein it in or there would be consequences to pay.

"'Me and my ilk'? And what exactly do you mean by that, Dr. Singer? What exactly are 'me and my ilk'?"

"Fuck it." Dr. Joanne Singer waved her hand dismissively: end of discussion. *Where the fuck was Agent Hawksworth?* She wondered if she was becoming an alcoholic. This job did things to a woman, especially if she was single...

"Magdalena is good," Miguel said. He sipped his second shot of Patron. "She just recorded a demo. Some producer heard her sing at an open mic and told her she's got real talent. Like maybe she could be the next J-Lo."

"Just what the world needs: another cheap Latina shaking her big-assed booty for a buck. Wasn't Charo enough?"

"Sorry I'm late." Spencer Hawksworth appeared in the reflection of Dr. Joanne Singer's empty pint glass. He pulled up a stool between Singer and Miguel and sat down with a wobble. "You wouldn't believe the pandemonium I've just come from. Bingham, Guy, the whole bloody lot. And Tucker O'Donnell too...turned up like a bad penny. There was no way in hell I was adding you to that mix, Dr. Singer. The place would combust."

"Call me Joanne." Dr. Joanne Singer forced her most inviting smile, which she hoped didn't make her look too lecherous, or drunk. "We're all friends here, right?"

Spencer eyed Miguel suspiciously. The Chihuahua stared back.

"Pick your poison," Dr. Joanne Singer nodded to the barkeep. "Another round and get this man whatever he wants."

"A San Pellegrino, please," Spencer said. "I never drink during office hours."

"Well, lah-dee-fucking-dah!"

"What is this about anyway, Joanne? I know you Americans don't believe in following protocol but this seems to be cutting all sorts of corners that shouldn't be cut. Is this even a secured environment?"

"That's what the Chihuahua's for – security. Just look at those muscles. Flex for me, Miguel. You could bounce a bowling ball off those pecs."

The bartender poured their drinks. When he'd finished, Dr. Joanne Singer waved her hand at him. "Now scram," she said. "And don't come back until I tell you to. *Capeche?*"

He did as he was told. Dr. Joanne Singer loved nothing more than telling men what to do. It was good to remind them who was boss.

"The thing is, Spencer," she continued after a healthy quaff of Guinness, "as much as I wish that I could tell you we're just here having a friendly pint at the local, the fact is we have some rather unpleasant business to discuss."

"I figured as much," Spencer replied. "Your bedside manner – or rather your lack thereof – precedes you, Dr. Singer."

"Joanne...please."

"Joanne." He said it like a challenge.

"Miguel." She snapped her fingers at her deputy, an unnecessary gesture to be sure but it gave her a renewed sense that she was on top of things and in charge of the game, neither of which she was at all sure of but every little bit helped. Things had gotten off to a rocky start. She needed to right the ship.

Miguel produced an envelope from the inside pocket of his jacket. He placed it down on the bar in front of them. Dr. Joanne Singer tried to gauge Spencer's reaction, but the British agent's face was a blank. Unlike her, he'd mastered the art of the poker face.

"Well?" she prodded. "Aren't you going to open it?"

Spencer picked up the envelope and appeared to weigh it in his palm. He looked first at Miguel and then at Dr. Joanne Singer, his eyes remaining as dead as his countenance. "What is this, Joanne?" he asked. "Are you blackmailing me?"

"Open it," Miguel growled.

"What's a little blackmail between old friends?" Dr. Joanne Singer laughed.

Spencer tore open the envelope and spread its contents out onto the bar. Dr. Joanne Singer leaned in until her chin was almost resting on Spencer's shoulder. She winked at Miguel who curled his lip in response.

"Photographs," Spencer said. "How very old school of you, Joanne."

"Old school but effective," Dr. Joanne Singer quipped. "Do you recognize yourself in them?"

Spencer gave the photos – a half-dozen or so – a cursory look before pushing them away in disgust. "What do you want, Joanne?" he asked. "Who else have you shown these to?"

"No one," she said. "Miguel and I wanted you to have first dibs. It only seems fair."

"Okay, so you caught me with my trousers down..."

"Literally," Dr. Joanne Singer scoffed. She fought the urge to give Miguel a high-five.

"What do you want?"

Spencer's upper lip had begun to twitch. It beaded with sweat. Dr. Joanne Singer smiled to herself as she enjoyed the last delicious briny drops of her Guinness.

"You and Agent Devereux," she said. "Whatever you think you had with her, it's over. Finished. Finito. Caput. *Capeche?*"

"You don't have the right."

"Oh, but I do. You see, Agent Devereux works for me. I'm the boss bitch. I know that's a difficult concept for you public school boy types and your white male, grey-haired cronies at MI-6 to accept, that a woman like me who doesn't have a pedigree or a fancy-schmancy education could pick herself up by her bra straps and get to the top of her game on nothing but street smarts and *chutzpah*. But I'm here to tell you, Agent Hawksworth, when I get done with where I'm going, you'll be licking the blood red heels of my Louboutins while I fuck you in the ass with my strap-on. Although judging from these photos..."

Spencer spluttered into his San Pellegrino.

"Have I made myself perfectly clear, Agent Hawksworth?"

"That's *Lord* Hawksworth to you," Spencer said.

"I'm an American. I'll call you whatever the fuck I want."

"Why are you doing this?"

Dr. Joanne Singer shrugged. "Because I can. Because Agent Devereux is my most trusted agent. No offense, Miguel, but I gotta look after my girls first."

"None taken," the Chihuahua replied.

"It's nothing personal. Business is business. I'm sure you'll understand, once you get past your fragile toxic masculine pride, that we actually want the same thing, you and I. We both want Agent Devereux to succeed. *N'est-ce pas?*"

"Does she know?"

"About the photos?" Dr. Joanne Singer shook her head. She was feeling quite pleased with herself. The line about the strap-on had just come to her in the moment. She'd have to file it away for future use. "I told you. The only people who have seen them are sitting right here in this pub. Of course, that could easily change."

"And if I agree? If I end things with Yvette – Agent Devereux – they'll go away?"

Dr. Joanne Singer and Miguel exchanged knowing looks. "As much as anything can go away in the digital age," she said. "But, frankly, Agent Devereux will be the least of your concerns should these photos somehow leak."

"What do you mean?"

"Take a closer look." She spread the photos across the bar. "You're not the only one compromised here. Lives have been destroyed by lesser scandal than this."

Spencer gulped. He sat back on his stool and pinched the bridge of his nose. Dr. Joanne Singer nodded to Miguel who swept the offending photographs up from the bar and returned them to the envelope which he then stowed back into the inside pocket of his jacket.

"You're probably wishing you'd ordered something stronger than Pellegrino," she said with what she intended as a kinder, gentler, more sympathetic tone. Empathy didn't come naturally.

"Fuck me," Spencer exhaled.

"If there's nothing else, I think we're done here. Enjoy the Steeplechase, Spencer. I hear it's a helluva party."

She pushed off from the bar and motioned for Miguel to do the same. Spencer didn't move, just sat with his elbows on the counter and his face in his hands. Dr. Joanne Singer hoped he wasn't crying. She hated men who cried.

"I'm afraid Miguel and I are due back in London," she said in parting, "otherwise we'd have loved to join you for a drink. Next time, my treat. And please do send my regards to Rajeev the next time you see him. His sister needs to shit or get off the pot."

The Agency car was parked out front with its hazards on. Dr. Joanne Singer waited for the driver to open the door. She climbed into the plush leather of the back seat, leaned back and closed her eyes. Blackmail was exhausting, she thought, but someone had to do it. She felt Miguel slide in beside her.

"Agent Rodriguez," she said, "are you gonna fuck me, or do I have to do all the dirty work around here?"

As far as she and Miguel were concerned, there was only one right answer.

| 20 |

Spencer was at a loss. He felt as though he'd stepped out of his life – carefully (even obsessively) controlled, ever circumspect, and always at least outwardly upstanding – and into a parallel universe that ran counter to everything he had ever believed himself (and the world) to be. The existence of the photos was bad, their content even worse. But what upset Spencer was the glee Dr. Joanne Singer had appeared to take from destroying him. He had heard the menace in her voice, had seen the hate that sparkled in her blue eyes when the Chihuahua had emptied the envelope and spilled his guts out all over the bar. For that was how Spencer had felt: utterly eviscerated. It went beyond protecting a fellow agent in the field. It wasn't even about blackmail really. Spencer felt as though Dr. Joanne Singer had castrated him for no other reason – as she had said herself – than that she could. But to what end?

Of course, Spencer had always known the risks. He had chosen a career fraught with more illustrious spooks than him behaving badly and getting caught. When one entered a career contingent upon being able to live a double life, one had to expect that the secrets and lies of others (including oneself) could and would be used as leverage if and when convenient and necessary. But how easy it was to deceive oneself into believing one was impervious to the indelicacies and mistakes of others who had come before. There was a certain arrogance inherent to the spook mentality. There was a thrill in the cat-and-mouse chase where the rules constantly changed and the landscape shifted imperceptibly and then dramatically underfoot without so much as a moment's notice. But that was all well and good when it happened to others, and not nearly so satisfying when it happened to oneself, as Spencer had suddenly discovered.

He ordered a whisky from the barkeep, who mysteriously reappeared the moment Dr. Joanne Singer and her lapdog departed. It hadn't been easy slipping out of Templeton Manor. He'd wanted to take a nap after the exhausting business with Ambassador Bingham and Guy – or in the very least spend a few quality hours alone with Yvette in their room – but Dr. Joanne Singer's cryptic text had erased any hope of a little R&R before the evening's festivities, and now the thought of facing anyone – let alone Yvette – was more than Spencer thought he could be expected to bear. Perhaps he'd check himself into one of the rooms upstairs and drown his sorrows in booze and pills? Or he could retrieve the Grindr app from the Cloud and have one last reckless hook-up before ending the conflicted misery of it all once and forever? The appeal, however, was lacking.

In the end, Spencer paid the tab, remarking to the barkeep that it was bloody cheeky for Dr. Joanne Singer to have not only dropped a bomb on him but to also have left him with the tab, and stumbled the two or so miles from the village pub to Templeton Manor. He fell in a ditch when a lorry barreled past and worried that he'd twisted his ankle. By the time he arrived at the estate, he was feeling worse for wear, his ankle throbbed, and he had to stick his fingers down his throat to vomit before presenting himself to the gatekeeper and doing his best to convince the old geezer that he wasn't some riffraff but an actual invited guest.

In the end, he really didn't have to do that much convincing – the paranoia was all in his head – and he was able to slip into his room without running into anyone from whom he preferred to hide. Anyone that is, except Yvette, with whom he had conveniently forgotten he was sharing a room that weekend. When he opened the door and stumbled into their room, Yvette was sat on the four-poster bed painting her toenails, dressed in a fluffy white terrycloth robe with the Templeton crest embroidered on the front breast pocket. Her red hair was freshly washed, styled, and pinned into a high bouffant that accentuated the length of her neck and the appealing freckles across her high forehead. She looked up with a start.

"*Mon Dieu!*" she exclaimed. "Where have you been? You disappeared."

As much as he loved her – for now that he knew their love was forbidden it seemed Spencer loved her with a passion and an ache in his heart he hadn't experienced in years – Yvette Devereux was the last person in the world Spencer wanted to see at that moment.

"Oh, hullo," he stammered. He paused in the open doorway, one foot in the hall. "I...uh...went for a walk down to the village."

"On your own?" she asked, one eyebrow suspiciously cocked. She extended her leg out in front of her and admired her handiwork.

"I needed some fresh air," he said. "I've always found this house a bit claustrophobic."

"Come here and help me. I know how much you like to paint my toenails."

"Right now?"

"Well, I can't very well paint the nails on one foot and not the other. I'm wearing open-toed stilettos tonight. The Jimmy Choo's you admire so much."

"That's awfully thoughtful of you," he said. "I do love those shoes."

Spencer sat down beside her on the edge of the bed. She nestled her foot in his lap and held the polish out to him.

"Are you going to tell me where you really were this afternoon?" Yvette asked. "Or are we going to do what we always do and pretend like everything is okay when you and I both know that it is not?"

"*Quoi?*" Had she read his mind? Had Dr. Joanne Singer said something to her? Had Yvette been in on everything all along? Spencer's hand trembled as he applied the polish to the nail on Yvette's big toe. He didn't put it past Dr. Joanne Singer to speak out of both sides of her mouth.

"I told you," he said, "I walked down to the village and had a drink. I needed some Spencer time. That's all."

Yvette leaned back against the headboard and appraised him with an expression that both alarmed and – strangely – calmed Spencer at the same time. He bit down on the inside of his cheek and focused his concentration on applying the nail polish, careful not to get any on the delicate skin of her toe. Yvette was a stickler for such things. She hated sloppy.

"I think that perhaps we should take a break," she said. "*Tu et moi.*"

Spencer couldn't bring himself to look at her. The big toe finished, he moved on to the one beside it.

"Did you hear what I said, Spencer?"

"*Oui,*" he replied. "I heard you."

"*Et?*"

"If that's what you want."

"*Serieux?* Is that all you're going to say? I tell you that I think we should take a break and you say nothing but 'if that's what you want?' What kind of boyfriend are you?"

Spencer was happy for the diversion. He loved how petite Yvette's feet were. He had always loved her feet. He loved sucking her toes. It was his favorite form of foreplay. Sometimes that was all he needed. The physical act had never excited him as much as her toes. He'd miss her toes, especially in her Jimmy Choo's. Yvette had always had an exquisite selection of shoes.

"I just think that maybe you and I need to focus on our careers right now," Yvette labored on, more to herself it seemed than to Spencer, who was perfectly happy painting her toenails and letting her talk herself out. "I don't think Dr. Joanne Singer approves of us. She's very possessive."

"She's your boss."

"*Oui.*"

"Has she said something to you?" he asked.

"Like what?"

"About me?"

"She's never liked you, if that's what you mean."

"Well, I've never liked her." Spencer felt himself begin to panic. The rumbling started in the pit of his stomach, the bile churned into his throat. His heart burned. He licked his lips and focused on each stroke of the brush. He couldn't bring himself to look at Yvette. He knew this was the end – for what else could it be? – and while a part of him was relieved, he also chided himself for not being more assertive, for not standing up to Dr. Joanne Singer and her Chihuahua, for allowing the brassy American to dictate the tenets of his life. But the photographs stacked the deck against him. He couldn't deny what they showed and he knew that if those photos got into the wrong hands – or any hands, for that matter – his career (the only thing he had ever really cared about) would be over. And without his career, what else did he have? Spencer didn't know how to be anything else. The prospect of a middle-age reinvention lacked any appeal. And as for what the photos revealed of him – of what they proved him to be – Spencer Hawksworth wasn't prepared to acknowledge that his life for nearly forty-five years had been predicated on a lie. It was one thing to lie as an agent of the State – he was a spook, after all, deceit was part of the job – but to recognize the lies he had told himself about himself was something Spencer didn't think he would ever be able to face. The photos proved nothing beyond that fact he had been extremely reckless. He'd find a way to spin it. There were no other options on the table.

"You don't like her because she's a strong woman," Yvette said. She pulled her foot free of his grasp and turned away from him on the bed. "Come to think of it, I don't think you like women at all."

"That's not true!" Spencer heard the fear in his voice and realized he had lost the upper hand, not that he'd ever really had it to begin with. Yvette had always been smarter than him, always one step ahead. She'd kept him on his toes. He'd thought it was one of the things he'd loved most about Yvette, but now he found himself questioning whether there had ever been love between them, whether for him it had all just been about the shoes. "I love you."

Yvette smiled. She cupped his face in her hand and looked at him with a mixture of sadness and pity. It's really over, Spencer thought. *She's moved on. When did it happen? When had she realized theirs was something not fated to last? How had he been so blind?*

"I know you love me in your way," she said, not unkindly. "As I have loved you in my way. But we are two different people, Spencer. We are both too driven by what we do. We are too alike in that way. There are things I have to do in the line of duty that I prefer not to have you on my conscience. It is too painful. Just as I am sure there are things you do that weigh heavy on your heart when you think of me. We're spooks, Spencer. We are not in control of our destiny. I think perhaps that is why we've both chosen this profession, because ultimately, we do not know our own identity. And in a way I suppose that's tragic, but I cannot help but find it liberating."

Yvette got up from the bed and opened the wardrobe. Spencer watched as she shrugged out of the bathrobe and enveloped herself in the grey Tom Ford sheath dress with the plunging neckline she had chosen for that evening's ball. He loved the way her breasts looked in that dress, but then wondered whether it was her breasts that attracted him or simply the fact that she was wearing Tom Ford.

"*C'est magnifique!*" he exclaimed.

Yvette smiled at him again in the reflection of the mirror. "Zip me up?" she asked.

"So that's it then?" Spencer said as he ran the zipper up her back. "We're over, just like that?"

"I don't do tears," Yvette said.

"What if I went down on one knee?"

"It's over, Spencer. *C'est finis.*"

"But we can still be friends?"

She shook her head and pulled him into an embrace that felt like a goodbye. He clenched his jaw and squeezed his eyes shut against the welling tears.

"Let's enjoy this weekend," she whispered. Her breath was hot in his ear.

"And after?"

Yvette shrugged. She stepped away from him and Spencer knew in that moment that he would never feel her in his arms again. She was present, but so far out of his grasp that the gap between them, he knew, would never be breached.

When they descended an hour later, hand in hand, to the main ballroom – Yvette in her Tom Ford gown, Spencer in his Tom Ford black tie and tux – and took their place in the reception line that was tradition for the opening ball of the Steeplechase Weekend, Spencer found himself wondering what it said of him that he wasn't incapacitated by mourning the death of what had heretofore been the most significant relationship of his adult life. In fact, now that the prospect of sex between he and Yvette had been all but rendered moot, Spencer found that he rather looked upon Yvette as more of a sisterly figure – the sister he had always wanted but had never had – than as an ex-girlfriend. In fact, this change in relationship status suited him rather well. It was almost as though he felt he could breathe again. He'd done what Dr. Joanne Singer had requested – or rather, it had been done for him by none other than Yvette herself – so the question of the photographs (if Dr. Joanne Singer kept her word) was now also moot.

Or at least, it should have been. Spencer knew it was naïve to trust anything Dr. Joanne Singer said. She had her own agenda, which she wasn't about to share, and in their line of work, it was always good to have something over on someone, even when that someone was hypothetically meant to be an ally – on paper at least. Of course, it wasn't as though the feisty director of The Agency didn't have shit of her own. Spencer knew for a fact that her hands weren't clean either. Espionage attracted a certain kind of person and Dr. Joanne Singer was nothing if not the epitome of this particular type.

Spencer had heard things from his colleagues at the U.S. State Department, and not all of it unsubstantiated: hotel rooms in Moscow, prostitutes on the payroll of the FSB, sex games that would have made even Christian Gray blush. And then her sidekick, Miguel Rodriguez a.k.a. "the Chihuahua," whose sister – the lovely Magdalena – had a reputation on both sides of the U.S. – Mexico border that went far beyond her aspirations as an up-and-coming chanteuse. Spencer had seen her file too – or at least a facsimile of it: sex, drugs, rock 'n' roll and one particular cartel that made the Zetas look like amateurs. But Spencer was nothing if not a gentleman. He'd never kiss and tell, unless Dr. Joanne Singer told first. It was a dangerous game they played.

And so Spencer found himself just going through the motions. There was no sense in attracting further drama by telling anyone that he and Yvette were no longer together. It was far easier to smile and nod and play Happy Families than behave otherwise. The copious amounts of champagne helped, as did the rather stiff, formal and thoroughly British pageantry of it all. Spencer was an ardent champion of tradition, and the Ball that officially heralded the opening of the annual Templeton Steeplechase Weekend was like a salve to a tortured soul. The fact that it was all flawlessly executed pomp and circumstance suited Spencer just fine. No one expected deep conversation; in fact, the shallower, the better. And judging from the parade of exquisitely turned-out plastic and muscle that seemed to be the hallmark of this year's Steeplechase, the eye candy alone was worth the price of admission. Spencer felt he had a certain license to play this year. It was a good thing he hadn't pursued an invitation for Dr. Joanne Singer.

The evening passed in a rather pleasant haze. After the reception line, the cocktails and small talk with a seemingly endless panoply of television presenters with big hair, big teeth, big tits and even bigger egos – though the standout for Spencer remained Cressida Parker, who at one time had been rather an obsession of his, if only things hadn't turned out so poorly with her and Guy – and a feast worthy of Henry the Eighth, Spencer decided to duck out for a bit of fresh air, a cigar, and a walk round the gardens between the house proper and the boathouse that serviced the canal that ran its winding course through the Templeton acreage. The pheasant, stuffed pork, roast beef, and caviar-encrusted salmon sat like a cannonball in Spencer's gut. He felt as though he had gained ten pounds just that evening and the buttons of his Tom Ford tuxedo strained against his engorged belly.

He needed a constitutional, but more than that, Spencer needed time alone to think, to process, and to digest all that had happened just that day. Ambassador Bingham was playing nice. Of course, Spencer had had to do a bit of maneuvering to make sure Bingham and Guy were never in close enough proximity to provoke another altercation, but as each were at heart civilized blokes, propriety took its course and made Spencer's job easier. But he knew that whatever rapprochement had been achieved that afternoon was likely to fall by the wayside come morning. The less time his best mate and the British Ambassador to Russia spent in each other's company, the better it was for world peace. At least for another twenty-four hours.

Spencer smoked his cigar and gazed out over the canal. The moon cast a pale glimmer over the placid waters that he found calming but sinister for reasons he couldn't articulate. The evening was still with nary a breeze. It felt good to be alone, to breathe, to recalibrate, to reassert a semblance of control, however fleeting. The cigar wasn't particularly satisfying, but it made Spencer feel manly, and to feel manly, Spencer found, was what he needed to feel most of all.

"It's all terribly tedious, isn't it?"

Spencer exhaled at the interruption.

"Tucker," he said.

"But I can't help but admire the tableau." Tucker O'Donnell emerged from the moonlit darkness and stood beside Spencer at the edge of the canal, cigarette in hand. "The Templetons are a dying breed, you know. Once Carleton croaks –

which, I hear, could be at any moment if it hasn't happened already – the world as they know it will simply cease to exist. Just like that. Poof! And then what?"

"They'll muddle through," Spencer said. "It's what they've done for centuries. Families like the Templetons are the backbone of this country. They're what make it great."

"Spoken like a true toff." Tucker gave Spencer a patronizing pat on the shoulder. "You're right, of course, which just makes it all that much more infuriating. But typical. Are there a more self-hating people than the Brits?"

"The Jews perhaps, though I suppose that makes me anti-Semitic."

"Fuck political correctness," Tucker O'Donnell said. "Strictly off the record, of course."

"Like our conversation this afternoon?"

Tucker shrugged. "I'm a journalist," he said. "Call me old school, but I live for the scoop."

"At the expense of integrity."

"Integrity, my boy, is in the eye of the beholder." Tucker winked. "And besides, in this business I learned long ago that to get the story – the true heart of darkness, if you will – you need not be afraid to sell yourself a wee bit. I should think it's not unlike being a spook."

"It's an honorable profession," Spencer replied. He felt himself on the defensive, but then that had always been the effect Tucker O'Donnell had had on him.

"There are varying degrees of honor, you know," Tucker said.

"Just as there are varying degrees of journalists."

"True. 'Tis a slippery slope."

"Indeed." Spencer took a generous puff from the cigar. Tucker's presence had somewhat dampened the pleasure of the moment as did the smell of the legendary newsman's cigarette. The problem with Tucker was that one never knew what the man might spring on you at any given moment. He never gave one time to prepare. And for Spencer, life was all about preparation, which was perhaps why – when he paused to think on it – his relationship with Yvette had never been destined for long-term success. Yvette was impetuous, to a fault perhaps, but nonetheless her spontaneity had always struck him as exciting if not, ultimately, rather exhausting. He'd never been able to keep up.

There was a certain parallel with Chloe, he supposed, although Spencer was loath to give either woman the slightest comparison. He sensed that Chloe had been giving him the slip all evening, at least since all the palaver with the ambassador. He couldn't help but wonder – no, he didn't dare consider it – if Chloe had her own suspicions about him, independent of whatever Dr. Joanne Singer's blackmail photos might reveal.

"I have to ask," Tucker's voice cut through the fog of Spencer's consciousness to a somewhat disorienting effect, "is Chloe seeing anyone these days, or is she too busy being an It Girl to give an old but very eligible bachelor the time of day?"

"Chloe? Why?"

"I thought she was looking rather fetching this afternoon is all. And very single."

Spencer tossed the butt of his cigar into the canal. He hadn't finished it but the conversation was rapidly becoming claustrophobic. He was desperate for an escape hatch.

"You know Chloe," he said rather lamely. "She's nothing if not mad for her cause. She's in a class of her own."

"Yes." Tucker leaned his head back and exhaled a string of perfectly executed smoke rings before flicking the end of his cigarette into the dark. "About that. You know there's chatter."

"About?"

"Her foundation: Sisters Against Sweat Shops. I've always thought that to be such a vulgar name!"

"What chatter?"

"You had a hand in that, didn't you?"

"Minimal. I helped Chloe with her business plan."

"You and I both know your contribution went far beyond a business plan."

Spencer shrugged. It really was time to remove himself from the conversation.

"I can't talk about it," he said.

"That factory fire in Dhaka a few years' back. The cause was never really resolved, was it? So many innocent lives lost too, I recall. Faulty electrical wiring: that was the reason given, yes?"

"Chloe started the foundation to protect against such tragedies from ever happening again. I'm not sure what you're implying, Tucker, but I am sure I don't like your tone."

"Pradesh Ranawat. Does the name ring a bell?"

"Should it?"

"I'm asking you."

Tucker produced a silver cigarette case from his inside jacket pocket and offered Spencer a cigarette before helping himself to another. Spencer shook his head but took one anyway. He needed something to calm his nerves. He was thankful for the dark as it masked the fact that he was now sweating rather profusely, something that he preferred Tucker not to see.

"Those sub-continental names all sound the same to me," Spencer said after a lengthy pause during which Tucker lit his cigarette and the two men took simultaneous first drags. "I can't keep track."

"Spoken like a true colonial," Tucker quipped. "But I don't hold it against you. You and I are, after all, cut from the same cloth. Pradesh Ranawat, for your information or perhaps to help jog your memory, is Bangladeshi."

"Ah, of course."

"So you do know of him?"

"I really can't tell you one way or the other."

Tucker was undeterred. "He runs a syndicate based mostly in the Near East and Southeast Asia: Dhaka, Mumbai, Goa, Phuket, Kuala Lumpur to name but a few locations where he's been spotted in the recent past. Goa, in particular."

Spencer flinched.

"What's your point, Tucker?" he said. "I'm catching a chill. I don't want to get sick before the big day."

"In fact, Pradesh was spotted just the other day in Goa – of all places! – in the vicinity of a certain five-star luxury beachside resort that I believe happens to be a rather favorite of yours and a certain Rajeev Gupta. And if I'm not mistaken – I have no reason not to trust my source in Goa but if I've been misinformed, you must be sure to tell me, as journalists we must fight against this trend of fake news before it destroys our integrity altogether – you've had some recent business in Goa yourself, with Guy Templeton, I believe."

"This is exactly what I don't like about you, Tucker," Spencer said through clenched teeth. He sucked too hard on the cigarette and nearly choked. "Your desperation to remain relevant in a dying industry. It's a losing battle, Tuck. Retire to the South of France or the Costa del Sol while you still have a shred of dignity."

"You can't run forever, Spencer."

"I'm not running."

"Your misdeeds are going to catch up with you sooner or later. I'm only here to warn you, as an old friend."

"We were never friends, Tucker."

Just as Spencer was about to take his leave – in as gentlemanly a way as possible, of course – he was arrested by the sight of Chloe walking along the dock toward them. She appeared oblivious to his and Tucker's presence. Tucker grabbed his forearm.

"Chloe!" he hissed at Spencer who tried to pull his arm away, but the old journalist's grip proved surprisingly strong. "She can't see us here together."

"Why ever not?" Spencer asked, though he offered little in the way of actual physical protest. Tucker's hand on his arm was insistent as he allowed himself to be led into the shadows beneath the overhanging eave of the boathouse.

"I can't risk my cover being blown," Tucker said. "She'll suspect you're a source."

Chloe passed Spencer and Tucker's not-so-hidden hiding place on her way to the front door of the boathouse. She paused before entering, sniffed as though detecting the residual aroma of tobacco. She glanced over her shoulder, thinking perhaps she wasn't alone or (more specifically) that Rebecca Hastings was already in wait for her in the shadows. Over the years, Chloe had become quite adept at sussing out paparazzi. The delicate hairs on the back of her neck triggered like gooseflesh whenever she sensed she was being watched. She rather loved the attention – for that's what being an It Girl was all about, wasn't it? – but she was loath to admit to anything that might even remotely smack of narcissism. A true philanthropist cared more for others than for herself. Chloe was ever mindful of the perception she gave to the press and her adoring (and not-so-adoring) public. The burden weighed heavy.

She glanced at her watch: a quarter-past-midnight. She was early. The lingering smell of cigarettes caused a craving that Chloe found she was helpless to resist. She opened her Chanel clutch and helped herself to a Gauloises. The fact that the cigarette was French somehow lessened the contradiction that she had always found smoking a disgusting and rather sordid habit, and yet in times of stress – which this certainly was – she found a well-timed Gauloises worked wonders for her perpetually shattered nerves, better even than alcohol. It burned as she inhaled.

"Chloe?" Rebecca Hastings emerged from the glow cast by the light of the full moon. "You came."

"I said I would, didn't I?" Chloe snapped. The words came out harsher than she had perhaps intended. "I'm nothing if not a girl of my word."

"Earnest to a fault." Rebecca Hastings strode towards Chloe with a confident swagger that reminded Chloe of a lioness on the hunt. It terrified and aroused her at the same time. "I used to find it irritating, but now it just makes me want to role play. Teacher and student. How about it, Chlo'? Do your knuckles need a good whack from my ruler?"

"Stop it!" Chloe stepped back and held her half-finished cigarette up in front of her like a weapon. "No more games, Rebecca. I'm serious."

"Then why invite me here?" Rebecca asked. She stood before Chloe, the burning tip of Chloe's cigarette separating them, but only just. Rebecca's dark eyes blazed in the orange embers. "The boathouse after midnight ... well, it positively reeks of the clandestine, doesn't it? All night, sitting there with those obnoxious dilettantes at dinner, I kept trying to catch your eye, but you wouldn't look at me. I suppose you thought you were being discreet, but it only made me want you more. You are so utterly delicious, Chloe, I almost can't stand it. Feel me." She grabbed Chloe's hand and put it between her legs. She wasn't wearing knickers. "That's what you do to me."

Chloe struggled against the temptation in spite of herself. How to make Rebecca Hastings understand? It wasn't that she was completely immune to Rebecca's seduction. She was a sexual woman, after all, and Rebecca Hastings was nothing if not sexy.

"I can't," she said, hoping there was more conviction in her voice than she felt. She pushed past Rebecca and went to the edge of the canal. She shivered against the breeze. "You have to understand, Rebecca. That wild and wanton girl you think you know, well, that girl isn't me."

"Who is she then?"

Chloe felt Rebecca's presence behind her. She tossed the cigarette butt into the canal and struggled against the trembling of her hands as she opened her clutch for another cigarette. This is what Rebecca Hastings had reduced her to: a chain smoker. Could the woman make her feel any more unattractive or not herself?

"I mean, she is me – of course – but what I meant was..."

"Are you going to offer me a ciggy or am I to stand here and inhale second-hand smoke all night while you grapple with your existential conundrum?"

"Sorry. I've forgotten my manners."

Rebecca Hastings stroked Chloe's hand as Chloe lit the woman's cigarette. She fought against the electrical impulse.

"Better," Rebecca said. "Gauloises too. *Tres chic*. I expect nothing less, of course."

"I'm not a lesbian!" Chloe blurted before she was aware of what she was saying. There was just no delicate way of putting it into words.

Rebecca Hastings tossed her head back and gave a low throaty laugh that made Chloe feel like a scolded child. This wasn't going well.

"Darling," Rebecca Hastings said, "whatever made you think that I thought you were? You're no more a lesbian than I am."

"You're not?"

"You really are quite the traditionalist, aren't you? I suppose that shouldn't surprise me. I mean look where we are...look where you come from...I can't hold your ignorance against you, darling, because you clearly don't know any better."

"I don't see what my family's got to do with it," Chloe snapped. She felt somewhat relieved but still just as at sea.

"You live in a bubble. Your unconscious bias is hereditary. You've never known anything else. You're really little more than a child."

This was too much. "I'm not a child!" Chloe protested. "I'm a grown woman. Just because I don't want to have sex with you, doesn't mean I'm somehow..." She was suddenly at a loss for words.

"Undeveloped?" Rebecca Hastings offered with a naughty twinkle in her eye. "Uninformed?"

"I don't want this," Chloe said. "I like things simple, uncomplicated. I have my foundation, my work for charity. I have my family and all the responsibilities that entails. It may seem like a walk in the park to you, but being a Templeton is a full-time job. One needs stamina to survive and razor-sharp focus so one isn't caught off-guard by those who wish to take you down. Take that nasty woman, for example."

"Which nasty woman?" Rebecca Hastings asked with a mischievous snarl that Chloe found annoyingly off-putting.

"Lady Eliza, of course! Whom else could I possibly be referring to?"

"I can think of a few."

"Well, you are rather nasty in your way, I suppose."

"It's good to be nasty," Rebecca Hastings growled. Chloe felt her conviction start to slip. "It's power."

"Don't."

Chloe debated the pros and cons of another cigarette, but decided that indulging in one more would only prolong the situation, which would only make her feel more vulnerable, which would only serve to give Rebecca Hastings ammunition that she didn't really need. But it was already too late. She felt Rebecca's hand work its way beneath the hem of her dress, her fingers toying the waist of her knickers, tugging them gently but insistently down. Rebecca was in her ear, in her head, her fingers working their way inside her. This is what Chloe loved, what she craved – yes, craved – but what she hated at the same time. Why did sex have to be so complicated? she wondered. Why did it matter whom she slept with (or didn't sleep with)? It shouldn't matter. But it did. Especially when you were Chloe Templeton with a foundation to run and worlds to change and a family that had had its share of bad press lately and another scandal – especially of the kind that Rebecca Hastings was suggesting – was the last thing Chloe or her family needed now, or ever.

"You feel so good," Rebecca Hastings moaned. "I've always wanted to fuck someone in a boathouse."

Chloe had reached the end of her tether. She shoved Rebecca Hastings out from in front of her and adjusted the hem of her dress. "No!" she cried with a dramatic flourish that was more for effect than from genuine anguish, though there was certainly some of that in there as well. "No means no. You're just like a man. If I wanted a man, I'd be with a man. Leave me alone."

Rebecca Hastings' eyes burned daggers. Her nostrils flared. She seethed. "Who the hell do you think you are?" she screamed. "What gives you the right to tell me to do anything? YOU came to ME! Remember? You went to my studio. You pretended to be all innocent and coy, like fucking butter wouldn't melt in your mouth. You led me on and then dropped me like yesterday's news, like I was nothing but one of your sweatshop workers. You did this to me! You violated me! If you think for a second that I'm going to let you get away with this, you've got another think coming."

Chloe wasn't sure how to react. It was clear to her – as if she had needed any clarification – that Rebecca Hastings was not dealing with a full deck. She knew the sensible thing to have done was walk away, block Rebecca Hastings' number from her phone, and tell security to remove the woman from the premises, with or without her husband. But Chloe found herself transfixed. No one had ever spoken to her in quite the way Rebecca Hastings spoke to her now. It was horrific and frightening and – yes – oddly flattering. To have such a passionate effect on another human was the ultimate validation, as satisfying in its way as the work she did with S.A.S.S., if not more so.

And yet, as she continued to stand there while Rebecca Hastings paced and ranted, Chloe experienced another emotion that was also new to her: Hate. She hated Rebecca Hastings, hated her with a virulence that made her stomach churn, that was even more intense than that which she felt for Lady Eliza, if such a hate was even possible. Chloe wanted to draw blood. She wanted to do bad things to Rebecca Hastings. She wanted to club the woman to death with one of the oars that hung from the ceiling inside the boathouse. Oh, the satisfaction such violence would bring! Chloe's palms tingled. She itched. She ceased to hear any of what Rebecca Hastings said, focusing instead on the movement of the woman's mouth, the way she tossed and flicked her hair like a stag in rutting season, the way her eyes flickered and flashed and raved in the moonlight.

But no. Such thoughts – fantasies – were unbecoming for a girl of Chloe's social stature. People like her hired others to do their dirty work. She didn't dare risk the taint of blood on her hands. She'd never get it off. No. Chloe's mind raced. Earlier that day, in the hallway, what had that little foreign toad – Edgar's loathsome personal assistant – said to her? What had he insinuated? About Rebecca Hastings...about what he could do to her...what he would do to her. Yes, the man was a lizard who made Chloe's skin crawl, but she supposed such people had their uses. The trick was knowing when and how to employ them and then when to cast them off so their stink never wafted in one's direction. It suddenly became very clear to Chloe what she needed to do.

"Are you even listening to me? Have you heard even one single word of what I've just said?"

Chloe snapped back to attention. She blinked. Any thought of bludgeoning Rebecca Hastings to death with an oar passed from her mind as though it had never even been under consideration. She felt very calm, very in control, very much a Templeton.

"Are you finished?" Chloe asked.

"Excuse me?"

"It's just that you're more interesting when you're not speaking."

Chloe arched her back ever so slightly as she prepared to make her exit. Now that she thought of it, Xander – the name just came to her – had been trying to make eye contact with her all through dinner. She'd been so put out by the very fact of him – an assistant! – sitting at the table that any thought that he might be trying to give her a signal hadn't entered her consciousness, until now. She had to find him. She had to give him the nod. She had to remove Rebecca Hastings from her life...and Edgar's too, for that matter. Chloe supposed she owed a certain grudging allegiance to her American sister-in-law.

"How DARE you?" Rebecca Hastings spluttered.

Chloe felt back in her element. She was a Templeton after all. That had to stand for something.

"I trust you can find your own way back to the house," Chloe said with a hauteur that felt so utterly natural it came as a relief. "But watch your step. I'd hate for you to fall into the canal. I hear it's very deep."

She felt liberated. Rebecca Hastings was a thing of the past now – utterly irrelevant – and whatever transpired between now and the Steeplechase, well, Chloe refused to give it (or her) a second thought. Whatever had happened between them – regardless of Rebecca Hastings' revisionist version of events, and in Chloe's mind, Rebecca Hastings was nothing if not revisionist – didn't exist, or had never existed except perhaps in RH's delusional imagination. The woman deserved to be locked up! Chloe had moved on. She looked forward to the next chapter of her life sans any and all encumbrance, or rather she'd pick and choose her encumbrances going forward. Tucker O'Donnell had looked awfully tempting, that horny old silver fox! She couldn't help but wax nostalgic about what she rather wistfully referred to as her New York Years. Tucker's Park Avenue 'boom boom room' had been their little secret, that and the dozens of luxury hotel rooms all across Manhattan – from the Plaza to the Four Seasons to the Helmsley. Chloe had found the intrigue delicious. She wondered whether the cheeky bastard still had it in him, or if he still had the key.

Her mobile buzzed. Xander. How the hell had he gotten her number?

Plan set all is. Not a thing must do you.

What was he doing, contacting her like this? The presumption! She couldn't be implicated. There couldn't be a trace, not even the slightest whiff of collusion between them.

How did you get my number?

Xander knows all.

I don't know what that means! Speak the King's English. I don't understand Euro.

Insult me must you not. Not if Xander's magic him you want to make.

Chloe thought she now understood why there was such a *furore* about open borders and the right of free migration. England had enough chaff without the likes of Xander and his fellow Middle-European Wild and Crazy Guys. She'd have to talk to Spencer and the powers that be at Whitehall.

But still, Xander had his uses.

Boathouse are you?

Yes...how do you know?

Xander sees. Xander knows.

Chloe paused. She peered into the dark on either side of her. Had he been watching her the whole time? She suddenly felt as though a million pairs of eyes were upon her.

Xander better get down to business if Xander knows what's good for him. And Xander better be discreet. I can't afford blood on my hands.

For nothing you worry, ma Cherie. Xander knows. Xander does.

The text bubble vanished.

Chloe fumbled in her clutch for the pack of Gauloises. She was going for broke. The stress was killing her. She couldn't help but feel as though she was being watched, and not necessarily by Edgar's reptilian assistant. She lit the cigarette and inhaled too quickly. The smoke burned her lungs. She coughed and choked and inhaled again. A sudden flicker on the murky water of the canal caught her attention...like a phantom wraith skipping stones. Chloe narrowed her eyes. She tried to see. Who was out there in the darkness? Had someone seen her with Rebecca Hastings? She thought she'd been so careful, discretion a necessity before all else.

But there was no one. Chloe smoked and counted back from five. She needed to get a grip. It somewhat alarmed her that Rebecca Hastings hadn't put up more of a fight. She'd expected drama, or at least more drama than what Rebecca Hastings had offered. Should she be concerned? Was RH planning something nefarious of her own? What if? Chloe banished the thought. It was inconceivable to her that Xander was playing both sides. He was an employee of the Templetons, after all. He should know on which side his bread was buttered. She didn't doubt Edgar paid him handsomely. Perhaps she needed to have a word with her brother? Perhaps she needed to suggest Xander get a raise?

"Well, I'll be! Fancy seeing you here at this time of night." Tucker. "If I didn't know you better, Miss Templeton, I'd suspect you were up to some rather risky business – or is the operative word *risqué?*"

The sound of his voice – chalky, cheeky, and very well-lubricated – made

Chloe's nerve endings melt.

"Not that there's anything wrong with that." Tucker appeared from the shadows, face flushed, cigarette in hand. His gait was unsteady. Chloe wondered whether Tucker O'Donnell had been sober a day in his storied life. "You know me. I like a naughty girl, especially when she pretends to be good. And you, Miss Templeton, are looking very naughty tonight. I meant to tell you that earlier."

"It's the moon," Chloe said. She felt her face flush. Tucker still had that affect on her. "Everyone looks naughty in the moonlight. What are you doing out here anyway, Tucker? I'd have thought it was well past your bedtime, old geezer that you are."

"You know me, Chlo'. It's not bedtime until I have someone to go to bed with."

"You're incorrigible."

"Horny more like."

"Well, I certainly don't know anything about that."

Chloe felt the pull of the past. She'd forgotten how much fun she'd had with him. There was truth to the adage that you never forgot your first...

"How's about it, Chlo'?"

He reeked of whisky and cheap cigarettes. Chloe turned her face from him. The alcoholic stench was overpowering.

"Give us a pull, love."

She slapped him. Not hard, but with force enough to remind him that she wasn't so easily swayed, even though they both knew that was a lie. Chloe could be very easy when it was convenient.

"That was for Stella," she said with a playful wink before taking his arm in hers and pulling him along the path back toward the house. The further away from Rebecca Hastings, the boathouse, and Xander for that matter, the better.

Tucker rubbed his cheek with a mischievous chortle. "Stella would have used her fist," he said. "She could have been a contender, that one."

"Is it true what they say? That everything's bigger in Texas?"

"Bigger, yes, but not necessarily better." Tucker squeezed Chloe's arm and patted her hand almost paternally as they walked. "The yellow rose of Texas has nothing on a true English rose."

"You flatter me, Tucker, though I fear Stella would have KO'd me in the first round."

"Why are we talking about my wife?"

Tucker swept Chloe up in his arms and pressed her close to his chest. He held her chin and forced her to look up at him. She tried to look away – something in the ardency of his stare made her nervous. It reminded her too much of the way Rebecca Hastings had looked at her just moments before. She wondered what it was about her that inspired such passion in others.

"How is Stella these days?" she asked.

"Alzheimer's is a terrible thing."

"You never divorced?"

"Stella gave me everything, Chloe," Tucker said. "I couldn't just abandon her. Despite my reputation, I'm not all bad."

"Stella's money, you mean," Chloe corrected. "Stella's money gave you everything."

She and Tucker had never spoken so openly before about his wife, Stella McIntosh, the formidable Texas heiress, mostly because Chloe had always preferred to remain ignorant of her. It annoyed her to be reminded of Tucker's wife now, and the fact that he still – after all these years – hadn't left her didn't bode well. And the fact the woman had Alzheimer's...well, it couldn't get more inconvenient than that, could it? Another inconvenient woman. Chloe shuddered against the sudden chill.

"Your reputation is well-deserved, Tuck," she said. "You're a scoundrel and a cad."

"And you love me for it." Tucker kissed her forehead, her neck, her lips: he devoured her. Chloe closed her eyes and found herself surrendering to him – to the memories of all that once was, and all that could have been – despite her conscience warning her well away. "I do love you, Chloe Templeton. My precious little Clo-Clo."

"Enough."

His grip was strong despite his age but he didn't resist when she wrestled free. His attention no longer excited her, but rather annoyed. Chloe still felt as though they were being watched. She needed to get back to the house. She would only feel safe once she was within the confines of her bedroom – with or without a nocturnal guest...preferably now without. She continued walking, more briskly than before but still at a relatively conversant pace. If anyone or anything were to jump out of the hedges or from behind a tree before she reached the manor, it was preferable to have Tucker there to protect her, not that he would prove much use. The geezer was drunk.

"Where is Stella now then?" she asked.

"At the ranch outside Austin. We've hired the best care money can buy. She's as comfortable as she can be, given the circumstances. Tanner and Mimi get there when they can."

"Ah yes, Tanner and Mimi." Somehow Chloe had forgotten Tucker had children. If she recalled correctly, they'd both be around her age. "And how are they?"

"Don't bother pretending you care."

"You're right," Chloe said with a petulant sniff. "I don't. It's a long way back to the house. I've never been much good at small talk."

Tucker was at her elbow now. He tried to touch it to make her slow down, but she pulled her arm ever so slightly away. Perhaps she didn't want him there after all? Perhaps it was best if he just left her alone?

"What's wrong, Chlo?" he asked.

The wicked edge had left his voice. He reminded her of Papa, but then he always had really. She stopped in spite of herself as she felt the familiar rise of tears. Not now! she excoriated herself. *No tears in front of Tucker. He'll only use them against you later because that's the kind of man he is. Remember what happened in New York? There's a reason you haven't seen or been in contact with him for all these years. Think, Chloe, think! Be strong. You're better than this. You're better than him.* His hand was on her back, stroking her with his deceptive tenderness.

"No!" Chloe said through her tears. "It's not right. It's not fair."

"What isn't, Clo-Clo? What isn't fair?" His strong hands were on her shoulders. He turned her around to face him. She allowed him to envelop her as the floodgates opened.

"Everything!" she exclaimed. "I can't take it anymore. You don't know how hard it's been, Tucker. You didn't see him last night at dinner."

"Who, dearest?"

"Papa!" Chloe wailed. She couldn't help herself. She'd jumped off the cliff. "I don't recognize him anymore! I kept thinking, that's not him. It's like she's taken over his body and sucked out his soul."

"Who, Chlo-Chlo?"

"That woman! Eliza!" It made her sick to say her name. "She tricked him into marrying her. He even converted, Tucker! I don't what's worse. She threatened me. She told me she was going to take away my foundation. My S.A.S.S.! It's the only thing that keeps me going. If that horrible woman takes away S.A.S.S., I might as well throw myself into the canal right now, for what else will I have to live for?"

"There, there, Chloe. Shhh. I'm here now. Daddy's here."

"And we have all these people at the house for this damn Steeplechase and Papa is probably going to die before we see the end of the weekend and Guy...and Guy..." She broke off. She wasn't too far-gone to realize that above and beyond all else, Tucker O'Donnell was more than an ex-lover. He was a journalist, one of the best, and with that came a certain mindset that anyone was fair game where a scoop was concerned, including her.

With that realization, the tears dried up almost as if on cue.

"I think I'd like to be alone now," she said. "I can manage from here."

"I don't think you're in any state to be alone," Tucker said. "There's still a long night ahead of us. And the thought of you all on your lonesome in that big four-poster bed with no one to protect you from the demons that only come at night, well, Chloe Templeton, I can't let that be your fate. It would be unchivalrous."

But Chloe had had enough. "The only demon I have to worry about is you," she said with a playful but dismissive wave of her finger. "The house is full of nymphs and naiads more willing than I to succumb to your satyr-like charms. But this damsel is definitely not in distress, which rather puts me off-limits. She's just due a full night's sleep. Run along, Caliban. Miranda needs her rest."

"I've always preferred Lady Macbeth."

Chloe paused. "There's only one Lady Macbeth in this house, and it isn't me," she said.

"Lady Eliza might yet surprise you."

He wasn't teasing her now. Chloe detected a faint edge in Tucker's voice that gave her cause for unease. Tucker's banter wasn't always kind. She remembered that about him now. Despite his rather avuncular demeanor, more often than not, Tucker O'Donnell was generally three steps ahead of everyone. It was a game to him, a game that Chloe preferred not to play.

"Is there something you're not telling me?" she asked.

Tucker shook his head and shrugged. Chloe peered at him through the dark. The moon was in shadow now, the light not nearly so bright.

"Far be it from me to interfere in family business," Tucker said.

"Your sudden restraint doesn't become you."

"Just keep your eyes peeled and your ear to the ground. I shall say no more."

With that, Tucker turned on his heel and stumbled off back in the direction from which they had come, leaving Chloe more betwixt and between than she'd been five minutes earlier. His parting words haunted her. She considered running after him and demanding he reveal to her what he knew – for Chloe wasn't so naïve as to believe there wasn't specific intent behind what Tucker had said – but the hour suddenly seemed so late and such an action would reek of desperation that Tucker would surely allude to it for years to come. (He could be so damnably insufferable when he wanted to be!)

No. Chloe would try her best to put any troubling thoughts from her mind, at least for a few hours. She was exhausted and the day ahead – only a few hours' hence – would surely prove all the more tiring. She needed to be on her A-game. Posh TV was covering the Steeplechase live for the first time in the event's history, and Maximilian Porter could be such a little cunt when he wanted to be, not to mention his rather all-too-obvious sidekick Bree Armstrong. Chloe shuddered at the very thought of them and kicked herself for allowing Cressida to convince her that it was her family's patriotic duty to allow the world (or at least Posh TV subscribers) a real-time glimpse into what it was like to be a Templeton. Chloe only hoped they didn't all embarrass themselves in the process. With Lady Eliza at the helm, who knew what madness might ensue? It didn't bode well for a restful night.

| 21 |

Lady Eliza awoke to the plaintive drone of a bagpipe outside her window down in the courtyard below. She hated bagpipes. The sound reminded her of Brookings Farm, or at least as Brookings Farm had been before it and her fortunes had changed. She used to think Lord Chester played the bagpipes just to torture her, for she knew the thrill his playing gave Dulcinea, who had loved nothing more than to dance around the great entrance hall in a kilt while their mother, Lady Josephine, accompanied them rather stiffly on her harp. Eliza, who had no musical talent to speak of, would obediently sit and watch the family festivities without daring to take part. How she hated those Sunday afternoon *musicales!* The bagpipes summed up everything she had ever loathed about life at Brookings Farm.

The fact that the bagpipes seemed to have followed her to Templeton Manor was enough to give Lady Eliza fits. She thrust herself out of bed and ran to the window. The bagpipes jarred in her head. She tried to open the windows but found the latch had frozen from age and years of disuse. She pressed her forehead against the glass and tried to see who it was that dared torture her at so early an hour. For a second she feared it might be Chester, come to haunt her from the grave, and was only somewhat relieved to discover that the offender was none other than Diana's husband, Duncan, whom Lady Eliza then remembered served as the official Steeplechase mascot and opened Steeplechase Saturday with the blowing of the bagpipes at dawn. Her new family was nothing if not archaic. Lady Eliza intended to bring them kicking and screaming into the 21st century, no matter the cost. But for the time being, Duncan and his bagpipes had to be endured.

Lady Eliza hadn't slept well. She rarely slept but last night had been particularly vexing. The ball the night before had gone about as well as could have been expected. She hadn't enjoyed it but then such frivolity had never really been her thing. Still, she felt she had handled herself rather admirably, despite the fact that Sister Francine had called in the afternoon to inform her the trains from London still weren't running due industrial action and she wouldn't be there until at least mid-morning on Saturday. The timing wasn't ideal. Lady Eliza depended on her spiritual advisor to be resolutely at her side when faced with all of these morally bankrupt sycophants over the course of the weekend. She drew strength from Sister Francine's rectitude. She took inspiration from Sister Francine's unfailing commitment to austerity. The fallen angel – for that was how Lady Eliza viewed her – was a bulwark against the debauchery Lady Eliza intended to smite to the ground even before Lord Carleton was finally laid to rest. The fact that he had died in his sleep not long after being wheeled back up to his room after the family dinner Thursday night was a slight inconvenience. Lady Eliza had hoped he might have held off until Sunday. But, as Sister Francine so often reminded her, the Lord worked in mysterious ways, and it seemed He had decided to once again test Lady Eliza's mettle by making her a widow just shy of twelve hours after becoming a bride, with a houseful of guests and a television network on site poised to broadcast the weekend's festivities to the shallow end of the gene pool all over the world.

Sitting at Lord Carleton's dressing bureau as Duncan blared his bagpipes and a surprisingly rosy dawn broke across the normally gloomy Dorset skies, Lady Eliza couldn't help but congratulate herself on her handling of Lord Carleton's death. Deep into the early morning hours, she had been hard at work hauling buckets of ice up from the basement pantry into the tub of her en-suite bathroom. Such arduous manual labor she hadn't experienced since her attempts at planting a vegetable garden on the grounds of Brookings Farm in the early years of her first marriage, as a distraction from her loneliness during Chester's extended absences in Kenya. But then Dulcinea had made a cruel game of pulling up each cabbage and carrot from the ground before their growth could reach completion, making a mess of Lady Eliza's efforts and an early feeding ground for the rabbits and deer that populated the estate. The fact that Eliza had succeeded in carting bucket after bucket of ice from the basement to her bedroom on the manor's top floor without detection was, she felt, a testament to her endurance, not to mention her stealth. Sister Francine would surely approve!

The ice, of course, was to preserve Lord Carleton's body in her bathtub until the last guests had departed from the estate after the Steeplechase on Monday morning. Her bedroom suite was (conveniently) isolated from the rest of the house by a private staircase that only she could access, for she was the only one in the household – including staff – who had possession of the key, save Sister Francine for whom she had secretly made a copy.

After the family dinner – and the nasty surprise arrival of the "impostor", the so-called Contessa Templeton – Eliza found she was so distraught by this latest development that she needed a quick roll in the proverbial hay to calm down and recalibrate. So beside herself was she that, at the time, it hadn't really entered her head that Carleton might not be up to the job. Their previous attempt at consummation hadn't been particularly satisfying, though it hadn't killed him either. Eliza felt a second round – however brief – was worth the risk if it allowed her to regain focus. She hadn't yet thought of a way in which to dispose of Contessa, but she knew an addled mind certainly wouldn't be helpful to the creative process.

So, once the staff had retired for the night and the family had gone on to their respective nocturnal activities – she supposed in this regard Contessa's arrival worked in her favor – Lady Eliza surprised Carleton in his bed and managed to work herself into such a frenzy that she failed to notice until after her climax that Carleton was no more. His erection had been somewhat limp but, for what Eliza needed, she'd found it more than serviceable. It wasn't until she had collapsed on top of him in a post-coital haze that she noticed his breathing – always labored even with his oxygen tank – was now non-existent. She panicked. Yes, even Lady Eliza conceded that she hadn't been at her best that night – too much champagne, too much family drama – and that the stress of her new circumstances (and the need to pull off her coup d'etat to perfection) was getting the better of her.

She tried calling and texting Sister Francine, but her right-hand woman didn't pick up. She even considered calling Francine's sister, Essie, but Eliza disliked Essie even more than most of her new stepchildren and wasn't about to give the woman anything to use against her when the power struggle between them commenced, as Eliza knew it inevitably would. It seemed to her at that moment of direst need that her first priority had to be hiding Carleton's body from staff, family, and even Dr. Raleigh and his nurses until they were all safely on the other side of the Steeplechase. Eliza needed time to strategize with Sister Francine. Every moment had to be perfectly choreographed. She couldn't afford to let anything – however minute – slip out of place. It was bad enough that her night of glory had been super-ceded (high-jacked rather) by an eighteen year-old upstart who looked better-suited for Glastonbury than the hallowed halls of Templeton Manor.

No, Lady Eliza couldn't endure another bombshell on her own, for that was very much how she felt. The harsh reality of her situation was that – with Carleton gone – Eliza had no one on her side. She cursed British Rail for separating her for so long from Sister Francine, the only person Lady Eliza knew whose loyalty to her was unquestionable. If news of Carleton's death broke during the Steeplechase, Eliza feared what fate might hold for her. Her grasp on power was tenuous at best. She needed Sister Francine's iron fist and steel resolve.

So it became of paramount importance that she hide Carleton's corpse from one and all until the following Monday morning (or, in a pinch, Sunday night). Her bedroom suite – with its private staircase and entrance – was her only option. She knew no one would dare venture into her inner sanctum without her invitation. If she could transport Carleton's body from his bedroom, up the staircase and into her suite, and keep him on ice through the weekend until she was ready (with Sister Francine's assistance, of course) to announce his death, she felt more confident of better securing her standing.

There was, of course, the slight issue of keeping Carleton's bedroom off limits in the meantime. She couldn't chance the not inconsiderable risk that someone might notice he was missing. This was something Eliza hadn't considered until after she'd expended her last iota of strength dragging Carleton to her bedroom (she'd underestimated how much even a frail corpse could weigh!) and packing the bathtub with enough ice to preserve him for seventy-two hours or more. But then it dawned on her. She'd move into Carleton's room in the meantime – she had his key in her possession as well – and tell all and sundry that the lord was not to be disturbed under any circumstances. And once Sister Francine arrived – God willing! – she would simply set her up outside the room as a sentry. No one would dare challenge the Fallen Angel, not even the pug-nosed Chloe!

The Friday following her Night of Trial had gone rather well, despite Sister Francine's continued delay. The estate was in such a festive whirl that Lady Eliza's confidence slowly returned. No one, it seemed, gave a thought to Lord Carleton's well-being (or her own, for that matter) that Eliza found she was able to go through the motions of overseeing the set-up and arrival of their guests with an aplomb that surprised even her. She had allowed herself a momentary meltdown in front of Diana and Penelope in regards to the presence of Contessa, whom – it irked her to no end – seemed to have been readily embraced by Chloe, though she supposed that shouldn't have surprised her. Chloe was a spiteful little brat and, with Sister Francine's help, would soon be neutralized. She knew there had been some palaver between Guy and Ambassador Bingham, that none other than the buffoon Spencer Hawksworth seemed to have successfully contained, at least for the moment.

Guy was front and center in her thoughts that day. Of any of the Templetons – real or fake – Guy was the one Lady Eliza had determined must be dealt with first and with expediency. The rest would follow in good time, though she continued to have high hopes for Diana. Her bagpipe-playing husband, Duncan, might have to be removed from the equation, but Diana herself had potential.

Lady Eliza rose from the dressing bureau after putting her morning face on. It was Saturday morning. The Steeplechase was officially set to commence at nine sharp. She had just under three hours to perfect her look for the day – Hunter riding boots, polo shirt and jodhpurs by Joules (not the most high fashion but practical and suitably English) – and tie her wavy shoulder-length white hair back into a sensible ponytail before venturing out of Carleton's suite and downstairs to await Sister Francine's arrival in a taxi from the train station. She needed alone-time with Sister Francine before the Steeplechase kicked off. It felt like ages since she had last seen her bulwark – in that time she'd been both a blushing bride and a not-so-grieving new widow – and now that the Fallen Angel was going to be at Templeton Manor (at long last!), Lady Eliza had no intention of Sister Francine ever leaving her side again.

Even at so early an hour, the entrance hall was abuzz with last minute primps and preparations. The first person she saw was Elena Grimaldi barking orders to her faceless blonde and blue-eyed minions on where to place yet another festoon of tulips. "And remember," the Tulip Queen of Amsterdam cried with an enthusiasm that Eliza found especially cloying, "Never accept anything less than flawless!" Lady Eliza found herself mouthing the catchphrase in unison. She caught a glimpse of Cressida Parker in her periphery, adjusting a particularly blinding set of klieg lights while directing a team of cameramen with her network's slogan "It isn't posh if it's not on Posh TV" emblazoned on their crisp white t-shirts. And there was Bree Armstrong – tall, Black, and blazing in a red-and-yellow dashiki with dangling oversized earrings in the shape of the African continent – and her trumped-up little sidekick Maximilian Porter, dressed head to toe in Hermes: bright orange riding jacket, white shirt, yellow equestrian tie with a silver horseshoe clip, and a pair of the tightest riding trousers Eliza had ever seen. His Warby Parker glasses and architecturally-sculpted brown hair (shaved tight at the back and sides, long and swept back into something approximating a pompadour on top) made him look like an oversized Tin Tin cartoon, which of course she knew was exactly the look he was going for.

Maximilian Porter – "Maxie" to those in the know – was the last person she wanted to encounter that morning, or that weekend for that matter. Unlike Tucker O'Donnell, whom Eliza grudgingly respected for his old school style of journalism (even if it hadn't always been favorable to her), this new breed of social media Twats – or whatever they were called – were anathema to her. And Maximilian Porter, Lady Eliza knew, was the very worst of his kind.

She tried to duck past them on her way through the front entrance, but just as she stepped out onto the steps that led down to the gravel driveway in front of the house, Eliza smelled Maximilian Porter's hair gel and Aqua di Parma 'Colonia' cologne long before he'd caught up to her. His voice – slightly shrill but deeply raspy at the same time – clanged in her ear:

"Lady Brookings! May I have a word, Lady Brookings? It's Maximilian Porter from Posh TV. I'd love a moment if you've time to spare."

Lady Eliza stopped. She arranged her face into a semblance of a smile that she knew looked as insincere as she intended it to before slowly turning around as the intrepid Posh TV journo caught up to her on the last step above the driveway. From this position he was taller than she, which she knew was also intended.

"I know who you are, Maximilian," she said. "And no, I really don't have the time."

Maximilian was all smiles. Eliza hated the way his glasses perched ever-so-precociously on the end of his nose. She also hated his clipped public schoolboy accent that he milked to maximum effect.

"But you'll make the time, won't you, Lady Brookings?" he said. "You know the game."

"That's just it, Maximilian, I *do* know the game. And I'm not playing it."

She might as well have been speaking to a brick wall.

"One question." He paused to give her a dramatic once-over. "Who are you wearing?"

"Save that for the kiddies," Eliza quipped. "I'm not your demographic."

"Oh, but you are!"

He was nothing if not persistent. Lady Eliza wanted to knock the goddamned Warby Parkers off his face. (Glasses should never be worn as accessories.) She shrugged and kept walking. She had told Sister Francine she'd meet her at the gate. She didn't want the Fallen Angel to arrive at the house unaccompanied.

"Is it true?"

"Is what true?"

Lady Eliza felt the hairs rise on the back of her neck. He wouldn't leave her alone. He was going to follow her all the way to the gate and probably pester her until Sister Francine's taxi pulled up and then follow them both all the way back to the house. Classic ambush journalism. Detestable.

"That you married Lord Carleton in a secret Catholic ceremony two days ago? That you smuggled the priest into the house in a delivery lorry? That you didn't tell any of his children about it until after the marriage was consummated? And that you now intend to kick Lord Carleton's heirs out onto the street without a penny and turn Templeton Manor into a refuge for pedophile priests?"

Lady Eliza saw red. She stopped in spite of herself. Maximilian's expression was smug. *Oh, he thinks he's so fucking superior, doesn't he?* She couldn't wait to set Sister Francine on him.

"Gotcha!" he said. "Care to comment?"

Lady Eliza's mind raced. *Who leaked news of her marriage to the press?* Certainly not Diana. Chloe? Doubtful. The youngest legitimate Templeton sibling – the It Girl – relied too much on positive media to promote her image and her blessed foundation. She wouldn't peddle in scandal. Penelope? Contessa? Hmm...

"I'll be sure to invite you to the grand opening," she snarled after a brief moment to gather her verbal ammunition. "Dressed like that, Maximilian, you'll be the most popular belle at the pedophile's ball. I'll be sure to invite the Pope."

He flinched. Lady Eliza allowed herself the smallest flicker of satisfaction.

"Now if you'll excuse me," she said.

Maximilian didn't follow.

Lady Eliza felt she'd dodged a bullet, and while the Posh TV presenter's ultimate angle was inaccurate, the fact that he had known of her wedding so soon after its occurrence when an official statement hadn't yet been released, was troubling. Of anyone in the know, she determined, the most likely suspect was Penelope. These were, after all, Penelope's tribe: Bree Armstrong, Tamsin & Jack, and Maximilian Porter. The wannabe American heiress needed them to sustain her relevance. Lady Eliza knew enough about Penelope's life in London to know that this social media triumvirate had Penelope at their beck and call. She was a slave to the Buzz-feed. And while the others also had their acquaintances in the so-called It Crowd – Diana with Elena Grimaldi; Chloe with Cressida Parker – it was Penelope, as the most desperate striver of them all, who courted this milieu most assiduously.

This, Lady Eliza determined, made her dangerous. The others had nothing to prove. But the American, the former Miss Penny Danziger, needed the spotlight to prove to herself that she belonged, that she indeed was deserving of the Templeton surname and all that came with it. As for Contessa, well, Lady Eliza wasn't about to have the wool pulled over her eyes where that one was concerned. She would get to the bottom of the impostor – for she was convinced Contessa was nothing if not an imposter – in due time. It would help also, she felt, if she could find a way to put a muzzle on "Maxie" before he uncovered anything that was truly damaging.

Sister Francine was already waiting for her outside the gates, dressed in her customarily austere uniform of black sensible shoes, black stockings, shapeless grey knee-length wool skirt, and black turtleneck. Her only adornment: a single gold cross dangling over the rolled neck of the sweater. She carried a battered black leather carryall in one hand and a well-thumbed Bible in the other. Lady Eliza's heart surged at the sight of her. She could hardly contain herself as she fumbled with the latch on the iron gates and pulled them back to let her most trusted companion into what was now officially her new home. The Fallen Angel responded to Lady Eliza's embrace with a rather tepid pat on the shoulder. She looked thinner, Lady Eliza thought, her double chin less pronounced.

"You country people and your posh ways," Sister Francine mumbled as Lady Eliza bid her through the gates. "I always thought Watford was far out until I come here. The cost of train fare alone. Blimey!"

"Didn't you get the money I wired?" Lady Eliza asked. "To pay for your expenses?"

"Essie took most of it. On account of having more work on her hands at the daycare in me absence. She said she needed the extra compensation. The rest I spent at the pub."

Essie. Always something with Essie.

"I thought the doctor told you not to drink in your condition?"

"Doesn't mean I have to listen. When life gives you little but cold comfort, you take that comfort where you can."

"I suppose." Lady Eliza couldn't argue with Sister Francine's logic. Everything the Fallen Angel said made sense to her. It was Gospel. "How's Essie?"

Sister Francine shrugged. "Essie."

"That money was intended for you, to help towards your travel. I shall have a word with her."

"Wasted breath," Sister Francine said.

"At any rate, you're here now." Eliza suppressed the urge to grab Sister Francine's hand and squeeze it out of a need to affirm that Francine was actually there. She knew such a gesture wouldn't go over well. "We have so much to discuss. There's so much to do."

"There's no limit to the Lord's good work," Sister Francine intoned.

"Indeed," said Eliza, for who could argue with that? "I'm afraid you might find the weekend tiresome. It's the Steeplechase, you see, and as much as such wanton conspicuousness pains me, it's a bit of a fixture on the social calendar. Next year will be different, I assure you. But big change requires small measures. We can't bring the foundation down without starting on the roof."

"And the lord? The 'other' lord...not the one with a capital 'L'."

"On ice. About that. I'm going to need your help. I had to improvise. I panicked, you see. He's in the bathtub in my en suite. No one has a key, except me. And now you. I made a copy. The problem is everyone thinks he's resting...in his bedroom...not to be disturbed. If anyone goes into his room they'll notice he's missing and then of course I'll be accused of all sorts of ghastliness. This family is so quick to judge."

"Don't Judge lest ye be judged."

"Exactly. My chambers are separate from the rest of the house, accessible by a private staircase only to those with a key. I figured he'd be safer there, especially if he starts to smell."

"Very sage," Sister Francine said.

"It's not ideal," Lady Eliza continued. The words tumbled forth like a confession. "But I didn't expect him to die quite so soon. I thought he'd at least get through the weekend. He did love the Steeplechase so! And who could have predicted you'd have such a time of getting here? I needed you at my side before I announced his death. They were all rather horrible about the marriage. You should have heard the abuse they hurled at me. The names they called me! They accused me of trickery."

"What did you expect?" Sister Francine asked. "Sinners always cast the first stone. It is within yourself, and the Lord, that you must find strength."

"Oh, Sister Francine, it's so much harder than I imagined!"

"You knew it was never going to be easy."

"And then just now, this little twat of a man – a homosexual, mind you. Maximilian Porter he's called, who works for that cesspit network, Posh TV – tried to catch me off guard by asking me to comment on reports that I intend to turn Templeton Manor into a safe haven for pedophile priests. Can you imagine? He also knew that I'd secretly married Carleton in a Catholic ceremony. I didn't know what to do, Sister Francine. I needed you."

"What did you do?"

"I put him off with a pithy comment about his appearance and hurried to the gates as fast my wobbly knees would carry me."

"We will discuss."

"Yes. Yes. We have so much to discuss, Sister Francine. I hardly know where to begin."

"But tell me," Sister Francine said, "who is that child?"

"Child?"

Lady Eliza blinked and followed the direction of Sister Francine's finger as it pointed ahead of them toward the house. In the distance, amidst the chaos of the Steeplechase preparations, she saw the outline of what was unmistakably a young child – a girl – cartwheeling and frolicking with abandon.

"Do you see?"

"Oh. Perhaps it's one of Penelope and Edgar's brats? Those children wreak havoc wherever they go. Their parents don't know the meaning of discipline."

"No."

Sister Francine stopped. Her eyes took on a faraway cast that Lady Eliza found disconcerting. The child was running toward them. The closer she came, the greater Eliza's realization that she had never seen this child before. It certainly wasn't Rain or Charlotte. Who's brat was it then?

"Well, she certainly seems happy," Eliza said. "Oh, I don't know. The house is full of strangers this weekend. I can't keep track of them all."

The child spotted them and appeared to make a beeline. Sister Francine shook her head but otherwise remained stock-still.

"She's coming towards us," Eliza said. "She's certainly a pretty slip of a thing. Look at those curls!"

The girl – who couldn't have been more than seven or eight – ran up to them and then stopped a few feet away. She was dressed in a peasant blouse that shrugged just off her shoulder and a long flowing skirt embroidered with a floral pattern that brushed the ground around her bare feet. Eliza felt Sister Francine stiffen beside her.

"Hello, little girl," Eliza said. She crouched to eye level. "My, aren't you a pretty thing? I don't think we've met. What's your name?"

The girl laughed and tossed her head back and forth so her mess of perfect brown ringlets flounced and shone in the early morning sunlight.

"What's yours?" the girl asked in reply. She pointed at Eliza and Sister Francine and then covered her mouth with her pudgy little hand and giggled. "You're fat!' she squealed.

"Isn't she extraordinary?" Eliza asked Sister Francine.

"Satan's spawn," Sister Francine intoned.

The girl's smile suddenly vanished, replaced by a deathly pallor that Lady Eliza found more than a little disturbing. She glanced from Sister Francine to the child and back again, wondering if perhaps she had misheard her spiritual advisor's words. The Fallen Angel's eyes were dark, their focus narrow through squinted eyes. Sister Francine fingered the gold cross at her neck and then raised it to her forehead. Her lips moved. She muttered an incantation that Eliza couldn't understand. It didn't sound like English to her – or Latin either, for that matter. Eliza slowly rose up and took a step away from the child, whose cold, deeply forbidding stare remained fixated on Sister Francine's forehead.

"Frannie?" Eliza cleared her throat. She couldn't swallow. "Sister Francine? What is it? Are you having one of your visions? Please, please, tell me what you see! Is it the Apocalypse?"

The ground seemed to shift beneath Lady Eliza's feet. She reached out to steady herself but Sister Francine waved her off. For a brief terrifying moment, she feared the earth would open up and swallow her whole. But then the moment passed. The girl's face lit up. She tossed her bouncy ringlets about her head and let out the most innocent, endearing chortle Lady Eliza thought she had ever heard. It almost convinced her that she liked children.

The girl turned then and ran back toward the house, peasant skirt flying in the breeze, popping cartwheels and handstands as she went. Lady Eliza held her breath. She almost couldn't bring herself to look at Sister Francine whose breathing had become labored and her face pasty with sweat. Lady Eliza wondered whether she had become prone to visions as well. Had she merely imagined what had just happened? Surely, there weren't earthquakes in Dorset? A natural disaster was the last thing she needed.

"Francine?"

Sister Francine blinked. She touched the cross to her forehead, closed her eyes, and inhaled deeply before returning from wherever it was she had gone.

"I've seen that child before," she said. "We must be vigilant."

Lady Eliza felt as though the eyes of the world were upon her, behind every tree an aggressor. Sister Francine motioned for them to continue their walk. The child had disappeared into the horizon.

"The enemy is near," she said. "I feel a presence."

"The child?"

"Forget the child," Sister Francine snapped. "There is a far greater evil in our midst. We must work fast. We must put this house in order. The battle is near."

Lady Eliza knew better than to question the Fallen Angel's judgment.

| 22 |

Guy couldn't have asked for a better view of the festivities than that which greeted him from the verandah off his bedroom. He wasn't one for such gatherings. The pomp and circumstance, the ladies with their over-the-top designer dresses trying to outdo each other with their hats and fascinators, the gents in their double-breasted morning jackets and top hats: it was a goddamned horse race, yet no one seemed to be paying any attention to the race itself – except the stable-hands and jockeys – for very few of the guests would ever dare the unthinkable of climbing onto a saddle or taking a pair of reins in hand for fear of messing up their bespoke Bond and Jermyn Street togs. Bunch of posers, the lot of them!

As for himself, there had been a time when he'd ridden at the front of the pack, reveling in the adrenalin rush, the thrill of the chase, feeling the cold wind blowing hard against his face as he galloped with abandon across the hilly green dales of Templeton Manor: the faster, the muddier, the more dangerous the better. But it had been a few years since he'd had the pleasure. He was out of practice, couldn't even remember the last time he'd sat a horse. Standing there on the verandah with his first whisky of the morning in hand, Guy Templeton felt older than his years and much too weary to bother feeling like he was missing out.

When had it all become such a circus?

The French doors behind him opened. Guy knew without turning that it was Chloe. The lavender scent of her milk bath gave her away. She looked like all the others in her demure but edgy knee-length Alice Temperley frock with its oversized pussy bow and a fascinator that looked as though she had Mount Etna perched on top of her head. Or a bald eagle. Guy couldn't help but smile at the sight of her. If ever there was an It Girl who took the role seriously, it was his little sister: too precious by half. She warmed his ice-cold heart.

"Hiding?" Chloe asked by way of greeting. Guy pretended to ignore the tinge of petulance in her voice.

"Observing from a safe distance," he corrected. "You know I don't like all that puffery."

"Posh TV is here," Chloe said, choosing it seemed to ignore him. "There are cameras and lights everywhere. I'd find it annoying if it weren't for the fact that Cressida is doing us a world of good."

"How so?"

Chloe sighed and pulled her pouty face that Guy had always found endearing and irritating at the same time. Today though the balance was in favor of irritating.

"Now, Guy, I know you don't like Cressida," she began, launching into full-on breathless mode, "and while I don't necessarily approve of what she did to you – there are other, more 'discreet' ways of breaking off an engagement – you can't spend the rest of your life avoiding her! She's my best friend. She's family. And whatever jealousy you may feel toward Olivier, I can assure you, he's never had anything but the kindest things to say about you, despite the fact that you really aren't all that deserving of a kind word from anybody."

"I think I was hiding from you," Guy replied. He sipped his whisky.

"Don't you ever get tired of being mean? Would it really hurt you to smile every once in a while and actually engage in mundane but light-hearted banter with someone other than yourself like everyone else for a change? Why must the weight of the world always weigh on your shoulders? It's boring."

"You're in rare form this morning, Chlo." He helped himself to another pour. "Did Tucker leave his Viagra in London?"

Chloe's face flushed. How easy it was to fluster her, Guy thought.

"If I were the swearing type, I'd tell you to go fuck yourself."

"Go ahead," he replied. "You wouldn't be the first."

"Give me some of that." Chloe snatched the bottle from his hand and tipped it back before Guy could even offer her his glass. She drank long and hard and with an enthusiasm that was a little too exaggerated to be sincere. "You're going to drink yourself into delirium tremens," she said once the burn had subsided. "Maybe I'll join you?"

"You're in a mood," he said. "What's your excuse?"

Chloe took another sip, decided she didn't like the taste, and thrust the bottle back to Guy. "The older I get," she said with a woeful sigh, "the more I realize it's rather difficult being me."

"I hope you're in jest?"

"No! When have you ever known me to be 'in jest' about anything, let alone myself? It's really hard, Guy. I feel like everyone wants a piece of me, but no one wants to give me anything in return. Including you, I'll have you know."

Guy shrugged. As much as he loved his little sister – above and beyond what he felt for any of his other siblings – there were times (like now) where he all he wanted to do was throttle her. Her utter lack of introspection never failed to astonish him.

"You're a saint," he said. "A regular fucking Joan of Arc."

"You should be nicer to me. I'm the only one of us who has ever had your back."

"I can fight my own battles."

"Yes, and look how well that's turned out." Chloe sniffed. "You do know the others are gunning for you, don't you? Eliza hates you. I think she hates you even more than she does me, and that's saying a lot."

"I don't give a shit what Eliza or any of them think. The only one I've ever cared about is you."

"Yes, I know." Chloe motioned at him for the bottle. "Your eternal devotion is something of a burden. It makes the others suspect I'm in collusion with you."

"Are you?"

Chloe rolled her eyes and held the bottle to her lips. She drank and then spat the liquid out with contempt. "I don't know how you and Spencer can stand to drink this stuff. It's vile!"

Guy leaned against the verandah railing and surveyed the pageant before them. "The end of an era this," he said. "Good riddance."

"Now you sound like Eliza."

"Think about it, Chlo," he said. "What good has money ever really brought us? I mean, look at it all. Look at those people: our family and supposed friends. Sure, it's a spectacle, but scratch the surface, and what do you have? What do any of us really have? Are any of us happy? Are you happy?"

"Those people are your people," Chloe snapped. "*Our* people. Without money, without our name, without those people, we'd have nothing. It's rather disingenuous of you to turn your nose up at the very things that make us who we are, what *define* us. What gives you the right to such arrogance?"

"No one defines me," Guy replied. He was done with the conversation. Perhaps, though he wished it otherwise, he was done with Chloe. He'd always hoped she might be different. Clearly, he now realized, he had been mistaken.

"I should have left you to rot in India," Chloe said. "With all those horrible little brown children who don't wear shoes. I would hate to see the state of their feet."

Guy felt himself withdraw. He shielded his eyes from the sun and scanned the gathered crowd below and as far as the eye could see. The race was about start. In lieu of their father, it was Edgar who had stepped into the role of Master of Ceremonies. Dressed like a 19th century dandy in his top hat, crimson velvet riding jacket and khaki riding breeches, at that moment Edgar epitomized everything that Guy despised about his family and their entire social milieu. And Penelope, standing proudly beside her husband on the raised dais at the starting gate in her matching tweeds and out-of-the-box-perfect Hunter boots and riding helmet, was, in Guy's opinion, even worse. He could feel her desperation – her cloying, suffocating need for acceptance – all the way from his position on the verandah, and almost understood why the others – well, Chloe and Diana anyway– held their sister-in-law with such barely concealed contempt. No wonder their children were so insufferable! With Edgar and Penelope as parents, Rain, Walter, Charlotte, and George didn't stand a chance.

He was about to excuse himself in pursuit of a fresh bottle of Jameson when he caught sight of a child – a little girl – running toward the house from the direction of the paddock. She appeared unattached to any of the guests in her immediate vicinity. At first, Guy mistook her for Rain, but as the child grew closer, he realized she looked nothing like his eldest niece. And then it dawned on him. The awful realization. The recognition. The night of Cordelia Bingham's ravaging. Svetlana's after-party. The masked orgy. Images of that night in Moscow consumed him. He was suddenly overcome by a sensation like vertigo. He gripped the railing as the child came to a stop directly below the verandah. Her tousled mess of ringlets stood out from her head like a mini-Medusa. Her cheeks and nose were smudged with dirt, as was the front of her peasant blouse and skirt. She looked right up at him, pointed, and giggled rapturously. Guy thought he was going to be sick.

"Guy?" Chloe was at his elbow. He could hear the alarm in her voice. She gripped his arm so her fingernails dug through his shirt into his flesh. "Guy? Who is that child? Why is she looking at you and...and pointing like that? Guy? Answer me! Who is she?"

"No." Guy shrugged Chloe off and covered his face with his hands. He closed his eyes. The world was spinning out of control. He could hear nothing but the sound of the child's giddy and almost drunken laughter.

"WHO IS SHE? You know her, don't you? You've seen her before!" Chloe turned to the girl and waved her arms manically. "Go away!" she cried. "Go find your mother!"

"No, Chloe!" The world was turning upside-down. Guy reached out to grip the railing but fell on his knees instead. The horrors of that night in Moscow consumed him. "She's not...you can't..."

"For Heaven's sake, Guy! What's going on?"

Chloe clawed at his arm as her hysteria matched his. Her nails ripped through his shirt, drawing blood. He pushed her away. He couldn't bear her proximity, her need to know that which he could barely admit to himself. He heard the child's laughter – a choked kind of giggle that sounded more bird-like than human. He covered his ears with his hands, hoping to silence her, but it was if she was all around and within him. He needed to make her stop. He needed to put an end to the insanity.

Guy noticed then that his sleeve was torn, revealing the tattoo on his bicep.

"That!" Chloe exclaimed. Guy saw Chloe's horror – no, more than horror, it was something more closely akin to revulsion – as she pointed at the unmistakable inked profile of the Black Widow of Sochi on his left bicep. "It's her, isn't it? Svetlana. I didn't want to ... I couldn't believe what they said was true...but you... and her...how could you, Guy? HOW COULD YOU?"

The child was still standing beneath the verandah, looking up at him, her round dirt-smudged face beaming, her ringlets tossing hither and yon. Guy had to stop her. He had to get rid of her before anyone else saw her, or before Chloe could sound the alarm. He vaguely heard Edgar blow the horn to signal the official start of the Steeplechase. He heard the applause and the galloping of hooves as the riders and their mounts took to the course. There was still time.

Guy contemplated jumping over the balcony but the drop was too deep and he didn't want to risk the possibility that Chloe might jump over after him. He stumbled into the house, through the bedroom, and down the hall to the front staircase and the entrance foyer, abuzz with distinguished (and not-so-distinguished) guests. He was vaguely aware of Tucker O'Donnell and Ambassador Bingham standing by the front door knocking back shots and toasting each other's importance, of Cressida Parker directing an entourage of cameramen and their assistants while the Tulip Queen of Amsterdam celebrated her flawlessness in front of the cameras to two of the most ridiculously dressed television presenters Guy vaguely recognized as Bree Armstrong and Maximilian Porter. And there was Spencer leaning against the wall by the front door looking uncharacteristically disheveled. There were others too –faceless faces in a crowd that was both all too familiar and alien to him, mostly by design. He'd been away too long, or maybe not long enough?

He felt Chloe a half-step behind him. He would have been impressed by her tenacity if she weren't so suffocating. She called out his name in such a way that only served to further draw attention to them, which he supposed – knowing Chloe – was exactly her intent. But it was too late now. There was no turning back. He needed to reach the child. He needed to remove her from the premises. He needed to find out where the mother was, for he felt – he instinctively knew – she was close.

But he was too late. When Guy reached the spot where the girl had stood only moments before, she was gone. "No!" he bellowed, looking every which way for a glimpse of her. "It's not possible! She was right here. Right here. Where has she gone?"

Chloe collapsed into him, out of breath but no less determined. "Who is she?" she cried. "Is she yours, Guy?"

Guy turned to Chloe. Her eyes were sodden with tears. The fascinator was still affixed to her head but at such a skewed angle it would have been comical were the situation not so dire.

"Answer me, Guy!' Chloe screamed. "Does that child belong to you?"

Guy opened his mouth to reply, to offer – he didn't know what – a rebuttal perhaps. The fact that the child might be his hadn't been something he'd ever considered, or if he had he'd just locked it away in one of his mind's many compartments. But Svetlana had told him that the father was her husband, the businessman blown up on his boat in St. Tropez. Hadn't she? He couldn't remember. For Chloe to pounce on this, to confront him in this manner, was more than Guy could readily handle. But she had opened the door, and now the question slapped him in the face.

Think, Guy, think. Let's be logical here. You've known Svetlana a matter of months, not years. The child cannot possibly be yours. Biologically it's impossible. So why was he in so much doubt?

"Her name is Feminina," he said. "And yes, she is Svetlana's daughter." It felt strange to say her name, and yet oddly liberating.

"Why is she here, Guy?"

"I don't know."

"Don't tell me you don't know, Guy."

Chloe brushed the tears from her eyes. A crowd had begun to gather, not sizeable but comprised of the very worst of the worst, the ones Guy wanted nowhere near him, or privy to the truth, whatever that truth was (or wasn't). Of course, for Chloe, it was exactly what she wanted: an audience, a kangaroo court of their peers, a spotlight.

"I say, Guy...Chloe," Spencer stepped forward, blinking his bloodshot eyes in exaggerated befuddlement. "What the hell is going on?"

"My question exactly," Chloe declared, her previous hysteria replaced by an equally toxic, earnest hauteur. "Guy's secrets and lies are finally catching up to him. Of course, it shouldn't surprise me. Everyone's been saying for years that he's a scoundrel. But I've always believed – naively and foolishly it seems – in looking only for the good."

"It doesn't concern you, Chloe," Guy said.

"But it does! Everything you do concerns me, Guy. Don't you see? You're my bane."

Guy looked at Chloe and the crowd that had now gathered around them. The child – Feminina – was nowhere to be seen. Spencer took a step forward as though to make some useless offer of assistance, but Guy shook his head and Spencer backed off.

"There's nothing to see here!" Guy said. "Go away, all of you, and take those fucking cameras with you. This is a moment between me and my sister. A private moment."

He saw their hesitation, the weighted and knowing glances that passed between Bree and Maximilian and their entourage. He knew they wouldn't listen. The story – or what they perceived as the story – was just too enticing. Scandal meant blockbuster ratings, especially when it involved a family as storied as the Templetons. Guy understood how their business worked. He didn't agree with it. But he understood. The more he protested, the more determined they became. He couldn't fall into their trap. The longer he stood there, the less his chances of finding the girl Feminina and her mother, for he was certain Svetlana Slutskaya was near. He hoped the girl would lead him to her. He hoped to end this once and for all.

"Privacy is dead." Cressida Parker pushed herself through the gathering crowd to stand between her acolytes, Bree and Maximilian. She took their hands in hers so the three stood together as a united front: defiant and smug. "Isn't that right, Chloe?"

Chloe seemed to shrink into the ground. "I'd like a moment alone with Guy, if you please, Cressida," she mumbled.

"The story takes precedence," Cressida stood firm. "Come on, Guy. Spill the beans. This is your chance to control the narrative before other, less 'reputable,' networks do it for you. We've known each other for years. We have a shared history. We're practically family."

"You're nothing to me, Cressida!" Guy spat. "You lost any claim to me or this family the day you stood me up at the altar."

Cressida flinched. Her grip on Bree and Maximilian's hands tightened. Her bottom lip quivered, but her posture remained resolute.

"I had my reasons," she said, "which should be obvious to anyone who knows anything about you."

"There are things I know about you too." Guy walked slowly toward Cressida. "Things that I'm sure your viewers would be very keen to know."

He stopped in front of her so they stood with barely a space between them. He could smell her scent – lilac mixed with bergamot – and her underlying fear. This was the first time he had been so close to her since the morning before she was to have been his bride. Years had passed, but people never really changed.

"Guy!" Chloe behind him yet a safe distance away. "Please, Cressida, I promise to give you the full scoop later. The exclusive, I swear. Before *Hello!* Before *OK!* Before *Tatler*. I'll even make you an honorary chairwoman at S.A.S.S."

"This isn't about us, Chloe," Cressida said. "It appears your brother and I have some unfinished business. I've always been one to let bygones be bygones, but Guy it seems can't get over a grudge."

"A grudge?" Guy emitted a scathing laugh. "Is that what you call it?"

Cressida shrugged. Her stare wavered. She looked from Bree to Maximilian and pulled them both closer to her, as though forming a protective shield.

"You're a bully, Guy," she said. "I didn't see it then until it was almost too late. Thank God I got out when I did. I've moved on. I married the man of my dreams. I've got more money than I know what do with. A fabulous career, power, fame. I've broken through the glass ceiling and then some. I love my life. But I'm afraid the intervening years haven't been as kind to you. In fact, all I see when I look at you now, Guy, is an emasculated shell in desperate search of his trajectory."

"Olivier is a fool!"

Cressida gave Guy a pitying smile. "Oliver's more of a man than you ever were, Guy, or ever could be."

The words stung but the overall effect was less than what was surely intended. He looked beyond Cressida. His eyes squinted against the sun. And suddenly, there she was again: the girl called Feminina. She had camouflaged herself within a group of other children that included Rain and Walter, playing what looked to be a game of tag over by the fences near the stables. From this distance, there was nothing to distinguish her from any other seemingly innocent eight year-old girl. He could hear her merry laughter, see her ringlets toss with gay abandon as she ran about with his niece and nephew in their innocent child's play. But Guy knew Feminina was like no other child. Her very presence portended destruction no one could imagine, let alone foresee. He needed to stop her. He needed her to bring him to her mother. Nothing else mattered.

"She's there!" he cried with something like triumph. "I knew she was here somewhere. I knew it!"

"Where, Guy?" Chloe was back at his side, trying desperately to follow his wild gesticulations. Of course, he knew it behooved him to stay calm. It was better for all of them – the family – if he approached the child rationally and not attract too much attention, but with Cressida and her salivating posse standing right there, mobile phones and television cameras poised, it was already too late.

"You want a show?" He opened his arms wide as though to embrace Cressida, but opting instead for a theatrical bow of Shakespearian proportions. "I'll give you your fucking show."

"Guy, old chap, I think you've really stuck your foot in it this time." Spencer teetered on one foot and then the other. "I don't think I can help you, as much as it pains me to say it."

"Have you gone stark raving mad?" Cressida asked. All eyes turned and gaped as Guy tripped and stumbled past them. Her words sounded of horror, but her eyes lit up and her face beamed. Collectively they watched as Guy ran headlong toward the stables where Feminina hopped and skipped with Rain and Walter. "Follow that man!" Cressida barked at the cameramen. "I want it all on tape. And you, Maxie: get over there and show me what you're made of. Shake that moneymaker. Prove to me you're worthy of Hermes."

"Yes, Mum!" Maximilian Porter nearly tripped on himself in pursuit of his story.

"What about ME?" Bree shrieked. "Why do you ALWAYS give Maxie ALL the breaks? You can't be the ONLY WOMAN in this industry to break GLASS CEILINGS. What happened to GIRL POWER?"

Cressida drew Bree close, her lips pressed to her ear. "For every glass ceiling a woman breaks," she rasped, "there's always another bitch behind her waiting to cut her throat. I'm not going to let you be that bitch."

| 23 |

Chloe struggled to catch up to Guy in his mad dash across the grounds to the stables. Perhaps it was time she got back in touch with Adolfo, her posh London trainer with the lustrous long hair, thick beard, sexy pecs and delicious Italian accent? She had never been much for foreign men, but Adolfo had given a whole new meaning to the "personal" part of personal trainer. Or at least he'd done so in her imagination. In addition to being the sexiest man Chloe had ever seen, he was also among the gayest – inclusive even of Maximilian – though he claimed he and his Moroccan boyfriend, Tangier, were ambisexual polyamorists. (Whatever that meant!)

Regardless of the figure she presented for the glossies and the red carpet, Chloe found herself out of breath and unable to keep pace with her older brother, who despite his rather broken appearance, had always been the epitome of peak physical conditioning. She begrudged him this. It made her feel inferior, and if there was one thing Chloe Templeton hated almost more than anything in the world, it was feeling inferior to anyone...especially to a man. And while she hadn't appreciated Cressida Parker hijacking what she felt was rightly her moment, she couldn't help but admire the television executive's brass balls tactics and 'fuck you' confidence. Cressida was an inspiration even as, Chloe felt, her best friend needed a better sense of timing.

She reached the stables just as she felt on the verge of collapse. What right did Guy have to ruin what should have been a perfectly beautiful weekend with close friends and even closer admirers? It was bad enough that she'd had to endure all that unfortunate and – more to the point – inconvenient business with Rebecca Hastings who, it seemed, had yet to make an appearance that morning. Chloe thought of Xander – what he had said to her yesterday and what she had texted him late last night once she was safely ensconced (alone) in her four-poster bed – and wondered whether what she thought he had alluded to had actually been done. Come to think of it, she hadn't seen him skulking around the grounds yet that morning either. The notion of him made her shiver.

Chloe caught up to Guy just as he appeared in the midst of confronting the child. He was careful not to physically apprehend her, maintaining a safe distance lest he be provoked into anything untoward. The child – how Chloe loathed her! – seemed as intent as ever on being a cipher. She giggled and laughed and pointed and ran circles around him while Rain and Walter – equally loathsome – followed her lead. Oh, and look! There were the twins, Charlotte and George, toddling over to get in on the game. Where the hell were their parents? Chloe wondered. She caught a glimpse of Penelope then, preening and falling over herself in front of Cressida's husband, the entrepreneur and Formula One team owner, Olivier Thibault. Penelope cared more about securing her status than controlling her children. In Chloe's eyes, her American sister-in-law was every bit as much a carpetbagger as her new stepmother.

"Chloe, darling, you're looking a little worse for wear." Maximilian Porter jogged up beside her, looking like a fluorescent traffic pylon in his orange Hermes riding jacket. "Adolfo asked me about you just the other day when I told him I'd be seeing you here at the weekend."

Of course, Maximilian Porter would know Adolfo!

"He said he'd seen you in that *Vanity Fair* spread and thought you looked like a little chunky monkey," Maximilian continued. "He even asked me – and don't you DARE tell him I told you this! -- whether you'd been hitting the Ben & Jerry's harder than the yoga mat."

She'd have to find another personal trainer.

Maximilian's presence made the situation all the more fraught – not to mention the cameras and the klieg lights – but this was the reality within which she lived, and frankly she needed Maximilian Porter and his type as much as they needed her. Best to present herself as the aggrieved little sister – which wasn't stretching the truth – and give them a story that portrayed her as not just a crusading philanthropist but a real and relatable human being as well.

"Guy, this really has got to stop!" she said after pausing for another handful of seconds to catch her breath and regain a semblance of composure. The cameras were on, after all. "This is nonsense."

The girl was careening through a series of cartwheels which Rain was trying – unsuccessfully – to replicate. Chloe reached out and grabbed the child's arm mid-twirl. "Excuse me, little girl, but I need you to tell me whom you belong to."

Feminina hopped from one leg to another like an over-wound toy bunny, her gaze focused solely on Guy. Chloe found the vacant look in the girl's eyes unnerving.

"Listen here, you," Chloe said. "You look at your elders when they address you. Haven't you been taught any manners?"

"Let her go, Chloe," Guy said. His tone was uncompromising.

Chloe hesitated. The girl fidgeted beside her.

"We were playing," Rain whined. "Let her go, Auntie Chloe."

"We were playing," Walter chimed in.

"Let her go! Let her go! Let her go!" Rain, Walter, George, and Charlotte jumped up and down, chanting in unison. Their high-pitched voices were like nails on chalkboard.

"You're such a meanie," Rain said. "Auntie Chloe's a meanie. I'm going to tell Mummy on you."

"Please, Chloe." Guy again. "No good can from this. Let me deal with it."

Chloe felt the floodgates on the verge of bursting again. She bit hard on the inside of her cheek and swallowed back the tears as best she could.

"It's hers, isn't it?" she said, pointing to the tattoo on Guy's arm. "The Russian."

"The child is Svetlana's, yes," Guy acceded.

"Are you the...? I can hardly bring myself to ask it."

Guy held a finger to his lips. "Shhh," he said. His tone soothed Chloe in spite of herself.

"Is she here?"

"I don't know."

"Did you invite her?"

"No, Chloe, I didn't invite her."

"Really, Guy, after all I've done for you."

"Mistakes were made." He turned to Feminina. "Run along now. Tell your mother that I want no trouble with her. Tell her what's in the past is best left in the past."

The girl cocked her head to one side and peered up at him with an appraising look that seemed years beyond her age. "Papa?" she said and then, without another word, turned on her heel and scampered off in the direction of the woods.

The dam burst. "Papa?" Chloe cried.

"Chloe..."

"Don't touch me! I'm done. What everyone says about you is true. I can't do this anymore, Guy. I'm not going to defend you any longer. You're on your own. I'm finished. Done!"

And Chloe truly believed that she was. Guy's very presence – his existence even – had become a greater burden than she felt she could bear. His behavior was nothing short of a betrayal. It was one thing to engage in risky activity with characters of questionable intent on one's own time at a distance of thousands of miles away, and quite another to bring that shady activity onto one's home turf where other lives were affected and other reputations were at stake. But then, Guy had a history of only thinking of himself. He'd always been selfish. Even as a child, Chloe remembered, he preferred to strike his own course rather than defer to the norms to which his siblings were held accountable. She supposed a certain level of independence was one of the advantages of being Papa's favorite, for Papa had always had a double standard where Guy was concerned. Chloe had never really stopped to consider it until now. As the youngest, she'd been allowed a certain space to develop as she pleased – not overlooked exactly, but never the center of her parents' attention either. For Diana and Edgar, on the other hand, the experience had been different. Chloe had never really understood their resentment. She'd thought them petty, smug, the epitome of all that she hated about the class into which she had been born. And the fact that Guy had always been so kind to her gave Chloe a different perspective: sheltered her in a way.

Clearly, Chloe now thought as she ran blindly across the grounds, unsure and uncaring of where she was headed or even of how she looked, Guy had pulled the wool over her eyes. He was a traitor and he'd bring them all to ruin unless someone intervened. She'd prefer that person not to be her, but she didn't trust Diana or Edgar to do the job. If not her, then who? Such was the sorry state of affairs at

Templeton Manor. Such was the challenge of being Chloe Templeton.

"Oh my God, Chloe, is there a fire? Do we need to raise the alarm? Did one of the riders fall off their horse? Has Carleton died? Has there been a terrorist attack? God forbid, but you never know these days, do you?"

Chloe was in such a state that she failed to notice she had run straight into Penelope...literally. It was as though she and her sister-in-law were on a collision course in hell.

"Penelope!" Chloe gasped.

"Chloe?"

She didn't know why, but Chloe couldn't restrain herself. The burden was too severe. She fell into Penelope's unsuspecting arms and clung to her as though for dear life, choking on her injured sense of propriety, the egregious feeling of being wronged, the sensation that her righteousness was under attack...

"I can't do this anymore!" Chloe cried.

"Yes, darling? Oh my God, you poor baby." Penelope crushed Chloe to her bosom so hard Chloe couldn't breathe. "You poor, poor baby. You're positively traumatized."

"Yes, that's it! I am. I am traumatized."

"What happened?" Penelope kissed Chloe's forehead and adjusted her fascinator to a more acceptable angle. "Who did this to you?"

"Him!" Chloe bit down hard on her bottom lip until it bled. She reminded herself whom she was talking to. Penelope might give the impression of being sympathetic, but Chloe knew to be wary around her sister-in-law. The American was not to be trusted.

"Who, darling? You need to be more specific."

It pained Chloe to say his name: "Guy."

"Oh." Penelope stepped back and released Chloe from her grip. She cleared her throat and fussed with her hair, straightened the front of her costume.

"He's a rogue. I see that now. He has to be stopped, Penelope. He can't go on like this! He'll ruin us."

"Well, I don't want to be the one to say 'I told you so'..."

"What do we do, Penelope?"

Penelope thought for a moment. "I don't think there's anything you or I can do on our own," she said after some deliberation. "We're strong but your brother is rather a brute. He might overpower us."

"Yes! He pushed me, Penelope. He literally pushed me and I fell over and thank God I know how to fall."

"He pushed you? Oh my God, Chloe darling, are you hurt?"

"No, just very troubled."

"Why would he do a thing like that? And to you most especially!"

"I know." Chloe found Penelope's presence calming and begrudged her for it. She wiped away what remained of her tears and smoothed out the creases down the front of her mud-spattered frock. She'd have to change before she attracted too much unwanted attention – especially with Maximilian and Bree skulking about the premises. "It's the drink. Guy's always had his demons, but I'd thought... oh, Penelope, I don't know what I thought! I don't know what I think anymore! I don't know him. I don't think I even know myself."

"Oh, you poor, poor dear." Penelope made a dramatic show of flourishing a Chanel handkerchief and dabbing Chloe's nose with it. Chloe dutifully blew as she knew it made her sister-in-law feel somehow a part of the family, but she also knew that behind Penelope's concern there were ulterior motives, and it was for this reason that Chloe's better judgment demanded she maintain a certain reserve, yet at the same time, she couldn't help but wonder if Penelope might indeed be the ally – at least where Guy was concerned – that she needed?

"You have to be strong, darling Chloe," Penelope said. "And you *are* strong. I've never told you this, but I've always looked up to you."

"To *me*?" Chloe forced herself not to laugh.

"If I'd been born under a different set of circumstances, I'd want to be you."

Chloe allowed herself a modest grin. Flattery always worked wonders even when its provenance was dubious at best.

"Well, I don't know what to say!"

"I so want for us to be sisters," Penelope continued. She took Chloe's hands in hers and raised them to her lips. "I feel there's so much I can learn from you. Diana is different. She's cold. I know she only tolerates me – and barely at that – but you, on the other hand. I've always felt a certain kinship with you. From the moment I married into this family, Chloe, I knew you were special. I sensed right away that you have a caring soul."

"I do," Chloe acquiesced. She gently attempted to prize her hands free but Penelope seemed determined to keep her close. It was becoming annoying, but Chloe felt she had no other choice than to play along. "That's my problem, Penelope. I care too much."

"Let me help you," Penelope whispered. "Let us help each other."

"I think he's fathered a child." Chloe didn't know which startled her more: the fact of her suspicion or the fact that she was giving voice to it to Penelope.

Penelope's eyes widened. She leaned so close Chloe worried her sister-in-law might try to kiss her. She'd had enough of that with RH!

"Who?" Penelope asked.

"Guy, of course." Chloe shook her head. "May I have my hands back, please?"

"Oh, yes, of course!"

Penelope released her grip and Chloe stepped back to a distance more comfortably within her comfort zone.

"Based on what evidence?" Penelope persisted.

Chloe hesitated. In a way, she supposed it would be easier to relate her morning's misadventures in full because sooner or later she knew she would have to in order to maintain a certain level of credibility. Yet, because she hadn't been able to engage in a rational conversation with Guy about the child – rather improbably named Feminina – or how the child had come into existence in the first place – beyond the obvious biological processes, of course – it didn't feel right to bring Penelope so completely into the fold until she was on more solid factual footing. By disclosing too much too soon, what would differentiate her from the likes of Maximilian Porter or Bree Armstrong or Penelope, for that matter? With what little she had already shared, Chloe sensed she had her sister-in-law eating out of the palm of her hand. Perhaps it was best to test the waters first and see how far Penelope would go on her behalf before diving in headfirst?

"I have my suspicions," she said.

Penelope wagged her finger. "You know more than you're telling me. But I trust you. Sisters have to trust each other."

"Yes, they do," Chloe replied. "Now what are we going to do about Guy?"

"I think," Penelope pursed her lips and considered the situation. "I think an intervention is needed."

"Oh dear, that sounds a bit drastic, don't you think? Very American."

"But very effective, if it's handled the right way. Guy must never suspect."

"Of course not."

"Leave it to me."

"Really?" Chloe asked. She suddenly felt very uncomfortable.

"It's best he not know of your involvement."

"But I am involved."

"If you're going to dispute me, Chloe, this isn't going to work." Penelope's tone hardened. Chloe took another step back. "I need to know that you trust me."

"Implicitly."

Penelope emitted a sarcastic laugh. "Liar, liar, pants on fire," she said.

Chloe felt reprimanded. "I trust you." She was doing an awful lot of trusting these days.

"I think I'm really going to enjoy this," Penelope said. "Finally I'm going to be able to prove to all you Templetons that my loyalty is not only genuine, but blood deep. And I have you to thank for that, my dear, darling little sister-in-law. Thank you." She went for Chloe's hands again. "Thank you, Chloe, from the bottom of my heart."

"It remains to be seen, of course," Chloe replied.

Penelope's aggressive eagerness to please unnerved her, as did the rather dead vacancy in her sister-in-law's eyes. She'd heard the rumors, of course, about Penelope's drug use, heretofore never giving it much thought. But now she started to wonder whether Penelope might not be – for lack of a better phrase – a junkie. She was beginning to have serious doubts about the wisdom of bringing the woman into her confidence. It was too late to retract what she'd said. Chloe just hoped she wouldn't regret it.

"To be sure."

"I'll leave you to it then." Chloe pulled her hands free for the second time. "I just need to go freshen up. All this excitement, I'm feeling a little bedraggled. With all these media types around, you never know when one might call on you for a sound-bite."

Penelope's smile was pinched. The time for pleasantries had passed. "Yes, yes, of course," she said. "The cameras just love you so. England's favorite little 'It Girl'."

A sudden chill ran up Chloe's spine. Without another word, she turned and hurried toward the house, hoping Maximilian and his squad would leave her be until she'd changed into something that didn't look like she'd been dragged through a hedge backwards in it, which was exactly how Chloe felt. There were times – like these – where Chloe longed for an approximation of anonymity – not the real thing (of course), for what good did anonymity do anyone in the long run? – but space enough, breathing room, to adjust and contemplate and consider the very real responsibilities inherent to a woman of her stature. She often wondered whether her Instagram followers would envy her so much if they knew the difficulties she faced. If only she could filter her life like a photograph, Chloe thought with a wistful sigh. How much prettier and more palatable everything would be!

| 24 |

As Penelope watched her youngest sister-in-law (Tessa notwithstanding) disappear amid the effervescent hullabaloo of the Steeplechase revelers, she allowed herself a little pat on the back for playing Chloe so flawlessly. The woman really was rather stupid, she decided: too narcissistic to have any sense of how she presented herself to the outside world. It certainly had its advantages, Penelope thought, and gave her what couldn't have been a better opportunity to (finally!) establish herself within the family hierarchy. Diana ruled the roost, of that there was no question. Fair enough. Diana was the oldest, after all. And even though Penelope found Diana tiresome and rather myopically superior, she respected the woman's position and all that she had had to endure, both as Lord Carleton Templeton's first-born daughter and (perhaps most especially) Duncan's wife.

For the first several years of her marriage, Penelope had longed for a sisterly bond with Diana. The rarefied airs and graces that marked the Templeton legacy hadn't come naturally to the corn-fed Midwestern-born Penny Danziger, who had thought the very height of sophistication was doing Jell-o shots on a Saturday night with Ruthie and Yolanda at Excalibur in Chicago, when Cedar Rapids proved too provincial. Meeting Edgar, of course, had changed all that. And while the young and thoroughly British scion claimed to find Penny's 'down-to-earth' Midwestern charm 'a refreshing change of pace,' she suspected it had more to do with the fact that she had him bound and gagged on all fours when he said this – while being spanked with a studded Sorority paddle – than out of any genuine affection he might have had for her so-called Midwestern virtues. And for Penelope, Edgar (Lord Templeton) was her bus ticket out of Nowheresville, U.S.A. She fancied herself a real-life Cinderella success story, though – as she had soon found out – the reality was much harsher and more nuanced than any fairy tale could ever have been.

When Diana proved more preoccupied with preserving her own position within the family pecking order than giving the new girl a hand, Penelope had had to look elsewhere. Lady Fiona had been lovely but too reserved to ever make the American feel truly welcome. Guy was never around and, truth be told, Penelope feared she might not be able to trust herself alone in his company. He was just one of those men whose slightest look could feel like rape. As for Chloe, Penelope had taken an instant dislike to the Templeton's "gal about town." Too delicate, too precious, and too precocious by half.

Of course, it wasn't lost on Penelope that the dislike was mutual. The first thing Chloe had ever said to her, that Christmas at Templeton Manor the year before she and Edgar were married, was: "So, were your people liberated from Dachau or Auschwitz?" When Penelope hadn't been able to answer, Chloe had continued with: "You know, my grandfather was a great friend of Oswald Mosley. In fact, my sister Diana is named for Mosley's second wife, Diana Mitford."

"No, I didn't know that," Penelope had replied. On the flight over, to his credit, Edgar had tried to warn her that his family held onto certain consciously unconscious biases that were not atypical of the British gentry. He hadn't specified what exactly those biases were, but Penelope was nothing if not perceptive. She thought she'd be prepared, but Chloe had left her gob-smacked. So for all of Chloe's philanthropic aspirations, charitable red carpet appearances, and special ambassadorial speeches before the United Nations on the plight of child sex slaves and sweatshop workers, Penelope knew from their very first meeting that it was all an act. Chloe Templeton – humanitarian "It Girl" extraordinaire – was little more than an anti-Semitic hypocrite. And Chloe knew Penelope knew this too, which made Penelope all that more of a threat. Penelope had always known she'd get her comeuppance. It was only a question of when.

But how to set the proverbial ball in motion?

Then it struck her: Lady Eliza, of course! She had to get an audience with the new Templeton matriarch, the sooner the better. Chloe had given Penelope just enough to goad Eliza into action. The supposition that Guy had secretly fathered a child, who then just happened to turn up at the Steeplechase, surely was proof that Guy's place within the family was untenable. This coming so soon on the heels of The Bingham Affair, well, it was obvious to Penelope that Guy's only motive was to bring the greatest of shame to his family. His antics had been tolerated for too long. It was time to get serious. It was time for consequences.

"Hey you, got any of that stuff? And don't pretend you don't know what I'm talking about."

Penelope was so caught up in her daylight fantasies that she failed to notice the appearance of Tessa who was now standing in front of her, dressed in her denim cut-off shorts and a slashed and sleeveless oversized t-shirt emblazoned with the words "Bad Ass Bitch" on the front and "Fuck the Patriarchy!" on the back. A daisy chain encircled her head and knee-high tasseled leather boots adorned her feet, completing the rebel look.

"What on earth?" Penelope spluttered. "Go put some clothes on! This is Steeplechase Weekend not Glastonbury!"

"Oh, really?" Tessa rolled her eyes. "I hadn't fucking noticed."

"What do you want?"

"I'm bored."

"Then do us all a favor and skank back to whatever Soho dive you crawled out of. You're not wanted here."

"I could say the same of you," Tessa said. "The way I see it, you really should be showing me some love and not throwing so much shade."

"I have no idea what you're talking about."

"Please, spare me the fake fucking accent!" Tessa leaned in close and beckoned for Penelope to do the same. Penelope acquiesced as she lacked the wherewithal to do anything else. "Let me remind you. That problem you told me about yesterday?"

Penelope blinked. How long ago yesterday seemed! "Yes?"

"I don't think it's going to be a problem any more."

"How do you know?"

Tessa smiled. "Let's just say, I have a sneaky suspicion."

"What did you do to her?" Penelope gulped. Rebecca Hastings had been the last thing on her mind. "Did you?"

"Give me some Spice."

"I don't know what that is. How can I give you something if I don't know what it is?"

"You're the family's resident junkie," Tessa said. "It's like the biggest open secret here. I'm surprised Chloe doesn't run an intervention."

"Leave Chloe out of this!"

Tessa held her hand out, palm up. "Give me some Spice," she said.

"Or what?"

"Or I'll tell that orange-suited twat that you hired me to 'neutralize' the woman who was fucking your husband."

"Maxie?" Penelope could barely draw breath. "He adores me. He would never believe you, never in a million years."

"You'd be surprised."

Penelope tugged at the high-necked collar of her blouse. How had her moment of triumph turned into such a nightmare? She had lost control of the situation. She could feel it slipping through her fingers. She needed to get it back.

She needed to put this imposter back in her place. But how? After all, she couldn't deny – well, she could, but in the end, what purpose would it serve? – that a certain conversation had taken place about a certain woman who posed a certain threat to a certain other woman's marriage. Thank God, there hadn't been witnesses to her and Tessa's exchange of the day before, but this was Templeton Manor after all, where the walls were known to have ears. Penelope thought she was going to be sick. She needed a Spice Bomb.

"Okay," Penelope said. "You win. I'll give you what you want."

"It's no less than I deserve."

"On one condition."

An idea came to her then. Penelope exhaled her relief. The deeper she delved into these machinations, the more they seemed to spiral and weave in and on themselves.

"Blackmail?"

"Survival."

"What?"

Penelope beckoned Tessa close. She whispered in the girl's ear: "I'll bring you in on the Spice trade," she said, "if you'll do one more thing for me."

"I'm listening."

"I'm about to stage something of a coup."

"Talk to me."

"I need your help." Penelope wasn't sure how much to divulge. The idea was still very much in the germination stage. She needed to talk to Eliza, needed the matriarch's support and blessing, but the more she thought about it, the more she realized Tessa could prove a worthy soldier to the cause. "I need you to shadow Guy for me."

Tessa's eyebrows twitched. "Keep talking," she said.

"Let's just say," Penelope began, "that information has come to light that puts my brother-in-law in a certain position."

"'Position?'" Tessa asked. "What kind of position?"

"Compromising."

"The best position there is."

"We speak the same language," Penelope said. "But that doesn't mean I accept you. Not yet anyway. Consider this a test: of your loyalty to me, of your loyalty to this family. If you pass with flying colors, I may be convinced to keep an open mind. Or you may decide that we're not for you. In which case, no harm no foul."

"There's no chance of that," Tessa said. "I've been wanting my cut for years. I'm here now. Ain't no one gonna stop me."

Penelope had to admit – albeit grudgingly – that she admired the girl's spunk. Tessa reminded her in some ways of herself, or rather of herself as she wished she had been, or wished she could be. But she couldn't let Tessa see that she was being won over quite so easily, nor that she felt in desperate need of an ally. She wanted to tell the girl that being a Templeton wasn't all that the magazines and broadsheets would lead one to believe. It was damn hard work for so little reward. Not that Penelope would have traded it for anything, though she did wonder if things had turned out differently, if she'd never met Edgar in that sex club in Cedar Rapids, and had contented herself with wearing the Miss Bachelorette of Cedar Rapids sash and tiara with greater pride than she'd done, whether she might have been – if not happier – than perhaps more content settling down with a nice Jewish banker in Winnetka or Highland Park, shuttling the kids back and forth between their Montessori school and soccer practice, dance lessons, piano recitals, and Shabbat services at the local synagogue on Fridays. But that would have meant she'd forever be known as Penny Danziger, an identity Lady Penelope Templeton never wanted to be reminded of again.

No. Penelope refused to allow herself to go down that road. It was too demoralizing. She had to focus on the task at hand. She was on the ascent. She'd worked too hard to get where she was and she wasn't about to chuck it all in for some rose-tinted suburban fantasy of what might have been but wasn't. If Edgar preferred some Sloane cunt to the love and devotion Penelope had showered on him for years, well, that was his problem. Penelope had to rise above. She needed to keep her eyes on the prize. She needed to prove to the new Queen Bee– Lady Eliza: an outsider, like herself – that she was worth every penny of her name. And then, one by one, watch the dominos fall. Guy first, then Diana...Chloe...Edgar. Oh, the devastation! She almost shivered from the pleasure of it. Or perhaps she just needed a fix?

"So I shadow Guy," Tessa said. "Then what?"

"You report back to me."

"But what am I supposed to be reporting back to you about?"

Tessa's questions annoyed Penelope. She felt like she was being challenged.

"You strike me as a resourceful girl," Penelope replied. "I leave it to you."

Tessa's eyebrows twitched. "And how far can I go?" she asked.

"Go where?"

Tessa rolled her eyes and posed with her hands on her denim-clad hips in a stance that Penelope supposed was meant to be defiant but only came across as mannered and Generation-Zeddishly precocious.

"What if I find myself in some compromising positions of my own?" Tessa said. "Is that allowed?"

"Darling, in this game, there are no limits." Penelope wondered if perhaps she was falling a little bit in love with this girl. "Everything is allowed. All that counts is winning."

They were simpatico. She nodded and Tessa responded in kind. They were a team.

"Fab," Tessa said.

"Now run along. We've stood here too long. People might suspect we're conspiring or something."

"When do I get the Spice?"

"When you give me something I can use."

"You drive a hard bargain."

"A girl has to look out for herself," Penelope said. "I know it and I think you know it too. Now go. We've no time to waste."

Having thus dispatched Tessa, Penelope hurried into the house, hoping that no one had seen her *tete-a-tete* with Contessa, or hadn't paid it too much heed. Regardless of whatever information the girl provided, it would all prove useless if Lady Eliza wasn't firmly on their team. Penelope didn't as yet have a feel for the new Templeton matriarch. A part of her admired the woman, for it seemed to her that Eliza was the ultimate female success story, yet Penelope also knew that Eliza didn't suffer fools – which was probably why she had risen so prominently in the Templeton hierarchy – and Penelope still wasn't entirely convinced that she herself wasn't one of those fools.

She feared that Eliza didn't particularly like her, or rather that the woman disregarded her altogether. It irked her to no end that Diana seemed to have found a way into Eliza's confidence. Of course, everyone knew that the real gatekeeper was Sister Francine, as formidable an opponent if ever there was one. Sister Francine made Penelope quake. And while Penelope had hope that Eliza might eventually be won over, she didn't have the same expectation of the ex-nun.

In her darkest – most desperate – musings, Penelope tried to conjure schemes that might cast dirt on Eliza's right-hand woman. The problem though was that Sister Francine's past was well documented, at least as far as Penelope could tell.

All one had to do was a simple Google search to learn the sordid, dramatic details of the nun's fall. And how far she had fallen! What was most puzzling to Penelope – and downright disturbing if one paused long enough to think on it – was why Eliza would choose to align herself with someone whose background was not only rather distasteful, but (perhaps more to the point) criminal as well. It led one to wonder whether Sister Francine had something on Eliza that kept the Templeton's newest matriarch on her leash. There was certainly more to that story than any of them knew, but one thing at a time. Penelope needed Eliza too much to allow gossip and speculation to get in the way of unseating Diana from her perch on Eliza's other side. By the time Penelope was finished, if she had her druthers, Sister Francine wouldn't be the only one to have fallen. Penelope just needed to make sure her own position was secure and that she didn't end up among the victims on the cutting room floor.

The door that opened onto the private staircase leading to Eliza's tower suite was locked as per usual. Penelope chided herself for not going immediately to Carleton's chambers for surely, given that the poor man was on his literal deathbed, at his bedside was where Eliza should have been. It jarred her to find none other than Sister Francine sitting guard in front of the chambers' entrance, arms folded across her chest, double chin set, gold cross gleaming. Penelope's breath caught in her throat as she rounded the corner of the corridor and saw the fallen nun looking as mean and formidable as ever. It was most dismaying. Penelope rather wished she'd thought to go to her own rooms for a hit of Spice before venturing further. But it was too late. Time was wasting. She needed to speak to Eliza before anyone beat her to the punch.

"Sister," Penelope said as she approached Francine at what she hoped was a calm and conversational pace, "what a nice surprise! I didn't know we were expecting you."

Sister Francine's focus was forward. Her presence was stalwart and uncompromising. "I came down on the train from Watford this morning," she grunted. "There's industrial action or I would've been down sooner."

"Do you like horses then?" Penelope cringed, the question was so lame but she couldn't think of anything more appropriate. The cross at Sister Francine's neck made Penelope feel very much like Penny Danziger.

Sister Francine shrugged. "Never given 'em much thought," she said.

"I only asked because well, you know it is Steeplechase Weekend, and...well, if you don't like horses, then that rather defeats the whole purpose of being here, doesn't it? No disrespect intended, of course."

"None taken."

"You wouldn't happen to know where Eliza is, would you?" Penelope cleared her throat. She felt like she was at an audience before the Pope where only he spoke Latin or Italian (or whatever language it was that popes were supposed to speak) and she was stuck trying to communicate with him in pidgin English. "You see, it's most important – tantamount actually – that I speak to her."

"Hmh," Sister Francine said.

"Is she in there?" Penelope pointed at the door to Lord Carleton's rooms. "How's Lordy doing anyway? Have you seen him? I thought he looked rather peaked at dinner the other night, but then, he is dying, isn't he?"

"He died for our sins and on the third day he rose again in fulfillment of the Scriptures," Sister Francine intoned.

"Oh dear," Penelope gasped. "I meant, the other Lord. Carleton. Not *The* Lord. Your Lord. Whatever."

Sister Francine sighed and fiddled with the cross at her neck. "Lady Eliza is in a meeting," she said.

"Oh…any idea with whom?"

"A certain gentleman. Name of Hamish."

"Hamish?" Penelope frantically wracked her brains trying to place the name. It was on the tip of her tongue and yet utterly elusive. "You don't happen to know his surname, do you?"

"I didn't ask. I'm not me mistress's keeper."

"But you are, rather, aren't you? I mean, that is rather disingenuous of you to say that, don't you think? We all know Lady Eliza places great faith in your… spiritual guidance…"

"'Tis true. The Lord is my keeper," Sister Francine said. Penelope found it particularly disconcerting that the ex-nun never once looked at her, not even in her general direction. It was almost as though Sister Francine was blind. "My spiritual abilities are of no consequence to you."

Penelope sensed the hate. She stepped back and wished again for the umpteenth time since the conversation had begun that she'd possessed the forethought to hit the Spice before endeavoring upon this interview. It killed her that little Penny Danziger and all her insecurities were never very far away. All it took was one slight, one inference, and decades of self-help and recovery were flushed down the loo, just like that.

"I seem to be inconveniencing you," she stammered. "I just thought perhaps Lady Eliza was attending to Lord...I mean, Carleton...I mean, her husband...but it seems that perhaps I was mistaken. I do so apologize."

"She's downstairs. In the library. She asked that she not be disturbed."

"I'll knock first." Penelope coughed into her fist and curtsied in an awkward sort of obeisance that only served to enhance her overall discomfort. Then it came to her: "Hamish? Do you mean Hamish Tavistock?"

Sister Francine shrugged. "Hmh," she said.

"I didn't realize *he* was on the guest list."

"I don't know nothin' about no such frivolities."

"No, I don't suppose you would." Penelope paused. "Well, in any event, do give my regards to Carleton if you see him. I pray for his recovery and I'm sure he appreciates your sitting sentry so diligently outside his room. I shouldn't imagine that he'd care to be disturbed when there are so many *frivolous* people about the grounds this weekend. If I were certain people, I'd certainly think twice about crossing you. Thanks again, Sister."

Penelope did a mad dash down the corridor in the direction of the grand staircase at the front of the hall. HamishTavistock? she thought. Why on earth hadn't Diana told her that Hamish Tavistock was to be in attendance that weekend? Not that having such advance knowledge would have made a jot of difference, for there wasn't a chance in hell that Penelope would have begged off her responsibilities on Steeplechase Weekend. But the presence of Hamish Tavistock brought an almost imperceptible twist to how Penelope chose to carry herself.

It had been years...many years...a lifetime ago really...

She arrived at the library just as the doors were opening and Eliza appeared in the downstairs corridor with Hamish Tavistock at her side. Penelope suppressed the urge to blush. He was just as she remembered him – the jet black wavy hair (probably dyed at his age), the pencil mustache, the perpetual sun tan like he'd just stepped off the plane from Ibiza (he probably had), the open-necked dress shirt of Savile Row tailoring (probably Gieves & Hawkes, definitely Jermyn Street), the gold chain, the tuft of grey chest hair (he'd missed a spot while waxing). The mere sight of Hamish Tavistock after all these years brought a lump of unrequited longing to Penelope's throat. She'd (almost) forgotten how it felt...how his presence had once made her feel.

"Penelope." Eliza looked none-too-thrilled to see her.

"Eliza," Penelope struggled to form the syllables that comprised the name.

"Well, well, well," Hamish Tavistock said. "Do my eyes deceive me or is it none other than Lady Penelope Templeton? You're a lonely but longed-for mirage on a barren vista of Arabian desert sand."

"You've always had a way with hyperbole," Penelope choked as she felt the blood rise to her cheeks.

"What a sexy surprise!" Hamish exclaimed with a deep-throated laugh. "Eliza, you know how much I adore American women. It's been yonks since I've had the pleasure."

"Oh, Hamish," Penelope chortled, "it's all coming back to me now."

"The two of you are acquainted?" Eliza broke in. She arched her eyebrows and gave Penelope an inquisitive look, thin lips pursed together in a measured but not entirely disapproving half-pout.

Hamish winked. Penelope felt the blood rush to her neck and up into her cheeks.

"More than acquaintances," Hamish replied, "but sadly, less than friends. I do so hope we can amend that. Perhaps this weekend? Nothing like a good old-fashioned Steeplechase to ramp up the social lubrication, is there?"

"Pimms helps," Penelope added.

"Bloody stonking marvelous!" Hamish cried with a lubricious cackle that set Penelope's teeth on edge, but made her tingle all the same. "Well, I'm off to find Bings. He's in such a state, you know. Crying shame about his daughter and all that. Packed off to a convent in Quebec of all places! Can you imagine? Anyway, I'd better tend to him before he makes a ruddy arse of himself. Ever since the 'ravaging,' he's stinking blotto all the time. That's why I'll never have kids. I'm tight enough as it is. How about you, Penelope? You've got a whole tribe of them, I hear."

The last thing Penelope wanted to think about at that moment – let alone be reminded of in conversation with Hamish Tavistock – was motherhood. "The little darlings," she said. "How soon they grow."

"And how soon they become little monsters," Eliza interjected.

Penelope winced.

"Do keep me informed of developments in that matter we discussed." Eliza extended a rather limp hand for Hamish to take in parting. "And not a word of it to anyone. Especially not the Ambassador. I've waited so long for this. The last thing I want is for Bingham to stuff it up with his insufferable political blathering."

"Protocol is protocol, Eliza," Hamish said, giving Eliza's hand a perfunctory squeeze. "There are certain processes we must adhere to if we're going to keep things even moderately above board...and, well, you know...*legal*."

"I'm not interested in 'above board'," Eliza snapped. "I'm interested in getting my..." She stopped.

Penelope's ears perked, her interest aroused. *What could Eliza possibly have been referring to?* Was there an opportunity to be had here? Another way in? Penelope cleared her throat and made a show of pretending to examine the contents of her clutch while Eliza – visibly perturbed – quietly tried to take back control of the situation. Hamish stared at his espadrilles.

"Thank you, Hamish," Eliza said once she'd regained a semblance of composure. "Enjoy the afternoon and make sure the Ambassador behaves himself. The last thing any of us needs is a scene."

"Quite right!" Hamish seemed all too happy to have received his marching orders. "I shall now bid you two ravishing ladies a fond adieu. And you, my dear..." He took Penelope's hand and raised it to his lips. "The Pimms is on me."

His lips were rather sweaty, the kiss on her hand too moist, but Penelope felt her insides start to melt at his touch. She appreciated the attention more than she might have imagined. "I'll find you," she replied, hoping to sound coy but feeling all too characteristically awkward and very much Penny Danziger, the Bachelorette of Cedar Rapids.

"Does Edgar know of your past with Hamish?" Eliza asked as they watched the old cad saunter out into the sunshine.

"Excuse me?" Nothing was going according to plan. Penelope mentally kicked herself.

"Was Hamish your lover?"

"Eliza!" It took everything Penelope had within her not to run and hide. The craving for a Spice bomb – hell, she'd settle for just a hit! – was intense. "Whatever makes you suspect anything of me so...so...untoward as that? Hamish is old enough to be my father! Please, do not mistake me for Chloe. I'm not the one with Daddy issues. And anyway, Edgar and I are very happy. Very happy indeed."

"Methinks the lady doth protest too much," Eliza smirked.

"Hamish and I...Barbados...too much rum, sun, and the sound of steel drums...I was there with Edgar on holiday, not long after we married. There may have been a mild flirtation but Edgar was with me the whole time. Men of that generation...well, Eliza, you would know more about that than me. I'm half your age."

"I stop listening when you speak," Eliza said. "Needless to say – but I'll say it anyway – whatever you think you heard just now, you didn't."

And then it struck her. "Is it Trevor?" How she hadn't immediately connected the dots before was maddening. Another reason she needed a Spice Bomb. The drug had an uncanny way of making everything very clear.

Eliza's expression tightened. Her eyes narrowed. For a moment, Penelope feared she might be slapped. "My son is none of your concern," Eliza said. "Why are we standing here? Why am I talking to you? What were you doing lurking outside the library door? You look ridiculous in that fascinator. Is it one of your creations?"

Penelope thought it best to ignore the slight. "Sister Francine said you were down here," she began. The nerves had once more come to the fore. "I need a word with you."

"Whatever for?"

"Can we talk in private? In the library, perhaps? What I have to tell you is for your ears only, at least for now. What you choose to do with this information after is, well, up to you of course, though I would strongly encourage you to act."

Penelope paused to give herself a moment. She could tell she'd successfully peaked Eliza's interest, which she supposed was half the battle won. "The survival of this family may depend on the information I'm about to share with you," she said.

Eliza peered at Penelope with unabashed curiosity. Penelope forced herself to hold the other woman's gaze. "All right," Eliza said. "The library then."

| 25 |

What Tessa saw that morning by the boathouse was something she was unlikely ever to forget. Not only did it solidify her determination to remain a part of the Templeton saga for as long as she could convince them to keep her around, what she saw at the boathouse also made her realize that this was no ordinary run-of-the-mill aristocratic family, but one with secrets that not even she could have imagined, which was saying quite a lot. She supposed the appropriate response would have been to intervene, or at the very least make some attempt to bring assistance to the person who was in such obvious distress. But Tessa had never been someone to whom appropriate behavior came naturally, and as it soon became clear, that said person in distress was none other than Rebecca Hastings, whose fate Tessa found had inexplicably become wrapped up in her own. Such were the tangled webs the Templeton family – and their hangers-on – weaved. Tessa wouldn't have had it any other way. Life really had become rather delicious. She couldn't wait to see – and, where possible, influence – what came next.

But she did wonder whether, less than forty-eight hours after first announcing her arrival, she might perhaps have been a little over-zealous and spread herself a tad thin. It wasn't as though she had set out to dominate the narrative...well, at least not all at once. Her mission, at least as originally envisioned, had merely been to secure her rightful position as one of Lord Carleton Templeton's heirs: take the money she felt was owed to her and then hightail it to LA or the South of France and use the inheritance to set herself up as a model or a TikTok influencer or a recording artist, or better yet all three. She certainly had the look and a passable voice that any number of self-styled DJs she'd known in London said they'd be more than happy to filter. And her songwriting wasn't all that bad either even if she did feel it was a little derivative. Life experience would help. But none of her Super Pop dreams had a hope in hell of coming together without money, and there were only so many desperate and desperately horny sugar daddies she could entertain before she started feeling like a pop culture cliché and her aspirations little more than stardust.

No, Contessa Templeton (otherwise known as Tess Rivers) had come to Templeton Manor to make her mark. She'd gotten this far. She wasn't about to let anything get in her way. But a girl – no matter how resilient she might be – couldn't expect to get ahead without a little help, especially when she was coming into a situation where the odds were decidedly stacked against her. Allies, at this stage of the game, were key and could be shifted as needs required. However, Tessa had been the new girl on the block enough times in her short life to know that those first alliances were often of paramount importance as they set the stage for what was to come. Chloe had seemed an obvious choice, but the more time Tessa spent in the It Girl's company, the more she realized the girl's limitations. Chloe was simply too much an insider to be of much use. The girl suffered from such a shocking – if not debilitating – case of narcissistic myopia that Tessa worried what would happen to her when she turned forty. She also suspected that Chloe might not be very bright. Diana was a non-starter and Edgar just seemed like your typical public school twat, which left Guy...Guy...hmm...rotten to the core but oh so dreamy. Tessa thought it a shame that the others seemed so dead-set against him, although his loss definitely looked to be her gain.

And then, of course, there was the sister-in-law, Penelope. A bloody hot mess, if ever there was one, but the fact that she was an American – despite the tedious and rather embarrassing attempts to act and sound properly British – held, for Tessa, a certain appeal. Americans were rebels and Tessa had always fancied herself a rebel, better suited for the Stars and Stripes of the U.S. of A. than gloomy old Blighty. This wasn't even taking into account the fact that Penelope had her finger on the pulse of the Spice trade. Tessa was no stranger to mind-altering substances. They made life that much more interesting. And Spice was definitely The Bomb. It also helped that, like herself, Penelope was an outsider and all-too-eager for an ally of her own. Tessa could use this. She could bend Penelope to her will. If a little reconnaissance on Guy was all it took to secure Penelope's trust – and, most importantly, the Spice – Tessa was more than willing and able to twist herself into as many compromising positions with the errant Templeton as the role required. She'd do so with pleasure.

Further complicating the situation, however, was the involvement of the flaming-haired Frenchwoman who had asked – in rather uncompromising terms – that Tessa be her eyes and ears where Guy was concerned. Tessa felt she was being tested between two loyalties, and it was still too early to tell which allegiance might benefit her most in the long run. Although the interaction had been brief, Yvette Devereux excited her in a deeply visceral way. Tessa wanted to get to know her in whichever way possible. Penelope's appeal, on the other hand, ran no deeper than the Spice and inspired within her no comparable passion. Tessa supposed it best to wait before making any hasty decisions. Regardless of the path she took, Guy was still the quarry, and Tessa rather relished the notion of being a double agent. The danger of it all had a deliciously seductive appeal.

What was less appealing though was what she had witnessed at the boathouse that morning. She had gone there before dawn for an early morning cold-water swim in the canal and to gather her thoughts before the onslaught of the day's Steeplechase activities. Her last boyfriend in London – more a fuck buddy and lifestyle advisor than anything if truth be told – had been a part-time yoga instructor at the storefront gym across the road. Stuart – or Ram Chandra as he preferred to be called, having eschewed his Western name after a year spent backpacking and rejecting modern technology in a silent Buddhist retreat in Bhutan – had introduced Tessa to the benefits of all things tantric, a result of which was a morning routine that involved not only swimming in freezing temperatures but a series of sun salutations and warrior poses to help put her in better touch with her inner goddess, or "Devi" as Stuart aka Ram Chandra preferred to address her.

While she'd been skeptical at first, Tessa soon found herself feeling more empowered than ever and soon realized that she didn't need Stuart or Ram Chandra or whatever he called himself to make herself feel good. Stuart soon became yesterday's news and Tessa seriously considered for a time becoming a freelance body-and-mind counselor herself. Like everything else, unfortunately, the path she might eventually decide to take was dependent upon the reading of her late father's will. She acknowledged (albeit reluctantly) that there was a very real possibility that Lord Carleton had left her nothing, in which case, Tessa would have some weighty decisions to make, a further reason why she needed allies within the family.

It was fear of the unknown that made Tessa restless. Whatever the outcome, she didn't doubt her ability to survive. She'd been on her own for most of her life and, all things considered, had done rather well. But there were moments when Tessa found herself utterly bereft of a sense of hope or a clear idea of who or what she was meant to be. One needed money to achieve anything in life, but money – at least heretofore – was the one thing Tessa (or rather Tess Rivers) lacked in spades. She needed cash, and fast. Meditation and aquatic exercise helped ease the anxiety and soothe the mind, better even than sex, which Tessa also enjoyed but lately the act of shagging just seemed to her like so much hard work with very little payout at the end. One couldn't rely on money shots alone to pay the rent.

When she arrived at the boathouse just past six that morning, Tessa was first of all struck by how ridiculous it felt to her to be part of a family that had so much wealth and property that they'd have their own private canal and boathouse at their disposal. From the looks of it, Tessa surmised that boating was not a prioritized pastime. The second thing she noticed as she slipped out of her shorts and tee shirt was a somewhat disconcerting sense that she was being watched. She peeked in the windows and tried the door, but it was locked and looked as though it hadn't been opened in years. Tessa shrugged off the paranoia as best she could. Forty-eight hours at Templeton Manor had already proven to her that one could never be too assured of one's privacy. The walls really did have ears and the family and staff themselves all seemed to have eyes in the backs of their heads. Tessa didn't mind a little voyeurism, but what she experienced at the boathouse that morning felt to her more B-movie than A-list. She considered abandoning her routine, but the thought of another day with *those people* without time alone to center and manifest beforehand wasn't something she was willing to endure. She shook her head and gamely struck her first salutation.

As Tessa worked her way through the series of poses and tried to focus on her Third Eye, the increasingly creepy sensation that someone was looking at her – and possibly doing things to themselves while they looked at her – prevented Tessa from losing herself to her inner flow. Her mind raced. She couldn't focus or harness the energy. She stopped mid-routine and glanced about the premises, even leaning over to peer into the rather murky water of the canal.

"Hello?" she called out. "Is anyone there? Come out, come out, wherever you are. Hello? Look, I don't mind being perved but I'd rather have some control over it before finding myself online. Hello?"

Of course, there was no reply. Tessa hadn't really expected one. She sighed, counted back from five – in through the nose, out through the mouth – and eased herself into Downward Dog before sliding into the Cobra pose. Something just wasn't right.

"I'm serious!" Tessa said. "You're really skeeving me out. I'll give you five seconds to show yourself before I scream bloody murder."

She paused. Nothing.

"Okay, you've been warned." Tessa scrambled back onto her feet and went to the edge of the canal. "Five...four...three...two..."

And then she heard it: a barely perceptible whimper, but unmistakable all the same: "Help...me."

"What?"

Tessa shivered. She folded her arms across her breasts and held herself against the sudden chill.

"Help...me...please?"

"Where are you?" Fear gripped Tessa's throat. She threw on her tee shirt and shorts and jogged up and down the boardwalk along the canal. The voice sounded as though it was coming from the water's edge, close by and yet strangely almost out of earshot.

"Please..."

Instinct dictated that Tessa run back to the main house, but curiosity proved a more powerful force. She ran the perimeter of the boathouse, knocking on windows and pulling again at the door. The voice had grown silent. Tessa wondered if perhaps she had imagined it, her mind playing tricks on her anxiety. But just as she was about to leave, she heard the voice again, this time directly behind her, so close she didn't know how she had possibly missed it the first time.

"I'm begging you. Help me."

What confronted her was so horrific that Tessa might have been forgiven for thinking the creature that had crawled up from the depths of the canal (for where else had it possibly come from?) and onto the boardwalk was none other than a strange and terrifying anthropomorphic sea beast. Its clothes – what had the night before been a very chic, sheer white linen jumpsuit from Miu Miu – were sodden and coated with fluorescent green algae slime. Its hair was long, disheveled and ropy like seaweed. But what Tessa found most disturbing was its face. The hair could not hide the horror of blistered and bubbled flesh that extended from above its scalp all the way down the left side of its face, disappearing under its jawline. Its left eye was red and burned, the skin around its socket puckered and raw, and its mouth a twisted and melted kind of gash that seemed to droop and puddle beneath its chin. Tessa screamed and tried to turn away, but Rebecca Hastings (or rather, what had once been Rebecca Hastings) grabbed her ankle and held her with a surprisingly strong grip.

"Help me!" Rebecca Hastings groaned. "Please!"

"Get away! Get!" Tessa kicked out as she struggled to break free. The mere touch of Rebecca Hastings' hand on her foot was enough to throw Tessa into hysterics. Where was she? What the fuck was happening? She'd need at least a year of intense mindfulness training with Ram Chandra and a whole shitload of Spice to get over this. Tessa was convinced she'd be traumatized for life. She'd never be able to look at a body of water again, let alone go swimming.

"No, please!"

Tessa managed to pull free and landed a sound wallop under Rebecca Hastings' chin that sent the Foraged hostess rolling away in pain. Tessa's first instinct was to push the woman back into the canal but even the extreme jolt of adrenaline that now coursed through her veins wasn't enough to overcome her aversion. She staggered against the boathouse, hitting her head rather painfully on the wall. Rebecca Hastings squirmed and contorted at the edge of the canal and then suddenly – ominously – went still.

Tessa despaired of catching her breath. Her mind raced to recall Ram Chandra's breathing exercises but all she really wanted was a cigarette. She reached into the pocket of her shorts and was relieved to discover that she'd had the forethought to bring a fresh pack of Pall Malls before heading out to complete her morning ritual.

She fumbled with the plastic wrapper. Her hands wouldn't stop shaking. Once she'd managed to pull a cigarette from the pack, she couldn't get her fingers to work the lighter. What would she do if she couldn't get the fucking thing to work?

"Give that to me. Let me help you."

Tessa startled. Her heart jolted. She warily looked up to find the flaming-haired French woman standing at her side, looking immaculate in a crimson belted coat-dress and black beret. She released the lighter to Yvette who promptly lit the cigarette before lighting one of her own.

"Sonia Rykiel," Yvette said. "The dress. In case you were wondering."

Tessa sucked hard on the cigarette. The smoke filled her mouth and burned as it went down her throat. Yvette went to the edge of the canal and peered down at the now immobile figure of Rebecca Hastings.

"Is she dead?" Tessa stammered.

Yvette crouched down and placed two fingers on Rebecca Hastings' wrist. She waited a moment before shaking her head. "*Non*," she said. "Her heart beats. There's still a pulse."

"She scared the fucking shit out of me," Tessa said. "I didn't know what to do."

Yvette smiled. "I like your moves," she replied. "Earlier. Perfect form in those sun salutations. And your warrior pose...I think maybe you are like Boudicca, *n'est pas?*"

"Ram Chandra taught me everything I know." Tessa paused. "You were watching me?"

"You make it sound so sordid." Yvette walked slowly round Rebecca Hastings' limp body. Her heels clicked on the boardwalk. "I prefer to say 'observing', 'admiring' even...but *oui*, I suppose 'watching' works too, though less artful. You young people today are so brash."

"Did you do that to her?" Tessa couldn't bring herself to look at Rebecca Hastings. She took another fitful drag on her cigarette.

"*Non.* I never get my hands so dirty."

"What happened to her?"

Yvette shrugged. "Acid on the face," she said, almost nonchalantly. "Most probably sulfuric, judging from the extent of the burns. It is very common in places like India, Bangladesh, parts of the Middle East and Africa. Whoever did it to her then probably pushed her into the canal, hoping she would drown."

"Who would do such a thing?"

"I can think of several." Yvette came to a stop beside Tessa. They smoked in contemplative silence. "And I think you can too. Rebecca Hastings has very few friends around here, it seems. A shame but not terribly surprising."

"Will she be okay?"

"She'll never work front-of-house in a restaurant again, if that's what you mean. Don't worry about her. I'll call security and arrange for her to be transferred to a hospital. You have more important priorities."

"This isn't what I signed up for."

"*Non?*" Yvette turned so she stood facing Tessa, boxing her in against the boathouse wall. "So tell me, Tess Rivers, what *did* you sign up for?"

Tessa thought she was going to be sick. She finished the last of her cigarette and tossed it toward the canal. Yvette's presence consumed her.

"How do you know?" Tessa paused, gulped, desperate for another smoke.

Yvette tossed her head back and emitted a throaty laugh. "Why do you think The Agency pays me the big bucks?" she asked. "I know everything. And the sooner you realize that, the better off we'll all be."

"I thought I was being so careful. I didn't tell anyone I was coming here. I knew there could be trouble if anyone suspected or knew..."

"And Ram Chandra? You said nothing to him?" Yvette asked. "Or is it Stuart Abuja? I was on assignment in Nigeria years ago. He went by Stuart then."

There was nothing for Tessa to do but gawp.

Yvette smiled, not unkindly. "Stuart and I go way back," she said. "We shared a mutual friend whose life was cut short all too soon. *Quelle tragique!* But then we knew the risks of the profession when we entered this line of work."

"Stuart's a spook?"

"I have already said too much," Yvette replied. "So I shall say no more."

"Fuck."

Tessa lit another cigarette. She was confused and intrigued. There was so much she wanted to ask Yvette, so much that she felt she needed to know, but sensed that now perhaps wasn't the best time. Life hadn't always been kind to Tessa, not that she expected anyone to do her any favors or give her special treatment for having had a rough go of things. But every once in a while, it might be nice, she thought, to have a helping hand extended in her direction. She wondered if perhaps Yvette – herself an enigma – might provide that support, a lifeline even. She just lacked the words to ask. Tessa couldn't bring herself to make that cry for help.

"Stuart asked me to look out for you," Yvette said, as if reading Tessa's mind. "He made me promise on the loving memory of our mutual friend. He cares for you."

"Your friend," Tessa said. She felt tears well in her eyes and wiped them away with the back of her hand. "The one who died. What was his name?"

It was now Yvette's turn to suppress her sorrow. "Tahar," she whispered. "It still pains me to speak his name."

"Tahar," Tessa repeated.

Rebecca Hastings stirred behind them then, breaking each out of their reverie. A welcome relief, Tessa thought. How quickly one's perspective could change.

"And now I must deal with her," Yvette said, all business once again. "Go back to the house. You must not tell a soul what you have seen or that you and I have had this talk. *Comprenez vous?*"

"*Oui,*" Tessa said. She didn't understand, but what would have been the point of saying otherwise?

"Keep your eye on the prize...who we talked about...Guy Templeton."

"Yes...Guy..."

"It is most important that we do not let him out of our sights."

Yvette then did something that added to Tessa's confusion when she supposed the gesture was intended to comfort. The Frenchwoman leaned forward and planted a gentle kiss on Tessa's forehead.

"*Courage!*" she said. "*Aller!*"

Tessa didn't linger. She hurried back to the house with a renewed sense of purpose and a determination to be Yvette's eyes and ears and then some. Whatever the flaming-haired Frenchwoman asked of her, Tessa would do her best to deliver. But when she arrived back to the house and found herself once again amidst the pageantry of the Steeplechase, a gnawing sense of anxiety returned. Images of Rebecca Hastings sprung before her eyes like flashbacks of a particularly bad acid trip. She stumbled and felt as though she was losing her way. The ground beneath her feet was pitted and unsteady. It was all Tessa could do to keep herself from tumbling down. She needed a hit, a pick-me-up, something to calm her nerves and steady her mind. She needed Spice.

So it came as a bit of a disappointment to encounter the one person on the premises Tessa knew dealt in the Spice trade, only to find that Penelope wasn't going to share her stash without strings attached. Of course, the promise of a bigger cut was awfully attractive even if it meant delayed gratification. And how convenient that Penelope's assignment dovetailed so nicely with Yvette's. Tessa was all for killing two birds with one stone if it meant double the reward. At least Ram Chandra – or was it Stuart Abuja? – had taught her that much.

| 26 |

So, if I'm to understand what you're telling me," Eliza said as she paced about the library while Penelope sat on the edge of the chaise feeling very much like an errant schoolgirl caught telling lies by the headmistress, "Guy has fathered a bastard?"

"Yes." Penelope nodded perhaps a little too vigorously, desperately hoping Eliza wouldn't grill her for more information than she could provide. Her brow felt sweaty. Perspiration trickled down her back.

"And how have you come about this extraordinary information?"

"Chloe told me."

Eliza stopped but a few feet from where Penelope was sitting. Her grey eyes flashed. "Chloe?"

"Yes, she told me just now." Penelope wondered if she hadn't perhaps been a little over-hasty in bringing this information to Eliza's attention. "And you know Chloe would never speak against Guy unless she had solid grounds for doing so."

"Indeed," Eliza said. She continued to pace. Penelope counted her steps from one end of the room to the other and then back again. "What exactly did Chloe say to you?"

"She said...well...she said she feels Guy has gone to the drink..."

"And?"

"And...he pushed her."

"He pushed her?"

"Yes."

"One push does not a baby make," Eliza said. "If only it were so easy, imagine the tedium it would save the mothers of this world!"

"I mean...he pushed Chloe. I didn't mean to imply—"

"Do you take me for a fool, Penelope?" Eliza thundered.

"No." Penelope swallowed down the bile that rose in her throat. *This wasn't going well, not well at all.* "No, of course I don't, Eliza! I was just...well..."

"SPEAK!"

"You frighten me is all." *Oh, the humiliation!*

Eliza's laugh was harsh, cold, and utterly without mirth: the laugh of a woman without a heart.

"'You frighten me,' she says!" Eliza replied. "Well, fancy that. I am who I am,

Penelope. It's not for me to change who I am, but for you to toughen up. You've all been pampered and babied, allowed to behave like spoiled little snot-nosed rugrats. No wonder your own are so insufferable. Children only replicate the behavior they see in their parents. They don't know any better."

"My children have nothing to do with it," Penelope said, her voice too weak to be taken seriously.

"SILENCE!"

Penelope fought the urge to bolt from the room.

"Where is Chloe now?"

"I don't know. Outside somewhere...with our guests."

"And why have you come to me with this information, and not her?"

"I think she knows you don't like her...Mum."

"I don't like you, but that hasn't stopped you from coming to me."

"I volunteered." Penelope was desperate for Spice. She forced herself to sit up straight. There was no use in cowering, she decided. Eliza would only continue to eat her alive and spit out her carcass for the guard dogs that prowled outside the kitchen door waiting for scraps. "I want a place at the table."

"By betraying your brother-in-law?" Eliza's tone remained hard, but Penelope – optimistically – thought she detected the faintest glimmer in her eyes.

"His behavior is shameful," Penelope said. "Indefensible really. And if what Chloe says is true, about there being a child, well, the last thing this family – or Templeton Enterprises – needs is another scandal. You know as well as I do, Eliza, the damage another round of negative press would surely have on everything this family has built over generations. Stocks and shareholder value could plunge even further than they did after...well...after Abbey-gate."

"That was Lord Carleton's doing, not mine!" Eliza snapped. "But that being said, you are correct, Penelope. This family cannot afford to carry on as we've been doing. I've tried explaining this to the others, but..."

"I know how that feels, Eliza. In that we're the same. I've struggled for twenty years to be accepted, but not one of them will give me an inch. Even after all this time. And Edgar just tells me it's all in my head."

"Edgar's a fool."

"Yes. But you and me, Eliza...if I may be so presumptuous..."

"You may not."

"I'd like the opportunity to prove to you that not only am I worthy of the Templeton name, I can also be your ally."

"How so?"

Penelope saw an opening. "Shall we take a turn around the room?" she asked as she hopped up from the chaise and went to Eliza, relieved that the older woman didn't recoil when she hooked her arm through hers, and proceeded to lead them for a walk about the library.

"The thing is," Penelope continued, measuring the impact of each word before she spoke, "no one in this family takes me seriously. It's always bothered me, but now I've come to see it as an opportunity. I can get in under the radar, hide in plain sight. People in this family treat me like I'm not there, or they dismiss me as inconsequential or too stupid to understand what they're talking about."

"And what are they saying exactly?"

"The most hateful things."

"About?"

"You, for one."

Eliza laughed. "Believe me," she said, "sticks and stones may break my bones..."

"And even worse about Sister Francine."

"Sister Francine is unimpeachable!"

Penelope felt Eliza tremble. She knew the fallen nun was Eliza's weak spot, her greatest vulnerability and Penelope's ace to play.

"To hear them speak, one might think you and the good sister were planning some sort of Papist overthrow of the family," she continued. "They think you're poised to throw us all onto the street, take their inheritance and use it toward turning Templeton Manor into a nunnery or (worse yet) a sanctuary for pedophile priests."

"This is what they're saying?"

They stopped in front of the bay window overlooking the festivities. Penelope waited and watched with bated breath. She couldn't help but feel her future was dependent on the next few minutes. She willed Eliza to play along, to give her a chance the way no one in the family had ever seemed to want to, even after so many years, not to mention four children. Penelope felt she had sacrificed enough for the family. It was time for a little payback.

"And Diana?" Eliza asked. "Diana as well?"

"I'm afraid Diana's the worst of the lot," Penelope said. "She's a wolf in sheep's clothing that one. But it's Guy who poses the greatest threat. The others you can pick off one-by-one...in time."

"I need proof!" Eliza bellowed. Penelope stepped back and released her arm from her new mother-in-law's. "What you're telling me is nothing but hearsay. How can I act without real, documentary evidence? Without proof, Penelope, we have nothing but idle gossip, nothing that will hold up in court."

Penelope secretly thrilled to Eliza's use of the pronoun 'we'. It meant she was getting through. It meant the door was opening.

"I have an agent in the field," she said. "Someone who's an outsider like us. Someone with a lot to prove."

"Who?"

"Tessa," Penelope blurted. She sensed Eliza's skepticism. "Trust me, Eliza, I have a good feeling about that girl."

"She's an impostor. A carpetbagger."

"The same has been said of you," Penelope couldn't help herself.

Eliza bristled. "Well, as much as it pains me to say it, it seems I have no choice," she said. "But I'm warning you, Penelope. If I find you've played me for a fool, I will show no mercy. You'll need more than a treasury of shekels to extract one pound of my flesh."

"I won't disappoint you, Eliza. I promise." *Oh, the elation! Oh, the relief!* "But if I may, I'd like to offer a suggestion."

Eliza nodded. "I'm listening," she said.

"You need to call a family meeting."

"Why?"

"To establish yourself, to show that you're in charge now, to demonstrate that you've taken command."

"And?"

"It's important that Sister Francine be there."

"That goes without saying. Sister Francine is my most trusted advisor."

"Yes, but the others need to see that. You need to be strong, Eliza. You need to lay down the law. They need to know there's a new sheriff in town."

"Spoken like a true American!" Eliza laughed and patted Penelope's hand with something bordering on affection. "But you're right."

"And one last thing, if I may?"

"Speak."

Penelope took a deep breath. "I think it best if you call this meeting without Guy or Chloe present. They shouldn't even be aware of it."

"Why?"

"Think, Eliza. The two of them are a team. Chloe will always defend Guy, just as she always has. She'll veto any action you propose even as she knows it's in her best interest to vote for the benefit of the family."

"Wise counsel," Eliza said with an approving nod. "And when do you propose I call this meeting?"

"Tonight, after dinner, but late when our guests have retired for the night. I think by then we may have the evidence you require."

"And if we don't?"

"We'll think of something," Penelope said. Her nerve endings were all a-tingle. She felt as though she had passed through a ring of fire and emerged to fight another day. It was, admittedly, more than she had hoped for. "But right now, it's important that you go out there." She motioned toward the throng outside on the grounds. "They need to see you among them, of them. You're Lady Eliza Templeton now. You need to own that. You need to *be* that."

Eliza looked through the window. Penelope held her breath. She resisted the urge to squeeze Eliza's hand: too much, too soon. The odds were in her favor, but Penelope had been around the family long enough to recognize alliances were fickle and what was "in" one day was "out" the next. She needed to maintain her poker face at all times.

"Thank you, Penelope," Eliza said after a pause. "You surprise me. I may have underestimated you."

"I've been underestimated all my life," Penelope replied. "But it's the underdog who usually gets the bone in the end, wouldn't you say?"

"Quite," Eliza said. She patted Penelope's hand. "Quite."

| 27 |

All of this running hither and yon is exhausting, Tessa thought. She figured she'd clocked just as much distance that morning as the horses in the fucking Steeplechase. Thank God she was relatively fit. Being a double agent was nothing if not exhausting! But she wouldn't have changed a thing, except for the Creature from the Black Lagoon bit. That she could have done without. She supposed it was all part of the game, and it certainly was exciting, but Tessa still couldn't help but question whether she was biting off more than she could chew. The thing about Yvette and Ram Chandra freaked her out more than just a little. Sure, it was a small world and all, but that was just plain whack. How could she possibly trust anyone if around every corner was another spook or informant, or someone capable of doing whatever it was that had been done to Rebecca Hastings? Tessa shuddered at the thought. It helped, she supposed, that she had someone like Yvette Devereux looking out for her. The Frenchwoman attracted her in ways Tessa – who certainly wasn't without experience – had yet to even discover. She felt a magnetic pull, an almost obsessive need for the French spook's approval, but Tessa suspected the feeling went deeper. She was confused. The world as she had known it for twenty-one years had suddenly turned upside-down, and Tessa wasn't sure whether to jump off or cling on for dear life.

It didn't take long for Tessa to find Guy. She caught up to him in a wooded glen about a half-mile or so from the manor. She feared if she didn't tread carefully he'd see her and her cover would be blown, so she hid behind an ancient oak tree whose gnarled and knotty trunk provided more than adequate protection. Tessa wasn't sure what exactly she was meant to do once she found him. From what Penelope had said, she surmised she was meant to discover what she could about the child Chloe had accused him of fathering, and she supposed she was expected to do the same for Yvette. The fact that he was pursuing a child who looked to be of about seven or eight certainly gave credence to Chloe's accusation. The girl hopped and bounced from one foot to the next, spinning like a dervish one moment, then diving into cartwheels the next. She certainly seemed like a happy child if not a little manic. But what did Tessa know of children? She'd never been particularly well disposed toward them. She'd never wanted any of her own. Penelope's brood did nothing to influence Tessa's bias otherwise. But this one intrigued her.

"Feminina!" Guy called out to the girl. "Feminina, please! I'd like to talk to you. Feminina, wait!"

Tessa pressed herself against the tree trunk and held her breath. This was about to get good.

The child – Feminina – stopped. She appeared to consider Guy with a quizzical, almost cheeky, grin, before pointing a pudgy finger at him and giggling like a baby. "Papa!" she exclaimed gleefully. "Papa!"

"No!" Guy said, perhaps a tad too vociferously. Tessa leaned in closer to hear. "Where's your mother, Feminina? Is she here? Can I talk to her?"

Feminina tilted her head to one side. "*Maman?*" she asked.

"Yes, your mother...Svetlana...is she here?"

The girl popped a thumb into her mouth and nodded. Tessa was struck by the way the child's blue eyes sparkled and how the sun that cascaded through the arboreal canopy overhead highlighted the red in her impossible mess of perfectly curled ringlets.

"Feminina?"

The child nodded again and then turned with a dramatic flounce. She pointed to a space off in the distance amidst the trees and overgrown foliage. Tessa followed the direction of the girl's finger and squinted to focus.

"*Maman!*" Feminina cried.

From the sunshine and shadows, a woman appeared. She was dressed in a black cloak that swept the ground at her feet as she came towards Guy and the girl. The hood was pulled down low over her eyes, obscuring her features save for her mouth, which was painted a particularly severe shade of red. Tessa bit down on the inside of her cheek.

"Svetlana?" Guy said.

The woman stopped a few feet from where Guy stood. She opened her arms to welcome the child into a loose but protective embrace.

"I told you I would find you," the cloaked woman said.

"What are you doing here?"

Tessa could feel Guy's fear.

"You ran away from me," the woman replied. "You shirked your responsibility to me, to the child...to my poor, darling Feminina...to *our* Feminina."

"How can you say that?" Guy said. Tessa noticed his instinct seemed to be to go to the woman but something was holding him back. But what? "You told me... that night in Moscow...on your birthday...you said...the child's father was..."

"Lies!" Svetlana spat. "I speak to you now as a woman abandoned by her lover with an innocent child who longs to be close to her father. I speak to you now as a woman who seeks justice in this world. How can you fault me for wanting what is best for my daughter?"

"But she isn't mine!" Guy hissed. "She can't possibly be mine. How old is she? Seven? Eight? I didn't know you then. We met at the opera just months ago. With Cordelia...the ambassador's daughter..."

"Feminina, *babushka*, go run and play for a little while." Svetlana knelt down beside the child. She pushed the hood back to reveal her face. Tessa had never seen anyone so beautiful.

"Are you and Papa having a fight, *Maman*?" Feminina asked. Her innocence almost broke Tessa's heart.

"No, *babushka*," Svetlana replied. "Papa and I are just having an adult conversation. Do you know what that is, darling?"

Feminina nodded. "Not for little girls like me," she said.

Svetlana's smile could have launched a thousand ships. "Exactly," she said. "Now run along. There's a lovely field of the most gorgeous bluebells just over there, where the sunlight dances on the dew."

"Are there leprechauns, *Maman*?" Feminina asked. "Should I look for toadstools?"

Svetlana laughed. "And a pot of gold at the end of the rainbow?" she asked. "No, babushka, we're in England. There are no leprechauns here."

"Or pots of gold," Guy interjected.

"That remains to be seen," Svetlana said. The edge was unmistakable. "Run along then. Make *Maman* the most beautiful bouquet of bluebells. I think I saw some Queen Anne's lace too. And Baby's Breath."

The girl needed no further prompting. She ran off with a shriek and a gurgle.

"Svetlana," Guy said once the girl had disappeared into the sunlight.

"I warned you."

"What do you want?"

Svetlana drew herself up to her full height, straightening her back and gathering the cloak about her like a cobra on the verge of a strike.

"What I've always wanted," she said. "What you stole from me."

"I don't know what you're talking about. I didn't steal anything."

"My heart, for one. You stole my heart." Svetlana gathered the train of her cloak about her feet as she slowly circled Guy. Tessa feared she might burst from holding her breath in an effort not to miss a single word. "Does that count for nothing? What is this divine but mad pounding in my breast that I feel every day and every night that you and I are not together? What is this pain that pierces my soul like the sharpest Ottoman dagger whenever I gaze upon our child – my *babushka*, my sweetest, dearest Feminina – who asks me again and again and again, '*Maman*, where is my Papa? Why does he not want to be with us? Why does he not love me?' And so I ask you now, Guy Templeton, why have you forsaken your daughter? I do not ask for myself – I care not for ego or my own personal aggrandizement – but for the child, only for the child."

"This is impossible," Guy said.

He turned away as she approached him. The hem of her cloak rustled upon the forest floor. A single ray of sun cast its light through the leafy ceiling above, illuminating what to Tessa looked to be a million sparkles the size of pin pricks across the entire surface of the cloak. Svetlana seemed to be made of light. Tessa edged a cautious step closer, pressing her shoulders and back against the tree trunk, the rough edges of the bark pressing painfully into her skin.

"What am I to tell her?" Svetlana asked, her voice infused with such longing that it caused Tessa's breath to catch in her throat. "You do not know what it's like. The child deserves to know her father. It's her right to be acknowledged by her father. It's her right to be loved!"

"Her father died," Guy persisted. "You told me so yourself. In that explosion on his yacht. Surely, it's better to tell the girl the truth than to delude her with false hope that her father lives?"

"But her father does live. That is my truth. That is our daughter's truth."

"No!" Guy shook his head. He raised his hand as though to strike her. In response, Svetlana cowered at his feet. The hood fell low over her face as the cloak billowed all around her. Tessa had to bite down hard to keep from crying out.

"You've filled her head with lies," he said. "Yes, the child deserves to know her father, but I tell you that man is not me. She deserves to know the truth – the real truth – not only about her father, but about her mother as well."

"And what truth is that?" Svetlana cried as she raised her head up from the ground. The hood spilled back onto her shoulders. "That her mother is a strong, powerful woman at the helm of an army the likes of which the world has never seen? That her mother is a warrior goddess who one day will rule the world: a world in which men like you finally receive the punishment you deserve for centuries of keeping women oppressed? Is that the truth of which you speak, Guy? Because if so, I shall be proud to share that truth. Feminina will rise from my ashes, more empowered and stronger than I have ever been. She will rise and the world will tremble. Mark my words. The Female Apocalypse is upon us."

Tessa feared she wouldn't be able to keep her presence concealed for much longer. (Being a double agent was proving a lot harder than she'd expected.) Svetlana's words inflamed her. The Russian woman's passion was intoxicating. If such words had been spoken within the context of a recruitment video, Tessa would have been the first in line to enlist. But she sensed – despite the fiery and inspiring rhetoric – that there was something not quite right about Svetlana Slutskaya, just as the child – Feminina (Tessa totally dug the name) – had the same somewhat chilling effect. And while Tessa was more inclined than not to believe Guy was indeed the girl's father – especially if she intended to use this as evidence that Guy was intent on bringing the Templeton family to its knees, as she was meant to do – she couldn't help but wonder whether Svetlana's somewhat amateur theatrics might somehow run the risk of undermining the credibility of her claims. Of course, a simple paternity test would easily bring resolution, but Tessa suspected in this case hearsay would prove more powerful than science. Almost as an afterthought, Tessa reached into the back pocket of her denim cut-offs for her phone. She'd almost forgotten. She clicked the video button to record and hoped she wasn't too late.

"You're crazy," Guy said.

Svetlana was undeterred. "For thousands of years, women have been called crazy – and worse – for being visionaries," she intoned in an almost incantatory voice that Tessa found hypnotic. "We've been burned alive as heretics and witches. We've been called whores. We've been raped, imprisoned and stoned to death for speaking our minds, for giving voice to our intelligence, for taking ownership of our bodies, for demanding the equality we deserve, that we have always deserved, that has been denied us for all these years! But no more. No more will we be downtrodden."

She rose to her feet in a defiant flourish of sunlight and ferocity. Tessa hesitated and then chanced a tentative step closer, desperate that her feet not disturb a twig or a bramble that would betray her presence. She held the phone at arms' length, watching the scene unfold through the viewfinder.

"If that is the truth of which you speak, then beware my truth."

Svetlana paused. She gazed into the distance. Tessa feared she was on the verge of being discovered. But then Svetlana's severe countenance suddenly brightened into a smile of surprising radiance. Tessa allowed herself a breath of relief.

"Of course, there is a way you can save yourself," Svetlana said, her voice dropping into an almost whisper. "It is a rather shoddy likeness but I do recognize myself in that tattoo. Its presence betrays you."

"It was a mistake," Guy replied. He crossed his arms in front of his chest and covered the tattoo with his hand. "An act of drunken foolishness. I don't even remember getting it."

"You've always liked your drink," Svetlana replied. "So English."

"I'm having it removed."

Svetlana slowly walked toward Guy. From Tessa's vantage point, it looked as though the Black Widow of Sochi was floating across the forest floor on gossamer wings. Her cloak rippled like a magic carpet.

"I am under your skin," Svetlana cooed. "You'll never be rid of me. Even in death, I will always be there. You will never escape."

"Try me."

But even Tessa could tell Guy's resolve was failing him. He didn't seek to evade Svetlana's hand when she touched him. Her fingers traced the crudely inked tattoo on his arm.

"Let me save you, Guy," she whispered. "It would be such a shame for Feminina to grow up never knowing her father. She doesn't deserve this. She didn't ask to be born. She is an innocent. Why punish her for the impetuousness of her parents?"

"For the last time: that child is not mine."

Svetlana whirled round. She clapped her hands imperiously. "Feminina!" she called out. "Feminina, *babushka*, come show *Maman* the lovely bluebells you've picked for her."

The child appeared within moments, flushed and giggling and out of breath. Her hair was adorned with a garland crown of bluebells and baby's breath. She held a bouquet out in front of her.

Tessa experienced a chill. The girl unnerved her.

"*Maman!*" Feminina cried as she ran into her mother's outstretched arms. "Look what I made for you."

"Oh, darling, they are lovely! So lovely!" Svetlana crouched to her daughter's level and accepted the bouquet. "Isn't she lovely, Guy? She even looks like you."

"Enough!" Guy exclaimed, his rage explosive. "I'm not going to let you do this. Take the child and go before I tell the authorities you're here. You're a wanted woman, Svetlana. If you care about the child, you'll leave now and forget all about me. I can't give you what you want, even if the girl was mine...even if I still loved you."

What happened next was so unexpected and so upsetting that Tessa doubted she would ever forget the moment. Svetlana rose to her full height and pulled the child close to her. From the voluminous folds of her cloak, she produced a dagger whose blade glistened in the sunlight. She raised the dagger high above her head before bringing it dramatically to Feminina's neck. The razor edge hovered terribly. Tessa gasped and nearly dropped her phone.

"Do not provoke me!" Svetlana cried. "I swear to you, Guy Templeton. Turn your back on me – on this child – and you will do so at her peril."

"Put the knife down, Svetlana."

"Oh, so you care now?" she mocked. "You acknowledge your seed only when she is about to be sacrificed. What kind of father are you, Guy Templeton?"

"She's just a little girl."

"*Maman?*"

"I am so sorry, my darling *babushka*. It is not I who does this."

"Papa?"

Tessa wondered whether she ought to intervene.

"Yes, *babushka*," Svetlana said. "Behold your father. Behold the man who loved me and left me, the man who denies his responsibility, who would prefer you not exist than acknowledge he owes you your life."

"He looks very sad, *Maman*."

"He has no heart. He is like all men. He will perish in the hell of the Apocalypse."

"But his heart is sad, *Maman*," Feminina said.

"If he is sad, it is of his own doing."

"*Non, Maman*," the child replied. "Let me go to him. *Il me fait envie de pleure*r. If I show him love, *Maman*, maybe he will show me love in return?"

"Men don't love," Svetlana said. 'They only rape."

"But is it not right to show compassion to those who would wish us ill? Release me, *Maman*. I want to feel Papa's embrace."

Svetlana reluctantly withdrew the dagger and did as Feminina bade. The girl ran to Guy and, in a gesture that brought tears to Tessa's eyes – and caused her to turn off the camera and restore the phone to the back pocket of her denim cut-offs – embraced him with such an innocent exuberance that even Guy appeared to melt.

"See, *Maman?* Perhaps Papa is not so bad after all?"

"Please, Svetlana," Guy said. "Let the past be past. The child deserves better than me. Leave England. Return to Moscow. There are people here that would harm you. Ambassador Bingham..."

Svetlana tossed her head back and laughed. "You think that old goat scares me?" she asked. "I did him a favor."

"Cordelia's ruined because of what you did."

"That was Anatole. I had nothing to do with it. He's always been over-enthusiastic. I am not my brother's keeper."

"You can't run forever."

"Who's running? I'd look at yourself, Guy Templeton, before casting the first stone."

Guy stooped to Feminina's level. He stroked her hair. "Go to your mother," he said. "You belong with her. Look after her. She needs you."

"Come, *babushka*. We should go. Perhaps I have been mistaken. Perhaps this man is not your 'Papa' after all?"

"No, *Maman*," the girl said, "you are not mistaken. It is just not his time."

Tessa watched as Feminina returned to her mother. Svetlana gathered the cloak about her and led the girl back in the direction of the bluebells before pausing and turning to Guy for one last appeal.

"You will regret this," she said.

"I'm willing to take that chance," Guy replied.

"You're a fool."

"I'm doing you a favor, Svetlana. Believe me."

"Your arrogance suffocates me," she said. "I see the future. I offered you the chance to save yourself, to stand at my right hand and rule the world – the new world that I am creating in my image, in our daughter's image – but you have rejected me. You have rejected her. I have done all I can. There is nothing left for me to do. You are doomed, Guy Templeton, and your family with you."

Svetlana paused, as though granting Guy one last chance to accept her offer, but Guy didn't acknowledge her. His back was turned. The child, Feminina, gave him a timid wave before following her mother into the bluebell patch and disappearing into the gathering shadows of the early afternoon sun.

In the distance could be heard the sounds of the Steeplechase and the generous din of intoxication and merriment coming from the grounds around the house. Tessa was torn. She knew she had witnessed something extraordinary, and while she didn't understand the context of most of the exchange, the gravity of Svetlana's parting words haunted her, as did the woman's willingness to sacrifice her child in the grief of Guy's rejection. It was Tessa's duty to report what she had seen to Penelope and to Yvette, yet despite her somewhat jaded exterior, Tessa felt a wave of compassion: for the Russian woman whose language frightened and mystified her, for the beautiful and ethereal child, and for Guy.

In the aftermath of Svetlana's departure, he seemed broken. He covered his face with his hands and appeared overcome by something like guilt. Tessa fought the urge to go to him, to embrace him and offer comfort, but she held back. How would she explain her presence if she were to reveal herself to him? What could she possibly say without raising suspicion and jeopardizing her mission? No, Tessa felt she had lingered too long as it was. She needed to get back to the house without further delay. Perhaps there would be time for compassion later? Tessa hoped so. She rather liked the idea of comforting Guy.

And so Tessa found herself once again running back to the house and the colorful, decadent and increasingly robust gaiety that encompassed it. The sun had risen to its zenith and the lack of cloud cover provided very little respite from its heat. Tessa longed to take a dip in one of the estate's many fountains and pools but her experience at the boathouse that morning had spooked her against any and all bodies of water on the Templeton property, not to mention the fact that the video evidence she now had on her phone was hot property and had to be delivered post-haste. But to whom was her first priority?

Which of them – Penelope or Yvette – needed her more? Or perhaps the more accurate question was: from whom did Tessa stand most to gain? The Frenchwoman certainly elicited a *frisson* that excited her more than anyone she had known in recent memory – male or female. Yvette was the stuff of Tessa's wildest imaginings, and she sensed – Tessa had a knack for these things – that she attracted Yvette as well. And while sex had its appeal, Tessa had learned from all too frequent experience that the thrill of orgasm was fleeting and often left her dissatisfied. What Penelope offered, on the other hand, seemed not only more lucrative in the long run (no one had to convince Tessa that dealing in Spice could reap a girl a fortune) but would help secure her place in the family fold, which had been – lest she forget – the main reason she had left London for the genteel Dorset countryside. But Yvette also made Tessa paranoid. The French spook seemed to have eyes everywhere – including in the back of her head – and her ability to hide in plain sight was, frankly, more than a bit unsettling, although Tessa figured a hit or two of Spice (or, better yet, a full-on Spice Bomb) would soon alleviate any lingering fear of Yvette she might have.

So off to find Penelope she went. Mercifully – for she was feeling quite exhausted – it didn't take Tessa long to track Penelope down. The American-born wife of Lord Edgar Templeton emerged from the house and onto the front lawn just as Tessa was approaching. A quick glance over each shoulder proved Yvette wasn't in the immediate vicinity, though Tessa knew better than to take this for granted.

"Penelope!" Tessa called out in greeting. "I have something for you, something I think you can use."

"Quiet!" Penelope hissed. She grabbed Tessa's arm and yanked her behind one of the marquis tents. "No one can see us together, do you understand? No one can suspect."

"Ouch!" Tessa pulled her arm free and rubbed it where Penelope's nails had dug into flesh. "Get a fucking grip!"

"What is it? What did you find?"

"The Spice first, please."

Penelope peered round the corner of the tent. Her eyes were wide and overly alert. Tessa smirked. Penelope really did have all the hallmarks of a Spice addict. She wondered whether maybe she should have gone to Yvette first after all. In Tessa's experience, addicts could be tricky customers.

"You drive a hard bargain," Penelope said once she'd convinced herself they weren't being watched. "Do I really need to remind you of the importance of being discreet?"

"Speak for yourself," Tessa snapped. She held out her hand, palm up. "Now give me my Spice and I'll show you what I have for you."

With a dramatic sigh, Penelope opened her clutch and deposited a plastic sandwich bag onto Tessa's hand. Tessa appraised the light brown Spice granules – like cinnamon really – before tucking the bag into one of the front pockets of her denim cut-offs.

"Satisfied?" Penelope asked.

Tessa smiled and winked. "That remains to be seen, doesn't it?"

"Out with it. I don't have all day."

"There's no question the child is Guy's," Tessa said as she took out her phone and pressed the video icon on its screen.

"How do you know? I need proof!"

"Voila!"

Tessa watched Penelope watch the video. When it ended, Penelope tried to snatch the phone from Tessa's hand but Tessa proved too quick and safely restored the phone to her back pocket. Penelope's fingers twitched. The woman was a basket case, Tessa decided. She'd have to watch her back.

"Well?" Tessa said. "Did I do good or did I do good?"

"He denies it."

"Of course he denies it! That doesn't mean it isn't true. I'd be more suspicious if he didn't."

"And you're sure no one saw you?"

"I hid behind a very big tree."

"Hmm." Penelope tapped the screen to play the video a second time. Tessa held her breath. "Who else knows about this?"

"For your eyes only," Tessa lied. "Just like you said."

"WhatsApp it to me."

Tessa snatched the phone back and did as Penelope bade her. "Done," she said. "What are you going to do with it?"

"None of your business," Penelope snapped. "You can go now. People might suspect something."

"I don't think anyone can see us."

"Don't contradict me!"

Tessa shrugged. Truth was, she found Penelope rather tiring. She now regretted not going to Yvette first.

"I'll be in touch," Penelope said, almost it seemed to Tessa as an afterthought. "And yes, you've done well. This is useful."

"Happy to be of service."

"I suggested a family meeting," Penelope blurted as Tessa turned to leave. "To Eliza. I told her you were my agent in the field. On reconnaissance."

"Does that mean I'm in?" Tessa asked.

"Not exactly." Penelope paused. "But it means you're on call. Later tonight. Keep your dance card clear and keep a check on the Spice. I can't have you showing up bombed out of your mind."

"Personal experience?" Tessa asked with a mischievous wink.

Penelope flushed. "And not a word of this to Chloe or Guy," she whispered. "Obviously they're not invited."

"Top secret," Tessa said.

"Very."

As much as Tessa longed to prepare herself a Spice Bomb before taking on too much additional exertion, she knew Yvette was waiting, and she sensed the Frenchwoman didn't take too kindly to being kept in the dark. Tessa emerged from behind the tent just as the first stage of the Steeplechase was coming to an end and the jockeys were dismounting for their afternoon tea. She scanned the environs for a glimpse of Yvette's fiery red hair but found herself suddenly distracted by the very evident attention of a rather burly dark-haired chap whose eyes, Tessa could tell even from a distance, bore a distinctly faraway cast that Tessa instinctively knew was one of the hallmarks of PTSD. She recognized him from somewhere, but the where and the how evaded her. Whoever he was, Tessa decided, he looked like a good time of the 'more wild than mild' variety. She liked the way he filled out his morning jacket.

"Who do you think you're looking at?" Tessa asked as she sauntered rather loosely toward him.

"Excuse me?" he stammered.

Tessa cocked her hip and crossed her arms in front of her chest. She tossed her head so her hair fell appealingly down to her shoulders and partially obscured her brow.

"Don't play dumb," she vamped. "I've seen that look. Don't you think a woman knows when she's being objectified?"

He coughed. His wedding ring flashed as he covered his mouth.

"And married too!" Tessa said. "Typical. Does your wife know what a lech you are? Christ, I really mourn for my gender sometimes. Put a wedding ring on a chick's finger and her self-esteem goes out the fucking window."

"Disgraceful," he said.

Tessa loved how easily he flustered.

"Contessa," she said – with an emphasis on the "Cont" – as she thrust her right hand out to him. "Templeton."

"Jack," he said, taking her hand and giving it a rather overly vociferous pump. His palm was sweaty. Tessa decided to overlook this on account of the fact that he was so goddamned cute – and probably famous to boot, which of course always helped. "Jack," he repeated. "Nice to meet you."

"Jack," she said. "Just Jack?"

"Tamsin and Jack," he spluttered. "Or Jack and Tamsin. Or just Jack if you'd rather."

Bingo!

"I thought I recognized you," Tessa said with a playful wag of her finger. "Your sexy mug gave you away. That and the dreamy faraway look in your eyes."

"I was in Afghanistan. Kandahar to be exact."

"A true British hero."

"And Iraq. Basra. The things I saw..."

"PTSD's a bitch," Tessa said.

"How'd you know?"

Tessa caressed his cheek before taking his arm. "You're sweet," she said.

"I'm not gay," Jack said. "At least I don't think I'm gay."

"Okay."

"No one knows what it's like out there, not unless you're out there. The stress, the heat, the dust: going out on patrol, never knowing whether you or your mates will come back alive or in a body bag, or strewn across the desert floor."

"Terrible," Tessa sighed. She was beginning to lose patience.

"Your boys become your boys," Jack continued. "D'ya know what I mean?"

"Sure," Tessa said.

"Do you have any idea how nice it is to talk to a bird that gets it?" Jack squeezed her arm. Tessa tried her best not to flinch. The faraway look in his eyes was less dreamy now – less poetic – and more crazed. "I mean, like, really gets it? Tamsin hasn't a clue, not a fuckin' clue."

"Obviously," Tessa said. "Good thing for you, I'm not Tamsin."

"Bully for me."

"Yes," Tessa smirked, "bully for both of us."

"Luca Mariotti," Jack spat the name in disgust. "She's welcome to him, fucking poof. Fucking Euro-trash wanker."

"Luca Mariotti?" Tessa asked. Her interest sparked anew. "The Formula One driver?"

"What's it to you?" Jack asked. His eyes twitched and blinked. "What have you heard? D' you know something I don't know?"

Tessa thought it best to steer the conversation away from any further minefields – real, literal, metaphoric, or imagined. Jesus, she thought, *being a Templeton was fucking hard work. No wonder Chloe's so neurotic!*

"Luca Mariotti's got nothing on you," she soothed. "Forget I asked."

"He's not even Italian. From fucking Brixton. Bet you didn't know that, did ya? Speaks the King's English though like it ain't his first language. Fuck me."

Tessa's phone buzzed. Yvette. *How did she get my number?*

`I don't like to be kept waiting…`

"Everyone's exploiting the migrant experience," she said. "What is the world coming to?"

"The things I've seen," Jack said. "Who can blame me?"

"Indeed," Tessa said. She removed her hand from his arm. It was time to move on. Yvette was waiting.

"She doesn't get it." Jack stepped closer. His fingers pawed her forearm, not in a threatening way exactly, but the alcoholic stench of his breath was enough to give Tessa concern that if she didn't nip this particular situation in the bud, things could get a little awkward. "She just doesn't fucking get it. I'm a veteran, y'know? A real flesh-and-blood hero. And Tamsin…I mean she…she…fucking…"

Tessa's smile was fixed and as fake as Penelope trying to convince everyone that she wasn't a junkie. "She doesn't get it," she interjected with an exaggerated roll of her eyes. "I know. I get it. You said."

"Boom!" Jack snapped his fingers. Tessa jumped. "I like you. You're smart. I get that about you. I don't know you but I think I'd like to get to know you. D'you want to get to know me?"

His hand started to paw. His nails dug into the flesh of her arm.

"Maybe some other time," she said. "Now if you'll excuse me..."

"Then how's about a shag? Prove Tamsin wrong, if you know what I mean?"

Tessa peeled Jack's offending fingers from her arm. "I don't actually," she said. "Now if you'll please..."

She didn't know what happened, but something in Jack suddenly triggered. He released her arm. His hands flailed to his ears and his mouth opened in a silent scream. Tessa wasn't sure whether to be alarmed, amused, or to call for help. Although she'd recognized the symptoms of PTSD from afar, confronting it close-up was more than Tessa had reckoned on.

"Are you all right?" she asked even as it was more than obvious that Jack was anything but. "Can I get you anything? Some water perhaps? Or an adult beverage? Pimms?"

Jack shook his head. His hands clenched and unclenched his ears. He bowed and rocked and swayed like a sinner about to be saved. Tessa feared he was about to convulse and she really didn't want to be there when he did.

"Luca Mariotti!" Jack exclaimed. "Fucking Luca Mariotti! Tamsin's been fucking Luca Mariotti. And she's telling everyone about it. I'm a cuck...a cuckold...a fucking pussy boy...because my wife is fucking pregnant and it ain't my fucking baby...because, d'you know what she says?"

Tessa glanced around her, desperate for an escape route, an exit, a way out. There were teems of people about them but no one seemed to be paying either of them the slightest bit of attention: horses, fascinators, top hats and tails. Everyone was having a bloody good time...everyone that is except Tessa. She needed to make some changes before being a Templeton really became a chore.

"It's not such a bad thing really," she placated.

Her voice seemed to soothe. "What is?" he asked. Jack slowly removed his hands from his ears and straightened up. He stopped swaying. Tessa exhaled.

"You'll see. Maybe your wife..."

"Tamsin. I'm asking her for a divorce before she gives birth to that poser's bastard."

"Tamsin ... maybe she's doing you a favor. Sometimes it just happens late in life...when you realize..."

Her phone buzzed again. Yvette.

Où es-tu la bête? [Where the fuck are you?]

"I have to go," she said. It didn't feel right somehow, leaving him alone like this in his all-too-evident distress. And he really did seem like a sweet guy despite, well, everything.

Then she had an idea. "Let me give you something," she said. She shoved her hand into her denim cut-off shorts pocket and pulled out the plastic baggie with the Spice. Tessa hated to part with it, the shit was valuable and just moments ago she had been so desperate for a Bomb, but there were times when you had to look out for others before you looked out for yourself, and Tessa sensed this was one of those times.

"What's that?" Jack asked. His dark eyes bugged out just a bit too eagerly.

Tessa dangled the bag at eye level. "The answer to your prayers."

Jack snatched the bag from her hand.

"But don't use it all at once," she cautioned. "Especially if it's your first time."

Jack opened the bag. He dipped his finger in and rubbed the Spice on his gums. Tessa wondered whether she might need to intervene, but decided it was better to take advantage of his distraction and hightail it to Yvette before the Frenchwoman went all Gallic on her and Jack OD'd.

"What's it called?" he asked as he sucked his fingers clean.

"Spice."

| 28 |

Jack couldn't recall a time when he'd experienced such a rush. Sure, he and the lads had dabbled a bit in the local *kush* – you needed to every once in a while to prevent yourself from going stark raving mad, and the locals were only too happy to supply – but this shit, whatever it was, took him to another level entirely. He couldn't describe it. His gums tingled where he'd rubbed the powder and his nostrils burned and his perception of everything around him and his place within everything around him was electric and it made him want to take his clothes off and run naked and free and roll in the grass and splash in the fountains and shag and shag some more – anything and anyone in sight regardless of age or gender assignation or biome.

It was incredible. The girl was incredible. Her fucking eyebrows were incredible. But she was gone. Where was she? Jack needed to find her. He needed to find her now. He needed to find her now and tell her…and tell her…what did he need to tell her? He needed to tell her how she had saved him. How she had saved him and how she had restored his faith in himself, in life, in the world, in sex, in being a man, a hero, in just being. Jack was obsessed. And he wanted to tell the world just how obsessed he was. But first, he needed to find the girl and thank her and proclaim his love for her and shag her brains out and never ever let her out of his sight ever, never, ever again.

He started to run. He wasn't conscious of running exactly but his feet were moving beneath him and his breath panted and heaved and he was reminded of being out on patrol with the boys in Kandahar, in full combat gear (helmets and everything), ever mindful that any misstep could result in an IED going off and limbs flying every which way 'til Sunday and you never knew where the enemy was but those fucking Taliban were crafty motherfuckers and they were watching your every move and even though the landscape never changed those fuckers had their foxholes and their target points and they loved nothing more than seeing your best mate blown to kingdom come and they laughed and prayed to Allah and strapped themselves to fucking bombs and blew themselves up without a second thought and you were fucked and the world was fucked and your brain jarred concussively in your skull and it was such a fucking rush you never wanted it to end even though a part of you knew that it could be your guts heaving out of your flak jacket and your brains and viscera splashed and splattered all over the rocky, dusty desert floor. Just because you were lucky one day didn't mean they wouldn't get you the next. *Allahu Akbar* my motherfucking arse!

Jack ran and ran and ran. The landscape ahead was green and unfamiliar. It didn't look like Kandahar but then he didn't put it past the locals to paint the fucking rocks and sand green to trip him up, to disorientate him, to separate him from his platoon so they could isolate him and fuck him up and shove their Korans up his ass and accuse him of desecrating their fucking religion before they shoved pincers up his pisshole and sacrificed him to their fucking Allah.

For that's what had happened to Corporal Danny Trevonte. Well, okay, maybe not the Koran bit but those fucking fuckers had fucked Danny up right good before they dumped his headless corpse outside the gate of the outpost to make Jack and the boys clean up the mess. Those motherfuckers had even cut off the kid's cock and balls and shoved 'em in his mouth.. That's when Jack had known he'd had enough, that nothing – not even queen and country – was worth the pain, the agony, the torment of what the army had sent him out there to do. And fuck if he'd ever known what it was they were doing there in that Godforsaken place. It seemed no one learned from history. Afghanistan could not be conquered. Should've taken heed from the Soviets.

Jack was hot. The sun was beating down. Like fuckin' Kandahar. He kept running. Like that time when he and his mates – Josh and Lewis – had gotten so goddamned stir crazy they'd climbed over the walls of the outpost in the middle of the night – risking their hands being cut to shreds on the barbed wire – just so they could run wild for a few minutes in the brush and the rock outside the sandbagged confines of the outpost. Of course, they'd all been off their heads from the arak Josh had managed to smuggle into the camp from his leave in Abu Dhabi, not to mention the dope Jack had "commandeered" from the lorries they'd intercepted that morning on the road out of Kandahar before blowing the convoy up to high heaven. It just hadn't seemed right to let the good stuff go to waste.

And there he was – Jack and the boys – running wild in the scrub on the other side of the outpost perimeter with the stars twinkling overhead in that vast midnight blue Afghan sky. He had been so at peace with himself and the world around him that it only seemed natural to strip off and run naked, unencumbered by helmets or body armor or flak jackets or boots. With Josh and Lewis – Corporals Pearce and Tennyson – at his side, what need had he for the inconvenience of camouflage and ammo? He felt secure. He felt protected. He was as high as those fucking kites he'd seen the kids in Kabul flying from the rooftops across the cityscape of that ramshackle city, and he was feeling no pain. Beauty could be found in the most godforsaken of places if you opened your eyes and your heart to it.

They went swimming in the riverbed at the bottom of the gorge over which the outpost looked. The water was shallow and skimmed with a yellowish kind of algae that looked almost radioactive, but to Jack it might as well have been Nirvana. He and Josh and Lewis ran full bore into the water until they were up their chests in the tepid stuff. They splashed and tried to dunk each other under, whooping and hollering like a trio of laughing hyenas or (more like) fucked up bachelors on a stag bender. In the back of his mind, Jack knew nothing good would come of this. The dope alone was enough to get him court-martialed, not to mention sneaking off base. What the fuck had he been thinking? But sometimes it felt good not to think. Sometimes, when the darkness clouded his mind, Jack wished an IED would find him or a fucking Taliban sniper would lay him out with a bullet between the eyes – wham, bam, thank you mum – and it'd be over and the numb would take over and he'd be free.

POSH

Free. Jack had always been a slave of his own mind. When the dark took over, there was nothing Jack could do but ride out the storm. He'd learned to deal with it (somewhat) in school, after his father was put away for beating up his mother so bad her jaw had to be wired shut for six months and she'd lost the vision in her right eye. Although he supposed his mum hadn't helped matters any by attacking his dad with an electric carving knife she'd been meant to use on the Easter lamb. Oh, what a fucking ruckus there had been! Jack preferred not to think about it. He'd gone out back by the garden shed and gotten fucked up on glue and his dad's bottle of homebrew and then had run amok in the neighborhood smashing telephone boxes with his cricket bat until he'd run himself out and his arms hurt from swinging and he vomited against the wall of the Paki newsagents down the end of the road by the roundabout.

Yeah, it seemed Jack was always running – never to anywhere, mostly just from himself, if he stopped to think about it. But Jack didn't like to think, at least not if he could help it, and his mind would keep racing even if he was standing still. Finally it all caught up to him. He ran himself into juvenile detention for picking on some refugee kid at the bus stop...right, so he did more than just pick on the kid, more like bash his face in with said cricket bat. Like father like son. He couldn't really be blamed though if he didn't have any positive male role models around. At least that's the reason he gave the warrant officer who wasn't at all amused. He was given a choice: jail or the army.

Jack chose the army. At eighteen he left everything he had ever known behind him to begin the process of reinventing (and rehabilitating) himself. And he loved it. He found he loved the discipline and the overall laddishness of it. For the first time in his life, Jack felt he had a reason for waking up in the morning and went to bed each night satisfied that he'd done something worthwhile even if it was only mopping up the barrack lavatories before lights-out.

The physicality of it appealed to him as well. He soon found himself in the best shape of his life. The endurance runs during training, where the heat and the pace and the weight of his kit on his back would surely have caused someone of lesser mettle to collapse from exhaustion, were what Jack lived for, that and the feel of cold hard steel in his hands and the power it afforded him by just taking aim and pulling a trigger. It was nothing if not an improvement over the wooden cricket bat back home.

None of this is to say, however, that all was strawberries and cream. Jack's demons ran deep and he could only run so far. There were dark forces at work, forces over which he felt he had very little control. Lala had helped, but look what had happened to her. He'd loved her and, by necessity, had had to leave her. Theirs had been a modern day fairy tale, a cross-cultural love story for the times, a Romeo and Juliet-style tragedy where Quetta, Pakistan had served as a stand-in for fair Verona. Jack had hoped for a time that Lala would be his salvation, his salve against the darkness, the madness, and rage of his mind. But religion and a culture he didn't understand – or, quite honestly, care to understand – got in the way and fucked things up in such a way that Jack knew he'd never recover.

He didn't want to think about Lala. Because when he thought about Lala he could only think about the video that was sent to his phone. He'd watched it again and again – rapt and horrified and perversely fascinated. Her own father and uncle, the villagers, the baby-faced but extremist Ali – the boy to whom she'd been betrothed from the age of eight – united against her in their ritual of death. Jack had probably watched the seven-minute clip a hundred times if not more. He'd memorized it: how her father had cast the first stone, then her uncle, then Ali, and then one-by-one the village elders while the women ululated and wailed and rent the cloth of their burkas. Jack would close his eyes and the scene would play out before him, forever etched into the remotest corners of his consciousness. It drove him mad. And all because he'd been careless.

Tamsin didn't understand...couldn't understand...*wouldn't* understand. When they'd first met, his future wife had been a breath of fresh air, frivolous, vapid and carefree, a willow-the-wisp flitting hither and yon in the breeze. She was *Made in Chelsea* through-and-through, a true Sloane Ranger born and bred. He'd received an honorable discharge three months previous on account of the trauma. He and his story were profiled in a *Sunday Times* piece that in his opinion was TLDR, but it had caught the eye of one Cressida Parker – not to mention the Heartbreak of a Nation – who had invited him to a fundraiser she was hosting at the Posh TV studios for PTSD-afflicted veterans of the Iraq and Afghanistan wars. Thus Jack found himself a poster boy for a cause he preferred to forget, touted as a National Treasure, and thrust before television cameras on breakfast morning shows and drive-time talk radio stations around the country. NPR in America even picked up the story and the fucking *New York Times*. Suddenly, Jack was a celebrity. Every star and starlet and YouTube personality wanted him, but no one had wanted him more than Tamsin.

He'd been blinded by the lights, cameras, and action, seduced by Tamsin's aura and her impossibly perfect teeth. Sure, she was a hot lay but sex only got a bloke so far. Without love supporting it, there was actually very little to the fervid press of flesh against flesh. In fact, it was one of the things he had prized about Lala: her innocence and how it presented itself in equal measures to her surprising worldliness and pragmatism. For Lala had been a woman seemingly trapped inside a child's body, just turned fifteen when he'd met her. She was young but she was old. They had barely even kissed.

Before he knew it, he and Tamsin were married and the stars of a hit DIY program on Posh TV. Tamsin fancied herself an expert on interior design. Jack knew how to use a hammer on account of the post-discharge rehabilitation program for mentally fucked-up vets like him. Cressida was the puppet master behind-the-scenes. He'd enjoyed Series One: it was something new and shiny and distracting. It helped that he and Tamsin were still getting to know each other as newlyweds. Their on-camera repartee and sassy double *entrendre* charmed the country and helped put Posh TV on the map, not to mention lots of pound sterling into their joint bank account. Series Two brought the licensing deals and more *ker-ching!!!* But Jack found himself wanting. The bloom was off the rose. He'd look at Tamsin sometimes and see nothing but a blonde-haired spray-tanned (albeit fit) monster staring back at him with eyes and a mouth that looked as though they wanted to devour him if he didn't behave exactly as she (and Cressida) demanded. But the money was good – too good – and he couldn't deny that being a celebrity had epic appeal. And it was pretty fucking awesome when Bear Grylls called him up and asked him to do a celebrity guest spot on *The Island*. That in and of itself was like the ultimate validation. Eat yer fuckin' heart out, Ant Middleton!

But then things started to unravel during the filming of Series Three. Ratings were down on account of some Tweet storm involving Tamsin and a racially-charged exchange between her and Bree Armstrong, who had never forgiven Tamsin for eclipsing her popularity on the British News Network (BNN) before hightailing it over to Posh TV. Jack had tried to steer clear of the *furore*, preferring to let Tamsin and the network duke it out, but the gist of the situation as far as Jack could tell had to do with a tweet Tamsin posted claiming that the only reason Bree had been given a co-host spot at Posh TV with Maximilian Porter was because the network had been told – by whom, Jack didn't know – that it needed to "diversify" its roster of presenters, and not because Bree showed any particular promise as a rising new television talent. Tamsin had then gone on to say that Posh TV was merely looking for a "token Black" to pair alongside its "token gay" in its struggling Monday prime time line-up.

POSH

Behind the scenes, Tamsin had been given a brutal dressing down by Cressida – whose reputation, of course, was at stake as well as that of the network – but little was publicly done to address the issue. In private, Cressida had even confided to Jack that she strongly adhered to the adage that no publicity was bad publicity and was secretly thrilled by all the media coverage. The upshot though was that Bree and Maximilian were elevated to the Magic Circle of television presenters – their weekly celebrity cunt-fest became Monday night's ratings champion – while Jack and Tamsin's own ratings tanked, the endorsement deals started to dry up, and rumors of marital issues between them percolated on social media and the gossip and entertainment rags, perpetuated of course by Bree and Maximilian, who were only too happy to throw Tamsin – and Jack by association – on the slag heap.

And then along came Luca. Depending on how one looked at it, the arrival of Luca Mariotti was either a blessing or a curse. The fact that the introduction was quite blatantly scripted by Cressida – helped along by her husband and Luca's Formula One team owner Olivier Thibault – made Jack suspect another ratings push was in the works. Tamsin had started to get desperate. Her followers on Twitter, Instagram, Snapchat, and TikTok were dropping like flies – while Bree's rose like Kilimanjaro. And while Cressida assured them the show was going to be renewed for at least two more series – to fulfill the five-year commitment on their contracts – Tamsin lived in fear that she was soon to be rendered irrelevant. Her behavior – on and off camera, for they were still in the midst of shooting Series Three – became increasingly erratic. She was abusive to staff, accusing everyone from the assistant gaffer to her wardrobe consultant of leaking defamatory stories about her to the press. But it was Jack to whom she flung the most vitriol. Oh, the anger, the rages, the hysteria! The late-night alcohol- and pill-fueled screaming fests, the suicide threats!

It was the accusations that hurt Jack most. Tamsin's cruel, razor-edged tongue knew no bounds. Nothing was sacred where he was concerned. She attacked his army record, his mental illness – she even went so far as to call him a "PTSD Poser" – and, the worst cut of all, his manhood. Jack had tried his best to take it all in stride. He knew he couldn't risk the rage getting the better of him. He simply had too much at stake. But Tamsin was relentless, and one night, Jack just snapped.

In his defense, Jack felt reason was on his side. The "incident" occurred after they'd attended the British Grand Prix at Silverstone, courtesy of Cressida and Olivier, who put them up in style at the team's private VIP lounge overlooking the pit lane. The bubbly flowed and with it (inevitably) Tamsin's stream of consciousness. The way in which she threw herself at Luca after the race – Brixton's very own Italian Stallion (he'd come in third) – was cheap and vulgar and a total embarrassment to anyone present who had half a sense of propriety. Unfortunately for Jack, Cressida's crowd ran fast and loose. Propriety apparently wasn't a priority. Tamsin ran up to Luca when he entered the lounge after the podium presentations – soaked through and reeking of champagne – and declared in a voice as shrill as it was intoxicated:

"'C'mere, Signor Mariotti, and show Tam-Tam some of that famous Luca Love!"

She thrust herself into the racecar driver's unsuspecting arms and launched herself up so her legs straddled his waist. What choice had Luca but to respond to Tamsin's fervent kisses? None, it seemed. Despite the fact that Jack was standing right there with little more than his very emasculated dick in his hand, Luca and Tamsin went at it for all the world to see. And how the world saw!

"Now that's what I call *amore!*" Cressida bellowed in her throaty voice, raising her champagne flute high and toasting the cameras and paps, and thus providing the morning's papers with their front-page headlines.

Only Olivier showed Jack the slightest concern, and even then it wasn't much. Luca's boss turned to Jack with an apologetic little shrug and said, "What can I say? *C'est* Formula One. We go a little *loco* sometimes" before going over to Luca, putting his arm around him, and pouring a bottle of Brut over his head.

Needless to say, the drive home was long, silent, and tense. When they finally arrived at their Belgravia townhouse, Tamsin stumbled up the front steps and tried to bar Jack from following her inside, clawing and scratching at him with perfectly manicured nails while blocking his entry. (More fodder for the morning's tabloids and social media feeds!) Jack knew he was treading on thin ice. The darkness pressed on his mind, weighing him down like lead blocks. His vision blurred. He felt as though his veins would burst from the adrenalin. His instinct was to kill.

"Get away from me!" Tamsin screamed. "You moron, you monster, you fucking retard!"

Jack managed to push through the door and into the entrance hall, doing so however at the expense of Tamsin who fell to her knees on the black-and-white tiled floor with a howl fit to wake the neighbors and then some.

"Shut up!" he cried. "Shut up! Shut up! Shut up!"

Jack was only half-aware that his hands were wrapped around Tamsin's neck and he was throttling her. It was almost as though he was standing outside of himself observing, a passive bystander as opposed to an all-too-involved participant: a state of being not dissimilar to that which he had often experienced in Afghanistan when he and his boys were out on patrol and under enemy fire. The sound of Tamsin's voice grated in his ears. Images of her and Luca flashed in front of his eyes – distorted and menacing. The memory of her drunken laughter burned in his ears, egging him on, encouraging him to press down harder on her neck, crushing her windpipe, blocking the oxygen to her brain. And then he released her. He sprang back and crumpled into a heap on the floor beside her, curling himself into a fetal position, tucking his hands between his knees. What had he done? Where was he? What kind of monster had he become?

Jack was horrified, disgusted with himself, with the world, with whatever it was that had driven him to commit such an act of rage against the one person he loved more than anyone or anything else on the planet ... after Lala, for there was always Lala. There would always be Lala. Tamsin didn't understand. She'd never understand.

"Baby." Jack heard Tamsin's whisper, felt her breath humid in his ear, the wet of her tears on his face. He smelled her perfume mixed with the faint residue of cigarette smoke and champagne. He opened his eyes. Her face hovered over him, her sparkling blue eyes bleary, her cheeks smeared with her mascara.

"Baby," she repeated.

Jack pressed himself hard against her. Tamsin's arms cradled and rocked him like a babe. Her touch brought him comfort. Her warmth was like returning to the womb.

"Tam-Tam," he sniffled.

"Shhh...I'm here. I'm okay. We're okay, baby. It's okay."

"I can't..." Jack couldn't breathe. "I'm drowning."

"*We're* drowning, baby," Tamsin said. She buried her face in his neck. He wanted to kiss her. He wanted her to kiss him. His lips sought hers. "We're drowning, baby," she said. "We need help."

"I want you so much!"

"I want you so much."

Their lips found each other. Their bodies sought unity. The rage within Jack's head released as he pressed himself inside her. Thoughts of Lala – of what had been, of what might have been – were banished. He gave himself fully to Tamsin – the love of his life, his salvation, his rock – as she in turn gave herself to him. Sex with Tamsin was sacred. He needed to remind himself of that. He couldn't ever lose her. He couldn't afford to lose her.

When it was over, they fell asleep in each other's arms after vowing repeatedly – desperately – to combat the darkness together. But even in the heat of the moment, Jack knew Tamsin offered nothing but empty solace. And as the weeks and then months passed after "the incident," Jack found himself anticipating the day when he'd return home to find Tamsin gone. She was always there – nothing if not faithful to the façade – but he smelled the sex of another man on her – Luca Mariotti – and every day was like a slap in the face, a reminder that he was less than a man and that Tamsin only stayed with him to keep Cressida Parker, Posh TV, and her now-returning legion of social media followers, happy. He in turn kept the darkness at bay, but Jack wasn't stupid. Once their contract with the network was up, Jack knew he'd be cast off as too unpredictable, too much of a liability...and then what would happen to him? With his broken mind and his destroyed spirit, Jack envisioned a life on the streets, selling *Big Issue* on street corners, standing in endless lines outside homeless shelters at day's end, hoping for a bed to crash on, a hot meal, and a few hours' respite from the tragedy he had become, before it all started again come morning.

Now Tamsin was pregnant, or at least so she claimed. With another man's child. *Luca's* child. And she – his fucking wife, his goddamned little Tam-Tam – had outed him as a poof. He could try to deny it until he was blue in the face, but Jack knew enough about the media to recognize denial only further stacked the odds against him. Or maybe, just maybe, Tamsin knew him better than he knew himself? He certainly wouldn't put it past her.

The fountain was cold. The water splashed against his naked skin. Jack dove headfirst into the Capability Brown-designed fountain and swam like he and Josh and Lewis – dead because of him, his best mates dead because of his carelessness – were back in the riverbed on the other side of the outpost fence. He suddenly found that he wasn't alone. All around him was a whirl of brightly colored madness, laughter and gaiety as other of the Templeton's Steeplechase guests took to the fountain to cool off as well. He'd inspired a trend. He wasn't in Afghanistan. This was England. He wasn't a corporal in the British Army serving his third tour of duty in the back of beyond. He was Jack of Jack & Tamsin, the second most beloved presenting duo on Posh TV after Bree & Maximilian, of course.

He caught a glimpse of Tamsin hitching the hem of her LK Bennett dress up above her knees as she climbed over the 17th century stone and into the water with the other guests. Jack paused. He held his breath. He willed her to come to him. Their eyes met. Their gazes locked. Her skin glistened in the water and the sunlight.

"Baby." Her lips moved. She looked as though she was crying.

"Baby," he said in return.

She came to him and they were Jack & Tamsin again.

At least for another day.

| 29 |

I t felt good to keep them waiting. Lady Eliza stood in the antechamber off of the second floor conservatory, listening to the din of disgruntled chatter as the family assembled in the adjacent room. Penelope had proven herself surprisingly useful. The video was just the thing she needed to convince the others that Guy must be banished from the Templeton fold. Clearly he was plotting against them, and with the Russians no less! Had there ever been such an act of treachery in all Templeton history? Eliza thought not. Nor had there ever been such a coup – more importantly – as the one she was in the midst of carrying out. And while it was still too early to trust Penelope entirely – not that Eliza trusted anyone entirely, except perhaps Sister Francine whose loyalty and resourcefulness never failed to fill Eliza with an overwhelming sense of gratitude, awe, and dread – the former Miss Bachelorette of Cedar Rapids, nee Penny Danziger, certainly had the makings of a worthy foot soldier for the cause. She'd have to keep a close eye on her though. And as for Tessa – the imposter – the jury was still out. The girl had done well in securing the documentary evidence Eliza had asked for, but there was just something about her that Eliza still didn't trust. She would have to think of another test. Francine would know what to do.

"Listen to them," Eliza said. She squeezed Sister Francine's hand and pressed it hard against her thigh. "How utterly foolish they are! How totally self-consumed."

"Idolators!" Sister Francine hissed. "They must be smote."

"And smote them we shall." Lady Eliza smiled. A tingle of exhilaration zipped up her arm from the hand that held the Fallen Angel's and flooded her whole body with a sensation that was nothing short of orgasmic. "One by one."

"Until there are none." Sister Francine's dark eyes flashed.

Not for the first time, Lady Eliza thanked God she was in the Fallen Angel's good graces.

"Tell me, Sister, in your visions..."

"Yes, Mum?"

"Do you see anyone else, or is it just the child and her mother?"

"Are you asking if I see the child's father?"

"Guy? Hmm. Yes."

"No, Milady...at least, I haven't as of yet."

"But you will now?"

"I've always felt his presence, but he himself has remained out of focus."

"And you're convinced that the child and the Russian whore are the same as whom you've seen?"

"Yes, Milady." Lady Eliza felt Sister Francine start to tremble. She pressed the Fallen Angel's hand again to steady her. "They are the harbingers of the Apocalypse. I am sure of it."

"Good." She allowed herself a short exhalation of relief. "Very good."

"Do you have reason to doubt me?"

"No!" Lady Eliza declared perhaps a little too vociferously. "Never. I didn't mean to imply. Your visions are our beacon, Sister. Without them, we would be lost and without hope of ever finding the path of righteousness. I need you. I need you here at my side – always and forever."

"Always and forever," Sister Francine repeated.

"The Movement can't survive without you. You *are* The Movement. I am just a lowly disciple."

"With cash," Sister Francine said. "Lots of cash."

"With a lot more coming if everything goes to plan. Now you're sure that Chloe and Guy won't recover before morning?"

Sister Francine shook her head. "The tincture is guaranteed. Poppy for slumber and a trace of arsenic for stomach upset."

Lady Eliza couldn't help but smile. "They'll think it was the Oysters Rockefeller!" she laughed.

Even Sister Francine conceded a slight upward twitch at the corners of her mouth. "Indeed, Milady," she said. "Nothing like a bit of bad shellfish to roil the bowels but good."

"It's time."

The family turned as one when Lady Eliza and Sister Francine entered the conservatory, hand-in-hand, presenting a united front. Eliza felt their eyes upon them and sensed their revulsion at the sight of the Fallen Angel now stood at her right hand. There could be no doubt in any of their minds as to where the power had shifted and to whom they were expected to pay obeisance. Eliza knew the road ahead was fraught, but she hadn't the slightest shred of doubt that in the end she and Sister Francine – and, more importantly, The Movement – would come out as the ultimate victors over the pending Apocalypse.

"Thank you for tearing yourselves away from the weekend's debaucheries to be here tonight," she began. Her eyes cast an imperious gaze about the room. *How apprehensive they all look, she thought. How fearful! Good. It is right that they fear me.* "I will try to keep this brief."

"Where's Chloe?" Diana interrupted.

"And Guy?" Edgar added most unhelpfully.

"They've been taken ill," Eliza replied. She had prepared for this. "It seems the oysters this evening were a bit off."

"Blimey!" Duncan scoffed. "I helped myself to an entire tray-full and feel fit as a fiddle. They were absolutely scrumptious. Not as good as the Oysters Rockefeller I've et in N'Awlins, because of course you have to go to Antoine's to get the real thing – the damn dish originated there – but they were pretty darn good. My hat's off to the chef. Don't you agree, Diana?"

Diana gave her husband an arch look and took a rather mincing sip of her port. "The last time I checked, you're as English as I am," she snapped. "I believe those of us who aren't from Louisiana are – fortunately or unfortunately – relegated to calling it 'New Orleans.'"

"That's the problem with you, Diana," Duncan replied. "You've got no zest – no sense of fun. No adventure. No passion for life. *No joie de vivre!* It's probably a good thing we've never had children."

A collective gasp spilled across the room.

"Duncan!" Penelope led the charge.

"What?" Duncan shrugged as he helped himself to a generous pour of cognac from the sideboard along the wall. "Barren of spirit, barren of womb. The two go hand-in-hand, if you ask me. Why do you think I spend so much time away?"

"Oh no, no, no!" Diana exclaimed, wagging a disapproving finger while she reached for the bottle of cognac and snatched it from her husband. "Don't you start with me!" Following Duncan's example, she filled a glass just shy of overflow before knocking it back with an alcoholic's relish. "Not in this house. Not in front of my family."

"What are you doing, just standing there?" Eliza heard Sister Francine's voice in her ear, harsh, urgent and impatient. "This is intentional. They planned this. They're undermining you. It's all an act."

But Eliza didn't agree, at least, not entirely, for she had been around the family long enough to have witnessed such scenes play out in a more-or-less unvarying loop whenever they were together en masse for any extended length of time. The Templetons were, if nothing else, a well-lubricated lot. In other words, there wasn't one among them who didn't enjoy their tipple or could handle it very well. Before her first Christmas on Carleton's arm, he had taken her aside and warned her there would be fireworks. She'd assumed – with uncharacteristic naivete – that he was referring to the festive kind. It certainly hadn't taken her long to be disabused of this notion. In fact, Carleton even encouraged his children to act out against each other. Eliza had witnessed many an occasion where her new – and now late – husband even seemed to enjoy pitting one against the other. Templeton Manor was like the Colosseum, he once told her, his children but gladiators in the pit.

For Eliza, rather for The Movement to succeed, she knew she would have to use this internecine blood sport to her advantage. The most volatile – and enduring – hot spot of course was the ongoing dissolution of Diana and Duncan's marriage, which ran far deeper than the fact of Diana's miscarriage and subsequent inability to bear children. Eliza had information – on good authority – that she intended to use at the appropriate time. But the jury was still out where Diana was concerned, and Eliza wasn't sure whether what she knew should be used to secure Diana as an ally or render Carleton's oldest heir six feet into the ground. Eliza had a lot of thinking to do.

"*Your* family?" Duncan scoffed in his faux Scottish accent that only presented itself on the outer edges of his public school enunciation when he was several sheets to the wind. "It's only ever about possession with you, isn't it, Diana? *Your* family. *Your* money. *Your* dynasty. Whatever happened to what's mine is yours? Or, I suppose in this case, what's yours is mine? But then, hang on a minute, you don't really have anything because you're just a girl. Your father doesn't like girls very much, which I suppose is rather a shame and perplexing really because your mother was such a delightful creature – such an exemplar of the fairer sex – so it's all the more perplexing that you'd turn out to be such a colossal bore...and frigid to boot. No wonder your father detested you."

"Really, Duncan old chap, don't you think you might want to rein it in a little?" Edgar again, as useless as ever. "Even if what you say is true, Diana is my sister – and your wife – and I really won't stand to have her spoken to in that way."

"Assert yourself!" Sister Francine seethed in Eliza's ear. "The moment is slipping. They need to be reminded. They need to be told."

Sister Francine was right. She couldn't afford to let the situation slip further out of hand. As it was, they were already indisposed towards her and all too accustomed to fighting amongst themselves. And if this meeting – a meeting that she herself had called – was allowed to devolve further into the anarchy upon which Eliza knew they all thrived, she might never get another chance to present the evidence she needed for them to unite behind. Eliza wished she could ask Sister Francine to take the initiative. How much easier that would be! But if she wanted to truly assume her place at the head of the table – and win the most grudging respect from her husband's children (for as much as she loathed them, Eliza was nothing if not a pragmatist) – she couldn't be afraid to use her voice. Otherwise, all her careful and meticulous planning and plotting – her life's work these past several years – might soon be rendered all for naught.

Eliza clapped her hands. If she'd had a bell, she would have rung it. "Enough!" she declared in a voice of such uncompromising authority it surprised even her. All eyes turned to her as one. She paused, took a deep breath, and reminded herself of whom she was and where she had come from. "I know your father indulged your childish bickering, but I am here to remind you that this is not a sandbox and you are not schoolchildren at play."

"But you look awfully like a headmistress," Edgar interjected with a mocking glint in his eye. "The resemblance is uncanny really. Don't you think so, Donut?" ('Donut' was Edgar's pet name for Duncan, a not very clever play on the American Dunkin' Donuts chain. How Eliza loathed their privileged antics, their arch superiority, their disdain!)

"Indeed," Duncan said. He cocked his chin and appraised her down the length of his rugby-broken nose. "The kind that me and my mates used to have a good wank over after lights out – corporal punishment and a big stick. A very big stick, mind you. Every Etonian's wet dream. Not so very unlike you, Penelope."

"You're beastly!" Penelope exclaimed before turning back to Eliza and nodding for her to continue. "Carry on," she said. "Don't mind them. Boys will be boys and some boys never grow up. You were saying? Chloe and Guy were taken ill? How unfortunate! Although I must admit, the oysters did taste a little fishy to me."

"What on earth do you possibly know about oysters?" Diana said. Taking the bottle of cognac with her, she returned to her position on the chaise and lit a cigarette. True to form, Eliza thought: when an outsider dared assert themselves, the dynamic shifted. They were like vultures. The marital strife between Diana and Duncan would live to see another day.

"And what do you possibly know about art?" Penelope shot back. "Being an artist is more than striking avant-garde poses and throwing paint on a canvas."

Diana emitted a wry chuckle and blew a plume of smoke in her sister-in-law's general direction. "And being British is more than putting on a funny accent and using the Union Jack as your Twitter avatar."

Touché, Eliza thought. She was almost enjoying this.

"Blimey," Tessa said to no one in particular. "And I thought I was a bitch. Donut, darling, pass me the booze. I have a feeling it's going to be a long night."

"Right." Duncan was all too eager to comply. Tessa's smile of gratitude was something more than familial.

Eliza felt Sister Francine's fingernail cut through the cloth of her skirt, pressing painfully into the flesh on the back of her thigh: a warning, a reminder. It wasn't like Eliza to be so easily distracted!

"Where's Papa?" Edgar suddenly asked. He peered at Eliza through the wafting smoke of Diana's cigarette. "You said this is a family confab. Shouldn't the pater be here for this? Guy and Chloe are one thing, but Papa?"

"His Lordship is indisposed." Sister Francine's voice thundered and gave Eliza the necessary jolt out of her torpor.

"And you are again?" Duncan made a move as though to go head-to-head with the Fallen Angel, but Eliza shifted ever so slightly so she stood between them. In a battle of blows, Eliza had her bets on Francine, but she didn't want to risk a physical set-to.

"For heaven's sake, Duncan, sit down and have another drink," Diana said. "We'll share the bottle."

"For the record," Edgar spluttered, "this doesn't sit well with me. This doesn't sit well with me at all. I will not have my family addressed in such a tone by a bloody, blooming Papist!"

"Shut up, Edgar," Penelope replied with a dramatic roll of her eyes. "No one asked you. The least we can do is listen to what Eliza has to say. Whether we like it or not, she's part of this family now. We owe her a fair shake."

"Thank you, Penelope." Eliza nodded in acknowledgment. "Now, some information has come to me that I think will be of great interest – if not concern – to all of you. I can't tell you whereby I came upon this information. The source doesn't wish to be revealed for reasons I understand and you'll all just have to accept."

"Lies," Edgar said. "Fake news."

Eliza heard Sister Francine growl behind her.

"It seems Guy has been playing a rather dangerous game," Eliza continued, each word bringing with it mounting confidence and a greater sense of righteous conviction. "He's gotten himself into a situation that – unless we nip it in the bud and do so immediately – will undoubtedly have lasting and severe consequences for us all."

"What sort of game?" Edgar asked. "The best kinds of games are always dangerous and Guy has always been a bit of a player – a black sheep – if you know what I mean. What makes this game any more threatening?"

She had their attention now.

"I think perhaps it's best if I let the evidence speak for itself," Eliza said.

She took out her mobile and tapped the screen so Tessa's video popped up and loaded. While she waited for it to download, Eliza gave the phone to Penelope, who was nearest at hand. Penelope's posture and expression gave nothing away. She was proving herself a worthy accomplice. Duly noted.

"This video was taken just this afternoon in the wood by the bluebell grove," Eliza explained. "After seeing this, I am certain you will agree that it's incontrovertible proof that Guy poses a greater threat to the longevity of this family than certainly I or any other 'outsider.'" She gave a subtle nod to Tessa who acknowledged the gesture with a quick wink whose sass Eliza found strangely beguiling.

She waited and watched as the video played out and the phone was passed from Penelope to Tessa, then Edgar to Duncan and finally to Diana who looked up from the screen and at Eliza with a look of such quiet devastation that Eliza knew the video had made the impact she had hoped it would. Edgar snatched the phone from Diana and played the damning video again. Eliza held her breath. The atmosphere in the room was as oppressive as the smoke from Diana's freshly lit cigarette. Eliza chanced a glance back at Sister Francine who pursed her lips and nodded.

"Well, fuck me!" Edgar exclaimed after the video had played out a second time.

"Blimey!" Duncan added.

"I don't know what to say," Diana said. "I don't understand."

"Devastating," Penelope interjected. "Just devastating. My God, why would he do that? Has he no shame?"

"You gotta admit though," Tessa said, "she is kind of fit."

"She's Russian!" Edgar exploded. "A goddamned Commie pinko is what she is. A honeytrap. It disgusts me. I think I'm going to be sick. Take it away. I can't stand the sight of it!"

He tossed the phone at Eliza with a flailing arm as he paced about the room, rubbing his face with his hands and emoting amateur theatrics. It took everything in Eliza's willpower not to smile.

"Get a grip, Edgar," Penelope said. "And besides, what does it really prove anyway? We've always known Guy was a rogue. Should we really be all that surprised he's fathered a child out of wedlock? It's the twenty-first century. Come on, people!"

Nicely played, Eliza thought.

"And it's not as if this family doesn't have experience with bastards," Diana added, with a knowing look and a twitch of her eyebrows at Tessa.

"Watch who you're calling a bastard," Tessa said.

Diana shrugged. "I was speaking more generally."

"Just as long as this child – or whatever it is – doesn't try to make a claim. I want it stated for the record that Walter, Rain, George and Charlotte take precedence where inheritance is concerned." Edgar stopped pacing and hugged himself as though he were about to be sick. "Bloody hell. What a fine mess this is."

"A fine mess indeed," Sister Francine intoned.

"Sit down, Edgar, before you give yourself a turn," Penelope directed. She patted the space beside her on the sofa.

"It's all very well for us to stand around here and bemoan Guy's treachery." In a move that surprised Eliza and gave her pause to consider whether she had perhaps been too hasty in judging Diana's loyalty, the eldest Templeton sibling crossed the expanse of the conservatory from her position on the chaise to take up position at Eliza's side. The smell of Diana's cigarette made Eliza want to gag, but she thought it best to keep her aversions to herself. This was, after all, a time for building alliances, however short term. "The question is," Diana continued, "what are we going to do about it?"

Not wanting to be outdone by her sister-in-law, Penelope bolted up from the sofa to assume a stance on Eliza's other side. In doing so, she was forced to rather awkwardly squeeze herself between Eliza and Sister Francine, who was loath to cede any territory between her and her Ladyship. *They're like lemmings, Eliza thought. Just look how quickly they fall into line.*

"Exactly!" Penelope declared with an emphatic nod and a shake of her finger.

"What are we going to do about it?"

"If I may." Duncan cleared his throat in an all too obvious ploy at regaining the spotlight. "Playing the devil's advocate," he said, "for obviously a devil's advocate is needed in this situation, shouldn't we invite the perp himself into this dialog? It seems to me there are always two sides to every story – and if there aren't, well then, we wouldn't know that without a proper investigation. Right?"

"That video speaks for itself," Penelope said. "No further dialog needed."

"Guilty until proven innocent? How very un-American of you." Duncan shook his head disapprovingly. "I must say, Penelope darling, you never fail to surprise me."

"That girl is obviously Guy's child, that woman is obviously Guy's Russian whore, and they are obviously conspiring to destroy all that this family holds near and dear!" Penelope was edging closer and closer to being beside herself.

"Far be it from me to defend Guy," Duncan continued. He stretched his arm out and splayed his fingers to inspect his nails. "The man is a cad, and it really was only a matter of time before his antics caught up with him, but this is England after all. We're the oldest and certainly greatest democracy in the world. Surely, we shouldn't cast aspersions on one of our own without due jurisprudence."

"This is a dynasty, not a democracy." Edgar looked up from his hands. His eyes were bloodshot. Eliza had never seen Carleton's eldest son look quite so undone. She rather liked the look. "And who are you to talk, Donut? I think you're a fine chap and all and bloody good fun on a bender – and please don't take this in the spirit for which it isn't intended – but you're not a Templeton by blood. You don't really have skin in the game. So I think it's best if you keep your devil's advocacy to yourself and let those of us who genuinely have a legacy at stake here carry on and handle things our way. The Templeton way."

"I say, no need to be such a prick about it," Duncan said with a sniff. "You're like the ruddy Mafia."

Eliza felt Sister Francine's nail dig into her thigh.

"Penelope is right," she said, attempting once again to assert control. "Guy can't be allowed to continue. My fear is this is only the tip of the iceberg."

"And what exactly does she mean by Apocalypse?" Edgar asked. "It sounds rather dire, doesn't it? Like the Cold War all over again."

Sister Francine stirred. *Oh God,* Eliza thought, *this really isn't the time for another one of her visions.*

"Do you think Guy's a Russian spook?" Edgar said to no one in particular. "I mean, we all know he went to Russia, although we don't really know why he went to Russia. And the company he keeps – Spencer, for one: nice bloke but kind of a shifty fellow, if you ask me. And that Frenchwoman…"

"Va-va-voom!" Duncan said from the sideboard where he stood nursing a glass of port.

"Well, I was going to say more 'ooh-la-la' but you're not far off the mark, Donut. I'll give you that."

"And what exactly were Guy and Spencer doing in Goa?" Penelope cut in.

"I hear the beaches there are fab," Tessa said. "Come to think of it, I could really use some fun in the sun. Maybe when my share of the inheritance comes through."

"Chloe would know," Diana replied. "She was only all too eager to run off halfway across the world to 'rescue' him."

"Chloe hasn't said a word," Penelope said.

"Nor will she, which is why she can't be trusted."

"Still and all," Penelope continued, "we need her on our side if we're going to take action against Guy with any chance of success."

"What do you propose?" Eliza asked. She could hear Sister Francine's breathing change, becoming more rapid, more pronounced. If the Fallen Angel dug her nail any deeper, she'd draw blood. Time to wrap this up.

A heavy collective silence fell across the room. Then:

"I have an idea."

As though taking her cue from Diana and Penelope, Tessa came up to the front of the room to stand beside Penelope, further boxing Sister Francine out of what looked to be an all-female all-Templeton alliance. Eliza tried to keep her skepticism in check. Tessa had done good work for her. The video had been shot with a steady hand and had provided Eliza with exactly what she had needed. That had all been thanks to Tessa – credit where credit was due. It was only fair to hear her out.

"What if we stage like a kidnapping or something?" Tessa began. "Tomorrow afternoon during the second stage of the Steeplechase."

"Go on," Eliza said. "Who would be kidnapping whom?"

"Chloe. I mean, Chloe would be the one kidnapped. And we arrange it so she thinks it's the Russians."

"And how do you propose we do that?" Edgar asked. "If it's any of us she'll suspect an inside job. Chloe may be daft but she's not stupid."

"Obvs." Tessa rolled her eyes with an exasperated sigh. "I'm sure we can find somebody up for a bit of mischief. There are hundreds of people here."

"And I know just the person!" Penelope exclaimed.

"Who?" Edgar looked pained. He held his head in his hands with his elbows on his knees.

"Leave it to me," Penelope said. "I think it's a brilliant idea, Tessa. Well done! But if I may make a suggestion… if we only target Chloe it'll look suspicious."

"As if staging a fake kidnapping isn't suspicious enough," Duncan interjected from the depths of his port. "Oh, how the world has gone mad! Stop! Stop! Stop the world, I want to get off. Crikey, I think I'm rather drunk."

"But if we were kidnapped as a pair – Chloe and me, for example – Chloe might not so easily deduce the whole thing was a plot designed to expose Guy's betrayal."

"So you'd be like a decoy?" Edgar asked.

"Something like, yes."

"Well, I say, that's rather brave of you. Aren't you the least bit frightened of putting yourself at such risk?"

"But it's not real, Edgar," Penelope said with a trace of petulance. "That's the whole point of it being a fake kidnapping. It's fake!"

"Like fake news?"

"Yes, Edgar, like fake news."

"How extraordinary!" Edgar's red-tinged eyes lit up. He looked at Tessa as though seeing her for the first time and not quite sure what to make of her. "You're a little clever clogs, aren't you? I still don't trust you though. For all I know you're aligned with the woman in the cape and that creepy child of hers – *Guy's* child. When did this house become such a den of snakes and ladders?"

"Oh, do shut up, Edgar!" Diana groaned. "For what it's worth – and also because I have no original ideas of my own – I think we should give this a go. So, well done, Tessa."

She led the room in a round of scattered and somewhat begrudging applause.

"But once they're kidnapped," Duncan said, "what then? And where exactly are they being kidnapped to? I mean, you can't very well have a kidnapping without a destination, can you?"

"The boathouse," Penelope offered after a measured pause. "We'll go to the boathouse. No one's used it in years, and I should imagine it's quite derelict."

"The boathouse?" Tessa said. "Really?"

"Unless you have a better idea? With the Steeplechase going on, the stables are out of the question."

"How about the tower?" Edgar suggested.

"No!" Sister Francine suddenly bellowed. "That's her Ladyship's domain. No one may go to the tower. No one."

Eliza wondered how long she could keep Lord Carleton on ice. It had been nearly twenty-four hours. In the excitement of the day, she'd almost forgotten him. Yet another detail to drive her to distraction...

"Sister Francine is quite right," Eliza said. "The tower is off limits. I don't want that kind of blood on my hands. And we as a family can't afford to attract the slightest suspicion that we're behind this. It can't be anywhere in the house."

"The boathouse it is then," Diana declared. "It's settled."

"I'm really not sure how I feel about this," Duncan said. "Do you think we're capable of pulling this off? Will there be violence, do you know? Guns or knives or something? I mean, who's ever heard of a bloodless kidnapping? At the very least, Chloe should be slapped. Lord knows, I'd like to slap her sometimes. Or shall we leave that up to you as well, Penelope? I've heard you're quite handy in the slapping department. The grapevine has a way of talking."

And so, the meeting adjourned. Eliza waited for the Templeton brood to leave before dashing to the sideboard and pouring herself a generous tumbler of Carleton's single malt. She felt by turns overwhelmed and relieved. If they were indeed able to succeed with this wholly madcap scheme, it would be yet another jewel in her crown and her position at the helm of the Templeton dynasty would be further secured, or so she hoped. But Eliza also knew that nothing was pre-ordained and the road ahead was steep and heading into the deep unknown.

"I'm afraid, Sister," she said. The words sounded alien to her, yet she also knew they were true.

"It is natural to be afraid," Sister Francine replied. "It is in fear that we experience the depth of God's righteousness. It is through fear that we come to love Him."

Eliza tipped the glass back and drank the whisky in one gulp. The alcohol burned as it went down, nearly causing her to choke. She wiped her lips with the back of her hand.

"Pray with me, Sister!" she cried. "Pray with me so that I might experience forgiveness for whatever it is I might do and all that I've had to do to get here."

Sister Francine was at her side in a lightning flash. Their hands locked as they dropped to their knees on the floor. Sister Francine closed her eyes as she gripped Eliza's hand. Eliza watched the Fallen Angel's lips moving in a rapid succession of aspirated prayers, punctuated every so often with a "*Mea culpa, mea maxima culpa*" and a string of Latin-sounding words that Eliza didn't understand. As the good Sister swayed on her knees beside her, one hand gripping Eliza's hand while the other rather urgently caressed the gold cross at her neck, Eliza couldn't help but wonder (and not for the first time that weekend) whether she had bitten off more than she could chew. As evidenced by the family meeting, the Templeton children weren't exactly the brightest stars in the universe, yet they proved that despite their various grudges and targeted antipathy for each other, when required they would stand together. Even Edgar seemed to have come around. He was a twit and a buffoon, but he was still the eldest male heir, and given the rather archaic structure of the estate – not to mention the antiquated and sexist rules of primogeniture that ruled within these lofty circles – he wielded an awful amount of power for someone who appeared so dumb. They had united around her cause this once, but who was to say they would do so again?

Eliza felt Sister Francine shudder beside her as the ex-nun came to the end of her prayers and sank back on her haunches in a state of sweaty exhaustion. Perhaps the Rapture would come soon? Eliza had her doubts. This talk of the Apocalypse – as extreme as it sounded – had her more than a little spooked. The Sister seemed to take it seriously, what with her visions and all. And the fact of the girl's presence – what was her name? Feminina? – on the Templeton estate no less, caused Eliza more anxiety than she could ever let on. But the girl's mother, with her raven-haired almost medieval beauty and mystical way of speaking, was truly chilling. Eliza could tell, even from just the video, that in Svetlana Slutskaya she faced a formidable opponent, one that she would need every ounce of Sister Francine's strength and fervor to help her defeat.

Sister Francine's eyes suddenly opened. Her tongue flicked across the thin line of sweat that coated her upper lip. Her gaze was impenetrable.

"You're losing your faith," she said.

It never failed to unnerve Eliza how well Sister Francine was able to read her mind. "It's not that," Eliza demurred. "I just wonder whether faith alone will sustain me."

"You must pray harder then."

"But what if God..." Eliza struggled for the words. "What if God doesn't approve...of some of my...our...tactics? My husband is dead, Sister, and his body is up there in the tower…I don't know how long the ice will ward off decomposition. If they…if the children find out about what I've done, they'll unite against me…against *us*…against The Movement. And then what? How will we face the coming Apocalypse if we can't raise an army? If we don't have the resources to build and grow and sustain it? You've said Templeton Manor is the epicenter of the coming battle."

"Aye," Sister Francine said with a grave nod. "'Tis written across the heavens but 'tis more than a battle. 'Tis ground zero for the final fight."

"Which gives me even more cause for concern. You have to admit, Sister, that the success or failure of The Movement rests rather disproportionately on my shoulders. I am not as young as I once was. I have days where I feel quite frail."

"*Basta!* [Enough!]" Sister Francine exclaimed with a dismissive wave.

Eliza quaked. "I didn't meant to offend you, Sister," she whispered. She clutched Sister Francine's hands in hers and kissed them. "I apologize. I spoke out of turn. I am not as strong as you. Help me, Sister. Tell me what to do. Give me guidance, a path, a plan, something to keep me on track. I am plagued by the demons of self-doubt."

The Fallen Angel took a deep breath. Her chest expanded and she appeared to grow to twice her size. Her dark eyes burned. "Penance," she said.

"What?"

"You must repent."

"Yes, yes, of course. But how, Sister? Obviously my prayers alone aren't enough."

"Pain."

Eliza didn't like the sound of this. The room suddenly grew cold as though a window had been left open somewhere. She rose to her feet to check but more so to avoid Sister Francine's trance-like stare. She knew about which the ex-nun was referring. Essie had told her. It wasn't something Eliza had any interest in pursuing. She admired Sister Francine's devotion, but masochism was definitely not in the cards for her. She'd rather burn in the Apocalypse. However – and there always seemed to be a "however" where Sister Francine and The Movement was concerned – Eliza knew she might not have a choice.

"I don't know that I can do that, Sister," Eliza said.

"You must!"

As expected. "Will you help me?"

"Of course." Sister Francine's tone softened. Eliza turned from the window.

The Fallen Angel's expression was almost kind as she got unsteadily to her feet and came to stand beside Eliza. Her touch was warm and reassuring. "You must build up your tolerance," she said. "There is much pain on the path ahead. Your threshold must be high otherwise you will not endure. This is the best method I can offer you. It is the only method I can offer you at this time."

Eliza knew Sister Francine spoke the truth. "I know," she said. "Thank you, Sister."

"Let us go."

Hand-in-hand, Eliza and Sister Francine ascended the steps to the tower. They knelt side-by-side on the cold bathroom tile. Eliza couldn't bring herself to look at the bloated corpse of the late Lord Carleton as it appeared to float on its melting bed of ice. Together they undressed. Eliza fought the urge to scream as Sister Francine handed her the leather strap.

"Forgive me, Father, for I have sinned."

The first lash was the worst, as Sister Francine – in all her infinite wisdom – had said it would be.

| 30 |

Chloe awoke the next morning from her rather queasy slumber vowing never to return to India again if she could help it. The next time Guy needed rescuing, he'd bloody well have to save himself on his own. She was done playing Good Samaritan. The lot of good it had done her! Diana said something about her funny tummy being on account of the Oysters Rockefeller, but Chloe was having none of that. Her funny tummy was a classic case of Delhi Belly, end of. And if it really was a case of questionable shellfish, why was she the only one afflicted?

Of course, the notion had entered her head that it might be something more nefarious, especially if the Russians were involved. She'd read of Russian agents slipping polonium-B into unassuming cups of tea. Was it possible that her oysters had been laced with polonium? Was she on a Russian kill list? Chloe wouldn't have been at all surprised, though the idea of it made her seethe with an anger that took precedence over fear. The nerve of some people! She felt the need to have a word with someone, but whom that person was escaped her. The only thing about which Chloe was certain was that Guy had betrayed her – not to mention how he'd let the family down – and that dreadful child with the impossible ringlets and the devilish laugh was his daughter: a bad seed if ever there was one. Chloe had felt it. She'd seen the wicked gleam in the girl's eyes. It haunted her.

There came a knock on the door of her bedchamber. Chloe was loath to let anyone see her in her present state but before she could conjure the energy to protest, the door opened and Penelope appeared. And while her American sister-in-law typically made Chloe want to scream, she had been awfully accommodating the day before – effectively talking Chloe down off the ledge after that horrendous scene with Guy – that she didn't have the heart to ask her to leave. She tried to raise herself up from under the comforter to at least make an effort at pushing the vomit bucket under the bed, but Penelope proved quicker and took care of it with no questions asked.

"Poor dear," Penelope said once the aforementioned bucket had been kicked out of sight and she'd plopped herself down on the bed at Chloe's side. "Poor, poor dear. You look dreadful."

"I feel like death warmed over."

"There's a reason I don't eat shellfish," Penelope tut-tutted. "If I was the one in charge of this household, heads would be rolling in the kitchen right now."

"I don't think it was the oysters."

"You could have died!"

"There's still a chance." Chloe pressed her head back against her abundance of pillows and closed her eyes. "They tell you when you go to India not to drink the water. They should also tell you not to eat the food. Or breathe the air, for that matter."

"Horrors!" Penelope exclaimed as she patted Chloe's brow with a handkerchief.

"Although I'm not entirely unconvinced it isn't the Russians. Whatever. I'm done with Guy. From now on, he can fend for himself."

"Fancy pushing you like that! And that child..."

"Oh, Penelope, I can't tell you how awful it was!" Chloe felt the familiar tug of tears. She bit the inside of her cheek in an effort to suppress them. "He was so beastly. All these years, I've done nothing but support and make excuses for him, and that's how he treats me! Well, not anymore. I'm done, Penelope. I'm all used up. I have nothing left to give. It's time I put myself first."

"Oh, darling, I can't tell you how relieved I am to hear you say that!"

"And you know it isn't in my nature to be selfish," Chloe continued.

"Not at all. You're the most decidedly unselfish person I know."

"Thank you." Chloe forced herself to smile through her nausea. She took

Penelope's hand and squeezed it. "You really are like a sister to me."

Penelope placed Chloe's hand on her heart and held it there. "Sisters," she said.

Chloe let the moment pass. Then: "How are things this morning? I hear all the hullaballoo outside and hate the fact I'm missing out. I fear I may be sequestered in here all day."

"Nonsense!" Penelope's sudden fervor struck Chloe as more than a little unnerving. She wondered if it was the Spice acting out. Penelope's pupils did look a little dilated. "I mean, you can't. You simply mustn't! It's the last day of the Steeplechase. There's the trophy ceremony and the garden luncheon this afternoon. And you always present the trophies! That's what you do. And it's been quite a race this year...at least that's what I've been told, though to be honest, I've been a bit distracted that I haven't really been paying much attention."

"Yes, you're right," Chloe said after a pause. "If I don't at least make an appearance, people will start to wonder. Duty waits for no one. I just don't trust Maximilian and Bree. He was horrible to me yesterday. I was mortified."

"Maxie isn't horrible," Penelope replied. "He's just gay."

"Still, they're *your* friends, Penelope. You need to do a better job of controlling them."

"I do try."

"Try harder."

Chloe sank back against her pillows with a dramatic sigh. Penelope was starting to wear out her welcome. *How taxing she is*, Chloe thought, *even when she's just being nice.* Despite her pledge of sisterhood, Chloe knew she didn't really have it in her to allow herself to welcome her sister-in-law into her heart. She supposed she should have felt some guilt about this when in fact all she truly felt was a mild but cloying sense of irritation.

"Did I miss anything last night?" she asked, making a conscious effort to soften her tone. It wasn't Penelope's fault that she tried too hard to be ingratiating. She was just American. "I spent most of the night with my head in that bucket vomiting my guts out. A bomb could have gone off and I wouldn't have noticed."

"Well..."

"What is it, Penelope? What haven't you told me?"

Penelope pushed herself off the bed and went to the window. She pulled the curtains back to allow a stream of bright mid-morning sunshine into the room. Chloe shielded her eyes from the glare.

"You're not well," Penelope murmured. "You need rest. Perhaps it's best that you take the day off after all?"

"What's going on?"

"I wasn't going to say anything. I don't want to alarm you."

"Tell me, Penelope!"

"It's too horrific for words. It's probably best I just show you."

The video confirmed all of Chloe's worst suspicions, nightmares, and fears. When it was finished, Chloe pushed the phone aside and turned her head away to stare out the window, at the sun and the clear blue sky. *How deceiving nature is, she thought, and how unkind.* Her stomach heaved but she forced herself to swallow the sick back down. She couldn't let Penelope see her vulnerability or how savagely the video had affected her.

"I'm so sorry, Chloe," Penelope said.

"And the others? Have they seen it?"

"Everyone except Guy. You were so ill we didn't want to disturb you. And Guy was taken ill as well, or so it seems. Eliza called a family meeting."

"Eliza?"

"She is in charge now, Chloe."

"As long as my father still draws breath, that woman has no right." Chloe snapped her head back around and regarded Penelope with a cold stare. "Was Papa there? At this so-called family meeting, was Papa there?"

"No, Chloe. Your father hasn't come out of his room since the announcement."

Panic gripped her. She tugged at the front of her nightshirt. Penelope's words sent a charge through Chloe that propelled her to take action. She struggled out from under the comforter and attempted to climb out of the bed, but Penelope held her fast, her grip on her arm gentle but firm.

"Has anyone seen Papa?" Chloe asked, her hysteria growing to a crisis point. "How do we know he's not dead somewhere? How do we know he's still alive? I wouldn't put anything past that awful hateful woman. How do we know she hasn't killed him herself? I've seen those hands, Penelope. She has blood on them, if not Papa's, then someone else's. The circumstances of Lord Chester's death have always struck me as suspicious. And where is her son really?"

"I thought he was in prison in Africa somewhere."

"Yes, but why is he in prison?"

Penelope shrugged. "I thought it was drugs." She gulped.

"But how do we know Eliza wasn't involved? How do we know she and Trevor weren't complicit in Lord Chester's murder? How do we know she isn't the one behind the camera?"

"Because she isn't," Penelope said, and then stopped herself.

"You say that with such conviction. How do you know?"

"Well...I...I don't, I suppose. Oh, Chloe, you're getting yourself all worked up. It's not good for you. You need your rest."

"I need to be with my family." Chloe tried to push Penelope off, but again, her attempts were futile. With a defeated sigh, she threw herself back against the pillows and fought a losing battle against her tears. "I just...I just don't know what to do!" she cried. "How could Guy do this? I should go to him. I should ask him myself. It's bad enough that he's brought that child here...but that woman too? Who is she, Penelope? And what does she mean by the 'Apocalypse'?"

"There, there, dear."

Penelope's words were soothing but empty. Chloe was content at that moment though to allow her sister-in-law to comfort her. The stress was beyond her limited capacity to deal with it in any effective sort of manner. She felt Guy's betrayal to her core.

"I'm frightened, Penelope," she whispered.

"I shouldn't have shown you the video," Penelope said. "You're really in no state to process such things. That was wrong of me."

"No, it's good that I saw it, otherwise I'd continue to hope in ignorance that Guy might change. And the others? What did they say? How did they react?"

"Action will be taken."

"When?"

Penelope hesitated. "Soon," she said after a pause, "which is why it's important you build up your strength this morning so you can rejoin the festivities this afternoon. We can't have people thinking it was more than a little tummy ache, especially as you know we've our share of conspiracy theorists out there."

"Indeed." Chloe exhaled as Penelope smoothed the duvet over her knees. "I'm actually feeling better already. I think all that excitement just now broke my fever."

"I'll have Demelza bring up some tea."

"Thank you, Penelope." Chloe forced her brightest smile. "You've always been so kind to me. I suppose I should make more of an effort to be nice to you."

"Yes," Penelope agreed. "Perhaps you should. I'll be back to check on you shortly, once you've had your tea and a wash."

"Oh, and Penelope?"

This time Chloe felt Penelope's smile was less than sincere. "Yes, darling?"

"About that matter we spoke of yesterday...the Inconvenient Woman..."

"Taken care of," Penelope said.

"So we'll be inconvenienced no more?"

"Yes. I mean no. I mean..."

"Thank you, Penelope. You can go now. Find Demelza and tell her to bring my tea. I can draw my own bath."

When she was alone again, Chloe scrambled off the bed and went to the French doors that opened onto the balcony. She threw them open and stepped outside. The cool morning air felt good against her sweaty brow. Despite the video and the evidence of Guy's treachery, Chloe felt almost giddy. And as she watched the tableau of the final morning of Steeplechase weekend play out in front of her – extending as far as her eye could see – she was filled with a sense of profound well being. *What doesn't kill you makes you stronger,* she said to herself, for she felt as though she had just gone through the very worst kind of ordeal and had come out on the other side in a blaze of glory. She hugged herself against the breeze.

"I release you, Guy!" she said. Never had four words felt so empowering. "I release you."

And now it was time to choose an outfit for the afternoon. Chloe returned to her room with a renewed optimism and the realization that, despite its many complexities, she really rather enjoyed being a Templeton.

Penelope forgot all about finding Demelza the moment she stepped out of Chloe's room. Their conversation had gone to plan, though it did reiterate the fact that despite her best intentions, she didn't particularly care for her sister-in-law, and wouldn't have minded at all if the fake kidnapping planned for that afternoon actually evolved into something more real. She didn't doubt that Xander could pull it off and do so with zeal. But what would that get her? It wasn't as though bumping Chloe off would any further secure her position– if anything it might bring Tessa closer into the fold – not to mention that it might also disrupt whatever master scheme Eliza had in development, for she was certain the new Templeton matriarch had plenty up her sleeve. Best not to provoke Lady Eliza's wrath, at least not at this early stage of the game.

Xander had been all too eager to play his part, as Penelope had suspected he would be. They had met before dawn in a dark and little-used passageway behind the kitchen pantry. She had told him what she wanted – emphasizing the word 'fake' – without giving in to his request for greater context. She did however thank him when he intimated (in his all-too-peculiar way of speaking) that The Inconvenient Woman would "inconvenience again never."

In truth, she had almost forgotten about Rebecca Hastings. Had Chloe not reminded her of their conversation from the day before, for all Penelope cared, the Foraged hostess could be relegated to the dustbin of history. She had bigger fish to fry, not the least of which was making sure Chloe got her ass out of bed, bathed, and dressed, and in the VIP tent well in time for the presentation of the Templeton Cup and the awards luncheon. At the appointed hour (3pm) and location (somewhere along the path that ran from the manor house to the boathouse), Xander assured her he would appear and overwhelm Chloe with a handkerchief laced with chlorophyll (or its more modern equivalent) to render her unconscious. And thus together – Penelope and Xander – they would sequester the incapacitated Chloe to the boathouse, whereupon (an hour or so later) Chloe would awaken to find herself (and Penelope) tied up and (for all intents and purposes) kidnapped.

Of course the plan was fraught with unknowns. Penelope wasn't at all convinced Xander was trustworthy – he seemed to have his fingers in too many pies – but there didn't appear to be another alternative handy. This was new territory for her. What if Xander never showed up? What if Chloe really was too sick to leave her room? What if there were witnesses along the path to the boathouse or the boathouse itself was otherwise engaged? The more Penelope dwelled on the "what if's", the more she convinced herself that this was a terrible idea and that its chances of success were less than nil. She'd need a Spice Bomb or three just to make it through the next few hours. Whatever happened after – or didn't happen –was out of her control.

Penelope stationed herself at the punch bowl in the VIP tent. The vodka-enhanced sickly fruity goodness went down smooth – too smooth – and after a glass or two (or three or four, Penelope lost count) she started to relax and feel that she needed to start believing in herself more. It was all too easy to fall back on old habits and insecurities – despite her beauty queen status, Penny Danziger had been a neurotic basket case – rather than focus on all that she'd managed to accomplish since her Cedar Rapids days. She acknowledged that reinvention wasn't something that just happened once in a person's life. In order to stay relevant and au courant one needed to maintain one's process, which often meant putting oneself in situations that might cause one discomfort or fear. Penny

Danziger had been afraid of everything, so in order to overcome that fear, she'd introduced herself to the world of BDSM and, for a time, had thrived as Cedar Rapids' reigning bondage queen. If she hadn't mastered the art of paddling, she might very well have never met Edgar and, as they say, the rest was history.

Lately, however, Penelope had begun to think that perhaps she'd been too casual about her former persona. Short of self-enrolling in a witness protection program, it seemed there was no fail-safe way of completely separating oneself from one's past, as was all too evident by the utterly unwelcome (if not unlikely) appearance of Ruthie Peterson and Yolanda Fung. She'd never intended for them to pick up their Iowa stakes and move all the way to the UK after, early on in her new life as Lady Penelope Templeton, she'd once shown her weakness and admitted to feeling lonely. And while Penelope thought she'd done her best to separate herself from their company – the Templeton name was a natural fortress – her two sorority sisters were unfazed. They seemed to understand the protocol, if indeed they understood nothing else. The arrangement between them – such as it was – had lasted more-or-less without incident for years, both agreeing to keep their distance in deepest darkest Essex, to the point where Penelope had almost – but not quite – forgotten Ruthie and Yolanda were even in the country.

But, wholly without intending it, a recent moment of weakness seemed to have rendered the arrangement moot. Ruthie's husband – what was his name? Owen – cute in a corn-fed himbo kind of way – had certainly known what to do with his tool. Penelope was still undecided as to whether or not she regretted their spontaneous bathroom fuck-a-thon at Foraged, the night she'd discovered Edgar had been getting his up with the front of house staff. She certainly regretted the bruises on her lower back, which – no surprise – Edgar had failed to notice.

The thought of Owen and his all-too-impressive everything made Penelope feel wistful. Perhaps she might run off with him? She hadn't any contact with him since the night in question however many months ago, but a girl could dream, couldn't she? No, despite its many vicissitudes, Penelope wouldn't trade her life for anything. Not even for better sex...or (let's be honest here) sex of any kind. She owed Edgar too much. Besides, he really was rather good to her in his limited way and they had genuinely loved each other once. The children, on the other hand? Rain, Walter, George, and Charlotte she could easily do without. Perhaps Bipasha could cut her a good deal with a white slaver? Penelope hadn't a doubt the Spice Queen dealt in more than just Spice and fashion.

"There you are, Pen, I've been looking everywhere for you!" Edgar appeared suddenly at her elbow, causing Penelope to startle and nearly slosh punch all over herself. "I say, feeling a bit jumpy this morning, are we? I reckon you'd give some of those stallions out there a good run for their money!"

"Are you comparing me to a horse, Edgar?"

"Only in the very best possible way, of course. I mean, you always were rather good on your haunches."

Edgar poured himself a generous glass of punch.

"Is there something you want, Edgar, or are you just here to annoy me?"

"A man's allowed to check in with his wife, isn't he?" Edgar asked with an edge of truculence Penelope found tiresome. "Especially when she's but hours away from being kidnapped?"

"I wouldn't say that so loudly if I were you. It is supposed to be a secret."

"Right. Yes, of course."

"Was there anything else?" Penelope asked with a sigh. "It's just that you don't usually speak to me, Edgar, so pardon me if I find your sudden eagerness to engage rather disingenuous."

Penelope didn't have to look at him to know she'd struck a nerve. Edgar was nothing if not predictable and all too true to his class.

"Well, as a matter of fact, I did want to ask whether you've seen Rebecca."

"Rebecca?" Penelope fought the urge to throw what remained of her punch in Edgar's face. "You would dare ask me about her?"

"It's just that it appears she's gone missing. Nevin and I can't find her anywhere. We've looked high and low and everywhere in between. Nevin's quite beside himself. He says he hasn't seen her since Friday night. And it's Sunday today."

"Yes, Edgar, I know what day it is."

"And they're due to cater the awards luncheon in less than two hours' time."

"If I were Nevin, I'd do a better job of keeping an eye on my wife."

"Oh but, Pen, they aren't married. Everyone only thinks they're married."

"Whatever you need to tell yourself to alleviate your guilt."

"Well, you don't have to be a bitch about it. She once threw a bloody meat cleaver at my head, you know. I might have been decapitated."

"No, Edgar, I haven't seen Rebecca."

"It's tragic when you think about it."

"What is, Edgar?"

"We used to shag like rabbits. That paddle, your strap-on. I'm tight again, Penelope. I need pegging."

"So find yourself a hung stud and have at it."

"You're cruel."

"Yawn." Penelope rolled her eyes. "I only married you for your title."

"Cunt."

"Poof."

"Last time I checked, my name isn't Spencer."

She rolled her eyes again. "Sucks to be you."

"What's that supposed to mean? I hate when you talk American."

Penelope flicked him the middle finger.

"Are you implying?" Edgar asked. He paused. Penelope watched the glimmer of an idea flicker before his eyes, which then filled with horror. "You're not shagging him, are you?"

"Please."

"There seems to be an awful lot shagging going on around here. I wouldn't put it past you if you were."

"I'm not fucking Spencer."

"Anyone else then that I should know about?"

She thought of Owen in the toilets at Foraged. And then of how attentive Hamish Tavistock had been when she'd innocently and wholly unexpectedly encountered him in the library with Eliza. *If only you knew,* she thought. She wondered somewhat longingly whether she would ever see Owen again? Or, more immediately, whether to allow Hamish to sweep her off her feet once more with his old school charm. *The horny old T-Rex!*

"If there were, you'd be the first to know," she said.

"You confound me sometimes, Penelope. I am confounded."

Penelope shrugged and cast her gaze over the grounds. "This conversation is over," she replied. "Sorry I can't help you rescue your damsel in distress. My charity only runs so far."

She poured another glass of punch as Edgar marched off, sputtering a torrent of archaic curses under his breath. While she wouldn't allow herself to feel even the slightest shred of remorse over whatever may or may have not been the reason for Rebecca Hastings' apparent disappearance, the thought did occur to Penelope that perhaps she had placed too much blind trust in her husband's strange and reptilian PA. Calculated deception was relatively new to her and the deeper the lies, the more dangerous the machinations, the more Penelope feared she was putting herself at risk. How did she know that Xander wasn't playing her from multiple angles? He was, after all, in Edgar's employ more than hers. As Edgar cut the paychecks, it was only natural her husband commanded Xander's loyalty. But on the other hand, Xander was a chameleon – as she herself was becoming – and she didn't think she was necessarily wrong in believing that she and Edgar's PA shared a bond. After all, they were now accomplices.

"*Bonjour*, Penelope."

How quickly optimism turned to despair!

"Yvette." Penelope cast the Frenchwoman a sidelong glance. She swallowed the tension that rose in her throat.

"Would I be wrong if I was to say to you that I feel something is afoot?" Yvette asked. Her voice was like honey but its effect upon Penelope was the opposite of soothing.

"And why would anything be afoot?" Penelope replied. She hoped the French spook couldn't sense her anxiety. A bead of sweat formed on her forehead just above the edge of her fascinator.

"You forget where you are," Yvette said with a knowing smile. "Or perhaps you need me to give you another friendly reminder?"

"Just because we may have shared a spliff in the loo at Foraged once doesn't mean we're friends."

"*Absolutement!*" Yvette gave a spirited laugh. "But then I have always made it a habit to keep my friends at arms' length and my enemies closer."

Penelope resented how easily the Frenchwoman unnerved her.

"Less than friends, yes, but enemies? Surely an overstatement, *n'est ce pas?*" she asked.

Yvette shrugged, though the gesture was anything but casual. "I couldn't help but eavesdrop on your conversation with Edgar just now," she said.

The panic! Penelope gulped. The bead of sweat turned into a stream as it worked its way down her forehead and over her brow.

"I don't know what you're talking about!"

"You play dumb but I do not think you are so dumb," Yvette replied. "Or else I am really stupid but I do not think either you or I believe that to be the case, *non?*"

Penelope opened her mouth to protest, but words were sadly not forthcoming.

"*Sommes-nous rivaux amoureux?* [Are we love rivals?]" the Frenchwoman asked.

"*Excuse-moi?*" Penelope shuddered, whether from relief or anxiety she didn't know. The question was not what she had expected, though if taken at face value it could add a whole new complication to her life that would be most unwelcome. "Not you as well. Rebecca Hastings is one thing, but..." She turned to Yvette while attempting to summon a courage she didn't feel. "Are you fucking my husband too?"

"*Quelle?*" Now it seemed it was Yvette's turn to be shocked, but Penelope couldn't tell whether it was sincere or a ruse. "*Je ne comprends pas!* It was not Edgar of whom I was speaking. No offense, Penelope, but your husband is not to my taste."

"Then who?"

"*Mais oui!*" Yvette shook her head and poured a glass of punch, which she knocked back with gusto. "Do I have to spell it out for you? I fear the Spice has really gone to your brain. Perhaps you should be hospitalized, *non?*"

"You're going to have to clue me in here, Yvette," Penelope said. "We are not, nor have we ever been (at least to my knowledge) what you suggest. Love rivals? Well, if that were the case then that would mean I'm getting it off with Spencer and let me assure you, Yvette, that I share a similar sentiment about Spencer as you apparently do about my husband. Is Edgar really that unattractive?"

Yvette sniffed. "He is too short, for one," she said.

"I'm just very tall." Penelope found herself jumping to her husband's defense.

"He doesn't know the first thing about food, yet he calls himself a restaurateur."

This was hitting below the belt. "He's a businessman," Penelope said. "If you don't like the food at Foraged, blame Nevin and Rebecca Hastings, not my husband."

Yvette gave Penelope a searching look that just about sent Penelope further over the edge. Her fingers twitched for another glass of punch but she was loath to give the redheaded Frenchwoman any additional ammunition against her. She hated how inadequate Yvette made her feel in every department, and she knew Yvette knew it too. And although a part of her couldn't help but hold a certain grudging respect, if not admiration, for Yvette – the woman was, after all, sexy, smart, a master of the art of commanding attention, and an all-around bad-ass – in her presence, Penelope felt once again like mousy little Penny Danziger, an identity that no matter how concerted an effort she made to rid herself of it once and for good, the past just served as a reminder that reinvention only went so deep.

"Speaking of Rebecca Hastings," Yvette said after a pause too pregnant for Penelope's comfort.

"I don't know where she is!" Penelope squawked. "Why does everyone keep asking me that? I haven't seen her since dinner Friday night. For all I know, she could have fallen into the canal and drowned. She was certainly over-served that night. You were there, Yvette. You saw how she was practically tripping all over herself, making the most vulgar spectacle. I mean, did you see that dress? Her tits were practically busting out to here. She's definitely had implants. She looks like fucking Jessica Rabbit. Disgusting, classless Chav. Not to mention the fact that she's fucking my husband!"

Penelope felt like she was drowning. She couldn't breathe. For lack of access to a Spice Bomb, the punch was too tempting. She wanted to dive right in, pick up the bowl and chug it all down in one giant, greedy gulp. She wanted to backhand Yvette across her all-too-perfect, all-too-Gallic face, rip out her all-too-lustrous hair from the roots, and stab her to death with her stilettos. But instead, she merely poured another glass – albeit with near convulsive hands – and drank it with a determined slurp that she hoped established a final exclamation point to mark the end of the conversation. Of course, Penelope knew she was only making a fool of herself.

Yvette watched her with a bemused smile and a slight tilt of her chin. "It seems I have struck a nerve, non?" she said.

"I'm a woman on the verge," Penelope replied.

"*Oui.*" Yvette nodded. The smile remained: taunting, mocking, and too wise. "But, I suppose, if I were in your shoes and I knew that I was mere hours from being kidnapped, I would be...*je ne sais pas...*'on the verge' myself."

"What?"

Yvette shrugged. She took a step closer to Penelope and leaned in until her lips hovered by the American's ear. "*Je sais tout* [I know everything]," she whispered.

The punch roiled up into Penelope's throat like a tsunami.

"I have to say," Yvette continued, "it is rather brilliant in a thoroughly Templeton kind of way. Do you really think Chloe will be so easily persuaded?"

"I don't think I should say anything," Penelope replied. "Obviously someone has already said too much." She gulped. The urge to vomit took precedent over any attempt at denial. "How do you know? Who's the mole?"

"I never betray my sources."

Penelope wracked her brains trying to think of whom at the family meeting might have had a motive to derail everything she had so meticulously set in motion. Diana perhaps? It was doubtful. Her sister-in-law talked a good game but, from Penelope's perspective, really didn't care to work that hard. Duncan?

Possibly. He had after all been rather critical, but again, she didn't think he'd do much to stand in her way. Eliza? No. Getting Guy out of the picture served her purpose too well. Edgar? Too self-centered. Sister Francine? Too pious. That left Tessa. But why would Tessa double-cross when the idea for the fake kidnapping originated from her in the first place? It was too much. Penelope needed a Spice Bomb and she needed one fast.

"No comment," Penelope said.

"To tell you the truth, it works in my best interests as well."

"No comment."

"I have my reasons for wanting Guy out of the family," Yvette said. "He has been my quarry for quite some time now. And that woman, Svetlana Slutskaya..."

"You know her?"

"The Black Widow of Sochi. Evil incarnate."

"That's the Black Widow of Sochi?"

"I have seen her carnage. Words cannot even begin to describe the horror."

"The Apocalypse." Penelope paused as the gravity of what Svetlana Slutskaya represented hit home. "And Guy is the father of her child..."

"That remains to be verified."

"But you believe?"

"The Black Widow certainly seems adamant."

"Oh, Yvette, what has he done?"

"You must be brave, Penelope. You must be strong."

Penelope nodded. She gazed deep into Yvette's eyes and suddenly seemed to recognize truth for the very first time. Was it possible that she and the French spook were on the same side? That they might even be allies?

"The kidnapping," Penelope began.

Yvette shook her head and held a finger to her lips. "Shhh," she murmured, "of the kidnapping, not another word shall we speak."

"And you'll keep it secret?"

"I will even help you. Someone has to be the hero. And, in a way, I feel that I owe Chloe a rescue. I have always regretted Dhaka. I let my heart get in the way of reason."

"I suppose it's nice to know you have a heart," Penelope said. She was wary of being too taken in by Yvette's apparent confession, but it was somewhat reassuring that the Frenchwoman was confident enough in her strength to admit vulnerability. Penelope wasn't sure she was able to say the same about herself.

"Admitting one's shortcomings can be empowering," Yvette replied with a smile that wasn't entirely ironic. "A strong woman knows how and when to be vulnerable. We often expect more from our male counterparts in this regard than we do of ourselves. It is a double standard, non?"

"*Oui.*" *How seductive she is*, Penelope thought. *No wonder men can't take their eyes off of her.* "*Merci,*" she said. "*Merci beaucoup.*"

The twinkle in Yvette's eye was genuine. "For what?"

Penelope shrugged. She was at a loss for words. "For being a strong woman."

Apparently Yvette thought this was too much. She tossed her head back so her lustrous red hair glinted in the sunlight as she emitted a deep belly laugh that might have been interpreted as mocking, but Penelope was too bedazzled to take it for anything beyond face value.

"You flatter me," Yvette said. And then her expression became serious. She stepped closer to Penelope and took the American's hands in hers. Their gazes locked. Penelope felt the flush rise in her face. "But this is a dangerous game we play, a game that we face a very serious risk of losing. Do yourself a favor. Get yourself off the Spice. You need to be at the top of your game when the Apocalypse comes."

"I don't think I can." Penelope gasped. This was the first time she had ever admitted to herself – let alone another person – that she was an addict. It didn't sit well. She didn't feel empowered. "This is me being vulnerable to you, Yvette. I am in too deep."

"You must try."

"No." Penelope shook her head as she felt the tears start to flow. "I can't. You don't understand. You can't possibly understand."

She wanted to run as far away from Yvette as possible. The electricity that emanated from the Frenchwoman threatened to overwhelm her. Penelope felt trapped. She was angry. She feared Yvette had manipulated her into a corner from which she couldn't escape. Yet at the same time, she wanted to throw herself into Yvette's arms and beg for her assistance. It was all too much to bear. And even as she knew the Spice was killing her slowly from the inside, all she could think of at that moment was how desperately she wanted a Spice Bomb. How had things gotten to such a state? How had she allowed herself to become so dependent?

The warmth in Yvette's eyes faded. Penelope now felt their chill. Yvette released Penelope's hands with a curt nod.

"Right on cue," Yvette said.

POSH

Penelope turned as Bipasha Gupta swept into the tent with her retinue of her punky-haired assistant Cleopatra and Bipasha's too-sexy-by-half brother, Rajeev. The Queen of the Hussites was attired in Manish Malhotra haute couture that sheathed her perfect figure in an almost translucent satin studded with hundreds (if not thousands) of Swarovski crystals. But what was most stunning about the dress was its train, which swept out behind her to a staggering eight feet, attended by three of the most beautiful young girls Penelope had ever seen. They couldn't have been older than seven or eight. Their skin was the drenched color of a Goan beach at sunset and they were clad in flowing silken sundresses decorated with sunflowers. To complete the look, Bipasha's hair was piled high and adorned with more Swarovski crystal. Her entrance towered over everything and everyone, stopping all conversation, and provoking a hailstorm of camera clicks and unabashed awe and admiration.

"Bipasha!" Penelope exclaimed.

"Penelope," Bipasha replied with a smile that was more condescending than sincere. Her dark eyes swept dismissively over Penelope before coming to rest on Yvette. Penelope felt the Frenchwoman bristle. "Yvette."

"Bipasha."

"If I didn't know better," Bipasha said, "I'd think you were stalking me."

"C'est true. I am everywhere."

Bipasha pursed her lips. She glanced at Cleopatra on her left and then at Rajeev on her right. "Raj, baby, you're familiar with Miss Devereux, are you not?"

"I am indeed, though perhaps not as familiar as I'd like to be," Rajeev said with a leer and a wink that Penelope found both revolting and alluring at the same time. She hated that he had that affect on her.

"Well, perhaps, this is your lucky day. Get her out of my sight. I have some business to discuss with Lady Penelope."

Rajeev stepped forward with a slight bow. "With pleasure," he said. And then to Yvette as he extended his right hand: "Shall we?"

Penelope wanted to cry out to Yvette and beg her not to leave her alone with the Mistress of Spice, but to her dismay, Yvette took Rajeev's hand without so much as another look.

"I have my eye on you," Yvette said to Bipasha as she stepped around the perimeter of the Mistress of Spice's train.

"Don't step on my gown," Bipasha snapped.

Penelope helped herself to another glass of punch.

Bipasha clapped her hands. The three young girls gently pulled the train away from the bodice of the gown and worked as a unit to fold the voluminous fabric. Penelope was petrified.

"So sweet," Bipasha enthused. "My little Hussites-in-training. Orphans, you know. I pick them off the streets wherever I go – Cape Town, Dubai, Mumbai, Kinshasa. It's important to get them when they're young, otherwise you can never be assured of their loyalty. No one can ever accuse me of not being charitable."

"I believe the technical term for it is kidnapping," Penelope said. How easily the word seemed to trip off her tongue!

"Well, at least I'm not selling them into slavery. Indentured servitude perhaps, but it's for their own good. Most of these children don't even own a decent pair of shoes. I could give your sister-in-law a run for her philanthropy."

"What do you know about Chloe?"

Bipasha laughed. "I was an It Girl once myself, you know," she said. "It pays to keep tabs on the sisterhood."

"Is that a threat?"

"Have you spoken to your husband about our little arrangement?"

"I've not had the chance. " Penelope hoped Bipasha didn't hear the quaver in her voice. She wondered whether it would be bad form to ask the Mistress of Spice if she carried, though the gown was so form fitting it was all but a foregone conclusion that she didn't. Penelope really needed a fix. The punch was making her head spin.

"You're not getting cold feet, are you?"

"No!" *More like a cold sweat,* Penelope thought.

"Perhaps it's easier if I just introduce myself? He's around, you said?"

"Yes, but otherwise engaged."

"There's a shipment due next week from Cape Town," Bipasha said. The smile vanished. She was all business. "I need somewhere to store it."

"How much?"

"Don't be greedy. You have hungry eyes, Penelope. I don't like it. Perhaps Yvette is right? Perhaps I am a bad influence. I'll have Dr. Priscilla Chang write you a prescription for a Spice blocker."

Penelope had read about Spice blockers. She knew the effect they could have on an addict. She was loath to experience it firsthand.

"That won't be necessary," Penelope said perhaps a little too vociferously. "I've just been under a lot of stress lately. Steeplechase Weekend does that to me. Every year it's the same. You have nothing to fear, Bipasha. I have things under control."

"That isn't what Dr. Chang tells me."

"I think the good doctor has her own agenda where I'm concerned," Penelope snapped. "I don't like to accuse anyone of unethical behavior – especially when it concerns their profession – but in my experience, she's less a doctor than a pusher. I'd have her struck off the boards if I were you."

"Out of the question. Dr. Priscilla Chang is one of my most trusted agents. She's cunning and ruthless. I need more women like her."

"She's made me a slave to the Spice," Penelope said. "Surely, that's not good for business."

"Dr. Chang stays."

The vehemence with which Bipasha defended the Chinese doctor alarmed Penelope. She wondered whether there was something else to the relationship that she didn't know about. She wasn't sure she wanted to know. If she had known working for Bipasha Gupta was going to be so complicated, she might have told the woman to take a hike. But then, she hadn't really had much choice. Her craving for Spice was too strong. What was she going to tell Edgar? How was she going to break the news to him that she was selling off their business to a Narco? She could only hope he'd be as seduced by Bipasha as she had been. And while Penelope didn't relish the idea of Edgar fucking Bipasha, if it served to smooth the way, perhaps it might not be such a bad thing. Bipasha Gupta made Rebecca Hastings look positively low rent in comparison.

"I'll arrange a meeting," Penelope said as she watched Bipasha's eyes rove across the marquis and out over the grounds. "But not today. This afternoon is too fraught, what with the awards luncheon and..." Bipasha fixed her with an inquisitive stare that compelled an impulse within Penelope to tell the Mistress of Spice everything about the fake kidnapping, but she held back. This had nothing to do with Bipasha.

"Who's that?" Bipasha asked, her gaze coming to rest on a point over Penelope's shoulder.

Penelope turned, happy for the distraction.

"She's gorgeous," Bipasha enthused. "What do you think, Cleopatra?"

"I think it's lucky you spotted her before Rajeev," Cleopatra replied.

"Do you know her?"

Penelope squinted against the glare from the sun. "Tessa?"

"With a face and a body like that – not to mention those eyebrows! – she should be on magazine covers," Bipasha said.

"Or the star of your upcoming collection," Cleopatra suggested. "Gigi and Bella are booked. And Kendall's agent still hasn't gotten back to us. And London Fashion Week is only weeks away."

"As if I needed the reminder. Who is she?" Bipasha turned to Penelope.

"Tessa? Um...she's family. My sister-in-law..."

"Call her over. I want to see her up-close and personal."

Penelope waved. Tessa caught her eye and approached with her rambling, long-legged gait. Penelope couldn't help but wonder in that moment if Tessa was indeed the mole. It couldn't have been any of the others.

"Who represents you?" Bipasha asked in lieu of introduction.

"Huh?" Tessa said. Penelope thought the newest addition to the Templeton clan looked suspicious, like she was hiding a secret.

"Your manners leave something to be desired," Bipasha said. "I take it you're freelance?"

Tessa shrugged. She frowned at Penelope who shrugged and looked away.

"Walk for me," Bipasha said. "I need to see you move."

Tessa did as she was told.

"Again," Bipasha directed when Tessa returned to their cluster. "Your posture needs work, but then there's something kind of hot in your slouch. Like you don't give a fuck."

Tessa shrugged again. "I don't," she said.

"What do you think, Cleopatra?"

"She's very sexy..."

"But?"

"Maybe too undisciplined?"

Bipasha shook her head. "She's raw. I like that. And very, very English. She's perfect for the Blood of Roses collection."

"Doesn't it concern you that she's just another white girl?" Cleopatra asked. "Isn't Blood of Roses all about diversity? As a woman of color yourself – a powerful woman of color – shouldn't you highlight this in your London debut? Don't you want your collection to be represented by a woman who, well, looks like you?"

"No one looks like me, Cleopatra. Remind me next time never to ask your opinion about anything," Bipasha said. "I like you, Tessa Templeton. I'm going to make you a star."

"Crikey," Tessa said.

"My assistant Cleopatra will give you all the deets. I'll need you to come to my London atelier next week. We haven't a second to spare."

"But do you really think that's wise, Bipasha?" Cleopatra persisted. She gave Tessa an appraising look that was anything but approving. Tessa's nostrils flared. Penelope sensed a fight brewing. She wasn't sure she wanted to be there when things really turned nasty. "I shouldn't have to remind you that you've a lot riding on this collection. Surely, it should be trusted to a professional? We don't know anything about this girl."

"Remind me again," Bipasha said. "You're my assistant, yes?"

"Well, technically..."

"So assist."

"Yes, mum."

Bipasha took Tessa's chin in her hand and turned the young woman's head from one side to the other. She pinched the corners of Tessa's mouth before stepping back. "Turn for me," she commanded with an impatient wave.

Again, Tessa did as she was told. For a fleeting moment, Penelope feared she was about to be replaced in Bipasha's esteem.

"I don't know what it is about you," Bipasha said as Tessa faced forward with an impertinent cock of her hips, "but you excite me. I want to lick those eyebrows. Like Giselle St. John, but upmarket and without all this." She fluttered her hand in front of her face. "London. My atelier. Next week. Do not disappoint me."

With that, the Queen of the Hussites clapped her hands. Her three attendants snapped to attention and fell into place behind her. Cleopatra did the same, albeit with considerably less élan. Penelope wondered if she was expected to follow suit but couldn't bring herself to be quite so deferential. She was, after all, a Lady in her own right, perhaps of lesser royal stock than the Mistress of Spice, but still an aristocrat. More than anything though she just wanted to touch Cleopatra's hair.

"The queen has spoken," Bipasha said. "Now I'm off to find my brother. I don't trust Rajeev when he's out of my sight. You'll have to do a better job of keeping him in line, Cleopatra, when you're his wife. I can't always be my brother's keeper."

"Yes, Bipasha," Cleopatra replied through clenched teeth.

Trouble in paradise? Penelope thought.

"And don't ever contradict me like that again. If you know what's good for you..."

"Yes, Bipasha."

When Bipasha and her entourage were finally out of the tent and at a safe distance, Penelope withdrew a massive sigh of relief and hastily poured another glass of punch. She knocked it back and went to help herself again before remembering that Tessa – the suspected mole – was still standing there looking both gob-smacked and admiring in the wake of Bipasha's departure. She hoped she still had time for a Spice Bomb before the kidnapping. The day had suddenly gotten a whole lot more complicated.

"Who the holy fuck was that?" Tessa asked.

"The future," Penelope snapped.

"I've always wanted to be a model."

"Humpf."

"Her assistant's hot," Tessa enthused. "A total fucking bad ass. Like Cleopatra Jones. I love Blaxploitation."

"I love her hair," Penelope said. "I've always wanted to be a woman of color so I could have hair like that."

"I don't think she likes white people very much."

"She just doesn't like you." Penelope turned on Tessa. It struck her then how tall the newest addition to the Templeton family was. She felt small in comparison – small and mousy and inadequate. Penelope was reminded yet again of her outsider status, of the fact that she could never shake off Penny Danziger no matter how hard she tried or how concerted the effort. An urge welled up inside her – no doubt fueled in part by alcohol and Spice deprivation – to knock Tessa down a peg or two, to remind her that regardless of blood relation, there was a hierarchy – a pecking order – and that she was stepping dangerously out of line. Penelope opened her mouth to deliver what she imagined to be as cutting a remark as she could muster, but her efforts were stymied by the grating sound of a voice – flat, nasal, and all too Midwestern: a nuclear blast from the past and yet another harbinger (as if she needed any other) of the hold Penny Danziger still had upon her.

"Oh. My. GAWD!"

Penelope clenched her fists until her nails broke flesh.

"You really are a princess!" Ruthie Peterson. *Motherfucker*. "I mean, look at this place. Just like Anne Hathaway in *The Princess Diaries*."

"My favorite movie of all time," Yolanda Fung chimed in.

"Like I had no idea," Ruthie droned. "I mean, even when we met you at that club that night? In London? I mean, like, I had an idea? But, Gawd, Penny, you're so modest!"

"I think we were roofied that night," Yolanda Fung said. "In fact, I'm convinced we were roofied. I read about it in *Cosmo*? And that DJ, well, he totally fit the profile. I knew there was something shady about him. He kept bringing us drinks. I think I saw him here when we arrived."

"He was really friendly though," Ruthie concurred. "I mean, I guess if anyone was going to roofie me, I'm kind of glad it was him."

"Well, he certainly gave a whole new meaning to Conga Line," Yolanda added. "Even Joshua got in on the action and he's, like, so conservative? Not as conservative as Owen though."

"That's because Owen has sense. He doesn't pretend to be something he's not."

"He kept going to the restrooms though," Yolanda said. "Or what do you call it here? 'The loo?'"

Penelope felt her skin crawl. How was this happening? Why was she being punished? No, it was worse than punishment. It was torture. Why here? Why now? And how in God's name, after all these years, had Ruthie Peterson and Yolanda Fung found their way onto the Steeplechase Weekend invite list? It was meant to be sacred. Diana guarded it under lock and key. Diana. Of course. She would do this to her. It all made sense. A reminder: *You do not belong. You are not and will never be anyone other than dopey Penny Danziger from Bumblefuck, USA.* There was no escaping it. Not even a title could erase the past. How foolish and naïve she'd been to ever have allowed herself to believe it might. Penelope gripped the edge of the bar and willed herself into some semblance of calm. Surely, it was almost two o'clock? The kidnapping had to be near at hand or else this was just the longest morning of her life. She glanced at Tessa who looked just as traumatized as she felt. Perhaps Tessa was her way out? Payback for two-timing her with Yvette...

"There was definitely something going on in the men's bathrooms," Ruthie said. "I asked Owen but of course he just told me to shut up. Actually, his exact words were 'shut the fuck up.'"

"I don't like how Owen talks to you," Yolanda said. "He treats you like the little woman. He's a caveman. You're such a strong female, Ruthie. You shouldn't let any man talk to you that way."

"I mean, I guess we really can't be too shocked," Ruthie said, her tone becoming reflective. "The club was called Sodom, after all."

"I kind of feel like Lot's wife."

"Are you okay, Penny?"

"What?"

"You look like you're not very happy to see us," Ruthie said.

"I think she's drunk," Yolanda chimed in. "Or high."

"Or both."

"What?" Penelope glanced furtively about the tent for an escape route, but there seemed no such relief in sight. She gave Tessa an imploring look, who just shook her head and shrugged as if to say, "Leave me the fuck out of this." Penelope vowed she'd get her revenge – first for being a mole and second for not giving a sister a hand when she needed it most. Penelope could forgive, but she would never forget. Tessa was now doubly on her shit list.

It was clear Ruthie and Yolanda weren't going away. She was saddled with them for the duration, or at least until the kidnapping, after which perhaps none of it would matter anymore. Fighting the urge to pick up the punch bowl and slurp up what little remained – it seemed she had already imbibed most of it – Penelope mustered as much resolve as her shattered nerves could manage and turned to face the opposition. How she loathed and detested them! How Ruthie Peterson and Yolanda Fung made her stomach turn! Oh, the violence of it was severe...too severe...perhaps out of all logic and proportion, but it was genuine and infectious and it gripped Penelope as hard and as fast as the most potent Spice Bomb, but without the pleasurable effect.

They were dressed in matching equestrian outfits – pink and blue Joules polo shirts with numbered patches sewn into each short-sleeve, chocolate brown jodhpurs and DuBarrys. Yolanda even sported a riding crop and an Ariat riding helmet. Who the hell did they think they were? What the fuck were they even doing there? Their presence was like a slap in Penelope's face, their attire designed no doubt to mock her, to remind her that even though she was an English Lady, she would never be rid of her distinctly suburban, American origins. Penelope's stomach rumbled and roiled. She was going to be sick.

"What are you even doing here?" Penelope nearly shouted.

"Catch you later," Tessa said with a roll of her eyes and a twitch of her eyebrows. "This is more trouble than even I can handle."

Ruthie and Yolanda scowled at Tessa who scowled back as she left Penelope to face the recurring nightmare of her past on her own.

"Attitude," Ruthie said.

"She looks famous," Yolanda said. "Or almost famous."

"She looks like a stuck-up bitch is what she looks like," Ruthie said.

"A man-eater," Yolanda added with a knowing nod. "She probably eats men alive with her vagina. We'd better keep a close eye on Owen and Joshua."

"I repeat," Penelope didn't know how long she'd be able to keep the sick down. The acid burned in her throat. "What are you doing here?"

"You invited us," Ruthie said with an exasperated sigh.

"I never."

"You did," Yolanda replied. "Don't you remember? That night at the club."

"At *Sodom*."

"You were really wasted. You kept telling everyone you'd fucked Owen in the toilet."

"Yeah," Ruthie said, "you were really kind of vulgar."

"Of course, Owen denied it on account of him being a Mormon."

Penelope swallowed. Her vision went in and out of focus. *This is going to be bad,* she thought. *Dear God, I've got to get away from here. I've got to find Chloe. I've got a kidnapping to fake. I'm going to be sick.*

"That's why I know he'll never cheat on me," Ruthie added.

"That doesn't make any sense," Yolanda said.

Ruthie shrugged. "Owen knows if he ever cheated on me I'd castrate him. After that scare at my second-cousin-once-removed's bat mitzvah, he knows if he so much as makes eyes at another woman – or another man – he's toast."

"Yeah," Yolanda sniggered, "you really showed him who's boss."

"These boots are made for walking," Ruthie said.

Ruthie and Yolanda shared a cackle. Penelope blinked. She felt the sweat drip from her brow, down her neck, under her bra. She covered her mouth with her hands. It bubbled and churned. A tidal wave...

"Excuse me," she gurgled.

But it was too late. An ocean of vomit shot through her clenched jaws like a projectile, thoroughly and unsparingly covering Ruthie and Yolanda's matching riding outfits, their boots, their hair, their everything. Penelope tried to swallow what remained but wave after wave catapulted from her mouth, hitting all and sundry. *Oh, the humiliation! Her mind raced. I'll never live this down. Edgar will surely divorce me. It won't be Guy that's exiled from the family. It'll be me. What am I going to do? What the hell am I going to do?* She wanted to cry. She wanted to rage. She needed to get away.

Ruthie and Yolanda just stared at her, their expressions matching their ruined outfits. Penelope imagined the eyes of everyone at the Steeplechase on her, laughing at her, judging her. She couldn't cope.

"I'm sorry," she managed. "I'm so sorry. But...I can't talk to you right now... I have to go. I have to..."

She ran from the tent, one hand over her mouth, the other over her eyes as another onslaught of sick threatened to burst forth. She tripped and stumbled and fell and then picked herself up and tore toward the house. She was vaguely aware of staff offering assistance and of Hamish (as if the humiliation wasn't bad enough!) appearing out of nowhere to ask if she was all right. But Penelope couldn't, wouldn't stop. She clutched the bannister of the grand staircase and propelled herself up three steps at a time. It was imperative she got to her room before inflicting any more damage to herself or to others. *What time is it? I need to get Chloe to the path leading to the boathouse. Xander will be waiting...*

"Penelope?"

She looked up. Chloe was standing on the upstairs landing looking demure and picture-perfect in a floral pussy-bowed Stella McCartney frock and matching kitten heels.

"Are you all right?" Chloe asked. "What's happened? Did the oysters get you too?"

Chloe was like manna from the heavens. Penelope paused at the top of the landing to take a breath and ward off the urge to hyperventilate as Chloe put a comforting arm around her shoulders and dabbed at the sick around Penelope's mouth with a handkerchief she produced from out of nowhere.

"I'm a disaster," Penelope said.

"Oh, you poor dear." Chloe folded Penelope into her arms as Penelope let forth a stream of sobs that, had the roles been reversed, would surely have done Chloe proud. "You poor, poor dear. You've been in such a state this whole weekend it's no wonder that your hyperactivity finally caught up with you. But a funny tummy can defeat the best of us. I was literally at death's door just twelve hours ago."

Penelope snatched the handkerchief from Chloe's hand and blew her nose. There was nothing she could think of to say, except: "Would you happen to have the time?"

"The time?" Chloe's expression went from compassionate concern to bafflement. She stepped back – breaking the embrace – and regarded her sister-in-law with wary suspicion. "What a peculiar thing to ask. It's just gone past one. I was on my way down to the awards luncheon."

Penelope breathed a sigh of relief. "There's still time," she said.

Chloe's alarm was evident. "For what?"

Shit, Penelope thought. Pull yourself together. Step back away from the ledge. In her own hysteria, she'd quite forgotten her sister-in-law's penchant for amplifying the drama from zero to sixty in no time flat. *I can't blow this.*

Penelope forced a smile that she hoped was convincing though she knew from experience Chloe was rarely so easily swayed. "Time for me to change and clean myself up," she said. "I can't very well show up to the luncheon looking like I've pulled an all-nighter in Mile's End."

"Surely, you're not thinking of making an appearance in your present state?"

Penelope's gratitude turned to irritation. She wiped her mouth with the back of her hand in a gesture that she sensed Chloe would interpret as defiant. (And indeed Chloe flinched.) She needed to get herself dressed and back on track. She needed to get Chloe outside and on the footpath leading to the boathouse. There was no telling what might happen should she fail to deliver her quarry. But she supposed the unsuspecting Chloe meant well. Yet, as ever, Penelope couldn't help but see her sister-in-law's solicitude as tinged with an element of disapproval. After all, the young woman was a Templeton and Penelope knew all too well how the Templetons were prone to judge.

"I'm feeling much better now, actually," Penelope lied. "And once I've had a wash and changed my clothes I'll good as new. In fact, I'd be so appreciative, Chloe, if you might assist me?" *Best to lay the charm on thick.* "You have such an eye for fashion and frankly I've always struggled with what is and isn't appropriate attire for a garden luncheon." *If only to make sure Chloe never left her sight.* "I think I made rather a hash of it last year. Do you remember?"

Chloe shuddered. "As if any of us could ever forget?"

"Was it really that bad?"

"Ghastly."

The criticism still stung. "Perhaps you could choose an outfit for me?"

The charm offensive seemed to achieve the desired result. Chloe's face lit up like cupid. "I'll do you one better," she said with a twinkle in her eye. "I'll let you borrow one of my frocks. I've an Alexander McQueen that's just this side of edgy but tasteful. I've had it for yonks but haven't worn it yet. One of these days I really must sort my wardrobe. You should have a look. Perhaps I could hand a few items down to you, though you may need to let the waistlines out a bit."

Bitch.

"Like sisters," Penelope said.

The trace of a frown wrinkled Chloe's brow. "Yes," she said. "Like sisters."

And so, with just under twenty minutes to spare, Penelope was washed and cossetted and dressed in one of Chloe's haute couture hand-me-downs that, even though she was loath to admit it, was indeed a bit snug around the middle. When she had finished primping, Chloe stepped back to admire her handiwork and, deciding that she approved, clapped her hands together and gave a little cheer that Penelope found wholly demeaning. She clenched her teeth behind the smile.

"You know," Chloe said, "a proper image consultant would work wonders for you. If SASS goes under, perhaps I might set myself up in a nice little makeover business? You could be my first client."

"Thanks," Penelope said.

"I really should come up to your boutique next time I'm in London." Chloe's chatter was starting to grate, as was the proprietorial hand placed on the small of her back as they descended the grand staircase to rejoin the festivities. "How long has it been open now? It's just that Shoreditch is such a hike and, quite frankly – between sisters – the name of it scares me a bit. Naughty 'Nickers. It sounds, well, vaguely indecent. Who's idea was it to call it that? Yours or Edgar's?"

"Mine."

"I mean, the alliteration is cute I suppose, but if you want my opinion – and what do I know? I don't know anything about...retail – I do think it projects a certain, well, Shoreditch isn't Essex (at least as far as I know) and it has a very *Essex* sound to it. Of course, if footballers' wives and cast-offs from *Strictly* are the clientele you're after, then more power to you. But I think you may want to rethink your demographic, if you're in it for the long haul."

There was no point in arguing, Penelope thought. Best to just let Chloe run her course. They were nearly downstairs anyway. Her chatter would be cut short once they joined the luncheon, or so she hoped. And then to the footpath, and then the kidnapping, God willing...

"What does Edgar think about it?"

"About what?"

"About the boutique. About (gulp) Naughty 'Nickers. I feel as though I need to take a shower."

"What time is it?"

"I don't understand this sudden obsession with time," Chloe replied. "It's most peculiar."

They swept through the doors and out onto the front lawn where Elena Grimaldi and her army of faceless (but cheery) black-clad attendants were finalizing the flower arrangements – tulips, of course – on each table. Elena greeted them with her dazzling toothpaste smile.

"Are we feeling as fabulous as we look?" Elena asked.

"How about we go for a walk?" Penelope asked. "I'm not in the mood for Elena."

"She is rather fabulous though," Chloe said.

Penelope was just relieved that Chloe wasn't offering resistance to their little detour down the footpath.

"Cressida can't stand her," Chloe chattered. "Cressida told me Elena has all sorts of secrets waiting to see the light of day."

"Is there anyone Cressida can stand?" Penelope squinted against the sun as she scanned the path ahead for signs of Xander. In order to maintain a certain level of surprise, they hadn't discussed the exact when and where.

"Cressida doesn't suffer fools, although I have to admit – sister to sister – that I am rather relieved she stood Guy up at the altar. As awful as it was – and believe me, it was awful..."

"Yes, Chloe, I remember. I was there."

"Oh, yes, of course. I think that must have been in the time before I noticed you. You've come a long way in the interim. Anyway, as I was saying, I don't think I could handle Cressida as a full-time sister-in-law."

Cressida terrified Penelope, but she kept this to herself. "Cressida is definitely someone I'd not want to get on the bad side of," she said and pondered whether it was too soon to ask Chloe yet again for the time.

"She's a pussycat really," Chloe replied, "albeit with a lion's roar. But in order to get where she has, she's had to play up the 'difficult woman' bit. It's a shame that in this day and age, women continue to be criticized for being strong, powerful, and successful in business. It's still a man's world, no matter what anyone says."

"Well, she's definitely benefited from marrying a rich husband," Penelope said. She stopped and put her hand on Chloe's arm for her to wait.

"I can tell you a thing or two about Olivier."

"Shhh!"

"What?" Chloe's face registered alarm. "Why have we stopped?"

Despite the fact that she knew the kidnapping was fake – nothing more than a means to an end – Penelope was suddenly gripped by genuine fear. She pressed her finger to her lips and glanced about the path and its vicinity, peering into the upper boughs of the ancient elm trees and at the tall somewhat overgrown grass and shrubbery that bordered both sides of the path. Her pulse quickened. Xander could be anywhere, watching them, listening to Chloe's mindless chatter, preparing to strike at any moment. She wondered whether she might have been a little over-hasty in agreeing to the plan.

Who was Xander anyway? She barely knew anything about him. He frightened her. She hadn't liked the way he'd rubbed his hands together with a pervy kind of zeal when she'd met him that morning to work through the logistics. He'd been unabashed in his enthusiasm and had even licked his lips with all too evident zeal. But it was too late to back out now. She needed the kidnapping to succeed. She needed Guy out of the picture. It was of utmost importance that she prove herself to Lady Eliza and secure her position, if not at the matriarch's right hand – for it seemed Sister Francine had herself well locked-in – then securely at her left. But at what cost, she asked herself. She didn't want anything seriously bad to happen to Chloe, yet she hadn't specifically told Xander to treat this as a more-or-less benign game of hide and seek. *Oh God,* she thought to herself at that moment, *what have I gotten myself into?* She didn't think a hit of Spice would help.

"It's nothing," she said. She loosened her white-knuckle grip on Chloe's arm and forced herself to breathe. "I thought I saw something move in the underbrush."

Chloe's bottom lip trembled.

"I think we should go back now," Chloe said. "We can't be late for the luncheon. I have an award to present."

"Did you hear that?"

"Did I hear what?" Chloe tried to pull her arm free but Penelope held fast. "Penelope, you're frightening me. Please, let's go back to the house. They'll wonder where we are."

"Right." Penelope nodded. "We should go. It must only have been the wind."

It was at that moment that Xander struck. He came from above. Penelope didn't actually see his descent from the trees – where she had first detected movement – but he seemed to spring from the sky as he landed between her and Chloe, knocking her sister-in-law to the ground and forcing Penelope to stumble several feet back from the point of impact. Chloe screamed and struggled, but Xander – looking very un-Xander-like, Penelope thought, though how exactly she couldn't begin to articulate – overwhelmed her with a brutal efficiency that made Penelope want to run as far away from him as possible. She felt a desperate need to save herself. And while she hadn't known exactly what to expect, Penelope could already tell this was not going to be mere child's play.

"Shut up!" Xander screamed as he forced himself down on Chloe, pinning her flailing arms to the ground and straddling her. He raised his right hand high before slamming his fist into Chloe's jaw, instantly rendering her silent.

"What have you done?" Penelope cried. "It's not supposed to be like this. I didn't mean for you...what have you...is she dead?"

It was as though she suddenly lost control of her senses. The impulse to flee left her. She ran at Xander and tried to force him off of the now unconscious Chloe, but again, his strength and stealth surprised her. He stood up and shoved Penelope so she fell to the ground, hitting her head on a rock and causing her vision to blur. The last thing she remembered before fading to unconsciousness was Xander standing over her, his hands raised high above his head, his eyes blazing with an evil the likes of which Penelope had never seen before. His voice, when he spoke, sounded like it came from the darkest pit of hell. It was bestial:

"I AM NOT XANDER," he intoned.

Then all faded to black.

| 31 |

When Penelope came to, she opened her eyes to a sight that was both familiar yet oddly, ominously transformed. She recognized the boathouse, yet – like Xander – it didn't look like the boathouse, at least not as she had always known it. Her head felt heavy and she tasted the salty brine of blood in her mouth. She blinked as her vision gradually focused and then became aware that her arms were raised and pulled taut above her head and that her feet didn't quite touch the ground. She tried to pull her arms free but soon discovered her wrists were tightly bound with rope. She couldn't move save for turning her head ever so slightly from one side to the other.

As her eyes adjusted to the dimly lit interior of the boathouse, Penelope detected the shape of Chloe beside her, bound and suspended above the ground in similar fashion. Her sister-in-law appeared conscious, much to Penelope's vast, though decidedly not reassured, relief.

"Chloe?" she whispered. The boathouse was too dark to tell whether they were alone or whether Xander – or whoever he was – was present there, lurking in the shadows, watching them. "Chloe? Are you all right?"

"I can't feel my arms," Chloe replied. She emitted a belabored moan.

"But you're alive?"

"Unless I'm in a waking nightmare, then yes, I'm alive...at least for the time being. My head is throbbing...and my nose, is it...do you think it's broken? I can taste blood."

"It's too dark," Penelope said. "I can't see."

"Is he here?"

"Who?"

"That man, or whatever he is. He seemed less human than beast."

"What do you remember?"

"Nothing."

Penelope held her breath. A floorboard creaked. She detected the presence of another – Xander, perhaps? But he had said he wasn't Xander. He certainly hadn't looked like Xander. And then a fresh wave of panic gripped her. What if he betrayed her? What if he told Chloe that she had been behind the plot? What if, God forbid, Chloe recognized Xander as Edgar's PA? Why hadn't she thought of that before? Penelope's only hope was that Xander, when he next appeared, had had the forethought to wear a mas, and that Yvette would come to the rescue sooner than later.

"It's going to be okay," Penelope said, more to reassure herself than Chloe. "Someone will find us. I'm sure your absence – if not mine – from the awards luncheon will have been noticed. They'll send a search party. We'll be out of here in no time."

"I don't understand," Chloe said. Penelope could tell from the waver in her sister-in-law's voice that tears were looming. She supposed it was inevitable, given the circumstances and Chloe's natural temperament. But she wasn't in the mood to be consoling. "What's happening? Who's doing this to us? What have I done to deserve this?"

"What have you done to deserve this?" Penelope couldn't disguise the irritation. "What about me? I'm here just as much as you are. We're both in this predicament."

"I'm just worried about my nose," Chloe said. "I have more at stake than you. Who wants an It Girl with a broken nose?"

"There's more to life than magazine covers," Penelope snapped.

"You don't understand. This face launched SASS. Without it, well, I might as well sequester myself in a convent or some ashram in the Himalayas. Although I may do that anyway given *that woman's* intent. I wouldn't be at all surprised if she's behind this. I wouldn't put it past her – her and that fundamentalist psychopath."

Penelope once again found herself wanting to vomit.

There came another creak.

"Shhh!" Penelope hissed. "Who's there?"

"Reveal yourself!" Chloe piped in. "I demand you tell us what's going on. Do you have any idea who I am?"

Penelope felt hot breath on her neck. She strained away from it. The smell was vaguely sulfurous with an undercurrent of anise.

"Pretty," a voice said in the dark. "Pretty but not as pretty as the other. The other is very pretty. Pretty, pretty. So pretty. But maybe pretty not so more."

"Who are you?" Penelope asked for now she was convinced that whoever it was that had kidnapped her wasn't Xander after all.

Laughter. A match was struck. It flickered and dipped and in the moment that it shone, Penelope could see a black-hooded figure standing mere inches from where she was suspended. And then the flame died.

"Pretty is as pretty does," the voice continued. It was deep-pitched and oily. She might have found it seductive if the situation were different, or if she had been the one in control. "Pretty, pretty, she so pretty."

"I was pretty," Chloe said. "*Vanity Fair* called me the Perfect English Rose. But I don't know now. You've broken my nose. I can't bear to think about it."

"Quiet!" Penelope felt a breeze across her face as their captor slipped himself between her and Chloe. The smell of anise followed him. "Is it not you of whom I speak. There is another here with us. Perhaps you know her? Or perhaps you'd like to be introduced?"

Another match lit. Another flame.

Penelope thought she espied the outline of a female form hovering on the outskirts of the ray of light cast by the match. She squinted and tried to lean forward to get a better look, but the suspension of her arms prevented ease of movement. The effort wrenched her rotator cuffs, both of which were already sensitive on account of a particularly aggressive bit of fun with Edgar and a sling, back in the days when he had found her attractive and they'd played together. She'd told everyone else – and her doctor – that she'd injured her shoulders playing tennis, which seemed to convince the family even though Penelope had never picked up a tennis racket in all her life. She and Edgar used to have secrets like that, never mind the origins of their relationship. When she had first been introduced to Edgar's parents, he'd told them they had met at the East Bank Club in Chicago. He said she had been his aerobics instructor and it had been love at first squat.

Penelope knew from the get-go that neither Fiona nor Carleton believed a word of it, but both had been too discreet to question him, though Penelope also knew Carleton hadn't been at all pleased with his oldest son's choice of mate. And as for Lady Fiona, the mother-in-law Penelope had come to prize as a goddess incarnate, she had taken Penelope under her wing no questions asked and had made sure that the rest of the family accepted Penelope into their hearts as genuinely and as warmly as she had done, or rather in so far as public appearances were concerned. For this kindness, Penelope was eternally grateful.

Oh, how time and circumstance changed things! Penelope often found herself thinking of the late lamented Lady Fiona. She couldn't help but wonder though what Edgar's mother had really thought of her. A paragon of virtue – a living saint – Lady Fiona represented everything that Penelope had always dreamed for herself and had desperately hoped to become. But life was cruel. (So cruel!) And here she was now, thick in the middle of a fake kidnapping plot that looked to be going hopelessly, dangerously, awry. She no longer even remembered (or cared) how she had managed to get herself into this mess. Whatever Guy had done – or hadn't done, for what did Penelope truly know? – to deserve the antipathy of his siblings and new stepmother, what stake had Penelope really in the situation?

In retrospect, none of this made sense to her. She had hoped to ingratiate herself with the formidable Lady Eliza Brookings but in doing so Penelope felt she had made a deal with the devil. And this didn't even take into account the looming disaster of her secret agreement with Bipasha Gupta. Was her mind so addled on Spice that she could no longer conduct herself or her thought processes in a rational manner? Further to all of this – as if Penelope didn't already have more than enough on her plate – was the question of what to do about Ruthie and Yolanda, who seemed determined to wreak as much havoc in Penelope's life as two thoroughly Midwestern girls could possibly do. And was it really true what they had said? Had she really confessed to shagging Ruthie's husband in the loos at Foraged? Could she have stooped so low? How vulgar! Not even Penny Danziger would have behaved in such an uncouth way.

If she survived this ordeal – if Yvette came to the rescue as she had promised – Penelope vowed to get to the bottom of her life one way or another. And if that meant making some changes – or taking drastic measures – to secure her position in the family she needed to identify as hers, then so be it. Penelope hadn't made it this far to see it all go up in a cloud of Spice.

Yet, as Xander (or whoever the mystery man was behind the hooded cloak) beckoned this ill-defined third hostage into Penelope's slowly adjusting vision, she found herself the victim of another shock.

"Pretty is as pretty does," Xander-not-Xander repeated in his eerily reptilian hiss. "Pretty does as pretty did until pretty-pretty not so pretty anymore."

Penelope suppressed the urge to scream. Chloe had no such compunction. Penelope's ears rang. The vomit rose up from her stomach, burning her windpipe. She clenched her teeth and forced the bile back down.

Rebecca Hastings was almost unrecognizable. Her face looked as though it had melted. The skin under her right eye was puckered and pustulent. And what had once been her right eye was now little more than a reddish orb that seemed too small for the surrounding socket. Her hair was limp and matted. The right corner of her mouth hung down like a stroke victim's and her lips were little more than an incongruous gash that exposed her gums and made her teeth look twice the size they should have been. What had Xander done to her? What evil had Penelope set in motion? How had jealousy driven her to such madness?

'I hear music,' Xander-not-Xander said. "And how I do so love to dance. Care to take a twirl round the dance floor, Rebecca? A little music and dancing to liven up the party, yes? Let's show our guests how it's done."

"What have you done to her?" Chloe cried. She valiantly struggled against the rope that bound her wrists. "Rebecca, Rebecca, it's me, Chloe. I don't know what's going on but I can assure you that whoever it is behind this will pay. They'll pay with their life if it's the last thing I do!"

"Help me," Rebecca Hastings mewed as their captor spun her round and round the boathouse to a soundtrack that only he seemed to hear. The former front-of-house at Foraged was like a rag doll in his arms.

"Think, Chloe, think," Chloe said. "Penelope, make yourself useful and help me think."

"Think about what?" Penelope could hardly bring herself to speak. Perhaps it was best, she thought, if she didn't survive the ordeal. The aftermath didn't bear considering.

"Escape," Chloe replied. "This is untenable."

No, Penelope thought. *Escape isn't part of the plan. We're to be rescued. Yvette is on her way. Any minute now she'll burst through the doors in a halo of lustrous red hair and an attitude of Gallic sensibility. Maybe she'll brandish a gun. Penelope rather liked the idea of Yvette Devereux carrying a gun. It didn't have to be loaded – in fact, it would probably be best for everyone involved if it weren't. It just needed* to be present and perhaps waved around a bit in a threatening manner to show Yvette meant business, just enough to be convincing.

But she was taking too long. Penelope hadn't any concept of how long she'd been knocked out, although she suspected it had to have at least been more than an hour, given the logistics of Xander transporting both herself and Chloe from the footpath to the boathouse and then tying them up in this rather brutal fashion. Penelope felt like a trussed pig, and not in a good way. Her shoulders ached and she had lost all feeling in her hands and arms. She supposed she should credit Xander (if that's even who it was that held them captive) for playing his part so convincingly, but enough really was enough. His over-enthusiasm frightened her. And the longer she remained in this hostage situation with Chloe, the more insufferable her sister-in-law became. Perhaps she could encourage Xander to wallop Chloe one more time for good measure? But there was still the most inconvenient issue of Rebecca Hastings, a problem that was supposed to have gone away. Not only had RH not gone away, she'd become even more inconvenient. Penelope began to despair.

"I demand you untie me right this minute!" Chloe bellowed. Her voice was shrill and earnest in its intensity. "Do you have any idea who I am?"

"Pretty pretty likes to dance..."

"Well, I'll tell you who I am. My name is Chloe Templeton. Yes, you heard that correctly. Templeton. Of the Templeton dynasty. My family's been around for centuries. You should look us up if you're not familiar. We're even mentioned in Magna Carta. But then you've probably never heard of Magna Carta, have you? I can tell from your accent you're not English."

"Dance, dance, pretty pretty." Xander twirled and scooped Rebecca Hastings around and around the boathouse. Her head hung back, her hair swept the floor. She was limp in his arms.

"Where are your people from?" Chloe demanded.

"Chloe," Penelope whispered. "Helping or hurting?"

"I'm establishing a line of communication."

"Why?"

Chloe rolled her eyes. "Half the time in situations like these," she explained, "the culprit is acting from a position where he feels inferior to the captive, and usually that inferiority is derived from a certain financial or cultural imbalance that the culprit hopes to rectify through desperate criminal action."

"Thank you for the lesson in socio-economics."

"We live in a very unjust world," Chloe continued. "It's all too easy for people like us – or people like *me* anyway – to stay safely sequestered in our gilded cages and pretend like people who don't live like us – or like me – don't exist. Why do you think I founded SASS?"

Penelope's patience had run out. "Because you needed something to do," she snapped.

"Well, yes, I suppose that was part of the reason." Chloe paused. "I mean it's not as though I could very well go out and get a normal job. I'm not exactly a nine-to-fiver."

Xander stopped, the music in his head apparently having come to an end. He let Rebecca Hastings go with a flourish that Penelope suspected wouldn't have passed muster on *Strictly*. Rebecca Hastings fell to the floor with a jarring thud that only served to further remind her that things were definitely not going to plan. *Where the hell is Yvette?* Penelope feared she was about to see her life flash before her eyes.

"You want talk?" he asked.

"No," Penelope said. "I don't want talk. I want you to let us go."

"*Nyet*," Xander replied as he adjusted the hood. "That's not part of plan. We wait."

"But she needs medical attention." Despite her antipathy for the Foraged hostess – or perhaps it was guilt? – Penelope found herself rather concerned for Rebecca Hastings' well-being. "I don't even know how she's mixed up in this."

Xander's breath smelled of pickled beets. "Damage of the collateral."

"Russian," Chloe said. "You're Russian. It took me a while to place the accent, but that's it, isn't it? Oh my God."

"Chloe..."

"This is because of Guy, isn't it? You're connected to that woman and that horrible child."

"I not know anything."

"I can't breathe. Penelope, I'm...I can't...I..."

"Try, Chloe. Try. There's no sense in getting yourself worked up." Penelope cursed herself.

"I didn't want to believe it. Even now, even after all that happened yesterday, I was still holding out hope that perhaps it was all a bad dream. But it's not a dream, is it? It's real. Guy's sold himself to the Russians and he's selling us along with him."

"You talk too much," Xander said. He licked Chloe's cheek. "Pretty pretty make me hungry like wolf. Make me howl at moon."

Xander threw his head back and howled. Chloe screamed. The door blew open at that moment and Yvette appeared, armed with little more than a torch whose beam cut through the gathering darkness of the boathouse and momentarily blinded Penelope, who found herself too disoriented to comprehend what was going on around her. All she knew was that she was finally being "rescued."

"*J'arrive*!" Yvette declared. She took a moment to establish her presence and brush her hair over her shoulder before running to Penelope and Chloe and cutting the ropes that suspended them.

"You took your fucking time," Penelope said.

Chloe threw her arms around Yvette. "He was going to kill us!" she cried in a blitz of sobs and sniffles. "Because of Guy. Because of that woman and that bastard child. Because the Russians..."

"You need to conserve your energy," Yvette said. *In other words*, Penelope thought, *you need to shut the fuck up*. "You've been through a *très traumatique* experience – a matter of life or death. Thank God I arrived when I did."

"But where did he go?" Chloe stumbled around the boathouse. *How quickly she seems to have recovered*. "He was just here a moment ago and now he's gone. You let him escape." *And how quickly gratitude turns to accusation*. "He could be anywhere. He could strike again, only next time he might have reinforcements."

Yvette and Penelope exchanged glances. Penelope shook her head and rubbed her arms and shoulders. She was definitely going to feel it in the morning.

"My intelligence tells me your kidnapper was a lone wolf," Yvette replied, her tone tinged with impatience. "He won't get far."

"He's Russian, you know," Chloe said. "Did your 'intelligence' tell you that also? Did your 'intelligence' tell you that a Russian honey trap and her bastard child somehow managed to break through security and enter my family's inner sanctum? Although for all I know, Guy might have been in on it. This whole fiasco might very well have been Guy's doing. In fact, I'm convinced of it. I sense an inside job. I must have a word with Spencer. MI-6 is not going to get away with this! Heads will roll. I assure you."

"I would have settled for a *merci*," Yvette quipped.

"This doesn't settle the score between us," Chloe said, "lest you've deluded yourself into thinking that it did. Nothing will ever forgive Dhaka."

"*Merci*," Penelope offered. "*Merci beaucoup*."

"*De rien*," Yvette said with a tight-lipped smile. "Regardless, you should both see a doctor. Your wounds look superficial but you could still be concussed."

"I'm fine." Chloe ran her fingers through her hair and shook her head. "My nose may need surgical attention, however, but in spite of that, I'm as fine as can be expected. It seems I've become a human punching bag this weekend. I've been pushed. I've been punched. It's a good thing I've got pluck."

"This one, on the other hand," Yvette crouched beside Rebecca Hastings who lay quivering on the floor in a fetal position, "needs serious medical attention."

"Oh God!" Chloe threw herself down onto the floor and cradled Rebecca Hastings in her arms. "The poor dear. Just like Sunny Joy. How can people be so cruel? This is England, not Bangladesh. We're a civilized country. We're a *civilizing* country. We don't do this kind of thing to our own."

"She deserved it." Penelope couldn't resist.

"What a horrible thing to say!"

Penelope shrugged. "What goes around comes around. She was fucking my husband. Enough said."

"Amen," Yvette murmured.

"It's all right, Rebecca." Chloe brushed the matted hair from Rebecca Hastings' forehead. "I'm sorry if I've ever done anything to hurt you. We'll get to the bottom of this. I'll make sure you have the finest treatment money can buy. Private – no NHS incompetence for you. You'll be back to fighting spirit in no time." Chloe looked up at Yvette and Penelope, an expression of resolute determination burning through her tears. "I'm taking personal responsibility for Rebecca's recovery. It's the least I can do."

"Suit yourself," Yvette said. "*Et voila!* My role here *c'est finis.*"

"Thank you again." Penelope followed Yvette to the door. "I trust you'll keep this under wraps?"

"I'm a spy," Yvette said with a smile and a twinkle in her eye. "*Discretion jusqu'à la mort.* I'll have a quiet word with Spencer. He'll see that Rebecca Hastings is brought to the house and put to bed without fanfare. The rest I leave up to you."

She turned to leave and then stopped. Penelope held her breath.

"These are dangerous machinations," Yvette said. "I fear for you. I fear for your family."

The words choked in Penelope's throat: "I know what I'm doing."

Yvette cocked an eyebrow. "Do you?" she asked. "The things I have witnessed this weekend give me cause to believe otherwise. But what do I know? I'm just a simple French girl from the provinces. *A tout a l'heur, ma amie.*"

When Yvette was safely off in the distance, Penelope grabbed the boathouse door to steady herself and dry-heaved. There was nothing left inside her to vomit. She then bid Chloe return to the house with her, taking a rather indirect path so as to avoid drawing undue attention from the guests. Chloe resisted at first, insisting that she stay in the boathouse with Rebecca Hastings, but relented when Penelope assured her Spencer would take everything in hand. Her head throbbed from more than Xander's knockout punch. Penelope was disturbed. While it seemed the fake kidnapping plot had succeeded in achieving its goal – Chloe was convinced that Guy's collusion with the Russians had resulted in that afternoon's events and thus turned her against her brother once and for all – Penelope found herself questioning what exactly had transpired. The man in the hooded cloak could only have been Xander, but why – how – had he seemed so different? The voice was alien to her. And the violence – for yes, it had been violent – wasn't something she would have expected from someone of Xander's seemingly delicate, if not effete, nature, but rather the stuff of nightmares and bad horror films.

To Penelope, the man in the black hood was something akin to a demon, possessed of an evil that Penelope hadn't thought real. But there was nothing she could say and nothing she could do. For if she exposed Xander as her captor, she risked revealing her part in the plot to Chloe, which she didn't doubt would ultimately undermine her position within the family, even as all of them (save Chloe and Guy) had been in on it from the start. Added to this rather unnerving mix was the truth in Yvette's parting words. This was a dangerous game she was playing and Penelope wasn't at all certain of the outcome.

| 32 |

Chloe was mystified. She couldn't remember the last time when the world had stopped making sense. The kidnapping had almost driven her to a breaking point. It wasn't so much the kidnapping that upset her – although it had been one of the most traumatic experiences of her life – but the sobering reality that it revealed. Chloe couldn't help but take Guy's betrayal personally. Did he really think so little of her that his actions – thoughtless and unexplainable as they were – put her directly in harm's way? What if she had been killed? Or worse, what if the man in the black hood had done to her what he'd done to poor Rebecca Hastings? Chloe would surely have preferred death to a life as the survivor of an acid attack. And while just thirty-six hours ago (or however long it was) she had been actively conspiring to remove RH from her own personal equation, this horror – the monstrosity of it! – was not at all what she had envisioned. In truth, Chloe wasn't at all sure what she had envisioned. She'd just entrusted Xander to take care of it without risk of getting blood on her hands.

Now, however, she felt as though she was drowning in blood. Like Lady Macbeth, she couldn't rid herself of its taint. After Dr. Raleigh had examined her and declared that her nose most assuredly was not broken – in fact, he had gone so far as to praise her resilience – Chloe drew herself a hot bubble bath (so hot it practically scalded) and forced herself to endure the cleansing pain without flinching. She hoped that the extreme temperature would burn off the guilt when all it succeeded in doing was make her feel as though she was going to pass out. She feared the guilt would drive her mad. When Spencer knocked on her door an hour or so later to ask for her statement, Chloe pretended not to hear him. She wrapped herself in her terrycloth robe – stolen several years' back during an attempted romantic romp with Spencer at the Dorchester – and smoked cigarette after cigarette while curled up tight in her favorite reading chair. She doubted her ability to carry on.

It was late – the sky outside her bedroom windows was dark and lit by a seemingly impossible tapestry of stars – when a series of gentle but urgent knocks disturbed Chloe from her monastic contemplation.

"Go away!" she cried, assuming it was Spencer. "I'm not loving myself very much right now."

The voice on the other side of the door was most definitely not Spencer's. "This is no time for self-pity," Eliza said. "Open the door. We need to talk."

"Leave me alone. I have nothing to say to you or to anyone for that matter. I may very well take a vow of silence."

"Be my guest," Eliza replied. "But not until you've opened this door and we've spoken. If you don't in the count of five, I'll have Sister Francine break it down. She's here and she's ready upon my order."

Resistance was futile.

"What do you want?" Chloe asked as she opened the door to her new stepmother and her stepmother's henchwoman, both of whom were clad head-to-toe in black. Eliza even sported a black lace veil as one might wear to a funeral – or an audience with the Pope.

"Stand outside and keep watch," Eliza directed Sister Francine. "My step-daughter and I are not to be interrupted."

"Yes, Mum," the Fallen Angel said with a sneer that Chloe found almost more unnerving than Eliza's funereal attire.

"Self-pity is for weaklings and fools," Eliza said. She coughed. "I can't breathe in here. I don't abide cigarettes and I won't allow them in this house."

"I don't care," Chloe replied. If she hadn't already smoked the last one in the pack, she would have lit another in defiance. "What do you want? And why are you dressed like that? Has something happened to Papa?"

"Sit down and shut up." The words were so harsh and spoken so decisively that Chloe found herself stunned into silence. She sat with a thud in her chair as Eliza perched on the edge of her four-poster bed. "You may be surprised to discover, Chloe, that the world does not revolve around you."

"I've never said that it did."

Eliza emitted an ironic, throaty laugh. "You're so myopic it's almost retarded," she said. "Your mother did you no favors."

"Don't you dare talk about my mother!"

"I'll talk about whomever I please. I'm in control now. I call the shots. You and all your siblings will just have to fall in line or face the consequences, just as Guy will now have to face the consequences of what he's done."

Chloe knew she was beaten. She sank against the back of the chair and adjusted the robe more tightly about her frame. Eliza's gaze made her feel naked. "Guy is indeed a disappointment, I concede that," she said with a sigh. "My biggest fail. For too long I've given him the benefit of the doubt."

"Most of us are guilty without the inconvenience of being proven innocent," Eliza said. "That's why there are more sinners than saints in this world. I believe it is our true nature to be irredeemable. Only the chosen few are without sin. Thanks to Sister Francine I've learnt that the struggles of my life stem from the sin I have in my heart. I've reconciled this through prayer, sacrifice, and Sister Francine's steady counsel, but I will never be among the redeemed."

"You open your mouth and all I hear is mumbo-jumbo," Chloe replied with a trace – but only a trace – of her former fighting spirit. "You should join a convent if that's how you feel, like the Ambassador's daughter. Put us all out of our misery."

"I've called a family synod for eleven o'clock tonight. You have just enough time to get yourself cleaned up and to the library. I wanted to speak to you beforehand to make sure we are all on the same page about what's to be done."

"About Guy?"

"A vote will be taken. I trust you will vote with the family."

"I'll vote with my conscience."

"You'll vote as I tell you to vote." Eliza flipped the veil up and folded it back over her head. Her eyes narrowed, black as onyx. "Need I remind you that you were a victim today of Guy's treachery? If it weren't for that ridiculous Frenchwoman who play-acts at being a spy, your fate might very well have been the same as that other unfortunate woman's. I concede Mademoiselle Devereux surprised me."

"And how is Rebecca?"

"She was airlifted to Radcliffe Hospital for emergency surgery. Dr. Raleigh isn't optimistic about her prognosis."

"And the Steeplechase?"

Eliza gave her an incredulous look. "Because of course that's all you people care about," she said. "Diana proved her mettle yet again – her and that insufferable Dutch bitch with the goddamned tulips. They arranged spa treatments for the ladies and a pub-crawl for the gents down at the local inn. Rented the entire place out for the night. Deflects attention, you see, from our internal machinations. Of course, the more intrepid will ask questions, but I've entrusted Tucker O'Donnell to shut them down. Still, I'm sure we'll be tabloid fodder for a while. I suppose it can't be helped."

As loath as Chloe was to admit it, she couldn't help but be impressed by Eliza's apparent lock on the situation. It made her despise her stepmother even more.

"And the kidnapping?"

Eliza drew a line across her lips. "As far as anyone outside this family is concerned, there was an incident with one of the guests who was subsequently airlifted to the hospital. A riding accident, you see. If she recovers, I'll see to it that she's rewarded handsomely for her discretion. And if she refuses – again assuming she recovers – there will be consequences. I made that point very clear to Dr. Raleigh."

"Blackmail."

"Crisis control."

Eliza stood up from the bed. She adjusted the veil once more before pausing on her way to the door.

"You asked me why I'm dressed the way I am," she said. "Your father has died. He gave up the ghost this afternoon while we were dealing with 'the incident.' It shouldn't come as a surprise. He was little more than a vegetable. I've charged Sister Francine with handling the funeral arrangements. We'll mourn and then we'll move on."

A thunderclap exploded inside Chloe's head. "Papa?" she cried. "Papa's dead?"

Eliza shrugged. Her lips were pursed in a tight, unforgiving smile. "For once, please spare me your histrionics," she said. "Death is a part of life. None of us are exempt. Not even your darling Papa."

The words were spoken with such contempt that Chloe couldn't help but react to their chill. She threw herself at Lady Eliza – arms flailing, hitting and kicking out in all directions – with a force that knocked them both back against the door. She reached for her stepmother's neck, determined to throttle the life out of the older woman, and when Eliza's resistance proved stronger than she had anticipated, Chloe sought to drive her thumbs deep into Eliza's eye sockets, tearing the woman's veil in the process and throwing it to the floor. But the fight was short-lived. The door opened and Sister Francine appeared. She pulled Chloe off of the older woman and slammed her down onto the bed. Chloe felt she was suffocating as the full weight of Eliza's henchwoman forced herself upon her. She tried to push Sister Francine away, but Eliza's Fallen Angel soon overpowered her.

"If you're not careful, we'll send you to the place where the bad little girls and boys go." Eliza, now fully recovered from Chloe's attack, hovered over her. Chloe blinked in an attempt to clear her vision, but something was wrong. She felt the pinch of a needle in her arm and a soft sensation of melting. "I daresay you won't like it there very much," Eliza continued, "even though it might do you a world of good."

"You'll never break me," Chloe replied. The words felt thick on her tongue. For the second time in less than twelve hours, Chloe found herself losing consciousness very much against her will. "You'll never break this family."

| 33 |

When she came to, Chloe was seated on a chaise in the library. Penelope sat beside her, holding her hand and stroking it with an intensity that was less than reassuring. Chloe squinted as her surroundings gradually came into focus. A strange metallic taste polluted her mouth and her head felt as though it had somehow been separated from the rest of her body. The family was gathered about the room, standing and sitting in various uncomfortable poses that cast the scene in an atmosphere of artifice that, had Chloe been in a more normal state of mind, she would have found alarming. As it was, she felt like an observer in a dream, both a part of and separate from the world around her. She was awake and yet, strangely, felt as though she was in a deep slumber. She remembered very little of her conversation with Eliza other than that her father was dead and that Guy was in collusion with the Russians.

"Papa?"

"There, there, dear," Penelope was in her ear, "you've had a terrible shock. We've all had a terrible shock. You've just born the brunt of it."

"Dead?" Chloe couldn't bring herself to comprehend. "And that woman..." Eliza's face now loomed monstrous in front of her, Sister Francine – arms folded across her chest, gold cross gleaming – as ever at her side.

"This family is in a state of crisis," Eliza's voice cut through Chloe's narcotic haze like a finely honed razor. "But we must carry on. Carleton's death, while certainly a blow, is not nor can it be treated as a surprise by any of you. He was not a well man. He lived large but the stress of his disappointment is ultimately what did him in."

"Disappointment?" Edgar rasped. He blew his nose into a handkerchief. "What the fuck are you on about, you nasty old cow?"

"Edgar!" Penelope snapped. Her grip on Chloe's hand tightened.

"Yes," Eliza replied, "disappointment. You – each and every one of you – have failed him in myriad ways. It is up to you to come to terms with your individual and collective guilt. It is not my place to provide absolution. That is between you and the Lord our God."

"Amen," Sister Francine intoned.

"However, as recent events incontrovertibly attest, one of you bears the greatest onus of responsibility and therefore merits the greatest punishment. Guy, would you please come forward?"

Chloe noticed her brother there for the first time. The disappointment – the hurt and the betrayal – came rushing back in a tidal wave of nausea. Despite feeling sedated and out-of-body, Chloe could hardly bring herself to look at Guy. Of all the disillusions she had ever experienced in life, what she felt Guy had personally done to her was the worst cut of all. She tried to raise herself from the chaise, but Penelope's hand became a fist around her wrist that she didn't have the strength to resist. Chloe could only sit there and wonder how – and why – everything between her and Guy, always the nearest and dearest of all her siblings, had gone so wrong. His betrayal of the family was bad enough, but his betrayal of her was nothing short of a tragedy.

"Guy." Lady Eliza stood supreme. Her mouth was drawn in its customary tight uncompromising line. If there was any doubt before, it was now obvious to all who was commander-in-chief. "The charges this family puts before you are grave, and at their worst pose an existential threat to the survival and integrity of the Templeton legacy, not to mention its reputation. Do you have anything to say for yourself?"

"Fuck all if I know what's going on," Guy said.

"Then allow me to enlighten you," Eliza replied.

Chloe felt Guy's gaze. She covered her face with her hands but couldn't help peering through her fingers at him. How sad he looked, like a spoilt child. *Resist*, she said to herself. *This is what he does. This is what Guy has always done. I can't be that person to him anymore. I won't.*

"That attitude does you no favors," Eliza said. "Your father always said you had such potential but you get in your own way. You think you're above us, don't you? You think that rules don't apply like they do for the rest of us."

"I don't know what you're on about," Guy spat. He turned in a circle to take in the family gathered in the room, searching each of them out, hoping to catch their eye. "Would someone please tell me what the fuck this woman is talking about?"

"*This woman* is your stepmother." Eliza's voice was thick with a humorless gravity.

"You're nothing to me!"

"And you're less than nothing to me," Eliza said with a cold smile.

"Chloe?"

She heard his desperation. It tugged at her heart.

"Guy," Chloe murmured. She shook her head. "I can't. I'm sorry. I just can't."

"Will none of you speak in my behalf? Diana? Edgar?"

"Sorry, old chap," Edgar offered with a guilty shrug. "As much as I hate to say it, the proof is rather stacked against you."

"Proof? What proof? Proof of what? Someone, please, help me out here. I'm in the fucking Twilight Zone."

"I saw you." Tessa stepped forward, prompted by an encouraging nod from Penelope. "In the woods by the bluebells. You were with that woman and that child. I heard what she said to you. I filmed the whole thing."

"We've all seen it," Diana said.

"Not to mention the fact," Tessa added, "that you perved me by the fountain the other day. Total sicko. I'm your sister. Well, half-sister anyway and young enough to be your daughter."

"Don't dilute your credibility," Eliza said.

"But what really astounds me," Duncan piped up, "if I may, is not only the utter thoughtlessness of it but the sheer stupidity. There comes a point in a grown man's life when he needs to stop thinking with his cock and consider the implications of his actions on those with whom he's affiliated in a familial way."

"Oh shut up, Duncan," Diana snapped. "Go blow a bagpipe."

"I'm just saying." Duncan drew himself up in an indignant pose. "I have business interests – business interests on behalf of Templeton Enterprises – that could be severely jeopardized if it became publicly known that my brother-in-law is mixed up with the Russians."

"The Russians," Chloe said. It was all coming back to her: the kidnapping, Rebecca Hastings, the acid burn on RH's face, the dance of death between RH and their hooded captor, the child...

The child... "Oh, Guy," Chloe moaned, "how could you?"

Guy was on his knees at her feet. He wrestled her hands away from Penelope's grip and clasped them in his own. She couldn't bear to see the desperation in his eyes.

"Chloe," he said, "you've always been there for me. You've always looked out for me, even when I haven't always deserved it. I need you. I don't know what's going on. Perhaps I should be more aware, more attuned to whatever it is that's prompted the family to turn against me, but I'm not a bad person, Chloe. You of all people know that. I'd never consciously do anything to hurt this family. You know that, Chloe, don't you?"

"Do I?" Chloe asked. "You weren't there, Guy, in the boathouse today. He was going to kill me."

"And me," Penelope added. "I was there too."

"Who?" Guy asked.

"One of your Russian comrades, no doubt," Edgar said. "He probably wants his money. The money you stole."

"It was horrible, Guy," Chloe sniffed. She felt herself melting. She steeled herself against the impulse. "And what he did to Rebecca..."

"Poor girl," Edgar said. "No one deserves that."

"I wouldn't go that far," Penelope replied.

"What do you have to say for yourself, Guy?" Eliza intoned. "You've heard the charges against you. How do you plea?"

"I reject you!" Guy cried. "I reject you and this kangaroo court. You may have pulled the wool over my father's eyes, but I won't be so easily tricked. I swear on his grave."

Eliza and Sister Francine exchanged bemused smiles. Chloe thought she was going to be sick.

"You can swear all you want upon however many graves you choose," Eliza said, "but the verdict remains. You're a liability to this family. Your presence here is no longer welcome, nor will it be tolerated."

"What?" Guy threw himself up onto his feet, releasing Chloe's hands with such a look of disgust she sensed their relationship was destroyed forever. Chloe couldn't help but bury her face in Penelope's shoulder.

"Now there, old chap, let's not have a scene," Edgar said. "These things happen, especially in a family like ours. It's best that we all just try to move on in as civilized a manner as possible. This isn't pleasant for any of us."

"Move on?" Guy turned on Edgar with an incredulous gasp. "You're telling me to move on? Who the hell do you think you are?"

"*I'm* telling you to move on," Eliza said. "Spencer's waiting in the entrance hall with your bags."

"Spencer's in on this?"

"He offered to take you back to London," Diana said, looking pained. She fiddled with the pearls at her neck.

"Capital bloke that," Duncan added. "A nitwit but capital."

"And then what?" Guy asked.

"We let the lawyers do what lawyers are paid to do," Eliza said. "It's best to leave that sort of thing to the professionals."

"I'll fight you!"

"Hmm." Eliza shook her head. She exchanged another set of glances with Sister Francine whose expression remained stoic. The Fallen Angel didn't need to say anything. Her power transcended all human interaction.

"What about my father? You'd deny me a place at his funeral?"

"It's already been arranged," Sister Francine said.

"A small private gathering," Eliza added, "with only close friends and *select* family. The chapel can hardly hold the village let alone unwelcome hangers-on."

"That's a bit harsh," Edgar interjected with a sniff. "Even for you."

"Bitch," Guy spat.

"Yes," Eliza said with a smile. "I am a bitch. I am everything all of you have ever thought or said about me. But I've made peace with it. I am absolved and cleansed in the eyes of the Lord. I seek no one's approval but His."

"This is madness," Guy said, but the fight had left him. He staggered blindly about the room like a drunk, only pausing one last time in front of Chloe, whose face remained buried in Penelope's all-too-welcoming shoulder. "And you."

"Leave her alone, Guy," Penelope warned. "Don't make this more of an ordeal than it needs to be."

Chloe forced herself to look at her brother. She felt it was the least she could do. While none of it made sense, Chloe didn't have the will or the strength to challenge Eliza or her siblings' claims. It was the kidnapping that had done it, that and what had happened to Rebecca Hastings. Now Chloe didn't think she'd ever be able to forgive herself for rejecting the Foraged hostess. She couldn't help but feel somehow the acid attack and kidnapping were all her fault, but exactly how or why she couldn't ascertain. *Guy is right,* Chloe thought. *This is madness.*

"Please, Guy," she whispered. "It's best that you go."

"Even you?" There were tears in Guy's eyes now. "My little sister...my dearest, most precious little sister. We've always had each other's backs. Chlo', what's happened?"

"I grew up," Chloe said with a resolve that surprised her. She cleared her throat and looked him in the eye. "Goodbye, Guy."

"This isn't the end," Guy said.

It pained Chloe to watch Spencer escort Guy from the room. She felt as though she had thrown her cards in with the devil. But really, what other choice had she? The kidnapping had weakened her. Her sense of herself – her values, her very womanhood – was gone. Yet, strangely, Chloe also experienced something akin to resolution, a sense of pride and belonging. The Templetons were, after all, more than the sum of their individual parts. She had to remember that.

"Are you all right?" Penelope asked.

Chloe straightened her back and smoothed out the creases of her skirt. She gently (yet resolutely) shrugged off Penelope's hand.

"Yes," she said. "Or rather, I will be. I'm a Templeton. We always muddle through."

Diana watched and waited as her family disbanded from the library in the wake of Guy's banishment. She had something to say to Eliza that she didn't want expressed in front of the others, something that she felt might give her leverage in the battle she knew was to come, but thought it best for it not to become common knowledge as she was less sure now than ever of which lines had been drawn in the sand and whose alliances lay with whom. The news of her father's death hadn't come as a surprise, though its delivery left one lacking. She didn't even feel particularly mournful. In fact, Diana actually felt very little, at least where Lord Carleton's death was concerned. Her focus was set on her own survival. Lady Eliza's ascendancy troubled her, though if she played her cards right, Diana thought she might be able to play Eliza to her advantage. The eldest Templeton sibling had always been smarter than any of them had given her credit for. She looked forward to surprising them.

"Might I have a word with you, Eliza, before we retire?" she asked. Eliza had lingered with Sister Francine behind the others as though sensing Diana might want to speak to her. Eliza and Sister Francine turned as one. "Alone," she said. "It won't take but a moment."

Sister Francine bristled. Her hands clenched into knotty oversized fists at her side. She looked to Eliza as though for guidance. Eliza nodded and Sister Francine bowed her head and left without a word, though she did cast a leer in Diana's direction as she did so.

"All in all a successful weekend, wouldn't you say?" Eliza said once the doors were securely closed. She motioned for Diana to join her on the chaise, but Diana shook her head. It was important she remain standing, Diana felt, so as to maintain an upper hand, or at least give herself the power of her conviction. Eliza shrugged. "Suit yourself," she said. "I'd be remiss if I didn't mention I found your reticence somewhat troubling. I'd expected you to have a greater voice."

"In what?" Already Diana could feel Lady Eliza usurping control in that insidious way of hers. It was maddening and troubling. She wondered whether her strength might be better fortified with a nip of brandy, but decided against it as she didn't doubt such a move would be interpreted as an act of weakness on Eliza's part. Best to remain steady, cool, calm and collected. Or at least give an impression of such.

"If you want to be taken seriously in this organization, Diana, you need to assume a stronger leadership role," Eliza said. "You acted like a follower. I need a leader."

"We all have our part to play."

"Penelope surprised me," Eliza said. "And that Tessa is proving quite the whippersnapper. Whether her claims are legitimate or not, she impresses me. The kidnapping plot was ingenious – risky, but ingenious. I have to give the girl credit where it's due."

"It served its purpose," Diana conceded, "though I'm not sure I agree with its execution."

"How so?" Eliza's eyes flashed. She hated being challenged.

"It served its purpose," Diana repeated.

An uncomfortable silence descended. Diana coughed. She felt as though her stepmother's gaze penetrated into her soul.

"You said you wanted a word with me," Eliza said. "I assume it's serious given you asked me to dismiss my deputy."

"Is that what she is?" Diana couldn't help the sarcasm.

"Do NOT underestimate Sister Francine, or do so at your peril."

"That sounds like a threat."

"You tax me, Diana. Don't force me to reevaluate you. There are others who would all too readily assert themselves over you."

Diana snorted. She felt herself falling for Eliza's bait.

"You mean Penelope and Tessa?" she asked.

Eliza's silence was answer enough.

"I have something on you," Diana blurted. The force behind the words surprised her, causing her heart to race and sending a rush of blood to her face.

"Excuse me?" Eliza's lips drew into a thin line. Her countenance became ashen. Diana knew she'd struck a blow, just as she had hoped. Still, it was much too early to declare triumph.

"Information has come to light," she continued.

"Explain yourself."

Diana shook her head. "I'm not at liberty to say more at this time," she said. "Just know that it's out there. I'm watching your every move."

"Oh, Diana," Eliza said with a dramatic sigh, "how you disappoint me. In a family full of amateur theatrics, I had hoped at least one of you might be a pro, or at least show promise. Obviously I was mistaken."

"You've been warned."

Eliza laughed. The sound of it was like a slap in the face. Diana turned to leave, but then stopped. She had promised Spencer not to reveal too much – at least not yet with so much still up in the air – but she found she couldn't resist. Her revulsion for the new Templeton matriarch was too propulsive. It made her want to retch. One last jab and she'd make her exit...and hope she hadn't been too hasty.

"That's a nasty bit of business Trevor's gotten himself into, isn't it?" Diana said, her words spitting with venom. She could have choked.

Eliza drew herself up on the chaise like a cobra poised to strike. "What do you know about Trevor?" she asked. "What do you know about my son?"

"Just know that I know," Diana said. "And I'm not the only one. There are others."

With that, Diana opened the door and hurried out into the hallway, closing the door behind her, desperate that Eliza not follow her and force a confrontation. She gasped for breath and leaned against the wall. Her collar felt restrictive. She loosened it in an attempt to gain a rush of much-needed oxygen. *What am I doing?* she asked herself. *What have I done?*

It wasn't as though she regretted the thing that happened earlier that day with Spencer in the conservatory amidst the madness of the fake kidnapping and the diversion of guests to the village inn. (Thank God for Elena Grimaldi's ability to think quickly on her feet!) She felt somewhat comforted in the knowledge that her actions – while impulsive, yes, and not wholly in character with the woman she had become in her middle age – hadn't been premeditated. There wasn't a conscious will to cheat on Duncan, albeit given all that she'd had to endure because of him in these many thankless years of marriage, infidelity could almost have been excused, if not expected. No, Diana had no regrets. She even found she had rather enjoyed herself, and she couldn't remember the last time she'd taken pleasure from anything, sexual or otherwise. But she was also all too cognizant of the fact that actions had consequences – both personal and reputational – and it was in this that Diana found herself pondering whether she might have been a little too careless in throwing caution to the wind. Spencer came with a certain amount of baggage, not the least of which was Yvette Devereux, for whom Diana had always felt a certain amount of grudging respect even as she didn't really understand what it was exactly that Yvette did.

But no matter, the deed was done and to have pretended otherwise would have made her a hypocrite, which may have been fine for some in the family, but certainly not for Diana. Still, she had no intention of broadcasting the liaison out to the world. It had been a one-time thing. She'd made this clear to Spencer before he'd pinned her against the piano and ripped her knickers down to her ankles with a violence that, if nothing else, surprised even her, who had thought until that moment that she'd had Lord Hawksworth rather well-sussed. Just when you thought you knew someone, they surprise you. Truth be told, Diana could have used more surprises of the Spencer kind. It relieved her ennui. In fact, she'd said as much to him in the immediate aftermath.

"Well, that was something," Diana said as Spencer released himself into her with one almighty thrust that, had she been pre-menopausal, might have caused her alarm. "Thank you, Spencer, for delivering me – however temporarily – from my all too crushing ennui. You can't possibly imagine how bored I am. I've contemplated suicide from time to time, but that's not the Templeton way, is it? Cigarette?"

He spluttered and mumbled to himself as he hitched up his trousers and adjusted his tie in the reflection of the gilded mirror above the Victorian sideboard. Diana rolled her eyes and withdrew a luxuriant plume of post-coital smoke that made her rather feel like Greta Garbo. Sex had a way of making Diana feel glamorous, probably due to the fact that she rarely had it. Duncan had never been the amorous type...at least not with her.

"Don't worry," she said after a bemused pause as she watched Spencer furtively tidy himself up, "I'm not the possessive type. I had an analyst once – not long after my last miscarriage – who told me when he looked into my eyes all he saw was a barren road to Mexico. Mexico of all places! I applauded him for his use of metaphor but never went back to see him again. I think it may have been his way of telling me he wanted to fuck me. It's always stuck with me though. Duncan just thinks I'm a cunt."

"I don't think we should talk about spouses or partners right now," Spencer said, "if you wouldn't mind."

Diana sucked on her cigarette and leaned back against the curve of the piano. "No, I suppose not," she said. "I always assumed you were homosexual."

She saw him flinch.

"That seems to be the word on the street," Spencer replied. They made eye contact in the reflection of the mirror. He looked away.

Diana groaned. "Let's not be precious about this. I can't think of anything more boring."

"I've always been attracted to women."

"Mademoiselle Devereux I can understand," Diana said, "but my little sister? Darling Chloe would make the straightest man bent. At least, that's what I've heard. 'Word on the street...'"

"I thought we agreed not to talk about significant others."

"Your collar's crooked." Diana pushed herself off the piano and languidly made her way across the room to where Spencer stood, still fussing with his tie in the mirror, still refusing to make eye contact. "Give it here."

He relented.

"I'm going to force you to look at me," she said. "I've always thought you had pretty eyes. There, that's better." She stepped back and stood beside him. They regarded each other in the mirror. "We could run away together, you know. Live as fugitives like a very British Bonnie and Clyde. What do you say, Spencer?"

"Don't you think I'm a little young for you?" Spencer asked.

"Is that your way of telling me I'm too old?" Diana turned and blew a playful but pointed stream of smoke in Spencer's face. She was becoming annoyed. "Was I not too old for you when you forced yourself upon me on the piano? I never gave consent, you know."

"Diana..."

"Don't worry." Diana appraised him through the haze of her cigarette. "On second thought, yes, you are rather shockingly young. You've never really grown out of your school uniform, have you? I'd never have placed you in Guy's class, but then my dear benighted brother has always had an old soul, hasn't he?"

"I don't agree with what your family's doing to him."

"It's not the family so much as *her*."

"You're like the Mafia."

"*Donna* Eliza." Diana emitted a sardonic laugh. "The moniker rather suits her. Too bad we're not Italian."

"She needs to be stopped."

"Yes." Diana lit another cigarette and sat down to the piano. She ran her fingers across the keys. "The question is how. I think we've only scratched the surface of what that woman is capable of, and that beast that follows her around like an overgrown orangutan. I don't know which of them I despise more. And it has nothing to do with them being Catholic."

"I may be able to assistance."

Spencer took a cigarette from Diana's pack and began to pace the length and breadth of the conservatory while inhaling rather inexpertly from the cigarette. Diana suppressed the urge to laugh at him.

"This has to be, of course, in the strictest confidence," he said after a pause. "In other words, this conversation never happened."

"Just like our fuck never happened."

"Precisely."

"Well?"

"What do you know about Eliza's son?"

"Trevor?" Diana shrugged. "I get the feeling he's rather persona non grata, a ne'er-do-well. I've never heard her speak of him and Papa made a point of telling us never to mention him to her or to anyone. He's in prison, isn't he? Somewhere in South Africa or somewhere equally blighted?"

Spencer frowned. "You already know more than you should," he said. "MI-6 has been keeping tabs on him. He's – as the Americans would say – a bad dude, if you get my drift."

Diana hated any and all things American. She sniffed. "Not really, but I'll take your word for it."

"You had better."

"But mightn't you at least give me a clue?" Diana asked. "If we're going to be complicit in taking the carpetbagger down, then our intelligence should at least be in sync, wouldn't you say?"

"I can neither deny nor confirm that," Spencer said. "Off the record, however, I can tell you he's about to be released."

"From prison?"

Spencer nodded and then seemed to think better of it. He shook his head and turned away. "You didn't hear it from me," he said.

"Of course not." Diana contemplated lighting a third cigarette. She normally confined herself to two a day, at the very extreme, but today had been rather trying. "And what was it that got Trevor in trouble in the first place?"

"Diamonds," Spencer said.

"Blood diamonds," Diana inferred. "How unoriginal. And in the second place?"

"There's chat about illegal arms trading," Spencer added. "And soliciting drugs and children as young as seven for various warlords in the Congo and Sudan. None of it, of course, has been substantiated, but those are the claims."

"How delicious," Diana said. "What does Eliza know?"

Spencer shrugged. "She's not under investigation," he said, "but questions have been raised about her first husband. I'm sure you're familiar with the circumstances of his demise."

"Bum boys in Thailand?"

"In a manner of speaking."

"In case you haven't already guessed," Diana said with a cheeky laugh, "I'm not one to stand on ceremony."

"It's refreshing."

"And he's coming home to Mummy?"

"We're not sure, but..."

"You needn't say more."

"I shouldn't have said anything."

"But you did." Diana wagged her finger. "And now I own you."

"I rather get the impression you think this is a game."

"Isn't it?" she quipped, but the expression in her eyes was less than whimsical. "Call it a game of thrones, if that makes the situation more relatable, but I assure you, Spencer, my intent is irrevocably serious. That woman will not destroy what my father and his predecessors have achieved for the good of king, queen, and country and we – or should I say *I*? – will not let that Papist deviant compromise all that we as a family value and hold dear. Do I make myself clear?"

"Rather," Spencer said. He still couldn't meet Diana's gaze. "Can I rely on your discretion?" he asked.

Diana emitted a deep-throated saucy chuckle. "Only if you make me come the way you did ten minutes ago," she said, "and then I'm utterly at your disposal."

Gay or straight or fashionably gender-fluid, men are such boys, Diana thought as Spencer went down on her on the piano bench. No wonder Mademoiselle Devereux kept him around for as long as she had. Chloe's loss...

...Diana's gain.

And she intended to keep on winning until there was only one seat left.

| 34 |

"You believe me, don't you?" Guy mumbled deep into his beer later that night back in London at the Pauper & Moxie. "You have to believe me. You're me best mate. If I don't have you, old boy, I don't know what I have. I might as well pack it all in, call it a night, off meself, because for fuck's sake, what else is there?"

Spencer wasn't sure how best to respond. The drive up from Templeton Manor had been painful, to say the very least, and Guy wasn't making things any easier on him or himself, for that matter. And where were they? What was this pub in the godforsaken depths of Whitechapel, Petticoat Lane no less? Guy had been most insistent. Something to do with patronizing a friend's business establishment and sticking it to the Man. Spencer hadn't a fucking clue what Guy had been on about, but he thought it best – given present circumstance – that he keep his head down and play it cool. Guy continued to mystify. He was nothing if not an enigma.

"My impulse is to believe you," Spencer said, ever the diplomat, "but you certainly don't make it easy. You can't refute your connection with Svetlana Slutskaya. You've got her profile fucking tattooed on your arm!"

"A moment of weakness," Guy replied, unapologetic as always. "Surely you can relate?"

Spencer thought of Diana, of what they had done that afternoon in the conservatory, the taste of her. Yes, he thought, he could relate, but that didn't mean he was going to.

"The child," he said after a reflective pause. "It all comes down to the child."

"Feminina," Guy said. He slugged back the rest of his beer.

"Is she..." Spencer hesitated. "Pardon me for asking so indelicate a question but is the child yours?"

The look said it all, or rather, Spencer thought, it said nothing because Guy was as oblique as ever. He supposed he might have cut his best friend a bit of slack. Whatever had transpired at the Steeplechase – not to mention the rather unfortunate business with the Ambassador's daughter, which was turning out to be the gift that kept on giving – had backed Guy into a corner. His family – never the most congenial (or, for that matter, consistent) of folk – had turned on him and Guy was clearly feeling the full force of their rejection. Were he in Guy's shoes, Spencer would probably have wanted to tell the world to fuck off as well. In fact, up until his impromptu tryst with Diana in the conservatory, Spencer had been in the same boat. He was a spy and he was being compromised. And by the Americans no less, who were supposed to be allies, though Dr. Joanne Singer and her Chihuahua were of thoroughly dubious provenance, as was The Agency, whose mandate – at least from Spencer's perspective – was ill-defined if not entirely fabricated.

But that was neither here nor there. *Focus, damn it!* Spencer told himself as he ordered another round of stout from the barkeep, a sketchy looking geezer whom Guy had introduced as the old friend. It didn't help that Yvette had abruptly left that afternoon for parts unknown. "Agency business," she had said, kissing his cheek on the fly as she climbed into the limousine that had mysteriously appeared in the midst of all hell breaking loose in the aftermath of the boathouse rescue and Rebecca Hastings' emergency airlift. She'd not even given him so much as an estimated date of return. Such was the topsy-turvy world in which they lived, Spencer supposed. If he'd wanted stability, he wouldn't have gone to work for

MI-6...or given his heart to another spook, though post-Diana, Spencer wasn't even sure where his heart lay anymore. It was all most perplexing, most perplexing indeed.

"For fuck's sake, mate, what do you think?" Guy's voice was a controlled thunder. He accepted the beer and gulped it down with a greedy flourish. Spencer didn't like the way the barkeep kept eyeing him. He wanted to say something but the thought of getting into fisticuffs held little appeal. He'd already had too much drama for one day.

"The question had to be asked," Spencer said. "If I'm to help you, I need you to help me understand what we're dealing with here."

"No."

"Is that your final answer?"

Guy squirmed on his bar stool. Spencer sipped his beer. He'd have much preferred whisky but it seemed impolite to ask.

"Biologically it's impossible," Guy said after a labored pause. "I would have had to have known her six, seven years ago, however old the child is."

"You don't sound convinced."

"I'd never seen the child before that night, at Svetlana's birthday."

"The night of Cordelia's ravaging?"

Guy shrugged.

"She'd told me then the girl's father had been her husband."

Spencer nodded. "Miroslav Borosevic," he said. "The Chechen. Blown to smithereens in that boating accident. In St. Tropez, I believe it was. Of course, there was nothing accidental about it. Between you and me, of course."

"Always."

Spencer decided to change tact. "And what do you know about her brother?" he asked. "Anatole. Was he there that night?"

"To be honest, mate, I don't remember much about any of it. Russia's a blur. Clearly vodka and I don't mix."

"There's speculation," Spencer said.

"About?"

"Speculation. I daren't go deeper than that. Rumor is all."

"About Svetlana and Anatole?"

He'd said too much. "I suppose a simple paternity test would answer the question soon enough."

Guy shot him a look. "I'm not asking Svetlana for a paternity test," he said.

"No, I suppose not." Spencer gulped the rest of his beer. It tasted like swill. He suppressed the urge to gag. "Well, I don't know, old boy. It seems we're in a right spot of bother."

"I need to hit the head."

Spencer contemplated switching his drink order as Guy got up from the bar and headed to the gentlemen's loo, but not before stopping to exchange a faintly 'bro'-ish clasp of hands and a back slap with the barkeep who, the more Spencer sat there, the more distrustful of the guy Spencer became. He couldn't put his finger on exactly what it was other than a vague sort of unease and an intuition that the bloke – regardless of his apparent association with Guy – harbored a shifty kind of malice that instinctively made Spencer uncomfortable. Perhaps it was the tattoos, especially the one that snaked in black ink up from under the collar of his Land's End FC t-shirt and coiled around his neck, or the barbed wire motif that circled his ropy forearm? Spencer had a prejudice against body art and what he felt it said about the people who sported it. And this bruiser looked like a right yob. Although, Spencer had to admit Guy wasn't looking all that much better. Spencer supposed he shouldn't judge. He could only imagine – no, he preferred not to – what the barkeep thought of him.

But there was something else, a feeling that was equally intangible. From the moment he and Guy entered the pub, Spencer had the distinct sense that he was being watched. Of course, as a spook he had come to take it for granted that there wasn't a wall anywhere in the world that didn't have at least one set of eyes embedded in it, let alone a pair of ears. Add to this the fact that he'd just come from a particularly fraught three days at Templeton Manor, which was enough to drive even the sanest, most well-adjusted bloke batty and bug-eyed. As he sat and waited for Guy to finish his business, Spencer peered into the back area behind the bar as best he could without being too obvious. He thought he'd seen a flicker of movement, the widening of an eyeball, the sound of a door closing perhaps a little too abruptly, suggesting covert operations or subversive behavior.

"So you're the toff from MI-6?"

Spencer nearly startled off his stool. The barkeep slapped his dishrag down on the bar and wiped the counter directly in front of where Spencer sat. His gaze was hard and unwelcoming. He suddenly felt very hot under the collar.

"I don't think we've been properly introduced," Spencer stammered. "Er, or rather, I don't think I caught your name."

"Liam." Liam crushed Spencer's extended hand in his decidedly calloused paw.

"O'Halloran."

"Nice to meet you...er...Liam." Spencer gulped. He tried to pull his hand free from the barkeep's grasp without coming across as too toff-like – he had the impression Liam didn't take too kindly to toffs – but Liam held fast. It was like a tug of war, a game that Spencer had always particularly loathed during Field Day at Harrow and wasn't any more positively inclined towards it now. "I say, that's quite a grip you have. Crushing."

"You can tell a lot about a man based on how he shakes your hand," Liam replied. "And if he looks you in the eye when he does it."

"I daresay you must shake lots of hands." Spencer cringed at how lame he sounded. "Being a bartender and all, I mean. You must meet all sorts."

Liam released his hand. "You wouldn't be wrong," he said, though his expression remained suspicious.

Spencer nodded. He glanced at his watch. The feeling that someone – other than Liam – was keeping a steady eye on him had not dissipated. In fact, Spencer felt it even more acutely. *What the hell is taking Guy so long?*

"I say," he stammered. The silence had become unbearable. "Might I trouble you for a spot of whisky? Whatever you've got on the house is fine as long as it's smooth and burns as it goes down the old gullet. I'm not particular."

Liam nearly cracked a smile. "I couldn't call meself a true Scot if I didn't serve a wee dram. Does a twelve year old Glenfidditch suit?"

"Rather! That would be most exceptional. One never knows what to expect in places like these."

Liam cocked an eyebrow as he poured them each a tumbler full.

"Bottoms up!" he said as they clinked glasses. Spencer felt himself blush. The whisky didn't disappoint.

"That hits the spot," Spencer said with a hearty lip smack. "You and Guy...I take it you're mates? I don't think I knew you at school. Your name isn't familiar and I know I'd recognize that face."

"In a manner of speaking," Liam replied. He poured another round.

"Were you at Harrow?"

"Do I look like I went to Harrow, mate?"

"I suppose not. I meant no offense."

"I worked for Guy's Dad."

"Oh! Lord Carleton. On the estate? Doing what? Were you a gamekeeper?"

Spencer sensed he'd made another blunder. Liam scowled and whipped the dishtowel down on the bar with an intensity that was just this side of violent. Spencer looked at his watch again.

"Lands End FC," Liam said by way of explanation. He pointed to the logo on his shirt. "Came up the ranks in their youth squad and played for the team proper for a while. Even got meself a few England caps. You could say His Lordship discovered me."

"You're a footballer? Well done you!"

Spencer knew the moment the words passed his lips that he sounded patronizing. He really hadn't intended to. It's just that people like Liam made Spencer feel well outside his league. He didn't think it was a class thing – or maybe it was? Yvette was always on at him about being a snob and Chloe had once told him he needed to be more (what was the word she'd used?) *democratic*, though Spencer had found that quite rich coming from a *Tatler*-anointed It Girl who was arguably even more class conscious than he, and he'd told her that too. Needless to say, things hadn't gone well. In fact, if Spencer had at all been introspective, he might have credited that moment as the beginning of the end where he and Chloe were concerned. Or at least the beginning of many ends. One really never knew where one stood with Chloe Templeton. Fickle didn't even begin to describe her.

"In the end, it didn't work out," Liam said. His tone softened. His eyes assumed a far away almost misty cast. "But it afforded me this place and I've never looked back."

"Funny how Guy's never mentioned you. I would have looked you up. You've a nice establishment here. Just you?"

"And me girlfriend. She's away right now."

"Mine too." Spencer wondered why he suddenly felt disingenuous when he thought of Yvette. When he paused to think about it, the redheaded Frenchwoman had proven time and again surprisingly accepting of his many foibles – both diplomatic and personal. Her strength and ingenuity inspired him. Yet – and perhaps this was just as a result of the rather dispiriting meeting he'd had with Dr. Joanne Singer and the Chihuahua – Spencer couldn't help but suspect that Yvette's sudden and mysterious posting abroad (she couldn't even tell him where she was being sent) marked the end of something.

He didn't care to consider this as the end of their relationship, though if he was truly honest with himself that is exactly what it felt like, as it should have done, he supposed, considering the fact that they had indeed agreed to part ways just the night before. Perhaps he'd only imagined a certain coldness towards him in their leave-taking? Spencer had hoped for, at the very least, a farewell fuck in his well-appointed rooms at Templeton Manor, but with the fake kidnaping and the emergency airlifting of Rebecca Hastings (now *that* had been a surprise!) Spencer and Yvette had only been afforded a hasty and thoroughly chaste peck on the cheek, a dissatisfying (for him) and thoroughly insincere promise to keep in touch before the limousine whisked her off to wherever it was she was going and a future that suddenly felt all too uncertain.

At an earlier time, Spencer might have considered this separation a blessing of sorts – an opening that allowed him to once again pursue Chloe with the ardor and attention that he felt she deserved – but his dearly beloved English rose now appeared indifferent to him at best, preoccupied, and rather disturbingly under the influence of a family that was becoming more and more Byzantine in its ever-evolving and all-encompassing machinations. Spencer shuddered to think what might become of Chloe if Lady Eliza was allowed to have her way.

Spencer had read (eagerly and yet paradoxically with reluctance) the reports from the Home Office. The rumors circulating within certain diplomatic circles about Lady Eliza's son were – as he'd more than intimated to Diana – disturbing in the very least. Trevor Brookings was nothing if not a problem. Spencer welcomed the distraction for it served to somewhat distance himself from questions that he preferred not to address – questions of an extremely personal nature – though the liaison with Diana couldn't really be regarded by anyone as a smart move and, if he were perfectly honest with himself, would only further complicate what was already a thoroughly fraught set of circumstances.

Guy returned from the loo and settled himself on the barstool. Spencer couldn't help but admire his best mate's diffidence, as maddening (not to mention, counterproductive) as it often was.

"I thought you'd done a runner," Spencer said.

"I got side-tracked." Guy nodded to Liam, who had positioned himself at the opposite end of the bar, and motioned him over. "Question for you, mate," Guy said. "Who'd you have hidden in your broom closet just now?"

Liam squinted. Spencer found the barkeep's expression suspect.

"Not sure what you're on about, mate," Liam said, his voice a growl. *Too defensive by half,* Spencer thought.

"It's just that I don't like being peeped at whilst I piss."

Liam shrugged. "Beats me," he said.

Spencer didn't believe him for a second. "I wondered the same thing," he said.

"This whole time we've been sat here I've had the distinct impression we're being spied upon."

"I don't think I appreciate the accusation."

"I even knocked on the door," Guy continued. "Whoever it was backed away like it was up to something it had no business being up to, if you know what I mean."

"We go way back, mate," Liam said. Spencer noticed how he clenched and unclenched his fists. He found himself weirdly – and inappropriately – fascinated by the pattern of tattoos on Liam's hands and forearms. He forced himself to look away. "But it's always been more about your Pa than you and me. I appreciate what he done for me, but those days are over now. I done me time and I done me penance. I don't take kindly to you waltzing in here with your posh friends and your lah-dee-dah attitude casting aspersions on me establishment. Now if we didn't go back a ways – and out of loyalty to your Pa – I'd tell you to get the feck out of here and never come back. In fact, I'd do more 'n that. I'd throw you both out on your feckin' arses."

Spencer braced for a punch. His instinct was to grab Guy by the shoulder and beat a hasty retreat, but he could tell from the way Guy stood up from the barstool, nostrils flaring, that his mate was itching for a fight and wouldn't take kindly to Spencer steering him down a distinctly less confrontational path. Ever the diplomat, Spencer found himself stepping in between the two – and directly into their line of fire – praying for the best. If a punch was thrown, Spencer hoped it didn't land on his good side.

"Don't you be bringing my Dad into this," Guy said. His voice was quiet but strained. "He put a lot of faith in you and you fucked it up. It cost him a fortune and that's not even getting into the damage it did to the club."

"I was set up," Liam replied. "I said it back then and I maintain it now. We all of us make mistakes but not all of us is equal in the punishment that gets handed out. Some of us don't have advantages, if you know what I mean."

"Always the class thing with you," Guy snapped. Spencer could feel him getting hotter. "The problem with you, Liam, is the same as it's always been. You've got a chip on your shoulder that's bigger than your head. You fuck yourself up because you don't know when to shut the fuck up. And your footie was always second-rate, if you want my opinion."

"Now, gentlemen, please." Spencer coughed. "I don't think this is the time for the airing of historic grievances. With all due respect to you, Liam, and to your 'establishment,' our mutual friend here raised a valid question. Now I'm sure we can solve this like the civilized gentlemen we are and then we'll be on our way. Either answer Guy's question or we'll have to ask whoever it is to kindly present themselves to us. It doesn't have to be any more complicated than that."

Liam slowly lowered his fists. His eyes darted from Spencer to Guy and then back to Spencer again. Spencer thought he looked like a caged animal.

"There's a good man," Spencer soothed. "Deep breaths."

"I don't know what the feck you're talking about," Liam said.

"Fuck that," Guy said.

Spencer ducked for the punch that didn't come. Instead, Guy bounded over the bar with an agility that Spencer found rather breathtaking, and lunged toward the broom closet door. Spencer missed what transpired next – for it happened in such a blur and he kept his head down lest Liam act where Guy had not – but when Spencer regained his balance, he saw that the closet door was open and Guy was running out the back of the pub, through the kitchen, and out onto the street in pursuit of whomever had been hiding in the closet. Spencer followed suit, but at much less pace. When he arrived in the alley behind the pub, Guy had given up the chase and was already walking back. Something gold glistened in his closed fist.

"She got away," Guy said.

"She?"

Guy opened his palm to reveal the gold cross and chain.

"Oh dear," Spencer said. "What the hell is going on?"

"That's what I'd like to know," Guy replied. "And that's what I aim to find out."

| 35 |

Sister Francine threw herself down onto her knees in front of the crucifix in her room beneath the stairs, ignoring Essie's shrill admonishments against treating her house in Watford like a bed-and-breakfast from which she could come and go as she pleased. She closed her eyes as the leather strap flayed across the scarred flesh of her bare shoulders and back. Her sister's voice echoed in the far reaches of her consciousness, like a harpy hell-bent on driving her mad. For Sister Francine felt as though she was going mad, truly losing her marbles and not just in a figurative sense. She didn't know whether it was the tumor growing with alarming speed on her brain, the increasing frequency of her visions pre-ordaining the Female Apocalypse, the intensity of the drama at Templeton Manor, or most recently her all-too-close-call at the Pauper & Moxie, but Sister Francine feared she was at risk of jeopardizing all that she had worked for in these years of relative freedom since her release from prison.

It seemed that God was truly challenging her: that the path to salvation she sought wasn't nearly as straightforward or guaranteed as she had hoped for or planned. She had detected elements of resistance at Templeton Manor that didn't at all figure into her strategy, though she supposed this had less to do with Lady Eliza not delivering her end of the bargain and more to do with her own inability to construct a Plan B. She'd have to work harder going forward, be more ruthless, and more alert. If need be, she might even have to take action independent of Lady Eliza or call on outside resources, although what those might be, Sister Francine had yet to determine.

"Open the door, Frannie!" Essie's voice – harsh, breathless, and desperate – grated on Sister Francine's already frayed nerves. Each knock was like someone pounding her head against a wall. "Right this minute. You can't just come and go like some casual lodger. I'm your sister, Francine. I deserve respect."

"Go away!" Sister Francine cried. She lashed the strap across her back with greater intensity. The leather bit deep, cutting through her flesh like a razor. "This is God's work," she said. "I go where He leads me. I am not bound by terrestrial conformities or familial responsibility."

But Essie was persistent. "Three nights in a row I've waited up for you," she shrieked. "Three nights I've sat here and wondered what terrible things might have happened to you. You're in no condition to be traipsing about God knows where at God knows what hours of the day or night."

"But God does know and that's all that matters."

There came a pause. Through the door, Sister Francine heard Essie give a sharp intake of breath as though she had been chastised, which is exactly what Sister Francine had intended.

"Can you please open the door?" Essie's voice weakened, the quaver beneath it suggested she was crying or very nearly on the verge of tears. "I thought we were in this together. I thought this is the thing that would bring us closer...as sisters... as guardians of the Divine Light."

"We are." *Damn her*, Sister Francine thought. "It is."

"You were there this weekend, weren't you?" Essie persisted. "With them. With her. You've replaced me in your affection with her. But I remind you, Frannie, that the Movement was my idea long before Lady Eliza became involved. I won't let her take my place. I won't let her usurp me."

It was then that Sister Francine realized the gold cross was missing from around her neck. She frantically looked about the room for it, turning the bed upside down, the chair, pulling the drawers out of her dresser and tossing their contents every which way in a purple haze of rage. The gold cross was her beacon. It was her light, a totem to ward her against the evils with which she was already afflicted and the evils that she knew were yet to come. Without it, Sister Francine didn't know what she might do. Its absence, she felt, was a damning indictment against her.

"What are you doing in there?" Essie's voice was like a gong. She pounded against the door. "Do I have to ask Seamus to break down the door? He won't be but pleased. There's something different about him, Frannie. I don't know what it is, but I feel it. I feel a change in him. There's a moony look in his eyes now that wasn't there before. I think maybe all this stuff and nonsense with that band is going to his head, like he's putting on airs and graces like he's bloomin' Cliff Richard!"

Sister Francine's head felt as though it was in a vise. Her vision blurred. A tremendous and terrible pressure exerted itself upon her from above. Her throat closed. She couldn't breathe. And then it happened.

Later, after the inquest and after the insurance speculators had been and gone amid suspicion of arson that was never proved, Sister Francine would remember only that it was as though the ceiling split open and a rain of fire crashed down upon her. She fell back onto the floor, convulsing as the flames of Diyarbakir descended like Hell's furnace. And there, above it all, Sister Francine saw the child – Feminina – running blissfully through a field of fire, her hair a tangle of curls that glinted off the reds and oranges of the inferno. Sister Francine reached out to her. Feminina turned. Her eyes opened wide. Her mouth stretched into a horrific smile. She pointed at Sister Francine before laughing with demonic glee. Sister Francine screamed.

She remembered nothing else.

Printed in Great Britain
by Amazon